Eye

of the

Bear

For Mary —
Naida West
State Fair 2005

Eye

of the

Bear

A History Novel of Early California

Naida West

Bridge House Books
P.O. Box 809
Rancho Murieta, CA 95683

Second printing, 2002

Library of Congress Catalog Card No. 00-093111
ISBN 0-9653487-4-1

Interior design by Pete Masterson, Aeonix Publishing Group, www.aeonix.com
Cover art by Gayle Anita, 916-961-6912; email: ganita3@aol.com
Map by Mary Engbring Estep

Poem excerpts, "The Endangered Roots of a Person" by Wendy Rose and "Skin" by Linda Hogan, are from *Reinventing the Enemy's Language: Contemporary Native Women's Writings of North America*, edited by Joy Harjo and Gloria Bird (1997).

Printed in the United States of America

Dedicated in memory of Bill Franklin, Sr. (1913–May 4, 2000), an elder from my corner of California and a gentleman of both worlds.

Author's Note

In writing about the violence associated witt the mission era, Alan Brown mentions, almost as an aside, the "irreversible effect which even a short acquaintance with Europeanized mission life exerted on the natives" (*Pomponio's World*, 1979). That effect is the subject of this book. Broader than church or nation, it is the imprint of western civilization itself.

While digging in the orchard and garden of our little ranch in California's Gold Country, my husband and I uncovered native artifacts, rusty square nails, hand-blown bottles and what appeared to be the clay floor of a cabin. I researched the identities of those who lived here before us and wrote the story of how the Gold Rush affected them *(River of Red Gold)*. However, that only scratched the surface. Before that—just prior to their discovery that gold was valuable to the newcomers—the native people were affected by the Spanish-Mexican missions. Therein lurked a mystery.

My early teachers in Idaho had spoken in admiring tones of the vanished warriors of the mountains and plains as "proud and noble savages." But when I came to California in the 1950s, the natives were talked about as though they had been childlike and lacking something. Schoolbooks said they loved the missions and were entirely peaceful. My teacher said they hadn't fought for their land because they didn't have the ability to do anything "on that scale."

I was curious why they would be so different from the natives east of the Sierra. The mystery deepened when I read, later, about major native rebellions against the missions. Why hadn't that been taught in my school? Why had so few people heard of those rebellions? Why are the Modocs believed to be California's only native warriors? Now I realize that the answers lie within my own culture. Western civilization evolved in admiration of warriors and warfare, and since the California natives were perceived as giving up without a fight during the Gold Rush, they appeared to be less interesting as research subjects. Furthermore, "important" California history was presented as starting with the Gold Rush. The Modocs had fought the American newcomers, so that was interesting. In contrast, everything about the mission era tended to be seen as quaint and irrelevant. In short, California absorbed the ethnocentric attitudes of the Forty-niners, and that skewed history.

That the natives *did* organize across cultural divides and challenge the Mexican military is likely to change some people's estimation of them. However it is arguably more admirable that they lived for many long centuries without the conquering hegemonies and warfare that are endemic in other civilizations. For people to live independently within their societies, and for small societies to live independently surrounded by different societies with different languages seems beyond the ken of the modern world. Anthropologist Alfred L. Kroeber wrote in 1925: "In Europe and Asia, change succeeded change of the profoundest type. . . The permanence of California culture, therefore, is of far more than local interest. It is a fact of significance in the history of civilization." California natives had much to teach, but back then no one paid attention.

In recent decades public opinion about mission history has turned from a simplistic, over-romanticized version to, at times, an anti-mission version. Indeed, funding for needed mission restoration appears to be in jeopardy. It was not my purpose to denigrate the good-intentioned missionaries. As historian James Rawls shows so well, the native people were treated far better under that regime than by the U.S. government. Rather, I hope readers are inspired to reflect upon the effects of western civilization, which are still sweeping through the remote areas of the world.

Fact and Fiction

In most historical novels a fabricated plot is imposed upon an historical setting. Instead, I used documented events as story guideposts and stayed very close to the actual timeline. All italicized correspondence quoted in the text are verbatim translations of actual Mexican documents. I imagined what might have filled the gaps and fleshed out characters who were little more than names. I created native characters who unquestionably existed but left no trace in recorded history. This adds fiction, but to tell the story solely from the perspective of those who wrote the documents would have perpetuated the larger fiction that the constant role of the California native people was to be acted upon—distinctly not the case here. Further, I used the tools of fiction to better convey the truths of the heart and spirit. Sometimes you have to write fiction to tell the truth. Any errors of history, language or culture are my own. Readers interested in sources and more of the facts should read the endnotes.

Naida West
Cosumnes River
May 2002

Regarding The Map

The map on the next page is intended as a snapshot in time. Approximately 70 different native villages on the San Francisco Peninsula and around the north and east bay had disappeared by 1825 and were therefore left blank. Exceptions mapped are those that Grizzly Hair hears about in the story. The missing peoples had gone to the missions; only a small percentage of them remained alive in 1825. For the same reason the many Ohlone (Costanoan) peoples and villages along the coast south of San Francisco and south of Mt. Diablo down past Monterey have been omitted. Likewise the villages on the eastern slopes of the coastal range west of the San Joaquin River and south of Altamont Pass had disappeared—absorbed by the central missions, the Pacheco Pass being a primary military route. In the early 20th century Frank Latta concluded that the numerous villages (archeological evidence remained) of Yokuts peoples in that area, more than 300 miles long and averaging 25 miles wide, had been "annihilated" by 1790. The Taches were the only surviving name (Latta, 1977).

On streams east of the San Joaquin and Sacramento rivers, the native villages were about as numerous as along the Cosumnes River. However, being less central to the narrative and each presenting difficulties of nomenclature and precise location, most were left blank. Nonetheless, the reader should envision the banks of all those streams populated to the extent that the Cosumnes River was.

Spellings diverge in all reports. Latta uses the suffix umne instead of amni in the San Joaquin Valley. The Jauyomi of Santa Rosa are also the Gualomi, and the Volvon just east of Mt. Diablo are also the Bolbon. For more about inconsistencies caused by transliteration, see Endnotes, "SPELLING," p. 623.

Clockwise from north and west, the eight major languages of the mapped area are Pomo, Coast Miwok (San Rafael Peninsula), Wappo, Wintun, Maidu (south to Cosumnes River), Miwok, Yokuts, and Ohlone.

Detailed maps of the blank areas can be found in Latta (1977), Margolin (1978) and Milliken (1995). See Author's Acknowledgments, p. 611.

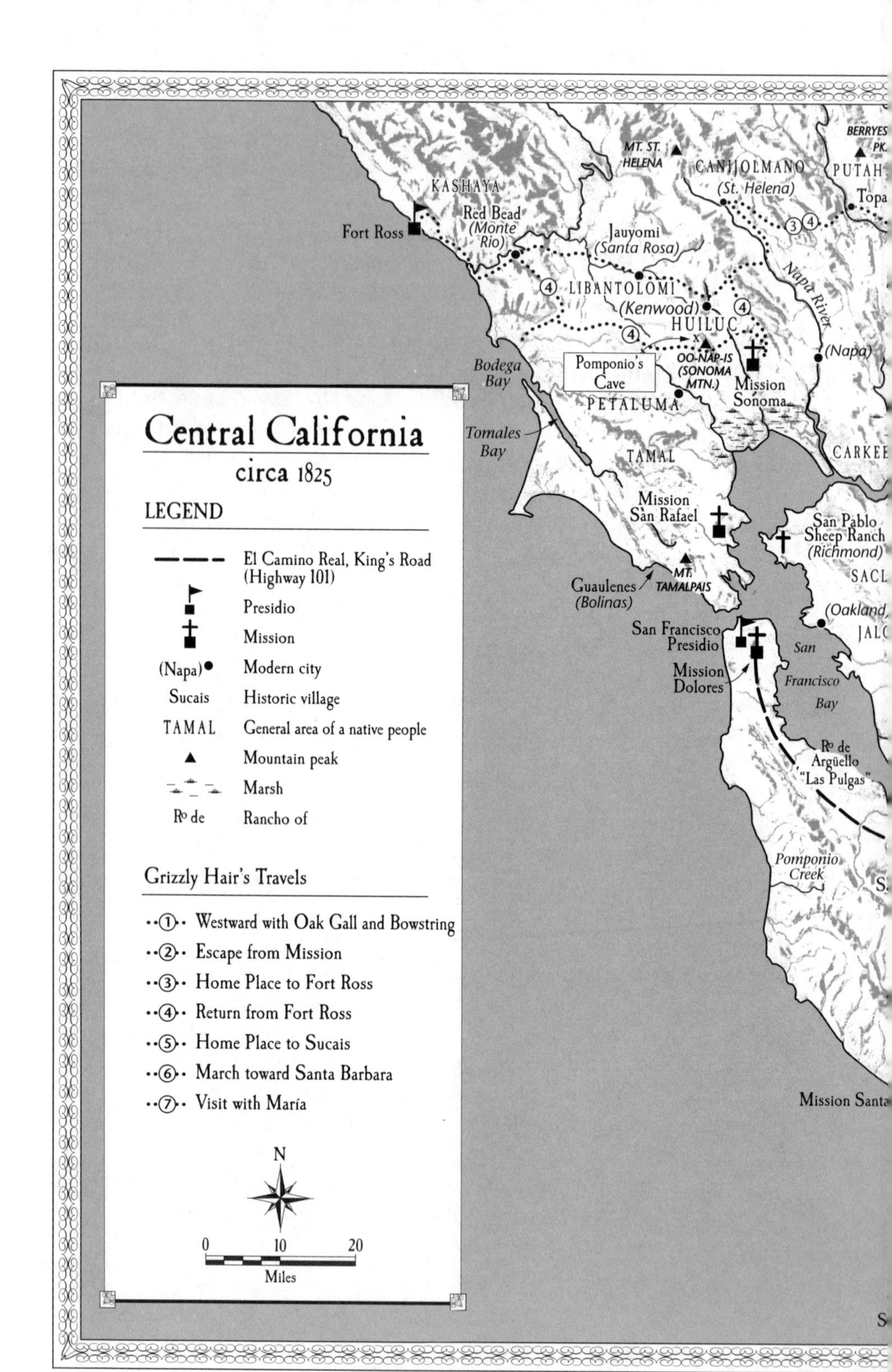
Central California
circa 1825
LEGEND
El Camino Real, King's Road (Highway 101)
Presidio
Mission
(Napa) Modern city
Sucais Historic village
TAMAL General area of a native people
Mountain peak
Marsh
Rº de Rancho of
Grizzly Hair's Travels
1 Westward with Oak Gall and Bowstring
2 Escape from Mission
3 Home Place to Fort Ross
4 Return from Fort Ross
5 Home Place to Sucais
6 March toward Santa Barbara
7 Visit with María
N
0
10
20
Miles
Fort Ross
KASHAYA
Red Bead
(Monte Rio)
Jauyomi
(Santa Rosa)
MT. ST. HELENA
CANJOLMANO
(St. Helena)
BERRYES PK.
PUTAH
Topa
LIBANTOLOMI
(Kenwood)
HUILUC
Napa River
(Napa)
Pomponio's Cave
OO-NAP-IS (SONOMA MTN.)
Mission Sonoma
Bodega Bay
Tomales Bay
PETALUMA
TAMAL
CARKEE
Mission San Rafael
San Pablo Sheep Ranch
(Richmond)
SACL
MT. TAMALPAIS
Guaulenes
(Bolinas)
(Oakland
JALC
San Francisco Presidio
Mission Dolores
San Francisco Bay
Rº de Argüello
"Las Pulgas"
Pomponio Creek
Mission Santa

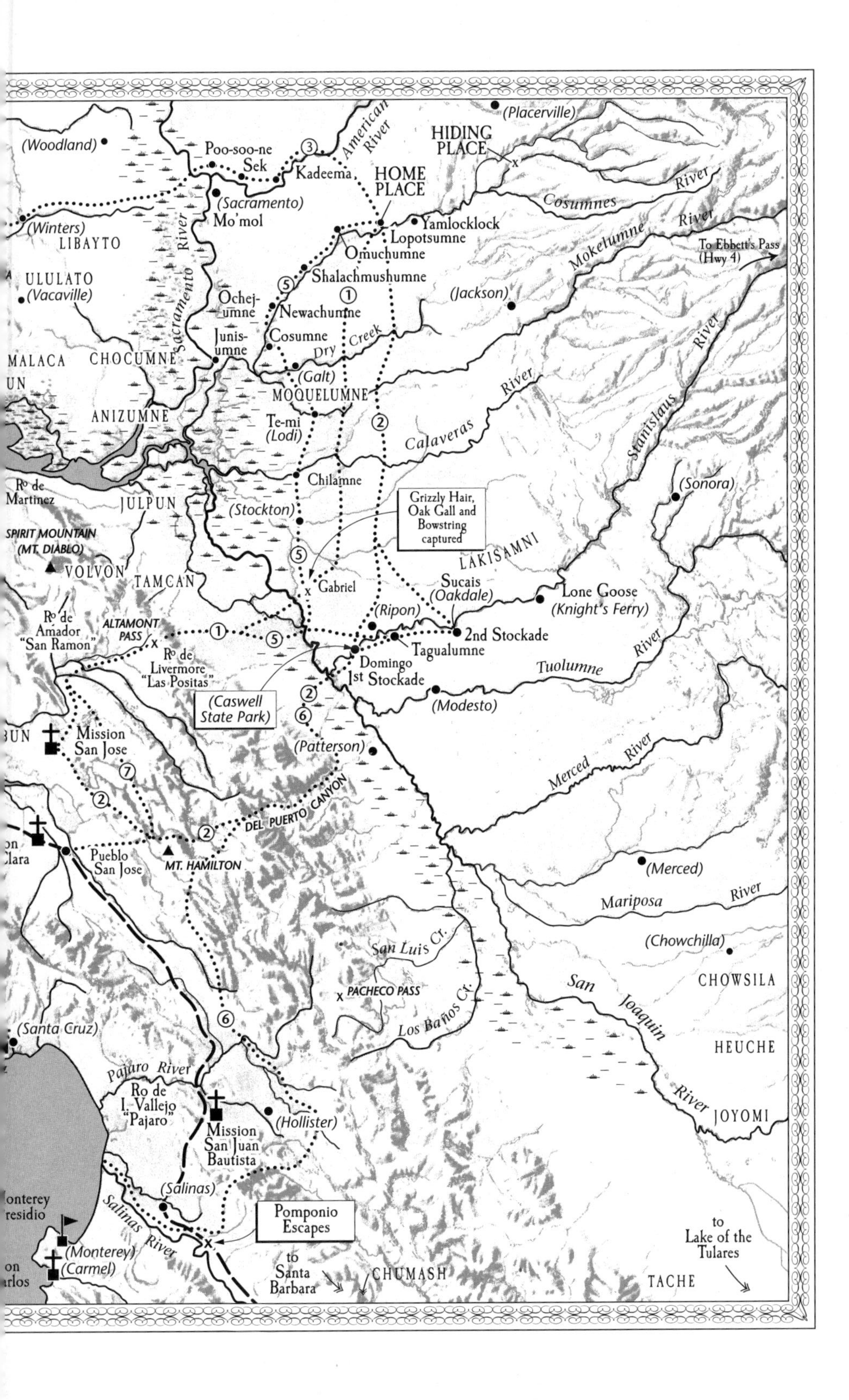

(Placerville)
(Woodland)
Poo-soo-ne
Sek
Kadeema
American River
HIDING PLACE
HOME PLACE
(Sacramento)
Mo'mol
(Winters)
LIBAYTO
Yamlocklock
Lopotsumne
Omuchumne
Shalachmushumne
Cosumnes River
Mokelumne River
To Ebbett's Pass (Hwy 4)
ULULATO
(Vacaville)
Sacramento River
Ochej-umne
Newachumne
Junis-umne
Cosumne
Dry Creek
(Jackson)
MALACA
CHOCUMNE
(Galt)
MOQUELUMNE
ANIZUMNE
Te-mi
(Lodi)
Calaveras River
Stanislaus River
Chilamne
(Sonora)
Ro de Martinez
JULPUN
(Stockton)
Grizzly Hair, Oak Gall and Bowstring captured
SPIRIT MOUNTAIN (MT. DIABLO)
VOLVON
TAMCAN
LAKISAMNI
Gabriel
Sucais
(Oakdale)
Lone Goose
(Knight's Ferry)
Ro de Amador "San Ramon"
ALTAMONT PASS
(Ripon)
2nd Stockade
Tagualumne
Ro de Livermore "Las Positas"
Domingo
1st Stockade
Tuolumne River
(Caswell State Park)
(Modesto)
Mission San Jose
(Patterson)
Merced River
DEL PUERTO CANYON
Pueblo San Jose
MT. HAMILTON
(Merced)
Mariposa River
San Luis Cr.
(Chowchilla)
CHOWSILA
PACHECO PASS
San Joaquin River
Los Baños Cr.
(Santa Cruz)
HEUCHE
Pajaro River
Ro de I. Vallejo "Pajaro"
Mission San Juan Bautista
(Hollister)
JOYOMI
(Salinas)
Salinas River
Pomponio Escapes
(Monterey)
(Carmel)
to Santa Barbara
CHUMASH
to Lake of the Tulares
TACHE

Prologue

Howchia Speaks

It is still, here in the blue oak forest. Heat hangs in the branches. The end of day holds its breath. No woman banks a supper fire. No child sings. My people are gone. But I am still here, tight within this oak.

In my roots I feel the faint tremor of approaching footsteps, then see the woman and her dog coming over the hill. They live nearby with their man, not in a village as we lived, but by themselves. She often comes here at the end of day and walks the path I once walked. Lately I have begun to imagine talking with her.

Her footsteps slow as she approaches. Then she stands still, maybe enjoying the first cool ground air rising around her bare legs. She looks at the softening colors in the forest and the wing people leaving one at a time for their nests. The large golden dog sniffs through the tall grass beside the path, detecting the crossed trails of rabbits, raccoons, deer, skunks, mountain lions and coyotes.

To my surprise I hear the woman's music. I have never heard it before. Like a theme from a once-familiar song, it flutes of her joy to be in the forest as one of its inhabitants. I can feel it opening the barrier between us, though she doesn't know I am here. I try to speak to her. Only a tremor in my upper leaves marks my effort, as though a phantom breeze blows upon them.

Hearing the rustle, she looks up and sees leaves moving against the sky. The dog returns and sits at her feet, also looking up. All other leaves in the forest are still. Darkness settles in the shadows, but she is not afraid. Her music continues to invite talk, head-to-head talk as my people used to say. The dog also knows a friendly presence is near.

"I am a mother," I say, hoping to convey much more.

"I think you are a woman who lived here a long time ago," the woman says. "Before people like me came."

Gently so as not to insult her, I point out, "Yes, I lived here long ago, but I am still here. When I died I looked back, unable to turn away from this home place that I love, and that is why my spirit lodged in this tree. It pleases me to come out of my solitude and talk with you."

"It pleases me too. Who were you?"

"Once I was Eagle Woman," I reply. "I am glad you want to know who walked this path before you." In a flash of clarity I realize that she could tell the story of my son, the story of my people. We didn't know our storytellers would die, and since the survivors didn't look back or speak the names of their dead, their grandchildren never heard the story. Next time I die, I shall look forward as they did, and walk the pathway of ghosts. I will sit at a campfire and tell my people how my son fought the *Españoles*. But that might be another three hundred tree-sleeps. The eagle in me grows impatient. "Tell the story of my son," I say to the woman.

She responds quickly. "I don't know you. I know nothing of your people. I know nothing of your son. How can I tell your story?"

"I think you can."

"But I am not of your people. One of your people should tell that story."

"They are gone now. But this is your home place too. You love the river and the hills and the boulders as I do. I hear your music. You are a spirit sister. Tell my son's story."

"I'm afraid I wouldn't tell it right."

"Defeat that fear and you will tell it well enough."

In the darkening shadows she is suddenly uncertain she has heard me, yet unwilling to break the link. "It would take a long time to do this well," she says, "It would change my life."

While she stands thinking, guessing correctly that my people left no records, I greet the dog. He says he enjoys these evening walks, especially the smells, and sometimes a chase. I tell him dogs have enjoyed walking here since the time of the Ancients.

"Maybe I can do it," the woman says. "But I will need to talk to you often. Will you be here?"

I smile in my grain. "I cannot leave until my roots wither and my wood dies. Sometimes these oaks live a thousand rainy seasons. We can talk whenever you come."

"I will be back," she says, turning toward her house, the dog at her side.

O-se-mai-ti, who has been standing in the shadows, steps onto the trail. It is nearly dark now and she blends with the umbels of the oaks on the hill behind, but I can smell the richness of her fur. "That will be interesting," says O-se-mai-ti, pointing her snout after the departing woman.

"I think she can do it," I say.

"Are the new people interested in our stories?"

"We shall see."

O-se-mai-ti ambles over and sits on her haunches beneath my branches. Her people are gone too and she often stops to visit on her lonely wanderings. She is known for her fierceness in defense of her cubs, but discernment is another of her strengths. She knows the magic of Silence and looks west toward the setting sun and shorter days. She rejuvenates herself in an earth den, and when she noses out, walks solid in her wisdom. I value her friendship. She helps when I grow impatient in my bond with earth, for even now Eagle remains in my nature—light-loving, soaring. Vision and moments of sparkling clarity are Eagle's strengths. Eagle looks east toward the rising sun and brighter, longer days. But now that my roots are entwined with the earth and the ashes and bones of my people, I reflect in silence during the long tree-sleeps and appreciate even more the meditative thoughtfulness of Bear.

"Have you ever wondered," Bear says, "whether the new people are different from your people?"

"You mean different in how they were made?"

"Yes."

"You called the council to make people. You should know."

"The new people came from far away. They could have been made at a different council. Horse and Cow would have been there, and other animals we didn't know. I have reflected upon this. We animals all wanted to make people in our own image. But we were all different, so Coyote tricked us and put a piece of each of us in Man. But if the new people were made by different animals, they would be different."

"I heard the music of that woman. I think we are the same."

We suddenly become aware of Coyote standing within earshot. He yips, "Maybe there is more to Man than you know."

O-se-mai-ti looks west, and we let the silence settle.

Mexico City, New Spain, 1774

Carefully barbered and powdered, Ensign Rafael Valdez arrived at the New Year's fiesta feeling lucky. The occasion presented a good opportunity to end a domestic problem, and considering that he wasn't directly involved with the principals, he had done well to wangle an invitation.

The viceroy had called the dinner to honor the famous explorer Captain Juan Bautista de Anza, the man Valdez needed to find. The dinner also celebrated the conclusion of a special council to address complaints by Junipero Serra, president of the Alta California missionaries, and had resulted in a new code of military conduct. It was adopted by the viceroy in time for the forthcoming emigration to a bay that some were already calling San Francisco. Captain de Anza would lead a company of soldier-pioneers and their families to that northern wilderness and establish a new presidio. Like the others, it would protect the missions from hostile Indians and provide internal policing for the missions, where thousands of natives would make their homes. Ensign Valdez hoped de Anza would enlist Pepe, his bastard son. However he hadn't yet seen the explorer in the pre-dinner crowd.

A forty-candle chandelier brightened the adobe hall and guitarists played lively Andalusian music. He steered his wife Consuela through the crowd of king's officers and their ladies who were working their careers and positioning themselves on the big floor tiles like so many chessmen. Valdez and his señora discretely joined a circle surrounding the most powerful man in New Spain, the host of the celebration.

Viceroy Bucareli's dark eyes peered from under a large blue tricorn and his cutaway jacket blazed with colorful insignia. In contrast, the governor of Alta California, with whom he was speaking, wore his dark blond braid unpowdered in the current French vogue. From what Valdez was hearing, the governor was expressing surprising ideas.

A handsome couple parted the circle. Doña Eulalia de Callis dazzled the eye in a blue satin frock embroidered with numerous pastel roses. It displayed nearly all of her bosom, which she presented with grand hauteur, and draped in loose pleats from her shoulders to a wide oval hoop. In the wake of this seeming apparition, the likes of which had rarely graced the shores of New Spain, eavesdroppers arrived by threes and fours.

"Doña Eulalia," exclaimed Viceroy Bucareli lifting her hand to his lips. "It is a privilege to have you in our midst." Everyone knew she had sailed from Spain to present her six-year-old son to his father for the first time, and would soon sail back. The viceroy nodded a greeting to her husband, the commander of Alta California military forces and the object of the complaints by Padre Junipero Serra.

"*Gracias*, Excellency," she lisped in patrician accents. "We didn't mean to interrupt. You were engaged in interesting conversation, something about civilizing the Indians."

"Nothing to bother a lady, I'm sure. Have you met don Felipe de Neve, Governor of Alta California?" In his introduction the viceroy mentioned Eulalia's connections to the court of King Carlos III and her grandfather's purchase of a strip of land from Madrid to the southern coast of Spain so the family could post guards along the route and travel more safely to their summer home. Valdez felt privileged to stand so near to this striking young woman of wealth and power.

Eulalia warmed to the fawning adoration all around. Her Castillian face with its somewhat vulpine nose would have delighted a portrait artist. Honey-colored curls bracketed her neck and touched her bare shoulders. Piled curls crowned her head, covered by a mantilla of white lace. Valdez saw that Consuela and the other women admired the cosmetic details. He knew they would feel suddenly out of date with their hair caught up under little cloth caps and their midsections whale-boned into heavy fabrics. No doubt every husband would be pressed to order new fabrics and patterns from Spain and France. However, more than bosom and hoops distanced Eulalia from those who crowded to hear her bon mots and tidbits about Spain.

The lady raised her nose, fixed her penetrating hazel eyes upon the viceroy, and lisped, "If I did not amuse myself with matters of the day, I should become even more weary of this utterly tiresome colony. Please continue with what you were saying about the savages." Wincing to hear his adopted land so described, Valdez reflected that the new viceroy, who had come to implement the royal order of 1772 to expand the conquest northward, probably shared her views. Doubtless the two would sail together back to Spain.

With a nod at Governor de Neve, the viceroy spoke in a tone of mocking disbelief. "Don Felipe here believes the natives in Alta California can be trusted with property and ought to be given the right to buy and sell goods. He would oust the Franciscans and make mission lands ordinary bishoprics. But there is little point in discussing it, now that accord has been reached by the council." As the King's representative, he had made the final decisions. His hooked nose and dark coloring suggested a trace of Arab blood, a circumstance that could not escape her ladyship. Surveying her from across the ruby pool of his wineglass, he continued in French, "Perhaps you are aware of the new regulations for Alta California?"

Eulalia's nostrils expanded as though she'd caught an interesting scent. "One can only admire how *long* such special councils draw out simple matters. As to the reforms, my husband is perfectly happy to send degenerate soldiers home for bad conduct, but if the military is to protect the missions from wild Indians, it must be allowed to locate the presidios."

Ensign Valdez marveled that she not only knew the details, but presented the opinions of Commander Fages without even glancing at him. Consuela would have died first. Captain Fages, however, appeared amused to have his wife spar with the dangerously powerful viceroy.

At that moment a voice boomed, "Well, if it isn't *Oso Viejo*, my old campfire *amigo*." A burly red-headed man elbowed through the crowd and clapped Commander Fages on the shoulders. "Pardon me, Excellency," he said, turning a contrite bow to the viceroy. "I am very honored to be part of the cause of this celebration. Honored more than I can say." He then lifted doña Eulalia's hand to his lips. Looking her up and down, he gave Fages a grin. "How did an ugly old bear like you attract such a lovely rose?"

Before anything could be said, Captain de Anza—clearly that's who he was—addressed the crowd in his frontier style. "Let me tell you how this worthy officer earned that name." He hiked a mischievous eyebrow at Fages. "It'll give you an idea what kind of man you're looking at. Mission San Luis Obispo had just started up, our farthest outpost at the time, north of Santa Barbara. So primitive a man could forget he was human. The Indians were half starved and sick in the mission. Some kind of trouble with the crops. The supply ships couldn't get through, as usual, and the holy fathers both had scurvy. They were about to let the Indians go back to their wilderness hovels to feed on bugs and snakes and whatever else they eat. Well, this old man here roared in with a handful of soldiers, took a good look around and rode for bear! He killed so many grizzly bears the Fathers could hardly believe it. He dragged them back and everyone feasted like kings." De Anza laughed his booming laugh and Ensign Valdez chuckled along with everyone else—except doña Eulalia. "Now the men in the ranks call him *El Oso*," de Anza continued, pounding Fages on the back, "I just came through there. They've named the place where he killed those bears *Los Osos*."

Flushed with pleasure, Commander Fages nodded.

Abruptly, de Anza turned to the viceroy and bowed, "Sorry to interrupt, Excellency. Again, I am honored." He vanished as quickly as he had arrived, and Valdez would have pursued him except for the unseemly impression it might have given.

Governor de Neve broke the silence. "I think the reforms will help, but they missed the point of the Council."

"Which was?" Eulalia demanded, obviously delighted to pick up where they had left off.

"We were deciding what kind of people we want the Indians to become," the governor said. "What kind of commonweal we are creating. Wasn't that the objective, Excellency?"

"That was certainly part of it."

The governor dipped his head. "Everyone agrees the objective is to transform the natives into useful citizens of Spain. But instead, I'm sorry to say, we're creating a stupid, docile population, the opposite of what we need. Look at Spain—the epitome of civilization, leading the world in education, economic philosophy, arts. . ."

"Of course, of course," Eulalia prodded impatiently.

De Neve shifted his weight, strong calves encased in white hose. "The Church should abandon all civil pursuits in Alta California and everywhere else. I disagree that priests are the only ones who can civilize Indians. On the contrary the missionaries will keep them in ignorance and poverty, unfit for enlightened citizenship. Governments should rule by councils of men pursuing a vibrant economy, as in Spain. Compare Spain's progress with the way it was when the Church controlled everything."

Boldly Eulalia parried, "It seems to be *de rigueur* for the young men of France and Britain to speak that philosophy. But it's quite naive, as anyone who has been in the north knows." Now she glanced at her husband, who had commanded its forces since the first mission, San Diego, was dedicated in Alta California five years earlier.

Eyes sparking in the brilliant candlelight, she continued, "The heathen are dull, ignorant, bestial, and appallingly barbarous. They lack any kind of organization or religion, except the worship of a wolf-like animal. They engage in behaviors about which no civilized person can speak." She barked a derisive laugh. "They prance about naked! Hardly to be compared with even the *lowest* elements of Europe."

"An opinion shared by most of the council," said the viceroy in a tone that signaled his wish to change the subject.

De Neve chose not to notice. "Unless we do much more than these little reforms, which only strengthen the Franciscans' control, the colony will remain an island of ignorance, belonging more to the sixteenth century than the eighteenth!" He added, "In actuality, the natives toil in serfdom. Slavery is perhaps a more apt description."

The viceroy glowered but the governor plowed on, "I know it is indelicate to say that, but it fits every definition I know. Yes, slavery is common in the world, but Spain ought to be moving forward, not stepping back to the Middle Ages." He looked at Eulalia's husband. "You have been the target of the friars more than I. Do you honestly think Indian alcaldes will have any real authority? Or will the padres control them like puppets?"

The reference to Captain Fages being a target of Junipero Serra subdued doña Eulalia not in the least. Color rose to the points of her cheeks and she looked as though she quite enjoyed conflict. "Don Pedro," she ordered her husband before he could respond, "Tell his Excellency if you think the California natives are ready to be citizens of Spain."

Valdez saw that she was using the occasion to contrast her husband's views against de Neve's unrealistic ideas. Intelligent, considering that the viceroy was the key to all their futures and Padre Serra was demanding that Fages be relieved of his command.

"Of course the Indians are not at all able," Fages began, "not by any means, to be citizens. I doubt they will ever be. Giving them alcaldes is a mistake. If those alcaldes are to be leaders, they will have followers." Clearing his throat, he made a soft roaring sound. "Can you imagine what would happen if the Indians united against us? We'd be outnumbered ten thousand to one." He leveled Bucareli a look. "They don't know how to organize now, and we shouldn't teach them. These new regulations mean that the military must be better equipped and increased in size. Mark my words, there will be trouble."

De Neve glanced briefly at the ceiling as though drawing strength. "All people are born with the ability to reason, including Indians. They want the same things we want, and their enlightened participation in the economy would lessen the hostilities. But they'll never be ready—nay, they'll be hostile—if we treat them as slaves and children. So would you and I be hostile if we were treated that way all our lives."

"Don Felipe," Viceroy Bucareli said, looking from the tops of his eyes, "we have been over this ground quite enough, and the weight of opinion is against you."

In front of so many people, especially Commander Fages, this would have landed like a musket ball. The governor brought his shiny heels together in a stiff bow. "I have been tiresome. Don and doña Fages, much happiness in the new year. Your Excellency, please extend my greetings to His Majesty." His braid hung motionless against his navy jacket as he walked away through the crowd.

Valdez felt excited to have witnessed that head-butting conflict between the losers of the council. The philosophies of both Fages and de Neve had succumbed to Padre Junipero Serra. Nevertheless, doña Eulalia would probably save her husband from losing position entirely. For such a wife, Valdez thought he would sell his soul.

Thirty minutes later the guests were seated and Padre Serra stood blessing the three long tables, the undyed habit of his order falling from his outspread arms. ". . . as Saint Peter brought light to the Ephesians, so we labor in the wilderness to light the childish minds and dark souls of the heathen, leading them from the sins of the world and the seduction of Evil to the discipline of the Church, where, as neophytes. . ."

The Indian servants knelt at the kitchen door with their foreheads on the floor. Ensign Valdez covertly regarded doña Eulalia de Callis, who, he was amused to see, glanced impatiently at the holy father from under her brows. Owing to the lack of place cards and a triumph of timing, he had secured a seat next to her while Captain de Anza was across the table within speaking range. Consuela sat across the table and down several more places.

"We ask Your blessing upon the brave pioneers who will soon depart for Alta California, that they. . ." A very small man in stature, Padre Serra had walked eight hundred miles from his mission on the Carmel River to present his opinions—a martyr's walk since he was infirm and could have ridden in a *carreta.* Everyone knew that most of the reforms, over forty in all, had flowed directly from his quill, virtually unchanged despite ardent discussion in the council. Among other things, he had accused Commander Fages of failure to discipline his soldiers for ravaging the native women. Padre Serra insisted that the missionaries needed the authority to have offenders deported. He succeeded by dint of his keen judgement, passionate nature and simple piety. On behalf of pious King Carlos, Viceroy Bucareli had approved nearly all of Serra's demands. Many officers now grumbled that the friars had seized control over the military and warned that it was a dangerous precedent for the Empire. But other officers said that if the cross ruled the sword, this was as it should be. Valdez didn't know which side was right.

Padre Serra concluded the *benedictus* and seated himself. Surveying the rich viands on the table, he took only a few spoonfuls of vinegared peppers and tomatoes.

"Captain de Anza," said Governor de Neve, inclining his head across the table toward that hearty explorer, "Will you be able to enlist enough men for the new presidio?" Valdez perked up. Under the reforms, married men with families were to be enlisted first, the purpose being to establish a settlement. But single men of good character were next in line, encouraged under the reforms to marry native women.

De Anza replied while helping himself to a steaming plate of diced goat, "We seem to have reached the end of the married volunteers."

"How many do you have now?"

"Nine wives. Twenty-eight children."

"In your opinion," the governor asked, "will those families stay in that inhospitable location?"

De Anza popped a fork-load of goat in his mouth, chewed thoughtfully and said, "It isn't always cold there. In fact during my last survey I found much of the larger area quite warm and fertile. In places it brings to mind the Garden of Eden." He threw back his head and chortled. "Who knows? They might find gold. Then everyone would want to go."

"That would help." De Neve smiled with him. "But I am glad this will not be a chase after a golden mirage like those that exhausted our treasury a century ago. You are to be commended for finding an overland route for the pioneers. The Devil himself blows the winds against our northbound ships. Spain is in your debt." He lifted his glass.

De Anza's rough face reddened with the compliment, and he began to entertain the table with stories of his recent explorations around that distant bay soon to be called San Francisco.

This competed with Ensign Valdez's desire to engage doña Eulalia in conversation on his right. "I visited family in Callis," he ventured, "just after I joined the Volunteer Light Infantry."

In a sharp tone she said, "I don't remember a Valdez in Callis."

"It was on my mother's side, Rubio."

She cut a brandied peach with her fork and slipped it between her rouged lips. In the pause Captain de Anza said, "You could shoot birds all day without taking a step."

"The Rubios related to the Zambraños?" Eulalia inquired.

"No, I don't think so." He knew perfectly well that those Rubios were several social rungs above his.

In a bored tone pitched more to others she said, "Apparently I don't know your family."

For some reason this felt like a gut hook in his innards. In need of fortification, Valdez reached for his glass of wine, which had been filled by the servant who plodded back and forth behind the row of chairs, but somehow the foot of the glass became entangled with the edge of his plate and catapulted to the front of Eulalia's bodice where it rolled down off her lap and shattered on the floor tiles.

Eulalia arched her back and sucked in her breath. In horror he watched the ruby stain spread through the blue satin and creep through the pastel roses, coloring them a muddy hue. He shook out his ruffled nosecloth and made as if to dab at the stain.

In a tone to break more glass, she said, "Don't touch me! Leave me alone. What is the matter with you!" The servant who had been reaching from behind with a towel withdrew his brown hand. In the profound silence of the table, the rush of blood to Valdez's face overwhelmed his wits and he sat in his chair like a dumb animal. Consuela gave him a stinging look. Only his need to talk to de Anza kept him from bolting for the door

The explorer ended the silence, awkwardly beginning a story about grizzly bears feeding on a beached whale. Stain blazing, Eulalia grimly turned her chair toward the man on her right. By the time de Anza's story ended, the heat had somewhat left Valdez's face, but not his ears.

"Captain," he said, "Are you signing up single men now?"

"I have enlisted a few. Why? Do you know someone?"

He lowered his voice. "My son." He mentioned his indiscretion with an *India*—actually a dalliance of over ten years, though he didn't say that. He added that he had established a new household and needed to distance the boy from it.

"How old is he?" de Anza asked.

"Fourteen." Pepe was thirteen, but Valdez imagined de Anza would prefer him a little older.

De Anza said age was no barrier. "A boy on horseback with a musket, armor and sword can take down a hundred Indians on foot with bows and arrows. But does he have enthusiasm for life on a wild frontier?"

Although not sure about that, Valdez pushed toward his goal. "He would love it."

"I'm sure you know that under the new regulations I can take only well-behaved recruits with vouchers of good character."

Valdez assured him Pepe was obedient and would have the vouchers.

"Send him to the presidio in Sonora. We'll leave from there. With luck, the journey should take about six months."

Dedication of San Francisco Presidio, Summer, 1776

A year and a half later, on a foggy bluff above the mouth of San Francisco Bay, twelve soldiers stood in formation. Homesick for his mother and the sunshine of New Spain, fourteen-year-old Pepe Valdez shivered among them. It had been a long journey filled with hardship and delay. They had camped for months at Mission San Gabriel while Captain de Anza took most of the soldiers to San Diego to help quell a violent uprising and conduct an inquisition into its causes. While they were gone, several men deserted with livestock. Pepe and others who had been assigned to guard the company were interrogated when the captain returned, but were absolved of guilt. The number of soldiers had shrunk, ten having been reassigned to San Diego Company. Another delay occurred in Monterey. El Oso's replacement was there, irate because the entire company didn't report to San Diego. De Anza exchanged angry words with him, then resigned his commission. He took several more soldiers on his return trip to Sonora. Pepe had wanted to go back too, but José Moraga, who now led the company, insisted he complete the last lap of the journey. Now only twelve soldiers remained. They had camped for a month waiting for the *San Carlos* to arrive with the artillery and other supplies, and find the best anchorage. Only then could Moraga pick the site for the presidio. Construction began with the help of the ship's crew and many curious Indians.

Now, a padre spoke about the significance of dedicating the new settlement to San Francisco de Asís, Guardian of Travelers. Moraga orated about the need to defend the bay against Russians and other intruders. Wind-driven fog was blowing from the ocean and Pepe tried to stop shivering. The wives and children of the five married soldiers huddled together, pulling at their shawls and rubbing their arms. The four priests—two from the Carmel mission, two assigned to this area—appeared to be warm in their woolen habits. The crew of the *San Carlos* stood at ease. Even the Indians, despite their nakedness, showed no sign of the cold. They appeared in awe of everything, including the crude mud-and-wattle buildings roofed with tulares—a tiny chapel, a three-sided garrison with compartments for families, a dwelling for the commander, and a storeroom for the guns, powder, artillery and cannonballs.

Moraga was ending on a high note, listing the benefits to be bestowed upon the natives—the arts of working in a civilized world and the salvation of their souls. He concluded, "This is an historic moment in the annals of the Spanish Empire."

The cannon boomed and swivel-guns fired. The terror-stricken Indians vanished into the fog. Only months later were they located and coaxed back to help build the first northern mission, also dedicated to Saint Francis. Thus commenced the northernmost conquest of the Spanish Empire in the New World.

I

Tracks To Another World

1

Between the Cosumnes and American Rivers

Badger Warrior heard his heart thudding. He felt almost as though he must uphold the honor of the umne all by himself. His excitement intensified when at last one of the enemy warriors stepped out of line and walked forward. He stopped within bowshot of the home warriors. Unlike his fellows, he wore no breastplate of oak branchlets and his hands were empty. He was young and strong and the muscles of his buttocks rippled as he crouched slightly forward, hands loose, eyes intent upon his headman.

The twenty home warriors positioned their arrows and aimed at the lone man, waiting for the signal from the enemy hy-apo. Badger Warrior could hardly believe he was witnessing a real war. Most people lived a lifetime without seeing one. Only Frogs-Eggs-Hatching, the most ancient person in the village, had seen a war, and he had been a young boy.

The enemy hy-apo raised a hand and the home men let fly. Arrows swarmed like hornets toward the enemy champion, some higher, some lower, some released a little later. Why didn't they shoot together, so they could kill him and win faster? That hadn't been explained in all the brave talk of the last ten sleeps. Badger Warrior began to realize that some of the rules of war were unspoken, just like some of the rules of living. No wonder wars lasted all day and people said stamina was the most important attribute of an arrow-dodger. This one jumped, twisted and ducked low, wiggling from side to side almost faster than the eye could see. He dodged all the arrows that hummed over the grass. Badger Warrior didn't know his mouth hung open. From his earliest memories he had practiced dodging the grass arrows of his friends, shot from toy bows. As they grew older the boys made real bows of willow and used arrows without points. He was now the best dodger among them, but realized how much he had to learn. Someday, he hoped, he would become the champion of the umne. Maybe then there would be another war and he could display his skill.

"Scared, little boy?" Nettles shouted.

"See how real men shoot," shouted another woman.

"The next one will get you," Badger Warrior yelled, joining in. Such taunts were part of war. Since the *pul*, the knotted string, had arrived announcing that the war would be held after ten sleeps, little else had been discussed.

"Wetting yourself yet?" Frogs-Eggs-Hatching shouted. That made the women titter and the children explode with laughter.

The last arrow was ducked and Badger Warrior raced with the other children across the grass and past the line of enemy warriors to retrieve the arrows. He was wary of the points, which had been dipped in deer liver saturated with rattlesnake venom. The doctors had captured many snakes and tricked them into biting the liver. Now, anxious for their side to shoot, some of the enemy children silently pointed at fallen arrows. Pretty Duck's chubby toddler ran in her awkward way back through the enemy line shouting, "Mamma, Mamma, look! I found one." Badger Warrior returned with an armload, proudly distributing the arrows, each marked with its owner's special dots and circles.

When the quivers were reloaded, Blue Snake stepped forward—the fastest runner, best ti-kel player and best arrow dodger among the umne. About to burst with excitement Badger Warrior stood back with the other children. Blue Snake had so much power he seemed to walk on air. Badger Warrior admired him above all other men. Now, about fifty paces from the drawn bows of the enemy, Blue Snake waited. It was almost more than Badger Warrior could bear.

At Morning Owl's signal, the enemy arrows hummed. Blue Snake floated like a heron—bounding, landing, bounding and landing, wings half out for balance. He was dancing! Blue Snake was a human wonder, so perfect a man that surely not even Coyote could have envisioned such balance and agility.

Many times the two dodgers took turns and the children of alternating sides retrieved the arrows. Shadows were coming from the west when red color suddenly sprang from Blue Snake's forearm. He had been nicked! He was visibly losing his power! Badger Warrior felt his stomach sink. Then an arrow pierced the stem of Blue Snake's topknot, the tightly bound column of hair that flounced over his head and normally looked so fashionable. The arrow stayed there. Enemy women and children pointed and jeered. Now this man of speeding legs and beautiful moves turned and ran. He ran full tilt though the arrows had stopped. He was running toward the home place with the arrow still in his topknot, and Badger Warrior suddenly saw him as he looked to the howling enemy—comical.

Crushing disappointment pushed tears from Badger Warrior's eyes. The shouts of the jubilant Kadeema-umne stabbed his ears. They had won the war. The shoulders of the home men slackened as they watched their champion vanish over the hill. A hand came down on Badger Warrior's shoulder and he glanced up to see his mother. "It's over," she said in her reasonable tone. "The quarrel has ended. It doesn't matter very much who won."

"Yes it does!" he all but shouted. Hadn't she helped weave the oak breastplates so the home warriors would look right? Didn't she see the care with which the arrow shafts were straightened and sanded with sacayak? Hadn't every last man, woman and child of the umne danced the War Dance, Wo-ke-lah, and beseeched their individual spirits to help them win? Why was she suddenly talking like this? He turned to his friends and found comfort in their wet eyes and crimped lips. In silent disgrace they trudged toward the home place, pushed, it seemed, by the jeers and taunts of the winners. They knew the enemy children would be running for firewood and the Kadeema-umne would dance and celebrate on the field of battle. For Badger Warrior it was a kind of death.

He could not eat his supper that night. To see his own mother applying drawing herbs to Blue Snake's wound somehow shamed him more, and he noticed that though she was doing it in the village center, no one watched. He thought maybe Blue Snake ought to die.

The next morning Blue Snake was gone. "His shame drove him away," people said. Trackers went out but never found him. His family wept because, as everyone knew, a man couldn't live alone. The young woman in the up-stream village, to whom he was half married, had witnessed his disgrace. She wept openly and her parents took her home.

A council was held to decide how many bows and baskets and blankets to ask for Blue Snake's life. Eagle Woman, being a doctor, played an important part in the joint council with the Kadeema-umne. After the first day she told Badger Warrior that the Kadeema-umne had rejected the demands. They claimed they had not taken Blue Snake's life. They said they owed the umne for only a piece of his arm and it was not their fault he ran away. Councils continued for several moons before the two hy-apos settled on reparations. The in-laws whose quarrels had provoked the war disliked the settlement, but the two peoples learned to speak to each other again, and after several seasons passed, most acted like the war had never happened.

But Badger Warrior never forgot. It changed his dreams, for he began to see the master hunter, not Blue Snake, as the man he wanted to be like. That is, if he ever became a man. Everything depended upon that.

2

Two Falcons, the master hunter, slit the belly of the buck and the entrails spilled into the waiting baskets. The women divided the steamy loops and cut them with sharp stone knives, hands black with the oozing matter.

"Boys stand back." It was Morning Owl, the hy-apo, motioning to Badger Warrior.

The other boys were already standing back. He had been singled out! A dry lump hurt his throat as he hid behind the women, shamed. Now he could hardly see the cuts. Many times he had seen a deer butchered, but each time he learned something new. Now all he saw was the distribution of the heart, liver and stomach. Then came the lung bags, bladder bag, antlers, small sinews and globs of precious fat. Each gift signified a debt paid or a promise of friendship. His mother accepted the forelegs and hooves, to make dance rattles.

He moved to a place where he could see the skillful, rhythmic cuts as Two Falcons removed the hide. Then the master hunter folded the hide and placed it on his outstretched forearms, presenting it ceremoniously to Morning Owl. Morning Owl accepted the hide with his usual look of pleasant surprise, though it was normal to offer it first to the hy-apo.

Next, Two Falcons took a hind leg and teased out the prized long sinew used for bowstrings. He presented it to Running Quail, who had helped bring in the buck. Then he sat back on his heels and watched the women butcher the animal for the family baskets, all but his own wife. Tonight the master hunter's family would have no meat. On another day she would accept meat from other hunters, in payment for favors done for them.

"The son of the singing doctor," said the master hunter, causing Badger Warrior to jump in his skin, "will hunt with me next time." He smiled at Badger Warrior.

Excitement flashed through him and he looked at Two Falcons for too long before remembering one didn't do that. He glanced at his mother and saw her pleasure that he had been honored. Lame Beaver, Bowstring, Oak Gall and Falls-off-House smiled too, but Sick Rat, the master hunter's son, gave him a flat stare and walked away.

Sick Rat hated his nickname and blamed Badger Warrior for it. The bad feelings had started a long time ago, when the boy had come running into the village proudly holding a rat by the tail. The kill was skinny and mangy. "It's a sick rat," Badger Warrior had said. The other boys laughed and the name stuck. Others had funny names too, but only Sick Rat resented his. Now Badger Warrior wished he had kept quiet. Once he had thought he should withdraw from the master hunter's attentions, but couldn't make himself do it. Maybe if Sick Rat would welcome his father's teaching, he too would be invited on a hunt.

Now Badger Warrior vowed silently to be worthy of the master hunter's teaching. This was the father he never had. Two Falcons had helped him get over Blue Snake's disgrace, telling him that war occurred very seldom and it would be better to learn more useful skills. Tracking was a prized skill, and now more than anything Badger Warrior wanted to become a tracker as great as Stalking Cougar, the father of Two Falcons. Men said old Stalking Cougar—long since gone to the spirit land—had been as tricky as Coyote himself and could approach any animal without its knowledge. Badger Warrior hungered to learn every trick and it honored him that Two Falcons seemed eager to teach him.

Just three sleeps ago Badger Warrior had asked, "How do you know striped woodpeckers will back down the tree and put their feet in the snares?"

The big man's voice had come low, interested. "To hunt anything you must understand its ways. Striped woodpeckers jump backwards down trees. So if you make many little loops, tying them on a cord like this"—he plucked several long hairs from his head, spun them against his thigh, made a loop and fastened the tiny slip-knot to the milkweed fiber spiraled around the tree trunk—"soon you will have a woodpecker by the foot." He smiled up from patient, hooded eyelids.

"But why do they jump backwards down the trees?"

Two Falcons gave him a teasing look, the same as when he'd named him Badger Warrior.

His face grew hot. People thought him overeager and too persistent. He tried not to be, though he didn't think the master hunter considered those traits entirely bad. He felt some shame about what people thought of him, yet was proud of his name because Two Falcons had given it to him. It was a name that could be spoken aloud, unlike his private name. The nickname reminded him every day that the master hunter treated him as a father would. It made him feel like other boys, but didn't stop his worry about becoming a man.

In the evening the supper fire snapped in the twilight and he sat against the rough bark of the u-macha hearing the murmur of talk at other fires. Howchia was cutting venison on a flat rock between her knees, her singed hair moving against her shoulders and eyebrows. He saw dignity and power in her posture and the set of her chin. Some people feared her because she was the singing doctor, though they feared Drum-in-Fog's magic more. Badger Warrior was proud of her, but a woman wasn't supposed to live in her home village. That wasn't proper. Only men lived in the places of their childhood, and that created the problem.

Most of the boys didn't seem to care who Badger Warrior's father had been, but he cared very much, for to become a man, he must be invited into the sweathouse. All the men of the umne were related through their fathers. He didn't know whether the home men would invite him. He didn't know whether an outsider had ever been accepted. He didn't even know whether he was an outsider, and couldn't ask the men for fear of drawing attention to his intensely private problem.

Quietly, so as not to be heard by people at the other fires, he asked Mother, "Will they invite me into the sweathouse?" If not, his life would be ruined. Even the best tracker in the world couldn't hunt without purifying himself in the sweathouse.

"You will become a man," Mother said, not looking up from the venison. It was the same each time he asked. He knew better than expect her to explain. A mother more like Bowstring's would make things easier, he thought, a mother more like a friend and less like a doctor.

Grandmother Dishi tottered hesitantly down the path toward them. Staring ahead, she stopped, turned toward the u-macha, raised her arms, took three steps, felt the wood and touched her way around the conical structure, plank by upright plank to where he sat. She poked and prodded him with her hard fingers, assuring herself he was the right person, then sat beside him. She stared at nothing, the skin of her face and body hanging in soft brown folds. The gaps in his family, he realized, had begun with her.

He leaned back on the dirt berm around the base of the house where the planks were planted, waiting for supper, and absently gazed at the other nine u-machas pointing at the sky. He couldn't ask Grandmother about this because she never spoke to people. His mother might have known something about Grandfather Crying Fox, but doctors were very careful to avoid speaking of the dead, as he must be. He couldn't ask. Nor could he ask about his own father's death.

Like him, Howchia had grown up without a father. That was the reason she hadn't married well. A father would have hunted and brought home nice things. Such a family might have attracted a suitor whose family tended good seed meadows and fished good holes, one who had learned to hunt from a skilled father. But Howchia had married a man who gambled too much and didn't care for his tools. As was proper, she had gone to live with him in his home place, but soon after Badger Warrior was born, his father had been killed by demons. Howchia returned from visiting upstream neighbors to find her man dead and his people gone, all but Eats Skunk, a distant uncle of her dead husband. She disliked him and refused to marry him, as might have been expected. Instead she brought her baby to her old home place and learned to be a singing doctor, thus not needing a man. So here he sat, a boy with no father and no real umne. But a boy needed paternal relatives like his very bones, and in his stomach he felt crippled, different from his friends, though he never let them see it.

Nudged by a basket, he looked up into Mother's smile and accepted the steaming nu-pah. The mush looked deliciously lumpy. Had she added grasshoppers? He scooped it up with three curved fingers and smashed a crunchy lump between his teeth. Yes! Roasted grasshoppers. Taking three more big scoops, he handed the basket to Grandmother, who lowered her chin and scooped hungrily.

Howchia added a red-hot cooking stone to the other cooking basket and stirred to keep the basket from burning. Almost immediately the venison stew bubbled.

"What did the demons look like, the ones that killed my father?" he asked Mother.

In a tone he knew all too well she said, "We do not speak of that."

"I speak of the demons, not the dead," he clarified, adding, "The demons might come here."

"No." She looked around to be sure no one else had heard. "Eagle told me in a dream. But son, the umne do not wish to hear more about this."

Badger Warrior trotted up the eastern hill where he had discovered an ongoing battle between ants and bees. "We learn from all creatures," Two Falcons had told him. Relentlessly the red ants marched toward the bee tree, never stopping and never changing course despite the swarming bees. Some ants made it all the way into the nest. Some came down the tree with amber drops in their mandibles, but he could tell they weren't fighting for a dab of stolen honey. They wanted the whole nest.

The bees were brave and so were the ants, their determined lines never slowing despite the diving bees. Ants and bees grappled in the dust, enemies armed at opposite ends—ants twisting to get their mandibles into the bees while the bees struggled to maneuver their big stingers into the thin, writhing ants. The oily stench of ant death clung to the air. Bees with multiple ants attached to their legs waded in the dust, too weak to fly. Every so often a bee emerged from the nest and dropped a dead bee. A heap of these bright yellow and black bodies lay at the foot of the pine. The pile was large and growing.

One morning he was about to go to the tree again when Two Falcons came from the sweathouse with his bow. Excitement flashed through Badger Warrior. For two sleeps he had heard the master hunter's muffled spirit-singing, and now he was ready to hunt deer. Badger Warrior would go with him. He could hardly contain his joy as he ran to the u-macha for amole root, then jumped into the river to purify himself. He scrubbed his scalp and underarms and all the parts that would smell, never mind that he wouldn't be able to use his bow—he hadn't been in the sweathouse. Still, he flew after Two Falcons too happy to feel the path beneath his feet.

Two Falcons carried the hollowed-out head and neck of a buck. An obsidian knife was tucked in his calf-thong and a small basket hung from his waist-thong. Trotting beside him, Badger Warrior glanced up at the big man. Would he remember?

The man's wide, straight lips pulled back in a little smile. Badger Warrior suppressed the urge to bound joyfully ahead, for deer hunting was a spiritual occasion. He tried to act like a man. Up the Omuchumne path they went to an ancient oxbow of the river. No deer were in sight, though in this season they often grazed near the little creek in the bottomland where even in the long dry, the grass retained some green. Two Falcons pointed at the ground. Badger Warrior had no need to be shown. The tracks headed north. He followed the hunter, slowing when he slowed, then, at Two Falcons's nod, crouched behind a tree.

Five does, several yearlings and three young bucks looked up, but after a time put their noses back in the grass. The fawns had lost their spots. Soon it would be rutting time. He could tell that these bucks hoped to befriend the does without their notice. Sometimes boys did that to girls.

"When you hunt deer," Two Falcons whispered, pulling the decoy over his head, "learn from the deer." The last words came muted from inside the decoy's throat. Black eyes sparkled through the parted deer mouth.

He watched Two Falcons approach the herd in bent posture. The bow in his hand dragged as he jerked his head forward and back exactly like a walking buck, his antlers turning this way and that. Often he pretended to graze and when he passed over a little rise that obscured his legs, Badger Warrior could no longer tell which one he was. A buck jerked and staggered and fell to its knees, then flopped on its side in the grass. One doe looked up then went back to grazing. None of the others seemed to notice.

Two Falcons stood up—the herd bounding away—took off the decoy head and beckoned Badger Warrior. The arrow was deep in the eye socket. The animal's spirit had not yet left, for the legs moved. As Badger Warrior stood in awe, Two Falcons drew out the arrow and went to the river. A short time later he returned with his small basket filled. He knelt beside the buck, tenderly lifted its head and poured water into its open mouth. Then he looked at the sky and sang in mystical tones:

Go deer.
Good journey, spirit deer.
Go and we thank you.

Two Falcons nodded to Badger Warrior and said casually, "You take the hind end."

His stomach expanded with pride as he struggled to balance the heavy animal on his head and keep his feet under him. With his nose in the stale urine-smelling underbelly, he walked behind the master hunter. Back in the village they lowered the kill. Never had he felt this proud.

Oak Gall brushed him with her glance. Behind her lash-veiled eyes he saw her new respect for him, and couldn't stop his lips from stretching in a smile. Bowstring, Lame Beaver and Falls-off-House looked at him with something new in their expressions. Exhilaration nearly lifted him from the earth and it didn't matter that Sick Rat ignored him. A little of the reverent aura of the hunt extended to him. Maybe now the men of the umne would invite him to the sweathouse.

Too happy to sit waiting for supper, he trotted up the east hill to the bee tree. Surprised, he examined the long furrows tamped by the ants' tiny feet, but the ants themselves were gone. He looked up thinking they had taken over the nest. A bee buzzed past him and landed in the entrance. Another emerged from inside and they talked with their feelers. The bees had held their home place! The ants had gone. He looked at the heap of dead bees and saw that it was covered with live bees walking and spitting all over their dead. Why were they doing that?

At supper time he went to Two Falcons's fire, squatted, and politely dipped his curved fingers into the nu-pah offered by the master hunter's wife. He told what he had seen, and asked, "What are the bees doing?"

"Covering their dead with a special coating."

"Why?"

Two Falcons nibbled a duck wing. "To stop the smell of their dead from passing. In this way they fool bears who search for weakened nests."

"They are clever," Badger Warrior said. Sick Rat ate quietly.

The master hunter nodded. "How long do you think the bees will be preserved?"

"Preserved?"

"How long before the dead bees decay?"

Sick Rat said, "They'll be gone by second grass."

Badger Warrior knew that wasn't long enough. "The next second grass?"

"Longer. Much longer," the hunter said. "Your children will see those bees under that coating, maybe your grandchildren."

Children! The joy ripping through him was not for the bees. Two Falcons expected him to have children. But only a man could become a father.

First grass sprouted in the time of rain, then second grass flourished in the lengthening suns. All grass withered in the long hot dry, then first grass came again. Badger Warrior grew taller. He hoped his calves were thickening too, for that was the part of a man most admired by women. One day it occurred to him that Two Falcons was teaching him less. Had he already learned all that the master hunter had to teach? He kept this question to himself. Besides, one hunting technique eluded him: spirit tracking.

"Spirit tracking is a gift," Two Falcons had explained. "It cannot be taught." He told of an old hunter who found a wounded man by *seeing* his location before looking for sign. "Drum-in-Fog can tell you more."

But the doctor, who understood magic better than anyone else, didn't like to talk. No one wanted to get on his wrong side, least of all Badger Warrior, so he didn't persist.

It was in the time of long nights and rain when a family of bears came in dream to Badger Warrior. They were having a good time dancing in the rain. Even the big male was there, the Old Man of the Forest, who was not normally seen with O-se-mai-ti when she had cubs. The Old Man looked at Badger Warrior kindly and the gaze warmed him, yet it also challenged and invited him. Badger Warrior walked toward the big bear. The eye drew him. He reached out, but before he could sink his hand into the thick fur he woke up.

In the profound dark he smelled the slightly damp earthen floor, the clean grass mat under him, the pungent medicine herbs hanging from the cordage strung across the inclined planks of the house and the comforting scent of his rabbit-skin blanket. He heard Dishi's snoring and his mother's even breathing, but mostly he felt the inviting gaze of the bear. He knew what it meant. He would do what few grown men had done. He would touch a living grizzly bear and take a piece of its spirit, as Stalking Cougar had done. Then the powerful O-se-mai-ti might become his spirit ally as well as his lineage ancestor, and even if he never became a man, the feat would distinguish him.

3

He waited until clover time, when the rains had ceased. He waited until mother moon would look down with full luminous light. After his morning swim he netted three fat ducks to fill his mother's cooking basket during his absence, and now he was ready to stalk the most feared and powerful of earth's creatures. It was bad luck to upset the local bears, so he would go east into the chaparral of the higher foothills of the eastern mountains—the home of many bears. He would leave his bow.

In the dim early light from the doorway Mother watched him tie a thong around his calf. "Take my obsidian knife with you, and some dried salmon," she said

He touched her forearm, appreciating that she respected his tracking ability and didn't try to stop him. However he suspected that part of her would go with him. He inserted her knife—payment for locating Lame Beaver's illness—into his calf-thong and pulled strips of dried salmon from the overhead cord, inserting them under his waist-thong.

He waded into the river swollen with snowmelt from the eastern mountains, then swam fast to the other side. The current swept him a little downstream, but when he climbed the opposite bank and looked back he could see Oak Gall approaching the bathing place. He always saw her first among people. He liked the way she settled into her steps. She was a woman now, in receipt of gifts from men, and that disturbed him, so he forced it from his mind as he trotted up the river trail. A tracker needed his calm.

Secretly he hoped to do more than touch a living grizzly; he wanted to take some of its hair. Even Stalking Cougar had not done that. It would test all he had learned, for the big bear was sensitive, nimble as a man and faster than a deer.

Father sun shown brightly as Badger Warrior walked on a deer trail through high green grass interspersed by masses of purple larkspur and golden poppies. The trail widened to a human path and led to the village of Yamlocklock's people who, three moons ago, had attended a big time at the home place. Here the river rested after its thrashing in the rocky canyon to the east. People stood watching his approach and dogs barked toward him. As the herald announced him, men came to greet him.

"Wu-meh? Where do you come from?" asked the headman, stepping forward, "and where are you going?"

"I come from Morning Owl's people," said Badger Warrior." I seek O-se-mai-ti in the hills."

The men looked at his lack of a bow, which everyone knew wouldn't kill a bear anyway, and his knife. "You are a brave boy," Yamlocklock said with raised brows, exchanging a quizzical and slightly amused expression with several of his people.

Anxious to be on his way and not drain his power by talking, he stayed only long enough to eat from the nu-pah basket offered by the hy-apo's wife. Then he headed east into the oak-studded hills. By the time the sun was low, he had left the home oaks behind. Black oaks were leafing out in pale halos. Swaths of pinkish manzanita bloom streaked the hillsides and a pine with darker needles and a spirit more direct than the gray pines of home grew in dense stands. Here bears roamed in large numbers.

It was after sundown. Colors deepened and the river baby spirit thrummed a splashier song. He followed it until he came to a place where another stream joined the river. There a grassy little meadow presented itself as a sleeping place. He knelt and scooped up ice-cold water, picked tangy watercress, then walked around to find a power spot, stopping here and there to feel the effect of the different places. A boy planning to steal hair from a grizzly bear needed as much power as he could glean from the earth. He knew his spot by the pull on his bones. It encouraged him to lie down. Settled into the accumulated needlefall against a pine, munching salmon strips and watercress, he looked up to find the mountain oriole that sang so well. It stood on a branch above him, thrusting out its yellow breast and trilling so hard it leaned forward on its toes.

"I know how you feel, little brother," he said.

The bird turned a curious eye down upon him, then resumed singing until the last of the twilight, when it flew to its nest. Still not ready to sleep, Badger Warrior sang too—songs of his people, some haunting, one that tripped high and low. Now the plant and animal people would know him and be friendlier. His newly lowered man's voice filled the place until mother moon floated into view and gave the world her peaceful light.

It was dark when he awoke from a dream. People had been walking across the sky. They never looked back and never spoke to one another—men and women in their prime, children and old people, all shuffling like sleepwalkers. They came in a steady stream from a place he couldn't see. It seemed he had been dreaming this all night, but no matter how many people crossed to the other side, they were replaced by new people and the sky trail was constantly crowded.

Moon had gone to her western house and the only light came from the milky pathway of ghosts across the sky. The number of people in the dream puzzled him. The most that had ever come to a big time was about five twenties, but many times that number had walked in his dream. What was the meaning of it? He searched his mind for all that Drum-in-Fog had told him, but couldn't understand the message his power place had given him. Then, turning over and over on the pine needles, he tried to forget the dream and go to sleep. He suddenly imagined the maw of a grizzly bear closing over his skull. Quickly he pushed away the bad-luck thought. Still, he couldn't sleep until the gray light of morning snuffed out the pathway of ghosts.

He was bathing when the fiery rim of the sun blazed across the eastern hill. Studying the ground for tracks, he began his search like a lost ant, circling in wider and wider arcs. He had no plan, except to follow a bear when he found sign. Whatever would happen would happen.

Father sun restored his high enthusiasm for the challenge ahead. In a short time he found the tracks of several mountain sheep. Normally he would have followed them to watch their nimble leaps from boulder to boulder. But not today. Circling wider, he climbed the steep canyon and moved through rough manzanita country. Bear scat lay everywhere. Deeply tamped bear paths crisscrossed the chaparral. It was tempting to follow a path, but he wanted no surprise encounter. He was looking for a single bear. At midday, crossing a gentle dip and a stream, he saw a track—twice the size of a man's foot and much the same shape, made about seven sleeps ago. The depth of the track in the damp ground told him the bear weighed as much as six big men.

He set off at a run following a trail of overturned rocks, plowed rodent burrows, slashed trees, and crushed manzanita. Before the sun reached his peak, he had followed O-se-mai-ti through an entire day of the bear's life. He stopped to study a place where the tracks doubled back on those of other grizzlies.

Not wanting to meet a mother bear, he moved away from the place of many tracks and finally found the tracks of the solitary animal again, fresher by several days. He was now where the bear had been that very morning.

He sat down to rest on a fallen tree, restored his calm, then began a fast stalk, circling to get downwind and testing the ground with the outsides of his feet before committing his weight. He must not snap twigs and alert the heralds of the forest—jays and squirrels. Two Falcons had taught him to use the hunting skills of other animals. He scanned the countryside with the wide, unfocused vision of animals whose eyes look from the sides of their heads and he used his flat human ears to pick up scattered sounds. But when he saw the flicker of something that might be a bear, he switched to sharp human vision and cupped his ears like a deer's.

Near the crest of a hill he lowered himself to his belly and slithered like a snake over fresh tracks. He heard snuffling and smelled the bear's scent on the incoming breeze. Creeping to the top, he saw the huge hind end a stone's throw away. The bear was digging in an ant hill. The reddish, silver-frosted fur was luxuriant. The testicles hung from the belly in separate pouches a hand's width apart.

The area was too open. He would follow the Old Man until he saw a better opportunity, for this bear could swat his head off with a single blow. The sharp curved foreclaws of a large grizzly—eight of which Morning Owl wore around his neck—were twice the length of Badger Warrior's first finger.

The bear ambled eastward and the breeze held. Feeling lucky, Badger Warrior stalked the bear to the river, where the animal scooped up a fish and clowned, rolling slowly in a backwater with his feet in the air. He enjoyed the river like a man. Badger Warrior smiled. Grizzly bears had no need to hide. They feared no other animal. All animals including humans gave them a wide berth. In rare instances when men hunted a grizzly bear, a team planned the hunt in advance and was led by a bear-hunter trained in special tricks.

From a distance Badger Warrior saw the bear stand on his hind feet against a pine. He took a bite of the bark and peeled it as he slid down the trunk to all fours. Passing the tree Badger Warrior saw the oozing scar two heads higher than his own. Farther along, the bear slammed and felled a dying tree to pick out termites. Eight men couldn't have done it.

Badger Warrior's chance came as the sun dropped. In a circle of pines and oaks undergrown with manzanita, the bear curled up to nap. As the shadows lengthened Badger Warrior waited patiently for sleep to fully overcome the giant. Then, knife between teeth, he snaked over sharp rocks and shrubs, ignoring the scratches. If the bear heard a sound, Badger Warrior would still himself while the bear searched above the ground. Only when he reached the manzanita—two arm-lengths from the bear's rump—did he rise to a squat from which he could spring and run. The bush was sparse and easy to see through. In his excitement he nearly forgot to breathe and when he did, the air was redolent with the sweetish odor of fur.

He took a squat-step around the manzanita, closing the gap between himself and the most powerful creature on earth. A grizzly's nose and ears were exceptionally keen. The giant grunted. To Badger Warrior's sensitive ears it sounded like a roar and nearly knocked him off balance. But a tracker maintained his calm. The animal didn't move, but the noise was a warning; he must act quickly.

He took the last squat-step. Now he was an arm's length away from a mountain of brown hair rising and falling in easy rhythm. He placed his left palm on the tips of the fur, applying no more pressure than a dragonfly. Absorbing the animal's power, he pressed slowly and gently until the fur surrounded his fingers. The hair felt coarse and soft at the same time.

He took one last squatting step and slowly closed his fist over a handful of fur. With his other hand he took the knife from his teeth. Holding the hair secure, he passed the blade over his fist. But the hair was tough and somewhat matted. It moved away from the blade.

He considered. The touch was coup enough, but he had come for the hair. Stone-still, heart pounding in his temples, he tried again. After what seemed an eternity of delicate cutting, almost hair by hair, he had what he wanted. It contained so much power it burned hot in his hand.

The mountain erupted to life. The bear emitted a loud coughing bark. It stopped his heart. He squat-jumped back behind the manzanita, gripping the knife. The bear rolled toward him, paws in the air. *Why am I behind a see-through bush? Why not running?* Had panic stopped him? He watched in horror, realizing that no matter where he stabbed the bear, the animal would kill him.

Successive thuds shook Badger Warrior's bones as the bear's legs, belly and head cascaded to a rolling stop, the reek of the nostrils blowing into Badger Warrior's face. He held the knife at the ready, but the mountain of fur settled and became still, snout resting on a paw like a huge dog, the dark slits of the eyes positioned to see Badger Warrior the instant they opened.

Had he run, the sound would have brought the bear into angry pursuit.

With his heart kicking in his ribs he slithered away as he had come, like a snake, one scale at a time. He looked back as often as forward, but felt growing elation to have avoided the mistake of most animals, who revealed their positions by running prematurely. Maybe he had absorbed enough power from the touch that he *saw* the bear's spirit. Maybe his own spirit had known the bear was only turning over in his sleep. He widened the distance, crouching, then straightened to a walk.

When he felt safe he exploded into a joyful run. With the knife in his calf-thong and the fistful of hair in his hand, he leaped over rocks, zig-zagged around trees and jumped from the tops of boulders, tearing downhill. He wouldn't step on a rattlesnake. He was lucky. He had succeeded beyond his dreams. The most powerful of all animals was his spirit ally! He could feel it in his stomach.

He came to a place where nothing obscured his view. Spread before him as far as he could see, north and south, was the great Valley of the Sun. The western mountains looked black in the distance with the fiery orb of father sun hanging over them. As he stood gasping for breath, sun showered a red haze down on the grasslands. Or was the verdant earth reaching toward the life-giver, pulling some of the sun's power back to itself? While he rested he too absorbed more power.

Then he resumed running. Moon rose above him and traveled across the sky, but he stopped only when he reached his lucky spot from the previous night and settled beneath the tree.

He bathed at sunrise, ate watercress, blooming clover and the last of his salmon, then ran downhill and west. The Yamlocklock-umne greeted him as before, and he couldn't not tell them what he had done. He enjoyed their new respect after seeing the wad of hair in his hand, but was anxious to get to the home place.

Trotting out of earshot, he broke into a run, laughing with abandon, prize in hand. He continued to feel new power in his stomach. At the home place people pretended to ignore him during the polite dead time extended to those who had been gone. Oak Gall sat on the boulder by the chaw'se, the singed line of her hair straight against the curve of her brown shoulders, her hips slightly mounded where they met the rock. Of all the beauties of the world, she was the loveliest.

Howchia broke the short quiet, for it had been only two sleeps since his departure. He opened his hand. She showed no surprise to see the hair, only pleasure to have him safely back. It was almost as though she had *seen.*

Boys and men collected around him. Two Falcons asked to hold the hair. Proudly he handed him the damp wad. The master hunter carefully examined the blunt cut and looked at him with an expression of respect. Thrilled, Badger Warrior watched as the hair was passed to Running Quail, who noted the cut and passed it on to other elders. With each person who held it, Badger Warrior felt more honored.

The hy-apo came from the east hill with a jackrabbit by the ears. He took the hair, studied it and dipped his head respectfully toward Badger Warrior. Then he sat in his accustomed place beneath the oak, straightened his back and said, "We will hear Badger Warrior's story."

Everyone sat in a talk circle. Little boys looked at him with wide eyes, and Oak Gall smiled from the back of the crowd. He told his story and as he talked, realized that even with the power of O-se-mai-ti, his need to become a man was all the more urgent.

4

Two sleeps later Morning Owl stopped him on the path and asked politely where he was going. "To the river to bathe," he said. At this perfunctory answer the headman said, "Come to the sweathouse tonight."

"Sweathouse?"

"Yes."

Sweathouse. "Ho!" he said with his voice breaking. He all but flew to the u-macha where Howchia was rising from her mat. He told her; she smiled knowingly. He ran to Bowstring's u-macha, stood before the doorway and waited on one foot then the other until Bowstring and Lame Beaver emerged from the dim interior, their hair standing up from the sleep. Lame Beaver rubbed his eyes.

"Morning Owl invited me to the sweathouse," Badger Warrior blurted out, "tonight!"

"Me too," said Bowstring.

That nipped his pride. "You didn't tell me."

"I just did."

"But you knew before the sleep."

"My father told me. It was late. You were sleeping."

Everything, Badger Warrior realized, was different when a boy had a father. The exuberance bubbled back. "Who else was invited?"

"Just us."

"I wonder if Sick Rat will be there."

"Maybe." Several moons ago Sick Rat had been invited to the sweathouse, but he had lacked the strength to withstand the heat. Maybe he wouldn't try again and risk humiliation in Badger Warrior's presence.

All day he struggled to keep his calm. By sundown he felt like a milkweed pod about to explode. Morning Owl sent him and Bowstring for seasoned oak wood and twigs from the gray pine, the fuel for the ritual fire. Then they were sent to collect fronds of the big-fringe fern. Returning, they joined the men who stood talking near the sweathouse.

Morning Owl pointed, indicating Badger Warrior should carry the ferns inside. Hunching forward, he entered the low door. He was alone, the men outside. Never had he been in the house of men. It was dim and smelled of ash and something different from any other house. The twilight at the doorway made his shadow fall on the unstrung bows standing against the encircling wall. The power of the place prickled his skin and the bows questioned his presence. He told them, "I will be a good man of the umne." Then he squatted before the pyramid of wood in the firepit and laid the ferns to the side.

Returning to the twilight and the gathered men—Sick Rat not among them—he went to the u-macha for his bow. Bowstring joined him and it felt odd to see Lame Beaver watch from a respectful distance, as though they were already men. Oak Gall was banking her family's supper fire. Seeing them, she gave Badger Warrior a sidelong smile. His belly warmed alarmingly. She swept up a basket and walked toward her u-macha on legs fleshed out a little but still too slim and long. They settled under her in a fascinating double-jointed walk that required an extra half-beat for each step. Bowstring cuffed him on the shoulder and motioned with his head toward the sweathouse.

Morning Owl led the men inside. All crouch-walked around the circular wall to their places, Bowstring settling beside his father on the west side. Two Falcons gestured Badger Warrior toward the north. He stood his bow against the wall and sat down. Morning Owl brought in a smoldering stick and lit the tinder. The pyramid crackled into flame. Smoke filled the conical structure and rose to the point. The lack of a smokehole tested men's strength.

Outside, a man who had elected to stay with his family hung buckskins over the entrance. Badger Warrior had seen this many times from a distance. Now, he unfocused his eyes and let his spirit come forth in this domain of men, where the glowing firelight changed the men's features and made them all magically the same.

After a lengthy silence, Morning Owl said in the formal cadence used by hy-apos, "Listen to, listen to, the fire transforming the wood."

The fire whispered of men's place in the world, so different from that of women and children. A dark silhouette crept forward to apply the first handful of ferns. They simmered and hissed and added their purifying smoke to the sweathouse. Sitting crosslegged, Badger Warrior inhaled the smoke and absorbed it into his pores. Time and space were one, the only sound the crackling, hissing fire. He melted into the communal masculine embrace, fused with the men of the umne and felt his spirit knotting into the twisted umbilical cord of patrilineal descent reaching all the way back to the Ancients. It meant nothing that his own father was of another umne. All had descended from the ancient fathers. Despite the thickening heat, the spirits gave him goosebumps. Like a caterpillar pushing through a cocoon, he could feel himself starting to become a man.

Perspiration trickled down his face and back and chest, purifying him for clearer vision. At last he permitted himself to lie down on the cooler earth, as others had been doing for some time, and breathed easier. Yet the accumulating heat and smoke continued to transform him as it boiled around him, seeking cracks.

"O-se-mai-ti honors us," Morning Owl, said, alluding to Badger Warrior's feat. But pride was gone. He wanted only to be one with the men.

After a time Morning Owl said, "Hear the music of second grass." Bowstring's talent with flutes would be heard at the coming big time. It was the hy-apo's way of welcoming Bowstring.

It had been quiet for a time when the reedy, seldom-heard voice of Drum-in-Fog came from the south wall, "Did you dream on your O-se-mai-ti quest?"

At first he couldn't speak and shame stung him, for he feared the heat had conquered him. Then he *saw* what stopped his tongue. Emerging from the smoke were the sad people shuffling across an arch over the sky. "I dreamed of many people walking on a bridge in the sky," he said. "They were high above me and I couldn't speak to them."

In the fireglow the doctor's deeply lined face looked like a demon. "Bear gave you a vision," he said. "Grizzly Hair has seen the dead on the pathway of ghosts."

Grizzly Hair. Drum-in-Fog had named him! For what he had done! And he had seen the dead, yet lived. He was not only a man, but one the doctor believed had power. It was almost more than he could absorb. The dream would guide him. But what did it mean? "Too many walked the pathway," he said, emboldened enough to ask questions of the doctor.

Drum-in-Fog spoke no answer to the riddle.

The heat intensified and two men crawled out beneath the hide. He and Bowstring remained. Following the example of the other men, they sang to their bows and handled them with reverence. A deer hunt would be needed for the big time feasts ahead, and they would hunt too. He learned the words on the second and third repetitions, and, as he sang, felt more impurities floating away with the smoke as it searched for and found little cracks.

Later, when the firelight dwindled, Morning Owl released the hide at the entrance. Cool night air washed over Grizzly Hair. He ran with the others to the river, pushing ahead, strong as a bear. In a running dive he skimmed into the cold black water and submerged. Hot on the inside, cool on the skin, he popped up and treaded water, grinning in the dark. The magic of the sweathouse bound him to the whooping, splashing men. A hand grabbed his ankle and pulled him under. He thrashed, broke free, rose to the surface and sputtered with laughter.

"Now you will smell the moss on the bottom," he said swimming determinedly toward his tormentor, but the culprit vanished into the black water. Side-arm splashing started, wild and fun. Men ran around the beach tackling and tumbling over each other. They yelled taunts like Shits-in-River and Vomits-in-Nu-pah, and slapped water into his face. Glad to see that men were much like boys, Grizzly Hair gave as good as he got.

The fun gradually subsided and men headed to their u-machas, many to the sweathouse. As Grizzly Hair stood wondering which way to go, footsteps approached from behind. He turned.

"I told Morning Owl I am tired of running for him." It was Yellow Jacket. "You are the fastest runner. He will ask you to be the runner."

Stunned and grateful that he would be the news-bringer, Grizzly Hair clasped the man's shoulders. He had no idea that his first running duty would show him the direction of his life.

5

The rains were gentle now; second grass had shot up in the lengthening suns, far outstripping first grass. Joy could be seen among the umne, but in none so much as Grizzly Hair, for he was a man. Soon he would invite the related villages to the Second Grass Festival. He awaited the festival and his first run with impatience.

Straightening arrow shafts in his stone ring, he wondered if he should give Oak Gall a gift—was that done before coupling? What would he give? Nothing of such significance that she would shrink away from him, yet something she wouldn't laugh at. What?

Nearby young boys lunged with sticks, showing how they planned to spear frogs for the feasts. Their fierceness made him smile. From the chaw'se came the eternal drumbeat of women pulverizing acorns, but Oak Gall wasn't there. She had gone with the women who dispersed over the hillsides to collect corms, onions and other root delicacies. She wasn't with the women on the west hill who sang as they pried the earth with digging sticks. A big baby suckled its mother's breast, which was stretched beneath her arm and around to her back where the baby could reach it from its bikoos. Toddlers romped and tumbled around the women.

He felt like running. Maybe he would see Oak Gall, maybe get an idea for a gift. He ran westward up and over the first hill, past Bobcat Ledge, up and over the second hill, searching the green hills, but saw only deer bounding away beneath the oaks and a golden eagle gliding low, hunting. He headed back, turning toward the river in the dip between hills. The big gravel bar spread before him and the river flowed in lazy abundance. Drifts of blue lupine perfumed the air peppery sweet, but Oak Gall was not there.

He went to check on Grandmother, who sat on her log with a heap of drilled clamshells at her feet. Singing to the river baby spirit, she moved her roughened hands up and down the delicate shell drill that twirled on a flat stone before her. Sunlight came through a tracery of branches and added more lines to her wrinkled body. She sang as if she were alone, staring past him, but he saw that she knew she was not alone.

He reassured her with a touch on the shoulder, then made his way through the waist-high lupine, alive with bees, toward the river. A wash of golden poppies blazed in bright contrast to the lavender. Underfoot, miniature purple and white lupine looked up from between the rocks asking not to be stepped on. Nearly lifted by joy, he came to the water and watched it part around the little island, the near stream purling over the rocks.

Movement caught his eye. Mother was watching him through a young pine. He made his way toward her over the sand and warm smooth rocks. "Where are you going," she said, politely avoiding his gaze.

Smiling for no reason, he shrugged.

She was rubbing her thumb over a gold nugget. Of all the umne, she alone found its glint and texture helpful. No doubt she had come to her power place to plan the details of the dances, as she did each moon. Rubbing gold gave her ideas.

"It's about time we danced the Rattlesnake," she said, "and some lighter dances. This will be fun." A bank swallow swooped past. "I'll include some special verses for the wing people. Have you ever heard them whistle so?"

About to take wing himself, he knew that the Rattlesnake Dance celebrated the mystery of coupling, which had fascinated him since his earliest memories.

"You are an attractive man, son. The young women will be interested in you." She raised her brows. "But I must tell you, some people are saying it is not right for you to be with the home women."

He felt his smile drop.

"They whisper about it."

"But none of them are my cousin-sisters."

"Maybe they think it is too easy for you, like catching fish in a basket. Your friends must find women from other places."

"Are you asking me not to couple with the home women?"

"No. I'm telling you what some people are saying."

He suddenly recalled Oak Gall's aunt looking at him coldly when he and Oak Gall walked past. Confusion replaced his joy. He wasn't related to Oak Gall closer than eight generations on his father's side or five on his mother's, which was the rule. Besides, she was Water and he was Land. So what was wrong with fishing in a basket?

After the sleep and a vigorous swim—certain now, having reviewed the rules of marriage with Morning Owl, that Oak Gall was an eligible woman for him—he waited on the riverbank until the hy-apo was finished talking to father sun. At last Morning Owl came toward him with knotted fibers swinging from his calf thong. He pulled them out and handed them to Grizzly Hair, each *pul* knotted five times, signifying five sleeps before the big time. He explained where to deliver the *puls*. Grizzly Hair felt a twinge of disappointment not to be inviting more distant villages.

"Tell them," said the hy-apo, "that we will perform the Rattlesnake Dance." He smiled.

At the mention of that dance, Grizzly Hair's mind raced over the many hiding places where he could go with Oak Gall. Like an arrow shot from a bow, he ran up the west path. The breeze of his running dried him and Dog bounded beside him, tongue lolling happily. With the life-giver at his back he watched his long shadow with its bouncing topknot. The ornaments of manhood moved his ears—plugs of polished heron leg bones—and the amulet containing the hair of the bear thudded softly on his chest. In the oaks a world of wing people whistled and trilled and cheeped.

Not yet winded, he approached the first little village, which, having no dancehouse, always relied on the home place. A herald with a resonant voice announced him. People gathered around. At the headman's invitation Grizzly Hair sat down, gave him a *pul*, and listened to the news, paying close attention to each item so he could repeat it later. In turn, he told of Yellow Jacket's retirement. The women, some of whom were sisters of the umne, asked whether Blue Butterfly and Hummingbird Tailfeather had given birth and if Eagle Woman intended to marry. Politely, he answered all questions, explaining that his mother was still the singing doctor and had no intention of remarrying.

Then he was off running again. This time the distance was greater. The next village had a dancehouse, but if the complaints of certain home women were true, these people liked to eat away from home as much as possible and didn't host enough festivals. Again a herald announced him and news was exchanged. He could hardly believe he was performing this important duty, which he had so often seen done in his own village.

On his way again, he ran to where Deer Creek ran parallel to the river, to the strong village of Omuch. He found himself standing before the ripe young woman who had flirted with him during the last big time. People crowded around and Omuch greeted him, but he saw only the full moon of the young woman's smiling face and the rich brown hills and valleys of her body. She was Water, an eligible woman for him.

He struggled to pull his gaze from her while an older woman brought a basket of nu-pah. He ate but didn't taste. He couldn't hear well because his heart was suddenly drumming in his ears. Realizing he wouldn't be able to repeat the news, he forced himself to listen. Omuch's wife was saying that a cousin-sister of Eagle Woman had left her husband for another man and moved into his house. She added, with a lift of her chin, that this had come as a surprise to no one. Moon Woman was pushing toward him through the crowd.

People looked at him, waiting for news of the home place. He cleared his throat and told about the expected births, but his tongue slowed and stopped. Moon Woman crowded so near that if he raised a hand from where he sat, he could touch her plump thigh. He smelled her interesting scent. His man's part stirred and his face heated like a cooking stone. He tried to think what he was supposed to say, but people were grinning, children pointing. All thought vanished. He felt more like a clown than a runner.

Omuch touched his shoulder and kindly thanked him for the *pul*, adding, "Tell Morning Owl that we will come to the big time."

The kindness intensified his embarrassment. He got up and left running. Would Omuch report to Morning Owl that his runner was a poor speaker? Would these people laugh at him when they arrived at the big time? He vowed to do better.

At the next village, the farthest south that he was supposed to visit, Shalachmush greeted him. Again Grizzly Hair presented a *pul*, seated himself, accepted food and exchanged news. All went well and he stood to go, but Shalachmush, still seated and loosely holding the *pul*, stared into the distance.

His unfocused eyes were underscored with puffy half moons. Knowing more would be said, Grizzly Hair sat down again.

"Spirit animals have come into the world," Shalachmush said at last. "The same ones that came with the demons at the time of the thunder deaths." All Grizzly Hair's senses focused. Shalachmush had been respectful, careful not to speak the name of his father. Impatient questions jumped to his tongue. "Did you see the spirit animals?"

Shalachmush looked down. "I saw their tracks."

That meant he hadn't followed them to their source, as a tracker would have. "What did the tracks look like?"

Shalachmush picked up a twig. Grizzly Hair and about twenty people watched as the hy-apo drew an unclosed circle, then a Y inside the circle. He asked a young boy to put his outstretched hand in it. Satisfied, he said, "The foot of the animal was about that size. It had no toes."

Then he drew the relationship of the prints to each other showing that the animal was a diagonal walker, one that planted opposite feet rather than stepping on same side like a cat. He stared over the river with an out-of-focus expression. Finished.

Grizzly Hair had been holding his breath, so significant was this news. "Show me where you saw the tracks."

"It has been a moon. The rains have washed them away."

"I would like to see the place."

Shalachmush glanced at the sun. "It is far."

Despite his impatience, he knew Shalachmush was right. He must run to the home place before dark. "I'll come back after the sleep. Then will you show me the place?"

Shalachmush pursed his lips reluctantly, then nodded.

By the time Grizzly Hair returned to the home place, father sun had gone over the western hill. He found Morning Owl with his long-handled duck net in a stand of willows. The hy-apo pointed downstream, signaling silence and making a "go" gesture.

Grizzly Hair circled downstream, then stamped and yelled and drove a frenzy of wood ducks into flight. Several caught themselves in Morning Owl's net. Morning Owl hauled them in and wrung three necks. He disentangled the fourth and tossed it into the air, where it rapidly quacked down river through the channel of cottonwoods.

Grizzly Hair told him, "The Shalachmush-umne have seen spirit tracks. Big animals with round feet and no toes."

A shadow flitted across Morning Owl's eyes. He stood with dripping poles on one shoulder and the limp necks of the colorful ducks in his other hand. His unfocused expression said the news troubled him and he wished to be alone.

Howchia was powdering bones at the chaw'se to add to her seed crackers. When he told her about the tracks, she stopped pounding. "Son," she said gravely, "the story was not imagined by the woman that Eats Skunk killed. I saw the wounds on the man I must not speak of." His father. "There is trouble in the west and I fear you will want to follow the tracks." She looked at him, knowing him well. "Those are dangerous spirits. I spirit-tracked the people who disappeared and I believe they were stolen by demons."

This chilled him. It was the first he'd heard of the trouble in the west being more than the murder of his father.

She picked up the pestle-rock and resumed powdering the deer vertebrae. "The demons could send sickness beyond my powers, beyond the powers of Drum-in-Fog to suck out. Those tracks are dangerous." She paused in her pounding. "This place has been good to us. We should stay here where it is safe. Forget about the tracks." Fingering the consistency of the bone meal, she looked down and he saw only the top of her woven cap. She had never spoken this forcefully to him before.

"I will think about this in the sweathouse," he said as gently as possible. But a man had to find his own way.

That evening, as the ritual smoke rolled upward, he told about the strange tracks.

Morning Owl spoke: "Our former headman said pranksters drew such tracks to make Newach think devils had killed his relatives."

"I remember that," Scorpion-on-Nose said. "The murders were properly avenged by Eats Skunk, so no ghosts should remain."

In the silence Grizzly Hair realized how little he'd been told. Mother hadn't mentioned pranksters. She said Eats Skunk had killed a woman for bringing the bad news. Some people still feared Eats Skunk because of it. Most thought the woman had been sent by the murderers to blame non-existent demons. Eats Skunk had held the small woman over the coals of a fire and roasted her feet before strangling her, and that was why Grizzly Hair had never wanted to live in the village of that paternal relative though he probably would have been welcomed.

"A long time ago," Drum-in-Fog said in his reedy way, "we talked about such tracks. Some people downstream said powerful doctors with thunder shooters came to the world. I worked my magic and kept them away."

Out of the smoke came a muffled voice. "Is your magic failing now, old man?"

The doctor didn't respond, but doubtless knew the accuser's identity. Now if that man fell ill, everyone would know why.

Grizzly Hair was thinking of what his mother had said about demons with rods that shot thunder and lightning. Apparently even Drum-in-Fog believed they were real, not the lies of pranksters. People here had more knowledge than they revealed. As the fire whispered in the murky silence he saw himself following the round tracks. He was a man now, and a tracker.

As if *seeing* his thoughts, Drum-in-Fog said, "We should learn what is real in the world." That penetrated Grizzly Hair's skin with the smoke. He had always pursued the real, not resting until he could understand the stories animals and birds left in the earth as they foraged and coupled and skirmished. The hair of a living grizzly bear hung in his amulet. He knew the touch and smell of a real bear. Now he would learn what was real in the world. "After the sleep," he said, "I will follow the tracks."

6

Father sun fired the world with power. Along every leaf and blade of grass dewdrops shimmered with brilliant rainbow colors. Amazed by the stunning sight, Grizzly Hair tingled from his cold swim. This was a good omen for his journey. He brushed dry with his bundle of vulture feathers, slung his weasel-skin quiver over his shoulder and trotted up the path, Dog bounding alongside.

In the southern village Shalachmush joined him and they trotted together, following the river trail through flatter land. Grizzly Hair recalled that a flood had drowned most of the Ancients and only a few had escaped by going to the low hills of the eastern mountains. A sea had formed in the big valley. Even Coyote had to swim to safety. Then much later a rip in the western mountains had drained the water. Every child knew that two large rivers, one from the north and one from the south, converged and flowed through the gap and into the western sea. He hoped to see that gap, which storytellers described so well.

The two of them trotted silently, Grizzly Hair deferentially in the rear. The river channel was deeper here, the earth softer. Unlike in the home place, no boulders jutted from the water or lay along its banks. On his right a continuous canopy of large oaks hid the Spirit Peak, which stood beside the gap. The shady grasslands beneath the trees were dotted with fresh ground squirrel mounds and the raucous birds swarmed between earth and sky.

They arrived at a village and were heralded. He looked back and couldn't see Dog, no doubt hunting rabbits with Shalachmush's dog. The polite hosts offered nu-pah, greens and dried salmon, and Shalachmush introduced Grizzly Hair to a small man, saying, "He showed me the tracks. He will come with us."

The three left the village trotting, the smallest man in the lead, Grizzly

Hair at the rear. Father sun rose to his zenith and even in the shade the air became unpleasantly warm.

Ahead, the two men stopped and pointed. "There. The tracks were there."

Excited, Grizzly Hair examined the sandy soil. Large and small tracks of varying ages were overlaid. He recalled the mildness of recent rains, the gentleness of the breezes and read the stories of the tracks. He saw which ones came first and what kind of damage the weather and smaller animals had done to the round impressions underneath. Wanting to avoid obscuring them with more tracks, he asked the men to hold the dogs when they arrived.

He pressed his ear on the sand. From that angle he could see the depth of the least disturbed impressions—an exceedingly heavy animal. With a finger he carefully flicked out the collapsed inside wall of a track and, with a mouthful of river water, lightly sprayed it as he reconstructed it to its former shape. He repeated this several times in different places and stood up to see the overall pattern.

Upstream a short distance was a dip in the opposite bank similar to the one on this side. He said, "Several animals entered the river there, came downstream and left here. Later they returned and went back the way they had come."

Shalachmush nodded. The other man said, "This is what we saw when the tracks were fresh." He smiled. "You are a tracker."

Swallowing a smile, Grizzly Hair declared, "I will follow the tracks." Seeing the men's uneasy expressions, he assured them, "There is no need for you to come."

They raised their brows and glanced at each other as if coming to a conclusion, then shrugged and left. Just then the dogs trotted down the trail.

"Go home," Grizzly Hair said to Dog, who was nearly as old as he was. It was too warm for him to run all day. But he came wagging his tail, slobbering happily and telling Grizzly Hair he would not leave. He looked into Dog's pleading eyes and scratched his ears. Mostly to himself he said, "Each of us finds his own way. You can come."

He swam the stream, bow dragging in the current. On the other side he walked a sandy cutbank ledge until he reached the swale where the big animals had entered. Climbing to the top he looked over land as flat as water and saw the faint southward trail. Had he not reconstructed the tracks, he would have mistaken it for an elk trail. The grass was recovering from being compacted under the weight of heavy animals moving in single file. He set off trotting, Dog at his heels.

The trail increasingly diverged from the river, which angled southwest toward the blue Spirit Peak where Condor had perched in First World. He ran effortlessly on the flat land. On either side, large oaks were spaced conveniently to shade his path about half the time. On his right the snout of the powerful blue mountain poked above the haze, and on his left, an indistinct white line marked the snowy eastern mountains.

He followed the trail until sundown when he came to a stream alive with bellowing frogs. With a sharpened stick he speared three bullfrogs that had been too intent on coupling. He wrapped them in grape leaves and buried them. With the help of a friendly elderberry tree he made a fire drill and soon had flames burning over the frogs. As his supper roasted, he made a makeshift shelter, bending and tying living willow branches into a loose dome, then picked sweet clover heads. The elderberry bushes were crawling with caterpillars. He caught and skewered about twenty and scorched the hair off. Reclining on an elbow he popped the juicy morsels into his mouth and tried to imagine the spirit animals he was tracking. Enormous sheep with curled horns for the demons to grasp as they rode? Bears with strange footwear? Never mind the danger, this journey excited him even more than the prospect of coupling. All men coupled but he was doing something no other man had done, none that he knew about. Maybe he would tell this story to his children and grandchildren, which, he constantly reminded himself, he would have after all.

He pushed the dying fire aside with a rotting branch and dug up the frogs—perfectly steamed. He nibbled every shred of tender meat, tossed the tiny bones over his shoulder and inched into his shelter. When Dog finally curled up beside him, it was so late the frogs and crickets were silent.

After the sleep he continued straight south on the trail. Troops of grizzly bears grazed here and there on the blooming clover, lifting their heads to see him. "Brothers and sisters," he greeted to them head-to-head, "enjoy the good clover." Hearing that, they returned to their feast.

The trail entered the trees and vines and flowering berry canes of a river somewhat wider than the one at home, judging by the depth of the thicket. At the place where the spirit animals had forded, he heard voices coming from the other side. Demons? His heart beat faster as he crept through the heavy foliage to where the alders and cottonwoods met over the water and grapevines trailed from them to the river. Hidden in the leaves and mostly underwater, he swam toward the voices.

He came up behind a gnarly alder and raised his eyes above water. Two ordinary women sat on the ground attaching feathers to netting—not demons that he could see, but their red skirts were far from ordinary. He had never seen such smooth, brightly colored material. Near them a skinny man sat straightening arrow shafts through a stone eye. Another man was making something small. A short distance upstream two little potbellied girls patted humps of damp sand. South through the trees, beyond the thick river vegetation, he got a glimpse of many u-machas made of tulares. People were walking around doing normal things. This village was even more populous than the Omuchumne. Not a single person that he could see appeared the least bit worried or afraid.

Concluding that the demons had departed, he pulled himself up and stood to his thighs in the river, water streaming down his head and shoulders.

Yelping, the people nearby ran and hid, including the little girls. People in the big village were suddenly running round and barking dogs rushed toward the riverbank.

In a friendly voice he called, "I come from the north. I am following—" An arrow hummed past his head.

He fell on his face and sank, knowing they hadn't meant to kill him. He had been an easy target. He moved toward shore where the shallows bumped his shins, and pushed up his head and said in a reasonable tone, "Friend."

Men with loaded bows were running toward him from the village.

"I am a friend," he called. He kneeled in the muddy bottom, showing his head and shoulders but keeping his bow underwater. No more arrows came. The skinny man with well-defined ribs stepped out from behind a tree with his bow drawn, no doubt the source of the arrow. With very strange pronunciation he said something that sounded like, "A meadowlark?"

Meadowlark sang anything that came to his mind. "I am telling the truth. My people live on the river north of here."

The skinny man lowered his bow, but the men from the town arrived with arrows pointing at him. Some looked upstream and downstream as if searching for someone else. With the attentiveness of a boy who had grown up dodging arrows, he watched the hands of those who had him in their sights, but no arrow was released.

"I am the runner from Morning Owl," he said. Realizing the umne engaged in little trade and tended to be aloof, he mentioned a better known people. "We are neighbors and relatives of the Omuchumne."

All the bows lowered. Breathing easier and smiling his friendliest smile, he put a foot under him and stood up. The people he'd seen first came out of hiding. Seeing no further alarm, he waded up the slope to shore and stood with water pouring through the openings in his quiver, his bow dripping in his hand. The little girls stepped closer and looked him over. Keeping an eye on the men with weapons, he nevertheless noticed that one of the red-skirted women had red scabby spots all over her face.

A dignified man arrived from the village, no doubt the headman. He motioned Grizzly Hair to sit and talk.

He sat a polite distance from this friendly looking hy-apo, and the other men formed a talk circle, though two stood watch, looking up and down the river as though expecting danger. In fear of demons, Grizzly Hair looked too, but realized they might be afraid he had brought other men. "I am alone. I come in friendship to ask about those big round tracks," he said, pointing toward the aging trail downstream. "Perhaps you have seen the animals. I am following them."

The skinny man said in his accented pronunciation, "Do not follow them. Bad."

Grizzly Hair looked at him. "Are they demons?"

The man talked fast, using words Grizzly Hair couldn't understand.

The hy-apo said, "He is talking about the *Españoles.*"

"What are *Esp—* " He couldn't pronounce it.

Muscles relaxed and some people smiled. The headman, whose speech was almost the same as Grizzly Hair's, said, "*Españoles* live in the west. They have great power." He paused to let that sink in. "They have excellent tools and shooters that make thunder. They kill from a distance more than twice as far as our bows. They ride on the backs of animals—*caballos*—who run them quickly wherever they want to go. You are tracking *caballos.* A little more than a moon ago *Españoles* came through here."

"Are they sorcerers?"

"We used to think so, but now we think only their doctors are sorcerers. I heard of men two rivers south who learned to ride *caballos* very well. I think anyone could learn to do it." He paused. "Many people on the southern rivers are going to the missions."

"Missions?"

"The homes of the long robes."

"I don't understand long robes."

"The doctors of the *Españoles.* They want people to live with them and become *Christianos.* Many do."

"*Christianos?*" He was learning many strange words.

"All *Españoles* are *Christianos,* and so are the people who went to live in the missions."

This talk was causing an odd sensation in Grizzly Hair, as though he was looking down to see himself sitting on the earth talking to strangers who told stories that had never been told before. Could he learn to ride on the back of a big animal? Would the long robes teach him to use a thunder shooter? Something inside him leapt at the thought. "Are the *Españoles* friendly?" He tried to pronounce it properly so they wouldn't smile.

"Sometimes." No smiles.

"I would like to hear more about them."

The spokesman obliged. "Only their men travel; we know nothing of their women. The men always wear costumes, from their hats to the bottoms of their feet. Some have very pale skin. Their yu-seh"—the word for hair sounded more like yoo-ze—"is different colors. My friend saw one with hair the color of a red-tailed hawk."

The thought prickled the back of Grizzly Hair's neck.

"Their doctors wear long robes and no hats. Their heads are bald on top. Sometimes they travel with the black hats."

"Black hats?"

"The men who have thunder shooters. They wear hats like this." He leaned forward and drew a block on the sand, colored it by ruffing the damp sand, then drew a straight line under it, so the block sat midway on the long line. "This is a red band." He broke a twig and laid it along the line, trimming the ends so it fit within the block. He tilted his head at the drawing, then drew a circle. "From the top, the hat looks like this." He drew a smaller circle inside the larger one.

Grizzly Hair nodded, seeing the hat in his mind. He wanted to follow the tracks to a mission, but first he would go back and report to the umne what he had heard.

The skinny man's companion stood up and turned around. On his back were long lumpy wounds laid over and over each other—stripes, some old scars, others fresh red scabs. It looked like a mountain lion had sharpened its claws on his back. The man turned to face him and said, "*Españoles* did that with *cuartas,* long leather thongs. They do it like this." He mimed striking someone repeatedly, wrist snapping. "They do this to people in the mission." He said something to the women, and one of them turned around. She too had long scabs and scars on her back.

Maybe he wouldn't go to the mission after all. A little girl peered up at him with round eyes and said something he couldn't understand. Her mother, the one with the spotted face, looked her to silence and said, "Many die in the mission. My son is dead. We make ready for a Cry. You dance?"

"Yes," agreed the spokesman in a genial tone. "It would honor us if you would stay and dance." He stood up in a strong posture, indicating that talk was about finished, adding, "These people are our guests." He gestured to the red-skirted women and their men. "They left the mission and found their old home place deserted." He opened his hand toward several younger men. "These are my sons."

"You honor me," Grizzly Hair said, "but I must go to my home place and tell my people what I have learned about the tracks. We are also planning a big time."

That evening he ate at the fire of the elder called Te-mi and learned that these were the people of Muquel, the Muquelumne being a strong people with four villages. When darkness crept over the lingering heat, he lay down to sleep in the u-macha of Te-mi's youngest son, a young man named Elk Calf, and his wife.

Long after the others began the even breathing of sleep, Grizzly Hair lay awake with his hands behind his head. Incomplete images of black hats, *cuartas*, long robes and thunder shooters consumed him.

All the village dogs suddenly began to bark.

Worried about black hats but guessing that Dog had finally arrived, he crawled to the entrance. In the light of mother moon he saw Dog cowering before the snarling snapping dogs of the village. Grizzly Hair stood up and whistled. In a display of extreme deference to the host dogs, Dog crept on his belly to Grizzly Hair and followed him into the house. It made him smile, and he lay down again. Dog curled up beside him with his tail thumping in the dark. He patted the wet ribs and told him, "You're too old for this. You should have stayed at the home place. Now you have run all this way just to turn around and run back."

Dog put his muzzle on Grizzly Hair's arm. He didn't care how far he had come. He only wanted to be with his man.

On the run home Grizzly Hair never stopped thinking about missions and black hats and *caballos*. The significance came in gusts, then receded, then nearly knocked him down again. His excitement made his legs churn faster. Nothing like this had ever happened in the world, not even in story. Taking the shortest route across the oak-grasslands, he headed northeast to intersect the home river at the start of the hills. Again Dog lagged behind, but his nose would find his man. Under a sky dome the shade of a robin's egg he ran on narrow traces that webbed the high grass. Startled from their naps, large groups of deer and elk and antelope bounded away. The traces meandered but were faster than pushing through waist-high grass and, with rattlesnakes awake, safer.

He knew now that the black hats had killed his father with their thunder shooters. A generation before that, Grandfather Crying Fox had gone to the western sea and never returned. Had he gone to a mission to get power? Had he died there? How long had this been going on? He suspected it connected somehow with his quest dream, but wasn't sure how. Where power resided one could find much that was healthful and strong, but one could also find death and bad luck. Many people had died in the mission. Many had been whipped. But some rode *caballos* and used thunder shooters. Bounding along the traces like the animals who scattered around him, he puzzled over his dream.

A shadow knifed across him. Instinctively he flinched, crouched. Condor swooped over his head, turning a cold yellow eye on him. He waved his arms and yelled, "Go away!" The condor flapped its wings and glided ahead. Why had this bird, who represented the power of the universe, examined him so closely? He assumed it held significance for him. But what? He resumed running, the bird already far ahead. With a flap of its enormous wings, it turned and circled and sailed over Grizzly Hair's head and down his back trail. He was young and didn't understand the spirits very well. Maybe Drum-in-Fog would explain it.

He arrived at the home place before supper, glanced around, and saw Bowstring and Lame Beaver, but everyone ignored him in the time-of-pretending, since he'd been gone for two sleeps. He caught sight of Mother at the chaw'se and went to her. She hid her emotions, but though they both pretended he wasn't there, he saw her pleasure that he had returned. Hummingbird Tailfeather scooped meal from a rock pocket and left the chaw'se. He sat where she had been, and looked politely past his mother, checking the trail for Dog. But a dog that old couldn't possibly arrive until much later, so he looked at the hills and inhaled the scent of elderberry trees in full bloom. Such sweetness suggested health and joy, not fear and agitation and big things happening in the world.

At last she stopped pounding and allowed her gaze to brush past his.

At this signal he said, "Powerful people live near the western sea. They speak the names of the dead."

She sucked in a puff of air.

"Men called black hats ride hornless animals the size of elk, and kill with shooters that make thunder. More people than you can count have gone there to learn. Many have weakened and died. Sometimes these powerful people come east away from their home places. I think they killed my father. Maybe my grandfather."

With a loud clatter she dropped her pestle. "Did the black hats see you?"

"No. I stopped following the tracks."

"Thank you, Eagle," she said looking up.

He followed her gaze to the reflection of the low sun on the river and waited, for he could tell she had something more to say. A cock quail called, *Ki-kágo, ki-kágo.*

"Son," she said at last, "after the sleep we will celebrate. The spirits must hear our joy and thanksgiving. Please do not speak of this until the dances are finished. Only Morning Owl must know, to prepare his final oration."

He had hoped to tell the men in the sweathouse this night, but she was a woman of knowledge. She understood the spirits. Dipping his head in respectful acquiescence, he consoled himself with the thought that he could relieve some of the burden by telling Morning Owl.

7

The secret separated him from his friends. He longed to see Oak Gall but her younger sister said she was in the woman's house. This was the way with women. Disappointed, he joined Bowstring and others preparing the outdoor dance circle. They were planting double posts and stuffing pine branches between them. But whatever he did, thoughts of big power jumped in his mind and the long scars made by the *cuartas* stayed before his eyes.

Bowstring, Falls-off-House and Lame Beaver gathered around—Sick Rat within earshot—and asked what he had learned from following the round tracks. Never before had he been evasive with his friends, so it pained him to say, "Morning Owl will speak of it in his final oration at the big time." Morning Owl had seemed distant when he heard about the tracks.

They returned to their tasks, but every once in a while he saw them looking his way. Groups of girls swished and clacked past in shredded willow-bark skirts and flower headbands. Oak Gall's little sister Etumu sashayed past, giggling with a girl from the walnut grove village. She stopped to pick a flower, turned and gave him a serious, adult look.

By midday almost everything was ready. Bunches of mallard feathers topped the four posts of the dancehouse—east, west, north and south—and lines of the purple and green feathers hung from the oak-trunk beams. Outside, acorn meal stood soaking in large baskets, ready to receive cooking rocks.

Grizzly Hair was in the playing field pushing a post into the damp earth when he heard faint singing. The herald called: "Our guests are coming. All pay attention. Our guests are coming. All go out and greet them."

He looked up and saw a line of dark figures cresting the western hill, the Omuchumne. The home people rushed toward them shouting greetings. Home dogs raced toward the visiting dogs barking furiously, except Dog, who hadn't returned. Perhaps Condor had taken him. The thought saddened Grizzly Hair, though it couldn't have been helped. It was Dog's fate. All was dreamed by Condor and nothing could change a dream. Still, the dog's absence seemed a bad omen.

The arriving visitors assumed the dance posture, forearms up, and playfully step-toed down the hill, singing, dancing and chorusing, "Hey, hey, hey-a, hey, hey, hey-a." Running to mingle with them, the home people linked arms with the guests and stepped down the hill singing with them in one long happy line. Distanced by what he knew, Grizzly Hair stood watching.

The visiting women set up camp near the dance circle, Moon Woman among them. They wanted to know where they should cut willows for shade shelters. Grizzly Hair showed them and Moon Woman, whose public name was Grasshopper Wing, followed.

As he helped the guests cut heaps of willow branches, her eyes teased. He tried not to look at her breasts, which were large and not the least bit slack, but she jiggled them at him and he felt a rush of heat. Back at the camping place he dropped his branches where the shade structures would be erected and turned away. Men didn't display their thoughts in their faces, but what about this? He had no father to advise him. People were looking and he felt like Coyote in the story, so full and stretched that he could hardly shut his eyes.

"She's a good-looking woman," Bowstring said with a salacious smile. Sick Rat turned away.

He left them all and headed for the cold river. On the way he passed Nettles, Oak Gall's mother, who was helping the visiting women unpack their gambling things. She cupped a whisper toward them. Their eyes followed him and he heard a tongue snick. But he was not like Coyote, scheming to seduce her daughter. Was he? The water cleared his mind and he thought about the great power in the west. It had broken his family and made him different. It even made some people think Oak Gall should not be his woman. But if he could get a piece of that power, it might change everything. It might be worth the danger.

During the day the people of the three other villages also arrived and set up camp near the outdoor dance circle. The mood of joyful expectation thickened with the crowd, but underneath something else simmered. He saw it in the eyes of the home men, when they glanced thoughtfully past him.

He was waiting for the feast to begin when Two Falcons, who had brought in much of the venison now roasting in the ground pit, walked toward him and said, "You are home."

Nodding, Grizzly Hair looked politely past him.

The master hunter seated himself and said, "You're not telling what you saw?"

It was one thing to be evasive with his friends, another with the man who had been like a father. "Morning Owl and Eagle Woman want no disturbing talk," he said. "They want the spirits to hear our thanksgiving first."

The vertical planes of the man's broad face remained impassive, his hooded eyes flat. His nod was almost imperceptible. "That is as it should be."

Shalachmush was coming toward them from a group of men talking under the trees. Acknowledging Two Falcons with his eyes, the visiting headman looked at Grizzly Hair, asking to be included in the talk. But Two Falcons rose to this feet and left. They watched him go.

Grizzly Hair wished he could explain it, but, feeling better about it after his mentor's words, he told Shalachmush the same thing he'd told Two Falcons. The man nodded and returned to his umne, obviously reporting to them.

The home women served a rich feast—roasted venison strips sprinkled with alit, salty herbs collected from low places, and rabbit stew with fifteen kinds of sweet bulbs. They served fresh greens with ant vinegar, a delicious spice daubed on the salad by red ants scurrying in and about leaves that had been heaped on the entrances to their mounds.

The opening dance was performed in the dancehouse. To Grizzly Hair, everything felt different. Not only was he a man now, but he carried a heavy secret. He went to his family's place and sat on the fresh pine boughs, old Dishi beside him. He watched the dancers, heard the dance doctor's chant, felt the throb of the log drum and tried to join with the spirits.

Hidden in the flickering shadows and the crowd, Moon Woman sat across the fire. She too distracted him. Still, he joined the men's line and danced around the fire with the others. It was important at this time to maintain the rituals that straightened the misaligned powers so chaos would not abound in the world. Only well-aligned power brought good luck, safety, good hunting and health.

Then he saw Moon Woman in the woman's line, dancing toward him. Her smile jolted him, and though it was shameful in the house of the spirits, he found himself dancing around the fire just to see her big sweaty bouncing breasts. But after only two more rounds, the drum started a new rhythm and people left the dance lines for the pine boughs.

The Molok dancer stepped into the dancehouse. Condor, big brother of Raven. His shiny feather robe glistened in the firelight as he strutted on stilts around the fire. His shadow on the wall doubled his size. His skinny bird legs and the opening and closing of the gigantic wings operated by strings beneath the robe made him appear to be the real spirit instead of the impersonator. A headdress of long-stemmed rushes radiated outward from Molok's netted hair, each stem tufted with a fluffy black breast feather—a huge seed thistle of a head. Below this, an anchoring hairnet was stuffed with white eagle down. It paled the "neck" like a real condor's and hid the dancer's face. Slowly and with great precision Molok enacted his part in the creation of the world, "hopping" with wide-winged landings around the fire. Whenever his shadow fell across the spectators, their faces reflected the awesome power, because the real Condor spirit was present inside the dancehouse, watching. Condor ate the dead and regurgitated the dreams that made the world. Now he was dreaming *Españoles* and *caballos* and long robes.

Then the bird-man stilted out the door, and once again dance lines formed around the fire, Grizzly Hair joining the men, stepping twice on one foot then the other. Singers chorused, "Blessings to the world, blessings to the world. Thank you spirits." Then everyone returned to the pine boughs, where dogs lay curled up at their masters' places.

More big-head dancers entered and performed the stories from the dawn of time. Coyote came through the smoke hole. Smeared with light ash, the performer slid down a post, and as Drum-in-Fog chanted the sacred liturgy, Coyote mocked the feared man, hilariously miming his dignified mannerisms. Only Coyote could do this. It reminded people that even the profound mysteries of life might not be what they seemed and people never knew what would happen next. Coyote made faces and interrupted the most sacred moments with laughing howls of "woo-woo-woo."

Coyote turned his teasing to other people. At the dance doctor's mention of O-se-mai-ti, Coyote feigned fear, stubbed his toe while trying to run, and fell on his face. In his outstretched arm he gripped an imaginary fistful of hair and grinned all around at the chortling audience. Grizzly Hair felt proud to find himself the butt of the joke. No boy would be so honored. Then Coyote climbed the post and hung by his knees from a beam, where he made comical faces as the visiting headmen took turns beseeching the spirits to help the ill. Coyote was teaching people that all events had their funny side.

The night deepened and the heat and rhythm of the dance peeled away the outer skin of the world. In the smoky firelight Grizzly Hair saw O-se-mai-ti dancing, and he saw the real Coyote up on his hind legs, nimbly dancing in and out among the people. The sharp cry of an infant could be heard now and then as the singers moved about shaking rattles. Like the sudden appearances of the spirits in everyday life, these rattles hissed unexpectedly here, there, low, high, suddenly buzzing like a rattlesnake beside Grizzly Hair's ear, the next moment far away.

The dance doctor held up his hands. The drum stopped and the spirit people vanished. Suddenly aware again of the heat and closeness and the identities of those around him, Grizzly Hair shuffled toward the entrance in the crush of perspiring people. As he passed into the cool night air, a soft hand traveled down his spine. He couldn't see who it was, yet was not in doubt.

She took his hand and pulled him toward the path to the eastern hill. He knew she would weaken his ability to *see* at the next dance, but went anyway. Here and there in the dark he could see other couples going into cover. His heart thumped strangely. Girls and boys who had followed whispered and giggled. Was Oak Gall's little sister among them? He couldn't be sure in the dark.

With a gesture Moon Woman-Grasshopper Wing sent the children into hiding. Then she kneeled and patted the thick cushion of old needles under a gray pine.

8

He awoke in the u-macha to the screaming roar of the crowds on the tikel field. The game had started without him. He rolled out from under his rabbit blanket and wobbled to his feet. It was true that coupling weakened a man. He squeezed his amulet, willing O-se-mai-ti to restore him, then scooped up all the leftover nu-pah from the basket and left for the game.

As he approached, about two twenties of people were on the field trying to run the connected deerskin balls—scrotum as it was jokingly called—to the opposing goal posts. The players fell in a heap of legs and poles and laughing people. "Find Grizzly Hair!" someone shouted. Then all were running again, a forest of poles waving, trying to snag the whirling bagballs at the tip of a woman's pole. She passed it to Grub Log.

A boy at the sideline offered his pole to Grizzly Hair. He accepted it and tore after Grub Log, champion of the Shalachmush-umne. Grizzly Hair caught up and pushed the tip of his pole into the whirl. Grub Log tried to push him away with an outstretched hand, but Grizzly Hair stole the scrotum and was off running the opposite direction, dodging players and whirling with his prize. A heady screaming roar propelled him down the field and the sounds of feet behind receded. He turned at the goal posts, caught the bagballs as they slid down the pole and held them triumphantly over his head. Coupling hadn't entirely weakened him.

After many more trips up and down the long field, Grub Log appeared out of nowhere and pushed him to the ground. Other players piled on. Grizzly Hair's neck was wrenched and a pole pressed hard into his back. Before he could get up, Grub Log was crossing the other goal line. Exhausted and slick with sweat, he couldn't make himself stop playing. It was always much more fun at a big time, with so many skilled players. Besides, it made him forget his secret.

The game continued into the hot part of the day as people napped and others joined in. At last, scratched, wet, dirty, bruised and happy, he felt he couldn't move another step and feared his mouth would stick shut without an immediate drink, so he handed his pole to a man on the sideline. Howchia was there plastering herb pastes on the injured players—children and Falls-off-House.

He went to the cold river and treaded quietly, feeling an unknown future pulling him away from life as it had always been. What fate was in store for him? Oblivious gamblers sat on the shore scowling in concentration and guessing which hand held the bone. Little children cavorted around them throwing fistfuls of sand, but the gamblers only waved at the sand as though it were gnats.

That night after the dance he felt Moon Woman's hand again, and again forgot all else. In first light they rose from the pine needles and his legs nearly buckled. She had the same trouble. Laughing at themselves, they staggered toward the river, but beneath the laughter he felt alarmed at his weakness. "After the dance tonight I will go to the sweathouse," he told her.

In the u-macha he fell on his mat.

"Does the big time please you?" Howchia asked from her mat, her voice raised above Grandmother Dishi's snore.

"Ummm, yes." Clothed men rode across his mind's eye, but he dropped into sleep.

Three sleeps and three more dances went by, all chores transformed into playfulness. No one asked about tracks or demons. He ran on the ti-kel field, rested in the river with his friends, gorged at meals until his belly hurt, danced in the outdoor circle and slept in the sweathouse. Oak Gall remained in the woman's house.

Now it was evening again and he sat eating with Bowstring, who had been quieter than usual. Across from them the five headmen sat together wearing their wealth. Omuch's chest was so covered with descending loops of shells that his skin was hardly visible. Morning Owl had only two strings of shells, mostly fresh water clams. It was a pity he was poor, but these days none of the umne chose to be traders and the few traders who came to the village said good shells were in short supply.

Grizzly Hair munched a mouthful of poison oak, boiled to remove the itch, and pointed with his head at Morning Owl. "We should get our headman more shell money." He didn't know how they would do it, but he felt lucky. Sooner or later something would present itself.

Nodding agreement, Bowstring nibbled a quail leg, then looked at him. "I think the round tracks stole a piece of you."

Maybe it was true.

With a voice roughening with emotion Bowstring continued, "We made our first bows together. We went to the sweathouse and became men together." He swallowed. "You can trust me to keep a secret."

"But— " Grizzly Hair stopped himself. This was the best friend of his boyhood. In two sleeps everyone would know, so what difference would it make if one more man danced with the knowledge that burdened him? "When you're finished with that," he nodded at the drumstick, "let's go to your family's fishing hole." The place was secluded.

It was the time before twilight when the plant people showed their richest hues and the water mosses released their scent. Flowering blackberry canes cascaded down the bank, lending sweetness to the rainbow of aromas. Grizzly Hair sat beside Bowstring on the cool sand and told his story. Listening, Bowstring watched fish jump, rings ebbing in the barely moving water.

Grizzly Hair was finishing when the hollow log drum started. "We could go see the mission for ourselves, a group of us," he said. "We could stay in hiding, then return and tell the umne what we see. Wouldn't you like to see the black hats for yourself? Maybe we could get some big power."

"I doubt any man would go."

"After they hear Morning Owl's oration I think they would. Two Falcons, I think he'd go, and other men would follow him."

Bowstring's burly shoulders rounded in stubborn disagreement. Quietly he said, "People want things to stay the way they've always been." Then a joking smile threatened. "You think they'd travel far from the home place to see men with powerful shooters who act like demons?" He pointed toward the drum.

"Would you go?"

Bowstring blew out air and shook his head. "I don't know."

That was to be expected. Still, with the secret shared, Grizzly Hair felt better. They pushed to their feet at the same time and walked toward the drum. "Been coupling?" Grizzly Hair asked. He'd heard about Straight Willow, a young woman from the Walnut Grove village.

Miming a face of ecstasy, Bowstring curved his fingers as though playing an imaginary flute, ending in a high flourish. Sly again, he looked over. "You like grasshoppers?"

Laughter boomed out of Grizzly Hair. "Let's talk about willows."

"Willow cures all pain," Bowstring allowed with a grin. His face was his downfall. Sometimes people tried to get him to play the gambling bones, but he refused, knowing his face would betray him.

The instant he opened his eyes on the last day of the big time, Grizzly Hair knew it was cool and overcast. He was glad for the rabbit blanket. Mother stood on her toes, reaching into the rafters. She pulled down her forked stick and snake basket. It was the day of the Rattlesnake Dance—a series of dances actually, that would last all day and half the night. Then, after the sleep, Morning Owl would orate about the *Españoles* and everyone would go home knowing the world had changed.

She saw that he was awake. "It's cool this morning," she said. "The snakes might stay in their den. Come and help me."

He'd never done that before. The thought of handling rattlesnakes sent a shiver through him, but a man didn't admit to fear. He sat up, laying the blanket aside.

She handed him the basket of cold nu-pah. "Here, this will give you courage." She chuckled softly.

Pretense was useless with Eagle Woman.

After bathing and nu-pah, she led him and four other doctors with sticks and snake baskets, each doctor with an assistant, over the hill. They came to an old, partly collapsed bear den at the foot of a boulder outcropping. Gray pines and cottonwoods shaded the place, and slim green sacayak spears poked out of the earth all around, a plant unlike any other. Sacayak could transform itself into rattlesnakes. In time of rain and frost an enormous tangle of rattlesnakes hibernated in the collapsed den. At all times people respected and feared this place. Children were told to stay clear of it. On a warm sunny morning the rattlers would have been slithering outside to hunt, but now, as Grizzly Hair, Eagle Woman and eight men stepped cautiously through the grass toward the opening, nothing moved.

They bent down and from a distance tried to see into the den, but no snake was visible. Eagle Woman went to the den mouth and began stamping, one foot then the other. "Help me wake them up," she said.

Keeping an eye on the hole, Grizzly Hair joined the strange dance. A gentle rain began to fall. Soon a snake head appeared, black forked tongue flashing in and out. He jumped back, faster than the others, and they all continued pounding with their feet. More snakes appeared, three, five, too many to count lying on top of each other—a mass of grey eyes in the cool morning light. He shivered under his skin. Slowly they emerged, testing the air with their tongues, so torpid the doctors walked among them with their sticks at the ready. Grizzly Hair admired their courage, for even a sleepy snake could strike fast.

Bent in concentration, Eagle Woman took her time inspecting the snakes. Lightning quick, she stabbed the forked stick down on a big one, grabbed it behind the head and picked it up. The thick muscular snake tried to leap from her grasp. She nodded Grizzly Hair toward the basket.

Jolted into action, he grabbed the odd-shaped basket with the narrow mouth and bulging belly, and held it before her, lid ready. She thrust the snake's head inside and quickly withdrew her hand as the body flowed into the dark opening. As the last rattle slipped inside he jammed on the lid and pushed the wooden peg through the loop.

Eagle Woman touched his arm in thanks. When all the doctors had their snakes, she led the way back to the dance circle. Grizzly Hair followed with the heavy basket, relieved that the snake lay still.

Festively dressed in feathers and flowers, many people waited at the dance circle. They watched while he and the other assistants dug a pit so people could view the snakes. The rain continued and the damp earth was easy to dig with the hollowed branch.

"Make it wider," Eagle Woman instructed.

When the pit was shaped to her satisfaction, she and the other doctors dumped their snakes into the muddy hole. Wide-eyed people crowded forward as the rattlesnakes lurched and flopped and caught each other in their loops and coils. They wove themselves into a blanket with five rattling tails standing erect in a loud, continuous buzz. Grizzly Hair stared until he felt people pushing forward, trying to see, and moved back from the pit.

The drum called and he went to the spectator circle. The fire had been lit and Drum-in-Fog, in a rain-soaked skirt of striped owl feathers, stood intoning the ancient verse. An elder added wood to the fire. Grizzly Hair seated himself between Bowstring and Falls-off-House; for this dance there was no need to sit with family. Some of the girls and women—placing collection baskets among the spectators—gave him long glances. He heard one say, "Let's choose him.

His face went hot. Bowstring elbowed him, chortling. At the end of the rattlesnake dances two men would be selected by the women.

Three Shalachmushumne women sang and the remaining girls and women dashed to the performing area. Each performed her version of lovely motion, demonstrating women's flexibility. The rain fell softly and the snakes quieted in their pit. Grizzly Hair lost himself in the mesmerizing movement of rain-slick feminine limbs and bodies. Moon Woman-Grasshopper Wing leaped, fell into a ball and slowly unfolded until her arms were over her head. Her hips and breasts swayed like river moss in a current. She whirled as if discovering some great pleasure, ran a few steps, leaped again and repeated the moves. Grizzly Hair noticed he wasn't the only one watching her.

He pulled his gaze away, searching for Oak Gall. Five sleeps had passed. She'd been in the woman's house before he returned from the southern river. Surely she wouldn't miss the entire big time. The women quickened their pace with the drumbeat, finishing in a grand leaping burst.

Bowstring, brows arched comically, nudged Grizzly Hair. "Get ready." Falls-off-House sat expectantly on his heels.

The drum started again, a slow voluptuous beat. Four women chanted in a throaty manner and flicked clapper sticks against their thighs. The song told of Coyote's sexual exploits. The rest of the women joined hands and circled the fire facing outward, stepping to the rhythm, seductively undulating their hips and breasts, wanting the men to want them. Jaws went slack, men's parts looked up. The drummer kept up the unbearable anticipation much longer than Grizzly Hair remembered from past Second Grass festivals. Behind the thinning clouds, father sun had climbed high and would see everything. The drumming stopped.

With a scream of laughter the women broke apart and rushed toward their men, throwing flowers from their hair and waists. Some didn't have men, which was why the unmarried men looked forward to this, and usually some went to the wrong men—trades having been worked out—and many would go to more than one man. But the complexities vanished when Moon Woman threw her blossoms at him, then her fullness. Before he could open his eyes another woman claimed him and Moon Woman had a different man. Bowstring's broad back was in motion, and beyond, people coupled all over the field. Coyote, up on his hind legs, ran across the field, pointing and howling, "Woo-oo-oo!"

Then it was over. Girls and women found their baskets and meandered through the men and boys, soliciting presents to pay the singers. Grizzly Hair went to the u-macha for his new beaverskin quiver and tossed it in a basket. His generosity would protect him from rattlesnake bites during the long dry.

Next came the doctor competition. This was always frightening, but it looked as though Eagle Woman had all her powers. She captured her snake and lifted it over her head, where it whipped and thrashed around her face and shoulders. With slow dignity she carried it to the center of the circle and pivoted so all could see the flicking tongue. This would help people understand the snakes and fear them less.

The snake's broad middle coiled around her neck, over her nose and chin and shoulders. The tail buzzed furiously before her nose. It seemed the snake would smother her or she would fall and lose her grip on it. Grizzly Hair held his breath as she pivoted around and around. The people fell silent. Even the rain stopped.

At last she put the snake in the pit as one would deposit a beloved puppy. A collective exhale sounded and Grizzly Hair breathed easier. The other three doctors demonstrated their power over the snakes, each taking a long time, but none matched the skill of Eagle Woman. Grizzly Hair felt proud to have such a mother.

Above, father sun broke through the clouds and shimmered on the green field and hills. To the east a blue-black veil of rain formed a backdrop for the sunlit colors and winking whites—egret feathers and polished bone ornaments against the men's dark faces, white and blue brodiaea blossoms against the women's hair. That the spirits were enjoying the festival could be seen in the sparkling beauty of these colors. Even the rattling in the pit quieted. He got up to dance—women and girls heading for the spectator seats—and the men singers took their places.

Now the men would display their special abilities: strength and stamina. Afterwards, two men would be chosen. The drummer stomped on the log and the song began, recounting the feats of the men of legend. The beat drove Grizzly Hair as he sprang, leaping into the air from a squat, arms high. Around and around he jumped, showing off for the women, his amulet flying and thumping against his chest. O-se-mai-ti was in him. He felt the strength. Even old Frogs-Eggs-Hatching, his sucked-in smile wide, ducked and swayed to the rhythm. With a happy look on his face, Running Quail twisted back and forth with each leap. Bowstring resembled his father, with his broad face and powerful build.

The pace slowly quickened. Faster and faster he danced until at last the drum stopped. Gasping for breath, he looked around and located Bowstring among the perspiring men, hands on his knees, sweat dripping from his nose. He went over.

"Now we'll show them!" Bowstring said with another salacious grin. The drum thumped and the men's chorus started the most erotic song of all. Boys bounded gleefully to the spectator area while the men's line formed again. With his hands on Bowstring's waist and Bowstring's father's hands on his, Grizzly Hair step-hopped around the fire. Wry smiles lit the men's faces. Women and girls pointed; he felt eyes on him.

The song came to the part where Coyote hid inside a hollow tree and pretended to be a branch poking through a hole, and the prettiest young woman came and sat there because he had convinced her all her troubles would disappear if she would marry the tree and all she had to do was to sit on that low branch for three sleeps. Bowstring wiggled his hips so outrageously Grizzly Hair had to let go of him.

Women screamed with laughter. Two Falcons, a normally sober hunter, wiggled his hips too. It was like a signal. Hands left waists. Grizzly Hair gyrated too—all the men did, including Sick Rat—and they all roared with laughter, turning toward the fire, then away, dipping and waggling, even shriveled old Frogs-Eggs-Hatching. Grizzly Hair felt his ribs about to break apart from laughing.

Women and girls were hugging each other and falling in heaps. Boys too. Tears rolled down Morning Owl's cheeks as he held onto Frogs-Eggs-Hatching, whose mouth was open wide in a toothless howl. That sight made Grizzly Hair's legs buckle. Men were dropping to the ground around him and rolling from side to side, squirming in silent laughter.

Suddenly hands were pulling him up, several laughing young women. He had been chosen, he realized with a shock, to perform the final dance. He saw Howchia smiling at him and old women cackling, all except Grandmother, who sat as if in a trance. He was glad she was blind. Oak Gall's father stood with his wife, both watching with flat eyes. They already thought him unrestrained. This would make it worse.

Embarrassment burned through him as he stood encircled by half the young women, their friends busy choosing a second man. For a moment he thought of sprinting up the western path. No one could catch him. But that would spoil the Rattlesnake Dance and he would not be allowed to forget it. Besides, this was an honor. Red Sun and Nettles knew that. He must behave as the umne expected.

The magic struck when Grub Log was selected and the dance began.

9

Half the young women danced around Grizzly Hair—a breeze cooling his perspiring body—while the other half danced around Grub Log. Men in the spectator circle were still wiping tears of laughter. The rain had darkened the eastern half of the sky, forming a background against which colorful double arches blazed across the world—two coyotes-making-water, the colors so brilliant it seemed a slice could be cut off and saved in a basket. Legs apart, head back, amulet rising and falling on his chest, he was admiring the astonishing sight when the knowledge came. As vivid as the sky it shot up from the ground into his feet and up to his stomach, where it lodged.

It had always been his fate to track the *Españoles* to their homes. He was chosen, born into a family that had been broken by those he would track. He was strong and young. He had accomplished everything he had ever tried. The spirits were with him and he would return to the home place with knowledge for his people. If necessary he would go alone.

The women sang a ribald song with a double meaning. The female spectators who slapped wooden clappers on their thighs knew nothing of the wider world, nor did the men and boys eyeing him, but they needed him to do this. Slowly the voluptuous beat accelerated, the dancers moving ever closer until they were an arm's length away. Over their heads he saw Grub Log standing at ease within his circle of dancing women.

A light stroke feathered across Grizzly Hair's calf. He whirled to see who had done it. All the faces looked guilty and delighted and the dance went on. A hand stroked his other calf and withdrew before he could see whose it was. A hand lingered beneath his left buttock, another touched his thigh. The soft strokes became more and more frequent as he twisted around to the obvious merriment of the women. He stopped giving them the sport of fooling him and stood in peace, allowing them to touch him from every direction as he watched the astonishing colors against the blue-black sky. He was chosen. He was of the bear's lineage. He welcomed the hands as he welcomed knowledge.

At a signal he didn't see, and with much giggling and scurrying about, the women switched men. Now Grub Log's former dancers fondled him. Meanwhile older men moved through the crowd soliciting donations for the singers. He noticed Howchia giving several new baskets to keep rattlesnakes from biting him during the long dry. A man was making a loud speech in front of Grasshopper Wing's older sister. With exaggerated moves he tossed down the offering basket, which he had been holding before her, and heaved her over his shoulder, yelling, "You are the donation."

Her husband yanked at her legs. Grizzly Hair was glad to see that their clowning drew attention away from him. Other married women were abducted and clumps of people staggered in mock battles, shrieking with laughter. Meanwhile, fingertips continued their butterfly dance and the arches stood astride the world—Coyote making water, a reminder that the most beautiful things on earth may not be what they seem.

The music stopped. Some spectators dashed to the snake pit and grabbed sticks that had been laid by for this purpose. They poked the snakes and provoked a steady angry rattling. Others stood on one leg holding a foot just out of reach of the snapping fangs—reminding the snakes why they had flat heads, ever since Coyote stepped on Rattlesnake. This bravado also prevented snake bites. Other people left in pairs.

Grizzly Hair lay on the ground vibrating with the loud buzzing, which he felt in his sinuses and lungs and loins, and the women took turns on him. The coyote-urine colors pulsed brighter and brighter until he roared from his chest and spurted purple and gold fire like the northern volcano of legend.

Again the women were fondling him but it was too much. Despite shrieks of "stay for me," he broke loose and sprinted to the river trailed by several women. Maybe they were diverted by other men or maybe they understood his need to be alone. They left him treading the quiet water and considering his fate.

That evening after gorging himself with succulent snake stew, Grizzly Hair gestured for Bowstring to follow to the secluded place at the downstream fishing hole. "I will go see for myself what is going on the west," Grizzly Hair told his friend.

A low whistle came from Bowstring.

"The spirits told me to go. Won't you go with me?"

After a silence: "Yes, I will go."

Moved by strong emotion, Grizzly Hair put a hand on his friend's thick shoulder. Bowstring laid a meaty hand on Grizzly Hair's shoulder, then they turned back toward the feast.

"Friend?"

Bowstring looked at him.

"Do the men think well of me, now that I was chosen for the Rattlesnake Dance?" It meant he was attractive to women, but how would the men see him?

"How would you feel about me if I'd been chosen?" Bowstring asked back.

"That you were a fine cock quail."

"Is that good?"

"Of course," Grizzly Hair had to admit. Seeing the smiling shrug, he probed, "Think your father feels the same way?"

Bowstring nodded.

"And the elders? Red Sun?" He didn't want to embarrass himself by asking Two Falcons.

"Yes."

They walked in silence, Grizzly Hair grateful for this good friend who would accompany him into the unknown. Singers, drummers, rattlers and flutists were also on their way to the dance circle. Bowstring trotted ahead to get his flutes from his u-macha. Later, Bowstring made the most haunting music of all the flute players. No spirit could fail to be lulled by it. Then the last dance began, with no purpose but fun. The festival had woven the peoples together and Grizzly Hair felt himself an invisible fiber in a blanket of motion and music, bouncing in the joy of the moment, the men's line dancing toward the women, the women step-hopping past them.

Suddenly in the firelight he was looking into Oak Gall's smiling face. He blinked to be sure, then turned and looked back as she danced away. Turning forward again, he waited for her face and the clacking strips of her willow-bark apron. She was dancing at last. Each time they passed in the warm glow of the fire, he told her mind-to-mind that she was beautiful and he wanted to be with her.

It was very late when the drum stopped. Other women touched him, but he looked over their heads and saw Oak Gall settling into her fascinating walk, coming toward him, smiling.

They must have seen this. Even Moon Woman left.

"Your family thinks I shouldn't be with you," he told Oak Gall, unable to see Nettles and Red Sun in the crowd. A short distance away, however, Etumu stood watching.

Oak Gall glanced at her little sister and moved her lips in silent talk. Etumu signed that her mouth was closed. Then Oak Gall and Grizzly Hair headed for the western hill. The misshapen moon lit their shortcut through the shadows to the boulder outcropping where they often talked. Up through the tangle of poison oak and buckeye they climbed, and he noticed the rippling of her long legs before him. She wasn't plump like Moon Woman, but made up for it with the confident grace with which she claimed the space around her. Despite her slimness there was nothing tentative about Oak Gall.

In the clearing overlooking the river, she kneeled in the tall feathery grass. Cupping her face, he kneeled and kissed one padded eyelid then the other. He slid his hand down the curve of her back to the softness of her hips resting on her heels, and gently laid her back in the grass, the earth's hair, and felt himself engulfed in sweetness, floating beyond manly conceit to a place he'd never gone before.

"You are a beautiful man," she said.

Inner lightning sparked, making him hoarse. "I have always wanted you."

"As I want you."

The night air was pure all the way to the campfires of the immortals. He joined her, and as a storm embraces the earth by intensifying degrees, gripped her with unintended fierceness. Later, they rolled to the side, all apertures of mind and body open to each other, and their spirits drifted like night birds together.

After a time she told him her fantasy of becoming a fish in the river. "Then I will swim beside you," he said nuzzling her neck, which smelled of peppermint. He could smell it in her amulet, though its contents were her secret.

She chuckled and breathed in his ear. "The other men should learn from you."

It didn't seem possible, but he was new again. Mother moon had gone all the way to the west when he told her of the people at the southern river. "I will go to the western sea," he said, "and observe the *Españoles*. Bowstring will go with me."

She sat up, the oaks dark behind her against a graying sky. "You always want to understand things," she said.

"I am a tracker."

She touched his cheek. "The best tracker since Stalking Cougar, the only man brave enough to cut hair off the Old Man of the Forest. Only you could bring knowledge of the *Españoles* to the umne." She seemed to smile. "And I am going with you."

It took his breath away. A woman traveled with a man only if they were married, and they had not mentioned marriage. But with Oak Gall at his side he felt he could do anything. His thinking expanded. She could hide in the bushes with Bowstring while he crept forward to observe the mission and the black hats. She would be safe. This too was fated—he and Oak Gall. "I want you to be my woman," he said. "Before we leave I will bring your parents the first marriage gift."

Hand in hand they walked to the river and waded into its cold embrace. Other couples were treading water in the early light, including Cranebill and his woman-man.

After what seemed a short nap in the u-macha and cold nu-pah, he went outside to see Oak Gall distributing the baskets of oo-lah to the crowd before the dancehouse. Morning Owl climbed the mound behind the roundhouse and walked out on the nearly flat roof. Now he would sound the alarm. He stood waiting for quiet, father sun glinting off his bear-claw necklace, shell money and long heron-bone earplugs. The young oak at the back of the dancehouse cast its shadow west.

Grizzly Hair sat among his friends on the ground before the dancehouse, saving a space for Oak Gall. She lowered herself beside him and clasped her knees. He scooted over so their hips were snug together. All around them people looked contented, except Howchia, who wore an expression of forced calm, and Nettles and Red Sun, who were glaring at Oak Gall. She boldly pretended not to notice. But it pained Grizzly Hair. Maybe they wouldn't accept his presents or allow him into their house to judge whether he was a good husband for their daughter. But she was fated to be his, so somehow he must overcome their resistence. A clowning woodpecker began violent drilling.

Morning Owl's voice rang out, instructing children to respect their elders and admonishing young men to walk away from arguments. With all the formal repetitions this lasted a long time. He came to the end of that part and stood in silence for a while. Then he said, "Pale-skinned men have come into the world." The audience looked puzzled.

He told how the black hats rode big animals. He told people to avoid being lured away, emphasizing that these were men, not spirits, and their *caballos* were mere animals that could be killed by arrows and spears. Gasps erupted from the listeners like steam from boiling nu-pah.

He took his time repeating all that Grizzly Hair had told him and emphasizing the dangers, all in formal speech. "Many seasons ago," he intoned, "some of us heard about this, but people said the story was invented. It was not. I tell you it was real. If you see costumed men riding animals, strange men on strange animals, run and hide. Hide in the hill boulders, where the Ancients hid from their enemies. Hide from your enemies."

Run and hide. Was that enough? Grizzly Hair looked at Oak Gall. She shrugged as if to ask, what else can we do? He wasn't sure. That's why he needed to observe the *Españoles.*

All gaiety had dropped from the peoples' faces. The hy-apo shifted to advice about living well so bad luck wouldn't strike. By the time he finished, Grizzly Hair's stomach was growling and the shadow of the oak pointed east.

After a quiet supper the guests departed in thoughtful lines. The umne, alone again, sat outside their u-machas, each in private thought. Red Sun and Nettles looked as though they had forgotten about Grizzly Hair and Oak Gall.

A loud voice came from the trees. "Don't hide from me! Come out and talk. Here I am, right here, waiting. Come out, come here!" It was Running Quail calling his spirit ally.

Grizzly Hair was wondering what to give Oak Gall's parents. The gift had to be something spectacular that they could not reject. Fleetingly it crossed his mind that they might never accept him, but that was so contrary to the love surging through him that it floated away.

10

Grizzly Hair and the men had slept in the sweathouse, each communing with his own spirits. Now it was the morning after the big time and nothing had changed. Men watched the young children and women gathered.

Grizzly Hair joined Morning Owl on his rounds of quail snares and sidled up to his talk. "The umne act the same as they did before they knew of the *Españoles.*"

"The frog doesn't stay in the mud shaking in fear when the heron nests nearby. He comes out and sings to the women."

It was time to speak his meaning. "I will go see the *Españoles* myself and return with knowledge for the umne."

Morning Owl pushed out his lips and said, "The frog presenting himself to the heron. I was afraid you'd do that."

"Am I a frog?"

"You are the one who talked to the southern people. You told us of the danger."

"I am a tracker."

"One who is too persistent."

He exhaled away the urge to be sharp. "I think it is important for us to have better knowledge about the *Españoles*."

The hy-apo opened and closed his arms as if gathering earth and sky to his bosom. "Anything of importance can be learned right here." He resumed stepping methodically through the grass, watching for snakes, adding, "People who search for trouble find it."

Grizzly Hair thought of responding, "Then you will step on a rattlesnake." Instead he said, "The quail knows whether the bobcat is stalking or merely sunning himself. Such knowledge keeps him alive."

"You told us all we need to know about the black hats."

"If you watch the badger only when he fights, you would think him aggressive and warlike. But he is reclusive and peaceful most of the time."

They came to an unsprung snare and Morning Owl sighed. "Be careful poking around in snake dens."

"I can observe the *Españoles* without being seen."

With a dismissive wave Morning Owl said, "Each man must find his own way."

Back in the village Eagle Woman said the same thing, but there was moisture in her eyes.

A little later, when he was pulling his net from the fishing hole, Hummingbird Tailfeather stepped from behind a tree—Bowstring's mother. She glanced past him with fierce eyes and her voice cracked. "Do not take my son to danger."

He recognized her courage in losing face like this, but had to say, "Bowstring wants to come with me." He didn't dishonor her by mentioning that Bowstring was a man.

She bit her knuckle and hurried up the path, waddling in her girth. He could only try to imagine the opposition Bowstring must be enduring in the privacy of his u-macha, and knew he must not further encourage his friend, though having him on the journey would be a comfort. He thought of Oak Gall and the struggle she would be facing.

With growing unease he returned to the u-macha with his net of blue gills and handed them to Howchia, who sat tying herbs before the doorway. Taking the fish, she glanced guardedly at Red Sun's u-macha and said in a low voice, "Nettles and Red Sun came here. They want me to make magic to stop you from taking Oak Gall. They offered ten new baskets and a full string of ocean shells." She took the fish inside, leaving him shaken.

Coyote had scrambled things. He could almost see Trickster's smug smile. For two sleeps he had pondered what to give Oak Gall's parents, and now, to keep her from him, they were offering a payment so rich as to render them destitute and beholden to relatives. He ducked into the dim u-macha, waited for his eyes to adjust and saw Howchia lying on her mat. "What did you tell them?"

She covered her eyes with a forearm. "I told them nothing."

That was good, but would she perform the magic?

"I wish you wouldn't go," she said.

Realizing that to linger would bring uncomfortable suspense to everyone, he decided to hurry straightening his new arrow-shafts and leave after the sleep. Quietly he said, "It is a path I must take."

"Then go, but don't take Oak Gall."

Stunned at that—Mother didn't make demands—he ducked back outside where father sun pressed upon his head and shoulders. The wing people were quiet in their shady roosts. No pounding could be heard from the chaw'se and men were drifting sleepily into the sweathouse for a nap. Oak Gall and Nettles sat beneath the willow porch of their u-macha winding basket-weaving roots into long skeins. Grizzly Hair looked at Oak Gall, who was looking at him, and received the distinct impression that she wanted to talk. He did too.

Heading up the western hill and down the other side, he took his time, then turned toward the river bottom. The sand and rocks felt hot even through his thick calluses. He went to Grandmother, who was drilling clamshells, and made his presence known. Not seeing Oak Gall yet, he went to the river and stood with his feet in shallow water. The gurgling of the river baby spirit soothed him, and he touched his amulet, asking O-se-mai-ti to restore his strength.

At last Oak Gall sauntered down the path, her bluntly singed hair swinging across her beautiful sloping shoulders. She settled into her steps with a sauciness that made him ache. He let her approach and stand in the water beside him, then cupped her shoulders and inhaled her scent along with the pepper-sweet lupine. She brought power of a different kind.

"I know what my parents told your mother," she said.

He couldn't let that disturb the moment—Oak Gall in his hands, the delicate aroma of lupine flowers. "Maybe I'll give your parents a pair of antelope hides," he said, "tanned in brains and chewed soft. Would they like that?"

Her crisply outlined lips turned up slowly and he smiled back, believing it meant yes, but she said, "They won't accept anything from you, so I've decided to go with you anyway." Her smile remained in place.

"But when we return," he said as gently as possible, "they will have me banished from the home place." Having her to himself during the journey would be a gift of the immortals, but that wasn't enough. He wanted her to be his woman in the proper way, wanted their children to dance with the related peoples, wanted to be a respected family man who would provide his daughters with fine gifts for their suitors and teach his sons to be men of the umne.

"I think they'd be so happy to see us that they would accept your gift then." She beamed him the smile he loved most, a young smile of confidence and enthusiasm. "Then you could move into our u-macha and they would see you as I do, a man unlike any other, the best man in the world."

It took his breath. He longed to swim with her then go ashore where the sand was cool and damp and lie with her in the shade of the black alders. But he had arrows to straighten. "I could start now by giving them the antelope hides." Antelope was a shy animal, fast and difficult to kill.

"I've talked to my parents. They will reject any gift from you now. This is the better way. I think they'll blame me more than you."

"I don't want them to blame you. And this has never been done before, a woman leaving with a man without any exchange of gifts."

"That's why it's the only way. None of this has been done before—you tracking the black hats. The world is different now." A tease bent her smile and she settled back on one hip with a hand on her waist. "That's funny, me telling you that—you of all men. You've always been different."

But the rules of marriage hadn't changed. Other things he could risk, but not her. "Maybe they would accept a gift so worthless it wouldn't mean anything, just start them thinking about. . . so our traveling together wouldn't. . ." He wound down like a drill on a played-out string.

"They absolutely won't accept any gift now and I am going with you." Her eyes said he was trapped.

But he wasn't. Knowing he must leave her in the home place, he gentled her to him and moaned, the emptiness of leaving her already hurting. Then quite suddenly he recalled a rumor he'd heard at a big time, that on the beaches of the western sea riches lay about on the sand—beautiful shells of all colors, unbroken abalone, tubular shells—and all you had to do was bend down and pick them up. There was also a sea animal with a pelt that kept people warm and dry in the wind and rain. He stroked Oak Gall's hair and admitted to himself that she would be safer here. He would return with a gift her parents could not reject; and he would bring knowledge to save the umne. Then Red Sun would be proud to be his father-in-law, and she would become his wife in the proper way.

He and Bowstring left at dawn. Every step pulled more distance between him and Oak Gall and he had to force himself to put one foot in front of the other. He reached inside but could not release the pain. He told himself he would be back in a moon or two and that she would remember him despite the fun of the big times. How many more big times would be held before be returned? He would have found it difficult, he realized, to leave the home place even if everyone had wanted him to go. But leaving her and knowing everyone wanted him and Bowstring to stay was the hardest thing he had ever done. It slowed his feet. Bowstring's silence and pained expression didn't help either.

When the sun sank into his western house they were making a bent-willow shelter on a creek, still far from the southern river. Without talk they roasted quail pullets and munched arrow-root and watercress. Bowstring pulled his flute from his waist-thong, went a distance away, sat against a cottonwood and blew sad music. Grizzly Hair crawled into the shelter and lay staring at the dark branches where a few campfires of the immortals winked through the willow leaves. The flute sang of the aloneness of men traveling far from their people. The low hollow tones bored into Grizzly Hair's spirit, and the rise and fall of tender notes told of happy love no longer present. In the privacy of the hut, warm tears ran down his temples.

Long into the night, dream people step-toed around and around a fire to the song of the flute. He felt a touch, assumed it was one of the dream people or Dog catching up, and continued dancing with the dream people.

Later the smell of willow came at him, mixed with her scent. He opened his eyes. It was dark. An owl whooed nearby—bad luck. He held his breath and listened. It seemed that two people were breathing in the hut. Heavy on his left, lighter on his right. Was this a trick of a sorcerer? Or was he still dreaming?

He moved his hand slightly and his fingers touched warm soft flesh. He blinked hard, trying to wake up. But he was awake. His thoughts swirled like leaves in a funnel wind. It was her scent. She had followed. Her father and uncles would assume he had arranged it. They would follow too. Or would fear of the black hats hold them back? It didn't matter. Banishment could await his return and he would lose her. Why hadn't she listened to him? With anger rising in his belly he lay stiff and silent, then carefully sat up and crawled outside without touching her. She had risked everything.

Beyond the dark willows and cottonwoods father sun was still in his eastern house, only a wash of gray light suggesting his coming. A night animal rustled. How much time before Red Sun and his brothers arrived? Fortunately, no reasonable person traveled at night.

He found a bush suitable for scattering urine and returned to the creek for a drink, kneeling and scooping cool water. Each handful clarified his thoughts more. He must take her back. She couldn't go by herself. She had already tempted the loose souls of the trail by coming this far alone. Then if Red Sun met them, he would see that Grizzly Hair was sincere about leaving her. Then he and Bowstring could go on their way. Relieved to be clear in his purpose, he stood up and faced the coming dawn.

A slim dark figure separated itself from the shadow of a tree. Oak

Gall. In a sudden tumult of tenderness—she had braved the night trail to be with him—he stepped toward her and all anger dissolved.

Her hands moved over him. Mother earth, transformed to airy softness, came up to meet them, and he joined Oak Gall in a magic dance of love, their moves as light and easy as two hawks on a thermal. He soared and soared with her into the salmon dawn, drumming with the power of joy and love. Then his pent-up breath came out in a rush and he let himself float in a feathery downward spiral, snug with the woman who made him whole, the air still beneath them. He never wanted to feel different from this moment.

A flicker erupted into song and blackbirds joined the chorus of life. He heard footsteps. Half ready to face Red Sun, he opened his eyes and saw that it was Bowstring coming toward them. Red Sun would be far back on the trail. Oak Gall smiled at him lazily and pulled away, halving him. She sauntered to the creek and lowered herself in it. Woodpecker clownbirds with comical round eyes and serious beaks emerged from holes in the cottonwoods and swooped and cackled to a nearby oak.

Sighing, Grizzly Hair sat up. "Did you know she was here?"

"She was in the little u-macha when I went to sleep."

He'd done the right thing, not waking him. Nothing could have been done about it at night. He looked at Oak Gall throwing water over herself and said, "We're taking her back."

Bowstring widened his eyes.

Grizzly Hair pointed with his head. "Better go find a bush." As Bowstring turned to leave, Grizzly Hair said after him. "Let me tell her."

He went to the creek, lowered himself in it and watched Oak Gall feather herself dry. Did she know how lovely she was? She turned and sauntered to the willows where she pulled out her carrying basket. By the time he finished bathing, she had a fire started, a cooking stone from the home place in it and a basket of acorn meal soaking in water. This was an unexpected treat, one that only a woman could supply. He gathered wood for a hotter fire, the sooner to feed his grumbling belly.

Bowstring bathed and sat on a fallen tree nearby. Oak Gall, with an expression of utter contentment, watched the fire. The cooking stone grew hotter and the unspoken talk felt white-hot on Grizzly Hair's tongue. "We're going back," he finally got out.

Her brows bunched. "You change your mind about tracking the black hats?"

"No."

She stared at the distance, the line of her jaw delicate but firm. "I won't go back." Bowstring looked innocently around like he couldn't hear.

Grizzly Hair forced out, "We will take you the whole way, unless we meet your father on the trail. Then we'll leave you with him."

"He won't come for me. And I didn't come this far to go back."

The sound of hurt tore at him. He wanted to please her and couldn't bear leaving her again. Yet he must. "We're going back as soon as we've eaten." It sounded strangled.

She looked past Bowstring, who was still pretending to be deaf, at Grizzly Hair for longer than was normally polite, and said with a tone of conviction, "I am not going back. You would have to carry me and I would fight you." The teasing corner of her mouth turned up. "Besides, I thought you'd like having nu-pah every morning." She took tongs from her basket and picked up the stone, now glowing red, and lowered it into the basket, stirring as the nu-pah boiled.

The coupling, he realized, had drained his ability to disagree. Besides, he knew her well, knew that her easy manner hid a fierce determination. What Oak Gall wanted, Oak Gall generally got. Would any other woman go out alone on a difficult night trail? Follow a man who was not her husband? Risk meeting bears and mountain lions and Bohemkulla—the bad spirit of night trails who overwhelmed travelers and made them crazy? Chin up, she moved the stone around. The bubbles of steam escaping from the thickening mush said, nu-pah, nu-pah. All around, the chorus of wing people swelled with the brightening day, but the humans were silent.

Until Bowstring said, "What makes you think your father won't come after us?"

"I told them Grizzly Hair didn't want me to go. I said I was sad and needed my power place. I went there and right away my spirit ally told me to follow you, so I tossed a pebble at Etumu to make her look at me. She came to where I was hiding and I told her to tell our parents I had followed you, but she promised not to tell them until after supper. By then it would have been too late for Father to leave." She gave them a little smile, "Etumu does what I tell her." Then her chin was up again. "I am a grown woman and I go where you go."

She lifted the stone from the nu-pah, set it aside, scooted over beside Grizzly Hair and placed her magic hand on his thigh. It sizzled to his man's core. "Don't you want me on your mat at night?"

Yes! Her spirit ally had told her to come. No doubt Red Sun knew her determination and would realize Grizzly Hair hadn't arranged this. Etumu had no reason to tell a falsehood. People didn't do that. Falsehoods weakened everyone. Sometimes plans changed, that's all. People had to adjust. Coyote's paw print was on this situation and nothing could be done about it.

Besides, he would bring back a spectacular gift for Nettles and Red Sun. But to avoid unnecessary surprises, he would lead his friends on a course of tricks that even trackers were unlikely to follow.

The sky was clear. Hawks circled and keened, and in the hazy distance dark animals took shape in the tan grassland. With growing excitement Grizzly Hair drew closer to the strange animals they had been tracking—*caballos.* No men sat on their backs and no people of any kind were in sight. Motioning Bowstring and Oak Gall to wait, he crept closer and hid behind the trunk of an oak, peering around it. Still no sign of people. But a herd of the magnificent animals grazed only two bowshots away.

In awe he watched them wind up mouthfuls of grass, bite and chew, then take one step forward to another mouthful. Their muscular bodies were sleek, haunches powerful, tails long and full. Most were brown or black. A black male—even from this distance that was visible—seemed to keep an eye on the others, the females. His swaying tail nearly touched his stonelike feet as he pranced on his rounds. Sometimes he approached a female and snorted to make her leave her grass. The female would trot away and quickly drop her head to new grass. After a while the male would nose her away again. He did this with many of the females, which kept him very busy.

Grizzly Hair gave Bowstring and Oak Gall a round arm to follow. They crouch-walked to him and Oak Gall sank back on her heels, clearly entranced by the animals. She looked him a tease and said, "Female *caballos* find better grass."

He had always liked her banter, and realized that three sleeps with her had made him feel like more of a man. She was fun to travel with.

Young horses with shiny brown coats frolicked and returned for their mothers' milk. Older youngsters got a toothy nip when they tried to suckle. Far in the distance, what appeared to be a group of young males grazed alone. Grizzly Hair felt like he could stay forever watching these animals.

But as father sun lowered, he felt restless to find water. The distant line of green vegetation beckoned. "Let's go back to the trail and camp at that river," he said.

"Yes, I'm tired of camping here," Oak Gall joked. She and Bowstring turned to leave.

The male *caballo* saw movement. He pointed his ears at them. To Grizzly Hair's horror the animal raised his head and emitted a piercing, quivering noise. For a moment it stopped his heart, accustomed as he was to the quiet grazers of the grasslands. The *caballo* then stood on his hind feet and pawed the air, calling again in his loud voice, then fell to the ground running, pounding hard at them with eyes like suns. Gasps of shock came from Bowstring and Oak Gall.

Grizzly Hair, who had one knee on the ground and the toes of his back foot digging in for balance, quickly slipped the loop over the bottom notch of his bow and pulled an arrow—Bowstring hurrying with his bow beside him. The animal thundered closer. Grizzly Hair aimed, realizing he knew nothing of a *caballo's* organs and had time for only one arrow. Between the front legs there had to be a collar bone that would shield the vital organs. He raised his aim to the big head coming at him. It shielded the throat and side-positioned eyes were impossible to hit from straight on. The arrow might only anger this animal more. Still, he was about to release it, hoping the skull wasn't too thick, when the *caballo* skidded to a halt in a cloud of dust. He snorted and flung his head up and down as if in warning, then wheeled around and galloped back to nip the flanks of several females, making the herd run north. He ran back and forth prodding those in the rear.

Watching them retreat, Grizzly Hair glanced at Bowstring—the horror still in his face—and blew out breath he hadn't known he'd stored. Oak Gall made a comical expression of disaster narrowly averted. Even this far away, mother earth shook beneath his knees because of the running of many *caballos*, tails drawing dark lines behind them. Feeling the power of the herd, he pressed his hands on the ground. Bowstring and Oak Gall did likewise. This had been a lesson in *caballo* behavior, Grizzly Hair realized, and something else. Bowstring or Oak Gall, or both, had been careless.

He said nothing about it as they walked single file up the trail they had abandoned earlier. They talked about the beautiful animals. Bowstring, who brought up the rear, spoke excitedly. "They didn't like people. How could a man ride them?"

In the middle, Oak Gall added, "And none wore seats on their backs."

"Someday I want to ride a *caballo*," Grizzly Hair said over his shoulder.

"Me too," Oak Gall said.

Bowstring made a whistling sound.

Grizzly Hair had a vision of them, each on a horse, riding with the herd across the grasslands, hair streaming like the tails and manes. If only Two Falcons could see these animals! "A man could hunt on a horse," he called back to Bowstring. "You wouldn't need to trick the deer to get within range." Lifted by the thought, he jumped and trotted ahead, the laughs and hoots of Bowstring and Oak Gall trailing close behind.

In the lavender twilight they made a bent-willow shelter and built a fire beneath a fire-hollowed cottonwood to disperse the smoke. Black hats could be near. This worried Grizzly Hair, especially now that Bowstring and Oak Gall had made a mistake. Still, he realized as he stalked a brush rabbit with a stone, he wouldn't mention it. They had seen the horse possessed of the fury of an aroused bear, and surely knew their error could have brought their deaths.

Later, when the rabbit was roasted and the greens steamed, he and Oak Gall sat close together, thighs touching, gnawing tender meat. With a lazy smile she tossed her bone and leaned back on grass that had been matted by reclining deer. He rolled with her, the stored warmth of the day coming up from the earth, and she chuckled low in her throat.

The purple sky deepened over the river jungle as the rhythms intensified around them, the insistent treep of crickets and the pumping bellow of frogs. Out on the balmy grassland a coyote sang. Another answered in a higher pitch. Bowstring took his flute and imitated the coyotes. An owl added its oo-ooo-oo. He imitated that too, and the lower hoots of other owls. Grizzly Hair hoped it would confuse the owls, and the black hats, if they happened to be within earshot. And, oh, Morning Owl was right. The frog came out of the mud and coupled with his mate in the presence of his enemies. Life flowed in balanced harmony. Black night came down and squeezed out the last of the purple, and layers and layers of campfires of the immortals winked and twinkled high above them.

It was morning. Judging from the depth of the vegetation as it had looked from the grassland, this would be a much larger river than he had seen before, likely the one from the south that had drained the ancient sea. The ground was damp, muddy in places. A forest of tulares dwarfed them—a hollow-stemmed plant that grew in big bunches. Redwings perched on the green tips, filling the world with their raucous song.

Searching for the actual river, they followed a meandering stream for some time, but backtracked after sinking to their knees in mud and crawling out with difficulty. Clouds of mosquitos rose from the mud and hovered around them. A startling roar of ducks blasted through the marsh and took wing, blanketing the sun—a flapping, squawking pandemonium.

Oak Gall shouted, "I didn't know there were so many ducks in the world."

"It's a wonder they find enough to eat," he yelled back.

They stood in the dark until the last duck crossed the sun and the world was bright and quiet and green again. Grizzly Hair lacked a counting word to express so many ducks; it was more, he thought, than any person could imagine.

"We feed the mosquitos," Oak Gall said with a grin, "and they feed the ducks. Smiling back, he and Bowstring followed her example, slathering themselves with mud against the insects.

The river remained hidden in the forest of marsh vegetation. A maze of large and small channels meandered in all directions, and the smell of stagnant mud was thick in their noses. Water snakes slithered in and out of view. At times they saw elk mothers and calves through the open channels, looking at them with vegetation dripping from their mouths.

Secretly Grizzly Hair was beginning to worry that they would be swallowed in mud. But at last he found firmer footing, higher ground, and saw a *caballo* trail. Relieved, he followed it southward, but after a short distance smelled the sweet oniony scent of Man.

11

Afraid this was a village of black hats, he stood behind the grapevines hanging from the trees, and watched. By no means was this the western sea, but the Muquelumne had said the mission wasn't on the sea either. Here, the dancehouse and u-machas were built entirely of tulares. Only the squat-legged cha'kas woven of grapevines resembled the granaries of the home place. Three young children shrieked with laughter as they ran about with sticks. Most of the women had skirts of cattail leaves, but several were made of the strange red material he had seen on the thin women. A squatting woman stirred something in a vessel placed, astoundingly, directly in the fire. It didn't burn despite the flames rising around it.

Almost as astonishing, four horses grazed at the edge of the village, not struggling though their front legs were hobbled in thongs. They nibbled quietly at leaves and grass that grew in the shade.

Stomach tightening with excitement, he gave Bowstring and Oak Gall a serious look and motioned them to stay hidden. Slitting his eyes to hide the whites, he used the trick of becoming invisible in the leaves, moving quickly when the quarry looked away, then stilling himself. He arrived at an oak a stone's toss from where most of the people sprawled in the shade of the high canopy. Bows and loaded quivers leaned on some of the u-machas. Dogs slept. There was no breeze but he and Oak Gall and Bowstring had taken the precaution of rubbing themselves with mint.

A big man in a stiff-brimmed black hat sat on a fallen log with his feet widely planted, elbows on his knees. He looked sleepy as he watched the woman stirring the unburning vessel. Not pale-skinned like *Españoles* were supposed to be, he wore a pale shirt that gaped open to his belly. On his chest was a large abalone shell shimmering with aqua, silver, lavender and coral. It was extremely valuable. Even broken pieces of such shells were valuable. His facial hair hadn't been plucked. Black hair bristled from his chin and drooped around his thick lips. Behind him, leaning against a tree, stood a long, dark thing. It was narrow and looked very smooth—like nothing Grizzly Hair had ever seen.

The other men of the village also had facial hair. Two wore the same kind of pale shirt hanging halfway to their knees.

For four sleeps they camped well beyond the village of the strangers and talked of little else. Each day Grizzly Hair observed the more than twenty men, five women, and three children, and in the evenings talked with Bowstring and Oak Gall about what he had seen. He refused to let them go closer than where they had hidden that first day. One question absorbed them: were these black hats? The headman wore a black hat, but their skin was normal in color. They spoke a strange tongue that he had never heard before, and Grizzly Hair wondered if the strange dark thing leaning against the tree could be a thunder shooter.

The three of them had discovered that this village lay near the big river they had been seeking—water that must be crossed. And Grizzly Hair realized that they needed help finding the best route to the western sea.

Increasingly, he was of the opinion that these people could be befriended, and hoped they would help with the route. He felt even more certain when he followed four men with fishing nets and spears to see where they would go. They overturned a structure made of bundled tulares and pushed it in the water—a boat similar to the ones used by the kadeema-umne. They picked up poles, waded into the river with the boat and climbed in. What convinced him was the way they joked with each other, as all normal people did. The boat drifted while the men trolled their nets, then a man stood up and pushed against the river bottom with the pole, moving them to another place on the river. Before long they had speared some very large fish.

Grizzly Hair made his way back to the mosquito-infested camp, where Bowstring and Oak Gall were standing knee-deep in the muck, and told them, "I am going to talk to these people."

Oak Gall looked up, three frogs speared on her sharpened stick, and said, "I am sure they are friendly."

He reminded himself that she was never in doubt.

Bowstring raised skeptical brows and high-stepped from the bog, two frogs decorating his spear.

"My stomach says they will help us," Grizzly Hair told him.

Bowstring shrugged and joked, "When do we herald ourselves?

The morning air was cool and fragrant. A dog lifted its head, pointed its ears and growled to its feet. Every large and small person looked at the dog then at Grizzly Hair as he stepped from the trees, bow held out from his body. In a flash he was surrounded by barking dogs.

Using the pronunciation of the Muquelumne, he said in a loud voice, "We come from the northeast. Can anyone speak my tongue?"

The dogs barked fiercely and most of the people ran out of sight. Only the *caballos* ignored him.

The man in the black hat stepped forward, clearly the headman. In his calf-thong was a knife made of strange material. He spoke the home tongue poorly, with an accent, "Where are you going?"

"To the mission to observe the *Españoles.* With my friends." For a while he wouldn't reveal how many.

The headman examined the trees, but Oak Gall and Bowstring were hiding well. "Why are you going to the mission?" A nasty smile tugged the man's thick lips.

Grizzly Hair spoke loud enough to be heard over the dogs. "We are curious about the people who ride on the backs of *caballos*." He nodded at the horses.

"They will chain you in *hierro*."

"What is ee-éro?"

With a harsh, unintelligible word to the dogs, which quieted them, the headman said, "Either you are stupid or you pretend to be stupid so I won't think you are spying neofi-tehs. That is iron." He pointed to the pot that didn't burn. "The black hats lock your feet together with it." He motioned for Grizzly Hair to sit down.

Relieved at this sign of hospitality, he sat on the ground facing the man who lowered himself on his log. Why would anyone, he wondered, stuff a man's feet in a cooking vessel? Some of the people were returning to the clearing, watching him and circling around to hear the talk.

The headman asked several questions about where Grizzly Hair's people lived, how many rivers to the north, how near the eastern mountains, and why he was tracking the black hats. Slowly and truthfully, Grizzly Hair answered everything and when the man seemed satisfied, asked, "Where did you get your hat?"

The man threw his head back in laughter, then spoke to the surrounding people in an alien tongue. They all laughed. Grizzly Hair waited. Then the man leaned forward and said, "It was when the black hats came up the northern river, your river. They brought many neo-fitehs and a cannon on a boat. You know what a cannon is?" Seeing Grizzly Hair's sign for no, he continued, "Many men rode with me. We hid in the trees and counted three twenties of black hats, all with *fusiles*—do you know what that is?"

At the "no" sign, he smiled in his unpleasant way and reached his hand back. Nearly falling off the log, his mud-caked feet in the air for balance, he pulled the strange long thing from its place against the tree—carefully, heavy for one hand. He turned the wooden end to his shoulder, raised it so his eye squinted along the top, one finger hooked over a curved piece, the other hand holding the long tube, then jerked back, making an explosive sound with his mouth. He smiled at Grizzly Hair. "This is a *fusil*. A cannon is bigger. Too big to carry."

Which explained why they transported it in a boat.

The headman continued, "The cannon kills better. Back to the story. My men and I watched the black hats make camp. We saw them cover the cannon with brush. When they were asleep, we pushed the cannon into deep mud. It sank. Then I went back and stole this hat and *fusil*." He looked extremely pleased.

Interested to hear this story of hostile action toward the black hats, Grizzly Hair thought it was clever to steal the hat that identified the *Españoles*. The man leaned the *fusil* against the log, careful as though standing his bow in the sweathouse, and spoke rapidly to his people. They nodded and smiled, clearly enjoying whatever was being said. Grizzly Hair felt pleased too, that he had trusted his feelings about these people.

The mood, however, changed. Smiles dropped and everyone went to their u-machas except the headman.

Grizzly Hair gave no hint of his alarm. "Is a *fusil* a thunder shooter?" he asked casually.

The headman smiled at him like a father whose infant doesn't know it has said something funny. "It shoots balls."

"And the balls kill men?"

He nodded almost imperceptibly, thick lips tight, bemused eyes high on the whites. "A cannon shoots balls this big." He held an imaginary object bigger than a cooking stone, then suddenly, as if coming out of a trance, straightened his back and said in a gruff voice. "Now give me your quiver."

Grizzly Hair looked around and saw eyes looking at him from the shadows of the u-machas, men with weapons. He told himself that the headman might fear an attack and that such a request was natural under those circumstances. In any case he and Bowstring wouldn't stand a chance in a fight. He reached back and lifted the otter-skin bag over his head, extricating his arm from it, and handed it to the headman. "I am a friend," he said loud enough for all to hear.

"Tell all your men to come out," the headman said, tossing the quiver to the entrance of the nearest u-macha, where a large hand reached out and retrieved it. He took the *fusil* into his arms and stood up, bracing his legs.

Still seated to show his friendly intent, Grizzly Hair beckoned Bowstring and Oak Gall to come forward. The vines moved and they stepped into the open and slowly approached. Again dogs sprang to barking life and rushed at them. Oak Gall followed behind Bowstring, and her face was hidden until they came into the clearing. She looked as confident as always—trusting him too much, he suddenly thought. Curious and expectant, she glanced around the village. Bowstring's face showed fear and he was lifting his quiver over his head.

Accepting the quiver, the headman looked at Oak Gall. His hat brim tipped down, then slowly came up level again, his eyes on her and his teeth clamping his lower lip as though to prevent the nasty smile. With the *fusil* in his arm and the tips of his brows disturbed, he looked like a demon hatching a plan.

He spoke over his shoulder to a man, and the man ducked out of the u-macha with Grizzly Hair's quiver and handed it back. They gave Bowstring's quiver back too. "I believe your story," the headman said. "Spies don't travel with pretty women. But only fools would go to the mission. Stay here with us. My name is Gabriel."

Relieved for the second time, Grizzly Hair was nevertheless shocked to hear a man speak his own name. Oak Gall and Bowstring stood open-mouthed. The three of them must have looked funny because Gabriel threw back his head and laughed loud and long. He wiped his tears and said, "I was right, you are *inocente.*"

"What is *inocente?*" Grizzly Hair asked.

"Stupid. Backward. Hill bunnies."

Some of the men came forward and tried to talk, a few knowing a little of the home tongue. The women let Oak Gall touch their red skirts, their iron bucket and their wonderful beads. Everyone wore necklaces more valuable than Morning Owl's.

Oak Gall touched the brown horse with a finger, then the palm of her hand. She turned to Grizzly Hair with an excited smile, motioned him and Bowstring. Impatient to touch the docile animal, Grizzly Hair approached. The horse scent was strong and strange, but not unpleasant. The big animal radiated a surprising amount of warmth. The short hair was slick, the muscles of her upper legs hard as a tree. With strangers petting her, she continued biting off grass and looking around with the huge brown globes of her eyes. Her friendliness seemed miraculous.

Later at Gabriel's supper fire, Grizzly Hair dipped his hand into a bucket of duck stew and asked, "Would the black hats shoot us if we walked into their village?"

Gabriel's answer was garbled by the food in his mouth, bits of food spraying. "If they think you are hostile gentiles, they will shoot."

"What is a gentile?"

"A wild *Indio.*"

"What is wild, what is *Indio?*"

"You are wild. You are *Indio,*" Gabriel chuckled.

"What does it mean to be wild?"

"Wild means not tame, not *domesticado.*"

He was getting the feeling of being laughed at. "What is *domesticado?*"

Gabriel smacked his lips on the meat and pointed with the duck leg toward the horse Grizzly Hair had petted. "She is tame. The horses on the plain are wild." He resumed the orderly gnawing of his duck.

Grizzly Hair exchanged a long glance with Bowstring, absorbing the fact that both animals and people were separated into wild and tame. He considered the headman and asked, "Are you tame?"

A burst of duck meat sprayed out as Gabriel laughed so hard he nearly fell off his log. Grizzly Hair wiped muck from his face and waited, only to watch Gabriel gobble one of the strange white flat cakes.

"I do not understand the joke," Grizzly Hair prompted. "The *Españoles* are afraid of wild, and you say I am wild. Please tell me what that means." For the journey ahead he needed to know.

"A gentile is not a *Christiano*, has not learned from the fathers, is not baptized by the fathers. He is wild."

"I know many things that fathers teach."

A snide grin. "You know nothing of the Spanish fathers, the *padres,* the long robes."

"Yes, you are right about that. I want to learn everything about them, their iron, their cloth, their *fusiles.* Can I get close enough to learn, without them killing me?" He slapped a mosquito behind his shoulder, another on his ankle.

Gabriel was earnestly chewing his fourth duck leg, juice dripping between his knees. Grizzly Hair waited until he tossed the bone to a waiting dog, wiped his face with his hand, looked up and said, "I wish I had understood the *Españoles* in the beginning like I do now. Do not go to them. Avoid the mistakes I made. Let me teach you. I can use two more men to ride with me."

"Ride?"

A smile and a nod toward the horses.

Excited, Grizzly Hair wanted Oak Gall and Bowstring to understand. Judging by their expressions, he assumed the mispronunciations had kept them from following the talk. He told them he would like to stay in this village for as long as it took to learn from these people, and that later they would resume their journey with knowledge of the *Españoles* as well as directions on how to find them. Besides, here was a chance to ride a horse.

Oak Gall and Bowstring readily agreed.

"If you will have us in your village," he said to Gabriel, "we would be happy to help you hunt."

Gabriel's thick lips turned up part way.

Grizzly Hair added, "I am ready to ride a horse at any time."

Gabriel spoke at length to his people in the alien tongue.

Later, in the privacy of the willow shelter the three of them had built, Grizzly Hair said to Oak Gall, "There's a little of Rattlesnake in Gabriel, but rattlers teach us too."

For three sleeps Gabriel waved him off when Grizzly Hair hinted that he'd like to ride a horse. Meanwhile he become fascinated with the skills that Gabriel's people had learned in the mission. They had knives made of *hierro,* a material that was heated and bent to any desired shape. They used braided rope of a tough hide from an animal he'd never seen and vessels made of an enormous hollow horn from that same animal. Some people in the village spoke of the long robes as good headmen of the mission. He talked often with those who understood a smattering of his tongue, and became increasingly curious about why the long robes had come and built the missions—several—far from their home places. He also wondered why, if they were good men, they commanded black hats to do bad things. The very notion of asking other men to do their will perplexed Grizzly Hair.

He also learned some of the tongue called *Español,* which was the common language here. It would likely be useful in the sleeps ahead. The people most at home here called people "yokuts," and he was learning a little of their talk too. But there were other peoples here too, all blended into a village of former strangers. From what he was able to understand, many different peoples lived in the mission, and when they escaped, started new villages instead of returning to their home places. They said their families were dead or gone.

In the mornings and evenings the mosquitos were so thick Grizzly Hair had to breath with care.

"You look like Coyote Man," he said coming up behind Oak Gall. He'd know that posture in any disguise. She had painted herself white with a paste of powdered cattail root, a mixture also used to make flatbread.

She took her time turning toward him, a smile cracking her mask.

"Did you save some of that for me?"

"Come."

He followed her through the shaded village to their shelter and waited while she fetched water in her smallest, tightly coiled basket. With a loose hand she stirred a line of powdered root into the water until the paste was smooth. She reached up to work it into his hairline, down over his face, neck and shoulders, cooling his itchy, bitten skin. She turned him around like a mother, working down his back and buttocks, turning him to the front again, circling the cool slick paste over his stomach and downward, circling, and he forgot about supper.

Every sleep it seemed the mosquitos grew thicker. Oak Gall dipped cattail heads in duck grease, lit them in the fire and pushed the butt ends into the soft earth around their shelter. The torches smoked late into the night. She also used the torches to banish lice and fleas from the shelter.

Each night they held each other, and even in his dreams Grizzly Hair played the games of these people: shooting arrows at a target hidden behind grapevines and, best of all, the game in which a small wooden burl was struck by a carefully fashioned club and made to roll into holes in the ground.

Whenever he could get anyone to explain about the long robes, he paid close attention. He learned the word neo-fee-teh, neophyte, understanding it to mean people who had allowed a long robe to put water on their heads. Once this occurred, people were tame, no longer free to leave the mission. If they left to go to their home places, they were hunted and punished with *cuartas*, and that's what had made the marks on the back of the man who was visiting Te-mi's people.

Gabriel said neophytes and gentiles were at war, especially when neophytes were sent to retrieve ci-mar-rón-ehs, runaways. Everyone who lived here was a *cimarrón*. This made it a dangerous place, Grizzly Hair realized, and he spoke to Oak Gall and Bowstring about that. "Should we leave now?" he asked.

Bowstring pointed out, "They say the black hats never walk. They ride on horses wherever they go. But horses make noise when they walk. I think we would hear them and have time to hide."

Oak Gall said she didn't want to leave until she had learned to ride a horse. Grizzly Hair agreed with both of them and was glad they were not afraid, because Gabriel had said that after the sleep he would let him ride a horse for the first time.

After nu-pah the next morning Gabriel, whose other name was Flies-with-Storm, nodded for Grizzly Hair to climb onto the back of a brown mare that had been brought for this purpose.

As instructed, he threw himself over her back, the pungent pelt in his nose, and, with the horse stepping anxiously around, pulled himself astride her. He sat grinning at the men, women and children looking up at him, Oak Gall tilting her head and smiling with a parted mouth. He felt so very high off the ground! Who would have believed this was possible? If only Two Falcons could see him now, and Mother and Morning Owl, and everybody else!

The horse was warm and wide between his thighs and Gabriel was explaining how to turn her with a tug of the thong that was threaded through a gap in her lower teeth and tied around her jaw. She shivered violently and Grizzly Hair shivered with her, leaning down to grab her neck.

"She's trying to shake me off," he worried aloud.

Gabriel mounted his black stallion. "No, just shaking off flies."

She tossed her head again and he realized that she was trying to make the flies leave her eyes. He felt thrilling strength in that tossing and quivering. And to think she allowed him to sit on her!

The spectators parted as Gabriel instructed Grizzly Hair to follow behind the stallion. The black horse walked and the brown horse followed without the prod of Grizzly Hair's heels, which was supposed to make her move. He passed by the people, smiling down on them like a man in a wondrous story.

He rode behind Gabriel on a winding trail through the river jungle. Out on the grasslands they followed a trail alongside the heavy vegetation. Riding quietly, Gabriel said without looking back at him, "I am surprised your people have no horses."

"How would we get horses?"

"I am a horse trader."

He wanted to say that they'd never known of Gabriel's existence, but the stallion was farther and farther ahead and he was completely occupied trying to keep his balance on the swaying animal. A little later, after he learned to adjust himself to the swaying, he asked, "What would a horse like this trade for?"

The man called back, "What do you have in your village? Kick her, make her walk faster."

Did he dare kick? Instead he bumped her sides gently.

She walked faster, which pleased him greatly. "Bone awls and fish hooks are our specialty," he said, "and we have plenty of snowy-egret and bald-eagle feathers."

Gabriel's laugh snarled back at him. "Don't be *inocente*. These are tame horses, trained. Feathers! Bone!" He made a loud farting noise with his mouth.

A harder bump with his heels made the horse trot, bouncing Grizzly Hair like a thing of little weight. He struggled to stay balanced and upright as the horse caught up to the stallion's tail and walked again. "What is *inocente?*"

"You," Gabriel snickered. "You don't know what's going on in the world."

It was irksome to be continually insulted, but he held himself in check to keep learning.

The stallion suddenly squealed and sidestepped. The mare stood on her hind legs. Grizzly Hair slid down over the rump and struck the ground hard. He jumped up and backed out of the horse's way. She was stepping around erratically. Then, as if suddenly making up her mind, she galloped toward the village.

Dreamlike, Gabriel and his horse fused into one flying animal, so lightly did the hooves tick the ground. They rapidly overtook the mare and Gabriel leaned far to the side and seized the reins. He yanked the runaway, the *cimarrón*, to a stop, spoke calmly to her and led her back. Gabriel was smiling, perhaps at Grizzly Hair's astonishment as he stood on the trail, having seen how well man and horse could blend in their purpose.

"Throw that away," Gabriel called, stopping the horses and pointing at a piece of a vine on the trail. "She thought it was a snake." Gabriel waited while he flung the vine away, then brought the mare up. "Watch for anything that will scare the horse, and be ready to control her fear."

"How can I control the fear of a horse?"

Gabriel handed him the reins. "Don't let her run wild. The horse feels safe when you guide her. Never let her make a move you didn't order."

"Is that what makes her tame? Not finding her own way, not thinking for herself?"

"Yes. Let's go back." The black stallion arched his neck and pawed the earth with a hoof.

"I think you are wild," said Grizzly Hair as he placed his arm over the horse's neck and threw himself up on its back.

Gabriel laughed appreciatively.

"But you have learned from the long robe fathers. They put water on your head. How can you be a neophyte and a wild man at the same time?"

Rollicking laughter rolled out. Then, as if tiring of it, Gabriel said, "Don't be so thick." With his stallion leading, he told Grizzly Hair to watch how to direct the animal without a rein, by using his knees. As Grizzly Hair tried to imitate him, Gabriel twisted around, nodded to the mare and said, "A horse like that is worth thirty to thirty-five strings of shell money."

Astonished at the high price—a string was measured from the tip of a man's middle finger to his shoulder—he said, "In our entire village there are probably only ten strings of shell money."

Gabriel snorted. "I can't believe people are still that backward."

That meant *inocente*, hill bunnies.

"Maybe," said Gabriel over his shoulder, "your people have one thing of value to trade for horses."

"What?"

"Women."

This shocked him. "Trading would be the same as gambling with people."

"So?"

"Remember Red Cloud."

"Who?"

"You must know the story of Red Cloud."

A torrent of laughter answered, and when it died down Gabriel twisted around with an expression of undisguised humor, "No, tell me about Red Cloud."

Had he actually never heard it? Or was he planning to laugh at the way it was told? He would make it short. "In ancient times a headman gambled with the Old Man of the Ice and lost everything, so he staked his people on the next play and lost them too. The Old Man of the Ice took the people to his home in the north, which was their ancient home. They cried and huddled together and tried to stay warm. Back in the Valley of the Sun, Red Cloud turned himself into a hummingbird and flew north to rescue them and bring them back to the Valley." The story meant that people were not to be used as items of trade.

"That was a stupid story."

"I didn't tell it right," he said, wondering why this man, who thought himself so cunning, was spending so much time talking to a hill bunny.

"No matter how you tell it, that story wouldn't make me fear trading women," Gabriel said, swaying gracefully on his horse.

"The story isn't about fear."

"Exactly. Most stories are stupid. You should laugh at them like I do. The only stories I care about have me in them, the things I did, the trouble I got into, the way I got out of it. I make my own stories."

Grizzly Hair was enjoying the horse more each moment.

"You must have women to spare in your village," Gabriel said amicably, "or you wouldn't bring a pretty one on a dangerous journey."

Recalling how Gabriel had looked at Oak Gall, he said, "My people would like this horse very much, as I do, but we would never trade a person for it."

Gabriel shrugged. "Want to run?"

Grizzly Hair was pondering the meaning of that when Gabriel's horse thundered away. The mare bounded into a leaping gait, nearly throwing him over her head. Thrill, fear and pain fused as he leaned into the mane, hugging the pumping neck with both arms, hips bouncing violently as he slipped more and more to one side. The trees blurred past in a miracle of speed as the animal stretched and contracted beneath him. He hoped she wouldn't see a snake because, contrary to Gabriel's instructions, she was following the stallion and utterly out of his control.

Ahead, Gabriel came to the village and dismounted in a swirl of dust. Grizzly Hair arrived clinging with all his might to the side of the horse, one leg hooked over her neck, a foot bouncing on the ground. He dropped gratefully to mother earth and rolled away breathing dust. His groin felt pulverized.

It took a while to hear the laughter. Even Oak Gall and Bowstring were laughing. He staggered to his feet and moved like an infant learning to walk. The earth seemed almost sticky, holding him back, making his steps slow. He glanced at Bowstring and Oak Gall and saw through their tears of laughter that they admired what he had done.

"I would like to ride with you again," he said to Gabriel.

Gabriel smiled like a fox.

12

Green acorns were already forming in their caps and Grizzly Hair was anxious to be on his way. This morning he was half finished with his boat, which would float them to where they were going. Despite what Gabriel had said, Grizzly Hair would observe the black hats and long robes for himself, as he had watched Gabriel's people. He wrapped twine around the big awkward bundle of tulares between his legs and cut the ends with the purple obsidian knife, thinking about the horses he had ridden on several occasions. Bowstring had ridden too, but not Oak Gall. Gabriel said women had no need to ride. That had upset Oak Gall, but this headman did more than bring people to agreement; he made decisions that in other villages would have been made by the people. He said Grizzly Hair, Bowstring and Oak Gall should stay here and be his people, that he didn't teach them to ride only to lose them. But this was not for Gabriel to decide. Besides, Gabriel, who coupled with most of the women, acted increasingly irritated at Bowstring for his attentions to a quiet young woman named Teresa—another reason to leave as soon as the boat was finished. After the sleep he and Bowstring would pole Oak Gall up the big *Rio de San Joaquin* to the place where the Suisunes and Carkeenes people had lived. From there they could float to *Misión San José* on the great body of water connected to the western sea—the *Bahía de San Francisco.* There might be a few of the skilled Carkeenes people left, old Matías said, to teach them to steer the boat on the choppy bay. Matías lived with Gabriel's people but Grizzly Hair could tell he did what he wished, not what Gabriel told him.

It was early in the day, but already father sun burned hotly into the unshaded spots of the village. People moved about as though slowed by the heat. Redwing blackbirds trilled far and near. Beside Grizzly Hair lay the skeleton of his boat—long willow poles with eight crosswise ribs, a long tule bundle lashed to one side of the bottom. Four more bundles were needed, two more on the bottom, one on each side. The bundles were as long as two men. Old Matías had instructed him.

The tulare stems made the boat float high on the water, tulares being flexible hollow tubes. They also made his sleeping mat soft, cloudlike. Wrapping the twine around the thick bundle, he looked across the shade to Oak Gall, who was pounding roots in a wooden bowl between her flexed legs. Feeling his gaze, she looked up and smiled. He smiled back. He had nothing to say, only that he couldn't live without her. As a boy he couldn't have imagined how full it would make him feel to be mated with a woman.

With a contented sigh he went back to his bundle, wrapping the twine looser in the middle, tighter fore and aft, tilting the points upward. He decided to make a smaller replica of this boat when he returned to the home place. The home river was unsuited to boats, being narrow and rocky, tulares not very plentiful, but the children of the umne would have fun bumping against the rocks and skimming over the small stretches of white water. Imagining their squeals of pleasure, he tied the tip off and wiped stinging sweat from his eyes. Bowstring wasn't in sight, perhaps gone with Teresa, with whom he spent the afternoons when he wasn't teaching people to play the flute like he did.

Besides the boat, Grizzly Hair would show his people the burl game, in which teams competed to be the first to get their ball into the last hole on the course. Someday, he thought, he would make the ball fly long and true as Gabriel did, instead of dribbling off his club. He imagined laying out a course on the rolling hills of the home place, which would be trickier to play than on flat land. The people here treasured their playing sticks as much as their bows. Old Matías had explained that the club must be weighted correctly, curved on the bottom, and polished.

Stuffing the bundle into the boat frame, he began the tedious tying of it to the ribs, when hoof beats sounded. Gabriel's friends often rode in and out of the village, so a rider was not unusual. He looked up, saw alarm in Oak Gall's face and followed her gaze to an owl jumping into flight from a tree branch. A tremor of fear passed through him, for owls did not fly at this time of day. It was a bad omen. Others saw it too, but appeared to ignore it.

The herald cried out and Grizzly Hair understood the Spanish word for runner. Crows cawed. Heads appeared at doorways. *Only a runner*, a runner on horseback.

In a cloud of dust a rider reined up shouting for Gabriel. The horse's sides expanded and contracted as its nostrils sucked and blew. White froth on its flanks slid down its legs. The herald bellowed Gabriel's name.

Grizzly Hair and Oak Gall joined the gathering crowd. Bowstring and Teresa came from the trees looking flushed. People made no attempt to sit, for the runner didn't sit, but spoke rapidly. To Grizzly Hair's surprise, the talk was close to his own tongue, though some of the words were unfamiliar.

"Sergeant Sanchez and ten black hats are at the river of the Muquelumne," he said, waiting while Gabriel repeated it in Spanish. "They captured women and children. One of the men was lassoed around his neck and dragged behind a horse. Muquel sent me for help."

"We will help," Gabriel said, turning to speak Spanish to his own runner. At the home place the men would have discussed what to do.

Gabriel's runner ran to his gray animal, jumped on, and without hesitation horse and man were galloping away. Gabriel flew about directing people. Men inserted knives, some stone, some iron into their calf-thongs and filled their quivers from a large cache of arrows.

Grizzly Hair felt pulled in opposite ways. A guest in a village should help his hosts, but he feared that becoming a known enemy of the black hats would endanger Oak Gall and Bowstring. He didn't want to be associated with *cimarrones*. And he didn't want to leave Oak Gall here alone, where Gabriel might return and he might not. He had promised himself he'd never do that.

Seeing Grizzly Hair standing like an island in a turbulent sea, Gabriel said, "You ride like a baby. You and Bowstring stay with the women and children." Then he ran toward the brush enclosure where they kept the best horses.

Grizzly Hair glanced at Bowstring, who stood hip to hip with Teresa, and saw that he too was relieved. Oak Gall's brows were knotted with worry. He touched her shoulder and was about to reassure her, but remembered the owl. The portent had been right: black hats were attacking people in the Valley of the Sun.

Gabriel pranced into the clearing on his black stallion, his head as high and haughty as the horse's, the *fusil* in one arm. About twenty men rode behind. They circled their horses, Gabriel talking to the men, then galloped away—more men running to the grasslands after their horses.

Quiet fell. Turning to Bowstring and Matías—the old man was also staying—Grizzly Hair said, "We should find a place to hide until Sanchez has left the Valley."

"*Sí*," said Matías. "We always hide in the mud of the tulares."

That they had done this before was comforting. Oak Gall and Teresa helped three sick women from their u-machas while the other two women of the village moved their children to the hiding place in a labyrinth of tulares. Grizzly Hair helped a sick man, one who had been constantly in his u-macha. He had a bad rash and bald spots on his head. Another man, blind and crying like a baby, refused to leave his house although Grizzly Hair offered to carry him.

"He is *loco,*" whispered Teresa. "Leave him or he'll scratch your eyes out and give our hiding place away." They left him on his lice-ridden mat—a sign that he, like most of the men of the village, had no woman.

The six women, the sick man and three children waited near the hiding place. Grizzly Hair, Bowstring and Matías hid in a thicket halfway between the village and the hiding place, where they could see both ways. From there they could wave to the women, who could rest comfortably on dry land until signaled.

Father sun moved slowly, beams of his light falling through the river jungle from straight overhead. Insects droned and old Matías nodded off to sleep. Grizzly Hair was resting his eyes when he heard the sound of horses. Expecting Gabriel and his men, he got up on his knees and stared through the foliage. But it was not Gabriel.

Shock stung his scalp. Strange horses and riders entered the clearing. Exchanging a horrified glance with Bowstring, he nudged Matías awake and signaled the women. Two riders were completely clothed from their black hats to their foot coverings, which had shiny spikes on the heels. With *fusiles* swinging from side to side, they directed the horses with their legs. A complex of thongs and shiny *hierro* was attached to the animals' mouths. Seven or eight more riders came across his line of vision, hatless, bootless, wearing pale wraps about their loins. Neophytes. He blinked, almost disbelieving.

The two black hats sat on thick hide seats, beneath which hung sheets of hide that hid the animals' bellies. The neophytes rode on the horses' bare backs and controlled them with simple thongs. More horses crossed his line of vision, each with a neophyte rider. Face-down over one horse hung a limp black hat, perhaps dead.

Grizzly Hair glanced at Bowstring and Matías, who were hiding their bows and quivers in a thicket of alders and berry canes. Then, with fear in their faces, they crept backwards toward the tulares, keeping their eyes on the village. Leaving their weapons! But Matías had done this before. A glance across the bare river-scoured land to the tulares told him Matías knew what he was doing. This was the last good hiding place for his bow. It would be awkward to have it in the mud. Besides, the weapons of the black hats had twice the range. He'd never seen Gabriel's *fusil* spit thunder, but that was well known. He concealed his bow and quiver in the thicket, pulled from his calf-thong the obsidian knife that Howchia had insisted he bring, and backed toward the tulares.

The black hats and neophytes were tearing into the u-machas like crazed demons. Grizzly Hair turned and crouch-ran to where the tulares grew lush and dense. Bowstring was sliding into the mud holding the greenstone knife his father had given him.

Grizzly Hair rolled in the mud. The hiss of air through teeth told him the lump he'd failed to recognize was Oak Gall. Afraid more than he'd ever imagined, now that the black hats were suddenly real, he pulled himself toward her, using hands and knife in the bottom muck. She held a mud-covered dog in her arms, muzzling it with her hand. Some of the other women held dogs too. They were to be drowned if they barked or tried to get away, Teresa had instructed.

All the way from the village he could hear the black hats, who seemed to be calling the hiding people. Then it was silent. Then came the snapping and crackling of fire. Above the village, up through the high trees the spots of blue became smudged with smoke. Mouth dry with mounting terror, he moved farther back into the mud, Oak Gall alongside with the dog. Others were going deeper too.

What had made him think the *Españoles* wouldn't look in the tulares? Of course they would! But if they could stay quiet and behind the tulares, they wouldn't be seen. "Don't let them see the whites of your eyes," he whispered. "Turn the dog the other way." Alone, he wouldn't have been half as afraid, but Oak Gall was here, and children and dogs. All he could see of her were her frightened eyes. Float-sinking in muck as warm as the day, he felt the rocking motion of his body as his heart pumped. He didn't know where the others were, no doubt too close. Why hadn't they separated? As a tracker, he should have insisted.

The fire roared like a troop of angry bears. At the thicket halfway between the village and marsh, the bushes moved. He thought the vines were catching fire, but a boot and black leg pushed through. A black hat, something wiggling in his arms.

A dog! A dog Grizzly Hair recognized, one they had missed. The black hat came nearer, the dog straining in his arms. Then, with the deliberation of a slow dream in which the dreamer knows what will happen next, the man placed the dog on the ground and it trotted straight to the hiding place wagging a friendly tail and looking at Grizzly Hair.

"Go away!" he silently beseeched the dog. But it stayed, tail wagging. This had been planned wrong, he realized. He should be back in the thicket armed with his bow, Bowstring and Matías aiming from different directions. Now they would be hunted like frogs. The mocking tone he'd used with Morning

Owl come back at him: *Am I a frog?* He had been young and stupid.

Raising his *fusil*, the black hat ran toward the dog, shouting, "*Muchachos, a los tulares!*"

Another black hat pushed through the thicket, followed by neophytes armed with heavy sticks. All rushed toward the tulares, iron protrusions jingling from the black hats' heels like the spurs of demon birds. Grizzly Hair's bladder released. To jump at them with his knife would be to invite the thunder of the *fusiles* and the deaths of others who might otherwise escape. He forced himself to lie still with his hair flowing in the green-brown moss, his nostrils and slit eyes at the surface. He was facing the same death his father had died.

The sudden sloshing mud-sucking noise of panicked people trying to run exploded in his ears, the turbulence washing over his nose and eyes. Then came the heart-compressing bang of a lightning strike. He half-inhaled, then clamped himself shut to stop a cough. Nearly exploding with the need to clear his breathing passage, his face tingled. It took all his strength.

The splashing intensified around him. Now and then a man shouted "*Aquí!*" and a terrified squeal rose from the mud. Silently he called on Mint to keep Oak Gall hidden, but he knew she might already be dead. He had brought her to danger, after her mother had begged him not to, after the owl had warned him. Now neophytes and black hats were tromping through the tulares hunting for her.

Pain stabbed into his upper arm, so intense it loosened his grip on the knife. He coughed, came up for air and blinked mud from his eyes. A big boot stood there, one that would have been deeper in the mud had the spur missed his arm. Blood reddened the muddy water. Looming above, the black hat twisted around and dug the spur in harder, and for an instant unmatched eyes in a sharp face connected with his, intimate in the giving of pain. "*Aquí! Aquí, hay otro aquí!*" the man yelled.

Grizzly Hair pushed the boot away with his free hand, his knife gone. The man stumbled, trying to regain his balance. Then O-se-mai-ti roared up and exploded from Grizzly Hair's chest. He lunged from the mud and easily knocked the man down in the muck with his *fusil*, which the *Español* clung to like a mother protecting her child.

Strong as a bear, Grizzly Hair fought for the weapon, to throw it into the tulares where it would be lost like his mother's beautiful knife. He slipped and struggled for leverage, spurs gouging his shins, the man kicking as he turned over and over, but the grip on the *fusil* was weakening.

Yelling and splashing, men converged from all sides. Just then the *fusil* gave way into Grizzly Hair's hands, throwing him on his back.

He scrambled to his feet so he could swing the *fusil* in an arc to drive them back, but hands grabbed his legs and yanked. He fell on his face. More hands closed on his arms, others jerked at the *fusil.* Hard blows pelted his head and shoulders—the clubs of the neophytes.

Slowly the *fusil* was wrenched from his fingers. Now he would meet his death.

He felt himself pulled face-down through the mud. For an instant he raised up, gasped air, saw a group of mud-covered people, a *fusil* pointed at them. He couldn't get his knees under him.

Hands grabbed his topknot and yanked him to firm ground. He saw two others being pulled the same way he had come. By their shapes he recognized Oak Gall and Bowstring. He nearly cried out with relief to see them alive, and sorrow that they had not escaped.

A dog shook himself, spattering mud in all directions. The black hat looked down at his mud-speckled shirt, turned the *fusil* at the dog. Thunder cracked. The dog fell to its side, the halved skull spilling pink brains, a leg twitching.

Stunned, Grizzly Hair stared at the dog. Had his father's head been blown away like that? He hardly noticed the neophytes pushing him to his feet, but when the hot end of the *fusil* jabbed his side he prepared to die.

Touching his amulet, he silently called upon O-se-mai-ti for the strength to die with dignity. But no thunder-bang sounded, only the rattle of Spanish talk. Before he knew what was happening, a neophyte grabbed the amulet, jerked it, the thong breaking, and threw it far out in the water where it made a tiny splash. Grizzly Hair stood looking after it, his power gone.

Between the shore and the amulet, the mud-covered black hat he had fought stared at him with a look of flat hatred, the muddy *fusil* in his arm, then stepped carefully to shore.

The end of the other *fusil* rammed into his side again, but still no thunder-bang. He stumbled forward, pushed by the hard iron until he stood with the other captured people. He recognized the thin legs and knobby knees of old Matías, and the three children. The black hat beckoned Oak Gall and Bowstring. They edged toward the group, the whites of their eyes large with terror as they watched the neophytes brandishing their sticks.

Now we are in a group and they will kill us, Grizzly Hair thought. He felt as powerless as the children. Needing Oak Gall's touch, he sidestepped until his thigh met her hip. She was trembling.

Arriving at dry land, the muddy black hat pointed his dripping *fusil* at Grizzly Hair, then at Oak Gall, then back at Grizzly Hair, eyeing him along its length as if enjoying their terror. His other eye was higher in his head.

Grizzly Hair couldn't bear to watch, so he emptied his mind and looked at a black hat pushing a rod inside the other *fusil,* pouring dark powder into it, ramming the rod down the weapon's throat. The black hat pointed it. Still no death blast. His tracker's mind returned. Gabriel had said black powder made a *fusil* spit lightning. How many times could it spit before it needed more powder? The feeding of the *fusil*, he realized, had taken a long time, much longer than loading an arrow in a bow. If he had known that, if he had known the *fusil* was empty after it killed the dog, if he had thrown the other *fusil* into the slough, they could have escaped. If, if, if—

Sudden Spanish yelling started everyone walking toward the village. The black hat covered with mud brought up the rear with his dripping *fusil*. Grizzly Hair hardly breathed, expecting a thunderball to blast into his back. His legs felt like cooked vines and his shins bled rivulets of blood through the mud. Oak Gall made a little whimpering sound. Shamed by his inability to save her, he nevertheless tried to prepare for an honorable death, as Two Falcons would have.

He was passing the thicket where his bow and arrows were hidden when, in the pit of his stomach, he felt a spot of calm. Some power remained, even without his amulet. Maybe he would die well after all. His fine brave bow called to him and he couldn't leave it alone in that bad-luck place, so he stepped out of line and reached for it.

A thunderclap felled him. He felt no pain, but calm spread through him and completely replaced the fear. Death felt good, if that's what it was, but it seemed strange that his soul was able to hear—Oak Gall weeping, the thudding of his heart no doubt an echo of how it had sounded moments before. There was a torrent of Spanish talk. He reminded himself that souls hovered until they were sung onward, so it seemed natural that his would remain here for a while seeing and hearing. No one had returned from the dead to explain it. In limp detachment he watched as a neophyte went into the thicket and gathered bows and quivers, then tossed them disrespectfully to the ground. Other neophytes stamped on the arrows, crunching and cracking them. They snapped the bows over their knees. It hurt to see that, but it hurt more to see Bowstring's tragic expression through the mud, and to hear Oak Gall's quiet weeping.

A jab from a *fusil* shocked him. They expected him to get up! His heart was still beating. Only his fear had died. Amazed, he pushed to his feet on strong legs and turned to Oak Gall, who was clinging to him. Glad to touch her again, he pulled a string of moss from her muddy hair and looked into her dark eyes. Tears had washed trails down her cheeks. *Fusiles,* he realized, were also used to frighten people. He had fallen in fright. What torture this was for her and Bowstring! But for him it would be easier next time. Now he knew how to die. He must sing his death song, as Oak Gall and Bowstring and any who would soon die should, so they could walk the pathway of ghosts and find the happy land. There they would dance and sing with the immortals for all time and not haunt the living.

At the first tone from his lips, neophytes and black hats looked at him as though puzzled. Shaking as she clung to him, Oak Gall began singing too, a scratchy whisper at first. Bowstring inhaled and from deep within him came the firm pure tones of a master singer. It strengthened Oak Gall's voice and by the time they walked into the scorched clearing where the u-machas had stood, their three voices blended in clear song.

Some of the treetops still burned, green leaves twisting with flame then drifting down like bright stars, but the trees would recover. The boat was a pile of cinders, and the crazy man smoked like charred meat in the ashes of his u-macha.

13

Grizzly Hair swam with Oak Gall, Bowstring and Teresa as they crossed the *Rio de San Joaquin,* and in those few guarded moments they stole a little talk. Teresa spit water and said they were being taken to Mission San José and that meant walking all day, then walking another day after the sleep. This gave him hope. There would be opportunities for escape.

The black hats herded the people at a fast pace up a trail into the western hills—golden hills he'd seen stretching north to south like a huge muscular mountain lion asleep in the sun. Dust from the forward horses blew back in his face, the trail deeply cut and powdered by the hooves of previous horses. It led toward a gap, a *paso* in the mountain called *Alta Monte,* High Forest, though it appeared low compared with the eastern mountains, and no forest was in sight. Dry bunch-grass covered the hills, cover for jackrabbits but not men.

With each step it became clearer that Teresa was right. The black hats intended to take all the captured people to the mission. Would some be killed there? Those who had fought? Besides the people from Gabriel's village, about fifteen others had been captured. Five more black hats rode alongside, seven all together, and many more mounted neophytes. Even with cover, escape would require speed, cunning and planning with Bowstring.

Bringing up the rear was the dead black hat hanging over a long-eared horse. Did that soul hover over the procession? What capricious havoc it could wreak!

Oak Gall leaned forward and whispered to Teresa, "What will they do to us at the mission?"

Teresa answered in Spanish and sobbed into Bowstring's neck, not explaining. Bowstring reached around her shoulder and patted it, his large calves bunching before Grizzly Hair as he pushed up the hill. A black hat turned on his horse and called out in Spanish. Moments later three women moved in between Bowstring and Grizzly Hair. Now they couldn't talk at all.

Behind, small children whimpered. Grizzly Hair turned, saw two young boys hoary with dust, arms upraised to their mother, pleading as they stumbled along. She was sick with rashy skin and could barely walk, much less carry them.

"Ride here?" Grizzly Hair said, squatting and pointing at his shoulders. The mother looked grateful as he swung the smaller boy to his neck, the chubby dust-covered feet astride his chin. He squatted before the bigger boy, signing for him to climb on too. But Bowstring was suddenly there swinging him to his own shoulders.

"Gracias, gracias," sobbed the mother, glancing worriedly at the black hat who trotted over to prod Bowstring back in line.

All walked silently, Grizzly Hair anxious for the cover of night. Could they avoid the soul of the dead black hat? He didn't dare look back for fear of seeing it, and escape would require running through the dark on trails where Bohemkulla might overtake them.

"Teach me talk," he said squeezing a fat little foot. He pointed at an old stunted tree on the rocky hillside, he asked, "What?" In his tongue the boy taught him to say "old oak," and he tried to repeat it. The boy corrected him, and he did better. In this way he distracted himself. But the dust thickened and father sun glared at them from the top of the mountain like a strange red being. The prevailing silence reclaimed him.

Could he escape with Oak Gall? She couldn't run very fast. He leaned over and whispered, "I shouldn't have brought you."

She frowned at him.

"Even when you begged to come, I shouldn't have. I was blinded by my pleasure. I am sorry." Remorse choked him more than the dust.

With warmth and admiration in her eyes she looked at him and the boy on his shoulders, and said in a low voice, "Gabriel's people were captured before, but they are alive. We will live too." She smiled his favorite smile, letting him see that her power had returned.

He whispered, "We will escape when mother moon is high."

She raised her brows in surprise and glanced at the nearest black hat. "Maybe. But whatever happens, I would rather be with you than waiting in the home place wondering if you are dead." She pressed her lips at him, teasing. "Stop being sorry we are together."

The tears behind his eyes hurt to break free. He was proud of her. She had made Gabriel's people laugh at her jokes. She learned Spanish quickly. She was brave and beautiful and he must keep her safe. Blinking, he counseled her gruffly, "If we don't escape, don't let the long robes put water on your head."

She gave him a look, "Am I that stupid?"

He patted her shoulder. "I talk too much."

She caught his hand, squeezed, and her warmth leapt through him.

The dust glowed like a storm of burning coals. The boy's exhales were beginning to sound like the high thin tones of distant flutes played in harmony. Near the windy summit he set the boy down, wiped gobs of mud from his eyes and turned to relieve himself, which was allowed if he hurried back from the bush. A black hat stopped his horse behind him, watching.

Far beyond his yellow stream the Valley of the Sun spread before him as the eagle would see it, the eastern mountains a jagged white-speckled line stretching north to south as far as could be seen. Far below, oaks blended with their long shadows and appeared as a sprinkling of dark sand on the pale background. Several condors sailed between him and the valley floor. Subtler movement caught his attention down near the dusty green line of a stream, as if the earth were shifting. Then he realized it was a moving herd—antelope? Deer? Elk? He couldn't tell, but felt the presence of the spirit that lived in all things, the power that gave each kind of animal their own food and made them hold to life beyond all expectation while struggling against those who would devour them. Condor dreamed a world where the dead nurtured the living: a magic circle. He recalled looking at the valley from the other direction after he had touched—

Stinging pain seared across his buttocks. Sucking air, he whirled and clutched the pain. Oak Gall and the children's mother made frightened noises; the black hat was swinging his *cuarta de hierro,* the iron-tipped whip that had struck him. Humiliated by this hateful man, Grizzly Hair hoisted the boy on his shoulders and pointed his feet into the sun and dust, the after-sting throbbing hard. He had never been intentionally struck until the black hats appeared. This one rode alongside as if to humiliate him more.

"After dark," he thought, "you will see me no more."

They followed father sun down the mountain and when he entered his western hole, the sky turned red. The sea still couldn't be seen, though it lay west of *Alta Monte.* Soon it would be dark. In this wooded place a fast runner could escape. Grizzly Hair was practiced in deceiving alert animals and could run large animals to exhaustion, but with Oak Gall at his side and a boy on his back, such thinking was useless.

The black hats called a halt. The neophytes, obviously having done this before, took long strips of hide from the pack horses and tied the people together by the ankles. Disheartened, Grizzly Hair had to step carefully so he wouldn't trip the woman in front or boy's mother behind. The procession slowed to half speed.

As the darkening trail fell steeply downward, the dust wafted like fog over the lopsided piece of mother moon, and the trail underfoot felt soft as rabbit fur. "Hungry," whimpered the little boy. "Water, Mamma." He twisted on Grizzly Hair's shoulders toward his mother.

Grizzly Hair was hungry and thirsty too, but nothing could be done about it as he walked in tandem with those before and those behind into a dark canyon of shadowy trees. At the bottom he heard the happy sound of water, the resuscitator of sad spirits. Teresa glanced back at him knowingly. This was the camping place.

His senses sharpened and he looked around to learn the features of the landscape. Moving with the others to the stream, he knelt and scooped water. He couldn't get enough. It cooled his throat and filled him. On the opposite bank, hands churned up and down in the shadows—neophytes slurping, sucking. The black hats took turns. One lay on his belly to suck from the stream while the others watched. At first Grizzly Hair couldn't believe what he was seeing, a man drinking like a snake.

It was very dark but he could see that people who had finished drinking were being herded into what looked like a small dark mountain. Puzzled, he stood tied to the women, then moved with them toward it, realizing at the entrance that it was not a hill but brush piled higher than his head. There was an opening, through which he shuffled with the others. It was an open enclosure with very thick brush walls. A strong, unpleasant odor wafted up around him. When the last of the captives were inside, men stuffed brush behind them to block the opening.

Grizzly Hair bent down and removed the strap from his chafed ankle, but hadn't taken more than two steps when his foot shot out from under him and he landed on a hip in a stinking wet pile.

Old Matías said, "Walk carefully in here." This, too, Matías had done before.

"What is that?" Grizzly Hair pointed at the pungent slime.

"The dung of *vacas,*" answered Matías.

The animals from whose hides horse seats and *cuartas* were made. Their dung lay all over the enclosure. He couldn't wipe off the smell, though he scraped himself in the brush. Orange firelight began to flicker through the cracks—the black hats preparing their supper.

Quietly he said to Bowstring, "We will tunnel through this brush when the black hats sleep." Oak Gall and Teresa had gone to help a woman comfort her children.

"I've been thinking the same thing," said Bowstring. "I'm sorry we lost our knives. It would be quieter to cut it than to break our way through."

Grizzly Hair agreed. It would require great care. But going over the top would make more noise. The brush was interwoven, big limbs and small, thick with twigs and dry leaves. Their legs would plunge through the rattling mass.

A thunder-bang sounded in the distance. Talk in the enclosure ceased, then resumed, a little at a time. Then another bang sounded. The black hats were hunting.

Oak Gall and Teresa came toward them, Teresa saying, "They're shooting deer." She cupped her hands at the brush and called, "*Los niños tienen hambre.*"

He recognized the Spanish for children and hunger.

Grizzly Hair whispered to her, "We will tunnel out of here when the black hats sleep, but your sisters cannot go with us." They had children.

"You can't escape," Teresa said flatly.

"I think we can."

"The neophytes," Teresa said, "surround the corral all night. They will hear you. People have tried before."

His tongue wouldn't move for the thoughts careening through him. He would be more careful than those who had tried before. He'd seen how vigilant the black hats were on the trail. They would tie their feet together again. There would be no other opportunity. But what would happen if they got caught?

There was a thud on the ground and the dark figures moved toward it. Grizzly Hair followed. On the dirt and dung lay the entrails, neck and head of a deer, butchered quickly. All had been thrown over the brush wall. Nevertheless, the meat made Grizzly Hair's stomach twist with anticipation.

A gossamer cloud veiled the moon and in her pale light the people tore into the raw meat. They bit the entrails apart and passed out sections. They tore back the hide with their teeth and ripped the neck muscles apart with their hands. Old Matías accepted the eyeballs, a treat often reserved for the headman. It would have been better, Grizzly Hair thought, if the black hats had thrown in a burning brand so they could make a cooking fire, but he realized they probably feared that the captives would somehow use the fire to escape. He squatted and sang to the deer's spirit, for no one had sung and the spirit could report to Deer that it had been disrespectfully handled and not thanked for its flesh. That would only add to the bad luck. Afterwards he inserted a finger into an eye hole, hooked the brain, carefully pulled out a handful and led Oak Gall to a place without dung.

Exhausted and famished, no doubt weak from the loss of his amulet, he dropped to the ground and ate the richly flavored brains in silence, then lay down and moaned with relief.

Oak Gall stretched out beside him.

Bowstring and Teresa joined them.

Bowstring whispered, "Teresa told me plenty. I don't think we should try to escape." Teresa leaned over and touched her forehead to Bowstring's face as a bobcat would show deference.

Quietly, Grizzly Hair tried to set him straight. "They might kill us at the mission, not the neophytes, but us, so we should escape tonight. It is a gamble, but the stakes are our lives."

"No," Teresa objected. "They won't kill you at the mission.

"But I fought one of them, and so did Bowstring. They kill gentiles who attack them. Remember? The runner from the Muquelumne said they dragged a man to his death behind a horse." His own father had been killed, maybe his grandfather. "We must escape tonight. Not you, if you are sure you will be safe in the mission, but us wild *Indios.*" Scowling into the dark, he locked his hands behind his head and looked up at the thin streak of cloud across the quarter moon.

Silence fell between them, the stench of dung overwhelming. Oak Gall's head was heavy on his shoulder. He could feel that she was rapidly losing herself to sleep. He knew that if he closed his eyes, sleep would suck him down too, but he would wake up in the night ready to flee, and Oak Gall would follow him.

Teresa whispered, "If they catch you escaping it will be very bad for you." She paused. "I don't want my man flayed by the *cuarta.*" She turned toward Bowstring and pleaded, "Please, don't do it."

Grizzly Hair wrapped his arms around Oak Gall, not wanting her flayed either. What should he do? Spanish talk came through the brush, black hats at supper, telling stories and laughing. He also heard Spanish talk in different places around the brush wall. Now that the people were quiet inside, the surrounding neophytes could be heard.

He closed his eyes and sank like a rock in a pond. When he awoke it was dark, mother moon out of sight. He put a hand on Bowstring's shoulder, felt him jerk awake.

"We must start tunneling," Grizzly Hair whispered. The silence was so profound it seemed the black hats would hear even that faint whisper.

"I'm not going," whispered Bowstring. No indecision there, unlike how he had sounded before.

Grizzly Hair blinked in the darkness, wondering if an evil doctor had bewitched him. Or was Bowstring the wiser one? Oak Gall moved her head. Awake. He touched her arm and asked, "Did you see where Matías went to sleep?"

Teresa answered. "Over by the entrance, on the other side."

"I'll be back." In need of wisdom, Grizzly Hair pushed his toes forward, feeling for sleeping people and *vaca* dung. The campfires of the immortals provided little light. Near the entrance he peered at the sleepers. Only Matías had white streaks in his hair. An owl hooed. A messenger from an evil doctor? The voice gave him goosebumps. Detecting white streaks in long hair, he squatted and laid a hand on the thin hard shoulder.

"Wha, who—"

"Shhh. I must talk."

Matías groaned.

"You know the ways of the *Españoles.* If we try to escape now and are caught, would they kill us? If we don't try to escape, will Bowstring and I be killed at the mission?" Matías hadn't fought, hadn't even carried a knife and

Grizzly Hair now suspected there had been a reason.

Matías was quiet for so long it seemed he had returned to his dream.

Grizzly Hair touched him gently.

"Don't try to go through the brush," said Matías, very much awake. "Wait. Escape at the mission. It's easier."

"But maybe they will kill us."

"If they wanted to, they would have killed you back at the *ranchería.*" That meant village in the tongue of the *Españoles.*

"If we try to escape now and they catch us? What will they do? What will they do to Oak Gall?"

"No doubt whip you both all the more, but I don't think they would kill you in the mission. The padres don't like killing, they say that to kill is a *pecado capital,* very bad, and killers go to the *Diablo's* fire in the ground. But I cannot hear their thoughts. I don't know what they will do. No one does."

"Thank you, Grandfather," he said. "Dream well."

He made his way back, lay down beside Oak Gall and said, "We will walk to the mission with the others." But it didn't feel right in his stomach.

"You will see," said Teresa with a quickening note of cheer, "it is not so bad at the mission."

Then why did she run away?

A thick plume of fog or smoke, he didn't know which, appeared in his dream. Having no tree or landmark for comparison, he didn't know its size. With smoky swirls along both sides, the plume rose in a straight column, fatter at the top. Then suddenly he *saw.* On one side stood a tiny bear, a perfect miniature of O-se-mai-ti looking at him. She appeared to have stepped from the—now he knew—smoke. Only the bear's front quarters and head showed. He realized that if she were life-sized, the smoke cloud would be enormously tall, high as the clouds.

Screaming horses jerked him awake.

Hooves punked as if the horses were jumping. Then came the huffing cough of a bear. Men's voices joined the din, everyone yelling at once. Within the compound people rushed to the brush wall, but the cracks were small and Grizzly Hair saw nothing.

A thunder-bang sounded, close up, then another. A bear roared and many horses screamed. Men continued to yell. Another thunder-bang sounded, farther away. The neophytes and black hats could be running after a bear to scare it away. A bear normally avoided a village and it seemed strange that this one would attack horses near this many men.

Then it hit him. His spirit ally had not deserted him after all. O-se-mai-ti had come to his dream to tell him something. What? That he could have tunneled and escaped under cover of the commotion? He should have had faith and started, he now realized. Maybe it wasn't too late.

He started breaking through the brush, the noise outside covering the sound, horses still thumping and squealing, men yelling. He came to a heavy tree trunk, which they could climb over, but the limbs on top were stuck. He kept pushing. "Get Bowstring," he whispered to Oak Gall.

Then the night was filled with the massive rattle of brush. The entrance was being cleared! He backed out of his narrow tunnel. Men were coming in. Quickly he drew loose brush across and backed away. Dark figures began to walk around the periphery, checking the brush. The eastern sky had lightened a faint gray. People talked excitedly, Oak Gall and Bowstring with them. A sharp snap sounded, a *cuarta*, a black hat standing at the entrance. "*Solamente Español*," he barked.

Soon they were back on the trail tied by the ankles and slowly walking toward the mission. In his quietest undertone Grizzly Hair sang thanks to O-se-mai-ti for attempting to help him, but that gave him little calm as he faced whatever waited at the mission. The sight of Oak Gall walking like a snared rabbit toward a cougar's den nearly undid him.

Later the trail stretched before them like a long dusty thread laid across the golden hills and down through gorges filled with poison oak and trees. Some bore small green acorns in neat canopies atop trunks that were strangely smooth and pale—little sisters of the oaks of the valley. Others were so tall their tips disappeared in the clouds. Grizzly Hair caught their subtle fragrance and, looking up, could hardly believe he wasn't dreaming. Wearing shaggy, reddish bark, their straight posture reminded him of the cedars of the eastern mountains. But those were baby brothers to these giants.

The tall trees disappeared as the trail cut steadily across the flanks of the golden hills. They passed ever larger herds of *vacas*—brown and white spotted animals with immense long horns and slim hips. The western sea remained out of sight, no doubt beyond the low ridge on the west. A while ago that ridge had cut a dark line against the blue sky, but a long cloudy fist had seized and smothered it beneath soft thick knuckles. A different smell came to his nose. Even the air spirits were strange.

The black hats called a halt at a pond that had been muddied by the split hooves of many *vacas*. The water smelled of their dung, but Grizzly Hair was so parched he drank deeply.

"Now we smell of *vacas* inside and out," Oak Gall joked as she hobbled past, her narrow ankle as raw as his. She gave him a brave smile.

He wished he had carried her, kicking and screaming, back to her father. The captives were removing their hobbles. All would walk freely, now that there was no cover. To calm himself he tried pretending they had come willingly to this place and were walking cheerfully behind Bowstring and Teresa, but *cuartas* snapped behind them and the illusion fled faster than the two neophytes who galloped ahead, long hair flying. *Vacas* trotted off the trail, turned and watched with huge black eyes while the human captives passed by. All were controlled by men on horseback.

Toward the end of the day a puzzling, distant sound came to his ears. He exchanged a glance with Oak Gall. Teresa turned and said, "*Las campanillas de la misión.*" Her face was tight with worry and she moved closer to Bowstring.

As they drew nearer to the chaotic clanging, Grizzly Hair was able to separate the sounds into four different pitches, each penetrating him with shivering echoes that seemed to reach to the ends of the earth.

14

The *campanillas* clanged inside his skull. Like a wary hunter entering dangerous territory he walked before Oak Gall and adjusted the boy on his shoulders. They crossed a neat bridge over a stream banked with stones, then passed a long structure with multiple doorways before which stood several twenties of people dressed in hip wraps and skirts—neophyte men, women and children. Even little children wore hip wraps. All stared as he passed, no greetings exchanged, no smiles, no song. The trail opened to a wide area before a much taller structure whose straight-up wall reflected the salmon light of father sun.

Grizzly Hair looked at the source of the clanging. High on the flat wall, within three square openings, three upside down iron pots swung back and forth. Clappers struck the pots as neophytes pulled ropes.

His attention fell down to where a wooden portion of the wall opened. An unearthly figure in a pale robe emerged and seemed to float to a stop. An identical figure followed and closed the wall-door. These long robes, for surely they were the long robes, stood with their arms folded like wings inside draping cloth, their hands hidden. Above their ears rings of short hair circled the pink-tan domes of their heads, bringing to mind the distinctive ruff around the bald neck of Condor. Their features seemed too close together—a trait they shared with the black hats—and their heads were too small for their bodies. Their narrow bony noses resembled beaks. Dangling from twine about their waists hung large shiny objects, identical in size, each a long bar crossed by a short bar.

Sick with apprehension that these headmen, who appeared to be allied with the big magic of birds, would become angry to be stared at, he couldn't stop looking. Was Molok their ally? Crow? Ravens and crows possessed so much power that human villages had sprung up wherever Coyote planted their feathers. Never had Grizzly Hair felt more like a man in a dream than he did looking at these birdmen with folded wings. He recalled that a giant bird had once terrorized the world by gripping the scalps of people and flying them up through a hole in the sky, where he ate them.

Forcing himself to stop staring, he turned toward the sound of running water. It poured from a perfect tube into a stone trough filled to the brim. On the lower end, the water flowed over a lip into a second, identical trough. The second trough received water but never gave any away. The downhill area was dry. The *Españoles* had even captured water.

He looked above the noisy *campanillas.* Against the coloring sky stood a white stick with a straight cross bar—the same as the talisman hanging from the long robes' waists.

"*La cruz,*" whispered old Matías, who stood beside him.

All the structures, even the chest-high walls flanking this tall building, were roofed with thick cakes of clay, humped and placed over each other like snake's scales. Coyote had shown these people how to make houses a different way.

Grizzly Hair swung the boy down from his shoulders and stood him at his mother's feet. The child gripped her legs and she staggered. The unhappy expression on her rashy face, he suddenly realized, could be seen on every captive and resident neophyte alike, the latter edging forward from the long building. Only the black hats, who remained on their horses, appeared pleased. The long robes' faces told nothing.

The taller long robe raised a wing and the pots stopped clanging. With the sudden silence and the smell of fear around him, Grizzly Hair tried to reassure himself with what Matías had said: the long robes did not kill people.

Sergeant Sanchez, the wiry headman of the black hats, threw a leg over his horse and dismounted, spurs jingling. He gave the horse to a neophyte, planted his boots and began speaking. His voice rose in vigor as he gestured toward the dead man across the horse, now being brought up the trail. Then he pointed at Grizzly Hair!

The eyes of the long robes followed the accusing finger. Grizzly Hair shrank in his skin.

The bigger long robe began orating, but only the word *cimarrones* had meaning. His voice rose and fell, his eyes shifting elsewhere at last, but Grizzly Hair couldn't find his calm looking at the sharp-edged houses and captive water.

Abruptly the talk ended. Everyone shuffled through an opening in the wall north of the tall structure. Grizzly Hair followed along a trodden path past a forest of wooden *cruzes.* He found himself entering an enormous house beneath a likeness of a grinning skull carved in stone. Goosebumps rippled up his neck and arms. It was unlucky to think of the dead, but to carve such a thing and place it where people walked defied all understanding. In the dim interior, smooth stones felt cool beneath his feet, the warmth of father sun excluded from this haunted place. Fortunately the people ahead were hurrying out the opposite door toward the light. As his eyes adjusted, he was horrified to see a man above that door, apparently dead and hanging by the backs of his hands from a large wooden *cruz.* He stopped in his tracks. The dead man's hands and feet had been pierced. Bright blood flowed from them, as well as from a big cut on his side. Blood also streaked the pale face, oozing from wounds, and it meandered down the pale torso into a loin wrap. The man appeared to have been dead for some time, yet magically all this blood remained suspended and bright in color. Grizzly Hair touched Oak Gall, horrified that they were expected to expose themselves to the possibility of instant death walking beneath the unburied body and hovering soul. The pale circle of over the man's head might well be the soul looking for someone to seize.

Behind, a man shouted, *"Prisa!"*

He couldn't take his eyes from the figure, yet the longer he stood there, the greater the chance that the ghost would spring upon him, so he took Oak Gall's hand and they dashed out the door.

Gasping with relief, he examined her and saw she was frightened, but healthy. From an enormous vessel water spurted mysteriously into the air, hung for an instant as a column, then fell onto two shallow bowls, one above the other, sheeting down over them into the chest-high vessel. Old Matías and the captive women stood at the rim, chins to the water, scooping. Beyond, neophytes walked around several long buildings and some came toward them. Their expressions conveyed hopelessness, not power and health.

Needing to restore his spirit, Grizzly Hair hoisted himself to the rim and was about to jump in the water when hands grabbed and pulled him. He fell back on the hard earth.

A black hat yelled down at him in rapid Spanish. When that stopped, he slowly rose to his feet. Old Matías came over and said with deliberate slowness, *"Esta agua para beber, solamente."*

"What does that mean?" For some reason Matías was not speaking the tongue they always shared.

"Solamente Español," a black hat barked. Matías looked down and repeated, *"Solamente Español."*

By now all the captured people were scooping water. Grizzly Hair approached the huge vessel cautiously, dipped in a hand, and when nothing happened, scooped the cold water over his dusty face and into his cottony mouth. It made trails down his chest through the sweat and dust of the walk.

Men in loin wraps staggered around a building carrying an immense iron pot filled with something that looked like oo-lah. They poured it into a hollowed-out tree trunk with the shaggy bark of the giants he had seen on the trail. A second vessel of gruel was brought and poured into another trough. Hungry, he and Oak Gall kneeled beside the others and scooped. The gruel tasted like boiled seeds, very delicious. Women in red skirts brought baskets of flat yellow bread.

"*Maiz,*" Teresa whispered from across the trough.

"They are polite hosts," Grizzly Hair whispered back. The hospitality surprised him, though it felt strange to eat under the gaze of powerful long robes who sat on four-legged wooden platforms with high back rests.

"*Solamente Español,*" Teresa said.

The yellow bread tasted wonderful. Now all he needed was nu-pah, the thick oily food Coyote had taught the Ancients to eat. But no nu-pah was brought. The gruel vanished quickly except for puddles in the uneven grooves of the wood. The boy he had carried climbed into the trough and, on his hands and knees, sucked the bottom. His big brother joined him, as did other children. It disturbed Grizzly Hair to see children drinking like that, as the black hats had done at the stream.

But his stomach felt better and his thirst was slaked. He realized his hosts deserved to have their good behavior noticed. Rising to his feet, he was about to tell the headmen "*gracias,*" but a single *campanilla* clanged. He turned, looked for it.

Black hats stepped forward and forced him down on all fours with his forehead on the ground. Bowstring was being held down too. Seeing that everyone except the black hats and long robes knelt in that posture, he remained down though the hands slowly released him. Perhaps by doing their bidding he could show that he was not a wild enemy and they would allow him to bathe and restore his spirit. He might even get some of their power.

A long robe stood, raised his draped arms and orated. Afterwards, the resident people handled their beads and spoke softly to them. Grizzly Hair remained kneeling even after the mumbling ended and the bell rang again—somewhere within the darkening symmetry of the buildings. Without talk, all the neophytes rose as one and walked away.

Black hats pulled him and Bowstring to their feet and prodded them to walk. Yanked from their mother, the two little boys screamed for her, but a *cuarta* snapped and they went tearfully away. Oak Gall was made to go with the woman, vanishing into the darkness in a different direction. Oak Gall! Where were they taking her and why wasn't he going there?

A jab in the buttocks jolted him forward. These men never tired of using their *fusil* barrels as prods. As he walked up the dark path through shadowy structures, a wavering light cast ghostly shadows. He turned to see the source. A tall man carried a waxy rod that burned only on the uppermost tip. More magic.

They stopped before a small square house. By the light of the little torch, a black hat fumbled with clinking iron implements and opened a door. Out belched the stench of human urine and excrement. Sickened, Grizzly Hair stared into the dim interior illuminated by the small flame, and saw a man caught in a trap. His forward-thrust head and hands were pushed through a slice of a tree trunk and he blinked in the unaccustomed light. The hair crawled on Grizzly Hair's neck.

The black hat went inside the house and returned with an armload of thongs, which he distributed to the neophyte who had accompanied them. With practiced speed a neophyte tied Grizzly Hair's and Bowstring's hands in front of them while the other stood by with what appeared to be many strands of thongs.

Suddenly Grizzly Hair understood. He was about to receive the flogging of which he had heard. In broken Spanish he tried to explain that he and Bowstring were not enemies.

The black hat showed no interest.

A neophyte passed a thong beneath the binding on his wrists, threw it through an iron ring embedded in a sturdy log over the doorway, then winched it down, yanking Grizzly Hair's hands over his head, nearly jerking him off his feet. Heartbeat quickening, he hung with the tips of his toes barely touching the ground, hands tingling and swelling. "No neh-o-fee-tes, no ci-mar-ron-es," he said to all around him.

Spanish talk gushed from the black hat, and the neophyte with the flame disappeared behind Grizzly Hair. Faintly lit, the trapped man stared at the ground, not meeting Grizzly Hair's glance. Bowstring watched in obvious dread.

A sudden swish and loud snap burned several tongues of fire into Grizzly Hair's back, throwing him off his toes. "*Uno*," said a voice.

A second blow made him bite his lip to keep from crying out. "*Dos*." He tried to yank his hands through the bindings, but they only throbbed more painfully. He must escape!

"*Tres*." He kicked and thrashed, desperate to leave this nightmare in which he, a strong man, was being injured like an insect in the hands of cruel children. Anger roared up through him. They had tricked him with their hospitality.

"*Quatro*." The exact lines of the whips seemed less defined because his back was a single mass of pain stinging with breathtaking intensity. He ached to kill the man with the whips, kill him with his bare hands. And kill the man who held the flame to make him an easy target.

Cinco. Seis. Siete. Ocho. Nueve, diez, diez y uno. . .

The lashes continued beyond imagination, beyond passion. He tried to distance himself the way the umne made their spirits float apart from their bodies, but returned again and again to the pain. When would it stop? Would it ever stop?

Cuarenta y uno, cuarenta y dos—he descended into the worst possible place, feverishly hoping, even expecting each blow to be the last. But the agony continued and the sounds accompanying the crack of hide upon his flesh were, he realized, his own unmanly cries.

Cincuenta y dos, cincuenta y tres. He became a frog beneath the foot of a giant blue heron ripping flesh from his back. Then a swirl of merciful darkness sucked him down.

He surfaced briefly, felt himself drop near the feet of the man in the trap. One thought came. It would be easier for Bowstring. He would know there was an end.

15

The earth cried out all around him as he clawed to climb up out of a bad hole. Stinking dirt clogged his nose and eyes and his arms felt too heavy to dig fast enough to stay ahead of the loose dirt falling back in the hole. A hump of pain rode his back like a turtle shell. But he kept trying to pull himself to the surface.

"Is your heart with me?"

Bowstring's voice jerked him to the top. It had been a dream. No dirt grated his eyes and he saw nothing but obsidian blackness blooming up out of a narrow bar of light. The stench remained and heavy iron rings weighed down his wrists and ankles, which were connected by iron links. "I think so."

Talk worsened the pain. He tried not to breathe, in part to avoid the smell but also because breathing moved his back muscles. He recalled the counting, the flogging, the swish and snap of the lashes, and his shameful loss of power. The night had been interminable. He had sat with his knees supporting his chin, but no change of position stopped the violent pulsing of his back. Something with sharp toenails scurried onto his foot and he waited for it to leave, preferring its warm weight to the pain of movement.

"Are you awake?" Bowstring asked.

"We've got to get out of here."

"I think they whipped you so long because they thought we were *cimarrones,* at first. The *cimarrones* were whipped like you."

He talked more easily than Grizzly Hair, and knew more. "But not as long as you. They talked, then cut me down sooner."

Good, he'd been spared some of the pain.

"As long as they've got us trapped here," Bowstring said, "we must make them believe we are friends."

The bear in Grizzly Hair growled, "Not friends."

With a sudden clank and rattle, the door opened. The weight on his foot leaped off as blinding light and healthy air flooded the little house. Grizzly

Hair wanted to shade his eyes, but it meant raising his arms. Black shapes stood before him and something soft stunned him, struck his chest. Spanish talk kicked at his ears and he felt nauseous.

By the time the talk stopped, his eyes had adjusted and he saw by the shapes that both long robes stood looking down at him. One uttered more talk. A black hat unlocked the iron rings from his wrists. At that moment sickness flew up his throat and he disgorged a flood of brown lumps and yellow grain.

The black hat jumped back and, when the spasms subsided, pointed to the pale wooly material before Grizzly Hair and Bowstring and signed that they were to wrap it around their hips. Afraid of more whipping—he didn't know if he could survive more—and lacking understanding how the vomit-soaked piece of cloth was to be looped and tied between his legs, he fumbled to arrange it, each tiny movement wracking him with intensified pain. Doing the same thing, Bowstring turned to the side. His back was a mass of red stripes, with some of the muscles shredded and swollen with crusted blood, red blood breaking free under the strain. Bowstring needed herbs. So did Grizzly Hair.

The black hat pointed insistently at the long tail of the cloth to be poked under Grizzly Hair's hip wrap, and after excruciating effort, he finally tied the thing to the black hat's satisfaction.

A long robe talked at him.

Kneeling with his heels on the spongy garment, Grizzly Hair said, "*No comprendo.*" Gabriel had taught him to say that when he didn't understand.

The long robes and black hat talked between themselves, then the shorter long robe spoke a word or two that sounded like Gabriel's tongue.

Grizzly Hair tried to say in that tongue that he and Bowstring were not fugitives from the mission, but he lapsed into his own tongue, then lost his thought beneath the drumming agony of his back.

Like a giant bird blocking the sunlight, the taller long robe asked, "*¿De donde vienes?*"

De donde meant where from, but Grizzly Hair couldn't form the answer. He lifted a heavy arm, gritting his teeth at the pain, pointed at the long robe and said, "*Padre.*" Teresa had instructed him to call them the Spanish word for father. He pointed at the black hat and said, "*soldado,*" then put his hand on his chest and said, "*Gentile. No cimarrón.*"

"*¿Cómo se llama?*"

Did they expect him to speak his name? No matter how much power they had, he wouldn't do that. He needed to follow the rules of good living as best he could, or he would lack the strength to fend off their magic.

"*¿De la ranchería de Gabriel?*"

"*No comprendo.*"

The padres and black hat turned and left. With a thunk of wood and rattle of iron they snuffed out the good air and sunlight. Grizzly Hair needed to drink. Bile sickened his tongue and tasted bad in his teeth. He also needed to pass water, as many others had done in the house, but he was not so delirious as to deposit more of himself where it could be seen and used against him. In agony he knee-walked to the door, reached a hand beneath it and pulled, but it held fast. In the after-pain of the effort, he lay down by stages and put his nose beneath the door. The vomit and excrement reeked and for a moment he expected more bad matter to spew out of his mouth. But his stomach quieted, and after a rest he said to Bowstring, "Come breathe with me."

Bowstring groaned. "I don't want to move."

He had brought the best friend of his childhood to pain. "Why did you come with me on this journey?" He'd often wanted to ask this question.

After a long silence, "To meet Teresa."

He meant that this was fated.

Footsteps and rattling returned to the door. Grizzly Hair scuttled out of the way as it pushed open. In the brilliant light framing a knot of shadows he caught the delicate scent of Oak Gall and his heart quickened. She left the other silhouettes and stepped toward him, but was jerked back.

Relieved to see her walking, but afraid for her, he watched the shapes—three besides Oak Gall, only one long robe this time—move to where the light fell on them instead of coming from behind. Oak Gall wore a red skirt to her knees. A black hat wearing a wide straw hat was gripping her upper arm. Covering her nose against the stench, she appeared to have been crying. Trails of tears ran down her dirty cheeks—a sight he hadn't seen since they were young children when she took a hard fall. He wished he could hold and comfort her.

Shamed by his weakness, he looked from her to the man beside the long robe. It was the man who had held the waxy torch, now wearing a suit of the same wooly material as the hip wraps. His hair lay long and black against the pale fabric. His handsome nose and normal skin color indicated that he was indeed a neophyte, but like the black hats, he left a bar of unplucked hair on his upper lip. The fire of knowledge burned in his eyes and Grizzly Hair found himself wanting to talk with him.

The long robe pointed at Oak Gall and asked, "*¿Tu esposa?*"

"*No comprendo.*"

The neophyte said in Gabriel's tongue, "Wife?"

"*No, no esposa.*" He didn't know how to say, Not yet.

The neophyte talked with the long robe, who turned his face into the light. His eyes looked like holes punched out of his head with pale sky coming through. Grizzly Hair tried to hold onto his strength, what little he had left. Fish, snakes and a few birds had eyes that color. Trickery was afoot and this man might transform himself into a demon at any moment.

The neophyte laid his palm on his shirt and said "Yokut," Human. Then he pointed at Grizzly Hair and looked him a question, "In your tongue."

"Mi-woh," he answered, trying to calm himself.

"Mee-wuk?"

Gabriel pronounced it like that, but it wasn't the way of the umne. "Mi-woh," he repeated.

"¿De donde vienes, miwok? De los Muquelumne?"

"No." He did not come from Muquel's people. "Lopotsumne. The people of Morning Owl."

The neophyte gestured at Bowstring and Oak Gall. "You were all in the *ranchería* of Gabriel."

"No cimarrones," Grizzly Hair said. Not fugitives.

"¿Por qué en la ranchería de Gabriel?"

Por qué meant why. Why had they been in Gabriel's village. He had asked himself the same question many times. Now he spoke in the tongue of his people, which this man seemed to understand a little. "We visited Gabriel's place. I wanted to learn about the *Españoles,* but didn't want to come inside the mission. We are not *cimarrones.*" He shifted to relieve the pull on his back, but it didn't help.

"¿Norte del río de los Muquelumne?" The neophyte pointed north.

He was beginning to understand. *"Sí."* His river was north of Muquel's river.

The neophyte turned and talked with the blue-eyed long robe. Grizzly Hair glanced at Oak Gall, her hand still covering her nose, the black hat gripping her arm. He felt sorry that she was forced to breathe the gagging stench. Then the black hat pushed her out the door. She looked over her shoulder as she walked into the sun. Would they hurt her? He couldn't stop them. He was like an infant that couldn't even walk.

The neophyte turned to Grizzly Hair, pointed at him and declared, *"Del Río de los Cosumne."* From the river of the Cosumne.

There was a headman named Cos somewhere on his river and the *Españoles* had named the river for those people.

In Gabriel's tongue the neophyte asked, "How far east on that river?"

He barely understood and could not form an answer.

"En las montañas altas?"

"No." Not in the high mountains. He wanted to say that his people lived where the first gray pines grew but not far enough up the mountains for the yellow pines, that he lived where the river tumbled down through boulders but hadn't yet spilled into the Valley of the Sun. But he came to his senses and knew he should hide the location of his people, as the bees had covered their dead.

"*En las montañas chicas?*" the neophyte probed.

"*No comprendo.*" He looked down, hoping his falsehood would not further drain his power.

The neophyte glanced at him then turned to talk with the long robe, but in that glance Grizzly Hair saw a spark of understanding.

"*Presento Padre Fortuni,*" said the neophyte, changing the subject and gesturing toward the long robe. Then he placed his large hand on his shirt and said, "Estanislao. I speak for my people in this mission. *Misión de San José.*"

He had spoken his name, obviously unafraid, and was acting as a headman.

"People say padres are headmen of the mission."

A smile cracked the vertical creases of Estanislao's face, though he was not old. "I speak for the *neofites* in council with the padres."

He also held the torch for floggings.

The padre and neophyte left, shutting the door and talking outside.

"Did you see the eyes," whispered Grizzly Hair in the dark.

"Yes," Bowstring croaked. "Maybe a demon, or a sorcerer."

Silence fell between them, during which Grizzly Hair wondered what magic could get them out of this bad place. The man in the trap coughed and moaned—not dead as Grizzly Hair had begun to suspect. "*Amigo,*" he said, "*hablas Español?*"

The door opened and Estanislao stood there in the light.

The man in the trap spoke rapid Spanish to him, and Estanislao talked to him with a kind voice. When they were finished, Grizzly Hair said, "We are in need of passing water." Having to say this felt bad. Even young children passed water without mentioning it.

Estanislao, a man Grizzly Hair's height, helped him and Bowstring to their feet, then led them, hobbled in heavy iron rings, behind the house. Sick, watery defecation lay all about. Grizzly Hair opened his mouth and let the remaining bad things buck up over his tongue. The throbbing after-pain of the muscular exertion made him grit his teeth, and when it subsided he was empty. Urine trickled down his leg through the spongy material, pushed out by the vomiting.

Holding back the threatening dark—though sunlight blazed upon him—and moving the thick wet material aside to pass more water, he told Estanislao, "My friend and I want to bathe in the stream we saw before the sleep."

Estanislao regarded them with sympathy and when they were finished, motioned the two to follow. Grizzly Hair clinked after him in mincing steps, the iron rings bruising his ankles, the reeking hip wrap chafing his thighs.

They passed a place littered with iron implements. Neophytes in loin wraps were removing logs from a large pile and tossing them inside a small, cylindrical mud house, the only house without corners he'd seen at the mission.

The fire burned brightly, yet they were making it hotter—a house of fire. With a sudden shock of recognition he knew this was the iron-bending place. Estanislao was saying, "In the mission we bathe in the troughs in front of the *iglésia*, and only on *Sábado por la tarde*."

"What is *Sábado?* What is *tarde?*"

"Here the days have names. After four sleeps it will be *Sábado*. After that comes *Domingo* and you will go to Mass in the *iglésia*." He pointed ahead toward the crowds of men and boys at the foot of the high wall.

How could anyone remember all the names of the days when they numbered like the sands of the river? Filthy from the journey, itchy with insect bites, smeared with blood and urine and vomit, he couldn't imagine waiting four sleeps to bathe. How much sicker would he be then? How many more bad things would lodge in him? Now he knew why the *Españoles* smelled bad, but how did they stay alive? Strong magic protected them, and he must use his opportunity inside the mission to locate that power, for they had stolen his. They had thrown away his amulet, broken his bow and kept him from bathing. Taking their power could be even more dangerous than stealing a piece of the bear's spirit, for these men were cunning and had extraordinary tools. He would watch for a chance to touch a long robe.

Estanislao stopped, turned toward him, his eyes alive with the understanding Grizzly Hair had seen before. "They shouldn't have whipped you that many times," he said in a quiet voice. "We thought you were someone else, bad *cimarrones*."

Grizzly Hair exchanged a look with Bowstring, then pointed to the iron rings. "Are these for someone else too?"

"No, Padre Durán wants you to stay in the *escuela* for eight sleeps, and he fears you would escape if we took the *hierro* off."

"For eight sleeps we walk like this?" Bowstring looked so horrified that if Grizzly Hair hadn't known him well, he might have thought he was playing the clown.

"Yes," Estanislao said, "but after eight sleeps, if you refuse the *bautismo* you can leave."

"Walk away?"

The tall man nodded solemnly.

"With my woman?"

"Yes. If she refuses the *bautismo* and wants to leave."

This was a crafty game, and he was trying hard to understand all the rules. With a glance back at the iron-making place, he followed Estanislao and Bowstring toward the open place with the food troughs, where many times more people than had ever attended a big time sat waiting to have someone else bring their food.

16

Morning bells woke him. The fourth sleep had passed and with it much of the throbbing pain in his back, except when he raised his hands, heavy in the irons, to scratch lice bumps on his scalp. As usual, unable to lie in his normal position, he had slept little. Estanislao had said that no gentile was allowed to sleep in the house of single men, so until they underwent the *bautismo,* they must endure this filthy place. But of course they would leave and never see the house of men.

"This is *Sábado,*" he said to Bowstring, his stomach rumbling. The pinole hadn't filled him before the sleep and he could never make himself eat curdled cheese—dead man's brains, Matías called it.

Another rumble in the dark, from the trapped man? But it was Bowstring who said, "Our stomachs are saying they are happy we will bathe today."

"I am hungrier for water and air, than food," Grizzly Hair said looking toward Bowstring's voice. He saw only a pair of tiny green eyes in the corner, reflecting light from under the door.

With a sudden clinking and clanking, the door flew back on its hide hinges and admitted strong light. Blinded, Grizzly Hair knew it would be the black hats who accompanied him and Bowstring each day. The one whose brown hair curled like the spent pods of the crane-beak plant would unlock their wrist irons and toss them into the corner. As he did this, Crane-beak said something to the two men who had been captured trying to escape in the night and received five twenties of lashes each at the door of the big house with the bleeding dead man. Now and then they moaned quietly. The man in the trap blinked. Punished for stealing food and not saying his prayers, he seemed to plead with Crane-beak. They paid no more attention to him than the mouse.

Grizzly Hair and Bowstring hobbled before Crane-beak, hurrying so he would not poke them with his sharp stick. Holding his breath as he relieved himself behind the *calabozo,* Grizzly Hair was careful not to splash on his raw ankles. Then they clinked as fast as possible toward the front patio, the place of eating. Oak Gall would be kept in the *monjería,* eating with the girls and unmarried women, so he wouldn't see her until later. But knowing he would see her made him lighter.

Moments after he arrived at the *iglésia* wall, the bell clanged five times. Everyone except black hats knelt with foreheads on the ground. Eyes slit, Grizzly Hair watched the west building where Padre Durán emerged from his door. Father sun, who now crested Mission Peak beamed directly into the long robe's face and glanced off the shiny *cruz* hanging from his waist. The padre raised his wings and orated in his usual monotone.

At the *amen* men and married women jumped up to wait at the troughs where people were bringing vats of pinole, vessels of milk, yellow flatbread called tortillas and curdled cheese. Old Matías bent toward the trough, his back a mass of swollen, shredded flesh caked with new and old blood. Each morning since their arrival he had received twenty-five lashes and would continue to receive that number for four more days. He received them at the door of the *iglésia.* Obviously accepting his fate, Matías was allowed to sleep in the men's house and walk without irons. He had not fought the black hats.

Quickly Grizzly Hair scooped the gruel, knowing he would be hungry before the evening meal. Too soon the trough was empty, and all the tortillas were gone before the basket came to him.

The bell clanged three times, signaling the time of *trabajar*. But first Bowstring and Grizzly Hair would join the children under the corridor roof, the place of teaching. Grizzly Hair looked forward to it because Oak Gall would be there. Each morning it seemed several seasons had passed since he had last seen her. He needed to talk to her.

Waiting, he sat on the packed earth with ten boys and Bowstring and recalled his talk with her the previous morning.

"The *monjería* is a bad place," she had whispered. Dark pouches normally seen on older women had appeared under her eyes. "I want to leave after the eight sleeps and bathe with you in a river. I want to lie with you in good air."

He had been momentarily silenced by the thought and had not yet responded when Padre Fortuni shook a finger and said, *"Solamente Español."* He hadn't been able to say that, assuming it wasn't a trick, they would leave at dawn after the eighth sleep. The previous day he had mentioned that one of the boys had said they might be taught to fly. "That's something I'd like to learn," he had told her. All night he had worried that she would think he had changed his mind about leaving. He ached to set it right. He needed her. She and water would heal him.

A door opened. Padre Fortuni rustled out and pushed a large thin sheaf onto a small iron spike protruding from a redwood pillar. Grizzly Hair said, *"Padre?"*

"Sí." The long robe turned toward him.

Avoiding the fish eyes, he said what he had practiced in his mind. *"Cómo hace hierro."* How make iron. He didn't know the word for fly.

"Primero, hijo mío, has de ser bautizado. Bautismo."

He understood only *bautismo* and was wondering what that had to do with iron, when girls and Oak Gall rounded the corner. She looked him love through tired eyes, and despite the dark circles she was the most beautiful sight in the mission. She came to sit beside him, but Padre Fortuni signaled her back with the boys two rows behind where he couldn't see her without turning around, and that was forbidden. All must face Father Fortuni. Now he wouldn't be able to talk with her unless they let her stay longer than usual after the teaching.

"Hoy aprendemos los siete pecados capitales," the padre began. They would learn about bad behavior. *"Entonces, contemos."*

The children chanted loudly: *Uno, dos, tres, quatro, cinco, seis, siete.* The counting sickened Grizzly Hair. The numbers took him back to the whipping and stuck in his teeth like pine gum.

"Otra vez," said the padre, and the children shouted, *"Uno, dos, tres, quatro, cinco, seis, siete."*

The padre pointed his stick to the sheaf on the pillar. *"Uno,"* he said, tapping one of the demons depicted there—all the demons leering, flying or holding their stomachs. "*Pereza,* he said. Sloth. This demon slouched horribly and her hair jutted out at all angles. Her vacant stare resembled the man in the trap. *"Otra vez."*

Everyone shouted, *"Pereza."*

As the padre pointed in turn to other monsters on the sheet, the hail of his talk pounded at Grizzly Hair: Lust, Greed, Pride, Avarice, Gluttony and Envy. Words without meaning. Threading through it came a woman's cry from the *iglésia*—Gabriel's women receiving their daily ten lashes for running away. By the look on Bowstring's face, he suffered each lash with Teresa and her friends and sister. Oak Gall had been spared because no *bautismo* water had been put on her head.

"Ojos aquí," said Fortuni, skewering Grizzly Hair with icy eyes.

The cries continued. A long time ago Grizzly Hair had heard of a mother slapping a very disrespectful child—one light slap to get the child's attention. But most parents never raised a hand against their children. Yet these self-styled fathers instructed other men to wound the people they called their children and, according to Estanislao, did it like *Español* fathers punishing their children. But Grizzly Hair and Bowstring were not children, the long robes not their fathers, and no father would use a *cuarta* on a child. The whippings defied all human experience, yet the long robes made no apology or restitution.

"Atención." Padre Fortuni scowled at Grizzly Hair and pointed his stick to the slouching monster. *"Cómo se llama este pecado."* What is the name of the bad behavior.

The soft brown eyes of the children fell on Grizzly Hair as he looked at his knees, shaking his head. *"No comprendo."* He wanted to say, "I forgot," but didn't know the word.

"Pereza," the padre said in an exasperated tone.

"Pereza." Grizzly Hair repeated. *"¿Qué es?"* What did that slouching she-demon mean?

"No trabajar," the long robe said, voice rising, *"No levantarse por la mañana,*

duermes cuando los otros trabajan." He let out his air and his eyes looked like those of a washed-up fish. "*¿Comprendes?*"

Anxious for the padre to look at someone else, Grizzly Hair nodded. He truly wanted to understand, for he believed that much of the power of the long robes lay in these teachings. But regarding *pereza* he understood only that *trabajar* meant people doing the same thing each day when the bell rang, starting at first light. Apparently sloth meant doing it badly or not at all. In the home place people made things when they felt lucky or when a spirit ally told them. Each man decided when to hunt or fish or make tools. The moment a woman awoke she knew if the time had come to begin a new basket. Sometimes she waited many seasons to feel the right moment. But no one rang a bell. Were the umne slothful? Would they burn in the big ground fire?

As Padre Fortuni rattled on, Grizzly Hair tried to make sense of the previous day's lesson. The padre had hung a different sheaf on the spike, one depicting many people in a big fire. They were falling over each other and screaming in pain. Their legs and arms were intertwined and their faces were twisted into terrified expressions. The padre said they were *muerto*. Dead. Magic must have made them suffer pain after death. It seemed the long robe was sharing a powerful secret, one that changed the way Coyote made people. Any doctor he'd heard of would have kept such a secret to himself. Big magic. But Fortuni was teaching it to children. If only Grizzly Hair could understand! At the end of the lesson the long robe gazed at the sky, opened his wings and mimed flying. The slack-jawed children stared in awe. Would he teach them to fly? That would be even more useful than iron-making.

His mind twisted through the confusion of the things that had been taught. On the first morning Padro Fortuni had seen the bloody wounds on his back and said "*bueno*." Good. He had talked a long time about padres flogging themselves and seemed to be trying hard to make him understand, but it was impossible. Pain and wounds were bad.

A gold striped cat peeked around the water cistern, dangling a cobweb from her whiskers. Her pupils were flat lines in the sunlight. A pride of these friendly miniature cats prowled the grounds, entering through special little doors hinged with hide thongs. They licked their paws, buried their feces and carried their young exactly like bobcats and mountain lions. How had they been made small? How had they been tamed? He wished he could ask.

The silky fur thrilled him as the cat rubbed his leg and the erect tail quivered on his knee. He stroked her back and she raised her haunches. The silence alerted him. Ice-blue eyes stared at him. He stared back, impolite behavior being expected, and the padre resumed his talk. The little cat left, perhaps to hunt mice that Oak Gall said nested in the granary.

A sudden yell startled him, a boy running toward them. "Padre! Padre Durán!" He skidded to a stop, dust rising from his feet. He was older than the boys in class, but not quite old enough to be a man. He pounded on Padre Durán's door.

Padre Durán cracked the door and peeked out. The boy spoke in excited tones. "*Una señorita está muerta en la monjería!*"

Girl dead in the *monjería.*

Padre Durán sounded gruff and upset. "*Tú me informas más tarde, Antonio. Tienes pereza. Además, sin las devociones finales, el espíritu de la señorita se quemará eternamente en los fuegos del Diablo.*"

Tarde meant late, *pereza,* sloth and *Diablo* was the demon who tended the fires in the ground. Otherwise Grizzly Hair understood nothing.

The boy wilted to his knees before the padre, forehead on the earth. He looked up, chin quivering, his soft cheeks wet. "*No, Padre, no tengo pereza. Trabajo mucho.* I am not slothful. I do much work. *Hay muchos inválidos en los dormitorios, en las casas, en la monjería, y en el campo. Cada día yo voy a ver a toda la gente, pero no sé si los inválidos tienen un mal pequeño o si se van a morir. Por favor, Padre, piedad.*" On his knees, he raised and lowered his outstretched arms, repeating, "*Piedad. Piedad.*"

Padre Durán glanced at Crane-beak. "*Diez,*" he said closing the redwood door. Ten.

The boy sat up and stared at the door, tears glistening. Crane-beak pulled him to his feet and directed his limp shoulders toward the door of the *iglésia.* He had obviously been trying to please the padre. Now he would receive ten strokes of the *cuarta.*

Rage rushed into Grizzly Hair's stomach. His ears burned hot and his breath came fast. He wanted to rise up and attack the black hat and stop him from hurting the boy. He wanted to whip the long robe who gave the order. Never had he felt so enraged, but he could do nothing.

Padre Fortuni removed his sheet of monsters, and the remaining black hat stepped forward to escort Grizzly Hair and Bowstring to the place of skinning. Still hot with anger, Grizzly Hair said to Oak Gall, "We'll leave after—"

"*Solamente Español,*" said the black hat, prodding him with the sharp stick.

A roar boomed up his throat but he stifled it to a groan, and it took all his strength to keep from leaping at the man and tearing out his eyes and smashing his bones. Oak Gall, being pulled by the old woman toward the *monjería,* looked back, puzzled.

The bear was in him, Grizzly Hair realized, and he must hold himself in check or be flogged more than last time and hobbled even longer. For the sake of Oak Gall and Bowstring, he must confine his rage. Did she know how much he wanted to take her away from here? Did she think he wanted to stay in the mission until he learned to fly? Now he wouldn't see her again until after the sleep.

17

The next day he waited in the place of learning, more anxious than ever to talk to Oak Gall, but when the old woman brought the unmarried women and girls, Oak Gall was not among them. Why was she not there? Had she committed a *pecado*? Was she being whipped? He could hardly listen, much less understand the padre, who was talking about the dead man on the *cruz*. *"Tres días despues del muerte de . . ."*

Was she ill? Maybe it was merely her time for the woman's house. Was the *monjería* also the woman's house? So many things he didn't know.

"Tres días," repeated the padre. Three days. Moon had argued with Coyote, saying the dead should be buried so their bodies could live again after three sleeps, as she herself was reborn after three dark nights. But Coyote insisted the dead stay dead to make room in the world for new people. And from that time on, the dead were burned to prevent their rebirth.

Muerte. Death. Why did this word push his reckless thoughts to Oak Gall? It invited danger.

Eternidad. A very long time, and that's how long it seemed until Padre Fortuni finished talking. Crane-beak and a black hat with hair the color of weathered iron nodded Grizzly Hair and Bowstring toward their *trabajar*. Bowstring didn't move. He was watching the musicians assemble with their flutes, portable drums and *violines*—wooden boxes with gut stretched over them.

Padre Durán took Padre Fortuni's place in the corridor and hung a large pale sheet filled with lines and square black and red marks, some with tails like polliwogs, all sitting on or wedged between the lines. The musicians stared at the marks. Padre Durán rapped the pillar with his stick and neophytes raised flutes to their lips and bows to their *violines*.

"Rapido," Crane-beak said, poking Bowstring in a buttock. Grizzly Hair left for the skinning place to the sound of haunting music that gave voice to his fears for Oak Gall.

"Un momento," said Padre Durán, stopping the music.

Grizzly Hair looked back. The padre was talking slowly at Bowstring. *"Quieres tocar en la orquestra?"*

Bowstring had a blank expression, and the long robe took a flute from a neophyte and handed it to him. Bowstring raised it and played a piece of a song as only Bowstring could. Clearly surprised and appreciative, the padre said something to the black hat and beckoned Bowstring to sit down.

This time when the instruments started, they sang of Grizzly Hair's sorrow to be going to his *trabajar* without Bowstring, and happiness for Bowstring. The music would last until midday, then surely Bowstring would join him at the place of skinning.

He clinked past the sun-speaker, an iron wedge embedded in a pedestal that pointed its shadow at scenes etched around the rim of the stone—now pointing at sheep and *vacas*. This signified the time of morning *trabajar*. When the shadow reached the *cruzes*, everyone knelt and talked to the spirits. When no shadow appeared, midday *devociones* would begin. The long robes had made even father sun speak for them.

The mission bustled like an anthill. Were the women as busy in their house? Passing the adobe-making place he saw many neophytes stomping mud in a pit while others tossed in straw and water. Beyond that, smooth pads of clay dried on tapered branches, neat rows of them lined up with several pads on each branch. These curved roof tiles were then baked in ovens that resembled beehives, and drawn out on long wooden paddles.

The dusty smell of hot clay gave way to the strong sulfur smoke of the iron-making place where sweating neophytes in headbands hammered long-knives for killing cattle. Next came fingers of wax hanging from crossed sticks over a vat filled with melted wax. Neophytes lowered the rack into the vat, held it there, then raised it slowly to drip, lengthening many tapers at the same time. The *Epañoles* were very clever.

He passed the square redwood-lined excavations where hides soaked in oak-bark water. Two hides he'd skinned before the sleep were soaking there now. Then came the big area where *vaca* fat bubbled over fires. Several vats were suspended from huge iron arms that could be swung back and forth. Neophytes fished with wire nets in the hot grease, catching bits of meat to be added to the supper pi-no-leh. A line of children and old people delivered wood to these fires that burned day and night like the everlasting fires of *el diablo*. Each day the wood collectors searched farther and farther beyond the mission walls.

He had walked through that denuded area with Oak Gall. Now he was destitute of her. Ankles chafing, he rounded the corner and the field opened before him, the sky swirling with vultures. Bloated carcasses littered the grass, ugly in their nakedness. These were the animals he and Bowstring had previously skinned. The scavengers couldn't keep up. Several grizzly bears, condors and a pack of dogs fed on the rotting meat. Briefly, the bears looked up, then returned to their feast. The world had gone awry. He felt a chilling foreboding, the smell of death putrefying the air. Yesterday's breeze had stopped.

The vaqueros were finished roping and killing the day's quota—forty bawling, struggling *vacas* brought to their knees, glaring wild-eyed as killers ran lances between their ribs. Fortunately, he wouldn't need to watch that today. Would he be expected to skin, stretch and salt all forty hides by himself?

The report of a *fusil* made him jump. White smoke and sulfur scent cut through the smell of death. Bears ran toward the hills and four condors whumped into the sky, the vultures giving them clear passage. The black hat handed Grizzly Hair his skinning knife.

He ran his thumb across the edge, the bluish circling marks along its sides. It had been sharpened on stone. He thought of escape, but must be patient. This constant thought disturbed his calm. He hobbled toward the nearest animal corpse and slashed the belly from throat to tail. A familiar pain shot up to his elbow, telling him the spirits were displeased with the disrespect to these animals, even if they were new to the world. Nevertheless he must continue skinning, placing the fat in the *carreta,* a cart with iron wheels which a neophyte pulled back and forth to the tallow vats. Heads, horns, hoofs, organs, entrails, bones and most of the muscle were to be left rotting in the field, though now and then a woman came for meat for the supper troughs and plates of the black hats and padres.

Sudden nausea overtook him. Swallowing, he thought he might control his lurching stomach, but it erupted and he whirled from the cow and vomited on earth that had been well fed by blood.

Crane-beak scowled at the field, hands on hips, then left. He reappeared with another *carreta.* "Load it," he ordered to Grizzly Hair, signing that he was to put the rotting meat into the cart. *"Allá."* He pointed at the field.

The fresher corpses weren't too bad, though they had to be butchered, but those that had been in the sun for several sleeps seethed with maggots. Greenish slime slid through his fingers when he tried to pick it up. He couldn't distinguish brains from entrails, liver from muscle. All was warm, nearly liquid and it slithered down his hip wrap and legs. His stomach twitched and he stuffed dry grass up his nose, but it couldn't keep out the death stench.

When his cart was full, he pulled it slowly across the field. The black hat shouted. Grizzly looked back and saw the signal to dump the load there. Back and forth he wheeled the cart until he had built a hill of rotten meat. The other black hat came to the field, relieved him of the cart and pointed at the freshly killed animals. *"A trabajar."*

Now, smelling like death, he must skin faster than ever to make twenty skins—or forty? Arm hurting, he was half finished with one hide when children pulled carts piled with brush into the field. They helped a black hat distribute the wood around the rotten pile and set it on fire. Before long, black smoke churned skyward. The vultures flapped away. This burning of the dead would have seemed respectful except that too many animals had given their lives for too little purpose.

He reminded himself that anger obscured clarity and invited weakness. Older men had the ability to confront bad situations and retain their calm. Would he forever burn with rage? Finished with his third hide, he was about to peg it beside the others when a neophyte from the tanning area came for it. Now and then this happened, and the "missing" hides wouldn't be counted at the end of the day.

Slashing a new cow belly, he glanced at Crane-beak, who lay across all three salt bags with his hat over his forehead, the *fusil* on his lap. The other black hat tended the fire in the field. More useless scenes filled Grizzly Hair's mind—slitting Crane-beak's throat and seizing the gun. But in irons he couldn't run and didn't know how to sneak Oak Gall out of the *monjería.*

After a while Crane-beak opened his eyes and sat up on the middle bag, leaning on the wall. Grizzly Hair yanked back the heavy skin and cut through the tough connecting tissue. His arm screamed at him, his spirit in conflict with his hands. The waste sickened him. Even the fat dogs quickly tired of the meat. After he pegged the skin, he hobbled over for salt, opened the heavy cowhide bag next to the black hat, scooped salt with the little basket, hobbled to the skin, sprinkled salt over it and returned the basket. Then he headed for a new animal.

Before the sleep, at supper, he had managed to ask old Matías why the *Españoles* didn't sing to the spirits of the killed animals. Matías had said, "The padres teach that animals don't have souls."

"But people are animals," Grizzly Hair had countered.

"*Españoles* say no." The old man regarded him with an unfathomable expression.

But anyone could see that animals were relatives. People's hands came from Lizard. Padre Durán's scowling eyes came from Hawk. People slept, played, coupled and cared for their young just like other animals. Old Matías had said more. The long robes believed everything on earth, including all animals and plants, existed solely for Man's use. Yet multitudes of creatures would never see a man. The water birds that darkened the sky near Gabriel's village lived for their own purposes. The long robes were wrong about that, yet they had knowledge about many things, and power. It was a mystery.

A steady line of neophytes in hip wraps came for the dried, three-day-old hides. Each man unpegged a hide, folded it, put it on his head and walked with measured steps toward the front of the mission. They came like disciplined ants and sometimes Grizzly Hair recognized the same men returning. Where were they taking the *vaca* skins? *Learn from the deer, learn from the ants,* Two Falcons had said. Learn from the black hats.

He caught Crane-beak's eye, nodded at a neophyte leaving with a hide, and asked, "*¿Dónde va?* Where go? *Habla lentamente,* talk slow." He quickened the pace of his skinning to show that talking wouldn't slow him.

To his surprise the guard talked. "*Al puerto en la Bahía.*"

Bahía was where the western sea came inland. The water he had seen that first evening was part of a large *bahía.* "*Puerto?*"

"*Para barcos grandes.*"

For big boats. They were taking the hides to big boats on the ocean.

"*¿Por qué mucho cuero?*" Why so much cowhide. He had wanted to ask who used it but couldn't say that.

The man remained friendly, perhaps weary of having nothing to do. He sucked smoke and blew it out and talked loudly and carefully as one would speak to a young child. *"Los barcos vienen en el verano."*

The boats came in the—*"No comprendo verano."*

The black hat smiled warmly at the sky and landscape and said, *"Cuándo hace buen calientito. Calor."* He crossed his black boots spurs jingling. *"Cuándo los barcos pueden navegar. Cuándo no hace frío. ¿Comprendes?"*

"No." he shook his head. He didn't understand, and the constant pain in his elbow sang shrilly.

Rubbing his thumb on his fingertips, the black hat said, *"Los capitánes de los barcos pagan mucho dinero por el cuero."* He pointed at the drying hides. *"Cuero. Mucho dinero."* He rubbed his thumb on his fingers.

But Grizzly Hair didn't understand. Spanish talk sounded like the gabbling of geese. The black hat fell silent.

The guard with rusty hair returned from the fire and joined Crane-beak on the salt bags; they joked and laughed and rolled tobacco. Out in the field smoke boiled into the sky. Grizzly Hair rubbed his arm and watched a condor sail around the worst of the smoke and land on a naked carcass. A heart-stopping blast of a *fusil* knocked the bird to the ground, its gigantic wings flailing the dust. Open-mouthed, knife at his side, he watched the most powerful of the wing people gradually stop moving. No one killed condors. No one dared.

The rusty-haired black hat trotted out for the bird. He held it up and spread its wings, smiling for Crane-beak to admire its size. Then he tossed the condor toward the fire and returned. *"A trabajar,"* he said to Grizzly Hair.

This disrespect for Molok would endanger everyone. How did the *Españoles* maintain their strength when they acted like this? They continued to talk, then broke into song.

Bowstring did not appear after midday *devociones.* Disappointed, Grizzly Hair continued skinning. Then surprisingly, before father sun had reached the horizon, the quitting bell clanged. Crane-beak extended his hand for the knife and motioned Grizzly Hair toward the front of the mission. Relief coursed through him as he straightened his aching back and rubbed his arm. They weren't counting hides.

Crane-beak wrinkled his nose at Grizzly Hair. *"Sábado,"* he said, *"Lava ahorita."* Pinching his nose, he chuckled for the rusty-haired black hat to notice the humor. *Lava* meant wash. The man was telling him to wash right away. As though he wouldn't.

With each step the irons rubbed his sore ankles, red and stinging with sweat, but he quickly covered the distance to the front of the mission, watching for Bowstring. No doubt Oak Gall wouldn't be there until after the sleep. Then it occurred to him that there would be no *trabajar* on Domingo, according to Matías, so maybe there would be no *escuela* either. On the other hand, he had the impression all people in the mission went to the *iglésia* on Domingo, so he would probably see her there.

Politely squeezing between the drinking neophytes who had returned from the seed fields, he lowered his mouth and scooped water from the cistern. But even in the presence of the healing water, his arm hurt and he knew he lacked power. Perhaps bathing would restore him.

The lines before the troughs were long, Oak Gall not in sight, nor was any girl or woman. But Bowstring came toward him, clinking in irons. They touched each other, smiling, then stood together in line. To Grizzly Hair it felt as though a severed limb had been restored. Talk wasn't needed. Glancing at his friend's chin-forward expression, he recalled that Bowstring was of the Turtle lineage, an uncomplaining animal who held the world on its back. Of such strength was Bowstring's friendship.

Quietly so the black hats lounging on the *iglésia* steps wouldn't hear their tongue, Grizzly Hair said, "The musicians are good."

Bowstring gave him a knowing sidelong look. "Very good. I will play with them every day."

"Until we leave," Grizzly Hair added.

Bowstring nodded.

Wondering where the women were, Grizzly Hair touched the shoulder of the neophyte in front and asked quietly, "*¿Mujeres no lavan?*" Women no wash?

"*Más tarde,*" the man said over his shoulder.

Tarde. Later. Patient men and boys held bundles of dirty clothing and lumps of shiny soap made from *vaca* fat and powdered shell, soap he'd seen being made.

At last they arrived at the troughs and Grizzly Hair was sorry to see that with so many washing, only those at the flowing tube got clean water, and no one could lie down in it. He and Bowstring, being new, deferred to the other men and washed at the bottom of the second trough where the water was dark and soapy. It was also shockingly warm and smelled of rotten eggs. Following the example of others, they unwound and dunked their hip wraps. Bowstring gingerly cleaned Grizzly Hair's wounds. He then did the same for Bowstring, though they were less severe. Even without soaproot the water eventually removed the old blood, vomit and rotten meat from Grizzly Hair's legs. He felt half restored, but when he wrapped the wool around his hips and between his legs, it stretched and felt so wet and heavy he feared it would slide to his feet. That would be a *pecado* anywhere but at the washing troughs.

The supper bell rang. Married women and children joined their men at the eating place, but as usual no unmarried women came and no girl old enough to make good baskets. Everyone kneeled with heads on the ground while Padre Durán beseeched the spirits.

When the prayer was finished, Grizzly Hair whispered to old Matías, "Will unmarried women come to the *iglésia a*fter the sleep?

"Yes."

Yes! He would see her in that dark place of power.

Matías seemed too weary for covert talk. With his wounds continually freshly opened, he had reaped seeds all day.

Neophytes poured *vaca* stew into the troughs. It contained squash and beans and onions from the mission garden. When the bell rang for the night prayer, all the children were inside the trough licking the bottom on their hands and knees. Afterwards, he and Bowstring hobbled back toward the stinking *calabozo.* Two other captured men and their black-hat guards joined them.

Crane-beak motioned the captives to bring the wrist irons from the corner, and turned the key on all four of them. Without looking at the man in the trap, the black hat unlocked and lifted half the heavy wooden frame from his neck, releasing him. The man took a staggering step, arched his back and rubbed his neck. The guard prodded him outside and the door slammed behind them.

Relieved that the man's torment was over, Grizzly Hair scooted to a clean spot against the wall. His shoulders sagged, and he felt tired enough to sleep immediately. It was the same every night, yet he'd hardly slept. As silence fell in the *calabozo,* his doubts about being released from this bad place sprang up and he would crawl around in the dark feeling the crease where the wall met the earth, checking for a hole or a weakness, or sit imagining how he would get Oak Gall out of the *monjería.* He would follow useless mental trails, changing course many times, thinking in circles. Then father sun would brighten the space under the door.

Bowstring broke his reverie. "I want to be with Teresa."

"I want that too, with Oak Gall." Grizzly Hair felt heavy, thick. "I have no idea what will happen next. Here it seems that good is bad and bad is good."

"What do you mean?"

"They say whipping is good. They say they are fathers, yet they hurt us. They eat rotten milk. They admire people who are thin and sickly. They say coupling is bad—the gift that makes children."

"I drank the cow milk this morning," Bowstring said. "Be glad you refused it. Now my stomach is sick."

"Oak Gall told me the grapes will be made into juice, then allowed to ferment. They drink it rotten." Anything rotten was abominable and not to be ingested.

Bowstring was quiet a while. "They say being naked is bad."

"Yes, that too. But Coyote didn't give us fur." The damp wool chafed his thighs and he struggled in his shackles to remove it.

"I talked to Teresa today," Bowstring said. He hadn't been able to see her until now; she'd been in the *monjería* since they arrived. "She wants me to stay."

Alarmed at the tone, Grizzly Hair almost reminded him of the many other women in the world, but thought better of it.

"She told me it can be good here."

They had just agreed that bad was good in the mission.

"She said the houses of married people are clean and snug."

"And the black hats are demons."

That quieted Bowstring for the night, but Grizzly Hair crawled around in the dark feeling the walls.

18

There were times when Friar Narciso Durán thought he was already in Paradise. The mild climate in this sun-drenched valley reminded him of Catalonia. The crops were bountiful. He liked to walk through the golden fields in the morning sun, as he was doing now, and inhale the aroma of ripe wheat. It restored his soul. He enjoyed watching the five hundred or so brown backs all moving to the rhythm of their swinging hoops and catching the grain in big leather bags. It made him smile to see the happy boys dashing about the fields scaring away birds.

Last night he had wrestled the Devil, but today God's glory shone around him. In many ways, he reminded himself, he had succeeded in his holy labors. Over seventeen hundred neophytes prayed and worked under his guidance. It was pointless to flagellate himself over the dead Indians; most of their souls had been saved. His work had born earthly fruit too. More neophytes lived here than in any other northern mission. No other mission produced as many finegas of wheat per annum or as many hides. The gardens and orchards flourished, feeding, in addition to the neophytes, about thirty-eight military men and their families at the presidio. Yes, His grace was evident.

At Mission Dolores fogs rusted the wheat and spoiled the root crops. Missions Santa Cruz and San Carlos Borromeo on the Carmelo River also lacked summer sun. Neophytes had to be sent inland to tend the fields—long walks that cut into their work hours and depressed crop tallies. Santa Clara, with the same climate and soil as San José, should produce more, but the brothers there didn't manage things as well. Remembering that pride was a mortal sin, he crossed himself.

Durán's success had been noticed by his monastic superiors and he hoped, one day, to serve as Padre Presidente of the Alta California missions, perhaps when Brother Fermin de Lasuén, Serra's successor, passed on. Presidente Lasuén was now elderly and infirm.

A military disaster of ominous portent, however, had recently reached his ears. A mob had seized control of the government in Mexico, and though Alta California was far from the minds of the combatants, the rebellion could jeopardize the future of the missions. Like a festering sore, secular interests here and in New Spain had been clamoring for control of the vast tracks of mission lands—necessary for the mission herds. Those scurrilous opponents of the Franciscans also coveted the neophyte labor force, caring nothing about their souls. Much work was needed. Durán had begun penning a letter to the Governor.

But that wasn't all that had kept him awake. Even if Spanish troops restored order, the future didn't look as bright as the morning. Durán had done calculations. Given the persistent neophyte death rate, the effort to transform hundreds of thousands of natives in Alta California into a Christian civilization could be in vain. In normal years ten percent of the adult neophytes died, and twenty percent of the children. In the worst epidemics a third of the mission population expired in a few weeks, seventy-five percent, or more, of the children. How long could such a high death rate be sustained?

That didn't even include the fugitive losses, which—it wrenched his heart—were greater here than at any other mission. He reminded himself that fugitivism was rampant everywhere and the natives of the San Joaquin Valley, his readiest source of new converts, were particularly troublesome. Reality had to be faced: the missions required an endless supply of new neophytes, as well as a steady supply of energetic, competent, patient missionaries. On both counts the numbers were limited. Few priests had the fortitude for this calling.

He bent down to dislodge a sharp piece of stubble from his sandal. Better than anyone he knew the limits on the supply of new converts, even in the enormous San Joaquin Valley. He kept track. He knew the locations of the gentile villages. Stung with failure every time the soldiers rode after fugitives, he drew maps of the interior. Saint Francis saw how hard he worked, testing every shred of diligence in his being, and still they ran away. He brought them back to save them from their heathen short-sightedness, only to see many run away again. The simple fact was, times had changed. Indians no longer came voluntarily to the missions, wide-eyed about rosary beads and paintings of saints, glad to accept the blessings of salvation. Some of his superiors harbored outdated notions.

In any case, *cimarrones* had to be hunted and new souls brought in. He hated those expeditions. He hated violence. With high ideals he had said his vows, but each autumn he was obliged to grit his teeth and accompany the soldiers and loyal neophytes as they navigated the gun boat through the channels of the San Joaquin. He well understood why his brethren stayed cloistered in their missions. Facing this worst aspect of his calling was, in an odd sort of way, a penance. It also allowed him to watch over the soldiers, whose behavior could be so appalling. As father confessor he heard from neophytes and solders alike.

He let his mind wander briefly to the only other source of new souls, the paltry trickle of infants born in the missions. Why was there such barrenness among neophyte women? And such fertility among the wives of soldiers and ranchers? Most of them were *Indias* too. Abortion explained it. Diabolical potions known to heathen women. Last night he had wept.

Saddened anew, he felt like talking to Estanislao, but hadn't seen him all morning. By the fresh whipping marks on the back of an old man working just ahead, he knew it was Matías, one of those recently re-captured. *"Buenos Días, Matías."* Without a moment's hesitation he would take the lashes on his own bared back if he thought it would improve the behavior of his charges.

The leathery little man straightened and faced him, a split-willow scythe hanging at his side. He looked past Durán in the way of natives and said, *"Buenos Días, Padre."*

"God has given us another pretty day."

"Sí."

"Have you seen Estanislao?"

The old man pointed.

"Gracias," Durán said, espying his favorite. He quickened his pace across the stubble.

Estanislao was a vaquero, the best mule trainer ever seen in the mission, but many hands were now needed in the harvest. Durán had prayed for direction when the neophytes had asked that Estanislao become their alcalde. Narciso already served in that position, but Estanislao, Cucunichi as he'd been named in the wild, represented a higher challenge. So he'd made him something of an unofficial alcalde. This tall, proud Lakisamni bore the marks of a natural leader, and Durán wanted him to become a Christian at a profounder level than the shallow acceptance of most neophytes. In some inexplicable way, this would quiet Durán's heart when he left this difficult work to meet the saints, or waited for that day with his brethren in the cloister in Spain. There was a practical reason too. Estanislao had ties with gentile leaders—indeed his heathen father still lived in his *ranchería*, though the remainder of that tribe were Christians here and in Mission Santa Clara. It added a measure of danger to grant a natural leader greater authority, but if all went as he hoped, Estanislao's leadership in the mission would discourage fugitivism. Thus far, Durán was pleased, and it had been only a year since Estanislao and his wife Estanislaa had been baptized.

"Buenos Días, mi hijo," he said with a heartfelt smile.

Estanislao turned toward him, his bare chest and flat abdomen rising and falling with exertion. Twenty-nine years old now and one of the better looking *Indios*, his sturdy legs were planted wide, his shoulders comfortably back, and he wore only his woolen loin cloth. *"Buenos Días, Padre."* The black eyes were intelligent but distant.

"Tomorrow afternoon we will have a special ceremony in the church plaza." Durán explained that all neophytes were to attend and added that a revolution in New Spain had prevailed.

"What is a revolution?"

"Rebel ranchers and their friends fought against the King's men. They won, apparently, so now a new man is giving orders, but the fight might not be finished. The King could send ships with more soldiers and guns." Would to God the shock of the rebellion would wake them to the military needs of their isolated colony.

Estanislao gazed thoughtfully across the fields toward the distant rectangle of mission buildings, which seemed so frail and white in the morning sun.

Wishing to strengthen the bond between them, Durán shared the matter that pierced his heart. *"Mi hijo,* I am weary of burials. It pains me that so many of your people are sick and dying." Before blowing out the candle last night he had penned in the margin of his Registry of Deaths that the neophytes' health was *"more fragile than glass."* In the twenty-five years since the mission's founding, the original natives of Mission Valley had died out and the coast-range peoples who replaced them were about gone too. Now the newer converts from the San Joaquin Valley seemed to be dying just as fast. In the last few days disease had claimed five and he feared another epidemic. He realized that the *Indios* must have survived better prior to the coming of the missionaries. That was the devil he had wrestled so long in the night.

"Yes, father. I am very weary of death too." He had lost his only child, little three-year-old Sexta, six months ago.

Durán said, "I have prayed, and asked our Father in heaven why he calls so many *Indios* to Him." Even the heathens were dying in their *rancherías.*

"Does *Díos* answer?"

He hesitated. "I am not sure. Not yet. Are your people praying for better health?"

"Every day."

They also practiced barbaric incantations, but he wouldn't trouble Estanislao with that now. "Is there anything I can help you with, my son?" He seemed troubled.

The large black eyes lingered on him longer than usual before they looked away. "Among my people a headman never hits or injures his people. I should not help with whippings."

Durán sighed, having heard this from every neophyte alcalde. "A leader must earn the respect of his followers," he explained. "If he allows them to break the rules, his words will be ignored. Without punishment there is no respect and no order. Order, my son, is the flesh and bone of a civilized Christian world."

His eyes flared. "My people fear the *cuarta* and the men who use it but that is not respect. The man from the Rio Cosumne, the one who received a hundred lashes, will not respect me, or you."

Durán stiffened at the impertinence. "That Indian was found in a nest of criminal fugitives." He took a breath and softened his tone. "I realize we made an error there. He looked a lot like Ulbicio. But what kind of order would we have if we let him get away with fighting and helping fugitives?"

The flat expression returned and Durán lowered his voice to a confidential tone. "Indians like you could become the governors and administrators some day." He let that sink in, and continued, "So you must learn to accept the unpleasant responsibilities that come with authority." He reminded him gently, "You are not required to wield the whip, only to assist those who do." This was a delicate point since all responsibility for punishment was supposed to have passed, by now, to neophyte leaders. He knew that the soldiers had complained to their majordomo that ten or more whippings each day, on average, added too much to their work load. Ridiculous! But the fragile political situation called for, if not praise for the missions, at least silence from the presidio. Estanislao would simply have to be a man about this.

"When my people first came here," Estanislao was saying, "you said you wanted to be my *amigo*. The *cuarta* and shackles and stocks, they make no friends. Among my people a headman with no friends is no headman."

"But your people, as they were, had nothing to govern, no rules to uphold. They had nothing to do." This was the great defect of the Alta California natives. They had no religion, no government, no ability to act in concert with other tribes, in short, no foundation for civilization. Each man lived according to his own wishes. But while many civil authorities argued that these deficiencies proved the native incapacity to advance to a higher state, Durán hoped to demonstrate exactly the opposite: that with the grace of God, a new and better world could be imposed upon a blank slate.

Estanislao said, "Our headmen do many things."

"Nothing important." Durán felt tempted to sit down with him in the shade along the creek and have Estanislao recite the slovenly daily routine of the gentile headmen. He would patiently point out that naps and obscene dances accomplished nothing—how right he'd been in demolishing that infernal roundhouse which his predecessors had allowed to stand near the mission! Today, however, he had no time for dallying. He hoped to finish his letters and ledgers before noon prayers.

"Someday you will look back," he told Estanislao, "and understand discipline. Twenty-five years isn't long, you know, to change so many people. In the future, when your race assumes the reins of government alongside mine, it is my sincere hope that no corporal punishment will be needed at all—except, of course, for young children, who always need the stern hand of correction. As he spread his arms to the horizons, uninvited emotion cracked through his words: "We have planted a precious seed here, my son, a very precious seed. It could bloom into the earthly City of God as envisioned by the saints and Padre Junipero Serra. With God's Grace it can come to pass." The idea was to bypass Europe, that cesspool of humanity steeped in centuries of pestilential sin, vengeance, intrigue, witchcraft, cruel punishments like boiling in oil and drawing and quartering, deceit, lust, lechery and ungodly greed everywhere right up into the highest levels of the Church—sin so thick that the pure and gentle influence of saints like Francis of Assisi could hardly penetrate. But here was a once-in-a-world chance to start over. He laid a hand on the strong brown shoulder, and said, "*Vaya con Díos.*"

The *adíos* came back pleasantly enough, but the eyes remained distant. Telling himself to be patient, Durán gathered his robe and strode back toward the orderly quadrangle of buildings.

19

The next morning, in the midst of a crowded stream of neophytes, Grizzly Hair and Bowstring clinked into the *iglésia.* His eyes quickly adjusted to the dark but he couldn't see Oak Gall among the many women and girls searching for places to sit on the floor, on the other side of the aisle from the men and boys. The *iglésia* was much lighter than when they'd passed through that first evening. In the light from the windows, brilliant colors came at him—the green of hummingbird necks, yellow of cat's eyes, dark blue of a warm sky in evening.

The guard motioned him down on the cool flat clay. He looked up and saw the man on the *cruz* with his shins flayed to the bone, the blood forever red. Real as it looked, he knew now that it was only a clever likeness, but the pain of being deliberately injured shouted from the brutal scene. Who had conjured up the idea—human or devil? This likeness and others in the *iglésia* astounded him as when he'd first seen a horse. No, astounded him more. A horse looked only a little different than an elk, but this suffering man at the moment of his death had no equal. No one had ever made men of wood and paint. Two other bleeding wooden men hung in the *iglesía*, one in front and one over the door to the yard of crosses. They all, he knew with a prickling sensation, harbored the souls of the dead. By walking among these horrors, the long robes and black hats displayed great power, as did the neophytes—all tempting fate.

Recessed into the north wall, two more wooden men stood on platforms, robed and unhurt. Beneath them, hundreds of real women and girls sat on the floor. Not even married women sat with their men. He couldn't see Oak Gall in the crowd of brown shoulders and black heads. He looked at the north wall close to the front where a golden-haired woman in a blue robe rose from the green heart of a large maguey plant. This likeness was beautiful, no doubt María flying to the sky. Not wooden, she was painted flat on the wall. The man in the trap had said María could fly because she was dead, and that the dead flew when they went to the sky. This was no different from the souls who left the bodies of the dead among Grizzly Hair's people. The trapped man said María could heal the sick if people prayed to her. Fearlessly they spoke her name every time they talked to their beads, opening themselves to bad luck and death. Yet many survived. They had acquired power.

Looking back at the many women, his eyes opened to Oak Gall, wedged in tightly and looking at him. Her gaze riveted him. He hoped she would understand that his need for her was greater than the need to be polite. Besides, *Españoles* looked into each other's eyes all the time. Perhaps he could speak to her without talk, and tell her they would leave after eight sleeps. She seemed to be drowning in his eyes, and her smile puzzled him. She looked tired, older. A poke in his arm reminded him of Crane-beak's constant attention. "*Mirada al frente,*" the man said, but the link with Oak Gall was hard to break. The next poke made him look to the front, feeling better for the smile but aching to touch her.

On a short wall standing by itself, many half-sized people with lazy expressions stood talking or looking about. They appeared to be painted on cloth, their shadows cleverly included to make them look real. Wearing gray and brown robes and cloth hats with feathers, they stood among stone pillars, stairs and walls, a scene from another world. The presence of unreal people enhanced the eeriness of this house of power.

Light shot from the back. Grizzly Hair twisted around to see the door open. Two white-robed boys walked up the aisle followed by the padres, one before the other. All stepped slowly forward to the haunting harmonies of men and boys singing in the first rows.

A-gnus Dei, A-gnus Dei
qui tol-lis
pec-ca-ta mundi
pec-ca-ta mundi

Padre Durán's robes whispered and shimmered as he passed near Grizzly Hair, golden threads forming a broad *cruz* on a bright red mantle. Next came Padre Fortuni in a golden mantle with a silver *cruz.* Under these spectacular robes hung gossamer material like the wings of the lacy hunting fly. The boy in front swung a silver vessel from side to side, letting out puffs of aromatic smoke, no doubt to help people contact their allies. Thick with ritual, Padre Durán flicked water from another small vessel, south and north, south and north. Meanwhile the chorus sang:

Sal-ve me
Sal-ve me

Save me. Arriving at the front rail, the padres turned toward the people and chanted. Hands dancing, the long robes opened little doors and removed things. By rows, neophytes stood and walked to the rail, accepting something to eat from Padre Durán. Then each took a sip from a vessel and passed it down the line. Matías had said this would be a Cry for eight people who had died during the last seven sleeps, mostly young children. The eating and sipping ritual was repeated again and again with every row of neophytes. Then the harmony of the singers shifted from bright and strong, then to a sobbing sadness:

Rex tremendae ma-jes-ta-tis
Sal-ve me fons pi-e-ta-tis
Sal-ve me, sal-ve me

Moisture streaked Bowstring's face, he was so moved by the music. No one keened. No one danced. All sat in silence as Padre Durán spoke the names of the dead. Grizzly Hair glanced around the room, afraid of ghosts or *el diablo,* who might grab everyone in his giant hand and throw them in his fire. Then suddenly the ceremony for the dead ended. Grizzly Hair was one of the first out the door.

He was drinking from the cistern when Oak Gall stepped beside him and leaned her head on his shoulder. He pulled her to him and closed his eyes, relishing the tender feel of her in his arms.

The old woman of the *monjería* took her hand and pulled her toward the gate. They hadn't talked.

He started to follow, saying, "We'll leave here as soon—"

"*Solamente Español,*" shouted a black hat, grabbing him by the hair and jerking him back. It forced him to drop Oak Gall's hand.

Padre Durán was suddenly there in the crowded patio scowling like a hawk. As Oak Gall disappeared toward the *monjería,* he said something and the black hat released Grizzly Hair's hair.

Two more black hats appeared with a sobbing woman stumbling between them. The crowd parted and they took her to the door of the *iglésía,* removed her skirt and shirt and tied her wrists in thongs which they looped through iron rings embedded on either side of the big doorway. One of the black hats orated for short time, then stood to the side as Narciso, the neophyte alcalde, came forward with a tool that resembled two sharp knives crossed. Holders at one end allowed him to make the sharp ends move and very efficiently cut all her hair so that it fell around her feet. Then Narciso put the strange tool in the waist band of his woolen *pantalones.* A black hat handed him *a cuarta.*

Grizzly Hair moved further back into the crowd and watched in horror as Narciso whipped the woman. *Uno, dos, tres, quatro. . ..* Fifteen lashes, most about her buttocks and thighs. When they untied her she was crying, trembling and looking down to avoid the eyes of the people in the crowd. Padre Durán handed her a robe of a coarse ropy weave. She put it on. Badly sewn at the sides, it hung at a loose, uneven slant above her knees. Padre Durán spoke sternly to her and thrust a crude doll into the bend of her elbow. The doll was made of cross sticks wound together with string, and it was painted the same red as the blood on the dead man in the *iglésia.* Holding the doll to her breast, still trembling and whimpering, the woman kneeled before the padre. He extended the back of his hand to her. She kissed it. He said a few words, gathered his robe and walked toward the back of the *iglésia.* She jumped to her feet and hurried away with the doll. A man from the crowd followed her, wiping tears from his face.

What did the doll mean? What did kissing the padre's hand mean? Most people were acting as though they had seen this ritual many times before—the expression of several woman indicating silent pain. But rituals had meanings—like the molah-gumsip, when a person knelt humbly and waited to be washed of mourning. Grizzly Hair wished he could ask what it meant.

A sudden urge came upon him to see if he could trick the padre and steal some of his power. First he would try to break down his guard by making him speak, not as a great doctor, but man to man. He caught up to the padre as he reached for the leather door-pull. "Padre?"

The long robe turned in surprise. "*Sí?*"

"How make—" He reached to touch the gold on the red mantle.

Vigilant as any good doctor should be, Padre Durán jerked back and held up an admonishing finger.

Acting innocent, Grizzly Hair pointed at the golden *cruz* and repeated, "How make?"

"Later you make cloth." The long robe wrapped his hand around the leather door pull.

"No. This." Grizzly Hair pointed at the golden threads without touching, and traced the cross in the air.

"Thread?"

Was thread the word for gold?

"First you do the *bautismo,*" said Durán in a friendly tone. Despite his impatience he seemed to be talking man to man. Or was he a man? There was hair above his knuckles.

"*¿Cómo se llama?*" Grizzly Hair reached for the gold again, thinking this time he might touch it.

Again the padre jerked back with a scowl. "*¿El oro?*"

"*Oro.*" Grizzly Hair repeated, feeling sure that was the word for gold.

"*Sí, oro,*" said the padre. "*Bonito, no?*" He smiled.

"*Sí, bonito.* How make?" If he got him to talk about how they made fine strands from rocks, maybe Durán would let down his guard.

Pulling the door open, the padre said, "*Solamente Dios puede hacer l'oro.*"

Only the chief spirit can make gold. Grizzly Hair was picking up a pebble to show that gold began as a rock, intending to say, "*Mucho oro* in the river of my people," but the long robe disappeared behind the door and it closed in his face.

On the day after Domingo, Oak Gall was not in the *escuela,* and Bowstring stayed to play music.

Worried and alone, Grizzly Hair skinned many *vacas,* thinking of nothing except why Oak Gall had not been present. Had they whipped her and given her a red doll? After the sleep this night they could leave the mission, unless they had been tricked. He needed to talk with Bowstring, but where was he? The distant music had long since stopped.

At last Bowstring came walking out on the bloody grass. He walked freely, unshackled! A black hat gave him a knife and he skinned silently, too far away for Grizzly Hair for talk.

Passing him on his way to get salt, Grizzly Hair said out of the side of his mouth, "One sleep more."

Bowstring grunted, his face a turtle mask.

Long before the sun had gone to his western house, bells rang. One of the black hats was passing water, the other sitting on a salt bag. "*¿Qué pasa?* said the black hat on the bag. The one passing water shrugged, shook himself and buttoned his flap. They retrieved the knives from Grizzly Hair and Bowstring and herded them back to the front of the mission, where hundreds of neophytes milled around, clearly happy about the unexpected break in the *trabajar.* Women and girls were present, including the woman with the red doll. Making his way through the crowd, Grizzly Hair looked for Oak Gall. He could see over most of the heads, but didn't see her.

A herald called something in Spanish and people stepped back to give more space to the headman of the black hats. He walked stiffly toward the pole in the center of the patio, a line of black hats following. Another black hat unfolded a cloth, attached it to the pole and repeatedly yanked the rope, which made the cloth jerk upward. A breeze caught it and for a moment the likeness of a catlike animal with a black mane waved atop the pole. Grizzly Hair looked around, but saw no Oak Gall.

"*Leo,*" somebody whispered.

With obvious respect, the black hat lowered the lion. Grizzly Hair was remembering Oak Gall's unusual warmth the day before, his stomach pulling into a tight knot. Padre Durán spoke briefly, the lines of his face hardening. Then his mouth snapped shut. The black hats folded the lion-cloth and one of them placed it under his arm and held it with his elbow.

Handed another banner, a black hat carelessly clipped it to the pole, hoisted it up, and a strange shape fluttered above the mission. *"Aguila,"* people whispered. Eagle.

Fusiles rang out, hurting Grizzly Hair's ears. Again and again, the black hats shifted their balance and shot thunder and lightning at nothing. Infants and young children screamed in fear. In flat tones Padre Durán spoke of a *"revolución"* in Mexico. He instructed everyone to repeat his talk after him. Grizzly Hair tried but couldn't. Bowstring, who had edged over to Teresa, moved his lips.

Padre Durán orated something about saying *devociones* for Emperor Iturbide of Mexico. "No more for the King of Spain," he said. "Now, *a trabajar.*" That meant go back to work. Whisking his robe around him, Durán walked, head-down, to his door.

Where was Oak Gall?

A neophyte said quietly, "Eagle defeated Lion." That was to be expected. It was the first sign that the *Españoles* understood the Animal People and recognized the greater power of Eagle.

On the way back to the skinning field, Bowstring caught up and looked as though he had something to say. Watched by the black hats, Grizzly Hair couldn't ask about his missing irons. He felt vaguely betrayed, though it was not Bowstring's fault that he was free of irons and Grizzly Hair was not.

As they passed the boiling fat and snapping fires, Bowstring stepped closer. His quiet talk struck like a *cuarta.* "I will stay at the mission."

It stopped his breath.

"Teresa and I will be married. Then they will treat us well."

Treat them well! He might learn to play the new instruments and understand the polliwog magic, but they hadn't been treated well since they arrived. Learning to fly might have been worth it, but Grizzly Hair had watched carefully and never yet seen anyone fly, and he'd seen no sign that it was being taught in the mission. Bowstring's thoughts had been scrambled. Stunned, all Grizzly Hair could do was keep walking.

"Tonight I sleep in the men's house," Bowstring said. "Then Teresa and I will get a room of our own."

The snapping vat fires covered Grizzly Hair's talk. "What of the umne? Your parents?" Bowstring could never go to the home place again, unless he ran away. But then a pack of black hats would come sniffing for him. He clanked his chains deliberately so Bowstring could answer.

"Teresa will be my family. The long robes' power will protect us."

"Bring her to the home place," Grizzly Hair said, suddenly preferring the threat of black hats to losing Bowstring.

The loud talk of neophytes at the tanning ponds overpowered Bowstring's whisper. "She is tired of hiding, tired of being captured. She wants to live the way of the *Christianos.*" After a pause, he added, "Our *orquestra* will travel to other missions to play for many people. I dreamed of such music before we came here."

That was it. One couldn't argue with dreams, but the umne would consider Bowstring dead and Grizzly Hair would be blamed. Rattling his chains he said, "Your mother begged me not to bring you here. Come and explain it to her and your father, your brother, Morning Owl, then return if you must." But surely the umne would straighten his thinking.

The voice came deep and steady, and Grizzly Hair could see the hard, underslung jaw of Turtle. "Someday they will understand."

"No they won't. I can't—"

"Solamente Español," shouted a black hat.

They took their skinning knives and worked in silence, until Bowstring finished pegging a skin and walked past Grizzly Hair on his way to the salt bags. He whispered, "Would you leave if Oak Gall stayed here?"

Later, when Grizzly Hair finished pegging his next skin, he passed Bowstring and whispered back, "Oak Gall would never stay."

That night in the airless room he was already mourning the best friend of his childhood. This was Bowstring's decision, his fate. But it deeply pained Grizzly Hair and he had trouble listening to the new man in the trap even though he spoke partly in Grizzly Hair's tongue, partly in Gabriel's, and used Spanish only rarely.

"After the sleep I think they will let me out of here," he said. "On feast days they have *piedad.*"

Piedad. The boy Antonio had begged for *piedad* as he knelt before Padre Durán, but he had been whipped. This man had been caught stealing grapes from the orchard and had received twenty-five lashes at the church door.

"We'll have a big time," the man said.

It was the end of eight sleeps and that was all Grizzly Hair cared about. How would he find Oak Gall? The fear that she was ill gnawed his stomach like an advancing worm. Almost to himself he said, "Evil gets into people here and they die. Don't you have healing herbs?"

"Sometimes women are allowed to go out and find medicine but they are tired after their *trabajo,* and don't gather much. Women born here don't know the plant people. Our doctors are forbidden to practice their magic, but I don't care. The padres are right. Those doctors don't know much."

"Maybe you haven't seen a good doctor perform."

The man sighed. "That's ignorant, those old ways."

"I think everyone could leave the mission at the same time and the black hats couldn't catch very many. Most of you would escape."

"They know you think like that. That's why you are in irons."

They saw his thoughts, as only sorcerers could. He didn't know why, but tears came to his eyes—a sign of lack of power. Merely being in the mission hadn't given him power, and for all the pain he could tell he hadn't acquired any. "Why did you come to the mission?"

"My wife and children were here. That's why I was stealing fruit, for my wife. I wanted to give her a present."

"Why did your wife come here?"

Air whooshed from the man in the dark, and he seemed to be thinking. Then he said, "She came with relatives to learn about the Devil."

Grizzly Hair reflected that the Devil was the spirit the padres feared the most and it was natural that people would want to learn about him.

"A few of us stayed at the home place," the man continued, "but we had no elders, no friends to gamble with and no one to dance with. There was no singing. It was too quiet. So we came to the mission too."

Again tears wet Grizzly Hair's eyes. "Do you miss your home place?"

A long pause. "No matter how long I live here, I will never forget our mother tree and our river, our hunting places and our playing field. I will never forget where the bones of my people are buried. No tongue could tell you how much I miss my home place, but I can never return." He chuckled dryly. "The black hats know where it is. It's not all bad here. We have big times. Then we eat *mucho.*"

"Now you stand in your urine."

"I shouldn't have picked the grapes."

Grizzly Hair shut his eyes. "It doesn't seem possible so many people can be held against their will."

"Most want to live here. They say Second World is ending and the *Españoles* are heralds of Third World. The padres are showing us how to live the new way. People have much to learn."

"I want to live the way Coyote showed us," Grizzly Hair said, "but with the tools and knowledge of the *Españoles.*"

"That is ignorant. We should live like Jesús and María and say our prayers so we won't go to the Devil's fire. A time is coming when no people will be left on earth. I feel it coming. We should learn from the padres. Learn to accept *castigo* and make *penitencia.* That's what I'm doing here."

"People don't laugh here, and there is too little water."

"We laugh on feast days. After the sleep you will see. We sing and eat meat until we fall down. And when the padres take siesta, we gamble and dance." He chuckled long and pleasurably. "I wish we had more feast days." His voice suddenly lost its joy. "When are you leaving?"

"After the sleep." Another of the unpredictable urges was coming into him, to kick his way out of the stinking house and run for Oak Gall, but he forced himself to be calm. He must wait and see whether the padres would keep their promise.

"That is good," the man said cheerfully, "the *fiesta* day for María, when she flew to the sky. It will be a lucky day."

20

Feast of the Assumption of Mary, August 15, 1823

The morning after the eighth sleep the black hat removed Grizzly Hair's irons. With his raw ankles cooling in the breeze of normal walking, he followed the black hat to the front of the mission. He had been summoned by Padre Durán. Estanislao accompanied them and that was good, because he could explain the talk. Father sun had already warmed the earth underfoot, and now it was time to stop mourning for Bowstring and take Oak Gall to the home place. Feeling luckier with the shackles off, and longing for the moment when he would be alone with her, he looked ahead at Padre Durán.

The long robe sat on his high-backed chair against the white wall of the *iglésia*, squinting into the sunlight. A small table stood on his right. The *cruz* that hung from his waist, now below his knee, dazzled Grizzly Hair's eyes. Carved into the tops of the chairback were twin lions, perhaps the defeated lions. The shade of a *palma* leaf darkened half of the padre's robe, beneath which the toes of one foot protruded. Around him, several boys on their hands and knees looked up expectantly. Grizzly Hair recognized them from the *escuela*. The padre acknowledged Estanislao with a nod and held up his hand in a wait signal.

Half smiling, the boys snarled and growled like dogs as the padre took a tortilla from the table, tore it and flicked a piece high over the boys. With bared teeth they leaped and snapped for it. Shiny spittle connected Padre Durán's open smile and he rocked forward as though afraid he would miss some detail as this or that dog edged out another. The padre patted the winner's head and tossed up another piece for them to fight over.

This went on until nothing remained on the plate. The padre dismissed the boys with a wave of his hand, turned to Grizzly Hair and talked. Estanislao repeated it in a mixture of his tongue and Grizzly Hair's. "Your friend will be baptized this afternoon with the Christian name José Francisco. After that he and Teresa will be married. You need to be baptized too."

Grizzly Hair said, "No baptize. I go Río Cosumne."

With a tired sigh, the long robe looked up at the *monjería* roof where a neophyte was crawling around replacing tiles. Alongside the building grew a row of tall *palma* trees that Matías had said were once used for roofing. Returning his gaze to Grizzly Hair, he said, "You understand that you will burn in the Devil's fire for all eternity?"

He felt himself scowl. Would he suffer agony for all time? The padres had knowledge of many things about which he knew nothing. They might even make it happen. But lately Grizzly Hair felt he was having trouble thinking straight. It seemed he had become a stupid, stumbling man. If he could just get away, maybe he could find his calm and explain the mission properly to the umne. He was Morning Owl's runner. Above all, he must take Oak Gall away. "I go to the home place," he said to the long robe. Estanislao spoke it in Spanish.

The padre spoke rapidly and gestured broadly. Estanislao translated, "You have seen too much here. Gentiles steal from us. Two years ago Sergeant Soto brought back seventy horses from the *Río de los Cosumnes*—horses stolen from us."

Grizzly Hair knew people stole things at the mission. If caught, they were whipped and locked in the man trap. The padre seemed to think stealing was to be expected, yet at home people left prized tools lying about and sometimes built granaries with more than a year's supply of acorns far from the village. These things were never touched by anyone except their owners, but fear of the powerful doctor kept him from saying that. "I go."

Padre Durán spoke again. Estanislao repeated it in the home tongue, the words settling around Grizzly Hair's shoulders like a lariat. "The woman who came with you is sick." The rest of his talk rolled past without meaning.

Frantic to get to her, he stuttered out in Spanish, "*Voy mi mujer ahorita.*" I see my woman right now.

"She is too sick."

His voice rose in volume, "Friend, woman, wife soon. I love, I see her."

The padre stared at him, then pushed himself to his feet and motioned all to follow as he walked toward the *monjería.*

Grizzly Hair checked himself from running, his long free strides outpacing Padre Durán and the black hat. The old woman sat on a redwood log beside the door. The padre spoke and she disappeared into the large dim room, which exuded a repellent odor. A ragged hole in the high ceiling and the open door provided enough light for Grizzly Hair to see women lying on floor mats in the center of the room. Around the walls, women and girls worked at tables, preparing tortillas.

The old woman lifted a limp figure—Oak Gall! She supported her as she walked on unsteady feet toward the door. Oak Gall's eyes burned brightly. Her face was unnaturally red and her hair was wet and matted.

With fear leaping in his stomach, Grizzly Hair spoke in his own tongue. "You need Eagle Woman and Drum-in-Fog."

"*Solamente Español, hijo mío,*" said Durán.

Oak Gall looked at the long robe as if he were invisible, and said weakly, "Drum-in-Fog will suck the bad out."

"I will take you to him."

"Español!" shouted the black hat.

Having difficulty supporting Oak Gall, the old woman turned back inside with her. Grizzly Hair stepped through the threshold where men weren't allowed and easily pulled her hot length to him, her face burning against his chest. The woman yanked her arm, but he held her firmly and spoke soothingly. "We will find medicine on the way to the home place."

Padre Durán's talk buzzed in his ears, something about "gentile."

The black hat came inside and tried to take Oak Gall, the old woman stepping out of his way. Grizzly Hair held on to her.

A powerful arm clamped across his throat, cutting off his breath while the black hat pulled Oak Gall. He fought the arm, lurching and staggering with a man on his back—Estanislao by the size—but without breath couldn't hold onto her. The black hat handed her to the woman, who took her away, away from the one who would take her home, away from his comfort, away to the unpurified place. He was about to throw Estanislao off, but the black hat stepped in front of him and slammed his knee into his groin. In agony he reflexed forward. Estanislao released his neck and pulled him backward, hardly able to stand, outside the woman's house.

Cupping his pain, he shut his eyes to Padre Durán's red face and closed his ears to the torrent of Spanish. Before he knew what was happening he was back in the *calabozo* clamped in the man trap. As the door shut out father sun, he roared his frustration from deep in his stomach and jerked his neck on the heavy wooden frame. It was silent and unmoving.

The heat of the house intensified the odor of suffering, unwashed men. Bowstring was lost. Oak Gall might die. He had acted recklessly and now he was locked up again. He felt like crying, but knew that he must find his power—if he still had any.

He detached himself from the morning and from the oak on his neck and wrists, and looked at the bar of light under the door. It was the same as when he watched the fire in the sweathouse. It helped him settle into his calm and let him float free of the dark house.

He felt himself running in long strides and breathing fresh air. Overhead an archway extended across the world and on it walked the same procession of people he had seen before. He stopped running. They shuffled sadly as before. Etched on their faces were the same furrows of sadness worn by mission neophytes. This time he knew they were dead. He watched for a long time, noticing their hands, hair, the babies on women's backs. They vanished at the opposite horizon, but from an unseen source renewed their ranks.

Even in deep reverie he was stunned to see Oak Gall in the crowd. Standing far below her, small as a gnat, he called up but couldn't make her hear him at that distance. He jumped up and down waving his arms but she didn't see him. She continued walking at the same pace. He yelled, "I am sorry I brought you to your death." She didn't hear. He ached for her and wanted her to know how much he loved her. Tears ran down his face. He wanted to touch her again and hear her laugh.

Wispy at first, something began to take shape over the sad procession. The background changed from black to brown. Then the tan was surrounded on three sides by black. Eyes emerged in the middle of the walking figures, lines angling diagonally from the corners. Above the mouth was a slight mustache. The people faded and he was looking directly into the face of Estanislao. He saw understanding and friendship.

Much later, when the door opened it was too bright. He covered his eyes and felt dampness on his face, tears. Someone unlocked the wood, lifted it. A hand belonging to a silhouetted figure guided him out the door and he realized his ankles were linked again by an iron chain. Estanislao and the curly haired guard had come for him.

Outside, no bird sang. Oak Gall's heart was gone. Father sun blazed painfully off the pale buildings and weighed down his head and shoulders. The heat intensified as he passed the tallow vats and everlasting fires. Patient old people and children with loads of wood watched him pass. All other places of *trabajar* were deserted. Grizzly Hair shuffled awkwardly but steadily, the soles of his feet warm on the packed earth, the chinking of the chain and the bootfalls of Crane-beak loud in the deserted mission grounds.

He stopped at the cistern, glanced at Estanislao, who nodded approval, and scooped cool water, sucking it down, splashing it over his face and neck, trying to wash away the tears.

Estanislao also leaned over to drink. "Your woman's heart is no longer with us," he whispered.

"I know," said Grizzly Hair, turning away to hide new tears.

"Padre Durán performed the baptism on her, and final absolution."

"*Bueno,*" he managed to say. Oak Gall would be spared the Devil's fire.

Inside the *iglésia* his spirit suspended itself in the eerie gloom. The neophytes were all sitting on the floor; that's why it had been quiet outside. Boys sang sad harmonies in the front rows, and before his wet eyes the yellow-green and dark blue of the place of magic swirled together. Bowstring stood before the rail, covered from chin to ankles in a woolen shirt and *pantalones.* In a shirt and red skirt Teresa stood beside him. Estanislao motioned Grizzly Hair down beside him, not far from where the black hats leaned against the wall with their *fusiles.*

Padres Durán and Fortuni paced up the aisle swinging their smoking vessels. The strange shifting harmonies of the chorus and the horror of Oak Gall's death blended with the eeriness. The ceremony was long. Bowstring bowed his head to the water that Padre Durán dipped from a stone bowl. Now and then the neophytes on the floor talked to their beads. Padre Durán looked directly at Grizzly Hair, then put his hand on Bowstring's wet head and said, "José Francisco." He lowered a string of beads around Bowstring's neck.

Estanislao nudged him, "Go forward and be baptized now. Then the irons will be removed and you will not be flogged for going in the *monjería* and fighting."

Nothing mattered anymore.

"It will be better for you to be baptized now," said Estanislao with the same kindly expression as in the vision. "I have been here a long time. I know. Go to the rail."

Staring unfocused across the heads of the neophytes, Grizzly Hair recalled the padre saying he might steal. Maybe he was already an enemy of the padres. Maybe it was no help to remain a gentile. Anyway it didn't matter. He stood up. A black hat leaned down and unlocked the ankle irons, and he walked like a dead man, shoulders low in sadness, the eyes of many strangers following him down the aisle. When the chanting was over and water trickled down his forehead, he hardly heard the name Juan Gustavus being said over him, or felt the beads lowered over his head or the folded shirt and blanket put in his arms. Returning to Estanislao, he stared with unfocused eyes at Bowstring and Teresa, still standing in front.

Pecatta mundi. Bad in the world. Bad in the world.

Then it was over. Bowstring and Teresa walked the short distance up the aisle toward Grizzly Hair, smiled at him, then went out the door beneath the suffering Jesús. *They don't know.* The padres followed, then the neophytes thronged out the door. Grizzly Hair went with them to the water.

In the confusion of the milling people, Estanislao leaned toward him and whispered, "Now I will help you escape."

21

Seeming to notice something of interest in the orchard beyond, Estanislao stood at the gate. Grizzly Hair went to him and asked, "When can I go?"

"Go before this *fiesta* day is over. When your spirit allies tell you. But I will stay with you and try to help. First, ask permission to help dig the grave. It will be permitted. Wait here." He walked around the patio, scooped water and stopped to talk with Padre Durán.

Grizzly Hair remembered that a bear had come in a dream and told him to leave the brush corral, and soon afterwards an earthly bear had come to help. Maybe O-se-mai-ti would appear again and tell him when to leave.

"My people must be burned," Grizzly Hair said when Estanislao returned. "I must take my woman's ashes and bones to the home place."

The crowd was noisy. Children dashed around as their parents talked. Estanislao spoke quietly, "*Christianos* believe it is bad to burn the dead."

"Then I will burn her away from here."

"You would travel slowly and make smoke. The soldiers would track you and you would be caught. They have iron tools to smash your thumbs. You would tell of my help."

Grizzly Hair tried to keep his thoughts straight, but they kept wandering away from death and smashed fingers.

Estanislao said, "Do your people tell the story, as my people do, that burial without burning was practiced long ago?"

"Yes."

"I think all our people once buried the dead. Think of burial as being proper among our ancestors." He lowered his voice. "All this land belongs to *Indios.* The padres teach that mission lands will belong to us someday. Your dead are therefore properly buried here. This is their proper home."

He had never heard anyone speak of *Indios* as one people, of the broad earth as one place, or of people owning land. But he shouldn't have been surprised. No one knew what Condor would dream next, and all dreams were unpredictable.

"I will not help you," Estanislao added, "if you insist on taking the dead."

In his pain Grizzly Hair made an effort to think, and knew he must not hurt one who was offering help. "I will not take her. I will remember what you said about 'our people' and someday I will return for my woman's—" he swallowed a painful lump in his throat—"bones."

"I'd like you to take a message to my people."

"I will."

"My people are the Lakisamni, on the river that enters the River San Joaquin."

He made himself silently repeat it.

Estanislao spoke in Spanish to a neophyte walking by, then continued, "Gabriel's people and mine have the same ancestors. He is back in his village now."

Estanislao knows what happens beyond the mission. "No women live there," Grizzly Hair said. They had been captured. *No woman.*

"Many villages lack women. Now, go mingle with the neophytes and talk to me later."

Grizzly Hair found Bowstring, now José Francisco, with Teresa in the crowd, but in his grief, couldn't speak. Bowstring asked, "Where is Oak Gall?" Instantly his broad dark face blurred behind the water in Grizzly Hair's eyes.

"Her heart is gone." The words fell like tears of stone.

They stood in awkward silence in the shade of the high *iglésia*, father sun starting to move behind it. Bowstring would escape the dangers of speaking the name because he hadn't known. There was moisture in Bowstring's eyes too and he said, "I am sad for my cousin-sister, and sad for you, my friend." He turned away, swallowed, and after a while murmured, "You let them perform the *bautismo* on you. Will you stay in the mission?"

Afraid to reveal anything to Teresa, Grizzly Hair stared ahead. Bowstring's brows pulled up like sad bows, but he said nothing. Grizzly Hair wanted real talk with this friend, with whom he might never talk again. Instead he mentioned the coolness of the water in the cistern, touched Bowstring's shoulder and walked back to Estanislao.

Still gazing toward the sunny orchard, Estanislao said, "Tell my people I think of them at this acorn time. Say to them the *Españoles* have lost a great war in their southern land and the fleas will soon jump off the wolf."

"I will say that."

"Now ask permission to help dig the grave. Padre Fortuni is sitting by the church wall."

Struck silent by the thought of burying her, he couldn't move. Then after a time, he turned toward the silence and Estanislao was gone.

Like a ram watching his flock, the padre sat smiling in the shade of the large building. From time to time neophytes went up to him and exchanged a few polite words. At a pause in these talks, Grizzly Hair stepped forward and said, partly in sign language, that he wanted to dig the grave of his woman.

"Muy triste que la mujer está muerta," the padre said. Sad that the woman is dead. "But it is good here at the mission." He looked around. "God will bless you." He beckoned Estanislao and a black hat. Of their rapid talk Grizzly Hair understood nothing.

Then Estanislao gave him the wait signal and took the big iron ring of keys from the black hat and walked toward the rear of the mission.

Grizzly Hair stood beside the padre, not knowing what was happening and caring little. The loin wrap felt heavy and awkward on his hips and he stared above the heads of the neophytes, who continued to mill around, or talk, or in some cases, bring baskets and musical instruments to the plaza. Some began painting each other with red paint.

Padre Fortuni spoke slowly and pleasantly about the *bailar*, dance. The fish eyes held no malice. He seemed to enjoy talking. He said the neophyte women were cooking and making things for the dance. He looked at Grizzly Hair as if inquiring whether he understood.

"Mi gente bailan." My people dance.

"Yes, all *Indios* dance. Here we permit dancing when it has no sacred meaning. We do not permit worship of your old spirits. Understand?"

Grizzly Hair tried to repeat it in Spanish. "*Solamente baile si no santo.*" Only dance if not for spirits.

"*Sí,*" the padre said, smiling as though Grizzly Hair were a child uttering his first words.

But dancing was always for the spirits. He suddenly saw himself dancing around the fire toward Oak Gall, her teasing smile and sparkling eyes in the midst of all the people. Later, on the western hill his spirit and hers had come together in a celebration of earth and river and grass and mother moon blessing them with her gentle light. Now, something collapsed inside him.

Estanislao approached, bearing two digging tools and herding a man in leg irons. He indicated Grizzly Hair should continue waiting with Padre Fortuni while he took the prisoner to start digging the grave. The padre agreed.

Grizzly Hair felt as wooden as the painted people in the *iglésia.* Meanwhile, women crossed the patio, some carrying wet clothing, some wringing their hair. Oak Gall would never wash her beautiful hair again. He saw Bowstring and Teresa sadly looking at him from their togetherness. It brought more tears for Oak Gall, who would never be his wife. Somehow he must stop thinking her name and empty his mind of her. He unfocused his eyes and gazed beyond the orchard, hardly aware of men passing before him painted in broad horizontal red stripes, the white of their hip wraps between the red of their stomachs and thighs. He hardly heard the clacking of charmstones with holy beads around many necks, or saw the musicians bringing *violines, trumpetas,* flutes and drums. He must not think of her until the Cry for her. When would that be? Would they banish him from the home place? Would he ever be able to speak her name again? Nothing of her would remain on the earth. He was hollow.

Estanislao came through the *iglésia* door with Padre Durán, and bells announced *devociones.* Vats of food were being brought for an early supper. Everyone knelt and Padre Durán began orating about the *asención* of María. In his hollowness, Grizzly Hair pretended to talk to his beads with everyone else. Drinking vessels and plates of food were set before the padres and the smell of moldy grape drink permeated the warm air. Pi-no-leh was poured and neophytes knelt at the troughs. Haunches of roasted meat were eaten and piles of tortillas, but he couldn't swallow any of it. Soon he would see his woman dead.

Later, Estanislao told him to leave the shirt and blanket there. He led him toward the rear of the mission until they came to a windowless building that Grizzly Hair had never particularly noticed before. Estanislao unlocked the door and the thick, choking smell of death gushed out. Grizzly Hair gagged and blinked against it. The house was heaped to the ceiling with human bones, many with bits of dirt and skin clinging to them. Jammed into the bones were two *carretas* with black crosses attached to their fronts. Estanislao took the handles of one, pulled it outside, locked the door and motioned Grizzly Hair to pull the cart. Estanislao headed toward the *monjería.* Following with the cart, Grizzly Hair swallowed over and over, to hold his stomach down.

After they had walked some distance, still trying not to breathe the death smell that clung to the *carreta,* he said, "You bury the dead. Why are the bones in that house?"

"The graveyard is too small. There are many deaths here, but *Christianos* must be buried in sacred ground. So now we bury them in layers, four to a hole, and when the ground is full we dig them up to make room." He nodded back at the house. "And put the bones there."

Pulling the cart over the packed earth, Grizzly Hair said, "You should burn the dead." Somehow he had to prevent Oak Gall's bones from being piled in that house.

At the open door of the *monjería,* the air coming from inside seemed to be tinged with the death smell too.

Estanislao, exchanging a signal with the old woman of the *monjería,* walked inside and gestured Grizzly Hair in. In the center of the huge room lay Oak Gall as though asleep on her mat. Flies walked on her eyelids. For the first time he couldn't hear her music. On the surrounding mats women moaned and shivered and perspired. Fighting to keep his calm, he looked up at the light angling down from holes in the roof. He looked at the tables where food was being prepared, and at the big grated firepit.

Estanislao took her feet, touching her without purification, and indicated Grizzly Hair should take her arms. Her soul would be hovering, but looking at her peaceful face he could not believe she would hurt him, even though he was unpurified. The final *devociones* had been said over her. Maybe she was a friendly ghost like María, and her soul could heal him of his weakness if he prayed. He told her in his mind, *Sweet woman, you have left me. Help me find the strength to leave you.* With tears streaming down his face and a noise buzzing in his ears, he squatted behind her head, reached beneath her arms and shoulders—cold, firm, unreal—and lifted her. They carried her outside, women and girls following with their eyes. Dead animals were stiff and heavy, but he had expected her to be different.

Feeling just as dead, the sound buzzing louder in his head, he helped lay her in the *carreta* with her stiff legs through the slats at the front, and pulled her like that through the patio before the eating people. Most didn't look up; perhaps they had seen this before. The cart fit neatly through the door of the deserted *iglésia,* and out the north door beneath the skull and crossbones.

Through the flood in his eyes he made out the wall encircling the yard of *cruzes*—shoulder high, roofed with tiles. Would he vault over it? Could he run feeling this weak? First he must see where she would be buried. Following Estanislao, he pulled the *carreta* on the path through the crosses and around a corner to where the shackled man was digging. The piled dirt contained small bones and a small skull with tiny teeth. He had dug up a young child.

Estanislao motioned Grizzly Hair and the other man to take Oak Gall from the *carreta* and lay her on the ground. He talked in slow, simple Spanish, then in Grizzly Hair's tongue. "Padre Durán wants all the bones dug out of this hole. Scrape them and put them in the cart. Then put the woman's body in the bottom of the hole."

Grizzly Hair gladly took the digging tool that Estanislao handed him and dug furiously, venting sorrow and revulsion. The roar in his head nearly covered the steady chink of cutting into the dirt, which was dry but loose. Graves had been dug here often. He could vault over the short wall and flee now, but still wasn't ready to leave her. He would see this finished and never forget where she lay.

The light shifted as the dirt pile grew larger. They found another skeleton, perhaps a woman. Cooler air from the hole came up and touched Grizzly Hair's soaked face and torso. His tears fell and sank into the earth that would press upon her face, earth that would contain something of him, something of the umne, and therefore be a friendlier resting place for her.

His shovel clanked on the last set of bones.

"Get down inside and dig," Estanislao told the prisoner. "You, Juan, stay on top and clean bones." *Juan, his new name.* The prisoner swung his shackled feet in, jumped down and resumed throwing dirt to the top.

Scraping bones with his shovel, Grizzly Hair let his spirit wander into the foggy place. He was only vaguely aware of the arrival of black hats and others. And then he was in the bottom of the deep hole laying Oak Gall straight with her hands crossed over her chest. He smoothed her hair and ran two fingers over her cool cheek. She would sleep, as Estanislao said. He couldn't take his eyes from the face that had been beside him since earliest childhood, the face that would remain in his mind until he drew his last breath.

"Mi hijo," said a voice.

Padre Durán was beckoning him out of the hole. Others had assembled around the grave—old Matías, Bowstring and Teresa, the old woman from the *monjería,* several young women and all the children from the *escuela.* Estanislao and the prisoner stood together with their heads bowed. The black hats held their hats in their hands. He pulled himself up from the hole and stood beside Bowstring, old Matías making room, but never took his eyes from her face.

Padre Durán uttered a long string of unintelligible talk, then quickly touched his forehead and chest on both sides. Everyone except Grizzly Hair made those same moves. He was hollow. Estanislao pointed to the shovels, which angled like awkward shoots from the heap of earth, handing one to Grizzly Hair. But he didn't want this dream to go forward.

A load of dirt pounded down on her face, pushing her hair askew. He tried to jump in to protect her, but hands held him. Gently Bowstring took the shovel from him, and added to the dirt. It piled and piled upon her in a remorseless cascade of sound until only a hint of her face remained, then only her toes, and then she was gone.

Now earth would consume her. Maybe that wasn't very different from fire. He took the shovel from Bowstring and vented his pain on the dirt, and as he shoveled, most of the people headed for the drumming and dance that was starting. Bowstring laid a hand on his shoulder, then left. A watchful black hat remained.

"*Bailar,*" Grizzly Hair said to Estanislao as the last shovels of dirt heaped upon the mound. We must dance.

"*Bailamos,*" said Estanislao, motioning the prisoner to pull the heaping *carreta* back to the bone house. Let's dance.

They went through the gate that she had entered only eight sleeps before, and saw several twenties of people dancing on the road before the church steps. People in all manner of dress and paint and feathers were singing, though he didn't know the song. The spirit of a big time prevailed, but he chose to think of it as a Cry for her. Bowstring's skillful flute sang out from the other instruments. Looking up where her soul might be, Grizzly Hair said quietly, "I am not afraid of you. Stay with me if you want."

"She is on her way to the sky, *el Cielo,*" said Estanislao, overhearing him. "We put her in holy ground and the holy words have been said. She is flying away now."

Empty, Grizzly Hair joined the dance circle, drumming upon Earth, seeking balance and alignment. Estanislao joined him. The musicians seemed more disjointed than they had been in the corridor under Padre Durán's direction. Here, no one rapped a pillar and no polliwog magic was used. Eagerly honoring her, Grizzly Hair realized these people came from many different home places and sang different songs. Yet all understood how to dance. The padres were absent and the black hats sat on the steps drinking moldy drink from *cuero* bags.

He had been dancing for some time when distant yells caught the attention of the dancers. With happy shouts the people hurried toward the sounds. Musicians followed, laying down their instruments on the church steps. Neophytes flowed like a human river past the warm-water troughs and toward the commotion at the back of the mission.

He felt annoyed to be jerked out of his reverie, and continued dancing. But after a while he realized he couldn't dance properly without music. Estanislao was beckoning. Reluctantly he joined him and they walked together among the people, past many deserted places of *trabajar*. Even the vats of fat were cooling and scumming over. Condor's dream had taken a new turn.

A small disturbance caused the river of people to part as though around an island—two neophytes beating a young man and woman with sticks, a black hat watching. The couple crouched, heads down, arms crossed over their faces. Estanislao stopped and asked in the voice of a hy-apo, "*¿Qué pasa?*"

The neophyte Narciso rattled out Spanish talk, of which Grizzly Hair understood nothing. Stepping in front of Narcisco, Estanislao talked to the black hat. Narciso lowered the stick and separated the man and woman. Then they were pulled away from where everyone was going and away from each other. They looked longingly after each other, exactly as Grizzly Hair and Oak Gall had done that first night in the mission. Estanislao and Grizzly Hair continued on their way.

"What did they do?" Grizzly Hair asked.

"They were together, but they are not married."

He had spoken for them. He was a hy-apo.

They rounded the corner to the skinning field. Everyone was there, more people in one place than Grizzly Hair had ever seen before. Men and boys had climbed a ladder over the salt bags and up to the roof of the building, where they sat tightly packed, knees up, looking over the *corral.* Sometimes it contained a cow and calf. Now it held an enormous long-horned bull that snorted and pawed the dust as if planning to run through the fence. The roof of the next building was equally crowded with women and girls. She would have sat there. Did one of those women hold her hand in the last moments? He examined their happy faces, wondering.

Riders galloped across the field at break-neck speeds. They circled the scorched grass where the putrid fire had burned, then raced back in front of the people. Watching them from the other side of the *corral,* about forty men in wide grass hats sat on horses, yelling and warbling high in their throats—neither neophytes nor soldiers by their dress. They drank from hide flasks. Accompanying them were *carretas* filled with laughing beings, apparently women, all clothed in strange, colorful garb—tight in the torso, wide and loose at the bottom. Their hair appeared to be propped up on top. Each *carreta* was attached to a saddled horse.

Dazed by grief and strangeness, Grizzly Hair moved into the crowd beside Estanislao. They were both tall enough to see over the high fence and watch the races, which appeared to be finishing. Out in the field, many men were kneeling and standing in a tight huddle. It was impossible to see what was happening but he didn't care. It would be more strangeness, and she was gone.

"They are burying a *gallo,*" Estanislao yelled over the noisy crowd.

"*Gallo?*"

"The bird that calls Roo, koo-koo, koo-kooooo."

Male birds with green-black feathers.

"They greased its neck."

Why bury a bird with a greased neck? But he lacked the curiosity to bring it to his tongue. Sorrow had drained his strength. He stood staring across the open land, vaguely aware of the vaqueros taking turns galloping past the bird. Each one slipped to the side, gripping the horse with his legs as he tried to grab the bird's head. The neck and head moved like a dancing snake. People yelled and cheered, but he was numb. Black hats stood around the crowd. In the distance there was a herd of horses and, on higher ground, patches of trees not yet cut for the everlasting fires. From the *carretas* came the strum of a stringed instrument and happy female voices as the vaqueros took turns trying to grab the bird's head.

A rider pulled the *gallo* from the dirt. To the roar of the crowd he high-stepped his horse holding a flapping, squawking plume of dust and feathers over his hat. Estanislao leaned over and said into Grizzly Hair's ear, "He lives in Pueblo San José. South of here. Do you know where it is?"

He didn't know and didn't care, though he knew Estanislao was drawing attention to that place.

The bull in the pen bellowed and pawed. Screams of excitement came from the huge crowd. People pointed. From the north, a large grizzly bear was being dragged by the neck—four lariats choking him—and for the first time his mind focused. This was for him.

The riders kept the lariats taut, the horses acting as though they had done this many times. The bear would have choked to death before now except for his great strength. His dragging rump and hind feet stirred up a large amount of dust. As they came closer to the *corral* Grizzly Hair saw the frantic look in the bear's eyes.

The Old Man of the Forest slashed at the ropes—each one plaited of many thongs. He bit through one, and the rope fell away. The man on the other end whipped a new lariat from his saddle, whirled it over the bear, and it settled around the thick neck. The horse stepped backwards, tightening the rope. The bear emitted a strained and terrible sound.

"What are they doing?" Grizzly Hair asked.

"The bear will fight *Toro*," Estanislao replied.

The gate was opened and three vaqueros rode inside the *corral*, one whirling a small low loop as the bull trotted around. Skillfully the man threw the loop around the bull's hind foot and the bull jerked to a standstill. He stood blowing angrily, his leg stretched out behind him. One of the vaqueros opened the gate to admit the four horsemen and the choking bear.

Jumping off his horse, a vaquero quickly tied the long ropes together so bull and bear were attached to each other. The remaining three ropes on the bear's neck were dropped and the vaqueros led their horses to the fence, watching what would surely be a violent fight.

Quickly rolling to all fours, the bear watched the bull. The bull stared at the bear—the crowd silent as the animals. Then the bull lowered his massive horns and charged, powerful haunches pushing. At the last instant before impact, the bear dropped to the ground in a ball of fur. Confused and losing his stride, the bull jumped over him and trotted to the end of the rope, jerking the bear to his feet.

People laughed and looked at each other. Estanislao gave Grizzly Hair a smile as if to say, this bear is clever.

Big black eyes glaring, the bull trotted around to face the bear again. He slashed a hoof though the dust, lowered his horns and charged. Again the bear rolled into a small pile of fur and the confused bull jumped over him.

Clawing the tight rope around his neck, the bear staggered to his hind feet and lurched toward his enemy—roaring, head rolling in massive anger, displaying a maw bristling with huge teeth. No doubt he would have preferred to fight those who had captured him, but he turned his rage on their champion.

Grizzly Hair noticed a flash of red on the bear's shoulder. "He is wounded," he said to Estanislao.

"The vaqueros shot him." Estanislao glanced over. "To even the fight. That is a big bear."

Horns lowered, the bull charged and the nimble bear, jumping out of the way, swiped bloody furrows along the bull's back. On the next charge, a horn scraped the bear's back and a tuft of brown hair waved from the tip. The bull bellowed, turned and pawed. The excited spectators screamed as one—all except Grizzly Hair. He was of the bear's lineage.

The wounded bear had to be tired after his fight with the vaqueros. How far had they dragged him? Now he had the disadvantage of being caught by the neck while three other ropes tangled around his feet as he danced for balance.

The bull charged again, viciously twisting into the standing bear. The tip of a longhorn caught the bear in the pit of a foreleg, lifting him into the air. For an instant he hung there—people gasping. Then he dropped to the ground. Recovering his footing, he whirled around but the foreleg hung limp. Dark and shiny in the late sunlight, blood pooled on the ground.

Obviously delighted, *Españoles* and their women peered into the *corral* on the opposite side of the fence. But it was cruel to tie these animals together so neither could run, and watch them fight to their deaths, like tying a man's hands and whipping him to death, or nailing him to a *cruz* and watching him die. *Españoles* acted like cruel children. "I don't like it," he said to Estanislao.

"I don't either." But he had smiled. This man talked from both sides of his mouth. Would he help Grizzly Hair escape or would that change too? Would he tell the black hats where to hunt for him?

Toro was resting, his huge tongue hanging out, sides heaving. Lightning quick, the bear ran to the bull, bit into the tongue and held it in his teeth. The bull's head hung low, the bear squatting on his hind legs. Nose to nose, they appeared to be kissing, the bear fondling the bull's head with his good paw, but the claws left bloody gashes. The silenced crowd leaned forward.

The bear took a crouching step back and the bull stepped forward, stiff-legged. The bear stepped to the side and the bull followed. They remained locked together so long that people resumed their chatter.

"Those people live in San José," said Estanislao, pointing at the men with the strange women, the men who passed hide flasks. "That's a town south of here, about a day's walk."

With a sudden mighty yank, the bull reared back and pulled loose. People ahh-ed as he staggered to the end of the rope and turned around. His tongue hung shredded in several bleeding strips. An eyeball dangled on the side of his gory head. But his good eye flashed. He charged.

It happened so suddenly that the three-footed bear failed to get out of the way. A horn ripped his haunch. The bear roared and whirled after the bull's tail, grabbed it in his teeth and with a mighty swing, helped by the momentum and the good paw, slammed the bull into the fence. On the other side of the fence women in *carretas* screamed and people closer to Grizzly Hair jumped up and down to see.

As the bull thrashed and tried to recover his feet, the lightning-fast bear bit into its belly then jumped away from the hooves, pink intestines trailing from his mouth. Bellowing in pain, *Toro* flopped toward the fence, which he kicked like a drum. More intestines slipped out.

Vaqueros who had been waiting inside the *corral* converged on their horses with whirling lariats. They quickly immobilized the bear while the crying bull sat in his intestines—a dazed and beaten animal with an eye hanging loose. He was lassoed and pulled out of the *corral* trailing his innards.

Now what would happen? The bear had won the fight, yet he stood fighting the loops around his neck. People were pointing. Grizzly Hair followed the fingers. Another bull was being brought! Pulled by the ropes around his horns, this bull was fresh and sleek and rested, his horns even wider and sharper.

Sickened by the unfairness and the bloodthirsty crowd, Grizzly Hair watched the skillful vaqueros tie the new bull to the bear, drop the lariats and back their horses to the fence.

The crowd went silent as the big bear, on three feet, gauged his new enemy. Yet the real enemy remained the same. This was a bad dream of Condor. Neither bear nor bull moved. People yelled. Men threw rocks over the fence, pelting both animals. Still nothing happened. A San José man hurled a flask, which landed on the bull's rump in a spray of red liquid.

Apparently driven by that and the thunderous crowd, the bull finally charged. The bear, rising to his hind feet, stepped aside and grabbed the bull's tail exactly as he had done to the previous bull. He threw him into the fence in exactly the same place. Grizzly Hair saw it shake loose from its posts, and knew what would happen. Estanislao was pushing into the crowd.

As the bull struggled for footing the bear bit into the bull's lassoed leg. Spitting out the hoof, he emitted a spine-tingling roar and hurled himself into the weakened fence. With a loud snapping and crackling, the timbers gave way and the bear rampaged into the *carretas.*

Horses reared and dumped riders. Carts turned upside down, wheels spinning. Women screamed. The pain-crazed bull also smashed through the fence behind the bear. With a twist of his horns, he charged into the scattering crowd and a woman flew up kicking in her billowing skirts. A *fusil* thundered amidst the screams and yells from the crowd.

Meanwhile, trailing ropes and parting the herd of horses, the bear loped for the hills on three legs. Excited neophytes ran after him, or the scattering horses. Grizzly Hair ran with them, hidden like a bird in a flock.

He glanced over his shoulder and saw a scene like the one Padre Fortuni had hung on the pillar—a mass of people in the Devil's fire. Here, father sun colored the people red. Men on rearing horses wheeled this way and that as they tried to chase the charging bull. Mouths were stretched wide in horror, and the screams were deafening though no individual could be heard.

In the fading light Three Legs vanished over a rise and disappeared in the trees. Thanking him for the message, Grizzly Hair veered away from the chase and followed him to freedom.

II
María

22

Oddly weightless as excitement covered his grief, Grizzly Hair unleashed his speed and flew south in long effortless strides. Evening dew settled upon the open grasslands and large herds of cattle grazed, but with luck he wouldn't slip in dung or trip in a ground-squirrel hole. The beads bumping his neck reminded him of the mission and he almost tossed them away, but such valuable beads could be traded, and he needed things.

To avoid Pueblo San José he ran in the contours of higher ground. Sheep, horses and cattle shied to see an intruder. With bears abroad, animals were sensitive to movement in the dark. He considered taking a horse, but had no reins and felt unsure about directing a horse with his thighs. Besides, horses were easily tracked and hard to conceal.

The campfires of the immortals twinkled through the night dome and a flat purple cloud lay on the western horizon. Faintly, as if from another world, he heard the untimely ringing of mission bells. His absence was known. He ran on, certain that the waning crescent of mother moon wouldn't give trackers enough light to follow him, and he would use tricks to confound the record of his passing.

Strangely perceptive and buoyed with mysterious strength, he seemed to float and didn't stop to rest for a long time. Then he sat on the flank of the hill and leaned back on a large ground-squirrel mound. The mountain stood behind him. Two pricks of light winked in the west—candles, the town of San José. How very far away tiny fires could be seen! What did people do this late at night that they needed light? Suddenly tired in the neck and shoulders, he decided this was a good place to turn east and climb the mountain. By daylight he would be sleeping on the mountaintop and impossible to track.

Instead, after only a short climb up a baffling, shadowy canyon filled with harsh brush—why was his skin so sensitive?—his mysterious strength abandoned him. He crawled into a hollow beneath a tree, some of its branches hanging over a gorge, and flopped on his back. He lay still but felt as though he were spinning like a rock rolling downhill. His entire body ached. Having been ill only once as a child, he had forgotten the feeling, yet the moment the thought occurred to him, he knew demons had jumped inside him. His earlier feeling of strength had been a trick. Now the evil ones poked him from head to toe with little spears. Had Bohemkulla ambushed him too? To make his thoughts spin so? He had hoped, despite traveling at night, that O-se-maiti would have blocked the night-trail demon. Then all thought fell to the bottom of darkness.

He awoke cold and thirsty. Earlier, the night had seemed warm. It was another trick of the demons who leaped around inside him, stabbing his neck, legs, shoulders and sides—unpredictable as the rattles of spirit dancers. He curled into a shivering ball, knowing he should have found water before lying down. If he searched in this weakened condition, he might leave sign for the black hats. His mouth felt like cattail fluff. Should he wait to find water until father sun came up? Would he be weaker or stronger then? He didn't know. He couldn't think. The night pulsed red whether his eyes were open or closed. He had done many things wrong in the last few sleeps, besides traveling at night. Now he was paying—teeth chattering, unable to remember what he was supposed to tell Estanislao's people. He forgot how he came to be under the tree. Long difficult dreams pinned him to the spot as he fended off the monsters Sloth and Gluttony and Pride with his bare hands, then stumbled into a snake pit and tried to kick away the snapping fangs.

Hands lifted his head. He sipped at a cup held to his lips and fell back down the hole. For a long time he struggled to get his head out of the mud, then popped up too high and floated into the sky above the Valley of the Sun. He soared over the oak grasslands all the way to the home place. The umne stared up in awe, recognizing him gazing down at them. His mother pointed and cried out in fear. He twisted around to see what she was pointing at and saw a giant bird looming behind him. He tucked in his arms and dove like a bank swallow, but the fierce bird dropped after him, easily closing the gap. Talons ripped into his neck and shoulders and the beak punched out his eyes. Blinded, he fought the bird with all his strength while tumbling from the sky. Just before he struck the ground his own hoarse yell wakened him and he sensed a gentle person holding his head, a cup at his lips. Then he was lowered to sleep.

A crow came in his next dream and told him to go to his home place. Slowly, he surfaced, opened his eyes to brilliant light stabbing through the canopy of the oak. He didn't know father sun's location; the pain in his head closed his eyes. Too weak to sit, he thought he must be dying. No, he remembered, he must die in the home place, not among strange spirits.

Something moved. With a sinking stomach, he knew it was the black hats. They would take him back to the mission and whip him and lock him in the *calabozo*. But he was too weak to move. The branches rattled and all he could do was watch.

A wrinkled yellowish face pushed through the foliage. It was the face of an old woman with the untattooed chin of a girl. She crawled toward him on her hands and knees with a sloshing metal vessel in one hand, the other hand yanking a woolen garment that impeded her motion. "*Buenos tardes, mi hijo,*" she said with a wide smile that exposed two missing front teeth.

He looked behind her, expecting the worst, but no one else appeared. She talked again. He shook his head at the Spanish babble. Then she spoke in the friendly tongue of the home place, but with a slight accent.

He thought he was dreaming. "You know how to talk," he said, wincing at the pain in his throat and wishing he could rise from the dirt and leaves and be polite.

The woman's smile folded her small face and curled back her upper lip. "From your sleep talk I guessed you were from the *Rio de los Cosumnes,*" she said. "Drink this." Somehow her kind expression said she understood that he was a fugitive.

The tea tasted of strong herbs. It cooled his mouth but swallowing burned and pinched his throat with agony so sharp he never wanted to swallow again.

"I must return to the pueblo now or my family will look for me," she said. "Drink all the medicine, sleep and get well." With a hand like fine doeskin she pushed the hair from his eyes.

"Are the black hats asking about me?" It hurt to talk.

"Yes. I didn't tell them."

He closed his eyes, tired of the pain. Maybe she wouldn't tell them. Outside the veil of leaves he heard the twinkle in her voice, "You must be a fox to find such a nest."

He slept and was surprised when the old woman returned, and so soon. It should have taken longer to walk to the pueblo and back.

"Good," she said feeling his forehead and cheeks, "You will live. I brought food and medicine."

He whispered, "You travel fast, Mother."

She grinned in a funny way. "I am María and I have been gone for one sleep and most of a sun."

María. Mother of God. A healer. He sat up for the first time, light-headed. Swallowing came a little easier. He felt hungry. From her burden-basket María took food that he had craved in the mission. His thoughts were straightening and he realized these greens wouldn't grow in this season unless she had channeled water to them like mission neophytes did. Her elixir of elderberry juice tasted so wonderful he nearly wept. "You saved my life," he whispered, allowing a bit of food to scrape down his injured throat. "How did you find me?"

She sat beside him under the tree, watching him eat. "I come often to this mountain to gather, where the cattle haven't trampled the bulb flowers. You can see the *bahía* from here. Mission Santa Clara too, if there is no smoke or fog. I found this place a long time ago." The smile on her flat face turned her upper lip back so it almost touched the tip of her nose. "I came here to take a nap and found you!"

He could hear her music, rich with the joy of the old, and knew he could trust her. "Magic brought you," he whispered. Touching the full bucket, he added, "There must be water nearby."

"Not far."

He drank again, his throat clenching like a ravaged fist, and lay back with a groan. "I've been sleeping too long. I must go over the mountain."

She tilted her head in a questioning way, the gray-streaked hair loose around her face. "Where on the river of my people is your home place?"

He whispered, "At the first pines."

"José y María, that far! My home place was not so far. It is where the river first leaves the tulares."

"How did you escape from the mission?" He coughed a gelatinous green mass onto the ground. Horrified to realize it was a nest of tiny demons, he threw it over the gorge and wiped his hand in clean dirt and leaves.

Unfazed, and with a hint of pride, she said, "I never lived in a mission." She told a story of being given to the black hats before she became a woman, which explained her lack of a tattoo. She had married a headman called Commander Pedro Fages. "He gave me a baby and I named her Angelita. Later he became Governor of Alta California and took us to Monterey. But his other wife, doña Eulalia de Callis, came from Spain on a big boat and said bad things about me, and my man lost his calm. He sent me north to the Presidio of San Francisco to *trabajar* for Commander Argüello's wife. There I met Pepe, a soldier with a place in the pueblo. The commander let me go with Pepe, so I took Angelita and moved into Pepe's house."

Grizzly Hair knew nothing of Monterey, governor, California or San Francisco, except. . . yes, someone had said that's where most of the black hats lived.

She sighed. "I talk too much. But hear me a little longer. I am old now. I want to visit the home place of my girlhood. I want to see people living as I once did. You make me think I could, if I traveled with you?" She tilted her head in her funny way, asking but not asking, and patted him on the shoulder. "Now I go to my house. Sleep now. Drink a cup of this whenever you wake up. I'll return after the sleep."

During the night he awoke several times, rearing up, heart thumping, sweat on his face. He listened until his ears rang, not sure if black hats were there. He would finally wear down into something like sleep only to sit up again, stare into the dark and wonder why they took so long to burst in. He almost wished they would get it over with. But surely, he would think, they couldn't track at night. Each time before lying down he drank the medicine.

Light pierced the canopy and he crawled out, pushing through the branches to see where he was. Far below and across the valley lay the tail of the shiny bay, enlarging northward until it joined the haze. Not far from the end of the tail, he made out the white buildings that had to be Mission Santa Clara. Mission San José was out of sight in the north. Closer to him, in the middle of the valley, stood more than twenty houses—miniature in the distance. This would be Pueblo San José. Beyond the green rectangles of land surrounding the village, beetle-sized cows grazed, as did two or three horses with riders.

Had an old woman actually come to him from one of those little houses? Except for the bucket and tortillas, which lay beside him, he would have thought her a dream. Had she said she wanted to travel with him? Surely not. Old women stayed at home. Young women too. Without warning Oak Gall's confident smile slammed into him. He covered his face and let himself cry, knees buckling as he sank into his nest of pain.

He would be forever marked, as the bear had been lamed, by the *Españoles*.

23

Awake again, he smelled moisture. He crawled out, looked down and nearly wept with relief to see First Rain dragging a large dark veil across the bay. Thunder growled and lightning winked through the blue-black clouds. He waited, absorbing the crackling power, and turned his face up to receive the first drops as they pattered on the leaves and beaded in the dust at his feet. First Rain would purify him; it would moisten the dry seeds waiting to grow and quench the thirst of the deep-rooted plant people—beaten, dusty and wilted but still alive. First Rain would give him the strength to shoulder his grief up the mountain.

He considered the route to the home place. He had promised to deliver Estanislao's message. He remembered it now. Estanislao seemed to know everything that happened inside and outside the mission. There could be danger. Would he send the black hats after him? He must be very cautious. Strange men might lurk along the trail, perhaps friends of the *Españoles*.

He needed a weapon. To make a bow he would need good willow and strips of split deerhide for backing. He would need either baked salmon heads or boiled soaproot to glue the overlapping layers, which meant he must make a cooking vessel. Only women knew how to make baskets, and he lacked a knife to make a wooden bowl. Would he find soaproot? Did it grow in places like this? Salmon were hard to find in this season, especially on a steep mountainside. He could catch a deer in a deadfall snare, and strangle it with his bare hands then use its long tendon for his bowstring, but where would he find the right material for arrowheads? Just finding the right hammer-stone would take a long time, and again, he'd need glue to bind stone to the shafts.

The lack of materials tired him. Mainly he needed a knife. He could trade beads, but many people around here had mission beads. Hill bunnies would value them more. María's bucket would be tradable, but it didn't belong to him. He would leave it for her. Even if she actually intended to travel with him, which he doubted, she must not. He needed the freedom to run fast. Even Oak Gall and Bowstring had encumbered him, but an old woman—

A clatter of hooves startled him. Soldiers? He ducked under the rain-pelted canopy and listened. One horse. And the quiet feet of neophyte trackers? He started crawling uphill through the low-hanging foliage, ready to flee, when the sound of the old woman's voice stopped him. "*Buen caballo.*" Good horse.

He peered back though tiny apertures in the branches. María was stroking a horse. He craned his neck to a bigger opening and concluded that she and a light brown horse with a nearly white mane and tail were alone. A bucket and several baskets were tied to the horse's rump. The woman was rich, and ready to travel. Such a woman would carry a knife. The spirits had sent her! He parted the canopy, pulled to his feet and stepped forward.

Her smile was nearly hidden by a scarf tied around her chin. She watched the rain washing streams down through the dirt and sweat on his body, then looked up asking, "Are you ready to go?" The lilt in her voice came from her friendly music, as did the sparkle in her eyes.

"Mother," he said, "does a sturgeon shit in the water?"

She chuckled. "Isn't the rain wonderful!" Her eyes spoke more than her words and he was almost in tears to have her there, someone who spoke the tongue of his people, to travel with and share First Rain.

She went to the horse, opened a basket and pulled out a metal knife and a fist-sized lump of dried meat. The knife easily sliced a curl of hard meat, which she handed him as she sat beside him. In thoughtful silence he ate that and the soggy corn bread from her basket. It was their own private First-Rain feast, while lightning danced in the valley.

When they were finished, she nodded at the horse and said, "You ride Amarillo. I'll walk."

"No, you ride. I am well now. But Mother, your people will worry about you. They might follow and take you back."

"I told Pepe and Angelita that I am traveling with a friend and will be safe. They say I am crazy, but will not follow." Her black eyes twinkled knowingly.

She rode the horse up the gorge that had baffled him when he was ill, and he followed behind the powerful haunches, slipping in mud and pushing through poison oak and scrubby growth. It wasn't long before his strength failed and he coughed in uninterrupted spasms. More demon nests jumped from his chest into his mouth. Ashamed of his weakness, he spat them out; but when María slid off the horse and sternly pointed for him to mount, he climbed on the horse.

Leading Amarillo, she extricated her dress when it caught underfoot or snagged in the branches, which happened continually. He knew the weight and discomfort of wet wool and was glad when she turned, eyed him naked on the horse, shook the scarf off her head, and said, "The rain is warm and I don't feel sinful with you." She pulled the dress over her head and stretched it over the baskets and buckets on the horse's rump, tucking the edges beneath the straps. Now as she led Amarillo the clothing of the *Españoles* no longer confined her. The long skin-flaps of her breasts swayed and her empty buttocks jiggled.

The gorge leveled into a high narrow valley. The rain lessened and the parting clouds revealed patches of washed blue sky. In a shaft of sunlight on the mountain crest ahead, Grizzly Hair saw three crude u-machas and several partially clothed men, no doubt *cimarrones.* "Mother," he said, "careful." He swung a leg over, to jump off the horse and hide.

"Don't worry, I will talk for us," she said with complete assurance, going to the rear to pull on her dress. "No soldiers have come this way. I watched the mountain."

When they arrived at the camping place, he saw what a good traveling companion she was. Her happy old smile and rapid Spanish made friends of these *cimarrones,* and they filled her skin bag at a spring.

"The black hats are at Alta Monte now," said a man in a woolen shirt, pointing north up a strong trail. "Don't go that way." He gestured toward a fainter path heading eastward down the mountain, a stream tumbling beside it from the spring. "This will take you to the Valley of the Sun."

"*¿Donde está la ranchería de los Lakisamni?*" Grizzly Hair managed in Spanish.

The response came fast and María translated. "The relatives of the Lakisamni, those who are not in the missions, have moved upstream. Sucais and Quinconul are there on that river, upstream from where it joins the San Joaquin."

Just where Estanislao had said it would be.

María smiled her thanks to the men and led the horse down the path, Grizzly Hair riding. Before long the trail steepened and the horse picked his way slowly, sometimes skating a little on rocky surfaces. María removed her dress again, and they entered a landscape of fractured rock walls. It looked like the turtle brothers who held the world on their backs had awakened long ago and moved around, smashing the rocks together in great upthrusting collisions. Stones that resembled bleached dog brains also lay about. This was a place of power and mystery.

Equally mysterious was the way Estanislao had found him in a dream, then offered to help him escape. Yet Padre Durán was Estanislao's friend. Was he trustworthy? What did it mean that the fleas would jump off the wolf? And that the black hats had lost a war in the southern land? Estanislao was respected by neophytes and black hats alike, yet he had chosen Grizzly Hair to deliver the message. On balance it seemed he should.

Other questions weighed on him too. Would the umne accept him back?

Red Sun could demand Grizzly Hair's life in retribution for his daughter's death. No one could deny that he took her to where the *Españoles* made her live in a bad house. They had also lured Bowstring with their powers. A nauseating sense of worthlessness sat on the back of his tongue and he wondered if he could ever face the umne again. But a man had to live in his home place. Even one who had never completely belonged there. His power place was there. He was rooted among those hills and boulders. If Red Sun killed him or paid Drum-in-Fog to do it, at least his bones would be in the right place; and if the songs were sung, his spirit would go to the happy land.

A vista opened. Below, the Valley of the Sun stretched far and wide, giving forth the wholesome life-promising aroma of washed grass. María stopped the horse and he slid off. Here and there rain hung in furry gray fingers. Some reached the valley floor, others not quite. Sunlight streamed between these clouds. Powerful spirits were putting on a display, perhaps telling him to stop looking back and honor the magic before him. The horse ambled away to browse.

María sat on a rock bench shot through with a wide vein of white quartz. Above her head in that same vein, a cluster of crystals caught his eye, bluer than the washed sky. He borrowed María's knife and pried them out, thinking to make a charmstone when he got home. The elongated, six-sided crystals were pointed and fused together in a jumbled way. From a narrower vein of quartz in another boulder, he removed a translucent red stone—for Morning Owl—then sat beside María as she looked over the valley.

"I don't know if the river of the Lakisamni is north or south from here," he said.

She pointed north.

He gave her an appreciative glance. "It is unusual," he said, thinking she might be keeping a secret, "for an old woman to leave her family and travel a long distance with a stranger."

She flashed him a teasing look. "I am not crippled yet."

He looked at her.

Her smile faded and she smoothed the wrinkles on her knees. "I want to meet your people and visit your home place. I want to know *inocentes* again, h'nteelehs." Gentiles

"Why?" He peered through the red stone at a red world.

She grinned a shrug. "Did I tell you I lived with the headman of the Spanish soldiers? He was my man for many *años.* My son-in-law is a soldier too. They haven't made *expediciones* very far up the rivers yet. The *cimarrones* usually hide closer to their old home places."

Años meant nothing, nor did *expediciones*, but he realized this old woman had much to teach.

She frowned through a sad smile, her lips wrinkled like a fine skin purse. "Did your friends die at the mission?"

He nodded, a barbed rock suddenly in his throat.

"Our people are dying." She patted his knee and looked at the rain squalls walking across the valley, then fingered her beads and began the long mission prayer that started with the name she shared with the headwoman of the *Español* spirits.

For a moment he thought it would be polite to pray with her—he had learned to mumble along—but she continued in the forthright way of Morning Owl beseeching the spirits, so he waited for her to finish, then said, "You say 'our people' too. Do you mean all who were here before the *Españoles* came?"

"Yes. Who else talks that way?"

"Estanislao, a neophyte at the mission."

"I've heard of him."

"What have you heard?"

"He is loyal to Padre Durán, a devout neophyte." She would return to her black hat in Pueblo San José, so he wouldn't mention Estanislao's offer to help, or his message. "I want to follow the river of the Lakisamni east to the foothills," he said, "then go north to my village." The men at the mountain spring had warned them not to travel on the valley trail.

She gave him a mischievous grin, her turned-out lip teasing the tip of her nose. "And you thought I'd be unhappy going the long way and missing my old place?"

He looked her the truth of it.

She whistled through the gap in her teeth. "It is better that way," she said as the horse came. "We will visit many villages and maybe one of them will still be celebrating Acorn Time." She added, "*Me gusta.*" It pleases me.

24

"That was the start of it," I tell Bear and Coyote, who has just trotted down the path and joined us. He stacks his forepaws and bends his back in a concave stretch until it cracks, then shakes a cloud of dirt-brown hair.

"You let your son suffer," he says, narrowing his eyes at my trunk. "Why didn't you use your powers?"

"Old Man," I reply, not a little perturbed, "I spirit-tracked my son. His pain was mine. I was mute with it. And I summoned the great black and white eagle to help me *see*."

"You took your time about it." Coyote circles and plops down.

"Who has perfect power? Even on the wings of Eagle? All around the mission we were buffeted by updrafts of strong magic. It swirled in circles and darted like hummingbirds. That my son survived at all proved his strength, and that of O-se-mai-ti."

The bear nods thankfully, sitting on her haunches.

"I found María to help him," I add, prickly with the memory of him alone and beset with bad spirits, fearing trackers. Coyote is smiling and I'm afraid I know why. "Did you know," I continue, hoping to change the subject, "that the *Españoles* look forward to death so they can live in a place where people walk on paths paved with gold and colored stones?"

The amber eyes look innocent. "Well then, the people over in the subdivision must be already dead. You should see those houses. They are so big the people could live there a lifetime without setting foot on the earth. They sweep away every crumb of it that sneaks inside. They fit stones together so they can walk to the water without touching anything alive, and that water is too sterile for moss. No swamp grass grows around it either."

The great she-bear asks, "Don't you worry about drinking from such dead pools?"

Coyote, who likes to brag about living under the noses of the new people, eating their pets and drinking their pool water, lays his snout on a paw and says, "Nothing can kill old Coyote." This is intended to remind O-se-mai-ti that she is extinct in California.

"Let's get back to the *Españoles,*" she growls.

"They were wanderers," I continue, "men who wept for a lost paradise—a lush and fertile land like ours when they found it—men who yearned to abandon the world of guns, yet taught my son the need for killing war. "Coyote," I suddenly realize, "you had a paw in that, didn't you!"

Heh-heh is heard from that curled heap of fur.

I sigh up through my boughs, for he has cleverly brought back the subject. "I played a part," I admit, "by summoning María to help my son. She taught him too. And not even a sorcerer knows where her magic will lead."

Eyes still closed, Grizzly Hair awoke to the sleepy, familiar song of a mourning dove stringing coos like beads, a high note trailed by three sad lower tones. With his eyes closed it seemed he floated above the woolen blanket María had let him use. Nothing touched him but the dove song and the fragrance of dewy grass and dank earth excavated during the night by ground squirrels—burrowers who carried earth to the surface one little mouthful at a time. They were not slothful. The mission had nearly broken him, but the earth and grass and wing people were starting to heal him.

He bathed lengthwise in the trickle of the stream from the mountaintop. The water hardly wet him. He rolled in it and María laughed. "Clean mud," he said.

After tangy watercress, hard jerky and tortillas, she filled her goat-stomach bag with water, stretched her dress over the baskets and buckets on Amarillo's rump, grabbed the horse's mane and scrambled on.

He rode behind her, holding her soft middle with one hand, the flap of a breast grazing it. Bantering emerged from his injured spirit. "This is a nice way to travel," he said. "I'm glad I thought to invite you along."

"How could I resist such a pretty man as you?"

"Oh, I am pretty all right, lying in a sweat with dirt on my face."

"And covered with mud."

"You're a sly old woman."

"Old women are sly."

"Then I'm glad you're old."

They were heading straight for the San Joaquin River. Although she, like the *Españoles*, postponed bathing, he could hardly wait. It felt good to banter again, and she had no qualms about talking. She talked about the *Españoles* as easily as about the horse. They had traveled for a long time when he asked about the man she had married.

"In a way I was married to Commander Fages," she said. "But the padres didn't consider us married. He was the father of my Angelita and gave me many presents. The padres said the big Papa in Roma didn't allow second wives. Doña Eulalia forced me out of Monterey. It was just as well. I was living in sin. I confessed each week." She crossed herself. "After that, Commander Argüello protected me from the *codicia* of the soldiers. Until I became Pepe's woman, then Pepe protected me."

"*Codicia*," Grizzly Hair repeated, trying to say it right. "I remember that, but not the meaning." It felt like father sun was sitting on his head, but the lice continued to crawl around on his scalp and, inside, the demons started hammering. He longed for the cool depths of the river, still far ahead.

"*Codicia* means joy of men in coupling with women against their wishes," María said, rocking with the horse, her flaccid rump tight against him.

Now he remembered. *Codicia* was another of the seven bad behaviors, the one Padre Fortuni barely mentioned. "Joy?" he questioned. "Men feel more joy when the woman desires it too."

"Christian women don't like coupling. I hate it." A cheerful tone.

"Is that possible?" He hoped she would take that as amazement, not disrespect.

"Oh, some like it," she said cheerfully, "but men won't marry them. The worst insult to a Spanish man is to call his mother such a woman."

The Rattlesnake Dance came back to him, and the many women who had desired him. *She* had wanted a baby. He struggled to banish her name and her face, and to find his calm.

María chattered happily. "I like talking to you. You are like I was a long time ago."

"How is that?"

"*Inocente*."

In Gabriel's mouth that was an insult.

"Of course I must return to a better way of life and confess to Padre Durán."

That landed like a rock slide. He pushed on the horse's back and vaulted over the big creamy rump, turning an ankle when he hit the ground. He rolled in the brittle grass.

Rearing, Amarillo danced on his hind legs while María scolded and struggled to control him. When the horse settled down, she asked, "Why did you do that?" The hoods of her eyes were peaked with astonishment.

He stood facing the horse, its ears flattened back. "You will talk to Padre Durán about me and he will find my people." He had forgotten that the long robes made people speak their secrets.

The drawstring in her lips tightened. "I must confess my sin of nakedness and talking about coupling," she said, "but I won't tell who I talked to. It is not part of the sin."

"It is a sin to be with a *cimarrón*." Gabriel had said so.

"Bad, but not a sin. Anyway, the holy fathers never repeat what they hear in confession."

Grizzly Hair doubted that. Besides, they could send black hats up the river without repeating what had been told to them. He stood in the crushing heat trying to think. Even if he left her and headed home by another route, she knew exactly where he was going. Why had he been so, yes, *inocente?* The world was different now. But María had saved his life and he wanted to trust her.

She reached back and brought out the goat-stomach bag. "Water?"

He accepted, letting it trickle refreshingly out the sides of his mouth and down his chest.

"Come, ride with me," she said.

His ankle hurt but he decided to walk until his stomach quieted. When his calm returned he'd know what to do. He followed the horse along a deer trail. The sky had bleached nearly white in the heat and the grass stretched in every direction as far he could see, dotted by oaks. In the shadows of an oak skirted by low limbs, the erect ears of resting deer rotated as they passed.

María talked as though nothing had happened. "Christian women want to go to heaven like the mother of Jesús, so they try not to couple."

"Then how do they get babies in their blood?"

"Many don't. Governor Fages used to complain about it. You see," she turned and looked at him over the horse's rump, "when women have babies everyone knows they have coupled, including God. Some take the babies out of their blood."

Men weren't supposed to ask about women's special knowledge, but this woman seemed willing to talk about anything, so, cautiously, he asked, "How do they stop babies from growing in their blood?"

"Oh, God save me, I have been secretly summoned to the mission by neophyte women who needed healing herbs after they tried to stab their babies in their wombs or ate too much black grass-fungus and became very sick. They didn't want their bellies to show their *pecado.* They wanted to be pure and strong like the padres and the *santos* in the sky." She put the reins in one hand and made the motions of the cross over herself.

The *Españoles* were in a puzzling predicament. Their women didn't want to couple. That, Grizzly Hair suddenly realized, must be the reason they left their home places without their women. The more he knew about the *Españoles,* the stranger they seemed. Old Matías had said the long robes strengthened themselves by never coupling, like sorcerers, but the long robes insisted people call them fathers. Maybe they were sorry they had no real children. It reminded him of a freak poppy he'd once seen with a bulging waxy stamen but no petals or pollen. He had felt sad for the poppy.

"But I think," María continued after a pause, "many babies come out in the blood by themselves, without any help. Padre Durán punishes the women. Did you see that?"

"He made a woman carry a wooden doll."

"Yes, painted red. That's supposed to make them sorry about the bloody baby they killed. They carry it around wherever they go, for many sleeps. Sometimes they stand in front of the altar in church so people can yell and jeer at them."

"But Padre Durán is a man. Men don't—" He couldn't express all that was in his mind about the place of men in the world and the secret knowledge of women.

"They are different from other men."

"Are they women-men?" Their clothing resembled hers rather than the *pantalones* of the black hats, and among most peoples women-men were thought to have mysterious powers.

"Oh, no!" She shifted the rein to one hand and crossed herself. "You must not say that. Coupling between men is the most sinful kind. The padres sacrifice all pleasure to keep themselves pure from the sins of the world."

He thought back to the mission, the many adults and few children. It was a life filled with *trabajar* and the threat of the *cuarta.* Bowstring and Teresa came to mind, then despite his utmost effort, he saw Oak Gall lying stiffly in her grave. He felt dizzy and suddenly choked with the smell of death.

Cheerfully, María was saying, "God forgave me for getting Angelita in my blood. Padre Junipero Serra washed my sin away, and hers too when she was a baby. I'm pretty sure I'll go to heaven." She wrinkled her nose and sniffed. "Something's dead."

He had thought it was a trick of the demons. A vulture stood, it seemed, on the tips of the grass heads, nervous wings half lifted. When they drew closer he saw that it stood on the hip of a young elk. Many more vultures walked around in the grass and others circled above—little brothers of Condor.

He examined the elk, vultures jumping into flight. By the size and depth of the slashes and the broken neck, it had been killed by a bear. The smell sickened him more than it should have. Sweat popped out. The clear day went dark and without warning the tortillas and jerky bucked up. He spewed them out and turned away from the mess on the ground, kneeled and put his forehead down in the posture of mission prayer. Demons hammered behind his eyes and ears. He had handled Oak Gall's body and could be killed at any moment, but must return and tell his people about the *Españoles.* He picked a handful of dry grass and wiped the bitterness from his tongue and teeth.

María waited, then said, "You're not well yet." She patted Amarillo's back. "Get on. I'll walk if you want." She extended the stomach-bag again, the question in her eyes.

He pushed to his feet and accepted the water, rinsed his mouth and climbed on the horse behind her. As the animal resumed walking, he noticed with the unconscious curiosity of a tracker, the disturbance in the tall grass where the heavy bear had stalked the elk. The bear had dragged a foreleg. O-se-mai-ti was giving him a message of hope. Three Legs had survived!

María asked, "Was it a close friend of yours who died in the mission?"

He caught his breath. Polite people didn't ask him to think about dead people he had loved, but she had learned Spanish ways. After a time, he said, "Yes."

"Louder. My ears are old and the hooves make noise."

He said, "My people may hate me. They may send us away."

She twisted and glanced back at him. "Because someone died in the mission?"

He groaned and María didn't probe further. After a while she said, "It wasn't your fault, you know. Every day people die in the missions. Young and old. I will tell them."

Wanting no more of that, he returned to a topic that seemed to interest her as much. "Do Spanish men hate coupling too?"

"Oh, no. They like it more than *Indios.* They like to remove a woman's dress and force her. They do it in the dark." She swayed easily on the horse while Grizzly Hair tried to imagine that. In the distance the seemingly low wall of dusty green beckoned.

"Spanish men are proud when they put a baby in a woman's blood," she continued. "The more children, the prouder they are. Some of their women have twenty children. I heard of one with almost thirty."

Aghast—he'd never heard of a woman having more than five—he was still thinking about the first surprising thing she'd said. "Have you coupled with an *Indio?*"

With noticeable pride she said, "Never."

Somewhat hurt by that, he pointed out a contradiction, gently so as not to seem disrespectful. "Then it might be hard for you to know whether Spanish men enjoy it more than *Indios.*"

She turned partway toward him, her lip turned back in a smile. "I guess I don't know what men think, only what they do."

She turned back, perspiration trickling down her back. They rode in silence, Grizzly Hair trying to fathom the ways of the *Españoles.* The heat stilled the land. Wise animals were napping.

At last they arrived at the Rio de San Joaquin. The smell of moss and water tugged him as he dismounted in the shade of a mother oak. He waded through warm mud and tulares and pushed through cattail spears glued together by the nests of white-stripe redwings. Clouds of them flew up. Frogs plopped in the shallow water and a thick rattlesnake swam out of his way.

Parting the last green cattail spears, he fell gratefully into the sparkling water—arms outstretched, face down. He'd missed water like a friend of his childhood. It cooled the ache in his head and tingled the scabs on his back. Turning for air, he stroked upstream to a bend in the river where black alders shaded the deep quiet water.

There he floated, legs buoyed and bent in the current. He made himself sink. Water mounted on his itchy scalp and pulled his thick hair upward like moss waving on the surface. The frantic lice would be abandoning their nests and scrambling up the hairs in search of air. He twisted downward, flooding all the little homes, every tip of his long hair under water. Kicking just enough to remain stationary, he waited for the current to carry them away. A blue-gill was staring at his knee, fanning its little tail to remain in place.

Hello, little brother, he said mind-to-mind. It seemed he might sleep like a fish, so calming was this return to water. When at last he exploded to the surface for air, María was beside him, cackling.

"This is nice," she said. "I feel like I never want to wear a dress again."

He needed silence to hear the spirits, but the look in her face told him it would be polite to talk. "Clothing is good when it is cold," he said.

"Sometimes I feel cold when I'm wearing my dress."

He shut his eyes and turned over on his back, light as a leaf, cupping the warm surface just enough to stay afloat. The sudden brightness and heat on his face meant he had floated beyond the shade. He was near sleep.

She followed, prattling beside him, "*Españolas* wear clothing to be *modesto.*" Her cackle was disturbingly loud. "My man, Commander Fages, used to tell this story. He asked a gentile how he could tolerate being naked in the time of cold fog. The man asked him, 'How can your face tolerate it?' My man said, 'My face is used to it.' The *Indio* was quiet. Then he said, 'I am all face.'"

He cracked an eye. In the blinding glare off the water he saw her hair slicked back, her skin fresher, something different in her eyes.

Quietly, she said, "You are the first man I have wanted to couple with in many *años*."

He gulped water and dropped his legs. "But you hate it."

She smiled, her fingertips brushing the side of his hip, and as they drifted in the current, she floated closer. Sunlight sparked off the rippling water and an iridescent blue dragonfly hovered beside them, whirring. Its face was all eyes, seeing what? He couldn't find his tongue to say that he couldn't—

She pulled him to her and the dragonfly zipped away. Her pink tongue bulged in the gap between her teeth. Stray white hairs reared up from her black brows. He jerked back. His feet hit rocks and he winced at the pain in his sore ankle.

"God forgive me," she cried. "I am a wicked, sinful old woman." She scrambled awkwardly up the muddy shore and disappeared into the green spears, the waving tips marking her passage toward firmer ground.

He stroked back to the shady hole, but his calm was gone. He swam to shore and slogged back to the little clearing beneath the oak, where the horse cropped grass, surrounding it with big lips, stepping forward, biting off more.

María arrived from the marsh, looking very upset. "Promise, if I ever do that, you'll stop me. Please promise. *El diablo* made me do it."

With Oak Gall's face threatening to come to mind, his voice came out gruffer than intended. "It is nothing."

"But I want to forget that I said it. I want you to forget." She called out to the sky, "I want María and *Dios* to forget."

"It is too unimportant to forget," he said. Strange, to have to say that to an old woman, who should be the wise one. It annoyed him that she attached so much significance to coupling. At the same time he felt a small conceit that he could attract a woman who hated coupling. Still, if he'd been the beaver-gnawed cottonwood stump beside them, he couldn't have felt less desire for her. Or any living woman.

María's face twisted into the half-frown, half-smile that he liked so much. "Can I ever be just an old woman to you again?"

Relieved, he said, "If I can be just an *inocente* to you."

"*Gracias, Madre del Cielo!*" she called to the sky. Looking back to him, "I am just an old woman who needs a siesta." She went to Amarillo for blankets, tossing him one.

Glad to flatten his riding-tired back on the friendly ground, he sighed and gazed up through the leafy oak. María lay down a distance away, and there was a joking lilt in her voice. "Pepe wouldn't believe I did that." She shook with spasms of suppressed laughter then later snored.

Oak Gall was in the branches. He heard her whisper, *I want to lie with you in the clean air on the bank of a river.* Her last lucid words to him.

He went to the horse, found María's flint, collected tinder and kindled a fire. He sat before it and when a suitable stick was burning well, removed it and singed his hair as short as possible. Now his grief was visible and people wouldn't ask him to talk about it.

25

On the trail outside the tulares they passed three deserted villages. Examination revealed that they had been deserted for some time; however the tracks told Grizzly Hair that the broken houses were sometimes used as sleeping places for occasional travelers. He and María shunned them, for the ghosts of the former occupants could remain. No doubt the original people had gone to the missions.

During the third sleep of the journey the remaining demons left his body. The green wall before them had grown larger and deeper, possibly indicating the juncture of the two rivers. Soon they must cross the San Joaquin and find the main stream of the inflowing river of the Lakisamni.

Toward the end of the day, the fluting of meadowlarks pierced through the clamor of the ubiquitous blackbirds. Shadowy within the cover of the trees, elk stood with marsh grass dripping from their mouths, watching them pass. Herds of deer and antelope rose from the stillness and bounded away, hooves tucked beneath their bellies.

The distant call of a horse caused Amarillo to lurch to a halt, throwing Grizzly Hair into María. Shocked, he saw riders rounding a bend, coming toward them from the north.

"I'll say you are my son," María said. "Give me my dress."

She threw it over her head and wriggled it down, tugging it under her. "Use my mantle for a loincloth."

He tied it around him and under a leg. Were it not that the riders would dimly see, he'd have jumped down and hidden in the trees. But only a fugitive would run, so he sat with his pounding heart.

"Don't say anything," María instructed firmly, pressing Amarillo into motion with her heels. "Keep your head down. I'll turn the horse so you'll be in my shadow.

He felt himself under her care like a hatchling in its mother's nest, yet measured with his eyes the distance to every tree and shrub they passed.

Five black hats halted before them, guns on their saddles. María said, *"Hola, señores."* Her voice sang as if they were old friends.

They shifted their horses to look at Grizzly Hair, but she deftly turned the horse and spoke in rapid Spanish, forcing them to look at her. He recognized, *hijo, pueblo, caballo,* and *Comandante* Argüello, the latter mentioned several times.

The black hats talked among themselves, constantly glancing at Grizzly Hair. He made his face calm but his calf muscles twitched in readiness to leap and run.

"*Vaya con Dios,*" said the spokesman, kicking his horse forward. The others followed and the sound of the hooves receded. Weak with the sudden release from fear, Grizzly Hair gripped María's middle like a drowning man. "You did that well, Mother," he said. The evil ones were buzzing in his head again.

"I know how to talk to *soldados.* They are from the presidio, so they haven't seen you before. They are looking for you, but they think you are a solitary *Indio* on foot. I told them you are my son and you have been mute since birth." She cackled, then added, "They said *Indios* are not permitted to own horses now."

He turned around to see his pursuers shrinking in the distance. "Then why did they let you go? You have a horse."

She talked through spilling laughter. "I told them Commander Argüello is my friend. It is true. He gave me this horse. That always makes soldiers careful what they say to me. I told them I never was a *neofite* and the rule wasn't meant for me. They can see my dress is better than a neophyte would wear."

"Why don't they want *Indios* to have horses?"

"*Cimarrones* use them to steal horses, herds of them."

A thrilling image. Gabriel had done it. People from the home river had done it. "I suppose the wild horses are too hard to catch." They had seen a herd of them a while ago.

"Oh yes," she said. "You know, I'm surprised so many horses survived in the valley, with no one looking after them, but I guess they don't need people if they have plenty of grass." She chuckled. "I remember when the *rancheros* were complaining about the *regla* that they kill so many horses."

"Excuse me, what is a *regla?*" He knew she wasn't finished.

"When an important person, commander or governor or commissioner, tells everyone what to do, and if they don't do it they are punished. Anyway, they had to kill seven thousand horses around the pueblo. More than once they had to kill that many."

"How many twenties is seven thousand."

She giggled. "I don't know. A person would need an abacus to figure it out."

He didn't understand that either, but he went back to the main thing he didn't understand. "What does killing horses have to do with wild horses in the valley?"

Again she laughed. "Instead of killing them, some of the *rancheros* quietly drove their horses over Alta Monte Pass and left them in the Valley of the Sun. The *Comisionador* knew, but he didn't care. The *rancheros* thought they would round them up later if they needed them, but never did. We still had so many horses around the pueblo that they destroyed the fruit trees and ate the grape vines. They ate the grass so short there wasn't enough for the cattle. And the hides of the cattle are our money, so that's why every few *años* the men were ordered to kill more horses."

It was becoming clearer why mission people skinned cattle in the mission, and why there were horses in the valley near Alta Monte Pass but not farther north, where the umne would have seen them.

They rode into the San Joaquin River and Amarillo swam the deep channel. On the other side the trail east was easy to see despite the deepening shadows and dense trees. The place smelled of earth magic. Mosquitos whined in their ears, and Amarillo nodded his head to keep them from his eyes.

Estanislao's people wouldn't be far. Grizzly Hair wanted to trust María completely before he talked to them. "Tell me about your man," he said, "not the one you left, but the one in the pueblo."

"I don't have a husband."

"You said you went to the pueblo to live with a black hat."

She cackled. "Old Pepe? He is my daughter's man. I coupled with him but never married him. He liked her better."

Shocked and disgusted that she had coupled with her son-in-law, he had trouble hearing as she prattled on. A proper man never even spoke to his mother-in-law, much less touched her. People of that relationship lived to the end of their sleeps without allowing their gazes to cross.

"Angelita has five children," she was saying. The first son has thirteen *años* now." She turned and must have seen his lingering shock, for she added, "Pepe never touched me after he married Angelita."

Embarrassed for her, he asked about *años*. She said it meant one complete cycle of seasons, and went on to talk about day-counters. *Españoles* celebrated the anniversaries of their birth and added a year to their age each time. "Most people know how many years they have."

He couldn't imagine a knotted string long enough to count the years of an old person. "*Españoles* are clever," he said. "How many years do you have?"

"About three twenties. I'm not exactly sure. We celebrate my birthday on the *Fiesta de la Natividad*, the day Jesús was born."

"How many *años* do you think I have?"

"I don't know. Maybe sixteen."

A large pale owl startled him, winging past the horse so low he felt the wind on his leg. His neck hairs bristled and he held tight to María as the frightened horse danced and she worked the reins. It appeared that horses also understood that owls were messengers of bad luck.

But no sooner had the owl disappeared than they passed a mother oak, gnarled and bleached with age. He was glad to see María's respect for the tree as she dismounted and touched the bark. Later, with the good-luck tree behind them, he asked, "Will the long robes and soldiers return to their home places across the eastern sea?" She had said that's where they came from, long ago.

"No. This is their home now."

"Not here!" A ground squirrel piped its alarm.

"No. Over there." She flapped a hand toward the western mountain range. "Pepe has a land paper that says a square of earth in the pueblo belongs to him. He won't leave. I wouldn't want him to because he would take Angelita and my grandchildren."

"Will they build missions in the Valley of the Sun?"

"Yes. Governor Fages talked of it—did I tell you he was my first man?" In stunned silence he listened to her talk. "He sent men to search for a good place, but they haven't built it yet." She turned her flat profile to him. "You see, a mission in the Valley of the Sun would need its own presidio to defend it against gentiles." She turned forward, her hair tickling his nose. "It would be too far from Presidio of San Francisco."

The trouble in the west would spread and engulf the umne. In his mind he saw his people whipped and locked in the *calabozo,* women dying in the *monjería. Españoles* were like marauding birds.

"Soldiers must be paid," María was saying as she guided Amarillo along the trail, "but the big headman in Spain, *el Rey,* didn't send enough men and guns so they lost the war in Mexico. I don't know. The new headman might have more money for a presidio and mission around here someplace, maybe north of here."

His own river was north. But wise birds avoided defended territories. Once he'd seen jays attack a young witabah, robin, as it sought the courage to fly from its nest. The bird's parents fought bravely against the jays, and the screeching uproar attracted many more witabahs, who normally stayed to themselves. Now, despite their normally peaceful natures, they all defended the young robin against the bigger jays. A jay seized the young robin and dropped it to the ground, where diving jays pecked the struggling little bird, but the adult robins attacked the jays on the ground and in the air, finally driving them away. Afterwards, he was surprised to see, the robins circled around the little bird in the grass. Looking outward, they stood there watching to make sure the jays didn't return. He had expected the young bird to die. Instead, it got to its feet and flew to a low branch, then to higher branches. Not only had it survived, it learned to fly.

Could the umne, the Muquelumne, Lakisamni, Omuchumne, Kadeema-umne, Shalachmushumne, Cosumne and others fight together like that? Peoples who spoke different tongues and sometimes accused neighboring doctors of casting fiendish spells? Peoples who lived for themselves? This would be no arrow-dodging war. Was the idea too farfetched?

Probably. Many *Indios* believed the missions made them powerful, and it might be true. The man in the trap had said Third World was coming and most people chose to live the new way. Estanislao believed the missions would be controlled by *Indio* people someday, then everyone would have iron knives and guns. Many *Indios* would be waiting for this. They wouldn't fight the *Españoles*. Bowstring came to mind. Would he?

Looking at it another way, however, powerful birds of prey had appeared in the land. They gathered *Indios* into the missions to build their houses, grow their food, skin their animals and even fight for them. María said the black hats wouldn't leave. Why would they? When they could sit and smoke while others exhausted themselves working on their behalf.

A shadowy trail began to thread through his mind. He had left the home place to learn what was happening in the world. Now, just as he had reconstructed those first horse prints in the sand, he saw where the tracks were leading—to a cooperative effort to drive the *Españoles* back whenever they tried to reach further into the Valley of the Sun, possibly back to where they came from. Clearly no single people could do it. The villages had too few men. He needed to think about it. Maybe it was impossible, being so contrary to people's beliefs about the proper way to live. Nonetheless, this mental trail suddenly seemed as important as cutting the bear's hair had once been. But there was much more to learn.

"How many missions are there?" he asked María.

"I don't know. Many," she said cheerfully. "Four in this northern area: Santa Clara, Dolores, San José and the one across the Bay for the sick people - San Rafael I think they call it. My neighbor told me they are talking about building a new mission up on the north side of the bay."

He listened with the nose of a bear sniffing the wind. "Do all those missions get their soldiers from Presidio San Francisco?"

"Yes."

"Did you say there were other presidios?"

"Yes, but that's the only one here in the north."

"How many presidios are there?"

"Well, our soldiers wear number four on their hats—remember that black mark on the red band, like the track of a deformed bird?—that's because San Francisco is the fourth presidio, the newest one. If they built one north of the bay, it would be number five, but they'd have to fight the Russians." Once before she had mentioned the powerful Russians, who sailed in huge wooden boats and traded fine goods. The Russians were feared by the *Españoles*. Such men would make good allies.

"Commander Argüello once went to Santa Barbara Presidio," she continued, "and said he visited the presidio in San Diego. I think his brother lives there. . ." She rattled on, and when she was finished, he counted:

"San Francisco, Monterey, Santa Barbara and San Diego. Four presidios."

"*Sí*. Four."

Ahead, something like steam rose from the tips of the highest oaks.

Dispersed smoke. No doubt Estanislao's people. He pointed past her cheek toward a path, indicating she should direct the horse that way.

Recalling that black hats also lived in the pueblo, he asked, "Are there more pueblos, besides Pueblo San José?"

"Yes, One near Mission Santa Cruz and I think one other. Yes, I remember now, *Pueblo de los Angeles.* Very far south."

Angeles were winged spirits. That could be dangerous. "How many soldiers live in the pueblos?"

"Mmm. Maybe two twenties in San José, but they are old and stiff, some crippled." She paused. "You ask many questions, my son."

Did she suspect the reason? At home her comment would have meant for him to be silent, but this wasn't home. "How many soldiers live in San Francisco Presidio?"

She inhaled loudly through her nose, but continued as before. "Well, I set out the food. I should know. Two twenties, I'd say, at most meals. More or less from time to time. Some were always out on expedition or at the missions." She halted the horse at a river crossing.

He slid off, thinking: *not many,* but they had *fusiles* and long-robe magic. The trail led down a steep cutbank. In both directions the river curved out of sight like a wide green snake slipping into a leafy burrow. Smoke came from the vine-festooned trees on the other side. Normally people would have come to greet them, but *Españoles* were in the world and everything was different.

26

They picked their way down the bank, pebbles splashing into the river from Amarillo's hooves, then swam across. The sand on the other side was still warm, though the sun was in his house. A path led into the dense heart of what seemed a large river island. Still no people appeared. The highest trees were so tall that even Amarillo seemed like a gnat. They walked soundlessly, except for the punk of Amarillo's hooves on spongy soil. Grizzly Hair sensed powerful spirits, like in the mission *iglésia.* Under heavy burdens of vines and berry canes, alders writhed toward the light. However, they would never reach the sun because the oaks and cottonwoods stood more than twice as high. Fragments of sky could be seen at the top, where a crow heralded them. Frogs bellowed and squeaked, mosquitos keened and somewhere a horse whinnied; but no people showed themselves.

"Amigos," he called, feeling the presence of hiding people.

The air was thick with the aroma of roasting meat and the fruity smell of ripe grapes. A clearing opened before them, filled with tule u-machas, each with a supper fire burning beside it, but no people.

Smoke seeped from an earth-covered pit. He looked at the bunches of purple grapes hanging in the trees. Some of their leaves were already bright red among the green. The rampant vines appeared to be strangling the trees, the alders straining at awkward angles under the loads. Many had fallen and died. It seemed everything would eventually collapse under the weight of the vines. Deadfall lay heaped around the village with green tendrils rearing up through it. Many small animals and birds would live here. He looked higher and saw green berry canes growing from the crotch of an oak—growing without earth, so strong was the life spirit. In the earth around the cleared village center roses, nettles, wormwood and many other healthful herbs crowded for space. Everywhere life trod upon life, uncaring what it pulled down—all surging toward father sun. He'd never seen the plant people this strong. Men would need to hack at them constantly to keep the u-machas from being smothered.

"Amigos," he called again, slapping a brace of mosquitos on his chest. His palm was bloody. Baskets of nu-pah steamed beside the fires, but not even dogs appeared.

María pulled on her dress against the mosquitos. "Let's unpack our food, then they'll know we're friendly." She added, "Maybe they think we're neophytes looking for *cimarrones.* This dress will show them I am no neophyte."

Perhaps they were afraid to shoot for fear of becoming *criminales de sangre.* María had said that men called by that name were locked in the Presidio *calabozo* to do the hardest *trabajar* with irons on their legs for the rest of their lives. He stood with his hands out, showing he had no weapon. María unpacked the food. Seeing a basket of cattail-root paste, Grizzly Hair slowly dipped his hand and smoothed it over his chest and arms.

Two dogs came running at them, barking and snarling. Three men, white with paste, stepped from the shadows, bows in hand. María jumped, then laughed nervously and sang out, *"Hola."*

Familiar with the tricks of hiding, Grizzly Hair had expected this. Two of the men wore hide aprons and bones through their topknots. The third wore a long mission shirt but no hip wrap. Their feet were bare and normal-looking, but with paste on their bodies and faces they looked like ghosts.

"¿Qué tal?" asked a man. Shell money hung over his shirt and he wore an astonishing hat—large and blue and three-cornered. Two points stuck out on either side of his head, the third in back. The hat was decorated with gold braid of the same thread that Padre Durán had on his special robe, and a variety of feathers jutted from the top. "My name is Domingo," the man said with stunning hubris. He spoke in Gabriel's tongue. "Where are you going?"

María explained in Spanish, referring to Grizzly Hair as *"mi hijo."*

Three women and many more men stepped from the trees, all painted white, about half in mourning. In addition to singed hair, the women wore black pitch on their heads and faces. But what seized Grizzly Hair's attention was a buckskin-clad man with a big belly, white eyes and a black beard frizzing out in every direction—an astonishing bush the likes of which Grizzly

Hair had never seen on man nor animal. Above the beard sloped a narrow nose that flattened into a shelf at the tip. This strange being wore hide down to the soles of his feet; fringes of it hung from his sleeves. He gripped the tallest *fusil* Grizzly Hair had ever seen. The butt end stood on the ground and the iron tip was level with the short man's floppy brown hat. He was smiling, or so it seemed, through the beard and paste. Perhaps he was a rotund spirit from the land of the immortals.

"Where is your home place?" Domingo asked Grizzly Hair.

"On the northern river."

"Which one?

"Rio de los Cosumne."

Domingo nodded and pointed, indicating Grizzly Hair and María should eat at his fire. Grizzly Hair sat down but couldn't stop looking at the strange man, though in politeness he covered his glances. María also stole looks at the man as she arranged her things at the host's fire. People returned to their fires. The bearded man tended a separate fire, apart from the others.

One of the women gestured for María to follow her with Amarillo. Judging from the whinnies, a horse corral wasn't far away. Grizzly Hair accepted the basket of nu-pah from Domingo's wife, a pleasantly plump woman in mourning who didn't talk.

"Are you Estanislao's people?" Grizzly Hair asked Domingo.

To his surprise Domingo said no. He spoke haltingly, half in Grizzly Hair's tongue, half in Spanish. "The Lakisamni are in the mission now, except Sucais and Quinconul and a few cousin-brothers. Sucais is father of one Estanislao. Which Estanislao do you mean?"

"One who acts as a headman in the mission."

"Ah, Cucunichi. Yes, his father is Sucais. Lives up river." He pointed east. "Half day walk."

Grizzly Hair nodded in thanks. That would be their next stop after the sleep. "Do you know Gabriel?"

Domingo narrowed an eye. "You ask many questions."

"I was only trying to remember where Gabriel's village is. I was visiting him when the black hats captured me. It was the first time I had seen *Españoles.*"

Domingo raised his brows. "The woman is not your *madre* then?"

"No, but she is like a mother to me." Grizzly Hair scooped a fingerload of nu-pah and smacked his lips so all could hear how much he liked it. He realized Domingo was a *cimarrón,* one who must have given thought to the problem of the *Españoles.* But allies had to talk first, to trust each other. Tonguing the oily goodness from the roof of his mouth, he explained, "She brought me medicine when I was sick, after I ran away from the mission. She wants to visit my home place." He paused and glanced at Domingo. "Her son-in-law is a black hat."

Domingo made a hum of wonderment. He lowered his chin to a bucket, scooped, wiped his lips with the back of his hand and remarked, "Maybe she will betray you." He raised his brows. "And us."

"I don't think so. She is an independent old woman. The horse is hers. She makes her own decisions. I trust her." Her songs were good.

Domingo pursed his lips, then pointed a corner of his hat at the women digging in the cooking pit. They were unwrapping huge steaming ribs from tule packages. *Vaca?* Elk? Grizzly Hair couldn't tell.

Domingo selected a rib as long as his arm. "You see the *soldados* ride by today?" He chewed along the rib, which formed a disembodied smile under his wide hat.

"Yes." Grizzly Hair picked up an equally long bone, bit into dark, sweet, loose-grained meat that he still couldn't identify, and explained how cleverly María had disposed of the black hats.

"How many black hats?" Clearly testing.

"Five."

Domingo glanced to the side, maybe speaking without words to his men.

"What meat is this?" Grizzly Hair asked. It was tender and delicious.

"Horse."

Horses were indeed fine animals. María returned and joined the headman's fire. As darkness fell, the flames brightened and she chattered happily of her life and their journey. Everyone except the man in buckskins crowded close to hear her talk. She held them in thrall with her casual mention of Governor Fages and Commander Argüello, and the people in San José. Even Domingo seemed to be more at ease. Her long woolen dress drew the women's glances, and it was clear that all admired her fluent Spanish. Their faces couldn't have been more rapt if she had been an immortal. Grizzly Hair felt pleased to be with her, though most of the Spanish talk rolled past him.

But mostly he looked at the fat man and wondered where he came from.

Domingo told an exciting story of another man's escape from the mission. Two black hats and many neophytes had come searching, but the man had hidden in a cave near Lone Goose's place—far up this river beyond Sucais's place.

Grizzly Hair looked at Domingo. "Will you keep hiding, next time and next time?"

Domingo smiled and bobbed his hat. "And next time."

"Maybe there is another way."

Smile fading, Domingo handed his cleaned rib to a waiting dog. "What do you mean?"

Realizing he shouldn't talk straight—Domingo's people might return to Padre Durán—he spoke obliquely. "Remember how Coyote hurled hot rocks at the Giant Ké-lok?"

At this mention of the giant bird who lived at the dawn of the earth, Domingo laughed. Then, he looked knowingly at Grizzly Hair and said,

"Coyote killed Ké-lok." His emphasis on Coyote implied that humans couldn't have hit the exact place under the white spot on the giant's arm, which was the only spot where the giant could be killed. Coyote's magic had done it. Mere men were not powerful enough.

"And do not forget," Domingo continued, "Ké-lok's fire jumped up and grew big the moment he died. It got bigger and hotter until it burned up the world." In the flickering firelight his broad face and out-turned hands expressed the enormity of the devastation, the strange hat somehow adding to it. "All men would have died." He lowered his hands and sat staring at the flames.

Grizzly Hair reflected on Domingo's fear of reprisals, for that was his fear too. But he knew that someday they would talk straight. In the meantime he appreciated that this man from another people seemed to understand the need for indirectness.

María, who had brought the blankets from Amarillo's packs, dropped Grizzly Hair's near him and took hers into the u-macha of Domingo's wife. Most of the people went to their sleeping mats, but some stayed to talk.

This village was similar to Gabriel's—mostly men without women. Some of their children were in Mission San José, others in Mission Santa Clara, and many of the women had died. Most had spoken different tongues until they learned Spanish. One man called his village Tamcan, a place near the base of Oó-yum-bé-le, his term for the Spirit Peak. Another man came from a big village called Saclan, beyond the peak and closer to the eastern shore of the bay. That village was deserted now, but at one time many twenties of people had lived there. Recently an *Español* had built a house nearby and herded longhorns on the Saclan-umne's old hunting grounds. Domingo's mother had come from the river of the Cosumne and that's how Domingo knew the northern tongue. His family had gone to the mission quite a long time ago, and his mother had died there.

The fat man was a different sort altogether. He was ramming a cloth-covered stick down the barrel of his *fusil.* "He is an *Americano* trader," Domingo said, following Grizzly Hair's glance. Domingo pulled a knife from his calf-thong and politely extended it on the palm of his hand. "I traded it for beaver skins."

Grizzly Hair felt the honed metal and the antler haft, which seemed to be secured without visible glue. It was the best knife he'd ever seen. Nodding appreciatively, he handed it back. "Is the *Americano* a worthy trader?"

Domingo dipped his hat. "*Sí.* Esteemed. He does not want the *Españoles* to know he is in the Valley of the Sun."

"Is he their enemy?"

"I think so."

"I will talk with him," Grizzly Hair got to his feet and went to the fat man's dying fire. Taking a branch from the fuel pile, he laid it on the fire, signaling that he wished to talk. Shreds of another strange meat emitted a sweetish odor from a flat iron pan, which lay smoking on the coals.

Lying on his side with his head propped on an elbow, the *Americano* removed his floppy hat, scratched his scalp until the hair stood on end, then pointed with the hat opposite him, indicating Grizzly Hair should sit there. He returned the hat to his head and stared impolitely. With firelight under the hat brim, his nose seemed extra long and his eyes horribly white, except for the small black pupils. Taking a breath, Grizzly Hair sat down and folded his legs.

The *Americano* slapped the buckskin on his chest, the fringe on his sleeve flying, and said loudly, "Missouri." He pointed at Grizzly Hair. "Your *nombre?*"

Understanding the request to speak his name, he dodged the question. *"No comprendo Español bueno."*

Missouri grinned broadly, but it didn't soften the terrible eyes. *"No comprendo Español bueno either. Comprendo?"* He talked loud and smiled so hard the wrinkles cracked the paste around his eyes. Dark wavy hair grew down the sides of his face and joined the bushy beard. With difficulty, given the size of his belly, he raised up to a sitting position, leaned across the small fire and surprised Grizzly Hair by poking him in the chest. Quickly withdrawing his hand, he demanded loudly. *"Nombre, muchacho."*

Men watched slyly from the other fire, hearing him called a boy and asked to speak his name. He answered, "Mi-wo." Person.

"Mewuk," repeated the fat man, falling heavily back on his elbows. "Mewuk."

Grizzly Hair recalled his Spanish name, a name that didn't feel like his. Even so he couldn't bring himself to say it much above a whisper. "Juan."

Missouri wrinkled his nose like he'd smelled something bad. The paste cracked in new places. "Mewuk," he insisted loudly, his smile falling back into its accustomed cracks.

Wanting to move beyond names, Grizzly Hair pointed to the antler haft protruding from a *cuero* sheath in the man's belt.

"Skinning knife," Missouri boomed. He flopped to a hip and struggled to retrieve the knife. *"Two hundred beaver skins,"* he shouted, perhaps believing extra volume would compensate for the problem of tongues. He handed the haft to Grizzly Hair, and he examined the fine tool.

Missouri drew a beaver in the dirt. Then he drew many, many lines in neat rows, possibly to show how many beaver skins. At last he circled the lines and pointed at the circle. Then he drew another circle beside it and said *"Comprendo? One hundred beaver."* He leaned back on his elbows and smiled.

Grizzly Hair started counting the lines, but a man at Domingo's fire said over his shoulder, *"Cien* means five twenties." That seemed a good bargain for such a valuable knife.

"Comprendo," Grizzly Hair said, handing it back. He wished he knew how

to say, "Maybe you would like to come and trade with my people too." Instead he said, *"Donde está su gente? Americanos? Familia?"*

Missouri pointed toward the eastern mountains and said, *"Family and Americanos over las montañas."*

Did he mean on the other side? No one crossed those treacherous mountains. He asked, *"Donde pasa?"* Where had he crossed? He pointed northeast, then east, then southeast, each time looking him the question.

With a huge grin, Missouri pointed north.

Was he teasing? He said he'd come from the east.

"Over the montañas in the north, from the Columbia River."

Grizzly Hair didn't understand. *"La familia?"* He pointed east.

"Sí. Family that way. Americanos there." He pointed east.

Had he come from the east, in the north, then come south over those mountains? *"Muchos Españoles?"* He pointed north.

"No Españoles in the north." Missouri kept smiling.

Grizzly Hair pointed east. *"Españoles?"*

Missouri thought, then said, *"No mucho."* Not many.

"Mucho Americanos?" He pointed north.

"No. Frenchmen and Englishmen, mostly. Besides Indians." He chuckled. *"No mucho Americanos."* He flashed all his fingers.

Grizzly Hair pointed east again and asked, *"Mucho Americanos?"*

"Oh sí, mucho, MUCHO *Americanos."*

"Cien?" He pointed at the circled lines.

Missouri threw back his head and laughed so hard his hat fell off. When he regained his composure he said, *"Thousands and thousands."* Seeing what must have been a blank look, he said very slowly and loudly, *"Comprendo, mil-ion?"*

Mil was very many. But it didn't matter exactly how many; the important thing was that Missouri's many people lived on the other side of the eastern mountains, but few *Españoles* did. He imagined villages teeming with short fat men in fringed buckskin, and fat women and children in buckskin. He pointed at the long gun lying beside the man. *"Todos Americanos tienen fusiles?"*

Missouri shrugged as if he didn't understand, then suddenly came alert and said in a halting way, *"Sí. Americanos have guns."* The white eyes smiled.

Americanos all had *fusiles.* Something new opened in his mind, as when the foliage is swept back on a vista. "We trade," he said mostly in sign language. *"Yo quiero . . ."* he pointed at the knife in Missouri's belt. He also wanted a *fusil* but decided to wait; men he didn't know were listening. But trading partners were friends and friends were allies. He didn't know what the future held but it couldn't hurt to have powerful friends.

"Bueno," said Missouri, grunting as he rolled to his knees, then hopped to an upright position. With his boot he rubbed out the parallel lines then picked

up a long stick and drew a wiggly line. "San Joaquin," he said. The line went south-north, the way of the river.

He drew another wiggly line running east-west, connecting it with the San Joaquin. "Rio Lakisamni," he said, pointing to this river. Where it ended in the east, he shoved a pile of dirt with the side of his boot. *"Las montañas."* He grinned.

Grizzly Hair was glad to see that earth pictures were used by *Americanos,* and it was good to know that *Americanos* existed in the world—potential enemies of the *Españoles.* Friendly to *Indios.* Missouri placed the stick in Grizzly Hair's hand and signed for him to draw. *"Your family,"* he said pointing at the dirt. *"¿Donde?"* Where.

As Grizzly Hair squatted to his task, Missouri signaled he would be back, and left. With surprising speed he returned with a roll of cloth and a *cuero* bag. The cloth was fine and white, like the material beneath the padres' robes. With clever moves Missouri made him understand that an arm's length of it could be had for ten beaver skins. From the bag he took tiny blue and red beads, the most valuable colors, and held up five fingers. Five skins each.

"Bueno," Grizzly Hair said, feeling lucky to be arranging trade with a man of marvelous goods and gun-bearing friends. He drew the route to the umne, and as Missouri studied it, hoped the trader's visit would help smooth his homecoming.

"I come in ten days. Comprendo?" Missouri held up ten fingers. Ten sleeps.

27

In first light the singing birds almost overpowered the snarl and wheeze emanating from Missouri's blankets. Getting an early start, Grizzly Hair and María bathed and carried their blankets to the brush corral. Dew sat heavy on the grass, a sign of the changing season. They rode up a well-traveled trail heading east. She said over her shoulder, "What did the *Americano* say?"

"He is a trader, wants to trade for beaver."

She twisted around and said in an admonishing tone, *"Indios* must not trade with *Americanos."*

"Why not?"

"The commanders get very angry about it. *Americanos* are not allowed in California. Neither are the Russians. No trade is allowed. I know Domingo's people did it, but that will make the soldiers even angrier at them." The worst of the bad *cimarrones* steal horses from the missions. People say they trade them to *Americanos* who come over the southern mountains. When those *cimarrones* are caught, they are whipped very long." She turned forward.

He nearly pointed out that the black hats wouldn't know if the umne traded with *Americanos*, but thought better of it. Her son-in-law was a black hat. Her presence made things complicated. This was something he'd have to think about. Should he and the home men meet Missouri some distance from the village?

For some time the land had been lifting into hills. They took the narrow, traveled footpath angling down a steep bank toward the river bottom, branches brushing the sides of the horses.

Five men came up the trail. The leader, an older man wearing nothing but his loose skin raised a hand in greeting. His eyes had the look of a man already partway in the happy land—distant and calm. No gray marred the heavy black hair that hung well past his shoulders. This would be Sucais.

Grizzly Hair slid off the horse and spoke the traditional greeting in his own tongue, "Where are you going?"

Answering in the same tongue, heavily accented, Sucais said, "I live here. We come to greet friends of Domingo." A stealthy runner had preceded them. "Where are you going?"

"I'd like to tell my story." The home tongue made him feel like a simple runner again. Sucais motioned and they all followed to the village center—ten or twelve pine u-machas of the type Grizzly Hair hadn't seen since leaving home. After María unpacked the meat and one of the men took Amarillo to a corral, they sat in a circle and exchanged niceties about the warm weather while María sliced her dried meat for each of the men. They accepted appreciatively. Grizzly Hair told how he'd been captured and had run away from the mission, not mentioning *her* death or Estanislao's offer to help.

Sucais listened with the quiet dignity of a man of knowledge. At the end of the story he ducked into his u-macha and returned with tobacco, which he stuffed into a small tulare-stem pipe. With the glowing end of a stick from a banked fire, he sucked and blew until the pipe was lit, and offered it to Grizzly Hair.

In politeness, he accepted, though tobacco made him sleepy and he needed to travel before sundown. Inhaling lightly, he passed it on. When María got up and seemed to be seeking a suitable bush, Grizzly Hair delivered his message. "Estanislao greets you at this acorn time and wants you to know the Spanish have lost a war in their southern land. He also says the fleas will soon jump off the wolf."

Sucais raised his brows and turned to his men. They spoke quietly in their own tongue, then the old man said, "A friend of my son is a friend of mine. My home place is yours." Calm music eminated from him.

"Has Estanislao ever run away from the mission?"

Sucais said proudly, "My son does not run or hide. The long robes give him *paseo*." Seeing the question, he asked, "You know what a *paseo* is?" At Grizzly Hair's shake of the head he explained, "*Papel* that talks with marks. It says my son can bring his wife and mother home to visit." Proudly he added, "My son is a friend of Padre Durán."

That was true. He helped whip people. The contradictions intrigued Grizzly Hair. Why was Estanislao's father in his home place when his son was in the mission? The old man intrigued him too and he knew straight talk was the only path. "Your son offered to help me escape," he said.

Sucais shifted and straightened one of his legs. He leaned toward his men and talked in their tongue. Smiles played at their lips and their eyes snapped. Sucais, who had received the pipe back, sucked on it and from his protruded lips blew discreet puffs of smoke. "My son's other name is Cucunichi," he said.

"What does it mean?"

"He who will be headman." He sat in his pride looking through the trees.

In a way, Estanislao already was a headman in the mission, to the *Indios.*

Returning, María asked, "Where are your women?"

"In the mission," said Quinconul.

"Were they captured?" Grizzly Hair asked.

"No. Cucunichi took them when he went to learn the ways of the *Españoles.* All our people went with him, except us. They offered themselves to the magic water that the long robes put on their heads."

This was courageous, Grizzly Hair reflected, and it also showed his influence over them. Yet some of the elders had stayed. More than ever he wished to talk freely with Estanislao. Did Padre Durán treat him like a friend because he had gone willingly to the mission? Did other *Indios* have *paseos?* "Someday," he said to Sucais. "I will come here and talk with your son."

Sucais nodded. "Come when he is on *paseo.*" He sucked on his pipe and blew smoke. "But your river is far."

"I am a runner. I will come." He glanced at his dignified host. "Will you and your men go to the mission?"

"No. This is our home place." Sucais glanced at his men, and their respect for him showed in the way they kept their eyes distant. Cucunichi had learned from his father.

Grizzly Hair wished to learn from him too. Someday he would. He explained that he and María needed to travel far while there was light.

With an understanding nod, Sucais said, "Come with me." Handing the pipe to his brother, he rose slowly to his feet, knees cracking, and showed Grizzly Hair and María the best place to ford the river. Then he led them through the trees to a corral of about ten horses of different colors. He untied the grape vines at the entrance and while María led Amarillo out, approached a brown horse with a rope around her lower jaw and petted and talked to her. Then he led the horse through the opening and gave the reins to Grizzly Hair while he secured the vines.

Grizzly Hair tried to give her back, but Sucais refused. "You are a friend of

Cucunichi," he said. "Morena will help you visit us. She is a strong runner." He stroked the horse's neck.

Stunned speechless, Grizzly Hair looked the man his deepest thanks. Estanislao had offered him freedom and now his father was giving him something almost as wonderful. The horse looked gentle, and it struck him as fantastic that any man had it in his power to make a gift of a big animal.

"Morena means Brown Girl," Sucais said. "She will teach you to ride." Gently he stroked her nose with the backs of two fingers. Morena blinked and seemed pleased. Then Sucais turned and walked away. María displayed open-mouthed wonder.

Still overwhelmed, Grizzly Hair called after Sucais, "I will come and visit."

The round rope around Morena's jaw was plaited in an intricate pattern from many strands taken from the tails of different colored horses—black, red-brown, tan and white. He put a leg over and hiked himself upright on the horse's back, unable to stop a boyish grin.

"Now you look like an *hombre,*" María joked. "On a stolen horse."

It was all the sweeter that the black hats didn't want *Indios* to have horses. It took a while to remember how to guide a horse, but Morena followed Amarillo with a calm demeanor, swam the river and allowed him to mount again. As the horses walked north on a traveled trail, she never took advantage of his ignorance. This gave him the leisure to think back on his visits with Domingo, Missouri and Sucais. Sucais hadn't revealed the meaning of fleas and wolf in the strange message, and in deference to his dignity Grizzly Hair hadn't asked. The fact that Sucais and Domingo were friends elevated Domingo in Grizzly Hair's estimation. Missouri excited him. A powerful network of allies might yet be possible, especially now that Grizzly Hair was a runner with four legs. Morena and Amarillo would help smooth his homecoming too, for none of the home people had ever seen a horse. They would be in awe.

The grassland stretched as far through the rolling hills as he could see. At this elevation gray pines stood among the oaks. These were the friendly pines of home, bushed out above long naked trunks. They brought health, purity and large juicy pine nuts. The sight of them leaning at jaunty angles above the oaks quickened his desire to see the umne, yet made him anxious about going home.

Father sun lingered long in the sky during this season, giving them plenty of time to travel before dark. Without talk they both knew they would eventually come to water. Everyone knew that many streams flowed out of the eastern mountains on their way to join the big north-south rivers. However, the smaller streams were dry in this season.

At twilight they arrived at a live stream and village. Again the u-machas were wooden cones. In other ways the village resembled Grizzly Hair's. Women were as numerous as men and many children watched their approach. Nobody ran to hide. Their talk sounded almost the same as the umne and no one spoke Spanish. They welcomed María and Grizzly Hair with great excitement about the horses.

The headman said, "Dance the Grasshopper with us tonight."

María clapped her hands together. "Oh, yes! Are you are having a grasshopper roundup after the sleep too?"

"We are, and you are welcome to join us." His woman smiled and added, "The more hands, the better."

Rubbing her hands together under her chin, María tilted her head at Grizzly Hair. "*Por favor,* let's stay and grasshopper with them after the sleep."

He reminded her gently, "If we rode all day instead, we'd get to my home place by dark."

"But grasshoppers!" Her sparkly glee defeated him. She had hoped to find a big time and hadn't complained about traveling the way he wanted to go, though another way would have taken them through her home place. Besides, the grasshoppers had seemed plentiful leaping out of the horses' way. So he agreed to stay. And the more he thought about it, the more he was glad to have another day to get ready to face the umne.

They ate with their hosts and danced in the roundhouse. Afterwards Grizzly Hair sat with María against an oak on a hill overlooking the valley. In the dark three distant grass fires flickered like bright orange caterpillars, two in the southwest, one in the northwest, all burning at the same angle. He knew they were racing through the sere grasses too fast to harm the oaks, but from this distance the bright fire-lines appeared stationary.

"*Bonita,*" María said.

"Yes, pretty. Did your people burn the grass?"

"Of course. All peoples did. My friends and I loved running over the scorched ground as soon as we could stand it, finding toasted hoppers." She cackled in her appealing way.

The umne had set fires to burn off the chaff and hasten the sprouting of First Grass after the rains. The deer and other grazers put on flesh sooner. Women claimed the burned areas brought a richer bounty of seeds. From his earliest memories a smokey haze had heralded the time of rain. He realized now that the smoke hadn't been only from the fires of the umne. "This whole land is a garden, *jardín,*" he said, opening his arms. He had learned the word from her.

She was silent, then said, "You are right. Many good things grow here. We work harder in the pueblo than you gentiles, but it seems to me we have less to eat."

He made a skeptical sound in the side of his mouth, recalling the abundance of cows and horses and greens.

"We have fewer kinds of food, and not enough help getting it. My granddaughters will not gather. They say that's for poor *Indias.* They don't help much with the gardens either, and the boys ride all day. Lazy as *cholos.* So I work hard. Somebody must. In my old home place everyone helped, like at the grasshopper roundups. Women and girls gathered roots together. People shared food too."

"What are *cholos?*"

"Bad men, drunk, trouble makers."

"What is drunk?"

"Ay, ay," she said, "you are *inocente.*" She patted him affectionately on the knee. "*Aguardiente* and *vino* make people drunk and crazy."

Anyone could have told her that rotten food and drink would bring bad luck. His thoughts returned to the season's delicacy. "Did your people form a big circle and beat grasshoppers into the center?"

"Yes, and sometimes we dug a big shallow pit and lined it with dry grass and herded the grasshoppers in and lit a fire to roast them. Did you?"

"Both ways." He remembered himself and Bowstring and Falls-off-House gleefully herding masses of hoppers. Rough feet stuck to his face, hair, arms and chest—every part of him—while the tobacco smell of the brown spittle was in his nose. Grown people stood behind the children beating back the escapees. Mostly he remembered the big time mood and his mother as she was then. "Children like being useful to their parents," he said, recalling how he'd loved helping her stuff her basket full of grasshoppers.

"Hah!" María barked, still looking at the fires, "We girls loved grasshoppering because the boys and men were there." She cackled fondly. "It was the only time they helped us gather." She paused. "You should see it when clouds of grasshoppers come to the pueblo." Suddenly she laughed harder and louder and her talk spurted through the laughter. "You can hear them chew, hear them from far away. There are so many. All chewing! They must smack their lips to make such. . . Ay!" Overwhelmed by laughter she tipped over on the ground holding her belly, trying to say more but writhing in pained silence. She finally got it out, "They laugh at us!" and went into a new fit.

He chuckled politely with her, but couldn't imagine why there were so many grasshoppers. He'd never seen anything like that.

"They look at us with those big eyes knowing we won't stop them," she laughed. "They say, 'You ate us. Now we eat your food.'" She wiped her hand across her eyes. "They have grasshopper big times." She burst into a new gale of laughter.

"Sounds like you should have a roast," he said when she slowed down. "You'd have grasshopper balls to last many seasons."

The cackling sputtered and died and she sat up, wiping tears from her face. "*Españoles* don't eat grasshoppers, and the *Comisionador* punishes anyone who sets fires. Many strokes of the *cuarta*. Fires burn the fences and scare the horses and cows, and those longhorns are hard to catch."

That was true. "Maybe some day," he said, "we'll all live like you people in the pueblo."

"Then you will work harder and eat the same thing every day.

He chuckled. "You are joking."

"No. I've thought about this. When you have cattle and horses, all the food plants grow inside fences, and you have nothing if the fence breaks. Except meat. Horses and cows lean hard on the fences and break them down so they have to be fixed. And besides that we're always spinning wool or making clothes or washing them." She paused. "Worms eat holes in them. We have to keep making new things. And we carry water instead of having it come to us. We plant seeds from Mexico and don't have the variety of greens and bulbs that grow here. I've tried to save wild seeds but they won't grow. I don't know why. We eat only three or four kinds of greens." She turned to him. "Only two kinds of bulbs."

He recalled the big onion rings in the mission stew, much bigger than home onions—the only kind of bulb he'd encountered in the mission. At home the umne ate more than twenty kinds of bulbs. His mother had counted once. The thought of the special bulbs she dug from her secret place made him salivate. But as he watched the distant fires and María prattled on about cooking and how the *Españoles* never ate moss or lichens or grubs and how much she looked forward to the food in his home place, his thoughts jumped like a spark to his mental trail.

He asked, "What was the name of the *Español* who lived in caves and fought the invaders? Earlier she had spoken of this much-storied ancestor of the black hats.

The gray of her hair streaked pale in the night as she rested her elbows on her knees, chin in hands, watching the fires. "El Cid?"

Yes. That's it. El Cid and his men had ridden from their hideaways and made attacks on strangers who had settled in their land. María had heard the story from her son-in-law. "Maybe it is a little like the grasshoppers," he said. "The *Moros* invaded the land of the *Españoles*, and now the *Españoles* do the same to us *Indios*." Us, he was learning to say.

She glanced at him, then looked back at the fires. "All I know is they were not Christian and they lived there a long time. But El Cid carried the cross. He defeated them for God and Jesús and María."

Earlier she had said they fought all their lives, as did their sons and grandsons and great-grandsons after them. When they finally drove the invaders back across a sea, everyone held the fighters in high esteem, especially El Cid. He was honored even now in this distant time and place.

Among the umne it was the opposite. People of quiet spiritual power were honored. People who argued and fought and caused disturbances were shunned, because their actions revealed a lack of power and invited bad luck.

They behaved like children. He couldn't think of a single story in which a person who physically attacked others was honored for it. Skilled arrow dodgers were honored, but not those whose arguments and skirmishes had caused the wars in the first place. They were best forgotten. This would, he knew, make it difficult to convince men to fight the black hats.

With a happy groan María lowered herself to the soft leaf debris under the oak and wiggled to get comfortable. The dance had tired her, and no blanket was needed on this warm night. He would let her sleep then wake her after a while, but for now he was enjoying the distant flames—streaks of excitement in the dark. By a nearby tree he could measure that the fires had crawled northward. As he watched he thought how he would tell the umne about the *Españoles.* It seemed he had a lifetime of stories to tell, assuming he wasn't driven out or killed by Red Sun and Running Quail.

He let out a woosh of air. First there would be a long time-of-pretending, during which they would become more and more agitated not seeing Bowstring and *her*. He had to hope Red Sun's sense of decorum would forestall his anger long enough to hear María explain that many young people died in the missions and what had happened wasn't Grizzly Hair's fault. But of course it was.

Then, if they didn't kill him, he would start with the wild horses they had seen, and Gabriel. He would let the umne ride Morena and tell them about the black hats who rode horses like dream-men—part horse, part man. He would ask María to tell about her grandson, Pedro, who had pulled the bird with a greased neck from the dirt.

Then he would tell about the mission. The familiar ache returned to his stomach. He stared at the bright orange lines and listened to a distant wolf. The breeze moved lightly over his skin, bringing the familiar scent of the sticky-yellow—late bloomers of the long dry, another sign of the season. Women of the home place would be adding those good black seeds to the crunchy flatbread. Being so near the home place stirred a great restlessness in him. It made his mind race like the grass fires. Learn what is real in the world, Drum-in-Fog had told him.

He would tell them that a presidio and mission were planned in the Valley of the Sun to help the black hats lure and capture people. A fire kicked up in his mind. It crackled and smoked in anguish for Oak Gall. It raged at the memory of the *cuarta*, the stinking *calabozo*, men in traps and irons, unburned dead people stacked in the dirt, bones heaped in the little house, Oak Gall's to be dumped there if he didn't go back for them. It roared like an angry bear at the thought of fighting the black hats and chasing them back to where they'd come from. It consumed him while María lay dreaming of grasshoppers.

28

Acquainted with every tree and bush and every root across the trail, Grizzly Hair leaned into Morena's mane and galloped to the top of the last hill. He pulled her to a stop, and as she blew and yawned, trying to work the rope from her mouth, he examined the deserted playing field below. Morning Owl had told the umne to hide if they saw men on the backs of animals. Someone must have seen them; the people were probably hiding half a bowshot to his right, in Hill Boulders—upthrust rocks surrounded by buckeye trees whose leaves had already turned crisp and brown.

They would be watching for Oak Gall and Bowstring, and would be worried after seeing his singed hair. Except for that, he might have felt like one of the mythical beings who in First World darted effortlessly around the sky. But he was changed; the joy he wanted to feel wasn't there. Instead, the ache sharpened. He was in the familiar place where *she* would never be again.

María stopped Amarillo beside him. He opened an arm to the vista below and said in a voice loud enough to be heard in Hill Boulders, "This is my home place." By now they would be alarmed about *her* and Bowstring, and wonder about the old woman.

"I don't see anyone," she said.

"They're afraid of the horses." He dismounted and led Morena down the hill. María followed atop Amarillo. Everyone would think the worst, and the worst was true. How long would the time-of-pretending last? He had no idea. No one had ever been gone this long.

They hobbled the horses to graze in a place still green near Berry Creek, then crossed the dry scummy pebbles of the streambed to the deserted village center. The supper fires weren't lit. His tracker's eyes knew immediately that there had been no trouble, no struggle. The sight of cooking stones piled neatly at each banked fire and the scent of the umne in the warm air brought tears to his eyes.

"Your place is pretty," María said gazing at the dancehouse, the steadfast u-machas and cha'kas, and the gentle land sloping down to the river.

Pretty. Was that the word for his soul's home—a place as intimate as his own hands? He caught the scent of river and willow, the scent of a lifetime of mornings and evenings and hot afternoons, of sand and wet stones and bubbly green-brown moss. But now that scent collided with hurtful pangs in his stomach—sorrow that *she* would not be here, impatience to see his mother and the umne, fear of Red Sun's anger and the uncomfortable sense of being a man apart from his own people.

"I thought the trees were bigger," he said at last, "and the river." After Domingo's place everything seemed small. Still, his spirit liked its home place. He could feel it resting as he stretched out where the soft mound tapered to near level at the side of the dancehouse. Sometimes this spot gave him power. "See that oak?" he said to María, pointing up at the tree on top of the mound. "Grandmother planted it." The big strong limbs sheltered the village.

"Do your people plant oak trees?"

"No." He smiled at the absurd thought. Squirrels and wing people did that. "When she was a little girl she played with an acorn, and later noticed it sprouting."

"In the pueblo some people plant oak trees on the graves of their dead."

He let the silence come. The ashes of his people's ancestors lay beneath him. Would he add Oak Gall's remains? Power wasn't coming. He rolled to his side and stood up. "I need to bathe," he told María. He went to his mother's u-macha. Among the baskets and neatly wound skeins of herbs hanging from the overhead cordage, he took two vulture feather tassels and on the way to the bathing place handed one to María. The things his mother had made deepened his sense of being home.

In the turbulence where the two streams plaited after tumbling over the rocky falls on either side of the island, he swam vigorously against the current. Then he and María lolled in the quieter water closer to shore. Downstream father sun played over the water as it surged westward into the trees, the patterns of the ripples always changing. People began to appear above the rise of the bank. First Morning Owl, then Howchia, then Nettles and Red Sun and Etumu, Running Quail and Hummingbird Tailfeather, Lame Beaver, Falls-off-House, Two Falcons and Pretty Duck and Sick Rat, Yellow Jacket, Sunshine-through-the-Mist, Drum-in-Fog, and the many others. Without speaking they returned to their tasks of fletching arrows, chewing skins or building fires, all without seeming to notice them treading in the river. Only two young children came to the bank and looked, until their mothers took them by the hand and led them away. Grizzly Hair was supposed to feel invisible, but it seemed the umne, though acutely familiar, were the unreal ones. They hadn't seen the realities of the world. They didn't know what he knew. Maybe migrating geese had that feeling when they looked at the jays and egrets, who lived their entire lives at the home place.

He swam to shore, María following, and they tasseled off. He kept his eyes straight ahead as he walked past the u-machas, past the fires where women chatted back and forth as though he were not between them. He went into Howchia's house and sat, María beside him, on his old sleeping mat. Waiting. She had apparently decided to stay with him during the time-of-pretending, and he was glad she didn't chatter. She seemed to respect his need to stay tight within the little power he had.

"I think people," Coyote interrupts with a wry twist of his snout, "ought to just run up and sniff each other's behinds."

Bear normally disagrees with Coyote, but in this instance nods her large head. "Your time-of-pretending made things awkward."

I cannot respond, so strongly does memory grip me. I see myself starting the supper fire and going into the u-macha, the scent of my son filling me with so much joy that I could hardly contain it. I reached above his mat where he sat staring politely through me, and untied a basket. Then I sat on my mat opposite them and, as if alone, sorted the goose feathers that I had piled there before the herald gave the message to hide. But I didn't need to look at my son for his presence to fill my empty places.

I stayed there a long time. The light from the smokehole and entryway dimmed and I couldn't see the feathers well. I knew the cooking rocks would be hot. Outside, people tried not to look at me too long—Red Sun, Nettles, Running Quail and Hummingbird Tailfeather. Did they wonder if I had broken tradition and talked to my son? Did they think I knew why their children had not returned? Glad that our ways allowed me to enjoy my son's return without upset from other people, I pretended not to notice. He was returning naturally to us, in the fullness of time.

At the other fires people ate in silence. My mother felt her way to her accustomed place and slurped her supper, and though she wouldn't have said a word, it took strength not to tell her that Grizzly Hair was in the u-macha. It took strength to carry the remains of the nu-pah and venison down into the u-macha and set it on the floor and leave without looking at those who sat there. After banking the fire I returned to my mat, happy to hear the sounds of eating, but I could not sleep in the presence of my son without continually waking up. I sensed that he and the old woman, whom I would later know as María, lay awake too. Not of the umne, she could have spoken to me but never said a word. I thought it just as well, for it would have made the wait harder.

After the sleep we continued pretending. Grizzly Hair and María went out and looked around the village, but no one appeared to notice. Love for my son warmed me and I was proud of his good behavior. Later in the day they returned to the u-macha when I was sorting the feathers—white down, black down, neck-ring down, small grey feathers, pin and wing feathers—and began folding the tips of the quills over my netting, clicking them into the cut slots. Some of our costumes had been damaged by insects and this cape was needed before the next dance. The light from the smokehole and doorway shifted too slowly but at last the u-macha darkened again. I decided enough time had passed. Quick as a minnow I glanced at Grizzly Hair—low nose tucked between generous brows, hair only a shadow on his bony head, shoulders sharp and wide, stomach nearly concave. He wore a string of spectacular beads around his neck, the same as around the old woman's neck. Across his eyes I detected a twitch of emotion. Regaining my calm, I sat staring at nothing.

He waited, then glanced quickly into my eyes. I shoved the feathers and netting aside and stood absorbing his presence, looking at him as much as any polite mother would. We were now together in our u-macha as we had been before his departure. Things had returned to normal.

His legs tensed as he slowly straightened under the sloping ceiling. He stepped to the center where he could stand erect. I went to him and touched his thin shoulders. He grasped my shoulders too and we stood like that, I marveling that so fine a young man had come from me. In the light from the smokehole, moisture glistened in his eyes and sadness twisted his smile. He pulled me gently to his chest where I felt the rise and fall of his breathing and his long, tentative arms around me. I pulled him to me with more firmness—I wouldn't dwell so long on it now except that it was our first embrace since he was a boy and our last in this world. He felt even thinner in my arms than in my eyes and, behind him, I ran my hands over the raised lumps and scabs on his back. In my spirit wandering I had seen this done to him. I reflected that the time of caring for him had seemed far too brief. When he was young I had healed the cuts and sores of his body, but now I couldn't heal his spirit.

María stood up and joined us, a threesome smiling at each other. "Son, you are rich," I said, touching the round clear beads.

"A gift of the padres," he said.

María explained that she hoped to stay and dance with us. Her wrinkled chin was grotesquely untattooed, and her smile folded her upper lip nearly to her nose. Children on all fours peered into the house like curious puppies, the feet of men and women not far behind.

"Our house is your house," I said to this grandmother who had saved my son's life. "Soon we will dance First Salmon and you will dance with us." I turned to him. "Son, you ride animals!"

"You must all come and see the horses," he said loud enough for all the umne to hear. He ducked through the entrance and walked among the people, who stared at the beads and the scabs on his back, and he saw the voids where Oak Gall and Bowstring should have been. As he walked across the dry creek toward the horses, it felt as though a boulder sat on the back of his neck.

Red Sun stepped before him blocking his way, his mouth a hard line. Nettles stood at her man's side with little Etumu, whose admiration for her big sister had known no bounds. Now it would come. Facing them but looking politely at the western hill, he said the words that had haunted him for so long. "Her heart is no longer with us."

Red Sun's face registered shock and horror, then anger and suspicion. "Then where are her remains?" Air rushed out his nose.

"At the mission. She was sick. I couldn't save her. They wouldn't let me take the body, but I'll go back for it someday."

Red Sun whirled and strode away, nearly colliding with Nettles, who looked like a woman rudely awakened from sleep. She walked after her man, and Etumu trailed sadly behind.

He wished his own heart were gone instead. Bowstring's parents and their son Lame Beaver looked as though they'd been struck in the face. Everyone stood staring into the distance or shaking their heads, Drum-in-Fog apart from the others. He had once told Grizzly Hair that malcontents who travel around all the time find only discontent. Two Falcons was the only one who, when their glances crossed, seemed to take some of Grizzly Hair's pain into himself.

Running Quail, a burly-chested man with no neck, stepped toward Grizzly Hair. Hummingbird Tailfeather joined him, the flesh on her arms and belly quivering. Lame Beaver stood to the side. The three were visibly afraid of what he would say.

"Your son is healthy. I couldn't make him come. He married a woman at the mission."

Hummingbird Tailfeather's fist went to her teeth and her eyes opened with joy. "When will he bring her home?"

"They want to stay at the mission."

The three looked stunned. Not far behind them, María was lifting a child to Amarillo's back but she too was watching and listening, as did everyone except the youngest children. Dangerously close to Morena's hooves, the children touched her legs with shy fingertips and looked their happy astonishment at one another.

"His woman insisted he stay at the mission." He started toward the children.

"A woman lives with her man," Running Quail nearly shouted through clenched teeth. "In the home place of her man's people." Blame burned in their eyes, just as he had known it would.

"The *Españoles* don't let people leave the mission," he said over his shoulder, moving the children from the horse's legs. "Bowstring's wife wanted him to stay so he wouldn't be beaten like this." He turned his back to them.

Hummingbird Tailfeather cried, "You took him from us! Go back and bring him home. His woman too."

"I couldn't make him come with me."

Running Quail raised his big head on his neckless shoulders and his cheeks shook with anger as he loudly announced: "My son is dead." He strode away, his woman waddling after him. They would not speak his name again except at a Cry. Lame Beaver closed his eyes.

Grizzly Hair felt like a stranger. People looked at him with indecipherable expressions, but they also watched María as she led Amarillo around the field with three laughing girls on his back.

Morning Owl broke the tension. "I want to ride on your horse," he said to Grizzly Hair. People bobbed their heads. "Yes," they said. And, "Me too."

Grizzly Hair nodded. "I would be honored if our esteemed hy-apo would ride my horse. Afterwards you can all ride." He motioned the children to stand back, unknotted the reins and gave them to the headman. To María, when she passed by with the children, he whispered, "Elders ride first."

She drew her chin into her shoulders scrunching her face into a mass of apologetic wrinkles, then reached up and removed the crestfallen girls. Grizzly Hair gestured to Two Falcons, and the master hunter went smiling to Amarillo.

Morning Owl, after patting Morena, hoisted himself across her back then pulled himself upright. He looked over his people like a proud ram on a high rock. His teeth blazed in white rows and the grin didn't fade as he ran a hand across her shoulders and turned and laid his palm on her brown rump as it rose and fell with her walk. A little dazed by what had occurred and not sure it was finished, Grizzly Hair led Morena around behind Amarillo, the umne closing in after the horses left and stepping back as they approached.

Suddenly Red Sun parted the crowd with his drawn bow.

Grizzly Hair fell to the ground. The arrow sang over his head. A sharp cry came from Scorpion-on-Nose's grandmother, who had an arrow sticking out of her thigh. Morena stepped around erratically, but Morning Owl jumped down to safety.

Red Sun aimed another arrow.

Grizzly Hair sprang like a frog, the arrow humming past his side. Red Sun was positioning another when Two Falcons, having jumped off Amarillo, ran and hit Red Sun from the side and wrestled him to the ground. Everyone watched as arms and legs and torsos churned, toes digging in, men grunting. Red Sun's strangled cry penetrated the thump and scuffle, "I won't live here . . . with . . . that . . . murderer."

Running Quail used the voice of a herald. "Grizzly Hair must leave and never come back. Unless he brings my son."

Howchia was attempting to remove the arrow from the old woman's leg. She gritted her teeth. This was the result of Grizzly Hair's return, that Red Sun, a respected elder, was sitting in the dirt with his head down, long mussed hair hiding his shame. Falls-off-House held his bow. One by one the umne looked at Grizzly Hair and their expressions turned cold.

He didn't belong among them. All through his boyhood he had questioned himself in situations that boys with fathers had taken for granted. Now he had led the children of respected elders to their deaths. He glanced at María—slack-jawed, rein in hand—and announced to her and his mother and everyone else, "I will go."

He went to his horse, mounted and after a struggle—Morena didn't want to leave Amarillo—headed up the same path he had so recently come down.

29

He rode at a gallop, then a trot, past places where as a boy he had practiced tracking. Once again he had no weapon and no tools, and now he had no people. All along the journey home he had seen this possibility in the back of his eyes. He didn't blame Red Sun or Running Quail. Any man would hate him.

He slowed to a walk—mother moon squashed on one side and whitening as daylight faded—and realized exile didn't feel as much like death as he'd expected. Though at times it seemed he could weep, strangely his power wasn't gone. He felt it in his stomach. Furthermore his vision had expanded. When had that happened? Elders said clarity came from defeating fear. He realized he had faced Red Sun and Running Quail, knowing they might kill him. He must have defeated fear. Now his *seeing* went farther and wider. He knew that back in the home place he wouldn't have been satisfied to hunt and fish like other men. Even running for Morning Owl wouldn't have seemed important. His fate was to save his people, though they didn't understand it. Even the perception of his people had widened. They lived in the mission and all over the land. They included Sucais's family, Domingo's village and what was left of Gabriel's. Broken as those villages were, those headmen would take him in, of this he was certain. He was luckier than other exiles.

He passed the boulders where he and Bowstring and Falls-off-House had long ago pretended to hunt bears. One tilted against another in a semblance of an u-macha. He stopped. There was no point in riding to the Omuchumne. They were closely related, and though they would allow him to sleep there for one or two nights, they wouldn't want him there for long after what had happened. A more dangerous and exciting possibility presented itself. He could go to the powerful Russians, enemies of the *Españoles*, and try to talk to them. But first he would sleep under the boulder and see whether a dream would direct him.

He dismounted, looped the rein around Morena's front legs, made a loose tie so she could graze, then broke a dead limb from an oak and swept under the boulder. Hearing no rattlesnake, he crawled in and made himself a nest. From time to time during the night he heard the sound of Morena's grazing and spoke to her.

But in the morning she was gone. Her mincing tracks led back to the home place. He followed from tree to tree, hiding to avoid the shame of being seen. At the top of the last hill—Hissik-stink!—he saw her grazing in the playing field with Amarillo, more than ten men and women petting her. Horses liked to be with their own kind. A dry chuckle popped out. This was the sort of thing that happened in Coyote stories. It taught children to laugh at themselves.

Young boys were taking turns dodging sticks shot from toy bows. They laughed and called back and forth, the novelty of the horses already worn off. He reflected that children saw many new animals. Horses were just one more. It seemed only a short time ago when he and his friends had dodged grass arrows. Now he was hiding from his own people.

The umne should have been snaring beaver, but they didn't know Missouri would arrive in about six sleeps. Sadly, he couldn't tell them, and sadder yet, he might never see his mother again. But that was useless self-pity. Deciding to return for the horse after dark, he went back up the trail.

He bathed near Tai Yokkel, the bow-shaped lowland where in ancient times the river had swung wide, where Two Falcons had allowed him to watch the deer hunt. After a breakfast of watercress, he sprinkled old leaves where he had slept and fluffed the dry grass—anyone could retrace the horse's tracks. Sweeping a stick behind him, he went to the steep bluff above the river and stepped down from rock to rock. Partway down he sat behind a boulder that would hide him from above. A tree trunk would keep him from rolling. Not having slept well the night before, it felt good to lie back and close his eyes, and in the warm late morning, it wasn't long before sleep carried him away.

He dreamed that he, Bowstring and Oak Gall were walking in a familiar woods, following the haunting tones of an elderberry flute. The familiar melody led them off the path. Father sun was bright and the wing people sang in the woods. Careless of where they were going, the three were drawn by the voice of the flute. Now and again Oak Gall would look at him with an expression he couldn't fathom. They entered a mist. The outlines of the trees grew fuzzy and the flute seemed to pull farther away from them. Rapidly the fog grew thicker. He saw only shrouded shapes of Oak Gall and Bowstring. He could hardly see his feet. The fog turned white and cold. He looked right and couldn't see Oak Gall. He looked left. Bowstring was gone. He called to them, but Little-blue-Lizard caught his voice and threw it back at him. He stopped, listened, but heard nothing. He put his hands before him like Grandmother Dishi, feeling for trees, hoping his feet would bump something. He stamped his foot. It met no resistance. Nothing was under him! Panicked, he cried out but only a weak croak came from his lips. Cold white terror encased him. He was lost between worlds.

Then he heard women's voices. He opened his eyes. Mother and María were bending over him like cousin sisters, María's beads and breast flaps hanging above him.

The women straightened and smiled. Still in the white silence of the dream, he rubbed his eyes and saw that father sun had moved west. How had they found him? Sitting up, he answered his own question. At the top of the bluff he saw Two Falcons looking at him with a wry expression. Grizzly Hair realized he could never outwit the master hunter.

He motioned for them all to sit with him. They did, Howchia saying, "Son, you left too quickly." She looked to Two Falcons.

"The men want you to return," Two Falcons said. "We talked in the sweathouse. They want to hear your story."

María added, "You didn't tell me what happened in the mission and I couldn't answer their questions."

Grizzly Hair looked at Two Falcons. "Red Sun and Running Quail? Do they want me back?"

"They want to hear everything that happened to their children," the big man said.

Howchia added, "Before the sleep they were sick with grief. There will be no more arrows."

Grizzly Hair wondered.

The dark planes of Two Falcons's face revealed nothing as he turned to Howchia. "If they don't like his story, they might pay Drum-in-Fog to kill him."

Howchia leveled him a look. "He'd have to overcome my magic and he knows it. For that he'd charge more than the two of them could pay. My son will be safe."

"Not if the doctor wants him dead too," the hunter mused.

Doctors were dangerous—men who could shoot magic long distances. Grizzly Hair couldn't forget the doctor competitions Drum-in-Fog had won. Still, he trusted his mother's powers. Besides, he needed to tell his story, needed the umne to know how much he'd wanted Oak Gall and Bowstring to come home with him.

María, who had followed this talk with her quick eyes, said, "*Españoles* say doctors have no powers."

Howchia gave her the same look she'd given Two Falcons. María shifted uncomfortably on the log and smoothed the wrinkles on her knees. "They believe," she said meekly, "that only *María en el Cielo* and *Dios* have power."

"What do you think?" Howchia asked.

She shrugged a sad smile. "I don't know but I will pray on my beads." She picked up the necklace from between her elongated breasts and rolled a bead between thumb and finger.

Eagle Woman said, "Then pray on the beads." She looked at Grizzly Hair. "You too, talk to your spirits. We'll use everything we have."

He would, but the fog had told him the old world was dissolving.

30

Etumu had been watching. She saw Grizzly Hair coming down the hill with the master hunter and the two women. His legs were long and thin, all of him thinner than when he'd left at the start of the long dry. He needed a woman to gather and cook for him. A familiar pain rushed to her throat and she grabbed a branch of the oak she stood beside to steady herself, squeezing tears from her eyes. But tears, she knew, would flow as dependably as the river whenever she thought of her sister and realized that Oak Gall would never embrace Grizzly Hair again or have his children. The fun and excitement that had been Oak Gall had passed forever from the world.

Since Etumu's first memory, her sister had told her things. Oak Gall was smarter than Spider and shared everything with Etumu. Not even Mother knew how much Oak Gall told her and Etumu protected her sister's intimate talk. This was how it happened that bit by bit Oak Gall's love for Grizzly Hair had climbed into Etumu and lived there and melted her at the sight of him just as it would have melted Oak Gall. This doubling of love between sisters couldn't be explained, but Etumu knew it honored her sister. It was her return gift for Oak Gall's secrets. And though Oak Gall's heart was gone, this rich part of her lived on. It couldn't be mentioned to a living soul, for talk drained that which was talked about, and Etumu held tight to every shred of her love for Grizzly Hair, as Oak Gall would have.

How excited she had been the day Oak Gall followed him against their parents' wishes! Afraid for her, yes, but it was Oak Gall's nature to do exciting things. Etumu had lain awake most of the night imagining the joy of their coming together. She had calculated how far ahead Grizzly Hair would be and how fast Oak Gall could travel. She knew it would have been late when they met. In the mystery of their double love, she too had felt his smooth warm skin and the gentle weight of him upon her and his sweet breath and felt the same exploding joy and rippling magic Oak Gall had described so well. Sharing Grizzly Hair in this way made Etumu different from her friends. She was not a child in her thoughts.

Now the joy of seeing him coming toward the village—not exiled after all!—met the horrific void where Oak Gall should have been. She kneeled and crawled quickly into the low bushes, hiding before he saw her, afraid he would guess her feelings. He might misunderstand and think it wrong of her to love him, as though she imagined herself somehow a beneficiary of her sister's death. She couldn't risk that. It wasn't like that at all. Not even a grown and beautiful woman, the most beautiful woman in the world, could compete with Oak Gall in any way and she—skinny, flat-ribbed Etumu—was so dull and insignificant and unimportant and young and ugly that when viewed against her exciting and eternally lovely sister, there could be no comparison and therefore no wrong. She would hold tight to the shining gift inside her and keep her secret.

People were gathering to hear his story. She went and sat between her parents to listen as though she were no different than anybody else.

Still feeling the fog of his dream, Grizzly Hair began his long tale. He talked all afternoon, pausing only to scoop peppermint water from the basket. Looking across his dripping hand, he saw the hard squint of Red Sun's eyes. Running Quail's head was turned away. Grizzly Hair continued his story, adding detail about how easily Oak Gall learned the tongue of Gabriel's people and how much she loved the horses—all without speaking her name. His throat clamped shut. He recovered, then told how happy Bowstring looked whenever Teresa was near. He told how the black hats captured them and how brave Oak Gall and Bowstring had been, and how Bowstring carried the little boy on his shoulders. He told how the black hats took Oak Gall to the women's house, where she didn't see the flogging. He paused and when he could go forward, explained that Bowstring hadn't been whipped as long.

As he talked he saw that even Red Sun and Nettles seemed to lose their angry expressions. He told of Jesús on the *cruz* and Padre Fortuni's school. He told of iron-making and skinning. They leaned forward as he said Oak Gall seemed sick after the ceremony in the *iglésia.* Twilight arrived and faded into shadows, and he tried to explain why Bowstring stayed in the mission. Why so many stayed. "They want to become new people who use metal tools and shoot with *fusiles.* They want mission power. People who go there don't want to be hill bunnies any more, like us. They play music on instruments that have never been seen before. My friend said he had dreamed that music before he went there." In deference to Running Quail he wouldn't use Bowstring's name.

No one brought wood for the supper fires, the umne listening like children to a storyteller. He continued, and when he came to the part where he went inside to take Oak Gall from the *monjería,* María, who sat beside him, elbowed him in the ribs. He nodded for her to talk.

"The padres protect unmarried women from the men," she explained. "When a girl reaches nine *años,* she goes to live there so she will stay pure. The old woman guards the house and calls the soldiers if men try to climb the walls to the windows." The umne exchanged puzzled glances.

"The house smelled bad," Grizzly Hair continued.

Sick Rat held up the palm of a hand. "She says the girls and women were pure in the house, but you say it smelled bad. Talk straight." People nodded. There had been a contradiction.

María explained, "To *Españoles,* pure means people don't couple."

Grizzly Hair continued. "I was trying to take my woman from the stinking house and bring her here to be cured by our esteemed doctor." He nodded at Drum-in-Fog. "But two strong men, Estanislao and a black hat, fought me. One put his arm here and stopped my breathing," he touched his neck, "and the other kneed me hard, here." He pointed. "They pulled me out and locked me in the *calabozo.*" He hung his head, his failure to rescue her crashing around him again. Battling the threatening tears, he said, "I never saw her alive again."

Hunger was ignored as the story went on—the burying of people in tiers, the house of bones, the improper dance and finally the bull and bear fight. It was dark when Grizzly Hair said, "I ran away. And I ran until I became ill."

María described how he had raved in his illness and how she had brought him healing teas and food. While she talked he decided that later, in the sweathouse beyond María's hearing, he would tell the men his idea of peoples joining together to keep the black hats from coming further up the rivers. But tonight he would sleep in his mother's u-macha, for the talk had unsettled his insides and he didn't want to face Red Sun and Running Quail until he had his calm.

The people ate dried meat and sat in their private thoughts. Grizzly Hair went to the u-macha, flopped down on his old mat, turned to the wall and let the tears come. María came in later and lay on the mat she and Howchia had made for her. Even later, old Dishi felt her way into the u-macha and settled on her mat.

For much of the next day the elders sat talking on the sandy bank, María and Howchia among them. From time to time individuals left and returned, but the steady talk continued. Purifying himself with amole root, Grizzly Hair bathed longer than usual. Then he took his snare materials and went to the hills to set them in quail and rabbit runs. He went to Scorpion-on-Nose's knapping place on the eastern hill to see what could be traded for arrow points. Hard shale would do, Grizzly Hair told the quiet man, no need for fine opal points of petrified wood or obsidian from the mountain of fire. Scorpion-on-Nose didn't knap arrow points from the plentiful greenstone, preferring to use that for large spear points. Grizzly Hair left in search of the ideal willow for a new bow, and the straightest alder branches he could find for the arrows. He had the good luck to find what he needed. From the doeskin in the u-macha he cut small oval pieces, split them carefully, and while his soap-root glue was cooling, sat listening at the edge of the circle of elders—Red Sun not present.

Sunshine-through-the-Mist, a woman in late middle life said, "Maybe the man in the trap spoke true. This could be the end of Second World." Everyone contemplated the stunning thought.

"What signs would there be?" Running Quail asked, glancing around the circle to Eagle Woman. When his gaze bumped into Grizzly Hair's, they both looked quickly away.

Eagle Woman gave her opinion. "I don't know the signs. I suppose this could be the end. But I am not sure that just because new people come to the world with new powers it means Man's time is over."

That brought María to life. "Ho. This is not the end but the beginning. The birth of Jesús made everything new. The bad is washed away. The padres came to California to tell us that."

"What is California?" somebody asked.

"All of this," María gestured widely. "To the western sea, over the mountains far to the east, south to the bottom of Mexico and north as far as men can go in boats."

"You mean earth," said Morning Owl. "It needs no other name."

María grinned and shrugged. "The Spanish call it California." Everyone agreed they should learn the tongue of powerful *Españoles.*

"Who is Jesús?" Sunshine-through-the-Mist asked.

María told the story of a baby in the blood of her namesake María without the help of a man. People made muffled noises of wonderment, that any woman had such power. María explained that María had been visited by *Dios*, the greatest of spirits. Now they nodded, understanding.

Drum-in-Fog, who had been sitting cross-legged and motionless, his walnut shell eyelids half closed, said, "The world continues." Heads turned toward him, for it was unusual to hear the doctor speak. "To say this is the beginning or the end means nothing," he said, "even if the rocks crumble to sand and Man is no longer here, it is not the end."

Uncomfortable with this talk, Grizzly Hair left to check the glue. It had cooled to a nice viscous consistency. With the shoulder blade of a young deer, he scooped a careful amount and applied it to the split doeskin, then pressed it on the peeled willow for the first layer of his hand-hold.

Morning Owl, who had also left the elders, came from his u-macha with a handful of knotted thongs. "I am happy to have my runner back," he said handing the *puls* to Grizzly Hair. "Twelve sleeps. Invite the related villages and tell them we will cry for their dead as we cry for our own." He returned to the circle of elders.

Grizzly Hair looked at the sun—too near his western home to start the run now. He would continue making his hunting equipment and run after a sleep, untying one knot in each *pul* before he left. As he pressed another layer of doeskin on the grip, he reflected that though his new clarity made him different in some ways, much of his strength came from the umne. He felt it in his stomach. If Red Sun and Running Quail traded beaver for rich goods and were therefore able to pay Drum-in-Fog to kill him, it was fated. Nevertheless, after the run, he would ride to intercept Missouri.

31

Now I *see* again something that Grizzly Hair never knew.

O-se-mai-ti rises to all fours and falls on her other haunch, groaning with pleasure at the change. Coyote appears to be napping, but he has an eye open.

The morning Grizzly Hair ran with the *puls*, María and I went to the u-macha for baskets, for we women needed to make acorn flour for the Cry feasts. I looked over and saw something new in María's face as she showed me a handful of my gold nuggets. "Is this *oro?*" She had found my old basket.

"Gold," I said, assuming *oro* was the Spanish word. Having been teased all my life about saving rocks, I had meant to throw them out but hadn't found the right moment.

"What do you do with gold," she asked in a strangely tremulous voice.

My embarrassment deepened. "Nothing." I hurried outside to the cha'ka, hoping she would lose interest.

But she followed, eyeing me like she expected me to catch on to a joke. I parted the woven vines to release a fall of acorns into my burden basket. "Do you use gold in the pueblo?"

Her hand moved rapidly across her head and chest. *"José y María,"* she said, "We have no gold in the pueblo and the people of my childhood had none at our home place, but I know about *oro."* A grin widened her mouth. I wanted to ask, What are you trying to say? But she was a talkative old woman and I knew she would get to it in her own way. The mortar holes in the village center were all in use, so I led the way to a secluded place downriver.

We climbed to the top of the big brown boulder, stacked our baskets, and scooped debris from the twin rock pockets. In times of flood the river polished the flat surface to a soapy smoothness and today father sun had heated it to the warmth of brown skin. It was amazing, I thought, that the quiet blue river so far below had the power to rise this high. I always wondered whether the water had scoured out the first little dimples and the women of the Ancients used them for so long that these holes eventually became as deep as any in the village center. I also wondered who those ancient women were but could never *see* them, having no object to connect me to them.

We took our acorn-breaking tools and began shelling—María, I realized with some surprise, still giving me that look—and tossed the meats into our respective holes. Across the river a large egret stalked the shoreline, dazzling white against the lush green of the shore grasses, reflected over the azure water—two necks, two heads. Even now I feel the joy I did then at the clarity of the air in the time of falling leaves.

"*Españoles* value gold above all else," María said.

I stopped mid-stroke with my shelling rock. "Whatever do they make with it?"

"Cups and ornaments, but mostly round flat pieces that they use for money. Gold makes them rich." Tapping an acorn she shot me a twinkly look.

"Like shell money?"

"Yes. They trade gold, not shells."

Very strange, I thought, that the *Españoles,* who possessed such power, honored those common twists and folds of rock more than the delicate symmetry of shells. I went back to my acorns. "What could I get in the pueblo in trade for my basket of gold?"

"Anything. The nicest house and maybe fifty excellent horses. I don't know. My first man would have known the trade value." Within the loose-hanging lids her eyes snapped with excitement. "But I know you are rich. Very rich." She tapped the next acorn and tucked back her girlish chin as though nipping off her excitement. "These beads," she said touching them, "are nothing at all compared to your basket of gold."

Testing, disbelieving though I had no reason to distrust her, I said, "I saved only the pieces that looked like little faces or animals or something. The rest I threw away."

She looked at me in open-mouthed wonder. This talk stuck me as preposterous. Since the time of the Ancients the souls of every kind of rock had been well known. Never had anyone noticed power in gold, except that it brought me ideas when I rubbed it. *Rich* repeated in my head. *Fifty excellent horses.* Then I suddenly realized my son would want to trade with the gold. "What would happen to Grizzly Hair," I asked, "if he went to the pueblo to trade my basket of gold?"

Her lips drew together like a purse. "I think the *Comisionador* would take the gold and have him flogged and locked up if he didn't tell where it came from. Then every soldier and *vecino* and *ranchero* would come here searching for more."

My insides were suddenly a mass of squirming tadpoles as the vision of the flogging filled my mind—the hopelessness, the horror. Above all, black hats must be kept away from the home place. Long ago I had returned to the place of my girlhood to avoid them, refusing to marry Eats Skunk. "If gold is valuable, why wouldn't the *Españoles* trade for it? Why would they hurt him?" It was Man's nature to trade.

"They don't trade with gentiles. It is against the *reglas.*"

"But the *padre* put water on my son. He is one of them."

"No. He is a *cimarrón* living in a gentile village. You are outlaws for harboring him."

"Those words have no meaning to me."

"They would see you as enemies." Deftly she flipped a peeled nut into her hole. "You see, the *Españoles* came across the eastern sea in search of gold. They found it in Mexico and fought the *Indios* there. They are still fighting. Many have died. Now the *Españoles* have all the gold and *Indios* have none. I think the same thing would happen here."

"Are you sure? Sure as that egret fishes?" I pointed to the bird, now standing on one leg, black toes dripping, expectant neck stretched and mirrored in the blue water.

"I am sure they won't trade with *Indios.*" She didn't look up from her shelling. "In San Francisco Presidio a long time ago, a doll with an oak gall head was found. My Pepe picked it out of a marsh and gave it as a gift to Commander Argüello's little daughter, Concepción. He didn't see the small gold nugget in the doll's mouth. The next morning when I was sweeping, I found the gold on the floor. Concepción must have pried it out. I gave it to Pepe and saw how excited he was. Pepe questioned me many times about dolls with oak gall heads and wanted to know where they came from, but I had never seen a doll like it before, with a body and legs of woven grass. For years he asked neophytes from every river about it. Later, after he married my Angelita and retired from the presidio, I felt sorry for her because that little piece of gold had stolen his calm. He still leaves her to look for gold."

"And you have found gold without looking."

She smiled at me and continued talking, and as she talked something like a dream began rising from my earliest memories.

"All the soldiers, even Commander Argüello," María was saying, "looked for gold back then, but Pepe never told them about the doll. Once in a while it seemed like the men went crazy digging in the hills, prying out rocks until their fingernails bled. They made the prisoners dig. Sometimes a runner came from Monterey and reported that some sample or other was not gold after all. Then the soldiers would look down at their plates and hardly talk at supper."

My own memory returned to me as I gazed across the golden hills mounding down to the blue river—some of the oaks already brown. I could see my mother, Dishi, as she had been then, when I played with my doll. Oak Gall Baby, I called her.

"I didn't like the way Pepe was always trying to get rich," María said, looking at me. Then, respectful of my silence, she stopped talking. Our first batch of acorns were shelled and we now pounded with our pestles, each in her own thoughts.

I was a young child on that cold evening long ago. Dishi was a young woman. Father sun was low when she left the u-macha, walking fast. I grabbed Oak Gall Baby and the small gold nugget I had found that day and hurried after her, knowing she would go to her power place as she often did at the end of the day. As I crossed the creek, cold water slashed on my stomach and I sucked in my breath. Mother stopped and turned and waited halfway up the hill. Against the darkening earth of the path, it was hard to see her. I hurried, hoping she would tell my favorite story. The wing people had gone to their nests and the frogs slept under the mud, so it was cold and quiet, except for the surging river.

When I caught up, Mother pointed with her head at Hill Boulders, all dark. I looked deeper and saw a motionless doe and two yearlings in the shadows. Quietly Mother said to them, "No need to fear." They did not run. She had that power. I felt safe with her, unafraid of mountain lions and grizzly bears, even Bohemkulla.

She took my hand into hers and squeezed my fingers, the ones not holding the gold. With my doll dangling in my other hand we walked down the hill and across the rocks, the river baby spirit rushing noisily before us.

"Tell how Coyote made people," I said, watching the clouds puff out of my mouth. She stopped at the shore, where smooth strands of water wove over the rocks and slid in a dark sheet under an overhanging branch. The aroma of moldering willow stood strong around us. "Look," she said, pointing down the river. "The color of clover blossoms."

A spot of pink-lavender hung low in the sky, the only color in a world of gray rocks, gray water, leafless willows and cottonwoods that reached gray fingers into the pearl-gray sky. But something was very white. I pointed across the river.

"Frost," she said. "The sun didn't melt it today."

"Why?"

She stood like stone. I knew I must keep her talking or she would fall back into her long silences.

"Why is that the color of clover blossoms?" I said pointing at the fuzzy spot.

"Father sun is at the happy western land," she said.

"Are the spirits dancing?"

"Yes, Little One. You can still see some of their fire. Sit. We will watch."

The sand was cold and I snuggled into her warm side, asking, "Does the river go to the sky?"

She put an arm around me and pulled me close. "It goes through the mountain. Remember the story?"

I didn't want that story. "Would my doll go all the way to the western sea if I put her in the water?"

She didn't move.

I nudged her with my elbow.

"Umm. Yes."

"And she might find the happy western land? And see the Animal People dancing?" I knew my doll baby could float a very long time. With an oak-gall head she was more buoyant than the lightest wood. I also knew that personal possessions carried a piece of their owner's spirit and she might find my father for me. He had gone to the western sea before I was born and never returned. "If I put her in the river, would you make me another doll?" I pushed my cold nose into the smooth warm breast that had until recently given sweet milk.

She glanced down. "Don't throw it away or I won't make another."

"But I'm NOT throwing her away. She will go see the happy land and find my father. Wouldn't you make me another?"

She stared at the fuzzy lavender spot and nodded, her eyes glistening with tears.

Relieved, I snuggled deeper into her warmth. "Now tell me the story of how Coyote made people."

She began in a monotone. "It was in the oak woodlands, to the north. The world was covered with grass and trees and bushes and the Animal People were enjoying themselves, but they knew it was time to make Man. No one knew what kind of animal that should be so they called a council." She sighed and stopped talking. I poked her and she said, "Your father told me this story. Did I tell you that?"

"Yes," I said. "Keep telling."

At last she continued. "The Animal People sat in a circle. O-se-mai-ti sat at the head. On her right sat Mountain Lion, then Deer and Mountain Sheep, Bob Cat, Ant, Salmon, and so on all around to Mouse—"

"You forgot Skunk, and Rabbit and—"

"If I name all the animals, the story will be too long and you will go to sleep."

I nodded glumly.

"Mountain Lion said people should have loud voices and fur and sharp claws so they could be mighty hunters. 'Nonsense,' said Deer. 'It is ridiculous to scare away the animals you are trying to catch.' O-se-mai-ti said, 'People should be brave and strong like me, and be able to stand up on their hind feet and kill their enemies with one swipe of a paw.'" She slapped the darkening air. "They should be willing to die to save their cubs." I felt happy that Mother was losing herself in the story and probably would not fall into her silence.

"Deer said a man would look foolish unless he had a magnificent pair of antlers on his head. He agreed that a loud roaring voice was unnecessary. He said people should have ears as sensitive as a spider's web and eyes that gleam like fire."

"Your eyes don't gleam like fire," I murmured, confused as always by that part.

She looked down and her voice touched me with love. "Your eyes do, Little One, and they warm like fire. Like your father's eyes." Her arm tightened around me and her voice came out scratchy. "Mountain Sheep said horns that tangle in the branches would be silly. 'If people had thick horns rolled up, they would be like a stone on each side of the head, giving it weight. With such horns people could butt hard.'"

Sad moisture spilled from her eyes. "Sandhill Crane said, 'People should mate for life—man and woman. They should dance all the dances together and share the feeding of their chicks.'

'That's ridiculous,' said Black Widow. 'People should put all their eggs in one sack and when they hatch let them go where they want.'

"Ant said, 'People should be very small so they won't be seen by birds. They should think only about others and carry heavy loads. They should be orderly. That way they can build nests much larger than any one person could build.' Bee agreed with that but added, 'And they should have sharp stingers.'

"And so it went around the circle. Each animal said people should be like them. After they had all spoken, Coyote, who had been standing apart from the talk circle, said, 'These are the stupidest speeches I ever heard. I could hardly stay awake. Every one of you thinks you are the best animal on earth. Woo-woo-oo. You might as well take your own young and call it Man. But you all have good parts.'"

I pointed at my foot, impatient for what came next.

"'Grizzly Bear is correct,' said Coyote. 'Standing upright on her hind legs allows her see over tall bushes. People should have big flat feet. Grizzly is right about having no tail too. She knows tails only harbor fleas. And Deer is right about eyes that gleam like fire, and sensitive ears.'"

"Sensitive as a spider's web," I corrected.

"Yes, and Coyote said Salmon was right that people should have no hair. 'My hair is a terrible nuisance,' Coyote whined. 'Burrs stick in it and I can hardly bite them out. Ticks and fleas hide in it and hair makes me too hot during the long dry. People should not—'"

"But people HAVE hair," I interrupted, "and lice do get in it."

Mother went on. "Coyote said, 'Eagle is right that people should be able to grip things with long strong fingers.'" She laughed in the teasing voice of Coyote, "But none of you mentioned my best quality. People should have my cunning. They should be clever and tricky."

"But the animals didn't agree. They began to argue and the council became noisier and noisier until it broke up in a loud fight. Fangs and claws were unsheathed. Owl jumped on Coyote's head and began to pull his scalp, Coyote took a nip of Beaver's cheek—"

"And Mountain Lion scratched a line down Racing Snake's—"

"I will not mention every animal tonight. All their roars and squeals and shrieks blended into the loudest noise that was ever heard on earth, and it continued for a long time. Then Coyote picked up his damp clay and began rolling it." She rubbed her palms together the way I made clay worms. "The animals stopped fighting and picked up clay and started making their own models of Man. But it grew dark and everyone was tired after the fight. Coyote told them they might as well mold their clay after the sleep. So they all lay down and slept. But not Coyote, the trickster. With the help of mother moon he worked all night. He tiptoed around and stole pieces of other models and folded them into his own. Then he poured water on all the remains of the other models, spoiling them, and in the morning when the animals awoke, First Man was standing there, made the way Coyote wanted."

I let out my breath, loving the story's end. I imagined a man as perfect as my father would have been, with muscled chest and strong arms to hold me and long shiny black hair. The small of my back felt cold where her arm didn't cover it, and the river baby spirit bubbled ever-changing songs over the rocks, sometimes a flutey sound. Owls called back and forth and the heavy dark had squeezed away the clover-blossom color. Mother moon hung above us, white as frost in the black sky dome.

Mother looked up and whispered, "Where is Crying Fox?"

But moon never answered. I brought my doll baby to my lips and whispered, "Go find Father." The journey would be long, so I put the gold nugget in her mouth to give her something to eat and pressed my thumb on it, wedging it in tight. Then I waded to my calves in the cold water and gently placed her in the current. Eagerly the water took her. "There she goes," I said, pointing at the small pale shape fast disappearing down the moonlit river. "Be brave," I called to her.

Now I was a grown woman with a grown son and María was pounding acorns beside me, the excitement still in her face. I felt my own sense of excitement; her Pepe had found my doll. That seemed as miraculous as the fact that my mother had once talked for human ears. Some people said Bohemkulla had overcome her on one of her night walks, and a few thought Bohemkulla had put me in her blood and that was the reason I had no father, but I never believed them. I knew my father had been a brave, handsome trader who went to the western sea.

I looked at María, understanding now what had connected my spirit to hers when Grizzly Hair lay sick. My doll and Pepe linked us through that gold nugget. "Are the black hats still looking for gold?"

Emphasizing her talk with pounding, she said almost all of them had stopped looking, except Pepe. He dreamed of returning to Mexico so rich that his father's family would respect him. Pepe's father, she said, had been ashamed of Pepe's mother because she was an *India.* Pepe had been little more than a boy when his father sent him away to San Francisco Presidio because of his Indian blood. And now, María said, the other soldiers teased Pepe because an *Indio* had shot off his ear with an arrow. She talked and talked and talked of her life while both of us pounded and transferred the meal to baskets. She was still talking when we shelled a new batch of nuts. Then she was silent.

"The doll was mine," I said. "I put the gold in its mouth."

She looked at me open-mouthed. A rustle in the leaves stopped my explanation. Grizzly Hair came from the alders lifting three cottontails by the ears, smiling up at us—a tinge of sadness always in his smile now. "Mother," he said, "your special bulbs would taste good with these tonight." We had been pounding for a long time and he was back from his run. The way María looked at him I knew they had talked of my bulbs, and was glad he liked my cooking. I suddenly realized María would tell him of the gold. "We are talking women's talk," I said.

Politely he vanished into the thicket and I exhaled. My entire life had been a struggle to keep him safe and now the knowledge of gold could kill him. Feeling strong resolve, as when I grabbed a rattlesnake by the head, I said, "He must not learn that gold is valuable to the *Españoles.* No one must learn of it. Please do not talk of it."

She sighed and looked down, pounding.

Then shame hit me. Fear had made me ask a big favor of the woman who had saved my son's life. "I misspoke," I said, "Your family and Pepe will want to know about the gold."

But she looked up and her voice was low and firm. "I will never speak of it, to them or anyone else." Her eyes snapped.

I reached across the mortar holes and touched her shoulder. "Sister, it is not for me to ask you to keep secrets from your own family. All I ask is that you not tell my son."

But her wrinkles were set.

Nonetheless, that evening I dumped my basket of gold at my power place and covered it with sand.

32

O-se-mai-ti remarks, "I often think of the Animal Council too. I would have made people more honest with each other."

"We talked straight most of the time," I say.

She disagrees. "Your son kept a secret about Missouri. You kept the secret of gold from him and everyone else, and María kept it from her people. Etumu didn't tell anyone what she was thinking. You thought Red Sun and Running Quail had secret dealings with Drum-in-Fog, and everything Drum-in-Fog did was secret. People would be better off living straight like bears."

Coyote elevates his snout and shines a grin at Bear. "Maybe you're beginning to understand why you're extinct."

"Bringing that up again!" the she-bear grumps. "And you're wrong—many of my kind still walk the earth." Rising to all fours, she falls on the other haunch. "You put your sneakiness into people, but there's a lot of me in them too."

"I'm surprised you two are still arguing about that," I comment quietly.

"Not arguing," the bear growls. "It's just that we'll never get another chance to make people."

"Would you really make them different, if you had it to do over?"

Reluctantly Bear shakes her head.

Coyote warbles high laughter. "You have to admit, it's fun to see the messes people get into. The Spanish thought they could change people." He hoots.

"Maybe they did," I say.

In a great noisy blur of a hind foot, Coyote scratches an ear, which makes him stutter. "That's absurd. Now let's see how the powerful Eagle Woman ended up in a tree."

Grizzly Hair took his arrow-straightening equipment and rode south to meet Missouri. He waited at a stream near the village that had held the grasshopper roundup and sat on the bank so he could soak his arrows before straightening them through the hollowed-out burl. At the end of the day the shafts were all straight but Missouri hadn't come. He rode back to the home place, deciding to go back the next day. Ten sleeps could mean anything from eight to twelve, and tomorrow was the ninth sleep.

At the playing field he was horrified to see three strange horses—two brown ones with straight backs and abnormally long ears, one normally shaped and dappled gray. Afraid for the umne, he ran around the brush of Berry Creek where he could see into the village center.

The umne sat calmly around their supper fires. Missouri was there sitting against the oak at Morning Owl's u-macha, legs outstretched with his boots crossed. He looked like a man settled in for long stay. A Coyote trick! Grizzly Hair put his things in the u-macha and went to the hy-apo's fire. Missouri's long gun lay beside him. The wide iron pan stood on the fire sizzling with the strange meat that gave off a sweetish odor.

The umne were trying not to stare at the fat man with the frizzy black beard and skin with the pinkish cast of underdone rabbit. María, who was eating at Scorpion-on-Nose's fire, nodded at Grizzly Hair like she had explained everything.

"Me-wuk," Missouri boomed, pointing and grinning at Grizzly Hair as though he'd come by a different route just to fool him. The antler haft of the knife protruded from his waist band, and the buckskin shirt bunched behind it as if the knife had just been inserted. A blanket was laid out with Missouri's roll of cloth and bag of beads upon it. Ready for trade.

"Sit with us," the hy-apo said, patting the ground.

Grizzly Hair sat down, picked up a twig and drew a beaver on the ground. He made hand signs meaning, "We have no beaver here now." Raven Feather, the headman's wife, handed Grizzly Hair a basket of nu-pah—gritty and tangy with ferrous earth.

Missouri pointed at the beaver in the dirt and said, "*Beaver no good now. No bueno. No bonita. Beaver in the winter. Comprendo? Beaver bonita in winter. Catch 'em in winter.*" He shouted louder and louder.

Grizzly Hair looked at María for help. She shrugged and said, "Maybe he wants the beaver when they are pretty." That made sense. Beaver pelts were full in the time of frost. She had a funny expression and he felt ashamed to have withheld the fact that he had invited Missouri to come here. But at least there would be no immediate trading.

Grizzly Hair pointed to the beaver and said slowly, "*Cuando hace frio.*"

"*Si, si, frio,*" shouted Missouri grabbing his leather-covered shoulders in a parody of being cold. He chattered his teeth and shook the long fringe on his sleeves. "*I come when it's frio.*"

"Sí, frio," repeated Grizzly Hair. He explained to Morning Owl that Missouri would return in the time of rain and frost. Or did he mean to camp here until then?

Missouri spraddled his thick buckskin-encased legs and leaned over the obstacle of his belly, turning his meat with a metal implement. An iron pot with a lid was steaming, the contents apparently not yet cooked. Falling back against the tree, Missouri pointed at an infant in a bikoos and said smilingly to the mother, *"Bonita muchacha."*

"Pretty girl," Grizzly Hair translated. He kept his smile inside, as did the polite umne, for it was a boy. Everywhere people looked at each other with humor.

"Muchacho?" asked Missouri, seeing the joke.

"Sí," Grizzly Hair said.

"Perdona me. Bonito muchacho," Missouri said, his smile crinkling to the temples. Grizzly Hair recalled his terror the first time he had seen blue eyes and knew how his people must feel to see them.

"He says he made a mistake," María was saying. "Now he says the baby is a pretty boy."

Everyone nodded and the mother ran a proud finger down the infant's brown cheek, four new white teeth showing.

Missouri, apparently enjoying the talk, said, *"No palaber bueno. Palaber with manos y. . ."* He pointed at his boot.

"He talks with hands and foot," María explained.

People chuckled and glanced between them as if to say, he knows how to joke. Grizzly Hair suddenly saw Red Sun's face. No joke there. Women came from their fires offering food and drink to the guest, though that was normally the headman's responsibility. Howchia gave him a basket of diluted elderberry juice. He honored her by swallowing several great gulps. *"Bueno. Good,"* he yelled.

Wiping the fringe of his sleeve across his nose and mouth, he coughed, turned to the side, pressed a thumb on one long nostril and blew out a string of yellow matter. He leaned to the side, grabbed a twig and made an earth map showing the upper part of the Valley of the Sun.

Grizzly Hair explained to the people where Missouri came from—his real home and where he had most recently come from. Brows elevated and people looked at each other in amazement.

"Why did you travel so far from your home place?" Morning Owl asked. But even María couldn't make the *Americano* understand.

Etumu used the word *gordo*, which she had learned from María, asking, "Did you grow that fat eating beaver? Is that why you want so many twenties of beaver?"

The people at the other fires waited as María attempted to translate the question into sign language and Spanish. It took a long time and many tries. Then Missouri threw back his head and laughed so hard his hat fell off. He rocked back and forth with his hands on his belly as if laughing pained him. Puzzled about the humor, Grizzly Hair smiled courteously with his people. When Missouri recovered, he made eating signs and said, "No eat beaver."

"He is not fat on beaver," María explained.

"What do you eat?" asked Etumu.

The man made incomprehensible sounds that no one could figure out and pointed to the pot. *"Frijoles."* He kicked the lid off the pot, sniffed the steam, stirred the contents with his iron implement and nodded as if satisfied. He dumped the entire mass of little brown lumps into the flat pan and stirred it into the sizzling meat. He spooned up the mixture, bared his teeth and nibbled a tiny amount. "Mmmm," he said, offering the spoon to everybody.

Several people came to taste, all the children interested.

In return, women offered baskets of their food. Missouri spooned his fingers into Howchia's quail stew and slurped politely. Seeing he liked it, other women brought their variously flavored nu-pah and he scooped generous amounts into the hairy hole of his mouth. He then gave each family more of his *frijoles* and meat, spooning it into each supper basket. Grizzly Hair savored the taste of the salty fat meat. He'd never tasted anything like it. The little brown lumps were interesting, though somewhat tasteless and dry. Only María declined to eat the food.

Raven Feather proudly presented her basket of red earthworm soup.

Missouri cocked an eye at the brown liquid.

"Sopa," María supplied. Soup.

He took the basket, put it under his nose, sniffed, tipped it to his mouth, smiled and swallowed a big gulp. His eyes widened and he grabbed his throat. Then he reached into the basket and brought out a handful of long red worms interlaced with his fingers. His lips pulled back and he flicked the worms at the soup and shoved the basket at Raven Feather with such force it splashed over the sides. He crawled a short distance away and gagged.

"He is sick," Raven Feather observed.

"His stomach," Howchia said. "I will make medicine."

Missouri waved a hand as if it were nothing and after a while came back and continued eating, confining himself to his own food. Then in the deepening twilight he signed that he wanted to sleep. He carried his *fusil* and saddle packs to the playing field near his hobbled horses. The umne followed and watched intently as he put down his things and sat heavily on his blankets, thumped to his back and said "ahh." He lay there for a few moments, then sat up and struggled around his cruelly belted abdomen to remove his boots, which he did with great difficulty. Panting and coughing he placed his hat on his standing boots, lay back, stretched out beneath the darkening sky and locked his fingers over his belly. His forehead and feet appeared completely white, and the umne couldn't stop staring at the *Americano.*

The next morning everyone watched Missouri lie in the sand and suck water like a bloated lizard. Then he picked up his gun, sprang to his feet and beamed his terrifying smile. The people stood shyly behind one another.

At a distance they followed him to the playing field and across it. He found two large pine cones that had fallen from a gray pine on the west hill and set them on top of a boulder. Everyone followed him half-way back across the field, where he raised the wooden end of the gun to his shoulder and winked along its length. He squeezed. The ear-splitting noise rocked him to his heels and the umne ran screaming. Only Grizzly Hair remained calm.

Missouri upended the gun as one would a walking stick and watched as Grizzly Hair and everyone else trotted to where the first pine cone had been. They poked through the grass, found pieces of it and carried them back. In admiration, they passed the freshly broken pieces among them. Missouri had hit the pine cone from twice the range of a bow, and now his expression resembled a dog looking at the umne without shame, mouth open, the tip of his tongue lying on his bottom teeth. Everyone watched him take the horn from around his neck, pour black powder into the gun's barrel, poke it down with a stick, insert a metal ball, and beckon Morning Owl. He handed him the gun, pantomiming that he should make it thunder.

Taking the gun, Morning Owl's face flickered between fear and painful trust, as when a child is told to jump from a tree into its father's arms. He squeezed. The explosion knocked him off balance and he fell to the ground. Howchia looked him over to see if he were injured, but he laughed, handed up the gun and got to his feet. People screamed with relieved laughter. He rubbed his shoulder and shook his head in wonder and admiration. The pine cone remained standing.

All the other men stepped forward, but Missouri reloaded and extended the gun to Grizzly Hair. Honored, he gave it to Two Falcons, who proudly accepted. Missouri made a show of bracing his feet—bouncing on them, looking pointedly at Two Falcons.

The master hunter braced himself, put the wooden part to his shoulder, pointed the gun at the remaining pine cone and made the gun thunder. In awe he smiled at his hand. Blood was seeping from a tear in the webbing of his thumb, but the pine cone had not moved. He nodded appreciation at the *Americano* and his magical weapon, one that clearly required practice.

Grizzly Hair and others stepped forward but Missouri held up a hand and said, "*No.*" He pushed his fingers in his pouch, brought out another ball, showed it to the crowd, pointed and said, "*Go. Look.*"

Everyone understood that valuable projectiles must be collected. Men, women and children ran toward the pine tree. They burrowed in the grass and dirt and it wasn't long before they returned with the three flattened balls. Missouri put them in his pouch and said, "*Gracias.*" Pronounced like he had mush in his mouth.

Two Falcons, in exaggerated sign language, invited Missouri to see his beaver snares.

"*No,*" he said, signing that he wanted to sleep.

Sleep? In the morning. Raven Feather said, "He IS sick."

Howchia went to examine him but he stopped her with the palm of his hand and went to his blankets.

33

For three sleeps Missouri ate nothing and moaned with pain. He refused to let anyone touch him, neither doctors nor women with herbs. "His stomach," women said, whispering as they walked past his blankets in the playing field. Often he could be seen writhing and holding his hands just under his ribs.

He felt better by the time the related peoples arrived on the first day of the Cry. In the pauses between dancing, people crowded around him in amazed wonder as he talked with the help of sign language and earth maps. Clearly he was pleased to show his goods, and all the men said they would trap beaver for him in the time of frost. Missouri's presence so fascinated the people that Grizzly Hair feared it detracted from the Cry. He worried that Oak Gall wouldn't hear the pounding feet and the special singing.

At nights in the sweathouse he continued to feel the unfriendly glances of Red Sun and Running Quail; however, the dancing pounded away some of his ache. The feasts were big and Missouri shared his food with all, as all shared with him.

On the last morning a Molah-gumsip was held to wash people of their mourning. A woman from the walnut grove village stepped forward and knelt. For two entire cycles of seasons she had worn blackface for her dead husband—twice as long as most people mourned. A long line formed and each person washed a part of her head. Waiting his turn, Grizzly Hair noticed that several of the umne appeared to be more exhausted than usual after the four nights of dancing, his own mother among them. She looked distressed as she stood in line, and after she dipped her hand in the basket of purified water and scrubbed a little on the woman's cheek, she went directly to her u-macha. This surprised him. Women were preparing peppermint water for Morning Owl's oration and Eagle Woman was in charge of all big time preparations. Lame Beaver washed the kneeling woman's forehead. María, who had participated in all the ceremonies, scrubbed under her chin. Two Falcons put water on her blackened head and rubbed. His daughter rubbed the woman's nose then went a few paces away and lay down with her eyes closed. Sick Rat washed the back of the woman's neck and went to look at his sister as though something were wrong. The old wife of Frogs-Eggs-Hatching stumbled as she perfunctorily swiped water on the kneeling woman's head, and nearly fell. Morning Owl caught her and they helped each other walk, then lay side by side on the ground, eyes closed. When every person had ministered to the kneeling woman, she stood up and smiled—restored to normal. However, something was not normal.

Grizzly Hair went to the u-macha and found Howchia lying on her mat with an arm over her eyes. He didn't know how to ask, for she was a woman of power and no one would suggest that she might be ill. "Are you coming to the oration?"

"Yes. Go on." she said, "I'm just resting a little."

Puzzled, he returned to the assembled peoples, sat between Lame Beaver and Falls-off-House and examined the packed crowd. Two of the home children looked listless as they lay in their mothers' arms, children old enough to be sitting up. Scorpion-on-Nose sat waiting for the oration with his knees up, head in his hands. His wife held a whimpering child in her arms. Running Quail rubbed thumb and fingers on his forehead. Sunshine-through-the-Mist lay on her back stretched out with her arm over her eyes, like Howchia. Oddly, none of the visiting peoples appeared particularly tired. They whispered cheerfully as they cast covert glances at Missouri, who stood leaning on a young oak, watching them as they watched him. Why would so many home people be more exhausted than the visitors?

Morning Owl climbed so slowly up the mound to the dancehouse roof, he didn't seem like a hy-apo. He walked across the roof and stood gazing down on the people below. Some were at the baskets scooping peppermint tea, for it would be a long day of listening. Etumu wasn't far from Grizzly Hair, hugging her knees and glancing sidelong at him, the whites of her eyes flashing in her blackface. She wasn't tired.

Morning Owl started to say something. His voice cracked and he coughed, and when he tried to speak, coughed again. He rubbed his temples and looked around the silent audience until his eyes came to Grizzly Hair. "My runner will speak about the trouble in the west," he said, walking carefully back across the roof.

It was so quiet the burbling of the river baby spirit could be heard. Then the crowd buzzed like a wasp nest. People looked at Grizzly Hair with surprise. No one was more shocked than he—a man too young and unimportant to orate at the culmination of a Cry. But he must save Morning Owl from embarrassment. He must speak well and give people something to think about after they returned to their home villages. María was looking at him too. Should he mention alliances with other peoples? His youth weighed upon him as he put his feet under him and walked toward the mound and climbed up past the trunk of the oak and across the rough bark of the planks. Why wasn't Two Falcons asked to speak, or Red Sun, any of the elders? Words flitted through his head like frightened quail and when he arrived at the edge of the roof and looked down at the people—so many—he heard only his whispering heart.

He reminded himself that Morning Owl believed he could speak well, and that none of the people looking up at him had seen what he had seen. He straightened his posture and assumed the dignified expression of an orator. He was, after all, a runner.

He told the story of his capture and the mission and what had happened to his friends. He told what he had learned from María, including the part about women wanting to hide evidence that they had coupled, and the way Padre Durán made the whipped woman carry a red doll. María's creased face looked serious, as though judging whether he had understood it right.

"The guns of the *Españoles*," he said, "kill at twice the range of our bows and they have even bigger guns on wheels." Men's eyebrows shot up.

He described the difference between wild and *domesticado*, and told how *Españoles* tended and ate special animals. He mentioned the few plants they grew and how they remembered their ages. He told of the mission sundial with little pictures showing what people were to do when the shadow pointed to each one.

"*Españoles* have great knowledge," he said, "but they do not purify themselves." People looked at each other in amazement. "The long robes insist people tell them their secrets." He told of the cruelties and compared them to when a child pulls the legs off a grasshopper to keep it from hopping away. He warned people not to go to the coast as he had, but advised them to stockpile beaver pelts for sale to the *Americano*. In that way they could trade for iron knives and perhaps guns. He told of a town of powerful Russians on the coast, enemies of the *Españoles*, and said he wanted to go talk with them. Red Sun squinted at him with an unfriendly nod—wanting him to leave.

"The black hats are few in number," he said. "They fear *Americanos* and Russians." He paused. Dry hacking coughs could be heard. All eyes focused upon him again, but he waited until even little children stopped playing and looked up with questioning faces. Then he assumed the cadence and repetition of a storyteller. He told of El Cid and his brave followers who lived in caves, riding on their horses to attack invaders who had made the land their home. He told of El Cid's success.

"And this is most important." He paused long. "There are many, many peoples besides us whom the *Españoles* call *Indios*. From the spine of the eastern mountains rivers cross the Valley of the Sun from east to west like this." He made an air map with arm gestures. "Rivers of people. Many peoples on the rivers. Together these peoples are much, much more numerous than the *Españoles*. The many peoples speak different tongues, many tongues, but they are all *Indios*, like us, even though they speak many different tongues. We are all *Indios*."

People puckered their lips in thoughtful poses and looked at each other in surprise. A few men, including Red Sun, laughed derisively.

"We should all learn the tongue of the *Españoles*," Grizzly Hair went on, suddenly in a hurry to get it all out. "Then we could talk to other *Indios* and help each other defend against the *Españoles*. Only three *años* ago, twelve seasons, the black hats came up this river." He pointed at the river and heads turned. "They didn't come this far east but sooner or later they will." Dogs panted at their masters' knees and no one moved, except Scorpion-on-Nose and Morning Owl, who were rubbing their foreheads. Two Falcons was listening intently. Grizzly Hair concluded, "We must protect our home places as bees protect their nests."

He started to leave but Eagle Woman had quietly come to the roof and joined him. Knowing an elder should give the concluding thoughts, she gave the advice Morning Owl would have, "Be joyful, for laughter keeps illness away. Also, as our esteemed hy-apo always tells us, many of you are gambling too much. You should not gamble more than you can afford to lose."

She turned to leave and he went with her, stepping over the uneven bark of the roof slats, down the soft dirt of the mound. Sweaty, lightheaded and thirsty, he headed for the river. It was suppertime and he had talked since morning. In the refreshing water he looked back to see children on the dancehouse roof puffing out their chests and pretending to orate. Over the rise of the bank he saw people talking or leaving in groups, visitors returning to their home villages.

He swam in place in the current. Had he said too much for María's ears? Nevertheless, he had spoken straight. What would happen would happen.

My head ached all night. After the sleep, though father sun favored us with his warmth, I shivered with cold. The pain in my head grew loud and spread through my body. María wrapped me in my rabbit blanket. Still I shivered and half-slept and murmured like old Dishi. Bad things jumped around inside my head and throat and stomach. I doubted I could cure myself, and when Drum-in-Fog came to see me, I couldn't tell him where to search for the spot where the bad things could be sucked out. Grizzly Hair offered to pay him, but the doctor said, "She helped me cure Sunshine-through-the-Mist's grandhild and now I will cure her. I owe it to her." He left to fetch his magic tool kit.

I was relieved to hear he wouldn't demand payment. I understood but could not talk coherently. I felt Grizzly Hair's fear as he knelt beside my mat and said, "You are too warm, Mother." I knew he wanted my counsel as he looked down the pathway of his life. He watched as María dipped her woolen dress into a basket of peppermint water, *yerba buena*, she called it. She washed me from head to toe. The mint cooled for a time but failed to staunch the fire that burned cold to me and hot to the hands of others. She brought healing tea and lifted my head to drink, exactly as she had done for my son on the mountainside.

María was in demand in other houses too. She came and went. I awakened as if in dream, no longer seeing or hearing, not even knowing if it were day or night. My thoughts were gone. I didn't know that every time pain racked my abdomen, liquid stool and blood leaked out on my mat. Others, however, could smell it.

The night was warm and dark. Grizzly Hair tended a small fire in the u-macha and watched Drum-in-Fog sing and dance to his allies. In the firelight Grizzly Hair saw that my face was dry and red like Oak Gall's had been. He hardly breathed as the doctor moved his elderberry tube over and over me, now and again leaning down to suck quickly at my neck or arm or chest. My mother lay on her mat as though oblivious to everything.

My spirit floated outside my body and stood beside Grizzly Hair as he squatted in the shadows trying to see the expression on the doctor's face each time he bent and sucked. The doctor saw a number of raised red spots on my upper abdomen. More intent, he aimed his tube just above the greatest concentration of spots and sucked hard.

He jerked up, dropped the tube, cheeks ballooned like a bullfrog's neck. Clapping his hands over his mouth to confine the demons, he hurried out the doorway and ran from the village. Hope roared up in Grizzly Hair as he surreptitiously trotted after the doctor and watched from a distance. In an explosive vomit, Drum-in-Fog expelled the demons into the air. Relieved and anxious to avoid the flying demons, Grizzly Hair raced back through the night.

He met Two Falcons, who held a string of shell money. "I need the doctor in my house right now," he said. "My daughter is sick."

"Wait here, see? He is coming," Grizzly Hair pointed at the returning doctor before ducking into the u-macha. I was on my mat the same as before. He put more wood on the fire then lay down on his own mat, waiting for me to recover. Sometimes doctors never did find the agents of illness and this was the reason for Grizzly Hair's relief. Drum-in-Fog had succeeded. He had found and removed the evil things. In the moving firelight his eyelids became heavy and after a while Grizzly Hair began to see an enormous amount of smoke billowing into the sky, fire all around. Inside the smoke stood O-se-mai-ti. "Follow me," the bear said. "I will show you the way."

He awoke honored, but wondering why the bear had been standing in fire. It was completely dark except for glowing coals in the fire pit. He crouch-walked to my mat and said softly, "Mother, you must be better now." I wanted to sit up and smile and reassure him, but as he put his hand lightly over my eyes, all I could do was open and close them.

Then as if a strange man occupied my body, a long low ugly exhalation pushed out of me. Grizzly Hair jerked back. No other breathing sounds were in the u-macha. He put a hand on my shoulder—hot and dry as the skin of an alder log left near a fire—and lowered his cheek to my nose, waiting for my breath. None came.

I floated up from my mat through the smokehole and hovered over the house. I looked down, feeling his pain and wishing I could stop it.

He shook my body's arm and yelled, "Come back!" He recalled that mission people believed the dead could be brought back to life. "María, come fast!" It was more like a roar, so loud everyone in the village heard.

Moments later María entered and squatted beside him.

"Make her live! Say the right prayer."

She lowered her cheek to my nose and stood that way waiting for breathing, then rocked back on her heels and clicked her beads and mumbled, *"Ave María, madre de Dios. . ."*

"Make her live!" he interrupted. "Tell God to make her live! Teach me to talk to God. I will do it. I am *Christiano.*" But her posture betrayed despair and she continued murmuring and shuffling her beads. He put a hand on my shoulder, a hand on hers and stood like a man trying to mend a broken thing. "No!" he shouted, "Don't go!" He shook my body with unintended strength.

This had happened too fast. I wasn't ready to leave the home place I loved and walk the pathway of ghosts, not when my son needed me. Then before I knew it, I swirled into this oak tree not a stone's toss from my u-macha and found myself tight within the grain, where I am until this day.

María touched his hand. He threw it off and left the house, running from the village. He was angry that the crafty doctor had pretended to suck out the evil. He thought about strangling him but remembered he hadn't paid for a cure and didn't have the right. Anger bloomed red before his eyes and he might have gone to kill the man anyway except he felt like he'd been gored in the stomach and everything was falling out.

Despite that, his legs seemed to run of their own accord. Through the dark night he followed the familiar trail. He ran for the endless motion, up and down the hills to Tai Yokkel then back to the village, the moans of the sick and dying and the wails of those who loved them driving him away again. He ran until the sky grayed behind the trees.

Crossing the creek between the hills the last time, he turned uncertainly toward my power place, feeling as though he didn't know how to stop running or that to stop would be to admit my death. At the place where I had dumped my gold nuggets, the place where Oak Gall had said she would go west with him, he finally stopped and listened.

I will never leave you, I said, but all he heard was his own gasping breath and the music of the water spirit. It had the moil and tone as if it might speak to him, but never did. With wide dry eyes he stood staring at the water. After a while his breath slowed but a convulsion exploded up his throat and he wept like a little child, from the belly. He didn't hear old Dishi rattle across the stones.

She leaned the withered sacks of her breasts against his bowed back, wrapped her arms around his chest and rocked him like a baby, forward and back. "I saw her spirit, Grandson," she croaked in a low voice. "A white wisp floated out of the smokehole. Do not ask her to stay. Let her go."

Though he had never heard her speak before, he said nothing. Grief stopped his tongue. She walked away, never to speak again except her muttering to the river spirit. That's when he began to believe he'd brought dangerous power from the mission—scrambled, disordered power that had killed Oak Gall and now his mother, power strong enough to make his grandmother talk. He recalled how self-assured and trusting he had been before his journey—even scornful of Morning Owl when he told him not to go. Since his return he'd never felt close to the men. That too was a sign. He had brought knowledge to the people, and death. He knew María might have brought the bad luck, or Missouri, but both of them had come here at his invitation, so he was the source. He must leave, as Red Sun and Running Quail had wanted. Then the sick might recover. This too was his fate.

The first blush of sunrise shimmered on the skin of the river. A bank swallow poked its head from its hole-nest, looked both ways and swooped over the water. The rocks clattered. He turned, expecting a deer. Instead he saw a slender upright figure with a round black head. Etumu in mourning, coming toward him. Girls didn't often put on blackface, but she had loved her sister very much. She resembled Oak Gall in her slimness and heavy eyelids, but lacked the saucy walk. No one would ever again duplicate Oak Gall in motion. When people died, some things left the world forever. He felt wooden.

Etumu sat in the sand beside him looking at the river. He sensed her sorrow—for Oak Gall, Howchia and him. She said nothing and he felt grateful that anyone wanted to be with him, especially from her family. Upstream the ball tree was blooming, balls of fuzzy white stamens hanging over the water. Their sweet fragrance would soon fade with the light. At last he managed to say, "Your parents might be looking for you." It came low and scratchy and seemed to stun her, as if she'd expected to sit forever in silence.

She shifted, turned her back, head down, and he let the silence return, relieved she couldn't see his tears. He had expected the home place to heal him. Instead he had torn it apart, killed his mother and brought his own exile.

Etumu was digging absently in the sand.

He started to say, "I'm sorry about your sist—"

In a child's voice laced with grief she blurted out: "After you left for the mission I told my father that my sister went with you and you didn't want her to. He was mad at me for not telling him while there was light, and after the sleep he and my uncles went tracking her. They were gone two sleeps and when they came back my father said he wouldn't ever talk to her again, even if she returned." She hiccoughed a sob, twice.

He took her warm little hand into his. "Thank you for telling me."

She looked at him, then down at his hand wrapped around hers and gave it an unexpected squeeze. "I'm sorry about your mother." She jumped to her feet and started walking back the way she had come. He had the strange sensation of his legs pushing under him without his volition. Like a puppy needing the wiggle and life of other puppies, he caught up and walked beside her over the rocks. She said nothing as they returned to the main path and turned up the hill. From the top he saw smoke rising behind the trees, though people didn't cook in the morning. Even from this distance he could smell burning hair. The wails nearly turned him back, but Etumu tugged his hand and they walked down the hill together. Father sun, now above the eastern hill, stabbed his swollen eyes.

He didn't drop Etumu's hand until they were across the playing field. Morena and Amarillo lightly nibbled each other's manes in a display of affection, and loud grinding snores came from the hump of blankets that was Missouri. He dropped her hand at Berry Creek. "Your father would not like you to be friendly with me," he said.

"My mother is sick. Father is with her in the u-macha."

He looked at her bowed neck, narrow where the blackened pitch met pale skin unaccustomed to sunlight. Would everyone die? The thought made him feel like he might collapse.

She turned toward him and said, "My best friend died." Two Falcons's daughter, Sick Rat's sister. "Father says we will burn the dead today and their houses. Morning Owl is too sick, so Raven Feather sent for the women-men. We will dance the Burn." She sniffed and looked at the distance, the streaks of tears on her black face shining in the glare.

They had just danced the Cry. Should he leave before the dance? Would that save other lives? Or should he dance to help Howchia and the others find the happy land? That would honor them more. Yes, he decided. He must exert himself strenuously to help mend the umne.

Etumu showed him her other hand, opened it. Sun glinted off a gold nugget the size of a quail's egg. She closed her fist around it and headed for the village center. He followed her slight figure across the dry creekbed into the village. The keening and the suffocating odor of burned hair enveloped him. Two Falcons's wife was on her knees singeing her hair.

Grizzly Hair ducked quickly into the bad-smelling u-macha and grabbed his bow, quiver, blue crystals and red stone. Eagle Woman's body had been removed by the women-men.

Outside, Drum-in-Fog was scooping black ash over his sticky face and head. This meant his wife had died. Did he hope this excessive display of grief—most men applied a simple black stripe across their foreheads—would make people pity him and not punish him? Anger boiled up again. Turning away, he saw Two Falcons with a black stripe across his forehead, also glaring at the doctor. His string of shells hadn't saved his daughter. Nettles and Hummingbird Tailfeather were already in blackface for Oak Gall and Bowstring.

Grizzly Hair found a bubble of translucent ooze on a gray pine, smeared it across his forehead and applied black soot to it.

Raven Feather was sitting against her u-macha in the posture of a woman absorbing the power of the sun. Her hair, he was relieved to see, fell thickly to her shoulders. He went to her.

She acknowledged him with a glance, her eyes dull like she hadn't slept for a long time. "My man is very ill," she said. "The doctor returned my payment, said he couldn't cure him."

"His medicine is no good. He pretended he found—" He had to turn away and wipe his eyes. Maybe the man in the trap was right, and María was right. Doctors had little power. "I found this for the hy-apo," he said. "Maybe Scorpion-on-Nose can drill a hole through it." *If he gets better.*

She accepted the pretty red stone and looked him her thanks.

Cranebill and his woman-man were removing things from Drum-in-Fog's u-macha. Women-men had the power to handle the dead and their possessions without harm to themselves. Some people complained that they became rich, but to Grizzly Hair that seemed small payment. He watched numbly as they entered his mother's u-macha and came out with two good baskets. Setting them aside, Cranebill took a brand from Two Falcons' fire and held it under the shade porch. Instantly the porch vanished in a crackling whoosh. A short time later the entire house was a flaming cone, the medicine herbs and new feather costume all devoured. They also set fire to Drum-in-Fog's house.

Missouri came from the river and watched with Grizzly Hair. Sadly he shook his head, pointed to himself and said, "*Jinx.*"

"*Jinx?*" Grizzly Hair repeated.

Missouri shrugged. "*Americano palaber.*"

Having little strength for difficult talk, Grizzly Hair headed for the playing field where the platform for the dead was being built. Eagerly he helped, then went to the hills to collect loads of fallen branches for the fire, welcoming the perspiration and the repetitive actions. The women-men positioned the dead with their strangled dogs and food baskets and feather capes and rabbit-skin blankets and all they might need on their spirit journey, then set fire to the underlying brush.

Drum-in-Fog, long staff in his right hand, the blackened ball of his head stiffly held, called out, "Now all cry." He began the short trotting steps of the dance. Setting aside anger so he could dance properly, Grizzly Hair joined the men's line behind the doctor, the women circling in the outer line, all stepping to the drummer's steady thump. Drum-in-Fog stopped. They all stopped and a prolonged sad wail came from Drum-in-Fog. The Burn had begun.

Everyone including María wailed, Grizzly Hair voicing his pent-up grief in the high-pitched ululation in which the wails of all blended. His chest vibrated but he heard nothing from his own mouth, so loud was the communal wail. The doctor and dancers repeated this in the four directions, then all beat their feet on the ground with the drum, calling the spirits to dance.

As he danced Grizzly Hair kept an eye on his mother's shriveling flesh as it pulled from the bone, and when the platform collapsed and her remains rolled, grabbed one of the staffs laid by for that purpose and respectfully poked it back toward the hot center, as others did for their dead. Missouri watched but people paid no attention to the disapproval on his face. Sometimes María took a stick and poked the remains back.

All during the heat of the day, the fire stirred hot wind around Grizzly Hair as he pounded the grief down with his feet. Smoke twisted in agony and rose in the blue afternoon, forming a black cloud of despair over the home place.

By nightfall the bodies were consumed and the pace of the dancing increased. Grizzly Hair and others threw on wood as they passed by the pile, and the fire burned hotly most of the night. The line broke and dancing became individual, jumping at random, wailing, flinging of arms, rolling of heads, black hair flying before the flames. He reserved nothing yet scarcely felt himself move. He danced even after father sun came up over the eastern hill. Others slept where they collapsed but he continued. Later, a dark claw came up and hooked him down to the ground, where sleep smothered his grief.

He felt sun on his back and opened an eye. The women-men were brushing charred bones into separate baskets, remembering which ones belonged together. They would bury them in the mound. Grateful, Grizzly Hair slept again.

Next time he awoke and saw, across the white circle of ash, Missouri tying a bundle on one of his strange horses. The animal stepped around like it didn't want the straps tightened. Its long brown ears lay flat against its head. "*Damned mule*," Missouri said, yanking the strap. The animal tried to run but Missouri held the reins.

Grizzly Hair got up and went to help. "Damned mule?" he asked, pointing to the animal.

Missouri smiled and said, "*Mule.*"

"Mule?" He pointed at Missouri's gray horse, who gently nudged Morena away from Amarillo.

"*Horse*," corrected Missouri. "*Horse. Caballo.*"

"Horse," Grizzly Hair repeated. It sounded like "horeh," deer in his tongue. He pointed up the path, looking the question.

"Yup, gittin on up the trail. Come back when it's frio."

Grizzly Hair nodded. *"Cuando hace frio."* By then the umne would have piles of beaver skins. But he wouldn't be present. *"Palaber,"* he said, squatting, patting the ground.

Missouri sat beside him with a questioning look while Grizzly Hair drew a map showing the northern mountains. He pointed north of the mountains and looked at him questioningly.

Missouri nodded and said, *"Sí. I go there."*

Grizzly Hair drew his finger along the sea coast. *"Donde Russians?"* A man who came from the north might know.

Missouri pressed a finger into a spot on the coast. "Fort Ross."

"Fort Ross," Grizzly Hair repeated, realizing that it would be an advantage to travel with a man who knew the way, a man with a gun. "You go Fort Ross now?"

"Sí."

"Russians, *amigos?*"

Seeing Missouri's nod, he signed the question, "I go with you? On my horse?"

The *Americano* removed his hat and scratched his rancid hair, the stench hitting Grizzly Hair's stomach. He put the hat on and said, *"Bueno."* Grunting to his feet, he held out a thick hand.

Thinking he meant to help him up, Grizzly Hair took the hand—hard with dirt and calluses—and stumbled up as Missouri moved his hand up and down. "Me-wuk *amigo,*" the trapper said, blue eyes crinkling at the corners.

Americanos apparently used hand pumping as a sign of friendship. He pumped back, feeling a bond. They were travelers heading together into strange territory.

III
The Circle Widens

Becoming strong on this earth is a lesson
in not floating, in becoming less transparent,
in becoming an animal shape against the sky.

From: "The Endangered Roots of a Person"
— Wendy Rose, Miwok

34

He pretended not to notice the eyes looking up from the gloom as he arranged the mission beads on the packed earth before Red Sun's u-macha—reparations for Oak Gall. Other people resting after the dance watched. Many were napping in the open.

With six beads remaining he went to Running Quail, who sat with his son against their u-macha. The elder rebuffed his glance. His chest and abdomen bore the same raised spots that had been on Howchia, and he appeared to be exhausted. Grizzly Hair showed him the beads and said, "I would like you to have them."

Running Quail blew out air and took the beads. Lame Beaver arched his brows, and it was indeed surprising that his father had accepted reparations. It meant the rift might mend.

"I am going with the *Americano*, to visit other peoples," Grizzly Hair said.

Lame Beaver looked amazed. Getting to his feet he beckoned Grizzly Hair with his head. When they were alone, he said, "You are not to blame that my brother stayed in the mission. But if you ever see him, tell him I want him to come home." His voice cracked. "Tell him I want to hunt with him again."

"Someday I will visit a man who knows him. I will give him the message."

Lame Beaver put his hands on Grizzly Hair's shoulders, each holding the other at arm's length.

Then Grizzly Hair went to Morning Owl's u-macha. Not looking at the ash where his mother's u-macha had stood, he waited before the entrance. María lay asleep on the riverbank. He decided not to wake her. That would only force them to struggle with parting. Raven Feather ducked outside, blinking in the sunlight. He was glad to see her hair still thick and full to the shoulders.

He explained, "Our *Americano* guest is leaving and I'm going with him." He nodded toward María. "She and Grandmother will need food and shelter." It was the hy-apo's duty to care for guests, but Grandmother was Grizzly Hair's responsibility.

The strong dark lines of Raven Feather's face conveyed warmth and friendship. "We are honored to look after Mariá. She finds good medicine. I am sure she will care for your Grandmother." She smiled. "Your red stone has power. Morning Owl is sweating now. I believe he will live."

Relieved that something good had come from him after all, he touched her arm in gratitude and turned to leave. "Wait," she said, going inside. She returned with a basket of acorn meal. "This will help you travel."

He accepted the basket from the hy-apo's wife, a sign of belonging, perhaps misplaced. As he crossed the dry bed of Berry Creek, Lame Beaver and Falls-off-House caught up. "We want to go with you," Falls-off-House said.

Had they been less eager, he would have laughed. "No, friends," he said, "I am going straight west. It will be dangerous." Their faces fell, but Grizzly Hair had learned a lesson on his last journey. "I will not risk other people's lives unless the umne ask me to." Even then he might not. "But if María needs you to travel with her and your parents agree, please help her. She could introduce you to Sucais and Domingo. Sucais is the father of the man who talks to Bowstring."

The two exchanged a surprised, happy look.

"You heard my story," Grizzly Hair cautioned, "and won't repeat my mistakes." They acknowledged that with nods and solemn faces, and followed him to the playing field.

Missouri had the last of his bundles on the mules and the animals roped together, one before the other. A rope also tied the front mule to the horse's saddle. About to put his boot into the leather sling, the *Americano* stopped, came over and took the basket of meal from Grizzly Hair. He removed a hide from his packs, covered the basket, wrapped a long thong around it and tied it firmly on the hind mule's load. Then he swung into his saddle and waited.

As Grizzly Hair bent to unhobble Morena, Amarillo came over and turned his rump. Just in time Grizzly Hair jumped to the side, avoiding the flashing hooves. The stallion didn't want his female taken away. Yelling, Missouri leapt off his horse and threw a rock. Amarillo squealed and bounded awkwardly away, hobbled forelegs together.

Missouri's actions made Morena skittish. "Easy, Brown Girl," Grizzly Hair crooned as he threaded the rope through the gaps in her teeth and knotted it around her jaw. Missouri continued lobbing rocks at Amarillo. Grizzly Hair was ready to mount when he saw Etumu.

"Falls-off-House said you were leaving," she said.

Basks, her name meant. It brought to mind Lizard Woman, who enjoyed basking in the sun. Lizard had given people her five-fingered hands. Etumu had been named for her competent hands—an honor for a girl. In the lumpy black of her face, all he saw were the whites of her eyes, moist reddish lips and white teeth. He could hear her sparking music. Her hands were clasped behind her back. "I brought you something."

"What?" He led Morena toward her.

"Something you might need." Glancing at him from beneath her padded eyelids, she opened a slim hand. On it lay a neat rabbit-skin pouch, the opening threaded with a thong to be worn around his neck—just what he needed to carry his blue crystals.

He accepted the pouch. There was something in it. He pushed in two fingers and brought out the gold nugget she had found at his mother's power place. The thought of his mother momentarily stole his strength. As though hearing his sorrow, Etumu turned and ran like a frighted deer.

"Wait," he called, slipping the gold into the pouch. "You sewed this very well. I like it. And the gold is pretty. Yellow as the sun, smooth as Lizard's belly."

She stopped, turned, gave him a little smile, then continued running. Was the gold supposed to remind him of the morning he'd held her hand? Did she admire him as a man? He hadn't thought of her as anything but a child. She was Water to his Land and, like her sister, an eligible mate, but he felt nothing for her. Fortunately she would become a woman before he returned—if he returned—and, as the daughter of a respected elder, would receive offers from good men and no doubt forget him. This was as it should be. Letting out a cynical chuckle, he realized her parents would prefer any living man to him.

They rode up the north trail through low rolling hills, the meager rain having brought only a hint of green. The oaks were brown and gold and ready to lose their leaves. Father sun was high when they came to the yellow cottonwoods marking the big river. A faint trail ran west along the river, but from story he knew more people lived on the north bank—the people of Kadeema, Sek and Poo-soo-ne. Perhaps also knowing this, Missouri angled his horse down the bank and plunged into the water, riding his swimming animal. The mules followed, noses up, packs mostly above the water. Grizzly Hair slid off Morena and swam before her, holding the reins. The current swept them all downstream before Missouri pulled up the steep slope of the north bank, the powerful wet haunches of his gray horse pushing west.

Grizzly Hair followed the dripping mules—bundles swaying with their gait. Aromas of oak and sagey wormwood rose up around him. The rabbit-skin pouch swung from his chest when he leaned forward to pass beneath oak limbs. Grapevines cascaded from the trees. The ripe fruit offered itself to a man on a horse, though it had been picked clean below. He savored the purple tart-sweet morsels. Squirrels moved through the trees like swift gray caterpillars, and from deep cover a coyote looked at him with slant eyes. On his left the water ran with power and depth. Great blue herons and snowy egrets fished the shallows, and the gabble of winging geese brought to mind the imminent arrival of salmon. The umne would dance and celebrate First Salmon. Racks of salmon would be hung to dry. He would miss that. And how many more festivals to come? Would he ever go back?

Sunlight flashed through the leaves and he momentarily saw his comical midday shadow, a squat four-legged monster with no hair. It made him smile. He was a new man, his bow across his chest, quiver crossed the opposite way. New heron leg-bones swung in his earlobes. He would use his broader vision to learn on this journey. There were many peoples to meet between here and where the Russians lived. Then maybe he'd go to Sucais' place and wait until Estanislao arrived on a *paseo.* They'd share their knowledge about what was happening in the world. By then something might have become clear about alliances. He'd learn from each village along the way.

Curious bears watched from the bushes, alert heads above the foliage, round ears erect—mother bears and cubs foraging on the ripe toyon berries. The number of them along the river told him that the salmon would be thick this season. As Morena rounded a bend, he saw three females running, but not from the horses. A male had to be nearby. Mother bears hurried their cubs away to prevent males from killing them; the half-grown bears knew to get out of the way.

Then he saw the male looking over the bushes a bowshot away, bigger than the others. The bear fascinated him as much as he appeared to fascinate the bear. He doubted any of these bears had ever seen horses. Missouri leaned down, took his gun from the sling and put it to his shoulder.

"No," Grizzly Hair blurted in his own tongue—too late.

The thunderclap resounded. Morena flinched, reared. Stunned, he grabbed her mane. They hadn't prepared for a bear hunt. Only special bear-men hunted bears, on rare occasions with a band of handpicked men, purified so the bear wouldn't seek retribution after its death. The mules were squealing and bucking. Deer crashed through the underbrush and croaking herons flapped over the water. Grizzly Hair watched the bear to see him fall.

Instead, as if confused and needing to see better, he stood up on his hind feet, exposing his wide pale chest. After being struck by the gun's magic, how could he stand? A man who could hit a pine cone farther away wouldn't have missed. The sharp scent of the smoke bespoke the gun's power, yet the brown eyes remained alert. Astounded that the bear continued to stand, Grizzly Hair struggled to control Morena.

Another explosion shocked him, and the horse. The bear flapped a paw as if at a mosquito but continued to stand. He rolled his head, revealing crimson fur on both sides of his nose, and uttered a grinding roar that clawed Grizzly Hair's innards.

Morena leaped and twisted, and Grizzly Hair flew through the air and landed painfully on a stiff, young tree. His horse galloped down the trail with the reins between her legs. Quickly he scrambled to his feet and untangled his bow from the crushed tree. The mules screamed and reared to break free. Missouri was off his remarkably still horse, calmly pouring powder into his gun barrel. Would the bear charge? Normally bears left people alone, but ordinary men spoke to them as brothers and assured them there was no threat. Hit three times, this one roared in pain.

To end the pain, Grizzly Hair positioned an arrow and aimed at the bear's eye. An intelligent brown eye looked back at him, saying, *Do not do this to your ally.* He lowered the bow.

The bear turned and looked at Missouri. As if understanding at last where the balls were coming from, he fell to all fours in a lunging charge—big pigeon-toed leaps over the bushes. He came with astonishing speed. Missouri fired again. The bear jerked a little to the side then continued straight for him. Grizzly Hair chinned himself into an oak and climbed two limbs higher.

The mules turned and kicked as the bear arrived. With the sharp crack of breaking bone, the bear's head was struck. Lightning quick, the bear slashed bloody furrows down the rump of one of the mules. The mule screamed like a dying man.

Then the hooves of the gray horse struck the giant's head and he sank slowly into a sitting position. His brown eyes searched, located Grizzly Hair—the expression of a kindly grandfather accepting his death. He had fought bravely. Grizzly Hair climbed down the tree and said, "Someday we will dance together in the happy land."

Missouri held his hand out as if to say, don't go near that bear until it's dead. Grizzly Hair turned to him. Did the man think he didn't know O-se-mai-ti?

Incomprehensible talk rattled out of Missouri. *"Why in tarnation didn't you help me kill the bugger? Now my mule's a goner."* He skewered Grizzly Hair with his white eyes, gun in hand, fringe swaying. By the tone and scowl, it was clear he was angry.

Grizzly Hair was angry too. The man had killed the most powerful animal on earth without ritual or purification—knowing there were limits to the gun's magic. His rash behavior could have killed them both. He gave Missouri a look to convey all of it. *Follow me,* the dream bear had told him. *I will show you the way.* Now this!

He stepped down the bank to fill the rabbit-skin pouch with water. Returning, he found Missouri sawing with his knife on the bear's foreleg, which was squeezed between his bent knees. Gently but firmly he pushed the man out of the way. The leg thudded to the ground and Missouri stepped back. He watched Grizzly Hair lift the heavy muzzle and pour water into the loose mouth, past the enormous incisors. Then he sang his brother's spirit onward.

Afterwards Missouri resumed cutting off the paws. When the second one fell, he gave Grizzly Hair what might have been an apologetic look, pointed to the bear claws on the ground and rubbed his belly. His tongue circled the hairy hole of his mouth and his grin challenged Grizzly Hair to smile back.

Everyone knew the tender feet were delicious, but Grizzly Hair couldn't smile. He signed that he was going after his horse. By the time he ran the long distance down the trail to where she had finally stopped, and subdued her, he could see Missouri coming, leading the two mules. The one in the rear limped badly. Something had been slathered on the wounds, and most of the bundles, including the basket of meal, were piled on the healthy animal. The four bear paws were tied together behind Missouri's saddle, a thong tight between the claws.

They continued single file toward Kadeema's village, sick sensations welling up in Grizzly Hair. He couldn't forget the bear's dying expression. What did it mean that he should follow O-se-mai-ti? This bear was dead and he was following its feet. Missouri killed the same way black hats killed cattle, the way they shot condors, without concern about the spirit. The mules were already loaded down and there was no way to carry the meat. He had killed the Old Man of the Forest for his feet. The longer Grizzly Hair watched the claws jiggle before him, the more uneasy his stomach felt.

35

No herald announced them when they arrived at Kadeema's place. The people were hiding. That was strange. Hadn't Missouri been here before? Grizzly Hair called out words of friendship. He spoke their tongue—all his people did, Nisenan their word for people. This was the home place of Pretty Duck, the wife of Scorpion-on-Nose and it had been the home of the wife of old Frogs-Eggs-Hatching. He announced that Missouri was a friend.

At last two men stepped out. The headman talked in careful tones and gave him guarded looks, never glancing at Missouri, though Missouri smiled at them. What was the matter here?

Kadeema spoke formally, solely to Grizzly Hair. "Where do you come from and where are you going?"

"Morning Owl's people, on the southern river. I go to the western sea."

A few more Kadeema-umne showed themselves. Maybe the unfriendly behavior lingered from the long-ago war. That seemed unlikely considering these people had given so little reparations—the umne grumbled about it to this day, always mentioning that Blue Snake had gone to his death. Still, it didn't explain why they didn't look at Missouri. Weren't they curious, as the umne had been?

Kadeema's women provided food, but it seemed less from duty than fear. This was not the time to speak about becoming allies. Grizzly Hair didn't ask. But he did ask whether they had seen black hats. None had ever seen them. He told them to hide if black hats came. As if considering the source, they looked at him with narrowed eyes. Missouri kept smiling but no one smiled back. He did not spread his goods before them or make sign language about trading. Instead he walked up to the injured mule and fired into the side of its head and gestured to Kadeema that the meat was a gift.

Everyone stared as the mule toppled to its side. The women didn't hurry to their u-machas for knives and baskets. Missouri removed his hat and scratched his hair into dark, greasy peaks. The people downwind turned or moved away to avoid the stench, and Grizzly Hair signed to Missouri that they must leave. Retrieving the remaining bundle from the dead mule, Missouri mounted his horse and they left.

On the way to Sek's place, Grizzly Hair considered how to tell Missouri he didn't want to ride with him. It would break the partnership they had so recently sealed with grasped hands. It would be impolite, and he needed to think about how to be impolite to a man with a gun.

The Sek-umne were no friendlier. Missouri seemed even more puzzled, gaping openly at the people who didn't ask them to sit and talk, or offer food. Grizzly Hair told them, "This man is an esteemed trader."

Sek responded formally. "The *Americano* is a sorcerer. Are you his assistant?"

Taken aback, Grizzly Hair said, "I am not his assistant and have never seen anything to indicate he is a doctor. Has he been here before?"

Sek gave him a lidded look. "He stayed for three sleeps and after he left, four of my people died. Ten were sick. We talked about him in council with Kadeema and Poo-soo-ne and the related villages. He tricks people by displaying tempting goods and pretending to be a trader. He does not purify himself, yet kills from a great distance. At any moment he could change into more of a monster and kill us all. We want him to leave."

This talk landed like a fist to Grizzly Hair's stomach. He recalled Missouri looking at him while the dead bodies were shriveling in the fire. If Sek was right, the *Americano* had killed the umne. His deceit far surpassed Drum-in-Fog's. Missouri must have killed Eagle Woman and Drum-in-Fog's wife, a woman whose husband could sling great injury. Had he killed these women of power to flaunt his powers? But he had also killed a powerless young girl, and no doubt more would die, perhaps Running Quail. No one could have paid him to kill those people. No one could talk to him; they hadn't known he was a sorcerer. This *Americano* stunk, too. He was unclean, so how could he be a doctor? It was a mystery. The word *jinx* came to mind. Missouri had called himself a *jinx* when he saw the people dying. Perhaps it meant doctor in his tongue.

The Sekumne obviously didn't want them around, so Grizzly Hair and Missouri mounted and left. Although Grizzly Hair had been anxious to get to

Poo-soo-ne's place by suppertime, he knew the reception would be the same. He must leave Missouri, but how? They were traveling the same trail. He caught up to the gray horse and signaled.

Missouri glanced over, the light striking his eyes, making them white. Grizzly Hair froze for a moment, thinking he had begun to transform himself to an inhuman form. However the change did not occur. "*Palaber,*" Grizzly Hair said.

With a nod the *Americano* stopped his horse and dismounted. As the animals chomped into the low limbs of cottonwoods, Grizzly Hair pointed back up the trail and tried to explain what Sek had said. He lay down and made himself look dead, tongue hanging out. He held his abdomen and made a vomiting motion. Then he pointed at Missouri. "*Jinx?*"

Missouri closed his horrible eyes and let air out of his long nostrils. "*No want that. No quiero.*" He made the sign of a dead person with tongue hanging out. "*No quiero. No quiero.*" It sounded as though he killed but didn't want to. That of course was impossible. A doctor knew perfectly well when he sent deadly missiles into people.

Missouri rested a fringed elbow on a knee and supported his forehead in his hand, like he was very tired of what was happening. This demeanor wasn't at all like a sorcerer, who would be proud of his exploits. Or was he cleverly pretending to be sorry? A man of strange features, pink skin, huge beard and unknown tongue was hard to judge. In the mission Grizzly Hair hadn't been able to make himself understood when Padre Durán said the people from his river were thieves. Could it be that Missouri was simply a man unable to explain himself? Still, even if he were the friendly trapper he pretended to be, accidentally killing people was unacceptable. Grizzly Hair could die too. And even if he lived, he would be shunned as Missouri's friend. This was the opposite of what he'd hoped, that people would honor him more for traveling with the *Americano.* Most important, O-se-mai-ti had told him not to travel with Missouri. He would obey that and treat bears as they ought to be treated. He wouldn't trade with Missouri either, when he returned.

Some of the heaviness he'd felt of late lifted. Yes, he had invited the *Americano* to the home place, but now he knew it wasn't his own bad power that had killed his people and his mother. Missouri had done it.

As he thought through the sign language to convey his intent to travel alone, Missouri grabbed his upper abdomen and made a toothy grimace of pain. At first Grizzly Hair thought he was pantomiming illness as part of talk. Instead this appeared to be real pain. After it subsided, Missouri grunted to his feet, went to the mule, opened a pack and brought Grizzly Hair a double handful of blue beads. His expression said, "Take them."

Reparations for Howchia's death? Grizzly Hair opened his otterskin quiver to receive the sparkling crystalline beads, which were even more valuable than mission beads. People along the route would recognize them as coming from Missouri and Grizzly Hair would be respected more for having taken them from a doctor.

The *Americano* went to the mule's pack and fished out a knife like the one he'd given Domingo. He also brought the long thong and basket of meal to Grizzly Hair.

He looked at Missouri's sad smile and realized that he too planned to travel alone. Maybe Grizzly Hair's song had conveyed his intent without talk. Gladly he accepted the wonderful knife as further reparations. He would need it in his travels.

Missouri chuckled like he was laughing at himself. "*Injuns won't touch me with a hundred-foot pole. I'm done with Californy. But that don't mean I won't tell other trappers bout the pickings here. I know you don't know a word I'm saying, but anyhow I'm sorry.*" He knelt down and began drawing an earth map, showing the river they were following and the river it would soon meet. Poo-soo-ne's place would be there. He drew the south-flowing river wiggling northward and made it clear that he intended to follow it to the mountains and go over them to the river he called Columbia.

"Fort Ross?" Grizzly Hair asked, pointing at him.

"No." Missouri looked at him with the concentric rings of his eyes, black points in the center. "*You,*" he said touching a crusty finger to Grizzly Hair's chest, "you *go to Fort Ross.*" He struggled to his feet, rubbed his belly and pointed down his throat. "*Eat?*" He went to his horse and pointed at the bear claws.

Grizzly Hair shook his head, never again wanting to see those callused pads that had walked so far on this earth. Besides, bear feet had to be slow-roasted in an earth pit, and that would take a long time. Poo-soo-ne's women would have food.

Missouri stuck out his hand. "*I go. Adios.*"

Grizzly Hair pumped the dirty hand. "*Vaya con Dios.*"

Missouri jammed his boot into the leather sling, threw his leg over the saddle, tipped his hat and plunged into the bushes. As the leaves closed over the mule's rump, Morena cried and struggled to follow. Delighted with his good luck and feeling the beckon of the river spirit, Grizzly Hair tied her to a tree. He removed his pouch and ear ornaments and fell gratefully into the water.

The surface was warm. He let himself slip down the steep underwater slope to where it was cool. He looked around at the moss and wary fish, then pushed off the bottom, popped up and scrubbed himself with fine sand at the bank. Exuberant in his good luck, he swam rapidly across the river and back. As he climbed up the bank, heart pounding with exertion, the breeze in the deep shade chilled and prickled his skin. The season was changing. He brushed off with a tassel of grape leaves and reinserted his ear ornaments, then cut a piece of the long thong, tied it around his calf and inserted the beautiful knife in it. The rest of the thong he tied around Morena's chest, threading the basket through it. Feeling strong and unfettered, he picked several clusters of ripe grapes and rode west down the trail.

Through small openings in the cottonwoods and willows he noticed people watching him from the south shore. They trotted along with him on their side of the river, no doubt a village related to Poo-soo-ne. He sat tall, knowing he cut a strange and wonderful figure on the horse.

Two men suddenly stepped into his path then plunged back into the bushes. A short time later they reappeared, bodies taut, bows drawn. Poo-soo-ne's men. Younger than Grizzly Hair. They were afraid of the horse and him. No doubt afraid to kill him, afraid of his powerful songs and magical retribution.

He pulled the reins, swung down and gave the runner's password in their tongue. He smiled and beckoned, knowing they wanted to touch the horse. Slowly they let their bows slacken and stepped forward with extreme caution. With tentative fingers they touched Morena's shoulder. Speaking in the tongue of Sek and Kadeema, one asked, "Where do you come from?" His young voice cracked with excitement.

"Morning Owl's place on the southern river. I go to the western sea." He rubbed his belly. They looked at each other, then turned up the trail, motioning him to follow. He walked Morena behind their bouncing topknots, father sun golden through the trees in the west. Later the men suddenly loped ahead and vanished around a bend. Here the path was wide and deeply tamped, the scent of Man strong. A little while later he heard the herald.

Then an astonishing sight spread before him—a wide clearing filled with tule u-machas, a town large enough for half the population of the mission. Barking dogs and yipping puppies rushed at him from every direction. Morena shivered uneasily. He patted her neck. Thick stands of tulares lined the south and west sides of the town, the junction of the two rivers. Though the sun was in retreat, the wind blew stronger. Smoke from many supper fires streamed southward into the waving boughs of the oaks. Leaves flew across the town, stirring against the u-machas and cha'kas. The western sky colored the thatch of the roofs salmon, and the heng'a, dancehouse, was big enough to hold ten times the people of the home heng'a. Women put their heads together and pointed at him. Children came to him with the dogs. As the headman stepped forward, Grizzly Hair dismounted.

People of all sizes crowded around to examine him and Morena with obvious fascination. No one seemed afraid, a relief after the Sekumne and Kadeema-umne.

Poo-soo-ne's strong voice was polite and dignified. "Where do you come from?" He wore a polished nose ornament and many strings of shell money on his chest.

"Morning Owl's people on the southern river."

Poo-soo-ne acknowledged that with his eyes. "Where are you going?"

"The western sea. The Russians, the enemies of the *Españoles.*"

Poo-soo-ne raised his brows and signaled Grizzly Hair to follow.

The rumbling music of two big rivers added to Grizzly Hair's excitement about the talk to come. Leading Morena and the crowd of people, he followed his host to a house at the north edge of the town. An older woman at the fire regarded him with intelligent eyes. Assisting her were two younger women, no doubt the hy-apo's other wives. Poo-soo-ne's children, large and small, were seating themselves. The aromas of roasting fish and grass-seed wafers made his stomach speak. Grinning at the sound, Poo-soo-ne suggested he put the horse in the trees behind the house.

When she was hungrily tearing into the grapevines, he seated himself a comfortable distance from Poo-soo-ne's fire and looked across the large town where men and boys came through the trees with netted fish, handing them to women at cooking fires. They turned and looked at Grizzly Hair. Poo-soo-ne's wives served fish stew, roasted salted grasshoppers, steamed greens and delicious frog soup. Grizzly Hair smacked his lips. In the tongue of the host people he talked of the changing season and the coming of salmon. Poo-soo-ne's children listened intently to the banter, which sometimes shifted to Grizzly Hair's tongue. Perhaps someday Poo-soo-ne would invite the umne to a big time, and men from both places would find eligible women. This place was so far away that almost no one was related. Then he realized it would be hard to reciprocate with such a numerous people.

Deeper twilight brought colder wind and Grizzly Hair was glad that Poo-soo-ne's wives continued to feed the fire. As people finished eating they came to talk at the hy-apo's fire, arranging themselves on both sides of the smoke, young children with their mothers. In spite of his youth even the elders seemed to consider him an important guest, and he felt honored.

"Have the black hats come here?" he began. People turned and looked at two men, one on either side of the smoke, perhaps *cimarrones.* But it was Poo-soo-ne who spoke:

"Black hats came on a big wooden boat. It floated up the Big Mo'mol." Grizzly Hair recalled mo'mol was their word for water or drink. "The boat came upstream without men poling. The wind blew it, for it had pale wings attached to tall poles on the boat. We saw black hats on the boat. Thunder came from the boat and everyone ran away. Later this man found a ball," he pointed at a man, who got up and trotted to his u-macha. Poo-soo-ne waited until he returned. The man handed an iron ball the size of a cooking rock to Grizzly Hair. He turned it in his hands. Slightly pocked and rusted, it had a tiny straight ridge around it like the balls Missouri used in his gun. This was heavier than most rocks. No doubt from a *canón,* of which Gabriel and Domingo had spoken.

The twilight faded and Poo-soo-ne's youngest wife added wood to the fire, releasing a flurry of sparks into the wind. People leaned back out of the way, faces darkly shadowed. Poo-soo-ne continued his story.

"Some of the men followed the boat up the Big Mo'mol. They hid in the trees along the shore. The boat went to the next joint of the river." He pointed north. "Up the river of feathers." Seeing Grizzly Hair's puzzled look, he said, "Many birds live there. They leave a blanket of feathers on the water. The boat turned around and came back. It passed our town going south." People nodded, the exciting memory in their faces. "The black hats never came to shore here, as they did in the north. We never saw them again."

"But we are afraid they will come back," one of Poo-soo-ne's wives contributed.

"How many sleeps since then?" Grizzly Hair asked.

A young woman from the crowd pointed to her child and said, "He was in his bikoos."

About five *años,* Grizzly Hair figured, since that child was in a cradleboard. He addressed all the people. "Have any of you gone to the mission?"

Everyone looked at the same two men, one of whom talked in the tongue of Gabriel, strangely accented, "Maybe your eyes see for the long robes."

Grizzly Hair replied carefully. "My eyes see for myself. I think many peoples could join together to stop the *Españoles* from capturing people."

The man glanced at his friend across the smoke and everyone exchanged looks. The man with the strange accent said, "I know of people down this river," he flapped a hand toward the Big Mo'Mol, "who went to Mission San José."

Grizzly Hair figured both of them had been there. "I escaped from Mission San José." He turned around to show the scars on his back. They might tell the black hats about him, but if *Indios* were ever to cooperate, risks had to be taken. "I think different peoples should help each other escape when the black hats come for them."

An elder shrugged. "Each village finds its own way."

That strength was also a weakness. He told how the young robin had been attacked by jays and how the robin families had put aside their normal behavior and joined together to drive the jays away. As they discussed this, women took children to the u-machas, and soon only men remained.

"We will talk about this," Poo-soo-ne said, "when you are gone."

He dipped his head. "I will stop here on my way back. I will have much to tell about the peoples along the way."

Unfolding his legs, Poo-soo-ne got to his feet and motioned Grizzly Hair to come. They passed many dark u-machas and banked fires. Leaves torn from the trees swirled around them. He looked up between the oaks and saw the pathway of ghosts brighter than he'd ever seen it—a bridge arching high over the world. The groaning trees brought to mind the restless dead. But he was on the trail of a solution, and Poo-soo-ne had treated him as an esteemed visitor.

He followed the hy-apo down inside a thick clay-covered sweathouse. Dark shapes of men who had been sleeping turned over and looked at him. He sat where Poo-soo-ne showed him, the earth still warm to his backside from the previous sweat. Others entered and found their places. Fuel was brought, the hide dropped and a new sweat began.

It warmed his bones along with his spirit and he felt that he did indeed belong to a broad group of people called *Indios.* At an appropriate place in the laconic talk, he asked, "Do you know the story of El Cid?"

"No, I'd like to hear it," said a voice. The men turned toward him, settling on their sides or lying on their backs with their hands behind their heads, comfortable in their place.

He drew out the story and when he finished, the hide was lifted and he ran after the men and dove into the black river, now warmer than the air. Back in the cozy sweathouse he slept soundly and dreamed of strangers offering food. A good omen. In the chilly dawn he retraced his steps of the night before, seeing overturned tule boats, and swam with the current, allowing himself to be drawn into the bigger, browner river. He wished he could see where the Big Mo'mol merged with the Rio de San Joaquin, but that was south. The Russians lived straight west.

He gave the headman a bead in friendship, then he and Morena crossed the Big Mo'mol and headed into the unknown.

36

Patient, sensitive Morena trusted him enough to struggle through the mud. He got off and pulled her, lurching and jumping, up over the silty bank and down into a forest of tulares. The earth between the tall dry columns was crunchy, flaky scales upturned at the edges. Overhead, geese gossiped in long wedges—time of rain visitors, though almost no rain had fallen. That was just as well, for judging from the tulares, the river would flood farther than he could see, and this would be an enormous lake.

Even high on the horse, he couldn't see past the tulares. Many stood higher than his head. This frustrated him because, except for occasional glimpses, he couldn't see where he was going, the notch in the western mountains where a big creek flowed into the Valley of the Sun. Tulares also rubbed his legs uncomfortably as Morena wound her way through the maze.

Accept what is, and learn from it, Two Falcons had taught. So he recalled how clever these plant brothers were to move to many different places during their lives. They traveled farther than many men. The shallow roots of these hollow-stemmed marsh grasses detached readily in a flood. Giant bunches popped up and floated wherever the water took them. They rooted where they landed and grew new green blades over the dry ones. The Ancients had learned to make boats from them. But the shallow roots also detached in wind. Many clumps had blown down, making riding slow and difficult. Sometimes the way was blocked and he had to back Morena to find another route.

This was a land of voles, mice and roosting birds. Small animals felt safe here because wolves, coyotes and bobcats preferred to hunt in open ground. Clouds of blackbirds and sparrows rose up from the tops of the columns and settled again, and sometimes he and Morena were startled by owls and other night birds squawking into the air. A gopher snake streaked across their path. Morena shied. Steadying her, he realized he could have grabbed the snake for a supper offering at the first village; but by the time he calmed her down, the snake was gone. A horse was a noisy traveling companion.

The tulares continued farther west than he would have imagined, but vistas of the mountains were beginning to open more often. Then to his relief he saw them rising steeply from the oak grassland he was now entering. A herd of about four twenties of elk grazed to the north. The high-legged animals had nibbled everything within reach, pruning the trees. He rode over grazed land beneath bare spreading limbs. The sky was cloudless, the chilly breeze from the north. Walking would have kept him warmer. Patches of dusty earth showed here and there in the short brown grass, and he heard the earth's cry for water. His own throat and tongue felt dry. Morena had to be thirsty too, and he regretted not having brought a water bag.

The notch in the mountains showed clearly now. He adjusted his course. Pines could be seen in the dark creases of the mountains, which stretched north and south as far as he could see. Leaping jackrabbits popped into view and vanished into the now undulating land. He came to what he hoped was the stream, but it was only a big dry wash filled with ragged cattails. A solitary red-legged frog looked up at him, waiting for water. "Patience, little sister," he told her.

When he found the stream it was totally without water. Green grass in its bed indicated the water had been gone for some time. It looked like a wide green snake crawling through the brown grassland. He guided Morena down the bank and into the bottom to let her graze—about as wide as the home river. An elk herd grazed downstream, big-horned parasites on the snake. He looked the other way. Movement caught his eye.

Something was spraying out of the streambed. A wolf or coyote digging?

It seemed too much dirt to come from paws, even a bear's. But water could be found beneath dry streambeds. Perhaps a man was digging for water. He knew from story that if the right songs were sung, such pits could attract the retreating water and sustain a village until the rains came. No horse was in sight, which meant it probably wasn't a black hat. He nudged Morena.

It was indeed a man in a hole pitching dirt with a split oak branch, the center rotted out. Only the man's head and back showed, the hair long and full—not an *Español.* He wore no hat or shirt and the dark, burly shoulders gleamed with perspiration. Two baskets and a greenstone ax lay on the grass out of the range of the flying dirt. It would be polite to help dig, and the quickest way to get a drink.

Another head popped out of the hole. They saw him, scrambled out and stared at him. The smaller man held another stone ax. Both were covered with dirt. Slowly dismounting and keeping an eye on the ax, Grizzly Hair said, "I will help you dig."

They looked at Morena, who was ripping into the grass, and spoke alien sounds. Though he couldn't understand the talk, he knew they felt uneasy.

"*Yo ayudo,*" I help, he said in Spanish, bringing the first spark of understanding to their faces. This was a good sign. He could speak to them about the *Españoles,* about which they clearly had some knowledge. He picked up the extra ax, made digging motions and looked them the question.

The big-chested man spoke carefully.

He shook his head, unable to understand, even when the man repeated himself. "*¿De donde vienes?*" Grizzly Hair asked. Where are you from?

The slimmer man gestured upstream and said something that sounded like a dog choking. Then he said, "*¿De donde vienes?*"

"Morning Owl's umne," Grizzly Hair said, pointing east.

"*¿Donde va?*"

He pointed west. "*A la mar.*" To the sea.

"Ahhh." They raised their brows and opened their mouths. Then the big man pointed south and looked him the question. That was no doubt the way most men traveled west on the big water, but he had a horse who couldn't ride in a tule boat, and needed to stay out of the way of the *Españoles.*

He pointed west again.

They said something to each other in their tongue, then the bigger man smiled and nodded at the pit.

Grizzly Hair hesitated, not having heard their songs. Morena grazed only a few steps away and, in the pit, he would be even more vulnerable than she. They watched him look at her, then the bigger man jumped in the pit and resumed digging. Clearly they were friendly. He lowered himself in the hole and began cutting the damp earth with his knife, throwing it out or into the path of the scoop.

Tight as three fawns in a doe's womb, they exerted themselves in silence, Grizzly Hair gauging his rhythm so he didn't interfere with the scoop. How lucky the umne had been, he realized as he dug. For generations they hadn't needed to do this. The river spirit heard old Dishi's songs, but despite the river's faithfulness, every long dry Hummingbird Tailfeather predicted the river would run dry. People teased her about it.

Gradually the bottom grew soggy. The pit was likely to fill half full and could stay that way for a long time. Elk and deer would spread their forelegs and drink; some would fall in and drown if their death time had come. The men changed tools, the smaller one scooping out mud, spraying it over the three of them. They began to laugh—three mud-slick men. *Indios.*

The water seeped in fast. Still chuckling, they hoisted themselves out. Working together had made them cousin-brothers.

Father sun was high now and Grizzly Hair was tired. They all lay back on the grass absorbing strength and waiting for water. Grizzly Hair whistled to Morena, who had wandered toward the elk herd. She appeared small against them, their enormous horns making them look top-heavy. She looked up and came halfway back, but the juicy grass seized her attention again. He lay back and closed his eyes, appreciating the protection of the bank from the cold north wind on his muddy body.

When he awoke women and children were looking at him, Morena not in view. He jumped up and looked around. One of his new friends was lying on his belly dipping baskets in the water they had lured, handing the baskets to women and children. A big woman sat on his ankles to keep him from falling in, a stack of baskets at the side. The other digging-friend caught Grizzly Hair's attention and pointed toward the canyon, making horse ears with his cupped hands. She was there.

When all were loaded with water, Grizzly Hair and the others headed toward the mouth of the canyon, the notch in the mountains. They passed a deserted village on the way. Where were those people? His hosts followed the streambed around a couple of bends of the canyon, rapidly rising, and there stood Morena, grazing in the creek bottom. On a nearby shelf of land where the creek would overflow in time of rain perched several makeshift u-machas in the shade of the steeply rising mountain. Several small children held Morena's reins, stepping when she did. It made him smile to see their serious faces, as though knee-high children could control a horse.

Later he learned that these were the people of Libayto. Judging by their acquaintance with horses and Spanish, he figured they were mission escapees. But after-supper talk was slow and difficult, the familiarity with Spanish slight. It took a long time to understand that they had never been in a mission. They told the story of the rest of their people, who, when the stream dried up, went to live with their relatives to the south. Some of those relatives had gone to a mission.

"Did your relatives go—?" Willingly he wanted to ask, but didn't know the word. In frustration he said it in Poo-soo-ne's tongue.

A woman brightened, asking him in a tongue very like his whether he understood. He did. She said her home place was downstream of Poo-soo-ne on the Big Mo'mol. She had married an elder in Libayto's place. With her help, talk came easier.

She stunned him with the story of why this group, a small part of their people, had returned to their home place. They had been visiting the Ululato people, their relatives on the plain to the south, when a large number of neophytes arrived on a *lancha*.

Sorry to interrupt, Grizzly Hair asked, "What is a *lancha?*"

"A big flat boat made of *palos altos*—very tall trees."

"Red wood?"

Libayto nodded and Grizzly Hair recalled those trees. A very long raft could be made from them.

Libayto continued. "Men came from Mission San José. They captured Ululato's people and tied them up. Some had been baptized *Christianos*, others not, but that didn't matter to Ildefonso—the leader. He said Padre Durán had sent them to round up *cimarrones* and *gentiles* alike. The fugitives among them were to be punished severely. Ululato's people fought them and tried to run, but Ildefonso's men had bows, spears and two guns, and knew how to use them. The Ululato people were beaten with sticks and gun stocks, and made to wait while Ildefonso's men robbed their houses.

"We were afraid they would catch us too," said Libayto. Everyone nodded agreement. The bigger digging friend added, "We ran back here and escaped."

Libayto continued the story, "We learned later that Ildefonso and his men went to Chemocoyt's place and tried to tie up more people. There was a big fight and five of Chemocoyt's men died. One was wounded. Then Ildefonso forced the captured people to go to Mission San José, but by the time they came back for our relatives, three sleeps after they tied them up, they had untied themselves and run to hide in the tulares. Ildefonso couldn't find them. The neophytes went to another village and killed everyone there." He paused long, during which Grizzly Hair, in growing horror, tried to imagine that.

"You must be afraid Padre Durán will send men here," he said at last, with the help of the woman.

Gravely people nodded around the circle. Libayto pointed south, "A long time ago they took the Suisun people, our distant relatives at the big water. Now they are taking our closer relatives. Next they will come here."

"*Indio* peoples should have a talk network to tell their friends when black hats come," he said, feeling the fire rekindling in his belly. "Special runners."

"What good is talk?" asked a man.

"Other people could help you fight."

"We'd be dead or captured before your men got here."

"But there must be closer people."

Libayto took a long breath. "They wouldn't help. Other people don't care as long as they are safe. That's how the people to the north and east would think of it."

"But no one is safe any more. You have seen that. Wouldn't you go if they needed help?" He recalled Gabriel's men leaving to do just that.

Libayto looked at his men, all of whom gazed at the guttering fire. At last one of the men said, "My wife wouldn't want me to die." The two men who had dug for water looked at each other and shrugged. The bigger man said, "We didn't want to stay in the south and fight the neophytes who captured Ululato's people, even though some of them were our relatives." A night bird shrieked.

Women herded their children inside the u-machas. Grizzly Hair looked at Libayto. "Will you help stop the *Españoles?*"

In the light of the red coals Libayto was barely visible. "If others help us—Topal, Putah, Poo-soo-ne and his relatives and Canijolma." He flicked his wrist west. "Then we might join together."

"I will talk to everyone I meet," Grizzly Hair said, "and I will talk to you on my way back from the Russians. Maybe your neighbors will join us if Russian guns are on our side."

The men perked up visibly. "Maybe," said Libayto.

In the sweathouse Grizzly Hair told the story of El Cid. Men hummed in quiet wonder to hear that a long time ago the home of the black hats had been invaded by a strong people. They chuckled when he said the *Españoles* had fought for many generations and finally chased the invaders away. He told the men what María had said: the invaders left things behind—rich cloth, good horses, clever devices and big decorated houses. "They left some of their power." This story, Grizzly Hair believed, would stay with Libayto's people. A story was like a man—capable of influencing all who heard him. The story of El Cid would make them think about a defensive pact.

After the sleep in the sweathouse, Grizzly Hair followed the men's example and sprinkled himself with water from the baskets, then stood absorbing father sun's faint warmth. One of the men yelled, no doubt telling father sun not to be angry, not to withdraw, telling him that no one had meant to upset him and he should rise sooner in the morning and not go to his western house so early. Grizzly Hair didn't need to understand the words; he had heard many such exhortations in the home place.

As he left, Grizzly Hair removed three beads from his quiver and offered them in trade for a stomach-bag filled with water. The beads were too much for the bag, but he was here to make friends. Libayto went behind his u-macha and returned with the large stomach of an elk tied off with thongs. Grizzly Hair nodded in thanks and filled the bag from one of the baskets.

With a lidded look, Libayto said, "I have seen these beads before."

Grizzly Hair gave him an enigmatic smile.

Later, as he rode up the somewhat grassy streambed that cut through the mountains toward Topal's place, he chuckled to himself. It was as he had hoped. People were impressed that he had acquired Missouri's beads. And he'd been glad to learn that the peoples from here to the Russians were spaced about a sleep apart. Luck willing, he would sleep in friendly sweathouses the entire way. Familiar plant people kept him company—oak, leafless buckeye, elderberry, redbud and the scent of wormwood coming to him on the stiff wind.

The souls of the rock people changed. No longer crumbly and yellow, they rose smooth, hard and dark on both sides of the steepening canyon. Inside the narrowing walls Grizzly Hair turned Libayto's story over in his mind, stopping now and then for Morena to graze on tufts of grass. Padre Durán's people were reaching far and wide. Ildefonso's attack had occurred only a few sleeps ago, while Missouri was in the home place. He urged Morena to walk faster. Libayto had said the people in the southern half of the next valley were mostly gone from their home places—all in the missions. Was it too late to form a defensive pact? Would Topal and Putah, Poo-soo-ne and Canijolma agree to it? Or would every village wait until it was too late, then fight by themselves, and lose?

Now he was heading to Topal's place at the top of the canyon. Putah's people lived in the higher mountains beyond that, but Grizzly Hair didn't want to go that far north. He would leave it to Topal to talk to them. Morena's hooves struck difficult rock in what seemed the bottom of the world. Ridges of rock ran vertically down the walls into the streambed, making the footing treacherous. The rockface on his left resembled a giant's flat chest with a head high above in the clear sky. Maybe it was the rock giant who sprang out of living rock and ate people and left their skulls in caves, or the giant Ké-lok, who had killed Falcon by throwing red hot stones at him. Coyote tricked and killed him with his own hot stones, then brought Wek-Wek back to life, but Ké-lok's fire escaped and burned the world. The colossal stone figure with cold wind swirling down from it made gooseflesh prickle on his arms. Would Grizzly Hair's own actions bring death to the umne? Could anyone bring them back to life?

He coaxed Morena up the suddenly steeper rocks. At the top, the land opened to a long meadow, through which the north wind blew. A streak of still water riffled in its bed, too low to spill down the canyon. In time of rain it would be a waterfall. Wooden u-machas and a dancehouse stood back from the stream. Wide-spaced oaks in the meadow seemed to wave at him, the limbs festooned with gray stringy moss like the long gray hair of old people. About two bowshots from Grizzly Hair, women sat coiling baskets while small children chased each other.

A child saw him and pointed.

Topal's people offered friendship and good food. Again a woman spoke Poo-soo-ne's tongue. After supper, the people gathered around the headman's fire and Grizzly Hair told them why he was there. A strange look crossed Topal's eyes and he leaned back against his u-macha. Talking slowly to allow for the woman's translation, he told a story:

"When my father's cousin was young, there was a headman named Malaca among the Suisun people. The Suisun people are our distant relatives who lived in the south along the big water."

Grizzly Hair understood more than the words—he heard emotion as deep as the Big Mo'mol. By their expressions, the people were settling down to hear an important story.

"Malaca was a respected headman with many people. One day a *lancha* came to his village carrying Padre Abella, some black hats and some distant relatives of Malaca's people who had once lived across the big water near the Spirit Peak. They were *Christianos* but Malaca's people didn't know what that meant yet. The visitors brought *mulas.* With big eyes the Suisun people stared at these animals, which they had never seen before. They touched the iron things on the animals and wondered what magic had made it. They touched the beads around the necks of their relatives and were respectful before people who possessed such things and made large animals do their will. The black hats made fire and thunder come from their *fusiles* and Malaca's people quaked with deepened respect. The relatives spoke Malaca's tongue and the tongue of Padre Abella, so everyone could talk. Padre Abella told Malaca's people that all these things would be theirs if they went to live in the mission. He said the Great Spirit in the sky would make them live forever and give them power. Padre Abella showed them a *pintura* of María with golden sunlight shining around her head. Malaca's people had never seen anything like it and their eyes grew bigger. They wanted to learn the ways of the strangers, the ways their relatives had learned.

"After the visitors left, the elders agreed that they would go to *Misión Dolores* on the other side of the big water. They made extra tule boats so all the people could go over there when the tide reversed."

Topal paused, the flames dancing in his eyes, then continued. "Malaca's people lived at the mission, but after a while they became sick for their sunny home place. Luck turned against them. A spotted death killed many of them, almost all of their children. They needed the protection of the home spirits.

So at night when the tide was right Malaca and his people got in their boats and returned to their home place. They danced the Cry. On the second day a runner told them Captain Moraga and many black hats were coming for them. Horses and guns and soldiers were coming on *lanchas*."

Topal looked beyond the fire with unfocused eyes and children leaned forward so as not to miss a word. "The elders decided not to go back with Captain Moraga. They knew they must fight. And men on horses would be hard to defeat. To make the black hats get down and fight on the ground, they dug a maze of pits and trenches around the village. And later when the black hats rode toward them, their horses refused to go farther. The soldiers got off and entered the village on foot.

"The fight was very bad. They ran out of arrows and many of Malaca's men died. The women and children were tied up. Everyone knew they would be punished severely. They had seen many whippings at the mission, and Malaca and his men decided never to go back. He raised a torch over his head and called to his men: 'Go to your houses. Let us die with dignity in our home place.'

"The men ran to their houses. The black hats thought they had quit fighting, but when they followed them into the houses, Malaca's men fought with their hands and feet. Malaca was running from house to house setting them on fire, his own house last. The dry tulares burned rapidly and the *Españoles* backed out of the heat."

Topal's eyes shone like black obsidian in the firelight. His voice came quiet and hard-punching. "The cousin of my father was a young boy then. He wanted to burn with his father, but the last he saw of him, his father stood inside the house with his hair a big ball of fire. He watched until nothing was left except the smell of cooked flesh. The women and children were taken to the mission and lived there until they died. They had nowhere else to go. A long time later my father's cousin told me that story when he was on *paseo*. I never saw him again."

Ash settled in the dying fire and wolves howled across the mountains. The crying spirits of Malaca's people? One cried higher than the others then slid down into the thickening darkness, but no one added more wood. Shivering children were carried to their u-machas. Men went to the sweathouse. The story had tripped a snare in Grizzly Hair's mind. It shot him back to the mission, to the bite of the whip and Oak Gall in the deep hole, to the last night of his journey with María. The fires on the valley floor had raced through the grass and touched his spirit. In his own way he had decided to burn rather than return to the mission.

He asked Topal, who was watching the coals crumble, "If black hats and neophytes invaded Libayto's place, would you and your men go down there and fight with them?"

Three more men grunted to their feet and went to the sweathouse. Men were carrying wood inside.

Grizzly Hair tried again. "If the men of Putah and Poo-soo-ne joined and helped Libayto, would you and your men fight with them?"

Topal spoke carefully. "Our men are brave. We help our relatives when we can—if they need food or water, or if men from the north hunt in their hunting grounds. When that happens the intruders look at our strong bows and turn back to their home. But black hats would not leave. Maybe my men will fight them some day, maybe not." Glancing at the smoke coming out the sweathouse entrance, Topal got to his feet. Talk was finished.

Later, despite the warmth of the sweathouse, Grizzly Hair lay awake thinking about the pits and trenches Malaca had dug to stop the horses. Malaca had been clever, but hadn't stopped the guns. With soft snoring around him, he lay thinking about the many seasons that had passed since Malaca had burned to death, and the many people still dying in the missions. He realized that Grandfather Crying Fox had gone to the western sea at about the time Malaca's men burned in their houses. That thought lingered in the heat and pulled him into bad dreams.

In the night he bolted up, startled. Where was he? The air smelled different. His heart pounded. But when he saw men asleep on all sides, he remembered he was in Topal's place. Perhaps his dream warned him that this journey would not always be as easy as his visits to the first three peoples.

After nu-pah the next morning, Topal drew an earth map showing the trail west. It went over the mountains then down into the valley home of Canijolma's people. Topal marked that with his thumb. He showed where Napa and his people had once lived on the river that flowed into the big water of the bay. "Napa and his people went to the mission a long time ago. The Caymus people are gone too."

Topal pressed his finger into the home place of Huiluc over the next mountain range. "Those hills are not as high as ours," he said, pouring handfuls of dirt west of the Canijolmas. "But I know nothing about the people and land beyond that."

Grizzly Hair thanked the hy-apo and his wife and rode west, still haunted by the story of Malaca. At first the trail was rocky and Morena walked as though her feet hurt, so when he could, he guided her to softer ground. Then the madrona, cedars and a pine he didn't know and bushes he didn't recognize grew so dense that little light penetrated.

Halfway down the mountain, the view opened and he saw the pretty valley of Napa's river. The air felt softer and he could tell the oaks and grasses of this valley would give generously. The gentle mountains on the other side, which he would cross after the sleep, were not very far away. In the north he saw more mountains. In the south the hills flattened into the horizon—the big water of the Bay of San Francisco. Captain Moraga and Ildefonso and his men had floated there on the incoming tide. On the other side of the big water, the blue Spirit Peak loomed precipitously. With the water before it, the peak appeared to float in the air. No wonder Molok had roosted there in the time of the big flood. Coyote's wife had given birth in that place of big power.

Strange trees with small lobed leaves crowded in among the oaks and laurel as he descended the mountain, and more poison oak than he'd ever seen twined up every vertical trunk, brushing his legs. "Your relatives in my home place are my friends," he told the powerful vine. "I am sorry to bother you but I cannot help it. I would appreciate your not giving me your itch." He never worried about that at home, but Poison Oak's cousins hadn't heard his music before.

On the floor of the little valley, father sun blazed directly in his eyes, yet the wind blew cold. It was the end of the day. He felt hungry enough to eat a whole elk, and his hind end hurt from riding. The water bag had satisfied his thirst, but Morena hadn't known how to drink from a bag. She would be anxious to get to the river. He was too. He could hardly wait to stretch and walk around. The path intersected a wide trail running north-south outside the thicket of the river. He turned north, then, a short distance up that trail, west on a path leading into the thicket—no doubt Canijolma's place.

An arrow flashed, thunked into a tree. It quivered there, having barely missed his head. Fear buzzed in his hands and feet. He looked right, saw nothing in the dense brush. Morena halted, ears back. Another arrow could have killed him by now. He was an easy target. It must have been meant to frighten, not kill. Should he call out the runner's password?

No. The arrow had spoken. Ildefonso's men might have come here and these people were afraid of visitors. He turned Morena around and galloped back to the wider trail. Relieved no arrow drove between his shoulder blades and no one followed, he turned south toward the deserted end of the valley where Napa's people had once lived.

As the fear of pursuit subsided, he realized with uncomfortable foreboding that he would sleep alone this night, exposed to loose souls and howling demons. The Huiluc people lived another sun's ride across the next mountain range. Adding to his worries, he had needed the Canijolmas to tell him how to find that trail. Now he must find it himself.

Morena's mane whipped in the north wind and the shadows of twilight deepened—a cold windy night ahead. A herd of pronghorn antelope looked up from beneath the trees, then bounded away. Hoping he was far enough from the arrow men and safely north of the deserted villages and dead souls of Napa's people, he reined Morena across trackless bunchgrass toward the river.

He guided her into the river bottom and let her find a drinking place in the low stream. He squatted to scoop water beside her. This secluded bend of the river seemed as good as any lonely place could be, abundant grape leaves for Morena—half-red now. He found a few shriveled grapes that hadn't been picked, for his nu-pah. Warm nu-pah would make him less lonely.

For fire, he gathered tinder and a dry elderberry stem, squatted against the cutbank and whirled Elderberry between his palms until the tinder smoked on the wooden platform. It would have been nice to sleep in a sweathouse, he thought, as the wind blew the ember to life, but he must not dwell on bad luck.

He took the bulb of soaproot that he had dug on the mountain and sliced it in half. Saving half for morning purification, he mashed the bulb in a curve of oak bark and stirred the froth into a river hole a little downstream. Shortly, the underbellies of two stupefied trout floated to the surface. He seized the slippery fish with his hands, thanking them for coming to him.

When the fire was whipping in the wind, he found a flat rock suitable to cook his fish, dry enough that it wouldn't explode, and placed it on the fire. While the fish cooked he found another dry stone for his nu-pah. He cooked a quarter of the acorn meal and saved the rest in the hide.

Singing softly, he took his time cooking. By the time he finished eating, the sky glittered with the campfires of the immortals. Night animals rustled in the bushes and coyotes sang. An owl swooped toward him from the other side of the river and landed only a little above his head. Big and pale on the branch, it watched him then softly hooed. Darkness dropped around Grizzly Hair and fear crept into him along with the cold. His small fire felt more and more isolated from the world, more a target for eyes—animals, loose souls, evil spirits. Fortunately, however, the arrow men would be in their warm sweathouses.

Oak Gall came to him, standing with a hand teasingly on her hip. He tossed another piece of wood on the fire and she mounted with the swarm of sparks on the wind. He hadn't meant to chase her away, but the sparks guided his uneasy thoughts to neophytes pounding iron. He recalled another metal being shaped in the mission—the orangish kind that was pounded into sheets and molded to make the huge vats. He touched the hard lump in his rabbit pouch. Gold was also dense and smooth. Could it be melted and pounded flat?

He added more wood and built up a small platform in the center of the fire. As the flames whipped around it, he turned the flat rock over, the one he'd cooked his fish on. It had an indentation into which he put the golden egg, then shoved the rock on the platform. This playing with gold would keep him warm and give him something to think about besides being alone. But though he continued to feed the fire, the egg held its shape.

Hearing a wet slurp, he jerked around. There stood a coyote in the firelight, practically at his elbow, nose in the nu-pah that he needed for morning.

He yelled and the Trickster bounded away. He threw a rock at the low, retreating tail, and smiled. Coyote was everywhere. Grizzly Hair climbed the cutback and selected a tree back far enough from his camp, tied a rock to the end of his long thong, threw it over a branch and threaded the ends through the basket so it would hang. Then he pulled the thong until the basket was high in the tree, and secured the rock-end to a branch. Now he felt safer from bears and their powerful noses. Coyote had warned him.

Morena would graze nearby during the night. He was her only company, as she was his. He left her free of hobbles and ropes so she could run from a bear, but nothing was certain. Earth's creatures could meet their deaths at any time.

The gold didn't melt and he couldn't get the fire any hotter. Thinking the wind cooled the gold too much, he laid another flat rock over it like a lid, and with a pair of crude wooden tongs pushed the covered gold deep inside the hottest coals. He left it there while he made his bed.

With a strong stick, he loosened and removed the silty earth in a narrow pit on the river bank above the fire. He put half the excavated dirt between his bed and the fire and half along the cold side. When the trench was level and as deep as from his fingertips to his shoulder, he took burning wood from the fire and started two more fires in the bed, like women heated earth beds for the sick—one fire where his chest would be, one at the knees. He fed the fires and let them burn hot, then stirred the red coals evenly over his bed and, tossing out all rocks, covered them with the dirt he'd dug up from the cold side of the bed. He fluffed and leveled the sand and dirt. His bed would be soft, warm and dry, not steamy as it would have been in the river bed. He laid his bow and quiver within reach of the bed.

The rocks in his fire glowed red-hot. He removed the gold with his tongs, but when he flipped off the lid he saw that the egg held its shape. Iron, he imagined, would have melted. He tried pounding the gold with a pestle rock, and to his pleasure it easily gave way and filled the stone indentation. Perhaps indeed the long robes had figured a way to spin gold into fine strands. He would look at this again after the sleep.

As he stretched out in his warm bed, a cold thought hit him—Oak Gall in her deep hole, narrow like this. He cleared his mind and pulled the heated earth down over him in a thick warm cover. The night had been long and he had ridden far since dawn. Now mother earth warmed his bones and pulled him into restful sleep. O-se-mai-ti came to his dream and the two of them walked in the woods together. A very good omen.

The bed remained warm even at first light, and he awoke rested and refreshed. Father sun was slow coming up, so he faced east and called to him, telling him to hurry, reminding him that earth's creatures needed his warmth and a man felt lonely without his light. The warm rays finally came through the trees, glancing off the moving water and striking the gold just as Grizzly Hair was prying it from its mold. He smiled to see that it had assumed the shape of a grape leaf, a thick, amusingly diseased leaf with perfect little creases to match the rock's indentation.

Someday, he realized, he might show this to Etumu. That meant returning. The thought felt neither repugnant nor pleasurable. He had no family there, except old Dishi, and at least one of the elders considered him a murderer. But for now he felt calm. Power had protected him from night demons. He put the gold in his rabbit-skin pouch, ate his remaining nu-pah and rode west into another mountain range.

On the other side of the hills, fortunately not steep, he found another main trail running north-south but unlike the last, this was pitted with many horse tracks. Black hats. He stopped to think. Huiluc's people had to be north, the way Topal had drawn the map, the Russians north then west. With signs of black hats all around, he must be stealthy.

Leading Morena back into the trees off the trail—how did *Españoles* tolerate the butt pain of riding all day?—he kept the trail in view. Sooner or later a stream would flow from the mountains he'd just crossed and the Huilucs would be located on it. He scanned the scattered north hills and a big mountain on the northeast that resembled a sleeping giant, the high point the shoulder, then the hip and slope of a long leg.

He came to the stream, mere puddles filled with nettles and peppermint. The dry stems of soaproot beckoned on the other side. Leaving Morena sipping a trickle of water, he crossed the creek and knelt to dig up a bulb that had wedged itself between buried rocks. He used his knife. When he had extricated it and was brushing the dirt off, something hit his shoulders, hard.

Shock jumped to his fingertips. He dropped the bulb, grabbed a thin rope tightening around his throat and turned around.

37

A man with the round eyes of a dog jerked the rope.

Grizzly Hair fell face down and was pulled by the neck, choking, through the grass. Morena had also been lassoed. Digging his fingers into his neck, he tried to pull the braided horsehair from his windpipe. He was dragged through mud and peppermint. Gasping for breath, he looked up, trying to blink the mud away, and saw two men in mission shirts. *Indio* faces. Neophytes.

When his eyes cleared better he saw a third man in the bushes, also wearing a mission shirt. He held a drawn bow with an arrow pointed at Grizzly Hair.

The man who had lassoed Morena jumped on her back and sat smiling at him. His unruly hair gave him a ferocious appearance and his sparse mustache moved as he spoke in soft deliberate Spanish, *"Gracias por el caballo."* Thank you for the horse. He pulled a knife from his calf-thong, flipped it high in the air and skillfully caught the tip, laying the haft over his muscular shoulder, elbow to Grizzly Hair. *Vaqueros* aimed knives like that and threw them with deadly accuracy. The man was a coiled snake, strong in its musculature, his face a hard flat mask, ready to strike.

"Tienes el caballo," Grizzly Hair choked out. *"No necesita mátame."* You have the horse, no need to kill me. His heart kicked like a horse in his chest. He wasn't prepared for his death.

The man in the bushes didn't slacken his bow, but the one holding the rope looked to the man with the knife. Spanish crackled back and forth between them. The man with dog eyes yanked again. His face hit the mud. Footsteps splashed toward him. He tried to raise up.

Pain flashed on the side of his head. He swirled with it and hardly felt his ankles being tied, or his body being rolled over and over while the rope was wrapped around him. Behind him, the rope was yanked through the tie around his ankles, knees bent back. He blinked mud, saw the man from the bushes straddling him and jamming a rolled cloth between his teeth. Something was wrong with the man's foot. The cloth was tied hard behind his head.

The two men picked him up, one by the shoulders, one by the rope around his ankles, and carried him like a bag of salt to the main trail. They stopped, swung him back and forth and threw him into the air. He landed in a bramble mound and bounced on springy canes bristling with thorns.

A man's voice called in Spanish: "I am Pomponio. Tell Captain Herrera next time not to send an *idioto.* Tell him to come find me himself. Tell him to take me if he's brave enough." Then Morena's hoofbeats pounded away and disappeared in the distance.

Her leaving cut him more deeply than the tight rope, deeper than the thorns. He cried out for her, yelling into his blocked mouth. It sounded more like the bellow of a mating elk. A wave of darkness threatened and he realized he could hardly breathe with the rope so tight around his neck. Yelling had taken all his strength. He couldn't move and saw nothing but tangles of canes and shriveled berry leaves speared by thorns. Most of the leaves had fallen to the ground, so father sun's light from the west penetrated to where he lay in a painful hammock with thorns piercing him from every direction. The cane against his nose was thick as a child's wrist. Pain throbbed in his head where he'd been struck. His face, abdomen, back, buttocks and legs stung in so many places it felt like he'd been skinned alive.

A cane gave way beneath him. His lower half dropped and another cane whipped across his face, grabbing his ear ornament. It pulled his ear. He closed his eyes, reminding himself that all plant and animal people suffered at one time or another. Some died slowly of hunger and thirst when the rains didn't come. Many were eaten alive. Several times he'd seen snakes thrashing and writhing while being hawked by slow stages into the bellies of herons. That would be worse than this. Some animals fought then died from infected wounds. Maggots ate their guts away in a single night while they lay helpless.

"Blackberry," he said, "I didn't mean to hurt you."

"Breaking my canes does me no harm," Blackberry seemed to say. "My roots are deep and each broken cane grows several more. I could grow up around you and no one would know the difference. My berries would be just as sweet." Then the voice urged, "You can track those men and get your horse and weapons back."

If someone cuts me out, thought Grizzly Hair. They had thrown him into the brambles at the crossing of two trails, which meant they expected him to be found. So he could give Captain Herrera the message?

The light hadn't changed but it seemed a long time before he heard human voices. They approached at the pace of walking women, coming from the east—maybe Huiluc's women. He saved his breath and when the women were very near, made his elk sound.

Silence.

He did it again, darkness momentarily washing over him.

They talked in a tongue he'd never heard, close by. Had he fallen the other way, he would see them. He spoke to them in his thoughts, asking for their help. Then heard splashing. Coming toward him! He wiggled, driving the thorns deeper into his body, so they would see him.

Their excited talk made his heart pound with hope. Maybe they would cut him out. No one liked to handle berry canes, not even for the sweetest berries. Many people suffered red itchy skin around the scratches. But maybe. . .

Splashes again, going the other way. He made his urgent noise. Were they going for help? Were they Pomponio's wives? Would their people laugh at his predicament? Would he lie here and die?

It was silent again, except for the wing people who sang just before dark, those who had dropped Blackberry's seeds over the countryside. He must not allow pain and fear to defeat him. He must keep his calm and not think about meat-eaters who roamed after dark looking for helpless creatures who presented themselves for supper.

He focused on the details of what had happened—Pomponio fearlessly speaking his own name, telling him to tell Captain Herrera to send somebody who was not an *idioto*. What did that mean? Who was Captain Herrera? It seemed to him that the word *Capitán* had been used in the mission. Then he remembered. At the ceremony when the eagle had replaced the lion, the name Capitán had been spoken as the black hats marched into the plaza. Perhaps

Pomponio had mistaken him for a friend of that black hat. Then he recalled that *Españoles* often shared the same name. There could be others with that name at other missions.

In any case Pomponio had to be very angry at Captain Herrera to do this to someone he thought was Captain Herrera's friend. This led him to the startling conclusion that Pomponio, who had seemed his mortal enemy, might actually be his ally.

Not much later he detected men's voices in the distance. He strained to hear. There were women's voices too. They came close. Many feet splashed in the creek. Excited, he wiggled, grimacing as the thorns drove into his flesh.

A man said, "*No hace. Pensamos que Pomponio hace.*" We didn't do this. We think Pomponio did.

"Hurry," he thought. Dark was coming. He made the elk noise.

Men talked back and forth in a strange tongue.

Putting more urgency into it, he groaned again.

At last he heard the rustling and cracking of brittle canes. Almost beyond patience, he waited. All his life he'd been too impatient, too eager. Some of the canes were pulled back from his head and shoulders. Then the rope around his ankles was pulled, dragging him across the thorns. He couldn't stop a moan. Then he was lifted by the ankle rope and waist rope and carried face down, three pairs of feet walking over a path of hides that had been laid over the canes. They carried him across the creek and dropped him on the ground. Though he had been very close to the ground, new pain rammed up his nose, but they were untying the rope. In a short time he was free, standing and smiling his thanks to these people, about ten. Women whispered and a man coiled the rope.

They didn't smile back and he couldn't understand their tongue. "*Ven,*" a man said in Spanish. Come.

He longed to follow Morena's tracks but couldn't do that until morning anyway, so he followed the unsmiling group. He smelled roasting venison before he saw the u-machas. Though larger than the home place, this village appeared to be half deserted. No supper fires burned at the vacant houses. Dogs peered out of them, apparently using the houses for dens. Everyone stopped whatever they were doing and stared at him. He looked down and saw that his entire body was a mesh of red scratches interlaced with streaks of drying blood. Drops of fresher blood ran down his chest. He wiped a hand across his nose and saw that it had been bleeding.

The men who rescued him didn't seem in a mood to eat, though others sat eating at their fires. Hard, suspicious faces were everywhere in the village. "*Sientese,*" ordered a half-toothless old man who seemed to be the headman. Sit.

Grizzly Hair sat before the u-macha and the old man stepped away, talking loudly to other people around the village and gesturing violently. The old woman of the house eyed him with contempt. She offered no medicine. After a while, the man returned with about ten elders, all of whom stood staring at Grizzly Hair.

"*Habla la lingua de su madre,*" said the old man, sitting across from him. Talk in your mother's tongue.

Unsure what good it would do, Grizzly Hair said, "Pomponio stole my horse and my bow and arrows. In the morning I will track him and get them back. He thought I was a friend of Captain Herrera, but I have never heard of that *Español.*"

They looked at each other and it was plain no one understood what he'd said. Some pointed at him and repeated the name Captain Herrera. A woman spoke to him in a language that sounded faintly like his own, but he couldn't pick out any meaning. She pointed to her ankle and said, "Nak." She pointed to the mountain under which they sat and said, "Tamal."

He repeated the words for ankle and mountain, pronouncing them as the umne did. Between that vague similarity of tongues and his broken Spanish, talk limped forward.

The reason for their unfriendliness became clear. They believed he was a friend of the headman of the black hats at Mission San Rafael. Captain Herrera and his men had come to this village and forced young women to couple with them. The men could not rescue them because the soldiers stood ready to shoot. When Captain Herrera started on the headman's niece, who was married to a respected elder, she scratched Captain Herrera's face. "He cut her throat," the speaker woman said in a low growl as she showed that in sign language. "Threw her there." She pointed.

Grizzly Hair's neck prickled. Neighboring peoples should have been here to help them. Magma's people stared vacantly, emptying their minds of the dead woman. Grizzly Hair glanced at the elder whose face showed the most anger, the man whose eyes people respectfully avoided—perhaps the husband of the dead woman—and realized these people might have rescued him from the blackberries so this man could kill him. Vengeance was the way of all people.

The woman continued the story in Spanish and sign language. "When the soldiers were finished with the women, they stood over there with Captain Herrera and their horses. The Captain said to us, 'Now you neophytes go to your mission and say your prayers with Padre Amarós. If you tell what happened here, you won't live through the whippings.'"

Hair moved at the back of his neck and his inner fire raged.

The woman pointed to a mound on the otherwise level floor of the village. "We put dirt on the blood."

He sat tall and spoke with the strength of O-se-mai-ti. "I do not know

Captain Herrera." People looked at each other with skeptical eyes, and he knew he must say something no friend of Captain Herrera would say. He drew an earth map. "My home place." He pointed, detecting their surprise at how far it was. He showed his scars, and said, "Mission San José. "Now I find *amigos* to help fight the *Españoles.* I go to talk to Russians. They have many guns. I want to make them war *amigos.*"

Suspicion left some of the faces, including that of the old hy-apo. Magma talked to his people in their tongue. Then he turned to Grizzly Hair and said with a large amount of gesturing and pointing, "You say *Indios* are one people. No. There are two: neophytes and gentiles. Pomponio thought you were a friend of Herrera. That was not correct, but you are a neophyte. He was right about that." The elder nodded, eyes terrible with hatred. Magma's people also seemed to be neophytes but Grizzly Hair didn't mention that. Pleased that Magma was talking to him as though he were the man he claimed to be, he continued in his power. "Is this Pomponio's home place?"

Several people gestured no—sharp and dismissive.

"Maybe you go with us after the sleep," Magma said with a sly tilt of his old chin, "help us teach Jauyomi's people a lesson." It seemed a challenge, a test of whether Grizzly Hair was actually on his side. Magma's people smiled without showing their teeth, but the mood of the village had changed for the better. The elder who had looked at Grizzly Hair with such hatred was now staring into the distance with a ravaged expression.

"Where are the Jauyomis?" Grizzly Hair asked Magma.

He pointed northwest.

The Russians were that way. "You teach them?"

People nodded and chuckled. Magma kept his sly expression, clearly not intending to say more.

They wanted him to go with them, but Grizzly Hair had to find his horse first, and he didn't like the sound of "teaching people." He didn't want to become ensnared in quarrels. But the story of Captain Herrera made him more certain than ever that he was on the right path, to find allies.

38

When first light brought the trees from hiding, he quietly left the sweathouse and backtracked the trail. The *Americano* knife lay waiting for him in the grass, but the bow and quiver were gone. Putting the knife in his calf-thong, he followed Morena's tracks on the northwest trail. Among the many hoof sizes and shapes, hers stood out plainly. Most of the other horse tracks were stale, with two exceptions. Two horses had joined Morena not far from where she was stolen. The three ran together, sometimes three abreast, sometimes two together and one behind, but always on the trail. Grizzly Hair ran well back from the trail but frequently checked to be sure the tracks were still there.

Father sun shone horizontally through the oaks, leaving long oak shadows, when it occurred to him that Magma and his men would come this way. Was that a coincidence? Or had Pomponio and Magma planned something together? That would be interesting. Magma had thought Grizzly Hair was a friend of the black hats, but had nevertheless saved him from the thorns. Was the sly old man trying to hedge a bet in case he was captured and returned to the mission? Maybe he hoped to escape some of the lashes by telling Captain Herrera he had saved his friend. Pomponio was angrier and more desperate, clearly not expecting to return to a mission. It seemed bad luck that Grizzly Hair had met Pomponio the way he had. He needed angry men. Now it would be dangerous to talk to him. Pomponio would think he'd come for revenge. He'd have to steal Morena back, then find a way to talk to Pomponio.

Sleeping-Man mountain lay behind him as the trail turned straight west into undulating, ever more wooded oak grasslands. Then the fresh tracks left the trail and headed toward a line of trees, no doubt a stream—tall trees, *palos altos,* laurel and willow. This would be the creek that gave water to Jauyomi's people. The trail he had left would cross the creek, probably at the village. He followed sign—broken brush, trampled grass, a red-brown hair from Morena on a willow tip. Pomponio and the two men had ridden here before the sleep.

He continued cautiously until he could see, beyond a stand of dry wormwood rasping in the wind, the edge of a low-running stream. On the bank sat a naked man, back hunched, long hair whipping around his shoulders. A twisted red cloth was tied at the back of his head. He hadn't yet grown into his bones—not much more than a boy. No horse was in sight.

He crept closer, searching for Morena, and saw Raven Feather's basket beside a cold fire. Beyond lay a tangled brown heap, possibly the thong. The young man, who was looking the other way, raised an arm and tossed a pebble into the water. A bow and quiver lay beside him.

A horse whickered. He moved toward the sound, circling past dry nettle to remain upwind. In a rough corral of brush he saw the three horses. Morena raised her head, ears forward, nostrils twitching—catching his scent? The other two kept their noses to the ground.

He wished he could simply leap on her back and ride away. At the thought a muscle jumped in his calf, but moving the brush would make too much noise, and the other horses would complain. Pomponio and his men were gone, but for how long? He crept back to where he could see the camp guard, whom he must immobilize.

This would have been easy with Pomponio's horsehair rope, but Missouri's thong would do. He straightened to nearly an upright stance, still unable to see whether the brown heap between the basket and man was the thong. He silently walked across the clearing. Yes, it was the thong. Carefully he lifted the loops from the grass, finding the ends and straightening the length.

The man turned his head.

Grizzly Hair lunged, throwing the thong over the smaller man's head and chest. They rolled off the bank into the gravel below. All his strength flowed as the man lurched and writhed. He finally managed to tie the thong in a double knot at the thin man's back, elbows pinned together. He tried to bind the feet with the long end, but the man flipped to his back and kicked violently. His eyes were black shields. Then his feet were under him and he jumped upright, bent legs braced as if about to butt Grizzly Hair with his head.

Grizzly Hair pulled the thong, urging him to walk up the bank. The young man kicked high with a long skinny leg, hooked it in the thong and nearly yanked it out of Grizzly Hair's grasp. He pulled his *Americano* knife from his calf and held it by the tip as Pomponio had done, threatening to throw it. Now the man walked up the bank and across the clearing.

Afraid Pomponio and his men would burst through the trees, Grizzly Hair strained to see or hear anything besides the thrashing branches. He must hurry. Luck wouldn't hold forever. Motioning the young man down to the base of a small oak, he quickly wrapped the thong twice again around chest, arms and tree, tying it firmly in the back. He removed the twisted cloth from the man's head and tied it between his teeth as Pomponio had done to him, then removed the stone knife from the youth's calf and put it behind a rock on the other side of the clearing. Picking up the bow and the quiver of arrows—not his—from the streambank, he started to leave.

The snapping eyes of the brave young man stopped him, and he knew he must try to explain. He replaced the knife on his calf, squatted before him and said, "I will not hurt you." The black shields glared.

Wishing he knew the Spanish word for hurt, he said, "*No mátete.*" No kill you. "*El caballo moreno esta de mío.*" The brown horse is mine. "*Despues, hablamos como hermanos. No soy amigo de soldados.*" Later, we talk like brothers. I am no friend of soldiers.

He went for his horse. The rein was around her jaw so it was easy to pull her out. The two males, one with a hoof-shaped gash on his rear, whinnied and snorted to go with her as he re-packed the brush against their aggressive noses.

He mounted, splashed across the creek and galloped north. When he came to the main east-west trail—big and well tamped—he realized Jauyomi's village would be only a little to the east. He reined to a stop. Part of him wanted to continue west to the Russians without delay; but if he did, he'd never know what would happen here, and something told him he needed to know. He tied Morena in a thicket of young redwoods north of the trail, well hidden.

"Horses are noisy," he told her. "I'll be back." He patted her neck, and took the precaution of brushing her tracks from the thicket to the trail. He also dropped dried redwood leaves and other debris and let the wind deposit it naturally over the brushed area.

He couldn't simply walk into the village to greet the headman, not with a bow that could be recognized as belonging to the young man. Keeping to the trees, he circled the village and hid in a stand of laurel behind the dancehouse. In the clearing, women worked with feathers or hides. At the stream they leached acorn meal. Men rested. No visitors seemed to be present, no talk was underway. He waited, aware for the first time of the pain and itch of the inflamed scratches all over his body. The sweat and scraping of the fight had made it worse.

Some time later he heard running horses. Two riders—Magma and Pomponio!—galloped into the village on the two male horses, one dark with a hoofprint on its rear, and stopped just short of trampling people. They sat in arrogant postures and shouted at the villagers. Following them, about twenty men arrived on foot, including the young man Grizzly Hair had tied up. They swaggered into the village center, one carrying Grizzly Hair's bow and quiver. Were the beads still in it? One of the men walked on the ball of his foot.

Obviously upset, the villagers pointed to particular u-machas. The invaders split up and went to those houses. After a while loud disputes could be heard in several parts of the village. People came out yelling angrily. Grizzly Hair had no idea what was happening. It didn't seem like anybody was teaching anybody anything, and none of this had any apparent connection to the *Españoles.*

Scuffles broke out. People pushed each other. But Magma and Pomponio had more men. Though some of the observing villagers took tentative steps toward the disturbances, they didn't help. Grizzly Hair recognized their reluctance—polite people didn't get involved with other people's problems. This was the same kind of thinking that stopped them from joining together to repel the black hats.

Pomponio ended arguments by skillfully throwing his knife past people's noses into the redwood planks of the houses. People quaked with fear. The two men who had helped ambush Grizzly Hair threw lariats around some of the people and jerked them around. At last the trouble stopped when people brought goods from their houses—baskets, shell money, dried meat and fish.

The men of Magma and Pomponio took piles of goods and left, heading back the way they had come. Disturbed by what he had seen, Grizzly Hair melted into the trees and followed. After a while he saw them stop and engage in heated discussion. Pomponio and the man with the round eyes dismounted and talked at each other with their hands as much as their tongues. Then talk stopped and Pomponio handed his reins to the man with whom he'd been arguing. Everyone continued walking and riding eastward with the goods, except Pomponio. He trotted south across trackless land with his bow in hand and his horsehair rope over his shoulder. He was heading toward the camp. To track Grizzly Hair.

Had Magma told him Grizzly Hair's story? Had he heard what Grizzly Hair told the young man? Would he apologize for hurting him? Did he want to become allies? Or did he simply want the horse—a man who didn't like to lose a fight. Maybe he wanted to see which way Grizzly Hair had gone: toward the Russians would verify Grizzly Hair's story; toward the south would confirm Pomponio's suspicion that he was from Mission San Rafael. Mulling over the possibilities, Grizzly Hair returned the way he had come, circling the Jauyomi village. Pomponio would quickly find the tracks; any man could track a horse. Either Grizzly Hair had to gallop ahead toward the Russians, worrying about an ambush, or surprise Pomponio. Could they talk? Should they? Why had they forced those people to give them valuable things?

Morena welcomed him with a nuzzle of her velvet nose. He scratched between her ears, thinking. To talk to Pomponio, he'd have to tie him up. He had no rope. A dead-fall snare would work; but too light a rock or limb wouldn't hold a man, and too heavy a weight would kill or injure him. And he had no time to build a good snare.

He galloped west on the beaten trail, watching for anything to help him capture Pomponio. Pomponio would know the tracks were fresh, but that didn't matter. It might intrigue him that Grizzly Hair hadn't immediately left after recovering his horse. If Pomponio was interested he would follow, if not he would turn back. Still, a trap of some kind was needed.

The trail led through a wide gap in the hills. For a while the land seemed to be rising, but changed its mind and fell steadily downward. He slowed to a fast walk and considered the heavy growth of willow, madrone, laurel, *palo alto* and oak, and a dry creek bed on his left. A little farther along he found what he needed, a tiny sunken meadow ringed by a dense woods, impossible to approach except through a narrow entrance—a natural trap. Morena would be the bait. He rode her inside and dismounted. As she happily tore into the slightly green grass, he explored a fallen redwood that lay alongside the entrance. The hollow, fire-blackened root end lay near Morena.

Satisfied that the place was perfect, he climbed in the tree trunk and lay down on the soft excreta of wood-eating insects. His senses filled with the aroma of must and decay, and he caught the sharp whiff of fox. This downed tree was big enough for a grizzly bear with two half-grown cubs to nest in comfortably during a storm.

He closed his eyes and was half into a dream when he heard what sounded like a distant drum. The hollow tree picked up the footsteps of a running human. It stopped. He crawled out, fitted an arrow in his bow and stood behind the trunk, the top of which he could barely see over. Shade and a tangle of dry limbs concealed him. Pomponio stood at the entrance to the meadow, alone and looking at Morena—bow in hand, rope over shoulder, knife on his calf. He had tied his mission shirt around his waist. His muscular chest was shiny with perspiration, rising and falling in steady rhythm. His rounded thighs rippled as he shifted his weight and his jaw looked as hard as before, a rattlesnake ready to strike. He looked in all directions, maybe realizing that to rope Morena, he would need both hands and that meant putting the bow down. "*¡Hola!*" he called.

Looking right and left, he walked slowly toward the horse, along the length of the downed redwood. His feet were visible through a break in the rotting bark—brown dusty feet moving carelessly, not with the noiseless roll that came so natural to Grizzly Hair. Grizzly Hair climbed back inside the tree and silently squat-walked past the fox smell all the way to the wide tree base. Through a plume of new saplings growing out of the old root-crown, he could see Pomponio's back.

Pomponio stopped, turned in all directions, called again, "*¡Hola!*" Morena, who was stepping away from the man, whinnied in nervous agitation. Her skin twitched.

Bow loose in his hand, Pomponio walked to Morena and petted her. By now he could have been on her back streaking past Grizzly Hair. He would know, however, that Grizzly Hair would have a clear shot at him. There was a place or two going the other way where a horse might get through the trees and undergrowth, but not with any speed. Grizzly Hair could shoot him from behind.

Pomponio gave Morena a final pat and lowered himself gracefully to the grass, folding his legs, coiling himself. He laid the lariat and bow beside him, no doubt to show how good he was with the knife on his calf. A small man, his danger filled the quiet meadow. Grizzly Hair doubted he'd last two blinks of a lizard's eye in a knife fight with that vaquero. But the man was looking the other way.

Grizzly Hair stepped to the ground at the base of the tree. From the crowded young redwoods that grew in the crumbled debris of the fallen giant, he walked noiselessly toward Pomponio with his loaded bow leading.

39

"*Hola,*" said Grizzly Hair.

Pomponio jerked perceptibly, turned his head and shoulders, but did not pull his knife. Instead a slow grin spread his thin mustache. "You been coupling with a blackberry?" The same soft, deliberate Spanish.

From the corner of his eye Grizzly Hair saw the swollen red slashes all over his body—he'd never had such a reaction to the thorns before. In no mood to banter with the man who had done this to him, he nevertheless said, "She wasn't very nice."

He could tell by the grin that Pomponio hoped to make him feel small and young. Keeping his distance, Grizzly Hair sat down facing him and, to suggest knife skill he didn't have, laid his own bow on the grass. He sat with his knees up, hands on knees. He could hardly believe he'd done that, but it seemed right.

As Pomponio's gaze slid to the magnificent *Americano* knife, the likes of which he had probably never seen, he uncoiled his legs and raised his knees too, resting his arms on the peaks, right hand hanging loosely near his mission knife. With a grin he said, "I could have killed you in that hollow tree."

Hiding his surprise, he gave back, "I could have killed you as you sat here."

"Maybe." Pomponio talked through a goading grin as if it were a natural impediment. "Why didn't you try?" Emphasis on try.

"You sat down."

"You were afraid?" The grin persisted.

"You saw a trap and came in anyway, to show me you wanted to talk."

"And I trapped you instead." He chuckled. "I can kill you any time I want."

"Why don't you try?" Emphasis on you. O-se-mai-ti flowed into Grizzly Hair, enlarging him in every way. Could he ever cooperate with such a man, even if they got beyond trading threats? He reminded himself that angry men made good warriors and he could not afford to limit himself to men he liked.

"I didn't kill you," Pomponio was saying, "because you are riding west. You talked straight to Magma." Even handing him that victory, he didn't wipe the insulting look off his face.

Now Grizzly Hair felt the calm of the supremely powerful hy-apo of the Animal People. He also realized that, even as a man, he was bigger, stronger, stealthier and faster than Pomponio—although somewhat younger. His back was straight and the fire inside burned hot. "You took things from Jauyomi's people."

The grin remained. "Nice things." Creeping into Pomponio's tone was a little boy who hoped the other boy had seen his stunt: "You saw us then? You were *curioso?*"

His Spanish was easy to follow, except for that last word. But the bear in Grizzly Hair didn't need to know it. "You and Magma took things from people who didn't want to give them."

"Ah, and you have eyes!" Like a father praising a child, but the power of O-se-mai-ti was affecting him.

Glancing at the long shadows, Grizzly Hair said, "*Hablamos.*" Let's talk.

"Oh," said Pomponio as if suddenly thinking of it, "thank you for the pretty beads. Women like them very much. Now I have a warm bed wherever I go."

Expressionless, Grizzly Hair waited.

At last Pomponio talked. "Magma says you want to make war on the *Españoles*. You should join me. I'm already fighting them."

"How does taking things from the Jauyomi people hurt the *Españoles?*"

"Those people are getting ready to trot like dogs to the long robes and kiss their hands. Then they'll do their dirty work—bullying people who want to live in peace."

"Those people"—Grizzly Hair pointed east—"didn't look like they were going anywhere."

"Maybe you didn't know that Padre Amarós traveled to Jauyomi's people and baptized some of the elders? Hm? Made them *Christianos*. You watch, it won't be long before all those families are saying prayers in Mission San Rafael. I teach people like that to leave the rest of us alone." Beneath the sarcastic smile burned a hot fire.

Even if they never rode together, and they couldn't unless Pomponio broadened his vision, Grizzly Hair wanted him to see things his way.

"*Christianos* are my enemies," Pomponio continued. "Are they your enemies too?" By that he meant all who had been baptized.

"No."

"Then you are my enemy." His thick fingers moved as if deciding, then not deciding to take the knife.

"Magma has a Christian name," Grizzly Hair pointed out, "but he is not your enemy."

"Magma is different. His people recognize their mistake in going to the Mission."

"Many people make mistakes. I am an enemy of *Españoles*, not *Indios*."

"For every *soldado* there are a hundred neophytes willing to go out and attack gentiles in their villages. And help the *soldados* to capture *cimarrones*." Pomponio looked at him. "How long have you known about the padres and black hats?"

He thought a moment. "Almost four moons."

Pomponio widened his eyes in a mock display of astonishment then hissed a snicker through his teeth. Quiet again, he said, "I have known them since I was this high." He held his hand to the height of a young child. "You know nothing."

In his strength, Grizzly Hair sat expressionless.

"Padre Amarós is luring the relatives of the Huiluc and Jauyomi peoples to the mission. He has invited them to the Easter Big Time. The Jauyomis say they will go. Listen to me. People who walk to the missions on their own become stickier shit than their teachers."

"*We Indios* cannot fight our common enemy if we are divided among ourselves."

Pomponio leveled him a flat look. "Exactly what I am trying to tell you. We are already divided. Better to scare the traitors who help the *soldados* than get killed provoking cannons."

"You are making sure we are divided."

"I?" He looked around as if he'd been called the wrong name. "They make of themselves *putas*. Pffft." He spat, and his hard eyes fixed on Grizzly Hair.

"Why are you talking with me?"

"I came to kill you and take your horse." He smiled.

"But you did not."

"I might yet. But for now you amuse me—a man with a horse traveling to the Russians. I like interesting men, unless they get in my way. My friends—you met them before the sleep—amuse me too. One escaped from Mission San Carlos Borromeo on the Rio Carmelo, the other from Mission San Gabriel. The other man came from Mission San Diego. You know where those places are?"

Grizzly Hair tried to recall all that María had said about the missions, but couldn't place those names. He shook his head.

The humor dropped from Pomponio's face. "Maybe you are too *inocente* to be amusing. You should be saying, 'Oh, Mission San Gabriel, San Diego, Mission San Carlos. Pomponio's men come from far away. He has loyal friends up and down this big land. He is a man I should listen to. He is a man I should ride with.'" He cocked his head. "Maybe you should not go to the Russians. You are too young."

Now Pomponio's motive in talking was coming clear. He wanted Grizzly Hair to ride with him and do his bidding. But no matter how he turned it in his mind, Pomponio was doing this wrong. Harassing *Indios* would discourage defensive pacts. Pomponio would have enemies on both sides. He would be a dangerous ally.

Still, Grizzly Hair sat in his bear-strength. "You say I know nothing, but I have felt the *cuarta*. I escaped from Padre Durán's black hats, and I also have interesting friends across this land. I know that only two twenties of black hats eat supper in Presidio San Francisco, and I know they are afraid of Russians and Russian guns. I will talk to the Russians, and when they are my allies, you will want to ride with me."

"Find me and we'll talk after that happens," Pomponio said. "Ask Magma or anyone around the mountain called Tamal-país where to find me." Tamal meant mountain in the home tongue; *País* meant land place in Spanish. "The first padre in San Rafael called my people Tamales. We lived along the inlet of the sea. We went to San Rafael Mission before black hats lived there, back when just one padre came only to visit." Wistfully he added, "It was nice then."

For a moment it seemed Pomponio felt like talking about old times, but his cocky arrogance returned. "Ask anyone. Everyone knows me." He looked at Grizzly Hair, who retained the strength of O-se-mai-ti. "Your tongue and mine are relatives. We should be allies."

"Yes, allies," Grizzly Hair said pressing his advantage. "To honor the start of friendship, I already gave you half of my blue beads. I will take back the other half now."

Pomponio narrowed his eyes. "I accept the beads and will also take the baby horse in your horse." He looked at Morena, hard-jawed.

A baby in her blood! He hadn't imagined. "If the baby horse lives," Grizzly Hair said thinking fast. "But not until it is old enough to leave its mother, and not unless we are of one mind about how to fight the *Españoles*. Then when we ride together our horses will be friends."

The flat eyes lingered on him too long and Grizzly Hair was surprised when Pomponio nodded in agreement.

Touching the bow with the red marks, Grizzly Hair said, "The spirit of this bow wants its man, as my bow wants me." They both knew weapons would shoot crooked as long as they were upset, and Pomponio's young helper would be of little use to him until the trade was made.

Pomponio sat as though thinking, then said, "Come with me back to Magma's place and sleep in the sweathouse. There I will return half your beads. They are not here with me."

Grizzly Hair disliked the idea of returning to the village of Pomponio's friends. But to display distrust would spoil whatever fragile bond existed. Was this a trap? He looked inside, felt his luck and his stomach told him there would be no danger. He gave a nod.

The next morning, after good dreams in the same sweathouse where he'd slept the previous night, Grizzly Hair faced father sun and absorbed more power. Before the sleep his scratched, swollen skin had been soothed by sprays of milk squeezed from the nipples of lactating mothers. The milk dried on his cleaned and purified skin and sealed out the itch. He had apologized to his bow and slept beside it. Pomponio had counted out the beads and six lay in the bottom of Grizzly Hair's own otterskin quiver.

Now he stood with Pomponio beneath the big cedar-like trees in Magma's village, ready to ride west again. Pomponio said, "I would go with you to make sure you say the right things to the Russians, but I'm going south to see what Padre Altimira is doing in Tso-noma. That's the earth home place of the East People." He didn't blink his flat dry eyes. "First I will visit a nice woman in Mission San Rafael."

"You visit women in missions?"

"All the time."

"What is Padre Altimira doing?"

"Building a new mission."

A new mission! "Where?"

"Down there." Pomponio waved south. "I don't know exactly where yet, but it won't be far from the big water of the Bay."

"I heard they wanted to build a mission in the Valley of the Sun, near my home place." The thought continued to sicken him, but a mission in this little valley would also be close to the home place.

"That's Padre Durán's territory," Pomponio was saying. "I don't know what he's doing." He flattened his eyes and looked south. "On your way back from the Russians, stop and talk. Ask the Cotati people or the people at Bodega. I'll be camping in the mountains around Oon-nah-pis."

"I will do that." He nudged Morena west. Despite the nagging shortness of time, he felt pleased with himself. With nothing but talk, he had befriended the skilled knifesman who had humiliated him. It was a coup, and he believed he could convince Pomponio to see all *Indios* as potential allies.

As Morena picked her way through the giant trees, skirting Jauyomi's village, he realized more than ever how difficult it would be to get so many different peoples to cooperate. Some were divided among themselves. He reflected that this ride across the countryside was also a ride toward knowledge. As a boy he hadn't grasped how defeating fear brought clarity, and clarity led to knowledge. He had noticed, however, that a man lacking clarity rarely seemed to know it. He'd had little when he went west with Oak Gall and Bowstring. But wise elders said that clarity shifted during a lifetime. Some day, he knew, his new-found clarity would become his enemy. But for now that would wait. For now he was traveling as fast as he could toward the Russians.

Riding past the same tiny meadow where he and Pomponio had talked, a question struck him. Had he defeated his fear in the mission? Looking back, it seemed fear had defeated him—when he was being whipped, when he feared more whippings, when he feared Oak Gall would die, when he butchered large animals without purification, when he feared the dead souls darting around the gruesome likeness of Jesús on the *cruz*. He had never stopped being afraid. Except once. He had defeated his fear of Oak Gall's soul. But that seemed a small victory compared to so much fear. So how could he have clarity about the *Españoles?*

Putting the question aside, he rode the trail steadily downward toward a wide brown river and stopped in a pool of sunlight. This was the river Magma had mentioned. Missouri had drawn it on his earth map. The Russians lived on the coast north of where the river flowed into the sea.

He nudged Morena through the redwoods hoping the peoples along this river were friendly with the Russians. He felt the nearness of his goal and wondered if Malaca could somehow see him. The death of that brave man who had burned in his house should be avenged. The other thing that had become clear was that a war would be necessary sooner or later, and it would mean killing, not arrow-dodging. The *Españoles* didn't care if people died; they offered no alternatives. Therefore, they must die. He saw that with the same brightness that shone in the eyes of Padre Fortuni when he told of Jesús rising from the dead.

He rode alongside the river on a well-tamped foot trail, and it wasn't long before he saw people running around. Still hidden, he moved Morena closer and saw men and women catching and throwing a ball in nets attached to sticks. Skirts of shredded bark whipped around the women's legs. A man tossed the ball from the sideline over the heads of the players and all struggled to hit it before it touched the ground. Men and women tumbled and shrieked with laughter.

He stepped Morena out of hiding. They saw him and stopped playing. Their bare chests rose and fell from exertion, not fear. He rode onto the field. People came toward him, a man speaking a strange tongue.

He shook his head. The spokesman said something else, also strange. Grizzly Hair got down to face them. The man tried again. Grizzly Hair tried Spanish. They shook their heads. He tried Sucais' tongue and words from various other places. They all shook their heads. Other people tried different tongues.

The headman turned and walked away, beckoning him to follow. He led the horse, and could tell that the people walking alongside had seen horses before.

Shaggy cone-shaped houses of *palo alto* bark stood in the village center. The cha'kas appeared much the same as at the home place, as did the dancehouse and sweathouse, except for the redwood bark on the roofs. For time of rain, the air felt warm and no breath of wind moved the graceful branches of the redwoods that stood like giants protecting the village. Their delicate aroma soothed his spirit. Shadow and sunlight were softer here than at the home place. This place made him feel peaceful.

He sat facing the headman, at ease among these curious people, even though he couldn't talk with them. He looked up through dizzying layers of branches of the largest tree he had ever seen. Its tip would penetrate the clouds, had there been any. Women brought baskets of nu-pah, which he gratefully sampled. The jelled mush of one crunched between his teeth—roasted beetles, shiny blue-green. The people watched him eat and smiled when he politely slurped.

He touched one of the stunning baskets. It seemed a fanciful piece of magic. Around the opening stood a row of quivering quail top-knot feathers. Below that, stripes of tiny yellow and blue feathers of mountain oriole and jay were woven into the pattern. On both sides of the basket was the likeness of a bird made from the bright red feathers of woodpecker scalps. The home women made fine baskets, but he'd never seen anything like this.

Noting his admiration, a large woman shoved the basket against his ankle, indicating it was now his. Shame shot through him. He shouldn't have admired it so openly, but it was too late. Her eyes ordered him to accept it. She had a high, unattractive nose and a disquieting chin tattoo—blue zig-zagged lines radiating from her lower lip to her chin and outward to her ears.

She appraised him like a fine kill.

40

"Miwok," he said, pounding his chest with his fist. He pointed at the headman's chest and looked him the question of how his people said people.

"Pomo," said the hy-apo, popping the first sound.

"Pomo," he repeated. He drew an earth map and pointed to his home place.

The headman studied it.

"Ross. Where?" Grizzly Hair asked.

"Rohsh," the headman corrected, drawing the river entering the ocean and a pathway north. He put his finger on the map.

They clearly knew of the Russians. "Rohsh friend?" He made the sign for friend and pointed at the headman.

The headman nodded pleasantly.

"Can you talk the tongue of the Russians?"

The headman smiled blandly.

"You trade with Russians?"

He smiled pleasantly, and his expression didn't change through several more questions.

At last he had found people acquainted with the Russians, but couldn't talk to them. Restless and impatient, he nevertheless knew he needed to hear their stories, because he would be useless dead or locked in a *calabozo*. He had no choice but to stay here long enough to talk with these people. That meant a long time, during which the black hats could be rounding up people closer to the home place. The thought tightened his stomach, but if he stayed calm and purified, luck would prevail. It was the best he could do.

He signed that he wanted to sleep here and help the men hunt.

The headman looked at him a little longer than was polite. The high-nosed woman smiled at everyone around the circle, her overly tattooed cheeks pulled wide. The headman nodded at him and turned to the other men. Talk bounced back and forth, then the headman gave him a deep nod. Women left the circle and went to prepare supper. Talk was finished. He would stay.

He walked along the loamy river bank under the bare branches of a tree he didn't know, and at night slept in the sweathouse. It was considerably more subterranean than the one at home, but otherwise similar. As the men spoke in quiet dignified tones, he lay back, inhaling the heat and smoke, restoring harmony and strength. He told himself that if little children could learn this strange tongue filled with clicks, pops and breathy aspirations, so could he.

Early each morning, when the birds chirped and sunlight filtered through the branches of the giant trees, he attended a strange likeness of Padre Fortuni's school. The teacher was the weaver of his woodpecker basket—Salmon Woman. Facing her, he sat with young boys and girls on one of two downed trees.

Surprisingly, two old men also attended each morning. More surprisingly, they were learning women's tasks. He wouldn't have believed it if he hadn't seen it. The home men would rather have died. When these old men prepared basket materials wrong, or leached acorn meal too little, Salmon Woman would scold them and say, "No, old fool! Like this." Then she would show them, and the children would cover their smiles. Under the sharp eye of Salmon Woman, the men coiled baskets and prepared food. They also joined the sing-song chorus of children when the young voices grew weak or tentative.

Salmon Woman taught from earth maps and stories. The chorusing of the children was helpful, and when Grizzly Hair was alone, he repeated the fragments he could remember. Thus he learned the rhythm of the speech before he knew what it meant, and he learned to make the popping and clicking sounds. After several sleeps the children stopped giggling to see a young man among them, and accepted him as one of them.

Finally he began to make out a few words: "Flea, eagle, acorn mush, crow. He learned as much out of school as in. Then he began to put words together: "Coyote walked north" or "Coyote fished at. . ."

One morning class was interrupted when traders came into the village—three men weighed down with strings of shell money, bundles of yew, bags of opalescent rock, salt, and a bag of red sandstone from which beads could be made. Everyone behaved as if the goods were ordinary, but when the trading was over and the traders were trotting up the trail, people turned to each other, obviously elated with the goods they had bargained for. Grizzly Hair heard a repeated fragment of their talk, and guessed it meant "esteemed traders." He repeated that to himself.

Adults spoke to him as they did the very young—loudly and clearly. That helped, as did spending time with children, who didn't sprinkle their talk with subtleties and puns. The children never tired of correcting him. They escorted him around the village and pointed out the names of things, like the drying racks where late salmon still hung. Playing teacher, they made him repeat the words. They also showed him little ditches that would bring water from the river. The ditches were dry now, the river low. Sometimes there was deep water here, they said.

A boy said the word Rohsh. He squatted down to his level. "Rohsh?" he asked, pointing at the ditches then making digging motions. Some said "yes;" others said "no."

Had Red Bead's people dug the ditches for the Russians? He tried to ask but couldn't. That evening as he ate at the fire of the headman, who had a metal cup, he asked again in sign language and a few words whether the people here were friends of the people at Rohsh. "Yes," Red Bead said. Also eating at the headman's fire were his wife, their nearly grown son and daughter, and the headman's father, an old man who sat as if in a trance.

"Rohsh esteemed traders?" Grizzly Hair asked.

Red Bead used another name for the Russians, a strange long name filled with clicks and pops, and said, "Esteemed traders."

Pleased to hear that, Grizzly Hair hoped one of Red Bead's people would accompany him to the Russians. For if the Russians were indeed esteemed traders, surely Red Bead's people would be deemed as such by the Russians. Such feelings were reciprocal, and Grizzly Hair would be seen in a good light to be their friend. "Rohsh come here?"

The entire family laughed, even the old man. When the laughter stopped, Red Bead drew an earth map with a leg bone of the goose he had been gnawing, then stood the bone in the dirt. "Rohsh," he said. "Rohsh no walk. Understand?"

Grizzly Hair thought about that and suddenly understood. Rohsh was a place, not a people. He must learn the complex series of sounds. He tried.

Everyone corrected him. The last part was clearly "pomo" with a big pop in front. Some complicated kind of people. With the help of the family he repeated it, and after four or five tries finally said it acceptably.

"They come here?" He pointed toward the ditches and field of young grass.

"Yes," they all said, smiling to have communicated.

The woman went inside the u-macha and brought out a fleshy but shriveled brown root. Pale juicy sprouts grew from it. "Kar-tof-eln," she said, letting him hold it. She said the sounds for Russians and pointed at the root.

He understood. They came here to grow those roots.

The old man lowered the salmon jaw he'd been nibbling and chuckled softly. The grown children exchanged words and began giggling. Red Bead's laughter sputtered through his flatbread, then they all laughed, the old man rocking back and forth—people smiling from other fires. Red Bead slapped the earth as if to make himself stop laughing. Grizzly Hair knew he wouldn't be able to understand what was funny, so he didn't ask. But he was pleased to have learned that Red Bead and the Russians were friends.

Another moon passed. In school one morning, as though debris blew away and clear tracks appeared, he realized he was understanding an entire story through the sing-song back-and-forth recitation of Salmon Woman and the children. The story was not about the Animal People, but a man whose face was covered with hair the color of fire. His exposed skin was red. Black Snake found him lying on his belly in the sand at the sea—"sea" being part of the word that meant Russians. The man looked dead. Black Snake lifted the man's shirt and saw that every rib could be seen under very white skin. Dark trousers were tied around the man's waist with a rope. That a man would starve in the midst of plenty, Salmon Woman said, was a wonder. Everyone repeated: "That a man would starve in the midst of plenty is a wonder."

She pointed to her earth map, showing where the man had been found, and chanted. The children and Grizzly Hair chanted after her: Black Snake saw that the man was alive. He picked him up and carried him toward the village, but grew tired and stopped to drink at a pool of water. The man opened his eyes. The children shouted, "THEY WERE BLUE!" The man crawled on his belly to the water and lay sucking like a lizard. He saw a frog. He grabbed and ate it. In unison Salmon Woman and the children repeated in an exaggerated whisper: "He ate the frog."

With great excitement they shouted: Black Snake ran into the forest, screaming like Eagle. He climbed up to the highest limb of the tallest redwood. Fear made him tremble and shake and he lost his grip and fell down through the burned-out stomach of the tree. With great zest the children yelled the last part. "He hit the earth." They stamped their feet to show what a noise it made, and all shouted: "BLACK SNAKE WAS DEAD."

Teaching ended for the day and Salmon Woman went to her u- macha. As the children scattered, Grizzly Hair asked one of the boys, "Why did Black Snake run from the skinny man?"

The boy said, "Big power scared him."

"Where was big power?"

The boy looked at him like he was crazy. "The man ate a frog."

That seemed sensible for a starving man. His puzzlement must have shown. The boy put a hand on his hip and repeated as if talking to an infant, "The man ate a frog."

"Yes. He ate a frog." Grizzly Hair rubbed his belly to show they tasted good.

"Eeeeew," the boy yelled, and ran after his friends.

It occurred to Grizzly Hair that though frogs were plentiful around this village, he'd never seen anyone eat them. Now he was glad he hadn't brought frogs to the headman's wife. Did these people know something about frogs that he should know? He'd thought only the eating of skunks brought bad luck. Perhaps the umne were mistaken. The thought bothered him in the place where dreams were born.

Other parts of the story puzzled him too. He had seen men with blue eyes and hair the color of a red-tailed hawk. Had an *Español* or *Americano* somehow washed in from the sea? Who had been left to tell the story after Black Snake died? How did Red Bead's people know what happened? Maybe the rhythm of an oft-repeated story robbed people of curiosity. Padre Fortuni told strange stories about which questions could have been asked, but were not. What about the stories of the umne? Would they seem strange to an outsider? One thing was certain, however. If Black Snake had defeated his fear of the frog-eating man and not fallen to his death, these people might have learned where the stranger came from.

The next day Salmon Woman left the two old men leaching acorns while she took her charges to view places outside the village—places they had chanted about in recitation. As usual Grizzly Hair had questions, and Salmon Woman enjoyed setting him right. She complimented him on learning her tongue and gave him frank looks of approval that made him uneasy.

On the way back to the village, the path was springy with the redwood debris from many seasons. Sunlight filtered through the trees, brightening the tender yellow-green tips. They brushed him like tiny velvet hands. Time of rain was leaving and it had not rained. This boded ill for earth mother, but the wing people flirted with each other as though all were well. Salmon Woman said to the children, "Run ahead to the village."

As the last of them bounded happily up the trail, she turned to him and said, "You have good legs and I want to couple with you."

He stammered, "Your man—"

"My man will not know." She looked at him directly, not shyly in the manner of the home women. Despite his uneasiness, excitement stirred. What would a woman this direct do?

She tickled him with her fingertips and all hesitation vanished. He followed her behind a wall of laurel to a little meadow. Deftly she coiled him around his raw senses and afterwards he lay turned inside out and disbelieving. She was as artful in coupling as basket weaving.

"Come," she said pulling him up.

The deep river returned his strength to him. As they walked back toward the village, she spoke carefully to help him understand. "My people love this home place as life itself."

"My people love their place as life itself," he repeated.

"Then why did you come here?"

"I talk with many peoples about the *Españoles*. We want them to go from this land."

She smiled in a correcting way. "They are not on this land."

"Yes they are. This big earth place is called Alta California. It is all one place. Your people and mine live on it together. All people whose grandfathers lived here before the *Españoles* came. We are called *Indios. Espanoles* want to make us *domesticado.*"

"What is *domesticado?*"

"Spanish talk. It means. . ." A key word eluded him. "Morena is *domesticado.* She goes where I want. She eats where I want her to eat. She lives to help me, not herself."

Salmon Woman laughed merrily. "No, no, no. Grown people don't obey other people."

"Yes they do." Obey was the word.

"Not we Kashaya. Every day our men try to make women obey them, but we do not." She smiled slightly.

He decided to ask the meaning of Kashaya later. "Old men obey you."

Her zig-zags stretched in a bigger smile. "Only old men, too old to hunt."

"All men are old if they live long." It pleased him to be able to banter, but her smile was undaunted.

They were entering the village. Her husband wasn't in sight, a man who, he supposed, had the right to kill him. Or was that different here too? He went beyond the village to a friendly spot at the transition between forest and grassland—they had a name for it here—and lay down among the angelica and fern people, knowing it was time to leave. He had been in Red Bead's village for two moons and could understand much. But first he needed to talk more with Red Bead about someone to talk for him with the Russians.

After the sleep he trekked up the river trail with Red Bead's people to attend a Cha-duel-keh, a special big time. He was walking with Cross-eyed Bear, the old arrow chief, a man with the happy spirit of a child. "Why are the people at Rohsh called Undersea People?" Grizzly Hair asked. "Do they live in the water?" Maybe Black Snake had found one who washed ashore.

With the help of his hands and expressive face, Cross-eyed Bear said it was just a funny name, that from the shore their baidarkas—boats—appeared to come from under the ocean. Grizzly Hair couldn't imagine that, but was anxious to see it.

"Are the Undersea People friendly?"

Cross-eyed Bear chuckled. "Sometimes."

"Esteemed traders?"

"Oh yes." Cackling to himself, he changed the subject. "Women don't like the Cha-duel-keh."

"Why?"

"You'll see."

"What does Kashaya mean?"

"Some people call us that—nimble, light, quick, good gamblers. Understand?" He laughed happily. "Don't gamble with my people."

Grizzly Hair looked around, saw Salmon Woman and her husband on the trail behind. Grizzly Hair had gambled. "I would like someone to help me talk to the Undersea People," he said.

"Look," Cross-eyed Bear said, pointing ahead as they rounded a bend, "a new dancehouse." He glanced at Grizzly Hair. "I will tell Red Bead to hold a council when we get back."

The dancehouse was even bigger than Poo-soo-ne's, and a huge crowd stood outside the door. On the roof a spokesman was orating and Grizzly Hair understood something repeated over and over again, in different ways: that wives should couple only with husbands. Dismayed to hear this topic, he watched as ropes were removed from the doorway and people surged inside. He followed Red Bead's people to the east wall, but stayed as far as he could from Salmon Woman. Having lost sight of Cross-eyed Bear, he sat beside Three Directions. The clean-smelling pine branches imparted good health and everyone sat as if expecting to wait a long time. Grizzly Hair asked Three Directions—a young man who didn't seem to have many friends—"What are we waiting for?"

"Dark. Yukukulla appears only in the dark. No moon."

Yukukulla, Grizzly Hair seemed to recall, was a demon spirit similar to Bohemkulla. Were they inviting a demon to the dance? Surely not. No one would sit and wait for that, would they?

Slowly the light faded from the smokehole and doorway and the spirit-house became very dark. He heard faint sounds like distant human wailing. People exchanged knowing glances. Men pulled their women outside. Three Directions went too, though he had no woman. Grizzly Hair followed. As the crowd spilled out the doorway he saw in the otherwise profound darkness, snakes of fire winding down the hills through the trees. Terror gripped him. Women screamed. Demons were coming toward the dancehouse! The women quailed behind their men.

Three Directions leaned over to Grizzly Hair and said, "Yukukulla comes."

Why weren't these people running? The fiery snakes would soon be upon them. He started to run, then stopped. Something was wrong. He looked at Salmon Woman, clinging to her husband like a little child, and saw her pretense as she begged him to protect her from the demons.

With a great flurry and stamping of feet the demons arrived, and he saw that they were holding flaming baskets on their heads. Horrible discordant patterns were painted on their faces. One grabbed Salmon Woman. Her husband bravely shoved the demon in the chest and yelled for her to save herself by going inside the dancehouse. Along with many shrieking women, she fled inside.

Then began a strange battle between the demons and husbands. They pushed and shoved each other. The fight seemed evenly matched, though the demons had only one free hand, the other holding a basket of flames on their heads. The husbands belligerently pushed them around, but not too hard.

Almost at Grizzly Hair's feet, a demon fell and the basket rolled on the ground, igniting the dry grass. Men and demons stamped out the fire together and, as the fallen demon squatted over a ball of flaming pitch, flipping it with rocks back into his clay-lined basket, a husband knelt to help. But the moment the demon was back on his feet with the flaming basket on his head, he shoved the man who had just helped him, and the battle continued. In the light of the fires Grizzly Hair saw, through the hideous paint of one of the demons, the distinctive grin of Cross-eyed Bear. What was the meaning of this?

After much posturing and pushing, the devils broke through the entrance and fighting continued inside. Grizzly Hair followed. The women's screams echoing in the wooden walls hurt his ears. In the jerky light of the basket fires, he saw Salmon Woman clutching her man as he defended her from the demon that looked like Cross-eyed Bear. Puzzled, Grizzly Hair sat beside Three Directions.

After strenuous exertion the husbands won the sham fight and the wailing demons ran for the hills. The dance fire was kindled. The dance doctor entered in a feather costume—petting and brandishing a live rattlesnake. Grandly announcing it as the spirit of Yukukulla, he admonished the women to control their sexual urges and be faithful to their men. One after the other, he thrust the snake at women's faces. They screamed and clamored over the seated people to get away. Salmon Woman pretended to faint when the snake was brought to her.

At last the snake was released outside and everyone danced. They danced until morning and fell exhausted in the playing field, Salmon Woman chastely beside her man. Had she been singled out for special attention in this ceremony? Obviously it was intended to frighten women into being faithful to their men. Maybe people knew about her and Grizzly Hair and didn't want to confront them. In any case, he wouldn't stay in Red Bead's village after the council.

41

He felt the men's curiosity as they seated themselves in the late morning sun. Red Bead passed an elderberry pipe. Wisps of smoke floated up and dispersed in the redwood branches, and noisy birds competed with the sing-song of Salmon Woman's class, which wasn't far away. Grizzly Hair asked, "Do the Undersea People pay for digging water ditches?"

Red Bead said, "My people help them in exchange for knives, cups, cloth and other things." Men nodded.

"Do all Undersea People give such goods?"

"No. Only the glav-nyi, the headman."

"Or his special helpers," a man added.

"Are any of you special helpers?" Grizzly Hair asked.

The men shook their heads.

"When your people plant the big-headed grass, do guards watch over you with guns?"

"No. They come and look at the grass, then pay us to collect the seed, unless orange fungus ruins it." Several men chuckled and Red Bead's old father laughed loudly.

Grizzly Hair recalled big-headed grass at the mission, but had never seen orange fungus on it. "You help them grow kar-to-feln too," he said, noticing wide smiles at the mention of it.

An elder gave a helpless expression and said, "We try our best to trap the ground squirrels, but—" Raucous laughter interrupted and Red Bead joined in. When it died down, the headman explained, "Undersea people coax weak plants to live where strong plants want to grow. Ground squirrels love to eat the kar-to-feln, but the Undersea People are surprised and unhappy when they do it." Tears of laughter were being wiped from faces around the circle.

Clearly, the Russians were something like the *Españoles*. "Do the Undersea People force people to work?"

Red Bead said, "Only those who steal from them."

Three Directions snorted disagreement and a heated exchange followed, the men raising their voices to be heard over the recitation of the children. Grizzly Hair understood little of what was being said, but it seemed Three Directions thought people had been forced to work. He also said the Undersea men took all the women. Grizzly Hair saw in the men's faces that Three Directions was not well respected.

Waiting politely for a pause to clear the air, Grizzly Hair asked Three Directions, "Did they force you to work?"

The response was hard to follow, with other men speaking out of turn and over him, but it sounded like he had argued with the Undersea People about whether they owed him more goods for his work. He had gone into the storehouse and taken things he said belonged to him, but they caught and whipped him.

"Do they take your people to Rohsh when they don't want to go?"

As the men shook their heads, Three Directions got up and walked away with rudeness in his gait. Red Bead repeated, "They are esteemed traders. We go to Rohsh when we want and return when we want."

Grizzly Hair's mind was unchanged about going to the Russians. Three

Directions behaved something like Sick Rat. "Do all of you talk the tongue of the Undersea People?"

Everyone nodded. "We are good at tongues," Red Bead said, drawing smoke from the pipe that had come back to him, then handed it on. "You talk well too."

Pleased at the reports of the Russians, and the compliment, Grizzly Hair accepted the pipe from Salmon Woman's husband, who had never displayed the slightest suspicion. He sucked the sweet smoke and noticed an immediate sharpening of his thoughts. Passing the pipe to Cross-eyed Bear, he asked, "Do the *Españoles* come here?"

Red Bead let out the smoke he'd been holding. "They have not come here," he said, "but relatives of the Jauyomis came and tried to make us go to Mission San Rafael."

"Did the long robes send them?"

"I talked to the headman," Red Bead said, "I think they wanted us to come to make the padre happy. Like bringing meat to a big time."

Grizzly Hair recalled that Estanislao had taken many people to the mission. "I think they do it to win favors from the long robes," Grizzly Hair said. "I think Jauyomi's relatives would live like neighbors in old times if the *Españoles* left this land."

The master storyteller shook his head. "We didn't like those people in old times either."

Red Bead added thoughtfully, "But in old times they didn't tell us they have more power than we do and can do anything they want to us." Most of the men appeared to be in deep thought.

"Are they more powerful now than they were before?" Grizzly Hair asked. "Did they get power at the mission?"

Several men nodded, others pursed their lips, all clearly interested.

"But they didn't take you." Grizzly Hair spoke from the strength in his stomach. "If they had big new power they would have captured you. So you have more power than they do."

Men looked skeptical. Cross-eyed Bear said, "We had to shoot arrows at them to make them leave."

"The black hats are your real enemies," Grizzly Hair said, "not neophytes who try to please them. And the black hats are afraid of the Undersea People, your trade allies." He told what María had said, that Commander Argüello feared the Russians would attack Presidio San Francisco.

The men waited for more.

He told how he had talked with men all along his journey about defensive pacts. "I have come here to ask you and the Undersea People to join us."

"But it is Jauyomi's relatives we want to stop," one of the elders said.

The father of Red Bead added, "The black hats have never come here. We have no quarrel with them. It is foolish to attack powerful men who have done us no harm."

"I keep the peace," Red Bead said—a peace chief like Morning Owl.

Cross-eyed Bear glanced around the circle and spoke with surprising power for an old man who often giggled like a woman: "We should wait until this young man talks to the Undersea People, then decide."

Red Bead sucked on the pipe and squinted up through the high trees. He handed the pipe to Grizzly Hair and said, "I agree with my arrow chief." Everyone else nodded.

Knowing that was the best he could do, Grizzly Hair said, "I will leave for the Undersea People's village now. Who will come and talk for me?"

The council broke into separate conversations. Finally, Cross-eyed Bear explained that he and two other men would accompany him to Rohsh. The trip would take a running man until midday to get to the camp on the sea, and another sun to get to Rohsh.

A man whose children spent most of their time petting and riding Morena suggested that he leave the horse in the village. By now everyone knew how to ride her and all were thoughtful of her needs. He looked around at the nodding men. Morena was his most valuable possession, but these people had been polite hosts and he would return their generosity. "I will leave her," he said.

Not long afterwards, with his bow across his back, he smiled at his former classmates, who vied to hold his hands and made sad faces as though they didn't want him to leave. Gently he freed his hands and followed Cross-eyed Bear and the two other men down the path. As the river took them westward, the canyon of redwood and laurel opened wider and the cooling wind brought a strange, fresh scent.

He rounded a hill and the horizon jumped out to the ends of the world. The river broke into small channels and fanned out over a big sandflat. Beyond that, at long last, Grizzly Hair saw the immense western sea. The breeze came briskly and he stood inhaling sharp new aromas and watching the glint of sunlight on the surface of the restless water—bright as the vessels in the mission *iglésia*. Gulls keened and circled above, landing and rising again. He ran across damp, pliant sand to the pulsing sea. It was more water than he could comprehend. He stopped and stared, barely noticing his three companions walking up the beach toward some makeshift u-machas.

The distances stunned him—sky blue married to sea blue with nothing between, a vast coupling. He felt tiny as a gnat. For the first time he knew in his bones how lonely it must have been out on the endless sea when Coyote, Raven and Turtle floated in their little boat, before Turtle dove to the bottom for land.

With the roar of the wind in his ears, he let out a whoop and ran along the water's edge toward the men and the u-machas. He laughed at the seabirds sailing over his head and leapt high over the surf when it ran up to catch his feet. The water splashed higher than his head. Tasting something, he stopped, cupped the foam and sipped. Salt! He recalled a story about salt in the sea. Salt was precious to all peoples. The umne traded fine bonework for salt. But here saltwater stretched as far as he could see.

Men and women and a few children stood in the camp. He vaguely recalled seeing them when he'd first found Red Bead's village. Red Bead explained that his people took turns fishing here. As the adults talked, fast and joking and impossible to understand, Grizzly Hair played with the laughing children, all trying to outrun the waves.

At supper he ate the sweet flat fish that had been caught in long-handled nets and steamed with greens. He also munched salty, crunchy kelp that had been baked in hot ashes. In the morning he and the three men trotted northward. Soon they slowed to a fast walk and lowered their heads as they climbed a mountain rising steeply from the sand. The sheer side of it plunged into the ocean. Exhilarating wind from the sea almost stopped his breath. If it hadn't been impolite, he would have run up the path ahead of the others, so filled with power was he.

A line of brown birds with huge beaks flew level with him. One by one they dove and splashed into the sea far below, emerging with dripping beaks—taking turns fishing. Then the trail turned landward, traversing back and forth as they climbed the steep short-grassed mountain. He was sorry to lose sight of the ocean. Keening hawks rode the wind. He smiled at the old pine people who leaned back to the rising mountain, their branches behind them like wind-blown hair, inviting the wind to sweep over them. They knew how to live here. Always rising, the trail headed into alternating gorges and ridges until it entered a forest of taller trees that protected each other from the wind.

In a friendly village well known to Cross-eyed Bear, they rested and ate, then continued. Father sun had moved to the west when, through the pine branches on a high ridge top, they looked far down upon the sea again. The blue-green expanse appeared entirely placid from this great distance, but Grizzly Hair knew it was filled with deep and restless power.

"Selenya Rohsh," said Cross-eyed Bear, pointing down.

Small in the distance Grizzly Hair made out a jumble of dark structures at the water's edge. The old arrow chief began his swinging walk down the steep incline and, with excitement building, Grizzly Hair followed, letting the fall of the land lengthen his strides. Down and down they went into dark, heavily wooded gorges on the winding trail. He knew he must speak well, for much depended on him. They passed a clearing with strange little trees similar to the fruit trees at Mission San José. A little beyond, the view opened again.

Now he could see brown square structures on a promontory over the ocean. As they continued walking downhill, a village of redwood u-machas, which had been hidden from above, suddenly stood before them. Smiling people came out to talk.

"These are the May-tee-neh people," said Cross-eyed Bear with his usual childish glee. "Top of the Land People. My relatives." He spoke to the headman, who wore a big metal medallion suspended by a red and black thong made of a tight, skillful weave. On the disk was the image of a face surrounded by strange marks. "He traded that," Cross-eyed bear explained, "for the use of his people's home place."

Impatient to get to the Russians, Grizzly Hair accepted food, talked politely with these hosts and looked at the huge wooden wall around the Russian houses. Excitement churned his stomach and he couldn't eat more than a scoop or two of nu-pah.

Leaving the May-tee-neh people, they went not to an opening in the wooden wall—there was none that he could see—but down into a sandy ocean cove where busy men scurried about. The selenya lay above on the bluff. Alongside the vertical earth wall stood a spindly structure of interlaced poles. Between that and the earth wall there was a wooden wall, perfectly cut boards slightly curved and fitted. Men in small leather aprons worked on three levels of the skeletal structure, walking back and forth with various implements, some sitting with their feet dangling while they hammered on the smooth wood.

Cross-eyed Bear said with the quiet pride of one who knows more about the world, "They are making a big boat."

A boat! Poo-soo-ne had told of a big boat that came up his river, but never had Grizzly Hair imagined anything as gigantic as that wall of wood. On the sand below it, two men pushed and pulled a toothed iron blade, one standing in a pit dug beneath a long slotted platform, the other on the platform with braced legs and back muscles moving as he pushed and pulled the blade up and down through the slot. As the blade chewed into oak, flakes flew in the stiff breeze. The great value of this tool jolted Grizzly Hair as when he had first seen iron pounded. A stack of oak trunks piled on the edge of the bluff would no doubt be rolled down on the sand where they would be cut by these men. Russians were as clever as *Españoles.*

He followed Cross-eyed Bear up a very steep switchback trail to the bluff top. There was another way to climb the bluff—a redwood trunk devoid of branches leaning from top to bottom, with steps carved in it, but it looked dangerously steep. On top, the flat land was dominated by the high walls made of vertical posts—more than twice Grizzly Hair's height.

He turned and looked toward the sea, the farthest protrusion of the promontory. A number of oblong houses stood there, and a square house with large dragonfly wings revolving so fast they blurred in the wind. A magical thing. He turned to look for his companions, who stood before the enormous iron-hinged doors that opened to the compound. They were talking in casual tones to a long-bearded man in a pale shirt and dark trousers who stood at the gate. He leaned on a gun like a walking stick.

Glad to see the friendliness of the Undersea People and their apparent lack of interest in him, Grizzly Hair listened to the alien tongue, which Cross-eyed Bear did indeed speak, and looked at the amazing wall of vertical poles, sharpened at the top, and the big houses inside. Built into the nearest corner of the wall was a house shaped like a giant cell of a bee-hive, with six or seven sides, the roof peaked and angled in as many directions. On it a banner whipped in the wind. In various places up and down this many-sided tower cannons poked through square holes. María had been right. The Russians had big guns.

The banner was red, white and black. He had to watch a while to make out a black bird against a white background—a bird with two heads looking opposite directions, something gold on each head. At a break in the talk, he pointed and quietly asked Cross-eyed Bear, "What ugly bird is that?"

"Eagle."

"But it has two beaks, two topknots and necks that look more like snakes."

"Hats, not topknots. The Tsar wears such a hat."

"*Tsar?*"

"Headman of the Undersea People."

"I thought he was called—" he meant to say glav-nyi, but the man at the gate motioned them through and Cross-eyed Bear was walking ahead. They passed men pounding hot metal. This too excited Grizzly Hair, as did the horses and cows in the surrounding pastures. The Russians were a strong and wealthy people, and friendly to *Indios.*

People of all descriptions converged upon Cross-eyed Bear, including two short, plump men—or were they women?—with laughing eyes and flat faces and heavy eye folds. They wore robes that had been sewn from horizontal strips of gut. The robes stood out stiffly from their legs and made them look like u-machas with handsome greasy faces coming out the smokeholes. The hair of some of the children was faded and unhealthy-looking, as was their skin. There were women, obviously women, wearing thin cloth tied around their hips. Their chin tattoos, though similar to those of Red Bead's women, zig-zagged differently, and by the way they looked at him, he knew they thought him attractive. The friendly reception heightened his expectations for the talks ahead.

Another man with a long black beard joined them. His pale shirt bloused down to his knees, roped in at the waist, and his dark *pantalones* were tucked inside knee-high boots. He talked with Cross-eyed Bear's friends and barely glanced at Grizzly Hair.

In a break in the talk, Grizzly Hair whispered to Cross-eyed Bear, "Is he the Tsar?"

The old arrow chief looked at him oddly. "You mean the glav-nyi?" He pointed at the tallest building, the one with clusters of glittering squares that reflected father sun's light. "The glav-nyi is in there."

Why didn't the headman come out to greet them?

"Ah, here is Katya," said Cross-eyed Bear. "She is the niece of my cousin."

Grizzly Hair turned to see a young woman with red-striped cloth tightly encasing her hips. Her brown breasts were draped in a wealth of shells, many nestled deep in her canyon. "She talks well with the Undersea People," the arrow chief said, "Her husband is one of them."

Her round face was framed by shining black hair that curved inward upon her shoulders and forehead. She had the same tattoo as Salmon Woman, and that produced a strong call to pleasure, especially to see her gazing at him in open appreciation. Katya was a plump ripe berry such as one was sometimes fortunate enough to find hanging in a protected area where the hot sun had neither dulled its skin nor shrunk its juicy parts. Her thick lips seemed to retain an excess of moisture. He felt an urge to touch their crisp, dark outlines, as well as the neat nose tucked into her darkly radiant face.

He asked in the Kashaya tongue, "Will you talk for me with the headman of the Undersea People?"

Color spread beneath her cheeks—tang beneath the sweetness. "I would love to talk for you." Her breasts held their roundness among the shells and her gaze touched him like fingers.

Cackling under his breath Cross-eyed Bear said, "You don't need me to talk for you."

In a low tone he asked the old man, "Where is the husband of your cousin's niece?"

The wily arrow chief whispered conspiratorially, "Hunting, far away." He waved an indifferent hand toward the sea, then spoke with several friendly men who were approaching, perhaps more relatives. Then they all left.

Katya turned to walk with the pale man toward the high house with the glistening squares, the motion beneath the striped cloth pulling Grizzly Hair like a rope. He began to understand why Spanish men liked to undress women.

Four cannons on wheels flanked the doorway of the big house, a sight thrilling in a different way than the struggle beneath the red stripes as Katya mounted the stairs ahead of him. Up and up between high wooden walls he followed her to another floor. The planks were flat and smooth beneath his feet as he followed Katya around a corner.

There, within a riot of goods and strange implements, which hung from rafters and stood piled on shelves, sat a man behind a spindly-legged table holding the wing-feather of a vulture. Hair the color of old straw grew on his cheeks in square patches. Lighter hair curled about his ears, the length of it tied in back. Pale hair rippled back from his forehead like wind-blown water, magically stilled. A knob of a pink chin asserted itself between the squares of facial hair. Perched on his high narrow nose was a wire device containing disks of the same transparent crystal that reflected father sun's brilliance outside and were now at the man's back, invisible except for slight reflections. Behind these disks the man's eyes were enlarged, distorted and very blue.

Trying not to stare, Grizzly Hair forced his gaze to the stacks of white sheaves on the table, then the big round thing on the wall with strange marks spaced around it. A short arrow pointed down at an angle, a longer one pointing at an angle toward the sky. It emitted the tapping noise of an angry beetle. The long arrow jumped a little. So did Grizzly Hair. Was it alive? A dangerous spirit?

The man at the table inserted the quill of the feather into a small, dark vessel. He pointed to the sitting platforms, then brought his hands together, pale fingers interlocked—pale hairs between the joints. He spoke in a tongue that sounded like bubbles rising from thick mud.

Katya said this was Karl Schmidt, the glav-nyi. The man who had accompanied them here dipped his head toward the glav-nyi and left. Glav-nyi Schmidt gestured again at the wooden platforms with four legs and square backs, similar to those the long robes had sat on. Katya—shells swinging around her large breasts, removed things from the sitting platforms and put them on the floor. As she bent over, the extreme difference between the width of her hips and waist overpowered even his fixation on the glav-nyi. Katya sat down and Grizzly Hair lowered himself slowly on the smoothest, shiniest surface he had ever sat upon. His feet rested on a nappy weave of purples and reds.

It would be difficult, he knew, to fasten his attention on what would be said in a house this alien, separated in every way from earth and sky and with Katya so near that her round toes lined up next to his. Yet fasten he would, for this was the most important moment of his journey, possibly his entire life.

42

As talk flowed from the glav-nyi, Grizzly Hair looked beneath the table at the man's narrow pointed boots and wondered if the feet inside had been shaped with an ax. The glav-nyi wore three layers of tight clothing. His white shirt appeared to be held together by a red band tied in a flourish around his neck. Over the shirt a layer of tan cloth patterned with bird tracks encased his stomach, tiny disks stepping up in a vertical column over his chest. On top of this was overlaid yet another garment, this one of dark blue cloth tight around his arms and hanging in swallowtails on either side of his sitting platform.

Katya said, "He wants to know who you are and why you come here." On the wall the arrow jumped—it jumped regularly, yet no one dropped dead.

He found his calm. "Tell him I am from Morning Owl's people, from beyond the Valley of the Sun. I come to talk with him."

As she told him this, Schmidt leaned forward, chin in hand, elbow on the stacked papers. His eyes were huge behind the disks and his head held the posture of an interested man. He talked again.

Katya said, "He sees that you are in mourning and says he is sorry about the death."

Relieved that the Russians were indeed polite people, Grizzly Hair nodded his appreciation. "Tell him I have come to talk with him about becoming allies."

Schmidt removed the hand holding up his head.

Grizzly Hair continued. "I have made friends among many *Indio* peoples. They tell stories about the warriors of the *Españoles* forcing them to go to the missions, as I was forced to go to Mission San José. Many have been injured in the missions. People say the *Españoles* are afraid of you Undersea People. They say you are their enemy. I came to invite you to be allies with me and many *Indio* peoples who need protection. Your enemies are our enemies."

Katya gave him a curious look. Grizzly Hair continued, "I have seen your big guns. Teach us to use them and together we will drive the *Españoles* from this land."

Glav-nyi Schmidt carefully removed the threadlike metal from behind his ears and examined the crystal disks. He rubbed the surfaces on the bird tracks on his chest and returned the disks to his face. His words flared and dipped, and when he was finished Katya said:

"This is a big surprise to him. The *Españoles* lost a war in Mexico. Things have changed. The missions and presidios belong to the *Mexicanos* now, not the *Españoles*. He doesn't know whether the *Mexicanos* will be enemies of Ross."

Grizzly Hair knew nothing about *Mexicanos* but believed that as long as the black hats and long robes lived in the missions and presidio, nothing had changed. He listened as the glav-nyi talked again.

Katya said, "He is surprised you came today. After the sleep, some headmen of the *Mexicanos* will visit him. He says you should stay in the selenya and he will talk to you after the *Mexicanos* leave. Then he will know if they are his enemies." Katya gave him a sidelong smile that, despite his alarm at what had just been said, touched his man's core.

Nevertheless, he kept his attention on the talk. "Tell him I am pleased to sleep here and talk later. But if black hats are coming, I am in danger."

Without speaking to the glav-nyi, Katya told him in a teasing voice, "You are the glav-nyi's guest, under his protection. The black hats behave politely when they are here; they are afraid of the guns of the Undersea People. My people have been safe here since I was born, all our guests too. You are in no danger."

"Say that to him. I want to know those are his words."

She repeated it in the glav-nyi's tongue. The glav-nyi smiled and nodded reassuringly, and invited Grizzly Hair to look around the selenya. He stood up and extended his hand.

Grizzly Hair reached across the table, grasped the soft fingers and pumped the cloth-encased arm up and down. He liked the custom. After the sleep he would know whether the glav-nyi would be his ally. In the meantime he would see the headman of the black hats. Now the danger excited him. It would be a coup to look upon the headman of the enemy he hoped to defeat, while the enemy knew nothing about him.

Outside, even the breeze felt excited. Everything was new and strange and heady, and he hoped he was about to change the world. He went with Katya to where men were making a big new house attached to the corner of the southeast wall. A man in a long shirt, roped at the waist, drove something into a redwood board with a hammer like the *Españoles* used. Grizzly Hair squatted and picked a small spike off the ground—pounded iron, square top, tapered to a sharp point. These spikes held the boards together. Nearly finished, the interesting house had a big round wart on the roof—as round as flat boards could make it—and if Katya hadn't been pulling him away, he would have stayed and watched longer.

"Thirsty?" she asked. Parched after the long walk, he nodded. She took him to the center of the courtyard where a redwood pole leaned through the crotch of an oak. At the high tip of the pole hung a bucket, poised over a deep water hole. She asked him to lift a big rock tied to the pole's butt end. As he did, the tip of the pole lowered enough to make the bucket fall into the hole, a rope unwinding. Leaning over, she looked down into the hole presenting her narrow waist and generous hips to him. Then she pulled the rope up, hand over hand, and the bucket came up, dripping and full. She drank, then brought the bucket to him. He gulped cold water, again admiring a clever device of a strange people. She poured the remainder down the hole, rearranged rope and bucket and ordered him to put the rock down. As he did, the bucket jumped back to the top of the pole.

Katya took him to a smaller house, the entrance flanked by two more cannons on wheels. For an instant he imagined these big guns at the home place, protecting the umne. Inside, the aroma of baking grain permeated the house. She showed him the polished table and benches where "important" guests ate, and he crossed gazes with a woman in a dress like María's. She was pulling a loaf from an oven with the same long-handled wooden tool that neophytes used in mission ovens. Two fragrant loaves steamed on a shelf.

Back in the dark part of the house, he saw several small compartments, each containing a raised sleeping platform and surrounded by three walls. These compartments opened to a central hallway. He touched one of the soft and wonderfully woven blankets. "Is this where I will sleep?"

Katya giggled, "No, no."

"You said I am the glav-nyi's guest, under his protection."

She looked at him with humorous admiration. "The *Mexicano* headmen sleep here, not people like you."

People like you. "What kind of people am I?"

"People who were here before the Big Noses came. People who do the hard work. People who sleep on mats on the ground and eat our own food."

Indios. Something was turning sour inside him.

"Commander Argüello always sleeps here," she continued. "He eats well too."

Commander Argüello, headman of the black hats. María had swept his floor and served his food. Argüello had given her a horse. "Have you seen that man?"

"Yes. He is big and wears many decorations on his coat and a feather on his hat from a bird no one has ever seen."

"Maybe we should all wear hats with feathers." He saw that she recognized the joke, but underneath it lay the cruel joke that in Rohsh enemies were treated like esteemed visitors. Or were they enemies? "I have seen no hand-held guns," he said.

"In the big house, locked in a room." Katya flicked her wrist toward the tall house they had just left. She went outside and beckoned him through the big gate. About twenty dark furs hung on a drying rack. He'd noticed them as he came in, but had been too overwhelmed with other sights to pay much attention. Now he squeezed a lush, soft pelt and realized this had to be the prized fur of which he had heard—otters that lived in the cold sea. Their fur made the finest of rain capes. Maybe he could get one for Morning Owl. Would the glav-nyi accept Missouri's beads in trade? Or would even those beads seem worthless to people who had so many marvelous things?

They walked along a trail toward the bluff edge, the wind blowing Katya's skirt between her thighs, the hair straight back from her forehead. They passed turtle-back rocks and blowing grass and oblong houses and saw mostly women and children. They passed the little house with whirring dragonfly wings. At the edge of the land he saw the ocean far below and understood why Katya's people were called Top of the Land People. Father sun lay before them half submerged in the sea, and for the first time Grizzly Hair saw the life-giver's western house. The bright mass that had always been round was squeezed into a wide flat rectangle—even he lived in a house with corners. Brilliant trails of gold and orange streamed from that bright house all the way across the shimmering water to the foot of the bluff. Magic pathways.

Katya's skin absorbed the warm bright colors as they watched the fiery house sink into the sea. He inhaled the sea air and she took his hand in hers—magic tingling to his core—and led him to the cove side of the promontory. They looked down at the men who were still working on the boat. Beyond them on the sand, he saw a wooden house he'd barely noticed before, tethered to the shore by poles and ropes. "That house floats," he said. It was bobbing on the swells in the most protected corner of the cove.

"That's the boathouse." She looked as though it gave her an idea.

Here, even boats slept in rectangular houses. Not far from that stood a sweathouse of a normal conical shape. Maybe he would sleep there. He pointed to the big boat the men were making. "Have you seen such boats on the ocean?"

"Yes. My man travels in them. When the Undersea People first came, they made them of redwood but they leaked, so now they use oak. These boats carry baidarkas to faraway hunting places, and bring back hides and grain from the missions."

The sour thing moved in his stomach. The Russians traded with the *Españoles.* María said they never traded, said they were enemies. He had trusted that. Yet trading bespoke friendship, as did the sleeping house. He shouldn't have spoken so quickly to the glav-nyi about war. Now he had to hope the friendship between those two powerful peoples would die, now that the black hats were called *Mexicanos.* The glav-nyi seemed to think it might. But how could a mere name spoil a friendship? Would Grizzly Hair be seen as an enemy of the glav-nyi as well as the *Españoles*? Would both of them ally against him? He had been *inocente,* ensnared by his own excessive enthusiasm, like Coyote in so many stories.

Katya walked around the curve of the bluff and stepped down on the first step of the notched pole. She turned and beckoned. He followed, stunned by his predicament as well as the steepness of the descent. Should he hide? Could he trust the glav-nyi's promise to protect him against the black hats? The notches were too small for his feet. Lacking anything to hold onto, it felt like the wind might blow him off. But he took care with his steps and followed Katya safely to the cove.

The moment his feet touched sand, a bell clanged above. The memory of mission bells made him jump in his skin, but he saw that the boat-makers began climbing down from the scaffolding, and the two men working the toothed blade quit pushing and pulling. The one on top pulled the blade up through the slot and laid it on the platform. The man below pulled himself out of the pit and they climbed up the redwood steps. Still, no one seemed to notice Grizzly Hair. Many strangers, he realized, must visit this place. He had questions but thought it best to stay observant and keep them to himself. He scooped a handful of warm sand and asked, "Name of this?"

She pronounced it, and he told her his word for the sand at the home river. "No," she laughed. "River sand is not sea sand." Her people had two words, but it seemed to him that sand wasn't on her mind any more than his. He went to the water, which perfectly reflected the astonishing reds of the sun's descent into his house. She followed and stood close beside him. Foamy water rushed past their feet and reversed directions, pulling sand from under their heels. She staggered against him.

He caught her—shells and breasts and the scent of madrone flowers—and it took his breath away that she clearly wanted him. "When will your husband return?" he asked in a hoarse whisper.

With a glance at the deserted bluff top she pulled away, the cold air erasing her warm imprint. "He comes when he comes. Maybe when the moon is gone." With a teasing smile she ran away, shells clattering, and disappeared into the boathouse. He followed. As for the *Mexicanos,* they wouldn't come until after the sleep.

Katya stood on a narrow floating raft running up the middle of the floating house. Boats were tied to the raft by means of iron rings embedded in the wood. He stepped on the raft, which dipped with his weight, and walked toward her, cautious of his balance. In this house the walls and roof would keep rain out of the boats and they wouldn't need to be pulled to shore and turned over. At the opposite end of the raft the wall opened to allow the boats to go directly out to sea. Seeing her interest in his fascination, he knelt down and touched the veined, hairless skin of which the slim boats were made—boats no wider than a man's two legs. The skin was stretched over the top of the boats too, except for two holes, one before the other, where men would sit.

"Baidarka," Katya said.

"The boat that comes from under the sea?"

She laughed. "They're too small to see from shore, except when they are on top of a swell, so it looks like they come from under the sea."

"Do men fish in these boats?"

"They hunt. You saw the pelts by the gate."

Sea otters. He touched the fine dark lashing on a bone stay inside one of the holes. "What is this?'"

"A whale whisker."

Whisker? He looked at her. She was making swimming motions, but he couldn't imagine what kind of animal or fish she was trying to describe, a very big ocean swimmer.

He touched the next boat, longer and much wider, no skin over the top.

"Baidara," she said, looking as though she were as acutely aware of their aloneness as he.

"Undersea People make good boats," he said, enjoying the prolonged teasing. "This baidara would hold ten or twelve men. What kind of skin is this?"

She said something he couldn't understand, then squatted, puffed out her cheeks, flapped her elbows and barked like a dog. "They live in the sea," she said, on her feet again. "Their bodies are fat and hairless."

"Like yours."

Her smile dazzled with the compliment, crisp lips turned out.

He laid his bow and quiver on the raft and stepped into a baidara, doing a quick dance for balance as the boat jumped and bounced. Katya's rich laughter echoed in the boathouse. He jumped a little on purpose and laughed again to feel the taut skin rebound beneath his feet and hear the delicate thunk of bumping boats amplified within the wooden walls. As the boat calmed to the normal rise and fall of the ocean, he admired the hills and valleys of Katya. "Come," he said.

She stepped into the boat, crying out in mock fear as it lurched. He pulled her to him. When the boat settled down he cupped a breast, mouthing one then the other, the firm dark berries tasting of sea salt and abundance. Careful not to excite the boat, he lowered himself until his knees rested on the dry, cold ocean. Breathing her fruity aroma, he ran his hands over the contours of her hips.

Full berry lips and dark eyes smiling, she kneeled; knees touching his knees. She rubbed her nose on his and her sweet breath mingled with the other scent as she murmured, "Kodiak men do this."

"Kodiak?"

"Undersea Men from the north."

His nose had never felt so sensitive, and he followed her as she lay back in her shells and untied her skirt. After a moment's hesitation to thank the spirits, he slipped in and they rose and fell on the breast of the great and powerful western sea.

"Your son was a randy man," Coyote says, licking his lips.

"You made people like that," I remind him.

Impatient at the excessive attention given to mating, O-se-mai-ti grumps, "People are as bad as you, Coyote. They should have an orderly schedule for copulating."

"We know, we know, only in second grass," says Coyote with a sly look.

But I am *seeing* my son's enemy.

43

Morning, North of San Francisco

Luis Argüello, Commander of San Francisco Presidio, thought he'd never seen such a perfectly wrong way to react to a shying horse. The sharp yelps of the Canon of Durángo Cathedral worsened the horse's state of mind as it sprang, four feet in the air, arching its back. The tooled leather drape of the Mochia saddle and the heavy wooden stirrups, no longer anchored by the canon's sandaled feet, whipped against the mustang's belly, further irritating the horse. Canon Fernandez gripped the big ball horn and his brown robe flapped up and down one beat behind his wide rump.

At last the horse succeeded and *Canónigo* Agustino Fernandez de San Vicente, who had been selected as the most capable diplomat to represent Emperor Iturbide, flew through the air and landed on his big middle. He exhaled like a down pillow and retched into the *arroyo* that fell away before him.

Padre Presidente Payeras trotted his horse courteously away, but the soldiers of the military escort stared. The red vomitus reminded Argüello of the canon's prodigious consumption of wine the previous night. *El Canónigo* rolled over and stared into the blue sky, small hands on the mound of his stomach as if to quiet it.

Waving the smiling men of the escort away, Argüello leaned toward his lieutenant, who held the reins of the canon's horse, and whispered. "Does that *arroyo* have a name?"

"I don't think we've named it yet, Captain."

"Did you see, ah," Argüello cleared his throat to staunch the chuckle, "the color of his face?"

"Green, *Capitán*," the lieutenant whispered.

"Enter it in the log. *Arroyo Verde*, Green Creek." Argüello twisted away to hide his smile as the lieutenant said in a soft voice, "*Si, Capitán.*"

On his hands and knees, the diplomat struggled to disentangle his feet from the ecclesiastical robe.

"Lieutenant Valle," Argüello said in his gruffest voice, "Change mounts with *el Canónigo*. That horse was improperly trained." Actually, it was the gentlest one.

"*Sí, Capitán.*" With catlike grace the lieutenant dismounted.

The canon accepted the lieutenant's cupped hand and mounted. As Valle subdued the agitated mustang, Argüello signaled the men to proceed toward the *castillo* of the Russians—a military fort despite Schmidt's insistence on calling it a settlement, selenya.

Thirty-eight years old, Argüello rode proudly under his new Chapeau de Bras with its ostrich plume and golden medallion. A talented Indian at Mission Dolores had made his silver inlaid saddle and three brass buttons twinkled from his maroon cuffs. Proud of the substantial figure he cut in the saddle, Argüello ruled San Francisco Presidio circumspectly. He'd made small improvements through trade with the Russians, though that was technically illegal. Before *el Canónigo* arrived several days earlier, announcing his intent to visit the Russian fort, Argüello had ordered the Russian goods hidden.

He'd also penned a letter to Karl Schmidt, business manager of the fort, notifying him of the impending visit. "He is the highest status person ever to visit Alta California, and wants *tout la monde* to know it," he had written.

"Your excellency," said Argüello slowing his horse beside the canon, "about the deputies' vote on a temporary gov—"

"Thank God he had the decency to resign. No regalist shall serve as governor." Under the brown habit, the canon's belly quivered with the horse's gait. "Sola is a friend of Spain."

"I'm guessing the deputies will elect Captain Guerr—"

"Stupid, unacceptable."

Argüello gave his horse its head crossing another *arroyo,* then waited for Canon Fernandez to catch up. "Guerra is very respected, and he has taken the oath to the Mexi—"

"He was born in Spain. We can't have such people in power." Luis Argüello, who'd been born in San Francisco, felt a ray of hope. Eliminating Guerra improved his chances of becoming governor. Casually he asked, "What qualities do you think a governor should have?"

"Unquestioned loyalty." He glanced at Padre Presidente Payeras on the *pinto* ahead and lowered his voice. "Ability to balance temporal and Church interests."

"For example?" One would think a canon would support the friars in all matters; however, this one's debauchery made Argüello wonder.

Canon Fernandez glanced at him. "Loyalty to the Emperor is most essential."

Cabron! Argüello looked ahead at his men and waited for *el Canónigo* to repeat the same, tired accusation.

The canon did not disappoint him. "You're so far away, it's hard to keep up with what goes on here. As I said yesterday, France might help Spain revive hostilities against us and reverse the revolution. We worry about the loyalty of you officers in Upper California." Argüello hid his irritation as e*l Canónigo* continued:

"Sorry to be blunt, but counterrevolution has already been attempted, so worry is only natural."

"Excellency, let me pledge to you once again, as I did in public ceremony last spring. My loyalty is totally with Emperor Iturbide. Mexico has nothing to fear from me or my officers. I, we, are your officers now." A demeaning thing to say to an upstart from a classless bunch of outlaws.

The canon nodded, apparently accepting the pledge again, but doubtless with no more sincerity than before. He glanced around to assure their privacy and murmured, "By the way, the woman you sent to my room was nice. *Gracias.*"

The pounding at Argüello's door last evening had startled him. Soledad Ortega, his young wife, had tried to soothe the quaking Indian servant at the door as she complained of the canon's drunkenness and cruelty. Soledad had dispatched another servant woman to help, and returned to bed.

Now, bouncing on his new mount, *el Canónigo* said, "We think it's time for, shall we say, the hard hand of ecclesiastical discipline to be moderated by acceptance in the Mexican family through participation in civil administration and the economy."

Argüello had trouble picking through that, but if it meant what he hoped, he was pleased. He kept his voice low and one eye on the back of the pious Padre Presidente of the Franciscans. "Under the new regime could the governor, for example, grant title to lands?" Until now he and others had run cattle on leased land. A cloud of impermanence hung over all ranchos, including his beloved Las Pulgas.

"The new regime will reward its friends with land; otherwise, how can we expect loyalty?"

"I agree, absolutely. Property is the glue that sticks people to their country, to their Emperor." *To their governor.*

"That is our belief."

"But the best land is claimed by the missions."

"That must change."

Ah, this was sounding better by the minute. Glimpsing the silver sea beyond the rounded hills, he felt his spirit rise like a boat on a wave. Riding to the crest of the steep, treeless incline and seeing the full expanse of the ocean, he inhaled deeply of the salt air and felt proud of this wild land of his birth. A soaring hawk cried in the cloudless sky.

The escort of soldiers dismounted, allowing the horses to graze on the short grass that had sprung up after the only rain. In a line facing inland the men urinated with the breeze, bright droplets flying before them. Argüello positioned himself next to Padre Presidente Payeras, who was listening to *el Canónigo.* "I thought you had fog on the northern ocean," the canon said. "But this is delightful."

Venerable old Payeras said, "Heaven is smiling upon us." He appeared sad, perhaps ill. Did he understand that the Franciscan star was declining in California? Or was he simply melancholy over the low character of Canon Fernandez?

The canon broached a delicate subject. "Padre Durán said he is opposed to closing Mission Dolores and opening a new mission over there." He gestured toward the east. "What do you think about that?"

Padre Payeras was circumspect. "Brother Altimira is weary of the weather in San Francisco." He smiled humbly at the canon, his wrinkles tracing a look of wisdom. "I have no opinion on such a move as yet."

"Why was the San Francisco site selected when the natives are so scarce there?" the canon asked.

Old Payeras said, "In 1776 the natives were numerous, but measles killed about half in 1806, and death from other diseases has, regrettably, remained high. Now we get the natives from this side of the bay and they often fall ill over there in the cold."

Argüello discreetly removed himself from the robed men. Padre Altimira, his friend and confessor, had appealed to him for support in closing both Mission Dolores and Mission San Rafael. If Argüello became governor, his first act would be to support Altimira. It would test his powers against the Church, for Altimira's request for a new mission had not been sanctioned by his ecclesiastical superiors. Old Payeras, who seemed to have one foot in Heaven, was not a strong adversary, but sooner or later Padre Durán would assume the presidency and everything would become more difficult.

He envisioned the rolling hills and incomparably fertile plain to the east, described by Altimira as a veritable Garden of Eden supplied by fresh springs. There was even a naturally warm spring and elk so fat they could hardly run. After the Indians were trained by Altimira, Argüello would grant those lands to ranchers. Settlement would discourage Russian encroachment and civilize the natives in their own area.

When the procession resumed, Argüello said as he rode alongside Canon Fernandez, "I'd be interested to hear whether His Imperial Highness has considered a matter vital to us."

"Do not hesitate."

"Trade with other countries." North American and British ship captains approached him every other week. The prosperity of Alta California depended on reversing the no-trade policy, which Spain had so stubbornly maintained.

"We think foreign trade should be encouraged, but taxed."

"Excellency, mark my words. Under those two policies, land grants and trade, this country will blossom." If taxation wasn't too high. He drew in a lungful of sea air and felt the world open to him. "I appreciate your candor in this early state of organization." He looked at the fat man and added, "In my opinion the potential of this country is absolutely unlimited."

The canon pulled a *bota* from his robe. "A little wine?"

"No, *gracias.*" How could the man drink this soon after vomiting?

At midday Argüello led the escort down the mountains toward Fort Ross. He was halfway to the cove when the full twenty-six cannon salute announced the power of Russia. In the cove he halted his nervous stallion and had to shout to get Lt. Valle to understand that he must assist Canon Fernandez off his horse and make the man walk. A mishap on the steep, narrow path up the bluff would be disastrous.

The barking of muskets and dogs joined the cannons as Argüello dismounted at the big open gate and handed his reins to a half-breed—Creoles,

Schmidt called them. Waiting for Fernandez and Payeras, Argüello noticed the *Indios* who crowded around were decently loinclothed except for one young man who was entirely naked, hair singed short. Something about his face looked more like the Valley Indians. By the build, Argüello knew he was one of those who could run all day without being fatigued. What was he doing here?

Karl Schmidt strode down the hill extending his soft hand and, at his signal, the booming cannonade ceased. The fort manager bowed toward Canon Fernandez and Padre Presidente Payeras, who had now caught up. After introductions, Argüello signaled his men to attend to the mounts.

Hungry from the long ride, he was glad to see a long outdoor table had been set, and a bubbling pot hung from a tripod over a fire. Schmidt said he'd already eaten but Argüello and his party should enjoy the meal. With a nod toward each of them, Schmidt said in French, "When you are finished, I look forward to our talk in my office."

Argüello arranged his white knee pants and square-toed boots under the bench as two Aleuts unhooked the steaming pot and staggered toward the board. They took obvious pride in the aromatic contents of the kettle—a thick soup. One Aleut stretched his arms to show how big the sea turtle had been. Turtle! The Aleut pointed to the southwest sea, no doubt to indicate where it had been caught. Argüello feared such barbaric food would taste bad, but it was surprisingly tender and savory.

As he ate, he marveled how those little dark-skinned men in fleets of two-man baidarkas could kill anything that swam in the deep, even whales. They spent days and nights without relief on the bitterly cold, rough sea, immobile in their narrow boats. Their bodies had to be different. No civilized man could tolerate it. That the Russians had harnessed these amazing hunters was the basis of much of Argüello's respect for them. Reaching for the peeled, cooked roots called *kartofeln*, Argüello noticed the glance of the naked Indian, who now reclined against the building with several others of the Kashaya tribe. There was something about him.

"Schmidt is a rude bird not to eat with us," said *el Canónigo*, chewing open-mouthed like the commoner he was.

Argüello sliced a piece of the round wheat loaf and spread it with butter, molded and sweet as always. Disliking the role of apologist for Schmidt, he merely raised an eyebrow. Indian women brought bowls of hazelnuts mixed with dried berries and clotted cream in redwood flasks. Mounding cream on his berries, Argüello turned away from *el Canónigo* so that he could enjoy his dessert. The tinware was new, reminding him that he must meet privately with Schmidt and order more for the Presidio. Lately the old cups had a bad taste as the tin gave way to the underlying copper.

In Schmidt's upstairs office, Canon Fernandez came rudely to the point. "Please show me the papers documenting your authority to establish this fortress on Mexican land, Señor Schmidt." Spoken in Spanish.

Argüello cringed inwardly. There were no such papers. Years ago his father, Brevit Captain José Dario Argüello, had dropped the formality of demanding evidence of Russian authority.

Schmidt pretended not to understand. In French he said, "If you please, I prefer to speak French. I do not speak Spanish." His gaze paused momentarily upon Argüello, asking for help in this ticklish situation. What he said wasn't entirely true. Schmidt spoke a Latinized, Frenchified Spanish.

The canon also looked to Argüello for help, claiming in Spanish that his French was inadequate. Argüello suppressed a smile at this proof that the canon, who had been selected as the best diplomat in the entire new regime, lacked the prerequisite education. "But my French must be worse than yours," Argüello protested in Spanish. "I was never good at it." José Dario, who had been from the old world, had forced Luis and his brothers to practice at the dinner table. *S'il vous plaît, donnez moi le lait.* But Luis' tongue had been unwilling. In his father's eyes, his poor French had been his only failing. Argüello added, "You might recall, Excellency, that we had no schools in Alta California when I was growing up." And only one poor excuse for a school since, taught by a one-legged sailor in Monterey.

"You read!" the canon challenged. Was it possible he didn't? Was the rabble that had taken over the government this bad? "When she had time," he said, "the wife of Sergeant Amador taught the presidio children to read, but no French."

Canon Fernandez attempted to shift his derriere, but it was imprisoned in the slats of the chair. He gazed out the glass windows—another item that could be imported from Russia if trade restrictions were lifted—and demanded, "Translate for me, Captain."

Not since his father had left him the command of the presidio had Luis taken a direct order. It galled even as it amused him, and he opened, "Monsieur Schmidt, *le canon* wants, ah, papers on your authority to have this establishment."

By now Schmidt had his reply ready. "Long ago the Spanish government requested such papers. We told them papers are unnecessary. Russia's right to this northern coast is the same as yours to California. We came here, we hunted, and when we saw the land was unoccupied, we built our establishment. We intend to stay."

Argüello translated readily from French to Spanish, but while the clock on the wall moved three hours, the messages back and forth were nothing more than repetitions. All amusement vanished as he tiredly translated the canon's insistence on papers, and Schmidt's refusal.

Pushing to his feet, Schmidt picked up an open book from his table and said he must see to his ship building. "I will show you to the visitors' quarters." Politely he authorized the canon to inspect the grounds.

Outside, while *el Canónigo* inspected the cannons, Schmidt nodded Argüello aside and said in a low tone, "*Comandante,* I have sad news for Concepción."

Did he know her? Then it hit him. "Word of Count Rezanov?"

"Unfortunately yes. I cannot verify this, but the captain of the most recent supply ship from Sitka said the Count is probably dead. His journal was found somewhere along the trail in the Siberian wilderness. The last entry was penned only weeks after he left here. I was told he died of illness while in the hut of a savage."

"He never even made it back to Russia?"

Sadly Schmidt shook his head.

Poor Concepción! Luis' beautiful little sister had never stopped waiting for Rezanov's return—how long? Twenty years? Tongues had wagged but the gossips didn't know the half of it. José Dario was the only one Luis ever told about the time he'd come upon the two of them while riding in the sand dunes behind the presidio. The sight of her unbuttoned frock still haunted him. Concepcíon was fifteen years old and the most eligible girl in the colony. Family honor being at stake, he'd told his father. After the anger and the hard punch on the Russian's aristocratic nose, José Dario, who had hated Russians even before the affair, drove the lovers in a frantic rush to Mission Dolores to be married. But the padre had said he couldn't marry a Catholic to a heretic from the Eastern Church. Only the Pope himself could grant an exception, so he betrothed them instead. Then Count Rezanov had left, supposedly to go to the Pope—a journey of at least a year before he could return. But the gossips said the wily friend of the Tsar had taken advantage of her to ally himself with Alta California's most distinguished family, ultimately plotting a Russian takeover of Alta California. Now the old worry could be laid to rest at last.

Sad as this news would be for Concepción, it was just as well, unless—"Does the journal mention my family by name?"

"I don't know." The low sun glinted harshly off the glav-nyi's glasses, and Argüello excused himself to heed *el Canónigo's* beckon. He wouldn't tell Concepción until he had more certain information. Why stir up grief on account of a rumor?

As he went after the canon, he noticed the same naked Indian in the shadow of the stockade wall, following his every move.

After supper, colorful fireworks exploded over the ocean, shot from the bluff. Argüello hoped Canon Fernandez and Padre Presidente Payeras felt honored. This was an exceptional display. The naked *Indio* stared in open-mouthed wonder at the flickering, cascading gunpowder. Obviously, all the other *Indios* had seen fireworks before. More proof that this one came from elsewhere.

Later, Argüello couldn't sleep. The grinding snore in the cubicle occupied by the Padre Presidente was amplified by the three wooden walls and unconfined by the missing fourth. The bed was also hard, so he pulled on his boots and tiptoed outside. He went to the bluff edge, the farthest point over the dark sea. There, to his surprise, he found the stout robed figure of Canon Fernandez.

"Couldn't sleep either?" Augüello inquired.

The canon whirled around but regained his composure. "I have no more wine and this cur hasn't offered us any."

"They have only vodka here. I learned that last year. Their grapes aren't producing yet."

"What kind of shit is vodka?"

"Powerful stuff made from fermented *kartofeln.* Maybe I can get you some."

"Yes, do. I'll try it."

Argüello left him at the bluff. Back inside the fort, he went to the big house and explained to the Creole guarding the door. The man shook his head. "No."

Drawing himself up to full height, Argüello pointed to his gold epaulets and made the universal sign for drinking. How dare this half-breed say no to him! The guard eyed him through narrowed Aleut-shaped eyes and pushed out his palm in the signal to wait, then unlocked the door, went inside and shut it in his face, the most powerful man in California left standing outside!

Still gnashing his teeth, he returned to the bluff with a bottle and cups.

"Schmidt is rude," said the canon after hearing the story.

"He doesn't come from noble people." Argüello took perverse pleasure in saying that to the similarly deficient canon. "He isn't even Russian. He's from Finland." He poured the vodka. "But I find him more agreeable than his predecessor."

"Well, he tries to flatter me with fireworks, but it won't get him anywhere."

"You don't actually expect him to vacate this fort, do you?"

"Not of his own accord."

"You've heard their twenty-six cannons fire. Who is going to make them leave?"

"You."

"But—"

"I know, you said you don't have enough men and your guns need repair, but that doesn't mean you can't bluff these squatters out of here. *José y María!* Look down there. Those *Indios* are going in that *temescal.* They use them this far north?"

"All *Indios* in Alta California use them."

"Loathsome to bathe in one's own sweat," said *el Canónigo*, gulping vodka like water. "Do all these *Indios* work for Schmidt?"

Irritating, Argüello thought, the way Fernandez spoke of the natives as though his own blood weren't obviously well diluted. "*Sí*," he said, "they work here. But Excellency, as the responsible military officer, I respectfully object to threats against Russia when we can't back them up. You are no doubt aware that the Russian army defeated Napoleon when all others failed." Not waiting for a response, he continued, "Russian strength is enormous. Russia is the most powerful country on earth. It would put my men at terrible risk, not to mention this whole Span— ah, Mexican colony."

The canon pretended to choke on his drink to let him know his slip had been noted. "Commander, surely you know that bluffing, when done with *finesse*, has always been a major weapon in the annals of warfare."

Showing he knows one French word, Argüello thought. He wished to be anywhere else but realized he must see this through. "It is my considered advice that we refrain from any threat. If we must make demands, we might ask them to stay north of Bodega Harbor, but your Excellency, with all respect, it is unrealistic to expect them to be bluffed into leaving."

"I have my instructions."

Stunned to hear weighty news in this tardy, insulting manner, Argüello fought to hold his voice steady. "May I inquire what those instructions are?"

"The Russians are to be given six months to clear out or the Mexican government will eject them."

Argüello's worst nightmare. Just when he had entered into a business agreement with Schmidt, just when it seemed certain he would become governor, Mexico would cause the colony to be defeated by Russia, perhaps assisted by Spain and France. His choices were: obey orders and fight a losing war or oppose the Emperor and destroy his career. Impossible. Iturbide shouldn't fear *Alta Californianos*, but his own ignorant henchmen.

It occurred to Argüello that a small push would send the canon tumbling to his death on the rocks below. No one would see, and Argüello's story of an unfortunate accident caused by the canon's drunkenness would be believed. He could tiptoe back to bed and feign ignorance and sorrow. But what unspeakable sin, to murder a cleric, never mind how debauched! Buying time for Alta California didn't justify even the thought. Could he ever bring himself to confess to Father Altimira? He turned and crossed himself in the dark. Besides, even if the canon were dead, the Emperor would send another diplomat with the same orders.

He turned back, determined to make this man see reason. "I would need artillery and supplies and back pay for the *presidios*. Immediately. I would need a hundred additional men to train for six months." For years his requests had gone unanswered, and—

"If you could see what is left of our treasury and army," said *el Canónigo*, chuckling as he refilled his cup from the bottle on the ground, "you wouldn't ask. The revolution was long and very costly."

Each word that came from the canon's mouth plunged Argüello into deeper gloom. He watched the smoke from the sweathouse below, took a last sip of the fiery liquid, and, trembling with anger, set his cup on the ground. "Why didn't your superiors wait to deliver this ultimatum after the treasury recovered enough to build up the military?" The low-born ignoramuses were bigger asses than he'd imagined.

"It's a matter of prinsh—principle. The new government will not tolerate squatters on its land. Period. Not Russians. Not English." He swallowed again. "Pay attention. If Emperor Iturbide allows foreign countries to build military forts on our land, and we tolerate that for any length of time at all, the entire world will see our weakness. Hic. We wouldn't last a year, not with Spain's conniving. Did I tell you the King is allying himself with France?"

Argüello stared at the streak of silver moonlight across the ocean and estimated that Canon Fernandez had told him this ten times. Had it not been for the infernal Spanish way of governing—layers of regulations capriciously administered—he would have considered a quiet alliance with France. The French ship captains who visited the presidio were invariably men of honor and substance. The canon's argument was absurd. In such a situation, one overlooked an offender rather than trumpeting a trespass and exposing one's inability to punish it. If there was one thing he had learned commanding the Presidio, it was that. His father used to say, "Respect is garnered more readily if untested." Besides, Mexico could prosper from an economic alliance with the Russian American Company. All of Europe and the Orient was crying for sea otter fur. But Argüello couldn't broach that without exposing his illegal deal. Oh, but those Aleuts were the key, in those cunning little baidarkas.

The canon was drinking vodka like wine, and Argüello knew he'd better reason with him while any reason remained. "If there were some resource of real value in this country, other than fur and produce, I could understand the policy better. But I know the mentality here." He jabbed a thumb back at the fort wall. "I don't think they *want* Alta California any more. They are just a trading company now." Thanks in part to Count Rezanov's demise.

"Like I said, it's the principle. If you don't have enough men, maybe you should ally yourself with the *Indios*. Hic. There's thousands everywhere." Gesturing widely, he nearly fell.

Exasperated, Argüello said, "The Indians are armed with bows and arrows. Surely you're not proposing to arm the heathens."

"No, but *Indios* could attack this bird from the inside, steal his artillery. Hic. I say we talk to these *Indios* right here." He pointed down the bluff. "Before we leave. NOW."

The nightmare was blowing up in his face. In Argüello's pact with Schmidt, neither would cause trouble within the other's labor force. Besides, strict Spanish discipline had made the neophytes unhappier than the Kashayas at Fort Ross. "I think the *Indios* like Schmidt," he said. "Asking them to rebel would be a mistake. They would tell Schmidt."

"Don't they want their liberty?"

"Nobody forces them to stay here. Schmidt pays them two *piastres* for every good fur."

"What's a *piastre?*"

"Two would buy a good Spanish shovel."

"Schpan—"

"The point is he pays for everything—construction, plowing, digging, harvesting. They dance their heathen dances whenever they want and are not forced to work."

"Think," the canon argued, trying to tap his forehead but missing, "this means these *Indios* can be bought." The canon headed abruptly toward the hovels on the point of the promontory, bottle in one hand, cup in the other.

Argüello followed in alarm.

Two Aleuts sat against their hut, the smoke from their stem pipes dissipating in the breeze. Canon Fernandez was already attempting to talk to them, but they smiled and shrugged—a shred of hope. The language barrier could salvage the night. But one of the men jumped up and made a wait signal. He trotted to the cove side of the bluff and vanished downward.

Argüello tried the only thing that came to mind. "Excellency, with all respect, please wait until morning. I implore you, let us talk about this later. I am weary. Surely you must be exhausted after such a ride. At breakfast we'll consider these matters."

Listing like a ship in high wind, Canon Fernandez brought the cup to his mouth, swallowed and said, "No."

The second time tonight that insulting word was directed to him. Argüello passed the time saying a silent Hail Mary.

A rich young baritone voice behind them said, *"Sí?"*

"Ah," the canon said, turning around.

It was the same tall, entirely naked Indian, his muscular frame evident in the moonlight, hair short and spiky, polished bones gleaming in his barbaric earlobes. Behind him stood a line of Kashaya Indians.

"See, they found one who schpeaks civilized Schpanisch. Are you a *cimarrón?*"

The *Indio* stared at the canon's robe, the silver cross hanging from his middle.

"Respondes!" Fernandez ordered, using the grammar of the lower classes.

Argüello said hopefully, "Perhaps he doesn't speak Spanish."

"Fool. They wouldn't have fetched him."

Argüello felt his face heat. His hands ached to drag this detritus to the edge of the cliff. The canon continued, "He's afraid he'll be whipped." To the *Indio* he said, "I won't have you punished, hic. I am no mission padre. I come from Emperor Iturbide of Mexico."

"What is emperor?"

"See, he can talk. The, hic, grrreat chief of this entire country."

The Indian looked at Argüello's epaulets and decorations. "Are you Commander Argüello of San Francisco Presidio?"

"Sí." Perhaps indeed he was a *cimarrón*, to know that.

"Glav-nyi Schmidt and his guns protect me in this place," said the *Indio.* The figures in the background stood their ground.

Argüello growled, "I won't hurt you."

The Indian looked at the canon. *"Tiene mal?* He sick?"

"Nothing's wrong with me! What is your name?" Hic.

The Indian stared seaward. Argüello was well acquainted with the reluctance of the natives to speak their names.

"Sit down and talk," said *el Canónigo* holding up the vodka. "Get a cup. You, don Luis, where's your cup?" He staggered to a hut and collapsed against it. The astonished occupants peered out. Argüello remained standing, as did the Indian. Looking up at them, the canon said, "I propose that you *Indios*, hic, help us fight for our government." Argüello held his breath.

"No comprendo. Fight *Mexicanos?"*

"No. Fight with us *Mexicanos*, against the Russians."

"Por qué? Why?"

The canon raised his voice. "This is your country. Don't you want a better position? Land? Hic. Trade goods?"

Argüello felt a creeping horror in the marrow of his bones.

"No comprendo," the Indian said.

"Simple. You help us fight the Russians and we give you protection, land, many beads." He held up the vodka in a gesture of a toast.

Argüello knew this would rapidly spread to all the *Indios* of the colony. But the canon outranked him and he was helpless.

The Indian stood quietly for a few moments, then spoke intently. "No catch us in our *rancherías?* Teach us to make iron and cloth? Trade things we make for things in big boats?"

Crudely spoken, Argüello thought, but this was what every colonist wanted: freedom and commerce without regulation. *Madre de Díos,* that's what he wanted. In a momentary fancy he saw the *Indio* as his ally and Mexico as the enemy. Was he losing his mind?

"Soon the Franciscan padres will lose power," the canon blurted. "Mission lands will belong to the people, you *Indios.*" He sloshed his vodka toward the fort. "Help us chase the Russians away and your people will own the mission lands, foundries, tallow vats, wheat fields, cattle, everything."

Argüello groaned inwardly. Those fields and herds would be the currency of his patrimony. *Indios* were to be the vaqueros, not the *rancheros*. Yes, Spanish law had always held that *Indios* would become full citizens with all rights, but not until they were deemed ready. Had the Mexicans proposed premature implementation? He prayed not. But even the rumor could foment rebellion.

44

In the sweathouse with Cross-eyed Bear and the many men who worked for the Undersea People, Grizzly Hair breathed the hot smoke of the local ferns until his nostrils stung and his lungs burned. When at last men crawled outside, he followed them into the misty night. Others came behind, happily whooping and yelling.

With huge strides he splashed through the shallow sheet and dove into an oncoming wall of water the instant before it crashed upon him. He kicked and pulled hard under the violent turbulence toward the quieter sea, and floated while his body cooled. Small hand movements kept his head above water. The dark water rose and fell like a cold, breathing giant and he was a tiny minnow riding on its breast. Tasting salt, he blinked water from his eyes and looked at the slip of a moon, but she remained pale and indistinct behind the fog. It was dark and he couldn't see the heads of the other men, yet felt their nearness and shared their joy in the bite of cold upon hot—the ancient ritual of fire and water.

He had always wanted to travel and meet other peoples; now he had done it. Fate had linked him to these Kashayas and the men of the north and the headman of the Russians. Now he had met the headmen of the *Mexicanos*. He was lucky. His music was strong. He had guessed correctly. Despite the special sleeping house, the glav-nyi and Commander Argüello were enemies after all. For a long time he floated in the cold water, his hot interior feeding him strength for the coming day.

Back on the heated sand in the sweathouse where all the other men seemed to sleep, he listened to the tireless ocean. It sounded tentative as it began pouring over itself, then fell faster and louder as it thundered toward him. At the other end of the cove it stopped quite suddenly, sucking back, gathering itself for another surge from its mysterious depths. The sea was worthy of man's profoundest respect. Learning to swim in it had been one of the joys of this place. And now, lying in the warm dark womb of men, he too was gathering strength for the surge that would come after the sleep. He would tell the glav-nyi what the *Españoles* were planning. Surely this would build an alliance.

"What did Commander Argüello say?" Schmidt demanded.

"Nothing."

"Did he agree with Canon Fernandez?"

"I don't think so. He said nothing. It was dark and I couldn't see his face."

The glav-nyi repeated these questions with variations. What did the long robe offer him for helping Mexico attack the Russian American Company? What part would Indians play? Schmidt was as persistent as Grizzly Hair had ever been. He hammered his questions like the man outside pounding iron spikes.

Grizzly Hair wondered if he had explained it badly. He told again how the long robe had seemed sicker as the moon traveled across the sky. He repeated what the long robe had said about Grizzly Hair planning the details with Commander Argüello, because he, the fleshy long robe, would return to Mexico.

"What did Argüello say to that?"

"Nothing."

Katya and Schmidt spoke back and forth, then Katya said, "He asks whether the Kashaya people would fight against the Russian people. I told him no."

"Tell him I talked to Red Bead's men before I came here, and they like the Undersea People. They call them esteemed traders." He repeated his main message. "Tell him I want the Undersea People to help the *Indio* peoples defeat the *Españoles.*"

Schmidt's shoulders slipped into a calmer posture. He smiled as if in mild pain. "You came here to get my support against the Mexicans, and the Mexicans ask you to make war against me. That is *ironique.*" He wiped a tear behind an eye-disk.

"What does that mean?" Grizzly Hair asked Katya.

"Like a Coyote trick." She smiled. "Not expected, funny."

He smiled wryly, for it was true, and asked Schmidt, "When do you think the Mexicans will attack?" During the night he'd decided an attack would be helpful; *Indio* allies would see the opportunity to strike while the black hats weakened themselves fighting a powerful enemy.

"I doubt they will. Luis Antonio Argüello is the highest ranking officer in California. I trust him. We have become, shall we say, economic friends."

That had been said before, but as Grizzly Hair understood it: "The long robes tell the black hats what to do."

Schmidt removed his transparent disks and rubbed them on the bird tracks. "I think he will make more of the decisions, but we must wait and see." Returning the device to his face, he said, "I don't think your people should do anything until the Mexican government quiets down. A different group could come to power. The missionaries could stop bothering you."

"Will they give the missions to the *Indios?*"

"I don't know. But if I were you, I'd hold off on war for now."

"Maybe this is the best time, while they are weak with indecision. You have many guns. We have brave men who can learn to shoot them."

"You are an interesting young man," Schmidt said. "Ten years ago we would have jumped at your offer. Their defenses have always been weak. They provoked us a number of times. The Tsar would have sent warships and taken Alta California, starting with San Francisco Bay."

Katya translated and Grizzly Hair groaned inwardly at the bad timing. Schmidt continued, "The ocean was teeming with otters. But today they are in decline. Some of our leaders are saying we might leave this settlement." He gestured around the cluttered room. "We are traders. We might switch to mining. Platinum has been discovered in the Ural Mountains, in Siberia."

"What is platinum?"

"Very white metal."

"Do Russians melt platinum and shape it?"

"Yes."

"We have much gold on my river," Grizzly Hair said. He used the home word. Katya looked at him, not understanding. He described gold in her tongue, but she couldn't think of a word, and then thought it was the greenish orange metal he'd seen being pounded outside. As they were talking, a man with a long beard rushed in, practically yelling at Schmidt. Their voices flared, each beginning rudely before the other had finished.

While this was going on, Grizzly Hair removed Etumu's nugget from the pouch and gave it to Katya. She turned it in her nicely shaped hand and gave it back, grazing his palm with her fingertips. "My people have no word for this," she said, "and I don't know what the Undersea People call it." She nodded at the glav-nyi. "Show it to him."

Grizzly Hair considered. The glav-nyi had just said he liked white metal. It was probably pointless to show him yellow metal, particularly when he was preoccupied with whatever the rude visitor wanted. Grizzly Hair decided to offer something of surer value, something Red Bead said the Russians always wanted. He dropped the gold in his pouch and waited for the heated exchange to conclude.

When Schmidt was gazing after the departing visitor, Grizzly Hair quietly asked Katya, "Does he want to continue the talk?"

Discreetly she replied, "The Undersea People speak rudely to each other all the time. It doesn't upset them."

"Is there trouble outside?" Grizzly Hair asked her.

"The man wanted to build the big boat a different way."

How very strange to be so upset over that. "Tell him I know he likes the fruits and maize and other garden plants that grow in the missions. If he helps us *Indios* chase away the *Españoles,* we will help him grow such plants all over California. We will trap the ground squirrels and dig ditches to water the plants during the long dry."

Katya translated and Schmidt responded, "No. I will not help you make war. I am not allowed to. Our agreement with the Imperial Military Command is that they will send troops and munitions only if we are attacked by another government or the Indians, and I doubt that will happen."

"But you have your own guns," Grizzly Hair countered. "You said you wanted Alta California."

"My guns are for defense only." Schmidt pointed toward at the doorway.

"Does that mean he wants us to leave?" Grizzly Hair asked Katya.

She nodded.

Grizzly Hair stood up, knowing he had persisted beyond the bounds of politeness, but he felt like a dog deprived of its bone. It would hurt to tell all the headmen along the trail that the Russians had rejected his request to become allies. Now the glav-nyi was talking to Katya.

She translated. "He says you and he should talk often. He will not leave this place in six moons, no matter the threats, and if the Mexicans attack, he will need you to help defend him. He also says to come and trade. He buys all kinds of fur."

"I will come back," Grizzly Hair said. He paused. "But before I leave, I want five sea otter pelts. Would you take blue beads in exchange for them?"

Schmidt's smile elevated the disks on his cheeks. "Your information has earned you two pelts." He extended his hand.

Grizzly Hair grasped the hand and moved it up and down, already planning to give one pelt to Morning Owl. Schmidt accompanied them down the stairs, and as they passed an open door, Grizzly Hair saw what he'd been looking for. A man was coming out and shutting the door, but not soon enough to block the stunning sight of a room full of guns. Side by side, the spear-tipped guns leaned on many racks at a uniform angle, close together like maize plants in a mission field. The glav-nyi had said the headman in Russia wouldn't send more guns unless Rohsh was attacked, but it was clear the glav-nyi had plenty right now.

Outside in the compound, where the fog had receded and sunlight pooled, the excitement of that glimpse lingered. It somehow added to his desire to be alone with Katya. Besides wanting her, he needed to ask her if the Undersea Men all followed the glav-nyi's wishes or, like most men, walked their own paths.

She hooked him with the sparkle in her eyes and sauntered out the big gates, shells jingling. They walked along a path north of the selenya, passing a large house built of redwood logs where two bearded men sat on the steps. Katya and Grizzly Hair followed the path uphill through a field of young trees and grapevines. At the place where the path joined the main trail to the May-tee-neh village, a baby boy toddled toward Katya, followed by an older woman. Katya picked up and hugged the child, who went straight for her nipple. She sat down beside the trail and let him suckle.

She was a mother! The infant's light brown eyes peered smugly over the mound that contained his milk and fixed on Grizzly Hair as though recognizing a rival. He stood a moment watching, then walked up the hill. This sudden evidence of her completed marriage disturbed him, and the presence of the woman who was undoubtedly her mother removed all vestige of desire. He walked a fair distance, then lowered himself beside a tree in a place where, when he turned to look, he saw the child's pale fingers toying with Katya's other nipple.

Some Undersea People were as pale as the long robes. Maybe the little fingers and eyes would never darken. It was as if some people never fully matured. Is that why the new people were rude, less patient and quick to injure others? Be that as it may, once again he had gotten himself in a dangerous position. He must not couple with Katya again. Perhaps he shouldn't even talk to her in private.

Hearing her voice, he looked back. She was handing the child to the older woman. The boy went willingly, as children go to their grandmothers, then Katya came up the trail.

He let her pass. She glanced sidelong to where his legs protruded behind the tree, and she beckoned with her head for him to follow as she continued beyond the fenced gardens and uphill around the bend. Maybe, he revised in his mind, he should talk to her. After all, she was his link to the Undersea Men.

In the place where the redwoods grew tall and uncut, she left the path and led him to where the selenya could be seen at a distance, small as an ant hill. She sat against a huge trunk looking seaward, and he joined her upon the springy debris of many seasons.

Her face seemed troubled, her voice quiet. "The glav-nyi said they might leave this place. My man said if that happened he would take our children across the sea. But I won't let him. I will hide the boys in the forest."

Boys. She was even more married than he'd thought. "Wouldn't you go with your husband to his home place?"

"No. Russians don't want Kashaya women in their homeland. Besides, I would never see my home place again if I went to Russia, and they would bury my bones in strange earth."

Grizzly Hair looked at the gray between sky blue and sea blue, the oncoming fog, and wondered why any man would take his young children but leave his wife. "How many boys?"

"One other. Not suckling any more. He plays with his friends all day. They pretend sticks are guns."

"You need your man," he said. "Maybe he and his friends would stay here even if most of the others leave. They could help us *Indios* chase the *Españoles* away." This would help everybody. Another thought came. "Then he could share the mission goods with us."

Sighing, she lay back with her hands under her head, her flattened stomach pulsing beneath the cloth. "Egorov told me about the missions, said they are rich places. He likes to go to Santa Barbara. The big boats take the hunters that far south."

"If the rest of the Undersea People left, would he stay here and help us fight the black hats?"

Katya, whose eyes touched like fingers, looked at his calves, thighs and higher, and said with a tease, "You want my husband to stay with me?"

She knew Man was weak. He reclined beside her, elbow supporting his head. A songbird fluted overhead, and he softened his voice. "I'd think you'd want him to stay. There would be no more trading at the fort. If he left, who would hunt for you and your boys?"

The tease left her face. "I've thought of that, and you're right. I need a man." She turned to him and drew an invisible map on his chest leaving hot pathways that connected to everything male in him.

"Your man is lucky," he murmured, running his hand up and down the length of this Deer Woman of all deer women, who had the power to lead a man wherever she wanted. "Do you soften your skin with kaba?" Salmon Woman had told him Kashaya women made love potions of madrone flowers and boiled the bark to soften their skin.

Her thick lips turned up. "Kaba is part of my real name." Then the smile dropped. "Undersea People say Egorov is not my husband. The Russian rituals were not said. My father says we did not marry in the way of my people either, so maybe I don't have a husband."

Did she want him to be her man? Could he take her to all the places he needed to go? With two young boys? No. He had learned his lesson with Oak Gall. And Katya's man was about to return from a hunting trip, with guns. Still, his resolve was quickly evaporating.

"Egorov finds his own way," she was saying. "He might stay in this land. The big boats are crowded, so maybe they would leave the cannons." She took him in her magic hand. "Big guns shoot strong."

Excited about the possibility of an alliance with Egorov and his friends—he trusted Katya to keep their secret rather than risk her life—Grizzly Hair stayed at the selenya three more sleeps. During that time Captain Argüello and the black hats rode away on their horses. The two long robes floated away in a baidara, rowed by several Undersea men, and Cross-eyed Bear and his friends left for their home place.

Grizzly Hair enjoyed watching the men work on the big boat and he often swam in the muscular surf. He also enjoyed Katya like a man feasting on soon-to-be-withdrawn meat, then restored his strength in the sweathouse.

Now the bell clanged and clanged. It was mid-morning, not a time for bells. People dropped what they were doing and ran to where they could see the ocean. Grizzly Hair, who had been talking with the old men of the May-tee-neh village, looked across the buildings of the selenya and saw something resembling a white moth on the blue-gray sea. Excited women and children ran down the path, including Katya and her mother, who held the younger boy in her arms. The older boy raced ahead with other children.

Katya's father said, "My daughter's man comes now."

Grizzly Hair invited him to come and watch the boat with him, but the old man waved a hand. "I've seen them many times."

Grizzly Hair walked down to the bluff to watch the approach of the winged boat. He could see tiny men climbing on the high poles and scurrying like ants through a web of ropes. The boat turned toward the cove, growing rapidly larger. The buzz of talk grew louder. Excited children ran in circles, even Katya's baby. Their fathers were returning. Three Directions had been right: the Russians hadn't brought their own women to the selenya. They married the May-tee-neh women. But soon they would leave them behind.

Several men on the boat pulled ropes to a soundless beat while others gathered piles of cloth as the big wings collapsed and fell. Meanwhile men on shore paddled baidaras to meet the boat, tossing ropes up to the men on deck. Then the paddlers towed the giant boat into the cove. More men tied the ropes to special poles driven into the sand.

At the front of the boat, men began throwing piles of skins into the surf while those in the water retrieved and brought them to dry sand. Narrow baidarkas were tossed down and taken into the boathouse. A rope ladder was dropped over the side and clothed men climbed down and waded ashore with guns over their heads. Brown men in loincloths dove off the back of the boat, then swam to shore through the crashing surf; their faces showed pleasure to be home. Gulls glided and cried above.

All the men carried goods and climbed up to the promontory. Grizzly Hair watched Katya to see which one was Egorov. It didn't take long. Her older boy ran to a man in dark trousers and a pale shirt roped at the waist. He tousled the boy's hair, then turned to Katya, grabbed her in his arms and pressed his lips against hers so hard it seemed it would hurt. He was smaller than Grizzly Hair.

Grizzly Hair left, following a deer trail beyond the cove, down across the creek and south to a secluded shelf partway down the bluff. He had been there with Katya. Now he gazed out to sea from the end of the land.

That evening while he was eating with the men of the May-tee-neh village, Katya jiggled up the trail in all her fullness. She came directly to him, touched his shoulder and said, "Egorov will talk with you now. I will take you there."

Alone on the pathway with her, heading toward the north side of the selenya, he asked, "What kind of man is Egorov?"

"Proud."

That was one of Padre Fortuni's seven monsters. Many men Grizzly Hair respected were proud. The incoming fog enhanced the pervasive cedar-like scent from the tall trees. Arriving at the house of logs, Katya lifted a clanking metal tongue and the door opened.

He followed her inside and was hit by the stench of unwashed bodies and cooking smells. Several men with pale skin, small heads, narrow faces and high noses came through the door behind them. Boots drumming on the wooden floor, they stared at Grizzly Hair as they walked past into an unseen room. Most of them had long black beards and the familiar long shirts and trousers. A man with normal skin color, wearing a robe of horizontal panels of gut sewn with tiny stitches, was just leaving—no doubt for his village on the promontory. This was a busy place.

A row of transparent squares reflected the candlelight. Through them he could see the fogged-in trees standing ghostlike, and the reflection of a naked man with short spiky hair beside Katya. He had never seen himself in anything but water, had never seen his length captured as well—a tall man slightly forward in the shoulders against the possibility of quick flight. A bench squatted below the startling reflection. Katya motioned him to sit there and wait. She went into the next room. He heard the clinking of metal against metal and wood scraping on wood. All the while his reflection stared back at him from another row of squares on the opposite side of the room.

He tried to quiet himself so his music would come out and protect him. He had coupled with Egorov's wife and now must seek the good will of the man who had the right to kill him. Two more Undersea People came through the door. They stared as they went into the other room. His pulse danced.

Katya returned with the man she had kissed. To Grizzly Hair's relief, he held no gun and the brown eyes looked at him the way a man looks at a harmless beetle, not an enemy. He spoke in firm, loud tones, and his thin mustache rode upon a wide upper lip. His skin was tan and flawless. His dark-brown hair, cut short like a woman's, showed white at the temples, and unlike most of the high-nosed Undersea men, his only facial hair was the mustache. His cheeks hadn't been plucked, but somehow the hairs were cut very close to the skin. Trying not to stare, Grizzly Hair looked down at the brown boots glistening with fat.

Katya was saying, "Egorov will eat his supper now, but he wants to talk to you afterwards, behind the house of horses."

"I will be there." He welcomed the extra time to strengthen himself.

Katya and Egorov talked back and forth much longer than necessary to convey the message. Jaw twitching in apparent anger, Egorov glanced at Grizzly Hair's man part.

Shocked, he stood up, ready to run or defend himself.

"He can't talk seriously with a naked man," Katya explained, "You must wear pantaloons."

That was odd, but a big relief. "Where can I get pantaloons?"

Katya and Egorov talked again, then Katya went behind a wall partition, leaving Egorov in obvious discomfort. As if unable to tolerate another moment, he clomped into the room from which came the smell of cooking meat, the babble of men and the clinking of implements.

Katya returned with the pantaloons and held them before him, two cloth tubes dangling down. Taking the garment, he tried to put a foot all the way through a tube, but caught a toe in a frayed hole, tripped and fell on the floor. An Undersea man entering the house laughed.

Giving back a grin, Grizzly Hair pointed at the pantaloons and said to Katya, "Tell him this is a trap." She didn't smile or repeat the joke. Her face had lost its friendliness.

On his feet again he told her, "I will put this on outside."

Thinking she must have disliked seeing him on the floor, he quickly lifted the metal tongue and went out into the misty evening. The solitude was comforting.

Waiting anxiously in the dark shadow behind the house of horses, he wondered if Egorov would come to kill him. Would he be nimble enough to dodge the ball and scramble to safety? He must defeat this fear, for this was his last hope of getting help from the Russians. Fortunately, the pantaloons felt smooth and supple, unlike the scratchy woolen hip wraps at the mission, and he was glad for the holes that allowed the cool mist to touch his knees and left buttock. The remains of the fading day tinted the fog pale lavender, and it blanketed half the mountain. Dark stands of redwoods poked up through it. The place looked unreal and felt chilly.

Hearing footsteps, he tensed. Egorov hove into view, straight as a yellow pine and without a gun. Greatly relieved, Grizzly Hair watched them approach, Katya somewhat behind. They stepped into the shadow with him.

Katya said, "Are you here?"

"Yes."

"Good. He wants you to tell him about the war the *Indios* are planning."

He told them about the many peoples he had visited across the land, and how they all wished the *Españoles* could be chased away. He said that with the guns from Rohsh on their side, the *Indios* would no doubt fight together against their common enemy.

He paused, suddenly realizing he should have invited them to sit down first. Now doing so seemed too awkward so he continued, "*Indios* want the black hats to stop capturing people. Many neophytes fight for the black hats, but they might join us if we had Undersea men on our side. Tell Egorov he and his friends should fight with us. Then when the *Españoles* leave, they can have one of the missions with all the goods in it." This was a gamble, since the people from those places might not want to share their home places. However from what he'd heard, few of the original people were left alive around the missions.

After a discussion, Katya said. "He wants to know if *Indios* will defeat the *Españoles.*"

"Tell him we would with Russian guns, and we probably will without them. The Spanish soldiers are few. *Indios* are many." Was that being too eager?

Egorov paced back and forth like a restless ghost, whirling at an invisible marker on either side of his course. His talk glided high and low, rapid, then slow, then rapid again, but seemingly not belligerent toward Grizzly Hair. Katya had been careful. Relieved, he sat down against the horse house and waited, watching the lavender mist go gray, then darker.

Still talking, Egorov sat facing Grizzly Hair, Katya beside him.

"Egorov is angry," she said, the familiar tongue startling him. "He says Glav-nyi Schmidt's father is not Russian and the Tsar should not have selected a German to be headman, one who does not love Russia. He says if the glav-nyi had loved Russia, he would have fought the Spanish soldiers long ago and driven a long knife into the ground, for Mother Russia."

More talk passed between them, during which Grizzly Hair tried to sort out that mystifying information. What was a German? Why would Russians drive a long knife into earth mother?

Katya spoke again. "Egorov said he will join you in war and will try to bring his friends." Joy erupted in Grizzly Hair's stomach and he struggled to understand what followed: "In exchange, he wants the mission on San Francisco Bay, Mission San José and Mission Santa Ynez and Santa Barbara and all the land in between. He will claim it for Holy Mother Russia."

Yes! Now the *Indios* would surely win and the disgraced *Españoles* would return to the land of their fathers. He wanted to leap and dance, but Egorov wanted four missions instead of one. He considered. The dead didn't mourn the loss of a home place, and Russians were fair traders who allowed people to live as they wished. The bones of the dead could be moved and buried in their home places. Wasn't that a good trade for so many lives? So many souls? For returning all the peoples safely to their villages?

As Egorov and Katya talked he found it increasingly difficult to sit still. At last she said, "He will know tomorrow night whether his friends will leave the Company with him. He says we must not speak a word of it to anyone. The glav-nyi must not hear of it or Egorov would be punished and locked up. Then he could not help you."

Egorov stood up brushing his pantaloons. Rising and extending his hand in the manner of Schmidt and Missouri, Grizzly Hair said, "I will not tell the glav-nyi."

Egorov hesitated but carefully took his hand, gave it a quick up and down, withdrew it and said through Katya, "We talk again after the sleep, after supper."

"Yes. Tell him if he and his friends help us make war, I will tell the headmen and arrow chiefs that Egorov should receive the four missions of which he speaks."

Talk the next night went even better. Egorov said several of his friends had agreed to fight with the *Indios.* They would steal guns from the storage room and a wheeled cannon from the yard. Then, dreamlike, Egorov and Katya receded into the dark mist—husband and wife. Grizzly Hair threw off the restraining pantaloons and ran down the bluff-hugging path to the beach. After being tight and anxious and watchful for so long, he unleashed his joy. He ran from one side of the cove to the other, his toes barely touching the sand. When boulders loomed through the fog, he circled and raced the other way. Drenched and gleeful and splashing through the foam, he chanted as the surf pounded: *We will win. We will win.*

His mind flew with his feet. As the ocean sucked back and gathered itself, Malaca's pits and trenches sprang to mind. Such trenches could also hide men who could pop up to shoot arrows, and with guns anything was possible. A killing war could be arranged like a spider web—a web of trenches into which to lure the black hats.

He continued running in the bracing fog as mother moon peeked over the mountain and floated upward, small, fogged-in and waning. He had often wondered how to fight a killing war. Now the spirits were showing him, perhaps O-se-mai-ti. A wave rose to an improbable height before it crashed. He heard O-se-mai-ti's roar in the thunder, and the same roar came out of his mouth—earth's fiercest fighter. The great bear's ferocity would bring victory. When the black hats discovered the trap, they would wet their *pantalones.* They would shake with fear and try to run away. They would shame themselves and know they could never again capture *Indios* and force them to go to the missions.

"*Malaca,*" he called as a curl of water gradually poured down the beach toward him, "we will win for you. We will avenge the deaths of your men. Father, can you see me? I will avenge your death. Oak Gall, never again will the black hats force women to live in big unpurified houses where they die far from their people. Once you told me to follow my spirits. I hear you saying that now. I feel you. After the war I will dig up your bones and bury them behind the dancehouse so you can go to the happy land. Then your parents will soften their faces when they look at me."

Gasping for breath, he joined the men in the sweathouse, but even then saw sudden, bright visions of *Indios* and Russians defeating the black hats. It would be in a place where the plant people could help, a place of dense trees and vines, a place where earth magic would be on their side.

45

Katya's parents gave him nu-pah the next morning. Her older boy smiled at him as Katya nursed the younger one. Then with an indifferent glance at him, she left for the selenya. Something had changed her. It seemed as though Egorov had brought her different eyes. This was just as well, for it simplified things. He was leaving.

All along the trail to Red Bead's village he *saw* how a killing war could be won. It would be much cleverer than El Cid's war. This wouldn't take generations to win. He hardly noticed the stunted, backward-leaning trees or the fog drifting past the guana-whitened boulders standing solid in the restless sea, and hardly felt the change of air as he turned inland along the river trail.

Morena whickered, happy to see him. He petted her, thought she'd grown a little fatter, and touched the heads of his former classmates as they gathered around. Later he told the men what he'd seen at the selenya—not revealing his talk with Egorov—and joy remained through it all, even when he ate supper with Red Bead and his wife, near where Salmon Woman ate with her man. The next morning before leaving the village he took Cross-eyed Bear aside and told him about his agreement with Egorov, and the web of trenches, and how they could lure the black hats into a trap.

Nodding throughout, Cross-eyed Bear cackled and said, "Ho, that would do it. I will keep your secret."

Grizzly Hair was in his power. He had no need to ask whether Cross-eyed Bear would bring men to the war. The old man was clearly sucked into the same funnel of strength. They parted with the understanding that he would appoint runners to carry news back and forth across the land, and convey messages to and from Egorov. They agreed that care must be taken in the selection of runners. Then he and Cross-eyed Bear clasped shoulders, silent brothers in a new kind of war.

Even Morena felt like running. They galloped south along a different trail, passing herds of deer, elk and antelope. Wing people streamed overhead on their way north and friendly plants waved at him from the rolling hills. This trail led to a protected bay called Bodega. More Undersea People were supposed to live there, together with people who spoke a tongue a little like his own. All along the hills, the flat-branched cousins of cedar welcomed him. A white cloud hung in the sky and O-se-mai-ti took shape in it, fluffy and determined in her stance—a powerful sign. As Grizzly Hair traveled, the bear stretched larger on every side, but never lost her shape.

Quite suddenly Morena slowed to a dignified walk, and something dark caught the corner of Grizzly Hair's eye. He was astounded to see O-se-mai-ti walking beside the horse in all the jouncing richness of her fur. She had come down from the clouds! Her curved black claws jiggled with each step—hind feet longer than a man's—and she bore herself as if it were nothing unusual to walk with a man and a horse. Pleasant music emanated from her along with the sweet, rich scent of fur. Morena kept a big eye on the bear as though to reassure herself that the music would not change.

"Where are you going?" O-se-mai-ti asked, looking over at Grizzly Hair.

In awe, and honored that she had shown herself, he answered, "To find Pomponio and tell him about Egorov. The people at Bodega might know where to find his camp. The *Españoles* are building a new mission near there. I'd like to see that."

"You have decided to strike out at the people who whipped you, and you want Pomponio to help?"

"Yes, and Egorov."

"Your enemies have strong weapons. They come from a people with a long tradition of killing war, and they honor men who do the killing. They vie to be the best warriors. They force men to fight for them, men who would rather not. This makes them fiercer than you can imagine. On your side, you have very few men willing to fight like cornered bears. And that's how you'd have to fight."

Grizzly Hair knew most of this, but he hoped the men of Poo-soo-ne, Libayto, Topal, Putah, Cross-eyed Bear, Sucais and Estanislao would help. And there would be many others. The euphoria that had buoyed him for two sleeps now recast itself into a colder assessment as he tried to explain it to his most powerful ally:

"The men I talked with on my way west might be ready to join me when I visit them again. I have planted the story of El Cid in their villages, where it will spread to the sweathouses of their relatives. I believe many who didn't talk to me the first time will join us, and together we will fight like the black hats of old who drove the invaders from their land. I have only begun. It takes a long time to do this. No one has ever done it before. The *Indio* peoples have never planned together. They never even talked to each other except in trade.

We didn't speak each other's tongues, unless we lived nearby and went to each other's big times. So this is difficult." He looked over at the bear and, seeing her thoughtful expression, continued:

"Now our enemy has given us a common tongue. He has given us horses so we can ride swiftly and talk to each other over long distances. I am grateful for the power that keeps me alive to acquire knowledge along the trail. I will spread my knowledge among the peoples in the Valley of the Sun. I have *seen* a way to fight the black hats. I have acquired a strong ally in Egorov and, perhaps, in Pomponio's men, who may themselves be cornered bears. I will introduce these allies to each other and help them *see* a killing war. I believe that together we will stop the black hats from forcing people to live in the missions. And if my luck holds, we will do it before the people of my home place are captured." He smiled at the bear. "I also hope to find a warm sweathouse in Bodega." This little joke was meant to cover his anxiety about whether the bear would agree with all his hopes and expectations.

The sober animal walked at a steady pace, the long fur of her underside bunching and separating. "It's always important to find a comfortable place to sleep," she said.

Healthy grass streaked with blooming clover presented itself and they stopped to graze, Grizzly Hair enjoying the sweet clover flowers as much as O-se-mai-ti. When they resumed their journey, the bear said, "You are doing this the only way it could be done, and you might well succeed."

Grizzly Hair's stomach felt calmer and he lost the need to talk. Simply being with the O-se-mai-ti gave him power, and he felt himself expand with the knowledge that he would have luck in the difficult talks ahead—starting at Bodega.

When father sun had disappeared in the fog in the west, the scent of salt infused the air and the thunder of the ocean could be heard again. The trail veered west into the wind, gulls soaring overhead, correcting their wing angles. In open country the bear walked resolutely before the horse, over dips and rises emblazoned with white and yellow flowers.

Then the land slid down to the wide gray sea and a bay shaped like a nearly closed hand. They stopped to look. In the crook of the hand two big boats rocked on the swells, their tall poles drawing zigzags in the gray sky. A few ropes connected the poles but the cloth wings had been removed. Two villages faced each other on opposite sides of the beach—one of log houses flying the banner of the two-headed eagle, the other with redwood u-machas and a dilapidated roundhouse. A few people moved around both villages. Near the log houses several men in pointed hats ran splashing alongside a baidara, then jumped into the boat and paddled toward the open sea.

But something else arrested Grizzly Hair's attention, and the bear's. Between the two villages bears of all sizes were feeding on something so enormous it couldn't have fit inside two dancehouses side by side. "Hello, brothers and sisters," Grizzly Hair said to the bear people.

Intent on their feast, they pretended not to hear.

"They are eating a whale," O-se-mai-ti explained, answering Grizzly Hair's question.

"Is that the giant fish Katya tried to tell me about? The one whose whiskers are used for the lashing on baidarka stays?"

"Yes, and the stays are carved from whale cartilage."

"Bears are good fishermen to catch such huge fish."

"We don't catch them. Whales are too big." Calmly watching her brothers and sisters, O-se-mai-ti sat down beside Morena. "But we swim in the surf for smaller fish."

To think of the bear people swimming in the breakers made Grizzly Hair smile. "Do you dive under the waves before they fall on you?" He imagined bears spinning like sticks in the harsh sand, nearly crushed under the violent, head-pounding weight, but realized their fur would keep them from being skinned as he had been.

"We like to play," answered O-se-mai-ti, a slight curve appearing in the furry line of her mouth. "Sometimes we get saltwater up our noses."

Grizzly Hair recalled the pain when the fist of the ocean had rammed up the cavities of his head. He watched the feeding bears. "People must have caught this whale then."

"No. This one saw her death, so she floated up on the sand with the tide and waited to die. They breathe air like we do. Maybe she breathed easier on land while her death overtook her."

Grizzly Hair waited in respectful silence, then asked, "Does whale meat taste good?"

She lifted the tufts of her eyebrows. "Oh yes. More fat than you've ever seen before."

"Well," Grizzly Hair said inhaling deeply, detecting a hint of putrification in the damp air, "I guess I've stalled long enough. It's time I went down there to talk to yet another village of strange people." This wearied him, this long journey alternating between fear and the grindingly difficult effort to communicate. These *Indios* worked for the Undersea People so he couldn't mention his alliance with Egorov, or the glav-nyi would hear of it. At the very least, he hoped to see an earth map to Pomponio's camp.

The bear, he was astonished to see, had changed into a thick knot of mist and was floating upward. Her voice came ever fainter, saying, "We'll walk together another day."

Two sleeps later he searched around the hills at the base of the peak Oon-nah-pis for a sign of Pomponio. The Bodega people hadn't known where he camped but knew where the peak was located, and that's where Pomponio said he'd be. Founts of fresh bubbling water pushed up from the earth by the power that pervaded this area. He kneelt beside them, asked permission and, when invited, drank the enchanted water. These springs nourished small forests of redwood, madrone, laurel, fern and other medicine plants. This was not suitable for a war, however, because the wooded areas were spaced too far apart to hide the large number of warriors that would be needed. The narrow forests accompanied the water down the hills to the horizon of the big bay, beyond which stood the amazing blue Spirit Peak. Magic abounded on every side. He would have expected many people to live in such a place, but saw only occasional deserted villages, places of dead souls from which he couldn't gallop away fast enough. Deer, elk, ground squirrels and quail parted before him. The missions had swallowed the people, but animals of every kind filled the void.

Searching from spring to spring as he rode east along the hills, he recalled a story told by the people of Bodega, in Spanish and a tongue very like his own. It happened back when there was nothing but deep water. Coyote had been floating in his tule boat for a very long time when the peak of Oon-ah-pis snagged the boat. Coyote got out and stood on the mountaintop, which was the only point of land, and tossed his boat over the water so the long part lay north and south, the narrow side east and west. This was why, when the waters receded, the land was longer from north to south than from west to east. Grizzly Hair believed the story was wrong. The Bodegans hadn't seen the wide Valley of the Sun or the high eastern mountains beyond, and didn't know *Americanos* lived beyond those mountains. The land was wide from west to east, but he had said nothing.

Something was also wrong in their story of why people spoke different tongues. From the peak of Oon-ah-pis Coyote had looked across the newly formed earth and bundled the feathers of blackbirds and ravens and tossed them north, west and east. In the north, human villages sprang up where the feathers landed and they spoke the language of Salmon Woman and Cross-eyed Bear. In the west and east the villages that sprang up spoke two entirely different tongues. Coyote threw the last bundle south across the big bay, and more villages appeared there, all speaking yet a different tongue. But, as Grizzly Hair searched through the spring-fed forests and intervening oak grasslands, he reflected that his people lived much farther east than the East People, who supposedly spoke the easternmost tongue, yet the home tongue was more like the westernmost Bodega people. It didn't fit the story.

The news that perplexed him more, however, as he rode near a herd of elk, had happened less than a moon ago. The Bodegans said the doors of Mission San Rafael had been closed and the neophytes had been allowed to go to their old homes. A few had returned to Bodega and remained there unmolested. Several sleeps later, however, the black hats went to the village of the Petaluma people. They jerked the strongest men from their u-machas and forced them at gunpoint to get on a *lancha.* They were made to row across the big bay and work at a mission sheep ranch called San Pablo, while the women and children stayed in their home place. What did it mean? Were all the missions closing? Would they be given to the *Indios* as the fleshy long robe had said? Maybe Pomponio could explain it. Regardless of the meaning, the black hats obviously remained in their presidio, warlike as ever.

The elk hardly noticed his approach. He estimated more than five twenties in the herd. They were so comically fat, he wondered if they could run. Playing a game, he galloped into their midst. They gave him the whites of their eyes and with shaking blubber bounded away like heavy jackrabbits. Laughing as Morena slowed to a walk, he caught sight of horse tracks under the fresher impressions of elk. He dismounted and knelt to examine them, then followed them to where no elk had crushed the grass. Three horses had been here, not more than a sleep ago.

The tracks crossed over each other and faded in a rock outcropping. An attempt to lose a tracker? Leading Morena, he found a faint trail of chipped rock and horse hairs—brown and buff and white, this being the season when horses lost hair. The prints were stronger in the grass. Stealthily he led Morena and, sure enough, came upon two familiar horses, one with a hoof-shaped gash in his rump, one a nondescript brown, and a nearly white horse that he'd never seen before. He glanced around.

Into the clearing stepped Pomponio. His hair was as bushy as ever and he now wore the tattered shirt that fell mid-thigh on his bare, slightly bowed legs. A fox quiver crossed his tightly muscled chest, and the bow in his right hand was strung. He went to Morena and patted her belly. "Taking good care of my horse's mother?" His white teeth blazed in the sunlight.

Grizzly Hair still couldn't hear his music, but he seemed as friendly as when they had parted at Magma's place. "You'll get the little one when it's weaned," he said. "I came to talk and to see the new mission."

"Come to my camp," Pomponio said, turning at a fast walk.

They descended through a rough, wooded gully filled with poison oak then came to a hole in the hillside that was hidden behind brush. Pomponio scanned the terrain, then motioned Grizzly Hair to follow as he crawled into the opening. Bear dens dotted the hills. In this old one, mother bears had given birth and suckled their young for many rainy seasons. It was a good omen that this place of rejuvenation was Pomponio's hiding place.

Grizzly Hair's eyes adjusted and the odor of old bear piss came at him. Three dark forms slouched against the back wall, possibly the men who had thrown him in the blackberry patch. He couldn't see well enough to be sure. Gnawed bones, scrapers, arrow-straighteners and other tools littered the cave floor. Two baskets of ground acorns stood there too, but no other sign of women. Pomponio reclined on his side, hand supporting his head.

Nearer the low entrance, Grizzly Hair sat hunched forward facing the four men. "What's happening at Mission San Rafael?" he asked, "I heard the neophytes are gone now."

Pomponio chuckled, "Padre Amarós was mad as a tickled hornet. You watch, those doors will open again."

"I thought they might be giving the missions to the *Indios.*"

Pomponio and his men laughed uproariously.

When the laughter died, Grizzly Hair asked, "Why are they building a new mission when they are closing the other one?"

Pomponio said, "I think it's because most of the peoples are dead over by San Rafael, so they're building one closer to the peoples who are still alive."

Including the umne. The need for war was as pressing as ever. He touched a basket of acorn meal. "Still stealing food?"

Light filtered dimly from the entrance but still caught Pomponio's teeth. "Men have to live. Those Petaluma women gladly gave me those baskets."

"They feared your knife."

"Tell us, Strange-Man-on-Horse," Pomponio sneered, "are the Undersea People your allies?"

Grizzly Hair let the attitude clear before he said, "Not the headman, but a man named Egorov and some of his friends. They have guns and will get a cannon."

The other men in the cave clapped each other's knees and shoulders, giving Grizzly Hair the impression that he had been the subject of discussion here. But Pomponio just looked at him. "So you think you're going to drive the *Españoles* away?"

"I hope Estanislao will lead the neophytes from Mission San José to fight alongside us." He gave a shrug. "But people don't want an ally who steals from them. That's a pity because when the fighting is over, we're going to divide up the goods in the missions—guns, pots, horses, everything."

"You'll need a lot more power than I smell around you to get neophytes to leave the missions," Pomponio said.

A voice came from the back of the den. "I've heard of Estanislao."

A louder voice said, "Yes. I think he could talk the neophytes out of the missions. And with the guns of the Undersea People, we could win. We could walk this land as our grandfathers did."

"Without fear of whips."

"Without fear of the *calabozo.*"

"We could move out of this nice house."

"A-iiii! We could find women." Shadowy hands clapped knees and shoulders.

Pomponio exhaled loudly. "All right. I will fight with you."

More than likely, Grizzly Hair thought, Pomponio had planned to do so all along. Chuckles and happy talk he couldn't understand swelled like an ocean wave, and Grizzly Hair rode it further. "You must stop stealing from our allies."

"Who do you mean by that?" Pomponio asked in an innocent tone.

"Neophytes, gentiles, *cimarrones—Indios.*"

A voice in the dark: "Listen to him, man. They won't help us if we steal from them."

Pomponio lay quietly.

"Soldiers are our only enemies," Grizzly Hair insisted.

"No, no," Pomponio countered, shaking his head, "so are the *rancheros* who ride and shoot with them."

Grizzly Hair went along with that. "Anyone who helps them."

"And the neophytes who hold their horses and hand them *amunición,*" added Pomponio.

"Ho!" cried the men at the back of the cave.

"But before war starts, you won't do anything to discourage the neophytes or gentiles from joining us?"

"I said I wouldn't," Pomponio hissed. "You want me to cut my wrist and say it in blood?"

"I heard you, man," Grizzly Hair gave.

"Well then," Pomponio said in all his former arrogance, "tell Estanislao to get started. The sooner this war starts, the better."

His men chorused happy *sí, sí's.*

"I will ride to Estanislao's father," Grizzly Hair said, "but I don't know how long it will take for his son to come from the mission on *paseo*. I must talk with him. Where will my runners find you when we are ready?"

"We are ready now. I will bring men and come to your home place. We'll ride from there."

Grizzly Hair didn't want to burden Morning Owl with feeding many guests for a long time, especially when the umne knew nothing of a war. "No," he said. "I won't be ready for a while. I'll send a runner for you." It might be two moons.

"Don't wait, *hombre*. Fight while the soldiers' guns are broken."

"Their guns aren't broken. I have seen them shoot." He recalled the dog's shattered head.

"You know nothing. Most of their guns are broken. A mule-breaker in the presidio told me the cannons are broken too. When the last *barca* came into the Bay they couldn't make them thunder. But they may be repaired soon. Now is the time to fight."

It was silent in the cave.

Grizzly Hair admitted, "The men in my home place are not ready to fight, and they wouldn't want their women to feed you while I waited to talk to Estanislao." He expected derisive remarks.

Instead, he heard Pomponio's tone of resignation. "We will watch from every tree and rock. Your runners can find us."

"How many men will you bring?"

"Plenty," said Pomponio.

"More than I see here?"

"Two twenties, all tough warriors."

"Good." Grizzly Hair felt well pleased, and Pomponio agreed to establish contact with Cross-eyed Bear and Egorov.

"Now," said Pomponio, "Let's go see the new mission."

At the thought, a sick thing sat up in Grizzly Hair's stomach. It stayed there while he crawled out of the den, and worsened when harsh light fell on a mutilated foot emerging from the cave behind him—no heel, only a mass of gnarled scars. This was the man who had helped throw him in the briars.

The man with round dog eyes was there too. He walked beside the one with no heel. They walked silently and purposefully—the heelless man straight-legged and on his toes.

Seeing his glance, Pomponio said, "Gonzalo is not the only man to escape from irons by cutting off his heel. I knew one who cut off both heels. But he couldn't hide the trail of blood. Gonzalo is lucky."

Appalled at the courage it would take to endure such self-inflicted pain, Grizzly Hair asked, "What did they use to saw through that big bone?" Black hats made sure *Indios* had no knives.

"Bone from the slaughter yard, hidden in the wool of a loincloth and sharpened on the *calabozo* stones."

They left the horses grazing and walked a distance, crossing a creek as warm as blood—a sign of great power—and approached cautiously. Motioning them down, Pomponio slithered to the top of a little hill into a clump of evergreen oaks with low-hanging limbs. He lay there a moment with only the calluses of his feet showing, then hooked an arm for them to join him.

On their bellies they looked south from the low hills. In the green distance, many men were making adobes at a steaming creek. Some stomped clay in a pit, others poured buckets of mud into molds, and still others carried the dried blocks to the knee-high wall that would become a long-sided structure. Black hats stood or sat around the work area smoking, reclining and playing a card game Grizzly Hair had seen in the mission. Upstream of the clay-making stood makeshift willow u-machas.

The spot in his stomach further sickened as he stared at the busy scene before him. Soon men, women and children would be brought here to live—

Topal's people, Libayto's, Poo-soo-ne's and the umne. It made no difference that *Españoles* were now called *Mexicanos,* or that they had closed a mission for whatever reason. These wolves were expanding their territory.

Something appeared on the horizon, too distant to make out.

They all watched a tiny shadowy blob move almost imperceptibly on the flat horizon. "A *lancha,*" said Pomponio. "Coming up the estuary." It disappeared for a while, then tiny figures sprouted. As they grew larger they became four riders on horseback. The men lay motionless, clearly as fascinated as Grizzly Hair. Below, the black hats who had been playing cards stood up.

The plume of a very large feather waved from a big hat of one of the riders. Captain Argüello? Had he ridden all the way to San Francisco and come back on a launch? As the riders reined to a stop, the black hats arranged themselves in a line. Something about the proud way the feathered man sat on his horse assured Grizzly Hair that it was indeed Captain Argüello. He and the other riders dismounted but held their reins as though not intending to stay. After a while, one of the black hats cupped his mouth and called out to the *indios.* All stopped what they were doing and came as a group to listen to Argüello.

"The East People," Pomponio explained confidentially. "They are building a mission so they can be trapped in it." No one laughed. Pomponio added, "The Petalumas were brought here to work too."

"But first they were dragged from their houses and made to tend *ovejas,* sheep."

Pomponio nodded. "That's what their women said."

The *Indios* turned and walked away, half toward the makeshift u-machas, the other half picking items off the ground and walking west. The ones who went to the u-machas retrieved goods and walked east. They were all leaving! Without resistance, seemingly under orders from the black hats.

Next the resident black hats went to a clump of trees, brought out horses and mules and strapped bags on the animals. They mounted and all the black hats rode toward the distant *lancha.* Puzzled, Grizzly Hair looked at Pomponio, who knew more about *Españoles,* but the man's mouth hung open and he appeared equally puzzled as the black hats grew smaller until they were nothing. Everyone was leaving, both *Indios* and black hats.

"Let's ask those men what's happening," Pomponio said, jumping to his feet. He ran after the Petalumas. Grizzly Hair and the others followed, Gonzalo stiff-legged on his toes, the long tendon of his leg useless without a heel to grip.

Hearing them, the Petalumas looked back and began to run.

Pomponio shouted after them, "*Amigos,*" but the neophytes continued running. The chase continued until quite suddenly the Petalumas stopped and half-crouched in their wooly hip wraps, facing their pursuers like cornered badgers. Pomponio walked up speaking their strange tongue.

Breathing heavily, they glowered, some leaning back as if from a demon. Could this fear and hatred of Pomponio ever be eliminated? Gonzalo caught up and Pomponio spoke in charming tones, clearly calming some of the fear. Talk bounced back and forth.

"What are they saying?" Grizzly Hair asked Gonzalo.

"The Captain told them to go home," Gonzalo gasped in Spanish. "He said to stop building the mission until the headmen of the padres talk about it in council. Maybe they don't want a mission here."

That displayed weakness, indecisiveness and lack of power, an invitation to strike. The bear roared from his mouth, "*Rompe los adobes!*" Break the adobes. He mimed the violent motion of throwing down an adobe, breaking it.

Pomponio wore a snake's smile.

"But," an older Petaluma man objected in Spanish. "We would have more *trabajo* when they make us work again."

"Does living in the mission please you?" Grizzly Hair asked.

"I like their food," the man said.

"Dead man's brains," huffed Grizzly Hair.

"Good bread," said a Petaluma man.

Grizzly Hair let out his disgust. "Arrrgh. Plant it yourself if you want their bread. Go in the night and take the seed. Do you like spending all your suns working for the *Españoles?* Saying their prayers? Fearing their *cuartas*, just to eat their bread?"

The sly older man added, "And waiting for Pomponio to steal it?"

Pomponio's eyes cut to Grizzly Hair.

"No more stealing, eh Pomponio?" Grizzly Hair said, head high.

Coiling his legs, Pomponio sat down and patted the earth to show he wanted to talk. A condor swooped over the grassy plain and the Petalumas seated themselves. So did Grizzly Hair. Pomponio's jaw was set, the dry stones of his eyes glaring at the neophytes in the way of the *Españoles.* "I used to tell you people to leave the mission and fight the *cabrones*, but you wouldn't, so I scared you into giving me little dabs of your spineless food. Now I say, change your ways. Become wolves! This man"—he nodded toward Grizzly Hair—"has made allies of the Undersea People and *Indios* across the land. He is my ally. I don't want your bad food anymore. Understand? Forget that. From now on, let us all eat nu-pah and make war on the *soldados.* But first, let's go back there and break those walls." A grin broke out over his face and he concluded as if to himself, "*Me lo gusta.*" I would enjoy that.

Gonzalo's eyes twinkled as he repeated, "*Me lo gusta.*"

The Petalumas were looking at each other with surprise, but not disagreement.

"A-iii," Grizzly Hair said, springing to his feet. He turned and ran toward the new mission, flying over the grass. If he had to do it alone, he would. No brick would be left intact.

By the time they arrived he had rolled a large rock from the warm stream and was standing over the short wall. Suffused with joy, he pummeled the short wall. The magic of the warm water strengthened his back and powered his arms. All around, chortles and cheers added to the music of the thuds and crashes, the smashing of the unborn mission.

In an exuberant sweat, Grizzly Hair realized he must return to the home place before going to Sucais and the Lakisumne, for how could he ask others to join him in war when he didn't have the support of his own men? He hadn't even talked to them yet.

Nothing but rubble remained when they silently parted. The Petalumas went west toward their women, Pomponio and his men toward their cave. Grizzly Hair fetched Morena and headed toward the home place.

46

Etumu had lain in the heated earth-bed sweating out the leavings of her girlhood. For an entire day and a sleep she had been under a blanket of warm earth, reminded of where all people came from. Father had dug the bed in the floor of the u-macha and filled it after she got up.

Now, on the second day of her womanhood, she opened her eyes in the dim u-macha still seeing the basket that had come to her dream, the basket that wanted to be made. This hadn't happened in a long time, so sad and empty she had felt since Grizzly Hair left. Her previous basket hung in the rafters looking childish and simple. The new basket would represent the life-sustaining river and the zigzag power of lightning. It would be a wide, flattened bowl with the top curved inward.

With calm purpose she headed down the path to the bathing place, walking among the umne with a straighter back and hands that felt even more capable than before. Father sun was only a promise, but he colored a streak of pink across the otherwise young blue sky, and he tinted pink the wisps of fog rising from Berry Creek and the river. The backs of her arms prickled at the sight, for these were families of ghosts twisting and stretching upward, slowly dancing their way to the sky—a powerful sign.

She stepped into the river. The water swirled around her ankle. Another sign of power, this one from the river spirit! Humbled to be so honored, she stroked respectfully through the cold water, out and back, then climbed the bank near where Morning Owl was chanting to father sun. She stood there and waited to absorb the strength of the life-giver. Then she saw Grizzly Hair among the dancing ghosts, his feet above the water. It was a message. Her heart bumped. Had he died? Was he in danger? Or did the presence of his spirit mean he was returning? When power abounded you never knew what would happen, but something would.

Determined not to let even the presence of Grizzly Hair's spirit deflect her from her purpose, she went to the u-macha for the purple obsidian knife her parents used on ceremonial occasions. Without eating, to keep her power, she returned to the riverbank to collect basket materials. The mist rose around her and she sat beside a budding red willow. After listening to its motherly song, she asked permission to cut shoots for her basket stays. The tree said, "I am honored to be part of your fine basket."

Thanking the tree, Etumu cut five shoots from the gnarled branches, then went to a second willow and listened. She repeated her request. Her basket would have ten smooth, shiny stays.

This was not the best season for collecting sedge root, but Etumu wanted their white color for the lightning, so she went to the gathering place across the river to check the quality. No flooding had occurred yet, so the sand remained disturbed from root-digging. She teased out a root and bent it back and forth. Too brittle. She reburied it and tried another and another until she found one that seemed to be at a the right stage of its life. Receiving permission of the sedge, she cut the long threadlike root, peeled a section, admired the whiteness of the inner root and cut it. She went to all the sedge plants in the sand by the river, repeating these steps until she had the right amount of material without inflicting too much injury on any one plant. Then she washed and separated the peeled white roots from the unpeeled buff roots.

Needing a background for the lightning, she went to the bullrushes and collected a bundle of their roots. Back in the village she peeled the bullrush roots and gathered a handful of black ash and coals, then scooped out a pit beside the river and mixed the ash with mud, spreading the bullrush roots in it so they would soak up the black color.

Now it was time to make the skeleton of the basket. She went to a place she trusted, not far from where Grizzly Hair's grandmother drilled holes in clamshells. She could just hear the old woman's sing-song, and she could see the dark boulders along the river with smooth water-carved indentations. The day was now bright and the mist had vanished. Split-tailed wing people swooped around in pairs, some of the males chasing each other. Crow people walked around poking for nesting material. They had been here from the dawn of the world. Everything was filled with meaning, as it must be for basket-making, and the willow stays bent graciously to her fingers.

She was well started when old María came down the pathway with a partially finished basket and several skeins of roots. She stopped, looked at Etumu, then stood silently questioning whether she might join her. Etumu smiled. A glance down at her work would have conveyed a polite "no," but Etumu had no reason to believe her power would be interrupted by this kindly old woman.

María made her way through the lupine and sat down, nesting her rump in the sandy soil beside Etumu, her back against the same downed oak. "I meant to sit with Grandmother, there"—she nodded toward Grizzly Hair's grandmother—"but thought you might like some company."

"I am honored."

María unwound two long skeins, removed the bone awl and arranged the black and tan roots in separate piles on the ground.

Noticing, as always, the untattooed chin, Etumu said, "Raven Feather will tattoo my chin after the sleep, if she dreams well." She was proud of that, but by the look on María's face wished she had not spoken until she had thought about it four times.

The old woman's brows peaked and sallow skin draped from the point. "Ahh," she said, "in the pueblo people say tattoos are ugly."

"Here we think it's ugly if—" She stopped

"—women have no tattoo," María completed.

"Yes, sorry." She gave an apologetic expression, bit off the tails of her knot and guided the root around the crossing of the next two stays.

María patted Etumu's knee, picked up a small basket and went to the river. While she was gone Etumu noticed the developing pattern in María's basket—different than anything she had seen before. When María returned and pushed her roots in the basket of water to soak, Etumu asked, "What are those blocks?"

"Hats."

Hats? Slowly the horror hit her. "Black hats of the *Españoles?*" The woman nodded casually. "On your basket? Why would you do that?" That basket could suck the power from Etumu's basket, from Etumu herself!

"My grandsons wear such hats. They wanted them from the time they could walk." Sadly she shook her head. "My old eyes want to see those boys again, so I make their hats." She glanced at Etumu, perhaps saw her shock. "They are good boys."

Etumu had almost forgotten that this woman came from a frightening place. Her good humor had lulled everyone. She had become one of them, like a woman marrying into the umne. She had taught them to speak Spanish and they had learned it as an ongoing challenge, not an enemy tongue. Etumu stared at the ugly shapes growing taller, the swollen knuckles pushing the awl and fine black root over and under the horizontal stay, connecting it to the previous row.

But then she realized María had faced the black hats and defeated her fear. She had sufficient strength to overpower the bad shapes. Slipping her root thread around the next stay-crossing, Etumu said, "I forgot how you say power in Spanish." She tied the knot.

María's awl arrived at the tan between hats. "Which kind? Bad or good?" She tied and bit off the excess.

The *Españoles* had two words for power. "Bad."

"*Diablo,*" María said, coiling the tan root.

"*Diablo,*" Etumu repeated. "Now say 'good power.'"

"*Dios y María y todos los santos.*"

A long tongue twister. She rehearsed it to herself, then repeated it aloud, slowly. The meaning was even more difficult. *Dios* meant the big father in the sky. María was the mother of Jesús, and all the saints had been people before they became souls. "How can the souls of dead people be power itself?"

A smile folded María's face so that the tip of her nose nearly touched her upper lip. "I don't know, but they are."

Pondering, Etumu continued knotting her stays.

"I think Grizzly Hair is coming back," María said.

It almost knocked Etumu over, and she waited for her calm before admitting, "I *saw* him in the mist this morning." Her voice sounded squeaky and timid to her ears.

María gave her a wise woman's nod.

Excited to realize that this woman of power must have *seen* him too, Etumu began to believe he wasn't dead after all. "Maybe he will come home soon."

"I think he will. You like him, don't you?"

More hopeful with each passing instant, yet troubled, Etumu tried to appear casual as she said what everyone already knew: "He was my sister's man." Under normal circumstances that meant he would likely marry Etumu, but her parents disapproved of him. No one knew that the memory of his warm hand around hers never left her, or that Oak Gall's love for him still lived in her. Ever since he had ridden away with the *Americano,* she had felt hollow and food had been tasteless. Now she looked through the moisture in her eyes and fumbled to tie the knot. A tear spilled loose. She turned away, her calm badly shattered, and lowered the skeleton basket between her legs. She must wait for *Dios y María y todos los santos* before continuing, or the basket would show the disturbance.

"Have you talked to your parents about him?"

She shook her head, seeing in her mind the way her father radiated anger at the mention of the name. Once he'd said he hoped the black hats had killed Grizzly Hair.

"Your sister's death was not his fault," María said—as she had before, when all the umne listened. But that had not lessened Father's anger.

Wiping her cheek with the back of her hand, Etumu turned to face her. "Am I foolish to think he could be my, my. . ." Gulping pain, she blurted out, "my man?"

The old woman looked at her with sympathy and somehow Etumu knew that since María would leave this place, she would be easier to talk to than anyone else. It poured out:

"People used to say my sister shouldn't touch him because he grew up here. They said it was too easy for him to be with her. They said it was improper, even though he is unrelated to my family. But he couldn't help it that his mother brought him back to her home place. Still, my aunties never liked him because of his being with her, even though," she couldn't quite swallow the lump in her throat, "even though he is the best man, the best tracker, the. . ." In too much pain, she changed directions. "People blamed him when my sister followed him to the mission. You saw Father try to kill him. That's why he was never really my sister's man. So it wasn't true what I said. So how could I. . ." Her tongue stopped.

Seemingly unperturbed, María coiled her root, making the hat taller. "I think you are mated with him in your heart. That's how the *Españoles* say it, that love between a man and woman lives in the heart, not the stomach. I think it's true. I remember how it felt to have a man in my heart when everyone said he was not for me. They said he was another woman's husband. I told him he had two wives, but he sent me away to work in San Francisco Presidio and never came to visit me or Angelita again, though he was her father. The pain in my heart pounded with hard fists and tried to tear me apart." She laid a gnarled hand on her ribs where the sack of her breast originated, then continued coiling the black root around the stays.

Arrested by this strange story, Etumu pointed at the pattern. "Did your man wear a hat like that?"

"No. He wore a big three-cornered hat with a plume on top. He was, as the *Españoles* say, *magnifico*, a fine man, and he was all mine until his other wife came from Spain with her son. From the moment she stepped off the boat she yelled at him and made everyone in Monterey hate me. He cowered before her and lacked the strength to tell her I was his wife too. My heart hurt for a long time."

"Were you angry at him?"

María pushed out her wrinkled lips. "Many strong feelings jumped around in me and I couldn't name them. He was of another people and they had different ways. I knew him to be a strong man and wondered if she was a sorcerer to hold such power over him. People said she came from an important family in Spain and he was governor because of her. Sometimes I thought I shouldn't blame him, but my heart hurt for a long time. I can never forget that. I think you have some of that pain."

In the presence of such sympathy, Etumu let silent tears flow. "Did you ever marry another man?"

"No."

"Did you see him again?"

"Never. Not long after I left he went away, maybe to Spain. Another man became governor."

Etumu looked across the chasm of age and considered such long-lasting hurt. "I am afraid Grizzly Hair will listen to what everyone says, just as your man listened to his other wife. I'm afraid he'll have nothing to do with me."

"Would you be willing to leave your people and go to a completely strange place? Persuade him to live with you in Pueblo San Jose? I'll be going back soon. You two could come with me. The *vecinos* and *rancheros* are always looking for *Indio* workers."

The conversation had veered off the earth into an alien place. "I. . . don't think I could. Besides, well, he. . . doesn't love me." The last part jumped out with a sob.

"Poor little one," María said, reaching over to pat her shoulder. "First we must make him love you."

"We? Can you help?"

The sparse brows peaked slightly. "I know some herbs." She continued coiling her root. "As for going to the pueblo, I can't blame you for fearing the *Españoles.* I wouldn't have gone either, except I was forced in the beginning, then Commander Fages—the man I loved—was kind to me. So I lived where he lived."

"Well, that would make it easier, and you are not dead, so it can't be all bad there. But first Grizzly Hair must come home and see me as his. . ." She changed course, letting the talk spill. "Mother says I am making a bed of thistles by thinking about him, but I can't stop. I have loved him since my sister did, since before I can remember. She made me notice the way he flies over the ground when he runs, the way he stands looking at things like he sees through them, the dark fire in his eyes, his face. Everything she loved about him, I do too."

"I know why you like him." Then, as if turning a corner and seeing a new vista, the old woman spoke more rapidly. "I'll make an elixir for him, and one for you. I'll speak to your aunties too, anyone I can. You and I are partners now. Understand?" She grinned her funny, wonderful grin. "I have seen your parents' love for you. You are their only child, so that helps you too. And remember, you are a woman now. People hear you better. Little One, use your powers."

Three sleeps later, the morning after black ash had been pressed into the tiny wounds that made lines of dots radiating from her lower lip to her chin, Etumu was still feeling twinges of pain when she heard dogs barking. The herald called, "Grizzly Hair comes on his horse."

She couldn't draw breath.

A woman hurried across the chaw'se in pursuit of her children. Time-of-pretending was starting. People were silencing the excited children and resuming whatever they had been doing, but Etumu's heart drummed for him and her stomach felt like a bull elk had stepped on it. She hurried behind one of the oaks that lined the riverbank. First he would hobble his horse in the playing field. She wanted to run and watch, but her legs might buckle. Anyway she must not let him see her. Too much was bursting inside her and she would fail to pretend.

As the pounding at the chaw'se resumed and people sat casually before their u-machas, she remained hidden, watching the path from around the dancehouse. She hoped Father wouldn't see her hiding, as several curious children did, or he would see her thoughts.

A foot and beautiful calf came into view, then his body. A small happy sound escaped from her closed lips. But he was slimmer than before. He needed her to gather and cook for him. Then she saw with joy the rabbit-skin pouch around his neck. He hadn't thrown it away! The long stubble of his hair stood up in patches and lay flat in other places like grass after a rainstorm. The heron bone earplugs swung from his ears. He stopped and glanced around the village. Was he wondering where María and his grandmother slept? Maybe he would sleep with them under the brush porch the hy-apo had erected against his u-macha. Or, more likely, in the sweathouse. Or would he sleep under the oaks until he built a house? Maybe she could slip out of the u-macha and lie with him. The thought tightened her heart. Mother might see, and then Father would kill him. No, she wouldn't do that.

He walked past the pretending people and headed for the river, toward her. She backed around the tree, then watched through the willows as he waded into the water and dove into the bathing place. Fortunately, time-of-pretending gave people time to regain their strength.

Also fortunate was the fact that María had gathered herbs for her brews. While Grizzly Hair swam, Etumu hurried to the hy-apo's u-macha, where María sat under the willow porch. "Grandmother," she whispered urgently, "Make your medicines. Make him love me." She thumped her shoulder and said, "If only I could cover these bones with flesh!"

Relieved to see most of the people in the home place, Grizzly Hair let himself float. Clearly, the *Españoles* had not been here. Still, all was not well. The river was too low. In the time of flowers it should have been full. The grass was too short too. And that wasn't all.

Walking up the path among the umne after the swim, he detected anger in Red Sun's face as they passed one another—anger restrained with difficulty, anger despite the pretending, anger not dissipated. A few steps farther, he passed another face that failed to hide its owner's contempt: Sick Rat. Sadly, he realized he wouldn't sleep in the sweathouse this night. His presence among the men would disturb the sweat, despite the pretending.

María had stayed, he was surprised to see. Some people were not present.

Away hunting or gathering? Dead of Missouri's sickness? What about Etumu? He addressed the spirits: *"Surely you didn't take the little lizard too, and leave her parents childless!"* Just after that left his mouth, he glimpsed her on the riverbank. Relieved, he found a place to sit and think outside the village but close enough to see what was happening.

Luck had ridden with him. O-se-mai-ti had protected him from many dangers. A network of runners was ready to spread messages and collect warriors. Topal's men, he'd been delighted to learn, had made a formal visit to the Putah people and told them everything, including the story of El Cid. Some of them would be allies. Libayto's men were less certain, but some gave their nods. Poo-soo-ne's men were also divided. Altogether it would be a strong fighting force, with Egorov and Pomponio's forty men, and many who wouldn't fight had agreed to make arrows.

He looked at the piles of beaverskins at almost every u-macha. The men had collected them for trade with Missouri, but Missouri had not returned. Grizzly Hair hoped he never would. Somehow he would see to it that these pelts were traded at Fort Ross. In any case he needed to go back there and talk with the glav-nyi.

A sleep passed and another sun before María stood before him with the smile he loved and said, "Well, the Russians didn't kill you." Fondly she touched his shoulder.

"And you are still here. Lame Beaver and Falls-off-House would have accompanied you most of the way."

"It wasn't time to leave. Anyway, your grandmother needed looking after."

In gratitude, he laid a hand on her shoulder. "A man likes to have someone waiting at the home place."

"I am not the only one." She gave him a twinkly smile.

Just then Two Falcons came up the path. He stopped and put a warm hand on Grizzly Hair's shoulder. "We are gathering wood for a sweat. Join me?"

In the sweathouse the men listened to his stories and heard about the people he had met, including the glav-nyi at the Top of the World and the fleshy long robe's offer to be allies. He told about Pomponio and Gonzalo and his mutilated heel. The smoke and heat had thickened by the time he explained his idea of luring the *Españoles* into a place of thick vegetation with hidden trenches, and how they could defeat them in spite of their guns and cannons. The coals settled in the whispering fire.

"I will leave in a sleep or two," he continued, "to visit Sucais and Gabriel, but will the men of my umne fight beside me? I want to tell my allies they will."

The men were quiet, too long quiet, and he felt the absence of a father who might have spoken for him.

Two Falcons' solid voice broke the stillness. "Grizzly Hair's eyes have always burned bright. He sees what is before him. Maybe we should listen to him."

"I agree with the esteemed master hunter," Lame Beaver said.

"So do I." That was Falls-off-House.

Someone grunted disapproval.

Drum-in-Fog's voice creaked through the smoke. "The umne have never done such a thing. We would be like squirrels fighting mountain lions. We shouldn't go. The spirits will protect us here."

Several grunts of agreement came through the smoke.

"How would we know where to get material for arrowheads in a strange place?" asked Scorpion-on-Nose, the knapper.

Red Sun's voice was ripe with anger. "Do not even listen to one whose rashness already brought death to our people."

As that settled, Morning Owl said in a summing-up tone, "I try to keep the umne safe. It would be a big gamble to go far away and fight powerful men who have powerful weapons."

No more talk came.

Aware again of the emptiness in the sweathouse where a father or uncles should have been, Grizzly Hair knew he would continue on his trail without the support of the umne. His own men didn't trust his vision. He was alone, too different from them. Maybe this was his last time here. Maybe Sucais would take him in. But what of Grandmother? He couldn't expect María to keep caring for her. She had a family in the pueblo.

At dawn after the sleep Grandmother left to drill holes in the small clamshells supplied by village children. Grizzly Hair ate nu-pah with María and Falls-off-House under the hy-apo's porch. "I will ride to the southern river today," he announced. Falls-off-House looked up.

"Why so soon?" María asked.

"I know what I came to learn." He didn't look at Morning Owl, who was then leaving, touching his wife.

María tipped her head inquiringly but didn't ask. "Here," she said, offering him a small basket of liquid. "It's a special tea I made you."

He accepted the tea—the likes of which he hadn't tasted before. The aftertaste seemed a little cloying at first, but he smacked his lips to show his appreciation.

María said, "I will ride with you."

Perhaps she hadn't wanted to travel with anyone but him. "I hope my grandmother isn't too much burden for you," he said to Raven Feather. Guests were temporary, Grandmother a never-ending responsibility. Imposing further hardship on Morning Owl's family was the last thing Grizzly Hair wanted to do, especially while he traveled around preparing for a war Morning Owl disagreed with. However, by the music and the look on Raven Feather's generous face, she seemed willing to assume the responsibility.

María said, “I think Etumu would like to do it. Did you notice? She is a woman.”

“I saw that. But why Etumu?” She should be free to dance and sing and receive gifts from men.

“Grandmother isn’t difficult to care for,” María said. “She goes her own way without needing to be led. She doesn’t eat much, and she pays for some of her food with her drilling.” Again Raven Feather seemed about to speak.

“My son,” said María with her wonderful smile, “I have been with your people for a long time, and I tell you Etumu is the perfect woman to care for her. Her hands are very capable, and I know she would want to do it.”

Astonished at this, Grizzly Hair glanced at Red Sun’s u-macha, where Etumu and her mother were skinning quail. It reminded him that he had wanted to show Etumu the flattened gold nugget. Leaving María, whose sly expression said she knew more than she let on, he ducked out from under the porch and strolled past Nettles, catching Etumu’s attention.

He went upstream to a forested stretch of bank where the river sometimes overflowed in time of rain and sat against a black walnut tree to wait. All around, new shoots of the old tree fanned up from the base, and in the fresh morning air the dips and ripples of the river shimmered in the morning sun. Thinking how complicated his life had become, he watched a golden eagle drop from the sky to the opposite shore, then labor upward with a snake writhing in its talons. That too was complicated. The eagle settled on a cottonwood snag, shifting from foot to foot atop its agitated quarry. Light footsteps approached.

He removed the gold from the pouch and turned to see Etumu standing a little beyond the polite distance. She looked at the gold on his palm. Sunlight streamed through the leaves behind him and lit the almost invisible hairs on her forearms and legs. Her feet were flattened by her scant weight and her toes looked like round buds, filling him unexpectedly with a hint of excitement.

“Look at the golden egg you gave me. I heated and pounded it.” He heard electrifying music and noticed her unusual scent—somewhat like lichens on boulders, or the sun-heated boulders themselves. What was this odd feeling?

She sat on his shady side, taking the proffered gold in her neat little hand. From this angle only her small, attractive toes were awash in sunlight. Her hair fell forward from her shoulders as she examined the gold, turning it, her padded eyelids giving her a distinctive appearance from the side, the lashes coming up from underneath. Why would he feel this excitement when he ought to be sad about the men’s lack of support?

She looked up and the black pools of her eyes contained all the mysteries of womanhood. She had been transformed.

He filled the awkward silence. "It looks like a sick grape leaf, doesn't it?"

She laughed in a way that reminded him of Oak Gall.

"Do you want it?" he asked. "I'll give it back."

Somehow her expression conveyed that she understood her gift to him had been worthless and that she knew he knew she must be embarrassed about it, but now thought the whole thing was funny. That tangle of friendly thoughts prompted him to put his arm around her shoulder. He had intended a joking comfort for her having given him a mere rock, but the instant his palm touched her tender shoulder and moved over the softest skin he'd ever felt, he wanted to pull her to him and protect her from all hurt that could ever befall her. She personified the *inocente* umne, and it seemed she became his reason to continue his quest to unify the *Indios.* Was that the origin of the excitement? A renewed vigor in his purpose?

There was a slight tremor in her shoulders, across which his arm rested. "Actually," he said, "I would like to keep the gold as a reminder of the pretty lizard who gave it to me."

She glanced over with misted eyes, her lashes casting a strange spell over him, and he recalled thinking, when he left the village with the *Americano,* that she was attracted to him as a man. He wanted to feel her newly peaked breasts against his chest, but the memory of Red Sun's glower returned. He took his arm from her. "I am leaving for the southern river."

"Going away again?" Alarm showed in her face.

"Yes, as soon as we are finished talking. I need to tell the people there many things. I feel I belong there more than here." The last part came out unbidden.

She scooted around to look at him and her toes brushed his calf, sending a strong sensation to his core. "You would be in danger in the west," she said. "They might capture you again." She caressed his calf with her perfect little hand. "Don't go."

"I am harder to catch now," he said, his voice breaking and cracking.

"I don't want you to go," she said urgently. "But if you do, please, please come back. You must."

Suddenly she was against him just as he had desired. He entered her music and felt its pleasant lightning. He wanted this little woman who had never attracted him until now. "Your father would kill me," he murmured.

"I'll change his mind about you." Small and interesting in his arms, she smiled up at him.

He rubbed his nose on hers and said, "The men of the north do this."

"Do it more. Oh, do it more," she said, her slim thigh moving across him.

"Your father. . ."

"He's not here. He's gone."

47

In wonderment over Etumu, he rode west with María. Etumu had agreed to care for Grandmother, and he knew she would be diligent. The thought of her made him smile, this former child. Yes, little Etumu loved him. That was as plain as the eternally blue sky. In payment for caring for Grandmother he had given her the baskėt Salmon Woman had given him, and Etumu had exclaimed over the red bird pattern made from the scalp feathers of woodpeckers, and the quail topknots standing in a line around the opening.

Could she change Red Sun's opinion of him? Could she change the prevailing attitude? That seemed impossible. He let out a chuckle, liking her determination. It was interesting the way she made him feel. More responsible than he'd felt with a woman before. He knew it would hurt her if he never returned, but he was obliged to return, especially since she was taking care of Grandmother. Where would this lead?

He had never been so far downstream on his own river, which was sad and little now. Where had the rains gone? Father sun burned at his zenith and Morena lagged, but María kneed Amarillo to move faster, passing him. Wearing her long woolen dress, she was prepared to return to the pueblo. In her haste to see her old home place, they had stopped for only short visits with the peoples along the river trail—five villages so far. The farther they came from the home place, the less people knew about Morning Owl's people. Grizzly Hair had wanted to stay longer in the last place and learn whether anyone there knew his father's people, but it was his turn to be patient. María had been patient last time they traveled together. Besides, something bothered him about suddenly exposing his patrilineage to strangers. He preferred to warm up to such talk. It would be better to stop on the way back, when María was gone. So now he merely observed that, unlike the villages on Estanislao's river, these were intact—men, women and children in the right proportion and the right number of people to fill the u-machas.

The Cosumne were said to be a strong and populous people, and he wondered how they would receive their long-lost daughter. Older generations would be dead and she had no children there, so only if her brother and cousins were left living would she be remembered by family. She disappeared around a bend. A horse whinnied. The Cosumne, being closer to the missions, were wary. Men stood watching from the trees. Grizzly Hair signed friendship, knowing runners from the previous villages had preceded them and told of their friendly intent.

Here the river meandered through the rich soil of the Valley of the Sun. Grass seed had been harvested and immense oak people stood thickly on the plain. Grizzly Hair followed María into a town almost as large Poo-soo-ne's.

It lay on the border of the vast tulare marsh. The herald announced them and people assembled, sleepy men coming from the dancehouse with mussed hair.

The headman came forward. "Where are you coming from?"

"A long time ago," María said with a twinkle in her eye.

Little Cos looked puzzled and glanced at Grizzly Hair.

"From the Lopotsumne, up beyond the Omuchumne."

"Ah yes," said Little Cos. Not very tall, he maintained erect posture. "Where are you going?"

"To visit the Lakisumne, including a few *cimarrones*."

Little Cos smiled as if at a quiet joke, no doubt because *cimarrones* also lived among the Cosumne, according to the upstream peoples. He looked at María's dress, horse, baskets and bucket. "It is not often we see a wealthy old woman on a good horse. What does it mean, you come from a long time ago?"

Dismounting, she glanced around. "This is my old home place."

Little Cos didn't hide his surprise. Several twenties of people had gathered, and the heat made it difficult to breathe. They went to a shady place overlooking an elbow of the lazy river, and talk began. Did María recognize anyone? No. Did anyone recognize her? People scowled and cocked their heads.

She told of the first time the *Españoles* had come and how excited and happy people had been to see friendly beings from another world. People buzzed with talk, and Grizzly Hair could tell that this story of a procession of *Españoles* on *mulas* and horses had been told many times.

"That was before we knew them," Little Cos said.

"I went with them when they left," María said.

Jaws dropped. Children hunched their shoulders, pointing at María as though their mothers weren't already looking. Obviously the story of a girl leaving with the strangers was well known. And now she sat before them, still untattooed despite the wrinkles of age.

María looked around but no brother or cousin came forward to welcome her. One old women looked at her with happiness, not the stunned wonder displayed by others. Cheerfully María said, "I never lived in a mission."

This produced surprised expressions. Talk tumbled over talk as people asked about her life.

She told them all the places she had lived. Everything she said brought more questions, and she answered them until the glow of sunlight faded behind the big oak people and shadows darkened the village. Women went late to their cooking.

María and Grizzly Hair ate at Little Cos's fire.

"My old place is beautiful," María told the headman, "You have taken good care of it."

The old woman with the happy expression shyly approached the hy-apo's fire and stood in the shadow. The hy-apo invited her to eat with them, and before long, the two old women were slapping their thighs and exclaiming in loud voices that they had dug basket roots together. They laughed like young girls.

Little Cos said quietly to Grizzly Hair, "Her people were poor. They accepted presents for her." The hy-apo continued in a lower voice. "People didn't like it when her father strutted around with beads of such skillful make."

"Now she is a woman with a house in Pueblo San José," Grizzly Hair said. "The *Españoles* changed her from poor to rich."

Little Cos gave him a troubled look. "We used to know whether people were worthy hunters and good guardians of the spirits. Now people are divided into those who have the goods of the *Españoles* and those who do not."

"*Christianos* and hill bunnies."

Little Cos let out a chuckle. "Hill bunnies."

"What happened to her parents?"

"They went to live with the Ochejumne. Independent people. Nobody goes to their dances. They lived on a big island."

"Island?"

"We call it that. There are several places like that over there." He gestured. "Big fingers of the river wrap all the way around the land. Places with good grass and much game. Her uncle stayed here with us until recently. His heart left last time we danced the O-se-mai-ti." He dipped his curved fingers into the nu-pah and passed the basket to Grizzly Hair.

"I am glad to be talking with you," Grizzly Hair said putting a scoop of delicious fish-flavored mush on his tongue. "I heard your people fought the black hats." Seeing the twinkle in the headman's eye, he lowered his voice. "I am on my way to the Lakisumne headmen to talk about a war to drive the *Españoles* away from this land."

Little Cos said, "I heard you were going around the country saying that. You must be careful." But the twinkle remained. "I have some men here you will want to know." He pointed through the trees toward a group of tule u-machas that stood by themselves in the western portion of the town.

Later, Grizzly Hair shared a pipe at Juan's fire. He was a big ugly man with long tangled hair and a torn woolen shirt. His older companion was small, naked and taciturn, but often smiled a mouthful of perfect teeth. Their badly built u-macha, like those of the neighboring men, were clearly temporary. Bones lay littered around these slouching u-machas, and the pack of village dogs gnawed upon them.

Juan seemed to be the spokesman of this bunch of *cimarrones* who had lived for some time with the Cosumne. None of them came from this village.

"Why do you live here?" Grizzly Hair asked.

Juan smiled.

The older man's lips opened to reveal his perfect teeth. "The big times are good here."

María came out of the night with Grizzly Hair's blanket. Handing it to him she smiled engagingly at Juan and his friends, and said she would sleep in the u-macha with her old friend. She turned to Juan and asked, "Who are you the son of? Maybe I knew your parents."

He looked past her, glassy-eyed. No doubt his parents were dead. The older man spoke up. "He is Juan. His parents lived over there by the Spirit Mountain." He waved his hand vaguely to the southwest. "Julpun."

María stepped to an oak and touched its bark. "I played in this tree." Her voice was matter of fact but her hands jumped to her beads. "God is here."

Laughing coarsely, Juan snarled, "You won't find me talking to those beads."

"Are you that angry?" Her deeply wrinkled brow showed tenderness and her head tilted as though questioning a child.

He gave the ground a thump, meaning she should sit down, then began a story. "In the time of falling leaves Padre Durán came to my home place in a *lancha* with black hats and plenty of *neofites.*" Juan spat in contempt. "It was their holiday, their hunt. Out on *paseo*. They lured our women and children to ride on the *lancha* and expected us to run along the shore begging for our families. They thought that would pull us to the mission. But some of us didn't go."

María asked, "Where are your wife and children now?"

Juan stared at nothing.

She made the sign of the cross over her head and shoulders.

"Did you fight the soldiers?" Grizzly Hair asked.

The unpleasant downward turn of his lips curved up, and he spoke through a gap-toothed smile. "We fought them here, didn't we?" He glanced at the older man. "One night, through the leaves, we saw the black hats tie the *lancha* over that way, between here and the Junizumne." He wiggled a finger toward the marsh. "They covered it with branches then lay down to sleep. We sneaked up with all our friends and pushed the cannon off the *lancha* into a water. It sank. Completely sank." He chuckled softly. "Then we herded away more than three twenties of horses, at a run—horses we had stolen before."

Grizzly Hair recalled Padre Durán mentioning the theft of that many horses on this river, and Gabriel's story about sinking a cannon. "I have heard this story," he told them.

Nodding appreciatively, Juan continued. "Later, Sergeant Soto came with many black hats and neophytes to get the horses. We gave them a good fight, but. . ." He shrugged.

María chimed in. "I know that story too. Old Pedro Amador tells it just about every day. He lives across the plaza from me. I could repeat his exact words." Almost a cheery tone.

"Sergeant Soto is proud of taking the horses back," Juan snarled. "I heard his talk in the pueblo. Some of us were listening in the shadows.

In a subdued tone María said, "You shouldn't fight the soldiers and you shouldn't steal horses."

Juan spat at the coals and the spit sizzled away.

"It is true," María insisted. "Many times I have heard *Españoles* say *Indios* behave like children. When they stop stealing and fighting they'll be treated like *gente de razón.*"

Grizzly Hair silently translated *gente de razón.* People of reason, people who think straight. No one ever meant *Indios* when they said it. He looked at Juan. Did he think straight? Maybe not, but he was angry enough to be a good warrior.

María was saying, "You're not old. You could marry another woman and have more children."

"There are no women left."

She twisted her mouth. "That's not true. Many women live here.

"None that want me."

She looked at him closely. "Many women live in the pueblo."

"Black hats get them all."

"But more *Indias* come from the interior all the time. They live on the outskirts of the town. They wash clothes for the *vecinos.* You could find a woman."

"They want presents for coupling, the kind I don't have."

The older man grinned. "But we like the *aguardiente* in the pueblo."

Neophytes talked of *aguardiente* as something precious. "Do you have some here?" Grizzly Hair asked, thinking it might not hurt to taste a little. Like the Kashaya story of frogs, maybe people were mistaken about rotten drink being harmful to health.

The old man shook his head, his smile slow. "*Aguardiente* never lasts. We have *fandangos* when we get it though. *Sí, sí!* We dance then."

"You should pray for your souls," María muttered, fingering her beads as she sagged back against the tree. Her wrinkles looked deeper, her eyes hidden in the yellow folds. She finished the prayer, then rose slowly to her feet and walked away.

Grizzly Hair whispered to Juan about the war he had in mind.

"Ho, I could die happy killing the black hats," said Juan.

"I am riding to talk with Gabriel. You know him. He helped sink the cannon." Seeing the nod, he went on. "I will send a runner when we are ready. We'd like you to fight with us." He looked at the old man. "And your friends."

"And Little Cos," said Juan. "He and his people will fight."

The next day as father sun blazed upon the parched western mountains, Grizzly Hair and María arrived at the foot of the *Paso de Alta Monte.* The powdery dust on the trail was even deeper than he remembered.

"I will go on from here by myself," María said, reining Amarillo to a stop.

"Will you be safe without me?"

Her look was a tease. "Safer. This is the land of Pepe's people, my daughter's people, my grandsons' people. I'll bet they told the soldiers to watch for me and escort me home."

"How would I get a message to you if I needed to?"

She studied him a long moment. "Come to the pueblo and say you're from the eastern mountains. *Indios* haven't yet come from that far. Tell people I met you on my *paseo.* Say I want you to help with the gardens and farm. Angelita and I are always looking for workers. But be careful. Don't let them know you escaped from a mission. Once a *cimarrón,* always a *cimarrón.*"

"How would I find your house?"

She described the pueblo as a square of about thirty-five houses with an adobe church on one end and a ditch running around the plaza. "My *casa* is in the middle on the south side of the plaza. My *casa* is made of adobe. It sits on a stone foundation about this high." She dropped the reins and held her hands apart, and he saw her pride that she lived in such a house.

"I will find it."

It was time to part. Custom told him to leave without making this difficult, but in his mind he saw his mother pounding acorns with María, the two talking and laughing. He couldn't quit looking at her as she frowned at him sorrowfully—also breaking custom.

"Our people enjoyed you," he murmured.

"Nettles told me you want to make war on the soldiers," she said, startling him. "Is that why you're going to the River of the Lakisumne? To plan a war? Is it true you are an *insurgente?*"

Red Sun must have told his wife what had been said in the sweathouse. Men weren't supposed to reveal that talk. "What is an *insurgente?*"

"*Indios* who fight against the soldiers. The commander always worries about insurgency."

"Has it happened before?"

"Many times. Little fights. *Indios* cannot win against guns and cannons. They might as well cut their own throats. Don't do it." She looked across the hills, sunlight glinting off a wet streak on her wrinkled cheek.

"I must."

She made the sign of the cross over her head and shoulders, closed her eyes and murmured to *Madre de Dios.*

This had turned out to be even more painful than he'd expected, but her wishes would not deter him. "I will come and tell you when it will happen," he said quietly, "so you can tell your grandsons not to fight. I don't want to shoot my arrows at them."

She blinked tears. "You don't believe me when I say the soldiers will kill you."

He realized she thought he didn't respect her talk. With her tears loosening his own, he nudged Morena in a circle to face her. Reaching over, he put his hand on her wool-covered shoulder. "Mother, you are the wise woman who saved my life. You always speak the truth to me as you know it." He let that sink in, then withdrew his hand. "I am sorry to ask a favor of one who has been so good to me, but I must, for the sake of my people. Please do not repeat what Nettles told you, not even to your daughter. She might tell her *Español* husband."

"What would I tell them?" She sounded hurt. "I know nothing. You tell me nothing."

"I can't tell you what will happen because there are no war plans now." *Not yet.* He blinked at the long mountain stretching southward, ashamed of his tears and his inability to ride away. She was like the only family he had left, and his insides were pulling into a knot.

After a long silence she raised her chin and said. "Etumu loves you. You should marry her and forget about fighting." Abruptly she kicked the horse forward. Amarillo's buff haunches pushed uphill and his long white tail danced behind, bucket and baskets jiggling. María swayed from side to side, the wings of dust from the hooves lengthening in the faint breath of the warm day. She never looked back. There was no hint of rain in the sky. The world seemed to be holding its breath.

The thong cut into Grizzly Hair's hands as he held Morena back, whinnying and tossing her head. The tan mountain looked more than ever like an enromous sleeping lion with the trail crossing its back. María would ride past the mission. Bowstring's face jumped vividly to mind, the ease with which they had walked together in life. Grizzly Hair missed him.

He would miss him in the talks with Sucais and Estanislao. But soon, he thought, Estanislao would bring Bowstring from the mission, and they would plan a war together as they had once planned hunting games.

48

Everything looked as it had the first time he'd wound his way back and forth down the switchback trail through the gray pines and oaks to the river bottom. Just as before, the loose-skinned old man came up the path to greet him. This was a relief, for Grizzly Hair had worried that Sucais had followed his son to the mission.

Quinconul was also there, the brother of Sucais. After greetings, they went to the village center and Grizzly Hair learned that Estanislao was expected home on a *paseo*, soon.

Pleased with his luck, he settled in to wait, hunting with Sucais, Quinconul and the other three men. Having no women, they cooked their own food. Sucais and his brother clearly welcomed his company, but Grizzly Hair didn't mention anything about a war, preferring to wait for Estanislao. As before, Sucais gave the impression that his son, whom he called Cucunichi, had gone to the mission on a scouting trip that would soon end.

The moon waxed and waned and still Estanislao didn't come. But Grizzly Hair enjoyed being around Sucais, a man of knowledge, and understood that this chance to learn some his wisdom was a gift. Meanwhile, up on the high ground the short grass withered. It crunched beneath his feet when he hunted. Large herds of elk, deer, antelope and many smaller animals crowded into the river bottom where they devoured everything within reach and became easy targets for men as well as wolves and mountain lions. The buckeye trees browned early, and the oaks produced a huge bounty of too-small acorns. The river sank lower than Sucais had ever seen it, and in places became a series of large pools. In his bare hands Grizzly Hair caught desperate, flopping blue gill.

Then one day a runner came and said many people were being released from the missions on *paseos* because the cattle were starving and the mission gardens had wilted and died. The neophytes had nothing to eat.

Two sleeps later Sucais squatted near the trail, watching. He never spoke until father sun was halfway across the sky. "Ho!" he said, creaking to his feet. Grizzly Hair and the other men followed him up the trail. Estanislao swung into view, bare-legged and bare-chested, leading many people. Thinner than before, he wore a woolly hip wrap like all the men behind him. As he drew nearer, Grizzly Hair noticed the cords on his neck and the lean muscles of his chest and limbs beneath his perspiring skin. Sucais put his hands on his son's shoulders and they smiled at one another.

Sucais turned to an older woman and clasped her shoulders. She leaned her forehead gently against his cheek—his wife. All the women looked tired. So did the people behind, small children and old people among them.

Estanislao finished greeting his elders, then nodded at Grizzly Hair, a hint of a smile pulling at his wide lips. "I hear you've been traveling."

"You have good ears." Nothing escaped Estanislao's runners.

"They tell me you have a horse."

"Your father gave her to me." He could tell by the look exchanged between father and son that this too had been known.

Sucais raised his arms to the weary crowd and announced, "Let's dance and celebrate the return of the people." As though instantly revived, the children jumped for joy.

Estanislao informed his father, "Cipriano and more people are coming from Mission Santa Clara." Spoken as a caution or disagreement?

"So much the better," declared Sucais. "Come, let us hunt and prepare food and drink. We need wood for a proper sweat. We have not danced since you left and it's already acorn time."

"Our dance doctor died in the mission," Estanislao said quietly.

Sucais appeared stunned, then his smile returned. "You be the dance doctor."

"I don't think I should." Estanislao looked over his father's head and said, "Maybe you should do it."

The smile dropped from Sucais as he looked up at his son. "From the time you were a boy, you heard the spirits better than I. And now you are the headman of these people."

Estanislao looked at him, "Let us talk later. The people need to swim and rest before they think about a big time."

Lips pushed out in thought, Sucais agreed.

Grizzly Hair thought he understood Estanislao's reluctance to be the dance doctor—he wouldn't want that responsibility either, without training. Conjuring up spirits without sufficient power could be the last thing a person ever did.

But as the long day cooked hotter, it became apparent that Estanisalao's hesitation was rooted in something more. He lay stretched on the ground near his old u-macha, his big hands pillowing his head. Sucais sat leaning against a nearby cottonwood, and Grizzly Hair lay nearby, curious about what would be said, for much depended upon Estanislao's mindset. It seemed he was essential to a successful war, not the small struggles María had mentioned.

"I have preserved the feather robe in herbs," Sucais offered quietly. "It is in good condition for a dance."

The irregular drumbeat of the mortar bowls was the only sound. Estanislao turned toward his father and said in a confidential tone, "It wouldn't be right for me to wear it."

"I am listening," said Sucais somewhat tensely.

Estanislao flopped to his back and looked up through the leafy canopy, his voice low and quiet. "I promised *Dios* I would not dance heathen dances any more."

Sucais pushed to his feet, knees cracking. He looked down at his son and declared, "They are poisoning you," then walked into the trees. Estanislaa, Estanislao's tall wife who had been watching from their u-macha, went to the river, giving Estanislao a significant look in passing.

When she was out of sight, Grizzly Hair asked Estanislao, "Doesn't *Dios* want you to dance?"

"Not gentile dances."

"Does *Dios* have his own kind of dances?"

"No. No dances."

A barren existence. "But we danced together at the mission, you and I." *After my woman was buried.*

"I'm through with that now. I want to go to the *Cielo* when I die."

"Where is that?"

"In the sky with María, José, Jesús and *Dios*, a place of power and riches and *gloria*."

"Are you still a friend of Padre Durán?"

"Yes." A speedy response, and not what Grizzly Hair wanted.

"Yet you offered to help me escape."

"I shouldn't have. I could lose my *paseos*." He closed his eyes. "It's good you left without my help."

"I delivered your message about the fleas jumping off the wolf. What did that mean?"

Estanislao looked at him. The sad lines down his cheeks spread as he smiled in his closed-lipped way. "It means you'd better keep that in your gullet."

Was that a threat? It seemed Estanislao had changed his mind about important matters. Discouragement percolated into Grizzly Hair along with the heat, like the fish giving up hope in the warm pools of the river. He had expected too much of Estanislao. This was no angry rebel, no *insurgente*. Would black hats arrive with Cipriano? Even the sleepy trees seemed to be conspirators in a waiting ambush. But no, he realized. A man wouldn't lay a trap for his own father.

Estanislaa returned to their u-macha with a dripping basket. Estanislao lay on his back as if asleep.

"How is my friend Bowstring?" Grizzly Hair asked him.

"You mean José Francisco? The one who married Teresa?"

"Yes."

"He is well. The best flute player I ever heard. Good singer too. Padre Durán features him. He sang for the Governor in Monterey."

Estanislaa said, "José and Teresa are like doves in a nest."

Bowstring was happy. He couldn't imagine that, in the mission, but it made him feel better. "Does she have a baby?"

"Maybe in her blood," Estanislaa poured water into another basket.

Suddenly recalling Lame Beaver's request, he turned to Estanislao. "I have a message for him. His brother misses him. He wants him to return to the home place so they can hunt together. Can you deliver that?"

"I will tell him. But Padre Durán doesn't grant *paseos* to people of questionable loyalty." He paused. "He was your friend and you are a fugitive. So I doubt José will get one."

Grizzly Hair realized that his escape had hurt Bowstring. "Was he questioned after I left?"

"For a long time."

"Did they use iron thumb squeezers on him?"

"No."

Greatly relieved, he said, "I'll bet they sent neophyte trackers to hunt for me."

"The next day. Then after several sleeps they sent Presidio soldiers to hunt along the trail of the Valley of the Sun. You are good. You hide well." Spoken without emotion.

"Will you tell Padre Durán I was here?"

"In confession."

That disgusted him. "I'll disappear again."

"Suit yourself, but I'm not going back until after First Rain."

Feeling bad in his stomach, Grizzly Hair went to the sweathouse, which, not having been heated for several sleeps, felt a little cooler than the outside air, and the flies weren't as numerous. The napping men shifted. Quinconul opened his eyes.

Grizzly Hair lay down beside him, and after a while said in a low voice, "Your nephew is an interesting man."

"Talk straight."

"Maybe he is too friendly with the *Españoles.*"

Quinconul grunted, turned away and said, "Talk after eating."

After supper, under a sickly yellow sky, they walked past stretches of stinking mud and dead river ponds that were pocked and punched by unfathomable numbers of hooves and paws. "Don't worry about my nephew," said Quinconul. "He is always this way when he first comes from the mission. Give him time. My brother shouldn't push him so fast."

Nevertheless Grizzly Hair watched to be sure no one left the village. He considered leaving, but an intriguing fragment of conversation came to his ears. Estanislao was speaking rapidly in a low voice to Sucais. Their tongue was difficult and they weren't enunciating well. The name Tuol came through more than once, a headman from the next river south, and "black hats." Then he heard Estanislao say in a firm tone, ". . . not let any injury be done to the padres."

Something was afoot. He couldn't leave now.

Then a runner—a man Grizzly Hair recognized, no friend of the black hats—invited them all to a big time at Domingo's place. Several sleeps later the entire village walked downstream, Estanislao ahead with his father. They swam the river, now so low that Grizzly Hair waded across, and entered the lush jungle that was almost an island. This was where he had first met Missouri. He felt the power of the place before he saw the people. Alders bowed under the weight of the grapevines. Mounds of berry canes and masses of deadfall teemed with hiding animals. The smell of earth magic enveloped him, and he realized this was the ideal place for war.

Several twenties of people were already there. Estanislao and Sucais greeted Cipriano, an *alcalde* from Mission Santa Clara. By the way they talked, Grizzly Hair knew they were related.

At first he didn't recognize the men standing around in the shadows. Then, to his surprise, he realized they were Gabriel's men—here with neophytes on *paseo.* It didn't seem possible that neophytes and *cimarrones* would celebrate the spirits together. In his faded black hat and thigh-length shirt, Gabriel stepped from the trees and came toward Grizzly Hair. Burly as ever, he slapped Grizzly Hair's shoulder and smiled into his face like an *Español.*

"*Cimarrones* dancing with mission neophytes?" Grizzly Hair said by way of greeting. "Something smells funny."

"Hah!" Gabriel barked. "You are not so *inocente* now. And you speak my tongue much better. I heard you lost your woman and had a bad time in the mission."

"Not good" was all he said. The man was as rude as ever, to mention that.

Gabriel's men gathered around and Grizzly Hair greeted each one. Old Matías was not among them—still in the mission, somebody said. There were many other people here too, some partly dressed in mission clothes, others naked. He met gentiles from south and eastward. Some of the men were hiding behind their smiles, as the animals hid in the trees. Fortunately, Grizzly Hair thought, the big time would likely loosen tongues.

The feast was huge and delicious. He had missed the kind of food women prepared. From the earth pit came herbed, salted meat. He got into a joking competition with some of the men over who could eat the most elk, and almost couldn't walk when the ceremonial fire was lit on the plain outside the river jungle.

Cipriano's dance doctor started the dance and, to Grizzly Hair's surprise, Estanislao danced along with everyone else. The power of this place had captured him. But would it last?

Much later, the dance doctor raised his arms and old people lay down on the pulverized grass to sleep where they collapsed. Hoping to talk with him alone, Grizzly Hair followed Estanislao down the path to the river, but Estanislaa stayed close beside him. The night was warm and a sliver of mother moon glinted faintly on the river. The welcoming scent of water and the breathing jungle pervaded all Grizzly Hair's senses. He waded in. As the river rose around his waist and caressed him, he suddenly remembered Oak Gall swimming with him at the home river and for a moment felt her limbs wrap fluidly around him. Her soul was here, still haunting him. Choked with loss and the effort to forget, he quietly beseeched mother moon to help him ignore her so she could leave. She needed to go to the land of the immortals, and maybe if he no longer welcomed her to follow him around, she could start on her spirit journey, though her bones lay in strange earth.

Other people splashed in and swam to the opposite shore. He swam toward their laughter. Except for the laughter and the scant moonlight and the campfires of the immortals brilliantly encrusting the night dome, he wouldn't have seen the men sitting on the ledge of a cutbank with their feet dangling in the dark water. He sat at the end of the line. The man beside him raised something to his lips, swallowed several times, touched Grizzly Hair's arm and offered the skin bag.

He took it and drank a swallow. Unprepared for the sting in his nose and throat as the fiery liquid burned into him, he coughed violently and stuck out his tongue, allowing air to pass. Handing the skin back, he asked in the tongue of the Lakisumne, "What is this?"

"*Agua diente,*" said the smiling voice. Water with teeth.

Well named, Grizzly Hair was thinking when the next man up the line said, "No. *Agua ardiente.*" Fiery water. Water of hot passion.

Aguardiente. His bones softened and he felt a release from the tight trembling that had overcome him during the encounter with Oak Gall. A voice up the line was saying, ". . .sold my mission blanket and shirt for this. It's good, no?"

They talked about the men who made *aguardiente* in a little house in the pueblo. Several men commented on how the honey enhanced the flavor. Appreciative grunts followed each utterance. After a while the *bota* came back to Grizzly Hair. He swallowed carefully this time and passed it back. If this drink came from rotten grapes, it didn't taste like it. It was clear and sharp and not at all scummy. The fierce fumes cleansed his nose and he smelled everything more keenly—the hair of the man next to him, the earth they sat on, and the sweet scent of the night-blooming flowers. He also felt a sudden bond with these laughing men. This drink had power. It made him laugh, and he looked forward to it each time the *bota* returned.

Talk shifted to the missions and the various punishments for various misdeeds. Sergeant Sanchez was mentioned. "Little Pile of Shit," somebody added.

"No," brayed another, "Big Pile of Shit."

"No," said the first, "he is a little man. I have seen him pee." Laughter crackled in the quiet night as Grizzly Hair recalled the headman of the soldiers who had herded him and Oak Gall and Bowstring to the mission.

Quiet returned to the riverbank, then a man growled, "I'd like to bury them all in sand and kick their heads off with their own boots."

Other brutal punishments were suggested.

Grizzly Hair joined in. "I think we should lay a trap for them. This is a good place, here at Domingo's. We could lure them in by sending runners to tell them exactly what we think of them, then when they come in for us, jump out of hiding and kill them.

Silence followed, then chuckles. Somebody said, "Ooo-weee!"

"I like it," said a quiet voice.

"He's one of us."

"Where do you come from?" asked a man leaning out of line to look at him.

"To the north. The river of the Cosumne." The *bota* returned and he prepared for a big swallow, but only a few drops landed on his tongue. "It's gone," he said, letting his disappointment be heard.

Groans moved up the line and he handed the bag back. A little later a man dove in the water. Others followed, swimming to the village side. They all did. Grizzly Hair sat alone listening to the river, seeing its dark dips and peaks in the starlight. Later he swam across and felt his way up the narrow trail, brushing past unseen leaves.

He bumped into somebody. A man said, "Who is it?" Estanislao's voice.

"Your friend from the mission, Juan." It didn't feel like a real name and he spoke it without discomfort.

"Aha, Juan Gustavus. You should get a woman."

That struck him wrong and he didn't feel like bantering. "Juan Gustavus is not my name."

"No?"

"No." The *aguardiente* spoke boldly. "I saw you dancing. Padre Durán wouldn't like that."

"Probably not."

"But you will tell him."

"Yes."

This seemed stupid, and equally stupid to expect such a man to be his ally. Intending to leave, he took a step past Estanislao, but stopped when he heard: "My uncle says you think I like the soldiers. But I do not like them. I hate what they do."

"But Padre Durán likes them and likes what they do."

"Not always. He tolerates them. Sometimes he is angry at them. He tries to cover his feelings, but an *Español* doesn't know how to do that."

This sounded deliberately confusing. "Did your friends tell you what I just said about a war?"

"Yes."

Of course. And he would tell Padre Durán. He took another step, determined to pass by Estanislao on this dark trail and all the other trails of his life.

Estanislao grabbed his arm with a grip that instantly brought to mind the way he'd held him while the black hat kneed him in the groin so he couldn't take Oak Gall from the woman's house. "Take your hand off me," he said.

Slowly releasing his grip, Estanislao said, "God wants *Christianos* to live like Jesús and María and Santo Francisco—gentle, kind spirits. They don't whip people. They don't force others to do it for them. My friend, we need to talk. Let us do it after the sleep when the *aguardiente* has gone through you."

"I don't talk to meadowlarks." Meadowlark sang whatever came to his silly mind. It made Grizzly Hair dizzy to listen to him.

Estanislao snorted at the insult. "Maybe we should talk now."

"No." He didn't want to talk now, not ever. He turned too quickly and his head reeled as though he'd been spinning. He needed to lie down. One more night in the sweathouse would feel good. Then, out of nowhere, he heard what Two Falcons would say: *If you want to hunt snakes, learn from the snakes.* "Talk after the sleep," he grumbled. Estanislao was as close as he was likely to get to the *Españoles,* without being whipped.

49

Hard light in the entrance of the sweathouse hurt his eyes as he cracked them open. He was not well. There had been a rumble—not the man in his dream slapping the ground, but horse hooves. Nauseating bile burped up his throat and his limbs tightened with fear. Had the loyal neophytes laid a trap?

He watched Estanislao, Cipriano, Gabriel and the other men grab their bows and quivers from the wall and crouch-walk toward the entrance, slipping the loops over the ends—just as fearful. No one was grabbing anyone else. Somewhat relieved, he took his bow and quiver and stayed in the midst of the crowd as they peered outside. Seeing nothing, he crept along with the men around the outside of the tule structure. By the time he got to a place where he could see the dripping horse, a naked rider with scant flesh on his bones was giving the runner's password. No other men or horses were there. Grizzly Hair breathed easier to see Domingo and Gabriel—surely wanted by the black hats more than he—rising to full height and stepping out to greet the *Indio.*

Dismounting, the skinny runner planted his feet and called out in the Spanish tongue—the voice of a herald: "The people of Andrés and Barnabé and others are fighting in three missions. They captured the guns and are holding off the soldiers in Santa Barbara, Santa Ynez and Purísimo."

Thunderstruck, Grizzly Hair stared at the man. How far south was Santa Barbara? That was the mission Egorov most wanted.

"Our peoples need your help," the runner shouted, turning back and forth so all could hear. "They would rather die than surrender. I have ridden all this way in six sleeps. My first horse died under me. He," he gestured to the blowing animal at the end of his reins, "was given to me at the Lake of the Tulares so I could come quickly to you." He glanced eagerly around at the men. "The battle is intense in all three missions. Our people are shooting with bows and guns from behind mission pillars. We need your help."

Women and children came from the u-machas. Estanislao asked levelly, "What started it?"

"People were hungry. Some were taking extra food. The guards whipped a man to death with the *cuarta de hierro*. Everyone was angry."

"Whipped him to death?" Estanislao repeated incredulously.

"Yes."

"Are you sure?"

"Everyone knows why he died."

Estanislao's expression of sorrow changed to anger. His nostrils visibly expanded with each breath and his eyes burned hot as coals.

Gabriel barked out, "It's stupid to fight in a mission where you are trapped. Why didn't they go to the hills where they could shoot from cover, and escape." His sleep-tangled hair gave him the look of Fadre Fortuni's angriest demon.

The runner shouted, "A Russian told us to take control of the missions."

Grizzly Hair's senses sat up.

Gabriel snorted, "And if he tells you to go out and kiss the soldiers, I suppose you'll do that too?"

"Egorov understands this kind of war," the runner shot back, stunning Grizzly Hair into the realization that Egorov had ridden south without notifying the runners. Pomponio would have sent word to Lame Beaver, who would have located Grizzly Hair.

"How long have your people been fighting?" Estanislao asked.

The runner looked up into the oaks, then around at the men. "At the half moon, we will be fighting about three moons." That long! Grizzly Hair figured the half moon would rise in about ten sleeps.

"Why didn't you ask for help earlier?" Estanislao asked.

"We were winning. Until the soldiers from Monterey Presidio arrived. We stole the guns from the guard house and Egorov taught us to shoot them. He said the soldiers from Monterey Presidio would be busy fighting you here in the north, so it was a perfect time. But I see you are having a big time instead." The accusative undertone silenced the crowd and they looked questions at one another.

Horrified, Grizzly Hair wondered if Egorov had revealed their talk about the missions and the land between them. He hadn't explained it.

There hadn't been time to figure out who could be trusted.

Estanislao was asking, "Why would a Russian think we were fighting here in the north?"

Grizzly Hair held his breath.

"He heard talk," the runner said. "Someone here must have tricked him."

"Who is this Egorov?" Tuol asked.

As the runner told about the Undersea People and their place on the northern coast, questions burned in Grizzly Hair's mind. Who had translated? Katya didn't speak Spanish. How many other Russians had gone to Santa Barbara?

In the sudden silence a dove sang three downward coos. The runner also lowered his voice, but every word cut into Grizzly Hair: "The soldiers from Monterey Presidio went to Santa Barbara with their guns and a terrible cannon, then everything went bad. I escaped in the night to come here. We were running out of food and *amunición*. Guns were exploding in the faces of our men. The cannons were chewing through the mission walls. All around people lay bleeding and dying. I rode all this way to ask for your help."

Would Grizzly Hair be blamed for those deaths? He wanted to step up beside the runner and say that Egorov had tricked him, not the reverse. But, many ears listened—people released from the missions because of the drought and because the padres trusted them, and for no other reason. Grizzly Hair stood quietly in the murmuring crowd as more questions were asked and answered. Hearing nothing to implicate him, he turned his thoughts to what should be done now. Andrés and Barnabé thought it was a good time to fight if there was war in the north. This reasoning held in the reverse. It was a good time to make war while they were fighting in the south. The black hats would be divided.

Gabriel barked over the crowd. "I will ride down there with my men and attack the *cabrones* from behind. Ride with me, all of you. Show you are *hombres!*"

Excitement sparked through the crowd. Acting as headman, Estanislao stepped up beside the runner and gave the nod to Tuol.

Tuol said, "Gabriel's men should go south. But maybe the rest of us should go to Monterey Presidio. The soldiers are gone. Their presidio is unguarded. Then when the San Francisco black hats go down there to see what's happening, we'll shoot them with their friends' cannons."

Domingo shouted, "Ho! That would pull the Monterey soldiers away from Santa Barbara, back to their own place. We would greet them with a good *canonado.*"

People laughed. Grizzly Hair could hardly believe their readiness for war. Were they serious? Sometimes people played elaborate hoaxs. His weak grasp of Spanish left him uncertain.

Estanislao's expression had changed to jaw-twitching resolve, and he spoke forcefully. "We'd be spread too thin, fighting in Monterey and Santa Barbara. But we should do something to help."

We, we, we. Amazed and surer with each statement that this was no hoax, Grizzly Hair spoke to Estanislao, but in a voice meant to be heard by the crowd:

"We could lure the black hats here, where there is good cover and soft earth to dig trenches." Hearing words of approval—the men of the *aguardiente?*—he continued, "Monterey is a strange place and we don't know how to shoot cannons. They might blow up in our faces. Here we can use our own weapons and the power of this place. The soldiers in San Francisco Presidio are very few. We could defeat them. That would draw the Monterey soldiers from Santa Barbara. We could defeat them too. Then if the southern people win, we *Indios* would have defeated three of the four presidios in Alta California."

"Ho!" sounded here and there.

"But man," the runner objected, "that would take too long. My people are dying now. Anybody left alive will be punished severely. Please go down there, all of you. We need you down there. Now."

"This is too sudden," said a hefty man with an impressive topknot pierced by a cannon bone. The villages related to me are not ready yet. Neither are our trading friends to the east."

Yet. War talk had indeed been underway—*the fleas will jump off the wolf*—but everyone had been careful, until now.

A man was saying, "You mission neophytes must stay here with us, or they'll force you to fight for them. Estanislao and Cipriano, tell the neophytes to steal horses and ride to Santa Barbara with us. They'll listen to you."

Estanislao appeared to be in deep thought. Cipriano, who was about Estanislao's age, cleared his throat. "First we should talk about whether to fight. We must not bring punishment to the neophytes for nothing. However, if we do fight, we must win. But I don't see how we can win now. From the time this runner left to the time anybody gets down there, they could all be dead. They should have talked to us first, not a Russian. Now the guards will reach for their *cuartas* very fast. In the north and the south. Our neophytes in Mission Santa Clara are not ready to make war. We must not make this worse for them." His gaunt face looked ever more pained, the lines pulling in two directions.

"He is right," said a man who until now had been quiet. "We must talk about whether to do this. This is very serious."

"Crazy talk," said another.

"No, not crazy," shouted the runner, his bony ribs expanding and contracting. "You must help, but help us down there where the fighting is. Don't waste time."

Burning with the knowledge that his meeting with Egorov had helped spark this war, Grizzly Hair looked inside the runner's expression and was persuaded. To the crowd he said, "Yes, we should go to Santa Barbara. I hope Estanislao and Cipriano convince the mission neophytes to fight with us, but we shouldn't wait for them. They'll join us faster if they hear we are fighting, just as some of you were more willing when you heard they were fighting in Santa Barbara. Gabriel, you and your men ride south. I will ride back to my place and send a runner to gather warriors from other places. I know where they are." His mind flew as he spoke. "I will return in five sleeps with men and arrows and we will follow Gabriel's tracks to Santa Barbara. Others will follow behind me. Pomponio will bring two twenties, and the Cosumne and Muquelumne will help."

The names of Pomponio and Little Cos bumped around the crowd as if they were known. Though some men looked skeptical, Grizzly Hair was relieved that the talk that followed was not about whether to fight, but how. Most agreed to go to Santa Barbara. Women brought cold nu-pah and as they all ate, the runner gulped it as though he hadn't eaten for many sleeps. Estanislaa pointed out that the neophytes in the northern missions were hungry too, as they were in Santa Barbara, and their tempers were also short. She said women were angry to see many barrels of maize and beans sent to the presidio. "We ask ourselves why we should work so hard to grow food only to give it to those who do not grow their own. We are told the black hats have large families and their children are hungry. But mission children are hungry too. I think many women would leave the mission and fight now."

Bravely spoken, Grizzly Hair thought. He hoped she would convince her husband.

Before he rode out, he motioned Estanislao into the trees. Time was short and Grizzly Hair couldn't hear Estanislao's music yet. At times he wondered if Estonislao was crazy. He needed to trust this ally better. He started with the Cosumne. "What kind of people are they?"

"They have resisted all attempts to get them to the mission."

"Good." He went to the problem. "You told me Padre Durán doesn't like the black hats to injure people. You said *Christianos* are gentle people who are sorry the soldiers tortured and killed Jesús. Then why does Padre Durán tell his black hats to whip people? Like the boy who was trying to please him?"

"Antonio? The boy who reports when neophytes are dying?" Seeing the nod he said, "Antonio was slow and a woman went to hell. Father had him whipped to make him hurry faster next time."

"Then Padre Durán thinks it's good to hurt people. Maybe the padre in Santa Barbara thought it was good to whip the man who died." This contradicted what Estanislao had said before.

Estanislao's eyes were level with his—a man his height—and his voice had a confidential, almost seductive tone, as though he were amused to be testing Grizzly Hair while Grizzly Hair tested him. "Punishment is good when it brings better behavior. God is displeased when a boy's slowness makes *Christianos* go to hell. Don't forget, Antonio can say his prayers later and go to heaven, but the souls in hell cannot. It's too late for them." His wide lips twitched in the ghost of a smile. "But if people are punished for no good reason, *Dios* is angry."

"You said *Dios* has all the power." He waited for the nod. "Then why can't he show people the way to heaven without depending on a boy to run faster?"

A slight flinch was followed by silence, then the amused, seductive tone continued. "The death-prayer wasn't said. And if God doesn't hear it, *el Diablo* grabs the dead and throws them into his fire. Then even God can't get them out."

"Then, *el Diablo* is more powerful."

"He fools people, shoots them with bad medicine and they do *pecados*, sins. He doesn't want people to go to heaven."

Like a clever doctor. *Dios*, on the other hand, seemed weak and stupid. A truly powerful spirit would outsmart *el Diablo*. Grizzly Hair returned to the main point. "Does Padre Durán decide who to punish and what kind of punishment?"

"All padres do, at their own missions. They do it for *Dios*. They do the *trabajo* of *Dios* on earth." Why did Estanislao seem slightly amused?

"Are the padres men of knowledge?"

"Isn't that obvious? They came to this land and showed people how to make things no human has ever seen before?"

"Do they talk to Condor? Raven?"

"Maybe. I don't ask people about their spirit allies. Why do you want to know?" An edge there.

It had been a prying question, but Grizzly Hair still wasn't sure whether to trust this man. "The long robes don't know that dancing brings power."

"Padre Durán says it brings no power."

"But you know better."

Estanislao turned his head to look at the distance and said in a quiet voice, "Yes." No amusement there.

"Then you know something he doesn't know. Maybe he's wrong about *Dios*. He makes mistakes when he decides whom to whip."

"Sometimes he makes mistakes, but he prays to *Dios* to forgive his sins."

"The Devil makes him sin too?"

"Everybody sins. They ask to be forgiven."

"Padre Durán didn't ask my forgiveness when he had me whipped."

Estanislao brows shot up. "I didn't either, did I?"

"No."

"Well, I am sorry. Forgive me. I'd like us to be friends."

But that wasn't enough. "If Padre Durán ordered me whipped again, would you tie me up for it?"

"No. Not if I knew it was a mistake."

If. "Mistake or not," he said with rising volume he couldn't stop, "my friends don't tie me up to be whipped. My friends don't pull my head back so a black hat can knee me in the groin. My friends don't whisper to Padre Durán where I can be found."

Looking down, Estanislao said softly, "I hate the floggings. I've told Father more than once. I refused to wield the *cuarta.*"

Grizzly Hair waited, but knew that was all he'd get. He went to the other matter. "I think *Dios* would be happy if we punished the black hats and scared them out of this land."

Estanislao blew air. "Padre Durán would be angry."

"*Dios,* I said. He would be happy."

"People like us don't know how *Dios* feels. But Padre Durán talks to Him. He knows."

"But he makes mistakes. *El Diablo* fools him and shoots him with bad medicine. He doesn't know dancing brings power. Look, man, you said *Christianos* want people punished so they'll behave better. I think only we *Indios* can punish the *soldados.* You said *Dios* and María want people to be kind. The *soldados* are not kind. Surely *Dios* and María want them to leave so the *Indio* peoples can live in peace. Then we could celebrate *Dios,* Jesús and María and the dead *santos* along with our own spirits. And the people in the missions could dance for them. We should help the Santa Barbara people punish the black hats and chase them away."

As Estanislao looked into the vine-laden trees, the amused look, which he seemed to wear as a kind of armor, dropped from his face. "I think *Dios* wants the missions and everything in them to belong to us *Indios,*" he said. "The padres want that too. Padre Durán told me this will happen. The governor says *Indios* should be free to come and go where they want, and not be forced to work in the missions if they don't want to. But all the time the black hats are ready with their *cuartas* and *fusiles* and that makes it too easy for things to stay the same." His normally steady voice rose with emotion. "But things are not the same; punishments and *expediciones* are getting worse. Sometimes the soldiers do not listen to the padres when they beg for *piedad and merced* toward the *Indios.* Sometimes the guards tell lies to the padres about what neophytes have done. Sometimes they bribe the old woman to let women out of the *monjería* for them, but not for *Indios.* Yes, I think we should chase the black hats from this land. That's why I'm going to Santa Barbara."

More than a little relieved, Grizzly Hair placed a hand on Estanislao's shoulder. "Are you my friend?"

Estanislao put a dry palm on Grizzly Hair's opposite shoulder. "I am your friend, and ally."

"Good. Will you lead the neophytes from the mission?"

Estanislao hesitated. "Yes. But we must not hurt Padre Durán in any way."

Grizzly Hair took back his hand and steadied his tone. "Then you must not tell him where to find me or any other *Indios.*"

Estanislao nodded. "I will not."

Was he singing like a meadowlark? He didn't seem crazy—difficult to understand, but not completely scrambled. And if no risks were taken, nothing would be accomplished. Sucais believed his son had power, and Estanislao certainly had strong influence with mission people. He also had good runners. Deciding to trust him, Grizzly Hair put out a hand and said, "This is how Russians make agreements."

As he showed Estanislao how to grasp hands and move them up and down, restraint returned to Estanislao's voice, and his wide lips straightened in amusement. "You know the Undersea People."

"I figured you knew that."

Estanislao scratched a leg. "Maybe." The twinkle deepened.

Had his informants heard the true story? Grizzly Hair explained, "Egorov said he'd wait to hear from me. We never talked about where the war should be held. I was waiting to tell you about him when you came from the mission. I didn't because you sounded too much like an *Español.* Now I've learned that Egorov went to Santa Barbara without telling my runners. He can't be trusted." Unable to hide his disappointment, he added, "I think we could have defeated the *soldados* in three *presidios* if he had."

"Maybe." The amusement left Estanislao's face. "But the missions should belong to *Indios,* not Undersea People." Clearly aware of that talk, he continued, "Undersea People dislike the padres. We must protect them from harm or *Dios* will strike us dead."

Grizzly Hair took a breath. "Egorov said he would bring friends to fight with us. How many did he take to Santa Barbara?"

"Only himself."

"I made no promises about giving him missions." He looked at this man, whom he needed as an ally. "*Hombre,* we are beginning a dangerous journey together—plenty dangerous without doubting each other. I was surprised to hear you had talked of war here, and did not tell me. I did some things you didn't know about. But now we must run together like wolves. We must trust each other. We both need to know what the other is doing, and what we are hearing from our runners. In the mission you told me *Indios* were one people. Let's you and I be brothers."

The wide straight lips parted slightly as Estanislao dipped his head, then thrust out a hand. "Wolf brothers." His large hand wrapped around Grizzly

Hair's and as they shook, he continued. "I knew you'd be a good warrior. You bring the gentiles to war and I'll bring the neophytes. Together we will teach the *soldados* a lesson, and the padres will see that they don't need black hats standing over *Indios* with *cuartas*."

Grizzly Hair would trust him because he had to, but he would remember that his wolf brother had a long-robed friend in the mission.

Making up for lost time, he galloped Morena up an old trail a little east of the line where the tulares met the oak-grasslands. A vast expanse of dancing sandhill cranes ignored the horse. Only those in danger of being struck by the hooves bothered to flutter up. After the horse passed, they settled back into their graceful dances, males and females paired. He crossed the first stream over a bridge of nearly dry mud between ponds, and when the trees thinned, saw the Spirit Peak floating in a blue haze on his left. It remained in his eyes as he continued north through more grazing cranes than could be seen by one man. This was a desperate effort, with so many people under siege by the black hats of two presidios. Santa Barbara was at least six sleeps away from Domingo's place. If only he could fly like Hummingbird! Twelve sleeps was a long time for the Santa Barbarans to hold out—if indeed they were still holding out—but a short time for Grizzly Hair to do all he needed. He and the men he collected would be exhausted after traveling so far, most of them running on foot. But if *Indios* were ever to fight together, it was now.

The Cosumne herald announced him. The trickle of a stream that came from the northeast was sad, yet the oak people stood dark and powerful. Father sun was high, and curious people gathered around.

Little Cos asked, "Where are you going?"

"Upstream to my home place to collect warriors. I'd like you and your men to join us."

The Cosumne invited him to sit and talk. They were eager listeners and before he left, twelve men agreed to go to Santa Barbara, Juan among them. Juan said he knew the way and they would start immediately. This pleased Grizzly Hair, for he and his warriors would be able to ride a more direct path south instead of veering west to the Cosumne. Older men agreed to make arrows.

At last he topped the hill overlooking the playing field. Morena was foaming with perspiration, mounds of lather standing on her flanks. He reined, got off and looked at her sucking, blowing nostrils. "Good horse," he told her, stroking her slick neck. Not a hair was dry, not even her ears. Her big sides swelled and contracted. Recalling that a horse had died beneath the runner from Santa Barbara, he realized he should be more careful. It was hot and she had a baby in her blood. He decided to let her rest while he ran on foot to Poo-soo-ne and Libayto.

Leading her down the hill, he also realized that time-of-pretending would slow him down. People would die because of a courtesy. There simply wasn't time. However he needn't shock those who wouldn't talk to him anyway—Red Sun, Nettles and Sick Rat—or those with whom he need not speak.

He walked into the village center, pretending to ignore everyone who happened to be there. Etumu, who had a lap full of feathers, was bending and snapping quills onto a netting. When she looked up, a feather whose quill she had partially bent came loose and, released from tension, flew like the duck from which it had been plucked. He walked past her and saw Falls-off-House's narrow shoulders through the oaks. Falls-off-House was honing a bone at the chaw'se in the special mortar that allowed a hand to grip a bone while turning the end of it in a narrow crevice. He pretended to be engrossed in what he was doing, though clearly he saw Grizzly Hair come around to face him. Pretty Duck, who had grown fleshier, was pounding acorns in the next mortar hole.

He finally caught Falls-off-House's attention and motioned him to follow. Relieved to hear footsteps behind, he walked upstream of the bathing place to the black walnut trees, and stopped. Falls-off-House came around, asking in amazement, "What are you doing, man?" He glanced back toward the village like a boy afraid of being caught.

Grizzly Hair explained the urgency of the situation and asked him to fetch Two Falcons and Lame Beaver. "Bring anyone else you think would join us."

By the time he had bathed in the slow-moving water, his three friends had assembled under the trees. Grizzly Hair explained what was happening in Santa Barbara and how important it was for *Indios* to join forces and fight together. Two Falcons questioned him on several points, but in the end the three agreed to go with him to Santa Barbara. They also agreed to talk for him with the other men and to prepare a cache of arrows. Meanwhile Grizzly Hair would run to Poo-see-ne and Libayto, who would send runners to Topal, Putah, Magma, Cross-eyed Bear and Pomponio.

He was leaving, crossing the playing field, when he saw Etumu combing Morena with a stick—pulling out old clumps of foamy hair. To his surprise she looked at him, not pretending, and trotted on the diagonal to meet him, still holding the nubby, hairy stick. "Leaving again?" she asked.

He felt embarrassed, talking to her when it wasn't necessary. "I will be back in two sleeps," he said, "but only long enough to collect the men of the umne. Ask Lame Beaver. He'll explain." There was something unfathomable in her eyes. "Is Grandmother well?"

Her voice was little. "She sings each day to the river baby spirit."

"Then she is well. Are *you* well?"

Her eyes flooded and she turned away.

Perhaps not. Again he felt the desire to protect her from all the hurts in the world. Yet he'd been foolhardy to ignore the way her parents felt about him. He touched her little shoulder and turned to leave.

"Wait," she said. "I will get you some traveling food." She ran back toward her u-macha. Already hungry, he realized that by the time he got to Poo-soo-ne's place, he'd be famished. Etumu was taking care of him. He wasn't sure how he felt about that. Quickly she returned with dried salmon, which he gratefully accepted.

Gasping for breath she said, "I won't let the children pester Morena too much." Children had gathered a few steps back from the horse.

"That would be nice," he said hearing Etumu's unusual music with its sparks of lightning. Awkwardly he said, "Morena has a baby in her blood." Then he recalled that Etumu already knew it.

She lingered in his mind on the way to the villages of Kadeema and Sek. Maybe he should have asked Lame Beaver to have his mother look at Etumu. Hummingbird Tailfeather was good with herbs, though not as good as. . . Stopping the image of his mother, he ran at a steady pace.

50

Twenty-two men and eight women bent under full carrying baskets accompanied Grizzly Hair when he returned to the home place. The women were determined that their men would have nu-pah to start each new sun. They swung the baskets off their backs and rubbed their foreheads where the thongs had made grooves despite the grass caps. Two Falcons, Lame Beaver and Falls-off-House walked toward him, not pretending. Nor was Etumu. She stood watching from the side of the field.

The visiting women removed cooking stones and food from their baskets while the men bent willows to make night shelters beside the field. Their women left in search of firewood.

Grizzly Hair was glad to see Morning Owl and Raven Feather coming to greet them too, followed by most of the umne. The time apart had been short, and everyone knew some hadn't followed custom the last time he'd been there, so it felt strange and loose. People looked around with questioning faces, unsure how to behave. Nothing like this had happened before.

Etumu stepped into the circle of home men, and said, "While you were gone, many arrows were made."

Grizzly Hair gave Two Falcons an appreciative nod.

Lame Beaver asked, "Is Pomponio here?"

"No. I didn't go that far. Topal's runner will contact him and Cross-eyed Bear and others. They will travel south by boat across the big bay. Pomponio's men know how to find Santa Barbara."

Running Quail inserted himself stiffly into the circle beside his son Lame Beaver. Despite the reparation beads, he obviously felt uncomfortable with Grizzly Hair, but his presence indicated he was trying, and Grizzly Hair appreciated it.

Sick Rat called over several heads, "Only idiots would travel to the end of the world to attack evil spirits with magic shooters."

Fortunately the visiting people didn't understand the home tongue.The hurt showed in Two Falcons' eyes, that his own son would call him an idiot. Or did Sick Rat know Two Falcons would go? The umne stood in confusion, watching the breakdown of polite behavior. Sick Rat, Grizzly Hair knew, would do all he could to make it hard to convince the home men to go to war. But then, when he thought of it, Santa Barbara was indeed like the other side of the world, and the reluctance of the umne was not Sick Rat's fault.

When suppers were ready, most of the umne returned by twos and threes to the fires by their u-machas. It was as if a giant had split the people; those who thought Grizzly Hair worthy of being followed ate with the guests. The others ate at the usual place. If this were evidence of how many his friends had recruited, few would join the warriors. Grizzly Hair ate with the water diggers from Libayto's place, as did Etumu, despite her mother's entreating glances. She had gathered bulbs of the kind Grizzly Hair liked and cooked them with duck in a fine new basket. The men took turns with the basket, scooping juicy handfuls, smacking with pleasure and handing it on. The stew tasted delicious, and Grizzly Hair felt proud to be hosting some of his warriors, though he had no claim to Etumu. When the basket came to her, she dipped her neatly curved fingers into the stew and inserted them into her mouth. Glancing sidelong at him from beneath her lashes, she took her time drawing her fingers out again.

He felt himself move, but couldn't entertain the thought with Red Sun so near. "How many of our men will go with us?" he asked Two Falcons, whose presence lent an air of importance to the fire.

"Most said they would wait and see."

"Wait and see what?"

"If you could actually persuade strange people to go with you. You have done that, but I still don't know how many will join us."

"I think my father will," Lame Beaver said.

Grizzly Hair showed his surprise. Running Quail was eating at his u-macha.

"This morning when he and I snared these ducks," Lame Beaver continued, "he said he'd like to kill the men who captured Bowstring. I think he wants to drive them away."

Could they succeed? It felt very strange to be eating supper on the playing field surrounded by people who spoke other tongues, yet were ready to die fighting with him. It seemed like a dream from which he would awaken. It was, of course, a dream of Condor, as everything was, but how would this piece of it end?

After the sleep, Grizzly Hair anxiously watched the home men come from the village center. Two Falcons, Lame Beaver, Running Quail, Falls-off-House, and the arrow knapper, Scorpion-on-Nose, all carried bows, quivers and extra bundles of arrows. Three good hunters and two strong young men joined him, but it was disappointing.

Morning Owl followed, but not with his bow. "Some of us are waiting to hear from our spirit allies," he explained. "Leave signs for us to follow, so we'll know where to go if we decide to come later." But Grizzly Hair knew they would not.

Again Etumu supplied him with traveling food. "Go with the protection of the spirits," she said, kneeling to rub his calf, apparently not worried who was watching. "I will watch over Morena and your grandmother."

Not knowing what to say, he petted her hair and listened to her music. "I will return," came out.

"This is a gamble," Grizzly Hair told the home men as they ran south across the dry grasslands, the others behind, all on foot. "The black hats could have won by now."

Trotting easily with his excess flesh jiggling, Two Falcons glanced over.

"It could all be for nothing," Grizzly Hair continued, "so many people going so far." Somehow it reminded him of Coyote's elaborate schemes, which tended to go sour. That's what made the stories funny. He ran in silence, reflecting that everyone had grown up hearing such tales. No wonder it was difficult to believe that something involving this many people could succeed. And yet here they were, all running with him.

One sleep later they arrived at Domingo's place. Earth magic and heavy vegetation quieted him as he walked the familiar pathway to the village center, the crows heralding. After the long run across brittle grass he felt tired to the bone, yet he'd only begun the journey. He looked at the women and the few older men who sat before their u-machas. They acknowledged him with their eyes, and acknowledged the strangers as they straggled in.

Addressing no one in particular he said, half in Spanish, half in Estanislao's tongue, "Did most of the men go right away, with the Santa Barbara runner?"

The women nodded, two of them pounding meal in wooden mortar bowls between their legs.

"Did Estanislao go to the mission?"

"They nodded."

"Has he led the mission neophytes out, to go to Santa Barbara?"

The women and two old men talked between themselves in their own tongue. He tried to distinguish the sounds. Then a woman jerked her head east and said, "Estanislao's people went back to his father's place, but Cucunichi stayed in the mission." She continued to pound.

"Stayed?"

The women nodded.

Grizzly Hair's stomach dropped. Did Padre Durán know of their war plans? Maybe black hats would be lying along the trail, like bobcats waiting for a line of quail. He caught Two Falcons' eye and motioned him into the trees. After explaining what he'd heard, he asked, "What do you think we should do? Send word to Estanislao to learn what he is doing? Run back to our homes and hide? Or continue to Santa Barbara?"

The master hunter turned his intelligent eyes upon him. "What would the black hats expect you to do?"

"Follow Gabriel's trail to Santa Barbara." But the real meaning came clear. "You think we should find another route."

"Yes. You told me that making war with the Santa Barbara people is important. You said it could drive the black hats from this land. Running Quail came with us to do that. He wants his son back."

"Maybe I depend too much on Estanislao."

"Maybe." Two Falcons looked at him fondly.

"I'm glad you are here with me," Grizzly Hair said.

Hunger slaked and aware of the quiet excitement that prevailed, Grizzly Hair and Two Falcons led the warriors and their women. All trotted away at a steady pace, following, at first, the tracks left by those who had gone before, but only long enough to see that it was the same trail Grizzly Hair had traveled with María. Eventually it would lead south to the Lake of the Tulares and over the southern mountains. According to an old man in Domingo's place, there was another way to Santa Barbara—a trail by the sea. Frequented by *Españoles*, it had good cover most of the way. They'd have to travel off the trail. The bundles of arrows would speak loudly if they were caught.

Leaving the valley trail, Grizzly Hair led the people at a fast pace up the path he had traveled down with María—through tilted, fractured rock faces streaked with veins of quartz, past the stones that resembled Coyote's brains, to the top of the mountain. They rested at the spring. A camp of *cimarrones* were there, two of whom picked up their bows and joined them as they trotted down the mountain.

Grizzly Hair recalled seeing Pueblo San José west of the mountain, so he turned south before it became visible, thus skirting the land of grazing longhorns. In the hills at the lower end of that valley, they turned west and entered a forest of *palos altos*. Ferns and herbs grew densely beneath the giants. They followed a trace through the dark forest, up and down difficult hills, until they looked down on a thin gray trail running north and south. West of that the trees and hills were backed by a profusion of coral and gold—father sun sinking. Pleased with the distance they had covered, Grizzly Hair stopped and pointed. "The sea isn't far over there. We should camp here."

Lame Beaver and Falls-off-House wanted to see the ocean, but heeded Grizzly Hair's warning not to run off at dusk. "You'll see it after the sleep," he promised.

The next morning, the excitement ever more palpable, Grizzly Hair led them southward along a rugged, wooded ridge within sight of the substantial trail below. A chilly mist shrouded everything. At times when he looked behind him, the fog obscured the women at the end of the line bent under their carrying baskets. "You won't see the ocean unless this fog clears," he told his friends. Below, the horse trail could be seen now and then, but rarely was anyone on it. A mission came into view in the distance. They skirted far around it and camped in the hills.

It was morning of the following day when three riders appeared on the trail. Grizzly Hair motioned the others back into the oaks and lay on his belly watching. The three horsemen rode slowly in and out of the fog. One was clearly a black hat. Naked men rode the other two horses, both of which appeared to be lame. The legs of one man hung south of his horse, the legs of the other hung north. Possibly *Indios* in leg irons.

Two Falcons and others lay watching beside him. The riders halted and a naked man slid off his horse. "What's happening?" Falls-off-House whispered, though a normal tone of voice would never be heard that far away.

"I don't know." The soldier dismounted and pulled his sword from its sheath. The other naked man also slid off his horse. From the stance, they were making water while the guard watched. When they were finished, the three talked. The soldier laid his sword on the ground and started to help one of the naked men get back on his horse—clearly the legs were shackled.

The prisoner put his shackled hands up as if to take the horse's mane, but turned and threw them over the soldier's head, hugging him tightly. He and the black hat staggered together. The other prisoner picked up the sword in two hands and ran it into the black hat's back. A cry pierced the distance, and the man pulled the sword out. All around, Grizzly Hair heard tongue clucks and other noises of astonishment. Never had he seen a person crumple to the ground who a moment before had been healthy.

The two shackled men now hopped around like frantic caterpillars—head and tail ends on the ground, midsections high. Finding what they were looking for, they quickly sat in the grass, one beating with a rock on what appeared to be the wrists of the other. The faint metallic ring of the blows could be heard.

Curiosity was getting the better of Grizzly Hair. "I'm going down," he told Two Falcons. "The rest of you should stay in hiding." Two Falcons agreed.

He carefully descended the low hill, around bushes and oaks, watching to be sure no riders appeared on the trail. The black hat lay still, possibly dead. The soul could be very dangerous. Drawing closer, he saw a thin man vigorously pounding with a rock upon the wrist irons of his bushy-haired companion. The latter stared down at his wrists, which were laid across an anvil rock. He resembled Pomponio, but that couldn't be. Forty men would have protected him, and Pomponio had the reputation of a man who could never be captured. The Bodega people had been definite about that.

Satisfied that no more black hats were in sight and keeping his ears attuned for the sound of hooves, he stepped from the trees and went nearer. It became obvious, he was horrified to see, that the man with the bushy hair was indeed Pomponio. A moment later Gonzalo succeeded in breaking the chain between Pomponio's hands. Gonzalo laid his wrists across the stone and Pomponio began beating on Gonzalo's irons—neither of them glancing Grizzly Hair's way.

Approaching by habit on the sides of his feet, Grizzly Hair asked, "Where are your other men?"

Their heads jerked up—faces streaked with sweat and dirt.

"*Hombre,*" Pomponio finally said, panting with shock. He pointed the stone at the dead man, then at the bushes beside the trail. "Hide that dung over there." He turned back and delivered a powerful blow to Gonzalo's shackles. The metal sprang open. Pomponio dropped the rock, scooted back on his hips and straightened his legs so his ankle irons lay over the flat rock.

In full agreement that the dead man should be quickly disposed of, Grizzly Hair swallowed his revulsion and fear of the soul and lifted the deadweight shoulders by the damp armpits, the thick black fabric of the foul-smelling coat. The head flopped back, open-mouthed, and the hat fell off. To the sound of hammering, he dragged the body through the bushes and scooped decaying leaves over it, breaking leafy branches to cover the terrified, glassy-eyed face with the trim mustache. Relieved to be back in the sunlight, he noticed muddy blood on his feet. He washed them in clean dirt and grass, scrubbing hard, then washed his hands. Circling Gonzalo and Pomponio—two determined men working fast—he squatted where he would see the soldier's soul when it rose, if it hadn't already done so, and heard his heart beating between the blows on the irons.

Pomponio said without looking up, "We were dancing at a nice fandango at Mission Soledad. Many pretty women. A neophyte coward betrayed us when we were coupling. What are you doing here?"

"Topal's runner went to your cave and told you."

The stone rang sharply off iron and stone. "I heard nothing from Topal."

Nada? It rang like the stone. Had Topal's man failed to run with the message? Then why was Pomponio at a fandango in Mission Soledad south of here? His stomach twisted, and consternation sounded in his voice. "I have twenty-four men and eight women with me. More than that ran ahead, and more are coming behind. We are going to Santa Barbara to help fight the black hats. You and your forty men were supposed to be on your way."

The irons sprang loose and Gonzalo—shackled below the knees—swung around and placed his knees over the anvil rock. Pomponio picked up the hammerstone, delivered a savage two-handed blow and said, "You might as well go home. The war's over. And that's my horse." He nodded at the saddled animal grazing with the two lame horses.

"What do you mean, the war's over?"

"The leaders have surrendered. Some of them are in irons doing hard labor. They'll sleep in the *calabozo* the rest of their lives."

They wouldn't live long. No man could. Believing yet disbelieving, he asked, "How do you know what happened in Santa Barbara?"

"I was there. The war had been going bad for a long time. We ran out of *amunición.* Gonzalo and I escaped in the night and started north."

We. Grizzly Hair felt the word as keenly as Gonzalo felt the pounding—gritting his teeth and gripping the grass on both sides of his hips. Pomponio had also gone to Santa Barbara without word to him. Neither he nor Egorov had respected him as a man, as an ally. He thought of Estanislao. This could explain why he hadn't led the neophytes south. His runners had told him what was happening.

"Those shits were good trackers," Pomponio continued, delivering another ringing blow. "They paid gentiles for information on the hiding places of the *insurgentes.* Gonzalo and I watched many people being herded back to the mission." He got up on his knees and came down harder with the rock. *Ching.* "They cried like children and begged the soldiers for *perdón* and *merced* and *piedad.*" Spat out like vomit.

It was over. He'd known this could happen, but hadn't expected to feel wrung out and empty. "I suppose all those people will be flogged."

Pomponio stopped to examine the stubborn iron chain, then came down on it again. "Padre Ripoll said he'd try to stop it, but. . ." He shrugged and struck. *Ching.* "From now on they'll be whipped if they have the wrong look in their eyes. Or speak to each other in secret." *Ching* "The *soldados* will tell lies." *Ching.*

It was as Cipriano had feared, a great loss for no gain. Now people would lose courage and the southerners might never go to war again. Their defeat damaged the prospects for any *Indio* victory. To prevent this Grizzly Hair had nearly run Morena to death. Feeling suddenly tired he said, "Egorov was down there too."

"Still is." *Ching.* The irons sprang loose. Pomponio jumped up, snatched the dead man's hat off the grass and said, "He's living with two women in the Santa Barbara hills." Jamming the hat onto his bushy head, he picked up the sword, ran across the trail and vaulted into the saddle, sword raised. Gonzalo trailed stiff-legged.

"You didn't send me a message about going to Santa Barbara," Grizzly Hair called as Gonzalo hoisted himself up behind Pomponio.

With a grin, Pomponio kicked the horse into a gallop. *"Adios,"* he yelled over his shoulder. The animal disappeared in a cloud of dust, the other horses limping toward it before they put their noses back in the grass.

Grizzly Hair headed up the hill toward the waiting people, and as he climbed, power drained down through his shoulders and arms and out his fingers. This had indeed been like a Coyote story—a joke, with him the butt. No wonder people didn't plan wars. Even the story of *El Cid* seemed silly now. *Indios* were not one people, but many private individuals accustomed to living for themselves and their families. Everyone kept secrets, starting with their given names and their spirit allies. The spirits were as private and individual as the people. Somehow he knew, from the little contact he'd had with them, that the *Españoles* were more like ants, allied with the same few spirits and following the wishes of other people. O-se-mai-ti had mentioned that as one of the things that made their warriors a strong fighting force.

No sooner had he thought about his ally than he saw her a short distance away, through the scrubby oaks. He stopped climbing and looked at the big bear, who sat on a shelf of disturbed earth in front of a shadowy den. She opened her mouth in a wide yawn, the huge incisors curving against her red throat and tongue. She smacked her lips together and said to Grizzly Hair, "Sometimes we need a good sleep."

He realized he hadn't slept well in a long time. He glanced up the hill but a rise blocked his view of the people. When he looked back the bear was gone. There hadn't been time for her to go inside the den. Nothing moved but squirrels harvesting acorns, woodpeckers swooping through the trees and jays banging the unshelled acorns on branches. Crows heralded him, woodpeckers argued and fly-catchers sang of good hunting. *Sometimes we need a good sleep.*

He noticed the beauty of the place. Probably the soul of the dead man had departed, for it to feel this peaceful. The ocean was nearby. His friends had wanted to see it. Two Falcons would love it. Maybe they could find a secluded beach and play in the surf. They could have some fun after all this running. Maybe there would be shells lying at their feet, possibly the iridescent abalones that made the Bodega people rich. He could find valuable shells for Morning Owl. Then, teasing through his disappointment, another thought stunned him: he might find Etumu's parents a gift they wouldn't reject.

Married, he would become a more respected man of the umne, not a ridiculous man trying to change the world. He could become a father. The thought moved something deep inside him. He had been a boy without a father. Now he could become a father with a son. That would repair the broken netting of his family and link him more firmly to the umne. It felt right. But the umne must make changes. During the long dry, when Padre Durán sent black hats and neophytes to search for fugitives, they must hide far upstream. Then, when the rains brought flooding in the Valley of the Sun they could return to the home place and find their spirits. He wouldn't lose touch with Estanislao either, or the other allies.

But it was the nature of a bear to hibernate.

IV
Los Americanos

51

The rains came again and the river rose and fell. During this time Grizzly Hair returned to Fort Ross with all the beaver pelts for trade. His friends went with him, carrying the pelts that couldn't be strapped to Morena, and the little fawn-colored colt trotted behind. The goods they brought back made people nearly fall down with wonder: buckets, tin cups, iron knives, ox-horn containers, iron arrow points, strings of translucent beads and striped cloth. Now the umne were seen as wealthy. Knowledge of them spread. From the north came traders with yew wood for strong bows and dark obsidian for fine sharp points. Grizzly Hair noticed that the umne and the related peoples asked for his opinions more often and waited longer to be sure he was finished speaking before they spoke. But he felt proudest at the big times, when Morning Owl walked among the headmen wearing many strings of rich seashells.

As a tough hide softens when chewed, so Etumu softened Red Sun's opinion of Grizzly Hair. Never again would Grizzly Hair doubt her persuasiveness and determination. Red Sun had accepted ten large abalone shells as a marriage present. Two of these he thinned into flat, oblong medallions. He strung and tied them, evenly spaced, on a buckskin thong and wore them during big times. They dazzled the eyes of all who looked at him. Nettles positioned the other shells around her u-macha and dusted them out every day so they would catch father sun's light.

During the long dry, the season of *expediciones*, the umne trusted Grizzly Hair's advice and traveled upstream to granite gorges and better hiding places. The black hats had never been known to go that far east. But in time of rain the umne returned gleefully to the home place, where they could talk to their spirit allies and be near their ancestor's bones.

Falls-off-House, Lame Beaver and Scorpion-on-Nose had been in awe the entire journey to Fort Ross. Everyone, including Grizzly Hair, learned many new things. Egorov had never returned from Santa Barbara, and Katya had married a respected Kashaya elder. Grizzly Hair was glad for her; she said Egorov would never take her children from her.

A new headman sat in the big house at the fort. Glav-nyi Schmidt had been replaced by the even more hospitable host, Glav-nyi Shelekhof. Shelekhof said Canónigo Fernandez was in a *calabozo* in Mexico and the Emperor had been cast out. It was puzzling why the *Mexicanos* had selected that headman in the first place, if they didn't like him. Nearer to the fort, Commander Argüello had moved his family to Monterey and become governor of Alta California, like María's first man. The glav-nyi didn't know Commander Martinez, the new headman of the black hats in San Francisco Presidio, but felt certain they would not attack Fort Ross and there would be no war. He and Grizzly Hair parted friends, each promising to send messages if anything changed. If talk had been easier, Grizzly Hair would have joked that everything had changed, yet nothing had changed.

The danger remained. The adobes of the new mission hadn't stayed broken for long. When Grizzly Hair and his friends passed by, big new buildings were being finished. From a distance they watched neophytes pounding iron and doing all that had been done at Mission San José. Cross-eyed Bear said the new mission was called San Francisco de Solano, or Tso-noma, which in the tongue of the local people meant Earth Home Place.

To make matters worse, Mission San Rafael had reopened. All neophytes north of the big bay were expected to live in one of three missions: Sonoma, San Rafael or San José. Invitations to fiestas were extended from those missions to all the gentile villages. In addition, the villagers received visits from belligerent gangs of neophytes on *paseo.* Even old Magma and his people were giving up the struggle; they were ready to go to a mission for protection. Elders in some villages said their families were tired of being regarded as h'nteelehs—stupid, unimportant people. They wanted their children to have the esteem of *Christianos.* Some of the Petaluma women, who were camping near their old home place when Grizzly Hair and his friends passed through, said mission life wasn't as bad as it had been. Whenever they needed a rest from too much *trabajo,* they told the padre they were going to one of the other two missions, and it was hard for the black hats to keep track of them. People were sneaking around like coyotes. Grizzly Hair thought that was an unpleasant way to live, but better than being entirely captive. In any case, the *Españoles* were enlarging their territory. That had not changed.

At Pomoponio's cave they learned that Gonzalo had died in a horse accident while escaping from the soldiers, and Pomponio had been captured by Corporal Herrera. Vultures had helped the *Españoles* find the soldier Grizzly Hair covered in leaves. They easily figured out who killed him, and now Pomponio was called a *criminal de sangre,* a blood criminal. While Grizzly Hair walked among the umne, Pomponio sat chained by the neck in the *calabozo* at San Francisco Presidio, waiting to hear what would be done to him. His punishment would be severe. Surely he would never walk free again, nor ride Morena's colt. Though he had proved unreliable, it upset Grizzly Hair to think of his plight, and he wondered if Pomponio would tell the soldiers about their war talk and Grizzly Hair's attempt to lead many men to fight in Santa Barbara. But all he could do about it was stay purified and open to power.

Every once in a while runners came from Grizzly Hair's network. One reported a rumor that when *Americanos* came to the Valley of the Sun, the time would be right for a killing war. That sounded like his own talk of Missouri coming back to his ears, changed in the telling. Missouri hadn't been heard from again, and *Indios* had no alliance with *Americanos* and no assurance they would fight on their side even if they did appear, so he ignored such talk.

The warrior bear slept, but Grizzly Hair never forgot the sting of the *cuarta* or the parade of dead souls on the pathway of ghosts.

Time of Early Flowers, 1826

Chilled and glancing at her distended abdomen, Etumu went to the cha'ka for acorns. Something deep inside was starting to hurt again. Thinking she had eaten too many of the abundant fresh greens, she turned her thoughts back to the happiest moment of her life—when Grizzly Hair placed the abalone shells before her parents' house. Nearly bursting with joy, she had overflowed with talk about how much she wanted him.

Now, letting acorns rattle into her basket, she recalled how it felt when he covered her with his strong, sensitive body and she stroked the moving muscles of his back. Never had she imagined anything so close and sweet, or imagined that she would lie weightless in the crook of his arm at sunrise. She closed the woven vines, shutting off the acorns, and went to the chaw'se.

He had behaved as an esteemed son-in-law while living with her parents for the proper length of time, and now, as she took the full basket to Mother, she recalled how politely he had refrained from talking to his mother-in-law, not even looking at her. Then, after the time of living there, he had built their own snug u-macha. Reaching over her big belly, she placed the basket before her mother and waited for the sharp cramp to end. This was worse than it had been during the sleep.

Nettles eyed her and patted her abdomen. "Bathe and go to the birth house."

A thrill tingled through her. Excitement and dread mixed badly with the cramp. Until recently she'd paid no attention when women talked about birthing. It was something that happened to others, and some women died. Now whenever she asked, "How does it feel to give birth?" women only smiled and said, "You will see." Maybe she would die.

In the river for the second time since dawn she lathered with soaproot, then rubbed every part of herself with fine sand. While the river spirit sang a happy song, she swam where the brisk currents tumbled together around the island, cold from the snow of the eastern mountains. Feeling purified, she stepped into the breeze.

Father sun hid behind a cloud. She hugged herself and hurried through the tall damp grass interspersed with flowers, up the eastern hill to the gully with the little pine-bark birth house. It was a place of women's power. No man or child could enter. Beside the entrance lay Mother's basket, woven with a feather design that had become fashionable of late. This new basket was full of acorn meal—payment for Sits-in-Tree, the birth helper. In the grass beside the basket lay a string of flat pink shells and a coil of braided thong, Grizzly Hair's payment. Her vision blurred with tears of love. How generously he had paid to keep her safe!

Bending to enter, she saw, in the middle of the floor, a pit filled with clean sand. What was it for? She kneeled beside it, careful, as always, not to look out the door lest the baby be born dead. All these months she had taken care, never looking at Dishi for fear the baby would be blind, never looking at a sick or dying animal, never speaking in a mocking way of any maimed or toothless person. Each day she drank the special tea Nettles gave her, and never backed out a door because the baby must come head first. Hard pain grabbed her. She gritted her teeth to keep from moaning. A woman showed strength by silence in childbirth, and she didn't want to shame herself before the female spirits who dwelled here. Soon Nettles would bring Sits-in-Tree and other experienced women. But now, alone and afraid, Etumu trembled and her teeth chattered. She wished they would hurry.

To calm herself she tried to imagine what Grizzly Hair was doing, but couldn't. He had been pleased about the baby in her blood. More than anything she wanted it to be strong. During the mounting pain, she recalled when he had ridden an entire sun to find the flat kind of fern she craved. And when they coupled he spoke in gentle tones and moved carefully, saying it was good for the child to receive more of his blood. As the hurtful cramp knifed upward she thought of the sad space between them. Occupied by Oak Gall? Runners from strange places? His eagerness at any moment to ride far away?

By stages the hurt stepped down from one plateau to the next and only one thing mattered: he was her man. He was good to her when he was there. Unlike most men who slept every night in the sweathouse, he spent many nights in the u-macha with her. The pain melted away and she thanked the spirits for her beautiful man.

Someone was entering, slowly crawling around to where Etumu could see her though she looked away from the doorway. Greatly relieved, she saw large, friendly Raven Feather with a steaming basket in one hand. "Breathe it," the headwoman ordered, putting the liquid under Etumu's nose. She had also brought Morning Owl's bearskin.

Thankful that someone was here to show her how to give birth, Etumu inhaled the cleansing pine essence. The rare fur was Morning Owl's most prized possession. This was an honor, and Etumu supposed the honor extended to Grizzly Hair.

She heard low talk as more women entered. Mother and two other women with packed carrying baskets crawled around where she could see. Sits-in-Tree came next. She rolled out the bearskin and arranged the little baskets of herb tea alongside it, speaking cheerfully of amusing things that happened during other births. More women entered and scooted around the wall, all chattering cheerfully. Now Etumu was ready to give birth in the proper way.

Sits-in-Tree lowered her on the soft clean bear rug. Never before had she received so much attention. Still, she felt jittery while Raven Feather massaged the special herb paste into her abdomen. She didn't know which plants had been used, but the mixture contained fat to be so smooth.

She felt the twinge again, deep inside. Knowing it would hike up and up the plateaus of pain, she tried to ignore it. "Where is Grizzly Hair?" she asked Mother.

"I think he went to lay a fish wier."

"Yes, but I thought he came back." It sounded impatient to her ears, but the pain was stabbing into her back, and if she didn't *see* exactly where he was she might cry out.

"I don't know," Mother said in a casual tone. "Maybe he came back."

Irritated at that and feeling as if she were being broken in two, she swallowed the medicine Sits-in-Tree held to her lips and managed not to cry out. The songs of the women around the wall told her this was normal. Again and again when agony seized her and she stanched the urge to scream, she told herself this pain wouldn't kill her; the women in the songs hadn't died. Then Sits-in-Tree said, "Let's put her over the pit now."

Sits-in-Tree and Mother took Etumu's elbows, supporting her on both sides. They helped her up from the bear rug as Raven Feather positioned herself at the edge of the sand pit facing the door. Raven Feather stretched out her large legs, resting her calves on the opposite edge. She patted her lap. "Here, you sit facing me, like you are riding your man's horse."

The women helped Etumu straddle Raven Feather's legs, toes dangling, distended belly against Raven Feather's large, pendulous breasts. The older woman looked at her, the irises of her eyes dark and deep, and embraced her as though she were a young child. "Do not worry," she murmured. "We will show you the way."

Still, she felt jittery. From behind, Sits-in-Tree massaged the slippery paste along her spine, kneading, circling, somewhat soothing the astonishing pain in her lower back while the women kept up their steady singing. Sits-in-Tree said firmly, "It is not pain you feel. First-time mothers are like children. They mistake all strong sensation for pain."

Etumu gritted her teeth so hard she could hardly talk, "What is it then?" A boulder with sharp edges pushing through her?

The birth helper rubbed the paste round and round, spacing her talk with soothing circles. "The baby is afraid to leave you. It is holding on, but will die unless it comes outside. You are the mother. You must talk to the baby mind-to-mind. Say you are glad for these good cramps and the baby must not be afraid. It is your strength, your power you are feeling. A woman with no power dies and her baby never comes. But you are strong. See that? Your belly is like rock." Reaching from behind she firmly massaged Etumu's huge lump downward. "This is joy and strength."

The women at the wall chorused: "The baby comes in joy."

Circling, circling and pressing down hard with the worst of the pain, the birth-helper murmured, "If a woman is afraid and cries, the baby will fear the world and take longer to come. Rest, Little One, you are doing well." She brought a different basket of tea to Etumu's lips as the strong sensation she had mistaken for pain slowly walked away.

Despite the longer cramps, the jittery feeling faded. So did the thoughts of death and worry about twins. Experienced women thought the birth was going well. Swallowing the bitter drink with the smell of wormwood, she felt her entire body rock with the massaging, and rested her cheek on Raven Feather's shoulder. Raven Feather stroked her hair and said, "Lizard Woman will bring her baby outside to the fresh air and the power-giver."

Yes. Etumu yearned for that. Never had she focused her mind more than now, hoping for the next cramp, talking mind-to-mind to the baby, coaxing it to come. Now she was glad the cramps were strong. The murmuring songs were also a salve and Etumu floated between strong sensations. Time passed and her strength flowed. Her belly hardened with deeper and deeper intensity, the birth-helper pressing her knees into Etumu's back for her to push against. Raven Feather hugged her in her big soft arms as a mother comforts a child, murmuring "Yes. Yes. You are strong. The baby is coming. This is good. Your baby will come out strong like its mother."

Etumu pushed against the knees and gripped the flesh of Raven Feather's shoulders, throwing her head back, teeth clenched, eyes closed, straining, no longer hearing the songs. But she was sure the baby heard them and was coming to the comfort of strong arms and the caress of breasts, where it would be held as lovingly as its mother was now, her damp hair stroked back to keep the stinging sweat from her eyes. She let out her breath and felt a shudder.

A tremulous little cry came from below. The women around the wall let out happy exclamations. "It's a boy!" Mother cried.

"Strong and whole," someone else said.

See, he's already looking around."

Tears washed the stinging sweat from Etumu's eyes and a sob of emotion pushed up her throat, for she had done it. The baby was born. Mother knelt beside Raven Feather's thigh, leaning into the pit. "She is biting the cord," Raven Feather explained confidentially into Etumu's ear.

Nettles brought up a wiggly little person covered with sand and blood and whitish streaks. The baby cried in his grandmother's arms. A purple thing jutted from his belly. Was that normal too? She wanted to count his fingers and toes, and had little patience for the birth-helper still massaging her tired abdomen from behind. Sits-in-Tree said, "No other baby is in there."

The women at the wall, sharing Etumu's relief, crept forward to see better. Nettles had a small basket and was rubbing the contents on the baby's pale waxy coating, rubbing him down to his tiny feet. He looked whiter than ever, like an infant clown. He threw wide his little arms and cried as loud as he could, but it was a tender sound.

"What are you putting on him?" Etumu asked.

"Oak ashes to keep his skin smooth and free of hair." Nettles then sprinkled pine water on his tiny penis to keep it small. "I'll be back after I wash him." She crawled out with him in one hand. Etumu looked after them—the first time in so very long she had looked out a doorway.

Since morning Grizzly Hair had stood on the riverbank waiting for Nettles to bring a baby—he had beseeched the spirits that it would be one. After all Etumu's discomfort and care, he prayed it wouldn't be twins—bad luck babies. If so he'd have to smother them. He could think of no reason for twins, but the size of Etumu's belly had made him worry. He hoped it was only that thin women appeared to be bigger.

From time to time people stopped to talk and give him a knowing look. Nearby, Lame Beaver, who was already a father, sat gluing feathers on arrow shafts. He kept the feathers under his foot to keep them from blowing away. "You look like a man about to jump off a cliff," he said with a wry look. Etumu was careful. She and the child will be fine."

No sooner had that cleared than Nettles appeared on the path with a single lump in her arms. It moved. Joy burst loose in Grizzly Hair's stomach and he stepped back into the willows to let his mother-in-law pass. He wouldn't endanger the child's health by pushing too close. Then, squinting into the wind and sun, he watched her wade to her waist and dunk the baby up and down in grand motions, four times facing east, west, north and south. He didn't care that Lame Beaver was grinning at him.

Nettles must have noticed his eagerness, for she suspended the dripping baby in the wind long enough for him to see. A cloud over the sun removed the glare and he saw the tiny legs with the suggestion of something between and thin little arms waving. He laughed to hear his son's mewling yells—First Water for him, First Wind.

Nettles gathered the baby in her arms and hurried back toward the birth hut. Proud new sensations expanded through Grizzly Hair. Crying Fox would be a good name, he thought. Many seasons had passed and it would be acceptable to put his grandfather's name back into use. Grandmother Dishi might be pleased too, even though people thought she didn't know what was happening. But she had comforted him when his mother died, so he believed she would understand. However, Grandfather's name must not be wasted. A child couldn't be named until it could talk and was strong and healthy and likely to live.

The four-sleep wait while Etumu and the baby remained in the birth hut would feel long. He wouldn't be able to see them, but would arrange for her favorite foods to be delivered. She liked quail eggs boiled and sprinkled with salty herbs, and they abounded in this season. He chided himself for his impatience, wanting to see his son.

Lame Beaver laid a hand on his shoulder. "Let's play Gabriel's game."

They found Falls-off-House and started playing, but for the first time Grizzly Hair felt silly hitting a little wooden burl around the hillsides. But his friends were trying to help. He used the club old Matías had shown him how to make, but could hardly pay attention to the game. As Lame Beaver hit his ball, Grizzly Hair stared at nothing, lost in visions of his son, imagining answering the boy's questions. He would help him in all things. This boy would not doubt that he belonged among the umne. He would marry a women from another people and bring her here.

Falls-off-House yelped. His club lay on the ground and he was hopping around holding his foot. "I hit my toe," he explained with a pained smile. On the journey to Fort Ross he had accidentally spilled a basket of nu-pah in Topal's u-macha, and at Fort Ross he had slipped off the redwood ladder, fortunately landing safely in the sand. He had earned his name, Grizzly Hair recalled with a smile, from another clumsy accident.

Grizzly Hair prepared to swing his club but stopped when he heard the rumble of hoof beats, maybe Two Falcons returning on Morena, the grown colt running behind. The colt's hair had changed from very pale fawn to a little darker—Milk they still called him. But the stallion that broke from the oaks was large and black and carried Domingo's runner.

Clubs in hand the three trotted to the village center. The man dismounted as the herald announced him, and Grizzly Hair led the horse to the river. The stallion buckled his legs and rolled on the leaching basins, angering several women, but soon everyone crowded around the dancehouse door, eager to hear the news.

The runner looked at the assembled people and said, "Neophytes are leaving the missions. They are allowed to go."

Astounded, Grizzly Hair knew second grass was tall; cattle would be fat and mission plants would be plentiful. There would be much *trabajo* in the missions and plenty to eat. So why were they allowed to leave?

"Only married neophytes who were born in the missions or have lived there a very long time are allowed to go," the runner added, "but many more are sneaking away. The black hats aren't stopping them."

Grizzly Hair couldn't understand it. Hadn't he just seen a new mission being built. Hadn't they just reopened another?

"People say it's a beginning. Soon all the neophytes will be free to leave," the runner said.

Grizzly Hair's joy was mixed with shock at the unexpected.

"The troubles in the west are over," declared Drum-in-Fog, the line of his mouth suggesting the satisfaction of a man who *sees* more clearly than others. "If we had fought a killing war, we would have died for nothing."

"Estanislao says the same thing," the runner said.

"Will the black hats stay in their presidio?" Grizzly Hair asked, believing the danger remained as long as they stayed.

The runner shrugged. "Do bears stop fishing?"

Hummingbird Tailfeather, who was touching Running Quail's shoulder, said in a voice everyone could hear, "Bowstring will bring his wife to the home place." It was the first time she had spoken her son's name aloud since Running Quail had pronounced him dead. Eyes glistening, Running Quail now looked over the heads of the umne.

Grizzly Hair felt something like the calm between a high wind and a rainstorm. Restless and needing more knowledge, he decided to ride to Domingo's place, a natural stopping place for neophytes coming over the *Paso de Alta Monte.* It would give him something to do while he waited to see his son.

52

After the sleep he rode south with several men. His friends also wanted to hear what was happening. The runner returned with them, not having ridden farther. He said Poo-soo-ne's people would hear the news from their friends along the Big Mo'mol. Two Falcons rode double with Grizzly Hair and Lame Beaver rode Milk, the feisty colt. Sick Rat, Scorpion-on-Nose and Falls-off-House trotted behind. At first Grizzly Hair hadn't wanted Sick Rat to come, but this was the first time Sick Rat had shown any interest in what his father did, and Grizzly Hair knew fathers and sons should be better friends than these two.

On the path to Muquel's place, Grizzly Hair wondered where married neophytes raised in a mission would live. Their old home places were deserted or overtaken by others. Would they even know where those villages had been? Could a man who rarely used a bow learn to hunt well? Could a woman acquainted only with mission gardens distinguish edible plants and find medicine herbs? Strangers would wander everywhere. They wouldn't know how to talk to the spirits. They wouldn't know how to sing. They hadn't learned to live the way Coyote taught people to live.

That night they slept in a Muquelumne village. In the morning some of Muquel's people joined them, also wanting to see and hear what was happening. Te-mi's sons, Elk Calf and his older brothers trotted along with Sick Rat and Falls-off-House.

Domingo's place swarmed with neophytes in mission beads and woolen hip wraps. Many were building houses of green tules, obviously planning to live here. Experienced men were showing them how. Women in red skirts sang as they harvested cattail root from the swamp by the river. Other women were skinning ducks. Men in loincloths slapped their thighs as they joked and passed tule-stem pipes. Children ran and played. It was the mood of a big time, and it seemed as though plenty of people were teaching the mission people how to live.

The men of the umne blended into the crowd, Scorpion-on-Nose joining those watching a red-hot bucket being cut into pieces for arrow points. Neophytes were teaching gentiles too. But wouldn't old hatreds from past raids divide them?

Gabriel, in his faded black hat and abalone medallion, was holding forth in the center of talk. Recognizing some of Gabriel's men, Grizzly Hair sat down. Sick Rat, surprisingly, sat beside him. Gabriel was finishing a long story about Hissik, Skunk, and the Animal People. Every time the animal hunters returned with their elk kill, Hissik tricked them and kept all the meat for himself. Finally, the animals tricked him into getting into a large pit they had dug, and before he knew what was happening, rolled a heavy boulder over the top. He yelled and pleaded to get out, but could not. After a long time Skunk gathered his strength and pushed out the biggest fart of his life, toward the east side of the pit. Gabriel scrunched up his face to illustrate the effort. "The land bunched up high on that side, but no hole opened. Hissik farted hard on the west, but no hole opened there either, and that's why," Gabriel concluded with a smile, "we have two mountain ranges and the higher one is on the east." Everyone laughed and a man handed Grizzly Hair a *bota.*

He took a swallow, passing the *aguardiente* to Sick Rat, who sipped, sputtered and coughed. Grizzly Hair's bones softened and after the bag returned a few more times, he laughed aloud at the slightest joke. The big time mood had captured him. Sick Rat smiled like a boy on the winning side of a ti-kel game.

"Will they send an *expedición* for us?" said a man slapping a mosquito on his thigh.

Several people talked at once. "They let us go."

"They've lost their power."

"They don't have enough soldiers."

"The headmen of the soldiers are weak."

Lame Beaver asked, "Have all the married neophytes left the missions?"

"No," a woman said, "Some don't know any other way to live."

"My brother is there," Lame Beaver replied, "and he knows how to live."

Grizzly Hair noticed a crowd at the upstream side of the village. "A runner," someone called casually. Apparently so many people were arriving all the time that heralding was no longer practiced. Grizzly Hair pushed to his feet but his legs refused to move smoothly. Sick Rat lurched into a man who then leaned on him, and the two staggered together toward the runner.

In the crowd everyone talked at once. It was hard to hear, but it sounded like a runner had come and gone. People were repeating the message they thought the runner had delivered. Pressed tightly on all sides, Grizzly Hair heard: "Pomponio is going to Monterey."

He shouted to be heard. "Did he escape?"

People shrugged and left, but one man seemed to have heard more. "Pomponio is in heavy chains from his neck to his feet. Twenty-five black hats and several ranchers are escorting him in a *carreta*."

"He will escape," someone declared.

"Let's help him escape," another yelled—exactly what Grizzly Hair was thinking.

"They are on *el camino real*," a man said. That was the trail to Monterey where Pomponio and Gonzalo had broken out of their irons. "By now they'd be almost there."

Grizzly Hair felt vertigo, as though he'd been spinning. Soon Pomponio would be inside another *calabozo*. Feeling sick in his stomach, he worked his way through the noisome crowd, many of whom obviously still hadn't bathed though they'd left the missions at least two sleeps ago and a river flowed within spitting distance. A voice in his head was saying Pomponio will die. Why did this bother him so? Maybe because Pomponio had a warrior's spirit, though he hadn't been reliable.

He found Gabriel where he'd left him, still sitting against the u-macha. Grizzly Hair told what he had heard, adding, "Why do you think they're taking him to Monterey?"

Gabriel said, "He is a *criminal de sangre*." A bad man of blood. "A *junta de guerra* has decided his fate."

"Junta de guerra?"

"Council of war." Gabriel shifted, making room for returning people, the big abalone shell on his chest iridescent in the spear of sunlight that penetrated the canopy.

"War?" Grizzly Hair repeated.

"Yes, war. But Pomponio is no warrior, just a fool."

One of the returning men said, "Señor Leebomo and his vaqueros are helping take him to Monterey."

Gabriel's eyebrows humped like bushy caterpillars, and he said softly, "Señor Leebomo keeps many trained horses in his big corral, and some of his vaqueros are gone."

"*Sí,* over two hundred horses," added the man swallowing from a new *bota* being circulated. More people were joining the crowd around Gabriel. Sick Rat sat down too.

"Vaqueros dance the fandango when they go to Monterey," Gabriel said.

Others contributed: "They couple with the pretty señoritas."

"They drink the good *aguardiente* of Monterey."

"They will have a big time."

"They will not return for two sleeps, maybe more."

Gabriel looked around the circle, his gaze lingering on Grizzly Hair. "Let's ride to Las Positas, the rancho of Señor Leebomo."

"Ho!" people shouted, slapping each other in happy accord. The women enjoyed it as much as the men. Grizzly Hair realized this was a chance for the umne to get trained horses. Wild horses were too hard to catch. They could hardly be hunted for meat, but here on the west side of the valley, many people rode trained horses stolen from missions and ranchos.

Feeling the dizzying effect of the *aguardiente,* Grizzly Hair repeated what María had said. "Some people say your raids delay the time when *Españoles* will respect *Indios.*"

Gabriel laughed so hard he fell on his side with his knees tucked up. His hat rolled off. People roared with him. At last Gabriel sat up, wiped the dirt off his face leaving a streak, and looked at Grizzly Hair through tears. "Perhaps you've been coupling with Señorita Concepción Argüello."

New howling erupted, longer and harder. The *aguardiente* inside him told him it was funny, although he had no idea who that was. He had been a hill bunny to say such a thing. He laughed with them, and the funniest part was seeing so many men falling to their sides laughing. Grizzly Hair reflected. Why was it wrong to steal horses from men who thought nothing of stealing people? This would be a vengeance coup on the *Españoles*, a kind of war. Meeting Gabriel's glance, he asked: "When do we ride?"

"Right away." Gabriel jumped to his feet with his chest puffed out in the manner of a big bird about to flap his wings and rise into flight—Flies-with-Storm his other name.

Sick Rat spoke boldly to Gabriel, though he didn't know him, "Lend me a horse and I will ride with you."

Gabriel cut a glance at Grizzly Hair and said, "You and the men of your people can ride my horses, and when we get to the horse fair, I'll sell them to you at a low price."

Sick Rat looked like a dog accepting meat. But Grizzly Hair felt doubt, not about Sick Rat's riding ability, for all the umne had learned to ride Morena. Gabriel had something in mind besides distributing horses among the thieves. Grizzly Hair tried to gather his wits, which the *aguardiente* kept scattering. He signaled with his eyes, directing his friends into the privacy of the tulares.

"The horse fair is at the Lake of the Tulares," he whispered. "*Americanos* come to buy horses. That place is many sleeps away, at the south end of the valley. We need the horses more than the goods that will be traded for them."

"What are you saying?" Lame Beaver whispered back, "Should we ride with him or not?"

"We should, but we should take the horses we need for the umne and not go to the horse fair."

"What would Gabriel's men do to us?" Sick Rat asked a little too loudly.

When he was sure no one was coming, Grizzly Hair whispered, "Let's pretend to go along with them and leave the first time they sleep. Gabriel would do the same thing to us. He would call us *inocente* if we didn't do this."

"But we'd be stealing the horses he's lending us," Scorpion- on-Nose protested.

Even through the haze of *aguardiente* Grizzly Hair realized how much he had changed, and understood that the men of the umne couldn't imagine the devious ways of a man like Gabriel. "He already has more horses than he can count," he explained. "He'd want to get to the fair as soon as possible. You could bring those three horses back here before he returns. And remember, we'll help him herd many twenties over the mountains, far more than we'll take."

Two Falcons, who well understood the importance of trained horses, said, "Let's do it, but bring the borrowed horses back."

All agreed, the shine of adventure in their eyes.

About ten and twenty riders in every manner of dress rode in close formation up the mountain toward Alta Monte Pass. At the rear, Grizzly Hair, Te-mi's sons and the men of the umne were the only ones riding naked. Their ear ornaments swung and their topknots flew straight back in the wind, which carried the scent of young grass, horses and men. Big ugly Juan rode before them in his greasy woolen shirt pinned down by his quiver.

They were nearing the top of the pass when father sun went to his western house, coloring the sky salmon and gold. Everyone rested and waited for dark, but the wind never slowed down. As the other men of the umne practiced their Spanish, Grizzly Hair stretched his back on the ground and let the wind skim over him. A piece of mother moon would rise early and he judged there would be no clouds. Enough light, but not too much. His hunger lay buried beneath the excitement, for the rancho of Señor Livermore wasn't far away, not nearly as far as the mission.

Gabriel suddenly stood over him, transformed by the lurid sky into a dark bird with long hair whipping beneath the brim of his hat. "You're coming to the horse fair, aren't you?" Apparently he worried that they'd do the more reasonable thing.

Grizzly Hair looked at the silhouette, aware of the loss of power that would flow from crooked talk. He gave a shrug. "We are riding with you to help you steal horses."

The hair flew but nothing else about the man moved. Nearby, a low velvet voice said, "At the Lake of the Tulares we have a big time with whee-sky."

Gabriel waited for an answer but Grizzly Hair addressed the voice. "What is whee-sky?"

"Hill bunnies!" Gabriel scoffed. "At the horse *fiesta* we'll trade for shell money and your friends can buy a horse for a low price. You can buy many more things too, maybe guns."

"Maybe not," said the other man in a skeptical tone.

"We're good riders," Grizzly Hair said, deciding to show his intent. "You'll have more horses for sale because of our help. We need ten horses besides the ones we're riding."

Gabriel sat down to face him, the magenta sky at his back. Now he talked like a kindly uncle. "*Hombre,* you've got to stop thinking of your entire village as family. They'll keep you poor, like a mother raccoon with too many babies. Stay free. Ride for yourselves. Trade with the *Americanos* and you'll get rich." He leaned forward, his tone suddenly gruff and impersonal. "On horse raids no one looks out for anyone else. *Comprendes?*" He drew back, pushed to his feet, adjusted his quiver strap and left. A warning?

"I like him," Sick Rat said. Two Falcons glanced at his son, then at the sky, his eyes reflecting the deepening red.

Grizzly Hair spoke in his own tongue, but quietly, for many men understood two or more languages. "We will need a little sleep before we go on with the rest of our journey. Understand?" They nodded, but Sick Rat had something new in his expression.

The procession continued down the other side of the mountain. In the midst of many walking horses, Grizzly Hair kept his legs tight to Morena's warm sides. It was dark and the wind seemed to be getting tired. Somebody said in Spanish that Roberto Livermore, the English rancher, had left a big *barca*, married the daughter of a *soldado* and allowed himself to be baptized by Padre Durán. His was the nearest rancho to the Valley of the Sun, the place where the *expediciones* stopped to make lead balls and iron shoes for horses, a place that deserved to be raided. He was their friend. He was not hunted as a *cimarrón.*

Ahead in the moonlight, the riders were bunched together. By the time Grizzly Hair caught up, the council was finished. "Half are circling this way," said a man pointing at a distant prick of light, possibly a candle in a house. "Follow me."

Grizzly Hair couldn't distinguish his own men from the others. Morena and other horses nickered softly as they approached a very large corral, where the sleek backs of many horses churned in mother moon's light like fish trapped in a drying pond.

A loud whinny from the corral was answered by the horse of one of the riders. Ahead, a dark figure slipped off his horse, opened the gate, and the sound of a hand slapping a rump could be heard. Instantly the horses stampeded out the gate and a pack of furious dogs barked across the distance from the house. Grizzly Hair kicked Morena, accompanying the running herd, the dogs yapping behind. Hundreds of hooves pounded dirt into his face. Behind, guns popped.

Fear and excitement thrilled him as he leaned forward; Morena's muscles and leaping strides seemed to be his own. She ran her fastest and he had to be careful to keep his balance. The other low-riding men were invisible, herders and herded one thundering mass drumming toward the saddle of the mountain. Gradually the dogs gave up and the gunshots grew fainter, but in their excitement, the horses continued to fly over the countryside. Grizzly Hair could feel luck surging through him as the dark trees flashed past.

But elation slowly changed to the monotonous pain of a sore behind as they drove the horses at a slower pace all the way down into the big valley. Mother moon retreated into her house and only the faraway campfires of the immortals lit the way. The *aguardiente* had long since worn off and Grizzly Hair felt so tired his eyelids hurt when he shut them. His tongue stuck to the roof of his mouth.

They continued to the tulares of the San Joaquin River, where the secret scent of moss came through the dark as they rode the sinuous trail. He dismounted with the others, swam the river and climbed out through the river jungle to a dark meadow. Leaving the horses there, they retired to the willows. Grizzly Hair helped tramp out a sleeping place for the umne inside the thicket. No fire was lit. He lay back, still feeling the pounding ride.

It was dark when he awoke. He reached over and touched Lame Beaver, Scorpion-on-Nose and Falls-off-House. Two Falcons was already awake. Sick Rat wasn't there. *I must have slept after all,* Grizzly Hair thought. He hadn't seen Sick Rat leave. Perhaps he'd gone to make water. The cool river cleared his head, and he was shocked to see a gray streak on the eastern horizon. He had slept too long. They hurried through the cattails to where the dark humps that were horses could be seen on the meadow. Softly he whistled for Morena, and was relieved to see two humps look up and come toward him. Milk still stayed close beside his mother.

Two Falcons said to the other men of the umne, "Get horses. It doesn't matter which ones." They trotted out to the meadow.

As Grizzly Hair hurried with him toward Morena and Milk, he said, "Maybe your son wants to go to the Lake of the Tulares."

The master hunter looked at him. "Maybe."

"Where are you going?" A harsh voice demanded.

Startled but recognizing Juan's voice, Grizzly Hair kept calm. "I'm getting my horse." Two Falcons disappeared in the willows.

"We're not ready to ride," Juan said. Barely visible in the dim light, he held an arrow between the fingers of his right hand, a bow in his left. He had been guarding the horses.

Grizzly Hair made his voice casual. "I'm taking ten horses, friend. Gabriel knows." Surely he did. The dewy world was silent, the frogs asleep, but the gray light in the east outlined the horse shapes ever more plainly. The snoring of Gabriel's men could be heard in the thicket.

"All the horses are for sale at the Lake of the Tulares," Juan said in a voice much too loud. "Where are your men?"

The comradery of their failed ride down the coast had vanished. Juan had to be silenced. Grizzly Hair lunged, pinned Juan's arms behind him and pressed his mouth into damp mossy ground. A mountain of fury, Juan flopped and kicked and tried to yell. Two Falcons piled on with a *riata* from Morena.

Even with two men it took all their strength to hold Juan and wrap the *riata* around his open mouth. They tied his head to a big willow tree, and wrapped the riata around his torso and arms in a sitting position. Gagging, honking noises came out of him, horrible sounds that were probably waking Gabriel and his men. They had to hurry.

Grizzly Hair snatched up his bow and quiver and ran and jumped on Morena. Two Falcons jumped on Milk. On the far side of the clearing a rider was galloping toward them. Riders were coming from the herd, probably men of the umne.

He kicked Morena into a full run, horses shying and galloping away, and helped Two Falcons cut out about ten. Another rider helped funnel them eastward—one of the umne. The race began.

An arrow whizzed past Grizzly Hair's ear. Shocked, he slid to Morena's other side.

Riders charged from the trees. The herded horses turned like water back toward Grizzly Hair and the others. A gun cracked. Men yelled. Morena whinnied and reared. It was the vaqueros from Livermore's place! Wild-eyed horses streamed by going the wrong way and Two Falcons yelled over the thunder, "Forget the horses. Ride for home!"

Just then Grizzly Hair saw, facing the lighter eastern sky, a familiar face behind a raised bow, a man on foot in the trees. Blinking to be sure he was seeing straight, he jerked confused, excited Morena to a stop and looked. It was Bowstring—thinner, but unmistakably Bowstring. The bow lowered and the mobile eyebrows elevated. He looked as bewildered as Grizzly Hair felt. Then, as though suddenly coming to life, Bowstring stepped back in the willows and motioned wildly for Grizzly Hair to go.

He leaned low, spanking Morena's haunch to make her outrun the arrows and balls that were raining after him, and the riders pounding toward him.

Something hit him in the left buttock. It nearly knocked him off the horse. He sucked in his breath with the pain, but kept his hold, lying forward as Morena galloped toward Two Falcons and Lame Beaver and Scorpion-on-Nose, who now had a wide lead. In agony, he never slowed until Two Falcons turned to look over his shoulder.

The master hunter decreased his speed to a slow lope and circled around. "They've gone back," he said, then looked over and frowned. "You're wearing an arrow. I'll cut it out when we get to that creek." He pointed toward cover ahead.

Grizzly Hair reached back and touched the wooden shaft embedded in his rump. It couldn't be pulled out without tearing through his flesh, and Morena's every step heightened the pain. Trying to take his mind off it, he gritted his teeth and said, "Sorry about Sick Rat."

Two Falcons scowled ahead. "I saw my son with Gabriel's men, shooting at the vaqueros. He is a man now. He does as he likes."

Grizzly Hair was glad Sick Rat would be under Gabriel's protection. But Bowstring concerned him more. Why had he gone to a rancho instead of returning to the home place? With the screaming hot pain in his buttock it was more than he could fathom. And they had acquired no horses for the umne.

In a creek thicket, Two Falcons cut out the arrow with Grizzly Hair's *Americano* knife. He also applied a mud and herb plaster to the wound. After that, exhausted by the adventure and the pain, Grizzly Hair tried to sleep along with the others. At daylight they continued their slow journey—slow for his benefit, as he lay along Morena's back. They slept again when dark fell, and continued at dawn.

He saw Etumu duck out of the u-macha as Two Falcons and Lame Beaver helped him walk into the village center. He answered her shocked expression with an apologetic smile. Trancelike, she came toward him, the amazingly tiny baby against her swollen breasts. She followed to where the umne were collecting to hear the story.

Two Falcons passed around the arrow he had removed from Grizzly Hair, pointing out its peculiar markings. Morning Owl had a twinkle in his eye when he said, "We ought to call him Shot-in-Ass." People tittered and Raven Feather motioned Grizzly Hair down on his stomach.

As Two Falcons told the story, Raven Feather washed away the temporary plaster, then went for herbs to draw out poison. Lame Beaver's little girl squatted on her plump legs, studied the wound, then toddled to Grizzly Hair's head end and whispered, "Ow?"

Grizzly Hair whispered back, so as not to disturb the story. "Yes, ow." Through the pain he smiled at Etumu, who looked just as worried. She amazed him, this little woman, with such power to make things happen the way she wanted. The baby amazed him too. He had to keep looking to assure himself the infant was real, was alive. His son!

When Raven Feather returned with soothing herbs, Two Falcons was finishing the most exciting part of the story—the vaqueros of Señor Livermore shooting. Grizzly Hair said nothing about Bowstring. When the story was over, the daughter of Scorpion-on-Nose asked, "Is Juan dead?"

Gently but firmly pulling her over, Pretty Duck gave her a disapproving look, which brought tears to the child's eyes. Children were not to speak first or ask questions.

Drum-in-Fog said, "Maybe Juan will sit against the tree until he dies."

The horror of such a death showed on many faces. Grizzly Hair, raising his head and wincing as he inadvertently tightened his hip muscle, said, "Gabriel couldn't have missed him. He was making loud noises. And they needed him."

People seemed to agree with that.

"When will Sick Rat come home?" his mother asked. Two Falcons looked into the distance and that was her only answer. Their son had chosen Gabriel over his own father, his own umne. But Two Falcons didn't pronounce him dead.

"Maybe Sick Rat is fighting the *Españoles* in his own way," Grizzly Hair said.

Two Falcons gave him a grateful look, then frowned. "People are leaving the missions. There is no need for war."

But there was. Bowstring was gone. Pomponio and many more were dead, and the Santa Barbara people were locked up and working in irons. The black hats had offered no reparations. The warrior bear kept an eye open.

53

When the marshes dried, the umne trekked up the river to their hiding place. They ate acorn meal that the women had carried from the home place. Deer and elk and water birds offered themselves, and when new acorns ripened, the people stashed half the harvest in cha'kas woven into oak branches.

Coyote's eyes have an amused slant. "Did your son's ass heal?"

"Old Man," I tell him, "the women of my people were skilled with herbs."

"His deceit got him into trouble," Coyote says.

"You of all animals saying that!"

Coyote dips his head, but quickly raises it again. "I think Scorpion-on-Nose and the others were stupid to take the borrowed horses back to Gabriel."

O-se-mai-ti speaks up, "Sometimes people try to be honest. And they needed Gabriel later, at the time of the battles against the *Españoles*, so it was best not to antagonize him."

"What finally woke up the bear in your son?" Coyote inquires.

My leaves rustle as I think. "The black hats became more aggressive. The horse raids played a part and maybe Concepción Argüello. Then the *Americanos* appeared." I stop to consider. "But in the end it was fate."

Monterey, Autumn 1826

Concepción Argüello turned down the blanket under the chin of the sleeping boy, felt his forehead and knew his fever had broken. She remembered the scourge of measles that killed half the Indians in the three northern missions. A child at the time, she had sickened with the red spots too, but her mother said not to worry, people with pure Spanish blood had stronger constitutions. Nevertheless, over her long life Concepción had seen many Spanish children die of the diseases that so quickly felled the Indians.

The boy's mother, the new Governor's wife, looked over the bed. "Doña Concepción," she said, "I'd be honored if you'd stay for a cup of hot chocolate." She turned to where her children stood in a ragged line, "Tell Josefina to make chocolate."

"*Sí*, Mama," they said in unison, but didn't leave. "Will Hector die?" the tallest daughter timidly inquired.

"Don't be silly," her mother replied. "Go now." Her thoughtful glance followed them, then she bent to look out the tunnel of a window toward the sound of a horse. Concepción caught a glimpse of boots, a dismounting rider.

"*Con su permiso,*" said Señora Echeandía, motioning Concepción before her. As they entered the parlor she called into the back of the house, "Don José, we have a visitor."

Concepción sat in a floral upholstered chair, accepting the steaming vanilla-flavored chocolate brought by the *India.* As Josefina left, Concepción admired the fragile porcelain cup, painted in shades of pink and aqua by a far-away oriental artist and imported on one of the trading ships. Señora Echeandía sat facing her, also sipping chocolate but obviously listening to the angry man with the English accent who was somewhat rudely addressing her husband at the door. The tails of the governor's topcoat were just visible to Concepción.

"There must have been over fifty of those savages," declared the Englishman. "Took all my horses again. The second time! Last time they struck Antonio Suñol. They've got to be stopped. In the name of heaven, if you don't order the *cimarrones* back to the missions, it won't be long before there isn't a horse left in all of Alta California. Call in the fugitives, sir. Punish the outlaws!"

Concepción assumed Governor Echeandía would be bristling at the implication that he wasn't acting in the best interests of Alta California. It would have angered her brother.

The governor was saying, "We're doing all we can, Señor Livermore. This very morning a firing squad dispatched Pomponio—one of the worst." He gestured toward the parlor. "Señor, if you please, be so good as to join us and our esteemed guest. Doña Concepción Argüello is here. Later we can discuss the particulars of the situation."

"*Perdón,* Excellency. I am on my way to see my wife's relatives, but tomorrow morning, if you find it convenient, I will come to discuss these disturbing matters."

The tails flicked outward as the governor bowed in dismissal. Accustomed to men in tattered uniforms, Concepción found this man of fashion interesting. Entering the parlor, he lifted her hand and brushed it with soft lips and a prickly mustache. "The pleasure is mine, doña Concepción." His hazel eyes looked at her and it took a minute, until he was sitting beside his wife on the French couch, before it hit her. Those eyes resembled eyes she had gazed into long ago with the yearning of a fifteen-year-old heart.

"I am honored to attend to your son," she said. That was true. A thirty-seven-year-old spinster had to busy herself with good works and charities.

He smiled in a way that made her remember what it was like to be called the Beauty of California. Why did this man, this political enemy of her older brother, bring Count Nikolai Rezanov to mind? His lean height and bearing? Or just those hazel eyes?

His voice resonated in somewhat the same way too, lacking, of course, the mesmerizing accent. "Your graciousness," he said, "is matched by your charity. Everyone in Monterey speaks of your many kindnesses. Is there anything we can do to repay you?"

She made a deprecatory gesture. "Don't even think of it." It somehow unnerved her to hear charming compliments from the man who had replaced Luis as governor. Luis had sputtered with resentment and, after drinking himself into a horrible stupor, left on an extended visit to their brother Santiago, who commanded Presidio San Diego. She assumed Luis would eventually return to his command in San Francisco. Then she would close the house in Monterey and follow him to that wilderness of white sand dunes and breathtaking memories of stolen moments with Count Rezanov, now forever cloaked in a gilded haze.

When the count sailed away, she was the only one who knew he intended to speak to the Tsar in Moscow and the King in Spain and negotiate the Russian acquisition of San Francisco Bay, maybe Alta California. Then he was to have gone to the Pope in Rome to get a special dispensation to marry her, since Russian Orthodox were considered heretics. He was to have returned in about a year. The tongues of the entire colony still wagged, claiming he had been false to her. They said he had compromised her father's honor. Luis had been scornful too, but the family had accepted the padre's compromise of a formal betrothal, and she had never stopped waiting. Had they known she shared Nicolai's view that Alta California would be ruled more graciously by Russia, people would have called the family traitors and her brothers most likely would not be presidio commanders. So it had been a secret, and a lonely twenty years. In the first years she cried herself to sleep almost every night. Her parents passed on, and Luis had been gentle with her. And now, here sat his replacement as governor, somehow reminding her of her lost love. She nevertheless made light talk.

Señora Echeandía excused herself to oversee matters in the kitchen. Governor Echeandía put down his cup and looked at Concepción. "If you wish I will drive you to your house."

"*Gracias,* but do not trouble yourself. I like to walk."

"My *carreta* is being readied. I am going to the mission. It would be no trouble to take you." He smiled and stood up.

She had meant to speak to the padre herself, to see if he might use her services. "In truth," she said, "I also have business there. Could I trouble you to drive me to the mission? "

Shortly afterward they were in the *carreta* hurtling up the wooded hill out of Monterey, leaving the adobe houses and pigs and chickens behind. Ahead, sunlight filtered through the tall dark pines.

"I marvel at this invention," said the governor, pointing at the straps connecting the cart to the horse's saddle.

"It's a little crude," Concepción allowed, smiling in a deprecatory manner. In Spain and Russia and other civilized lands people rode in carriages. Here the governor of Alta California sat in a high-sided box of woven willow that ran upon two enormous rounds of oak that served as wheels. They made a squeal that could wake the dead a league away.

"The Indians figured it out, didn't they," he said, "and trained the horses to pull these things?"

"Probably. They're good with their hands." Since her earliest memories they had made the gear and trained the horses.

Miguel, the Indian servant, spurred the horse. Governor Echeandía smiled over at her in a lopsided way that made him seem young. Or maybe they both seemed young, bouncing on the stacked hides. Sitting so near him filled her with unidentifiable sensations. She watched the passing trees and gripped the cart stakes to prevent falling against him. Despite the ungodly screeching, she liked going fast because the fluffy gray dust roiled behind in a long rooster tail instead of rising in their faces.

They bounced over the hilltop and down the long, winding road toward the mission. From a fair distance she saw the big Romanesque church with its round dome. The mission was nestled at the edge of the marsh of the Carmelo River, which fanned out and trickled into the bay in meandering streams. Today the marsh grasses were crowded with so many grazing birds that the underlying green was blanketed by gray and white plumage.

"We have good weather here this time of year," she remarked. It was the governor's first autumn in Upper California.

At first she thought he hadn't heard, so quietly he gazed at the distant promontory of *Punto de los Lobos*, Wolf Point, south of the mission. Then he said, "Oh, yes. Excuse me. It's lovely."

As the *carreta* screamed closer to the mission, she made out a procession of Indians carrying large *botas* toward one of the buildings—grapes grown in the Carmelo Valley and made into wine. Apparently not all the neophytes had deserted. At closer range she saw, however, that the garden around the big cistern looked untidier than usual.

The horse stopped and she put her hands over her face to keep out the dust. The governor didn't move to open the door. When the worst of the dust passed, he turned to her. "Come with me to the beach, if you can. I'd like to talk with you." He looked troubled.

Heart skipping, she pushed away the shameful notion of anything personal. This was Luis' enemy, and she was beyond the age of most chaperones, but if this old spinster was on earth for anything, it was to be of assistance. In this way a childless woman gave to the world. She nodded.

"To the beach," commanded the governor.

Miguel spurred the horse along the road beside the mission, then took a right-hand turn downhill through pines that stood like tall feather dusters against an azure sky. Pools of sunlight dazzled, reminding her of the lovely visions she'd once conjured of a Russian California in which she and Count Rezanov would have been the leading couple. There would have been elegant houses with glass windows lining these roads. There would have been grand balls. Friends like María Isidora Vallejo would have married noble Russians too, and worn fine jewelry. But those forbidden visions remained locked in her heart.

The road ended at the gleaming white scythe of a beach. The sun glancing off the Pacific nearly hurt her eyes. Twisted cypress along the bluffs added a subtle incense to the aromas of salt air and kelp.

The Governor tossed his jacket into the cart, strode around to her side, opened the gate on its leather hinges and stuck out an elbow, calling to Miguel, "Wait here."

She laid her hand on the warm linen, gathered her heavy black skirts and stepped down the rough natural stairs of yellow sandstone. Catching a strand of flyaway hair and tucking it into her bun, she grinned into the exhilarating breeze and felt an urge to lift her skirts and run freely through the sand as she had done in San Francisco with Nikolai Rezanov.

The governor sat on a block of sandstone to remove his shoes. He held up the first and smiled. "Why don't you take your shoes off?"

Wickedly thrilled by the idea of undressing her feet, she unfastened the buttons, careful not to show her wool-stockinged ankles, and when their shoes were lined up to the sandstone bluff looking for all the world as intimate as a married couple's, she gathered her skirts, pushed her stockinged toes into the powdery sand and headed past a pile of tangled amber seaweed toward the incoming waves. Walking beside her, the governor's turned-up pantlegs revealed hair on his arches, floured by the white sand. At the water's edge a crocheted sheet of foam slid down the incline of wet sand.

"Doña Concepción—"

"Concha," she corrected, emboldened by the expanse and the wind pressing her skirts from the front.

"Let's walk." There was an awkwardness in his bearing.

She fell in beside him just above the reach of the surf, where the damp sand had firmed to a soft, sensuous platform for their feet. With the ebb and flow of water, curlews ran up and down the slope, stopping often to poke for sand crabs. At the other end of the curved beach, waves crashed violently against enormous black rocks and threw white froth high into the air. Gulls and pelicans soared overhead, playing on the wind.

A wave came up and kissed her stockings. Jumping, she lightly bumped the governor, whose hands were clasped behind him. She murmured, "*Perdón.*"

He smiled at her, the wind mussing the hair that was too short for his brown braid. "You are a very special woman," he said, "Unassuming and pious."

A spark flared beneath the dry accumulation of years. Pushing down a ridiculous and inappropriate hope, she wondered if her disgrace had at last faded from collective memory.

"You are the daughter of the most powerful and respected family of Alta

California, and I have heard that you have a keen perception of matters of the day."

If he said anything inappropriate she would cut him short, this married man whose wife had just served her hot chocolate. A rising curl of water was taking on a pale aqua hue.

"I'd like you to tell me what you think about a matter."

The moment felt more fragile than the porcelain cup, more like the wave standing translucent before it crashed and dissolved into froth. She murmured, "Your honor, if I can be of service."

"José," he said. "Call me José."

Her heart stumbled.

"I am afraid I have made a mistake," he said. Maybe I acted too quickly in ordering the release of neophytes." He walked on, obviously preoccupied by that gubernatorial matter, and though half of her was relieved, a cold hand of disappointment slid across the other half, skimming off a joy that had no right to be born and removing the bright edge from the beauty of the day.

"Not that ultimately they shouldn't all be released," he added forcefully. "But maybe this was too soon to start. It was an action born of a philosophy that guides all enlightened countries—that citizens ought to be free and equal. Thomas Jefferson, a former President of the United States, articulated it well. Those principles fueled our separation from the Spanish king and the so-called emperor. Now we have elected men dedicated to a republican form of government. I was appointed by those men, and was trying to put the principles of liberty and freedom to work here." He was talking in an increasingly agitated manner. "This entire economy rests on the backs of Indians forced to labor in missions that resemble penal colonies. Sooner of later, and I'm supposed to make it sooner, that must change. It's just that I had no idea how backward these Indians were." He turned to her, hair blowing across his nose. "The people in Monterey distrust me. They are unfriendly toward liberal thinking. In truth, no one should hear this prematurely, but I came to tell Padre Sarría that I might be willing to rescind my order. Then I wasn't sure. I might appear too indecisive. I wanted to talk with you first." He left high-arched, long-toed tracks in the sand. "A man must recognize when he is swimming against too swift a current. Perhaps if I wait, things will look more favorable later." He glanced at her. "What do you think?"

Her thoughts were realigning.

"Perhaps I presume too much," he added, "confiding in you."

Old, never married, childless and therefore left with a freakishly young figure, she nevertheless looked at the bright side. He wanted reassurance. With a firm smile she said, "I will say nothing about this. Many men have told me secrets from their death beds. Yours is safe here." She put a fist over her pounding heart. He wanted to speak to her as he could not with any man, not even a priest. After all, they were the ones who raged against him and his orders. But what did *she* think of freeing the neophytes? Or forcing them all back to the missions? Would he look weak? Did it matter? Luis had marched into the woods, when he heard about the order, and killed a grizzly bear to vent his anger.

"It was an experiment really," the governor was saying. "Now I thank God I didn't free them all. It's going badly. I'm sure you heard Señor Livermore's complaint back at the house. A flood of unauthorized neophytes left the missions, and now they are begging and stealing." He stepped on a kelp bladder, popping it. "Originally I thought it was a mistake to allow the priests to write the rule determining which neophytes would be let go. But now I see how clever they were. To be released, married neophytes must demonstrate a means of making a living and prove they are individuals acting in their own behalf, not as members of their old heathen tribes. The Padre Presidente knew that few, if any, would qualify. So in truth, I could have them rounded up without actually changing my order. It just doesn't feel right."

Fully recovered, Concepción knew it was an honor for a woman to advise a governor. Even her brother hadn't asked her advice. She recalled the Saturday night fandangos and the jailing of the drunken Indians. She knew that most neophytes were skillful, polite workers, but maybe the problems caused by some of the fugitives outweighed that. The padres told tales of homelessness, drunkenness and neglected children. Luis would laugh if the holy fathers won the argument. It would show that the liberal ideas had been fluff and Luis Argüello should be governor. She realized she must be careful what she said, for brieflly it occurred to her that encouraging this governor to release all the neophytes might help Luis regain the governorship. But that was folly. He had drunk too much and behaved badly to important people. His chance had passed. Besides, he had few friends in Mexico City.

Echeandía watched a line of pelicans taking turns stabbing into the water. "Maybe these Indians need mission bells to order their days. You've known them longer than I. What do you think?"

"I have seen all kinds and heard many stor—"

"Are they childlike, as the padres insist? Do they need the friars telling them what to do every minute? People say if we didn't jail them they would hold non-stop parties until they starved." Tenderfooted, he picked his way over a profusion of pointed white caps, pink coils, black mussels, and pieces of jelly fish. "Perhaps I've assumed too much in speaking to you."

"No, no. Not at all."

"The whole idea here," he gestured widely, "was to train a citizenry. But it's been over fifty years. How long is it supposed to take?"

He reached down, picked up a shell and studied it as if it contained the answer. "The priests say I do the Indians a disservice in forcing freedom upon them, like a flock of lambs released in a city. But in Europe, economic progress followed the freeing of serfs from feudal obligations. When they took responsibility for their own livelihoods, the world prospered. "Here in Alta California," he said forcefully, "tens of thousands are detained and stripped of their freedom."

He hurled the shell out to sea, squinted after it, brushed his hands together and resumed walking. "Some of the ranchers hound me to release them all. The rest demand that I send them all back to the missions. I wanted to do the right thing for the country." His shoulders fell and he watched his sandy feet.

She knew nothing of serfs and economic progress, but she'd grown up in a family that had always supported the church despite widespread grumbling about its power. She had never doubted the priests, even when they refused to marry her to a man of the Eastern faith. How sad the Holy Virgin would have been a few minutes ago to see into Concepción's black heart! Maybe she should sew herself a *beata* and wear it in public. The Devil was everywhere. And if nuns came to Alta California, she should take the vow. She would live a blessed life as a bride of Jesús. Missions were like that, convents for *Indios*, places of spiritual discipline under the vigilant oversight of the Fathers.

She spoke with conviction. "I am just a woman, but I know that too much freedom can be an evil. It gives the Devil a playground. As for the ranchers, they want the neophytes working for them instead of the church. The ones that want the *cimarrones* back in the missions have made special arrangements with the Fathers to get plenty of labor when they need it. It think it's wrong to deprive *Indios* of heavenly blessings for the profit of landowners. Besides, the released neophytes have no land, no gardens, no cattle and no homes. No wonder they beg. And those that steal seem to me, well, like children who shouldn't have been allowed in the pantry. I think it would be more merciful to put them all back where their souls are safe in the hands of God."

He tilted his head as if afraid he'd miss something.

Her soul wasn't safe either, with shameful thoughts running rampant. "The bestial behavior at those fandangos," she added forcefully, "ought to be stopped. In the missions the women are locked up and can't, ah, be with men unless they're married." Feeling her face heating, she looked over the surf. "Maybe it does take more than fifty years to civilize people."

His attentiveness embarrassed her and she wanted to leave. He jumped back from a sheet of encroaching water, but she allowed the cold flood to run over her stockings. *No more surf kisses or any other kind.* She must confess to Padre Sarría. Perhaps he could hear her today.

"*Gracias,* Concha. You have been helpful."

54

Salmon Time, 1826

Old people said that in the old times you could walk across the river on the backs of salmon. The river looked that full that morning, when Morning Owl threw his spear and lifted First Salmon overhead, writhing and flipping water. It was the start of the Salmon Festival. Something else would start that morning too.

The hy-apo sang to Cos, the faithful sojourner who kept her promise to come when toyon berries were red and provide the umne with her valued red flesh. Cos meant birth, regeneration, a river of life wiggling magically from the rocks. This was the reason a man's well-turned calf, clearly shaped like Salmon with a belly full of eggs, sparked Woman's sexual desire. It was the reason Etumu couldn't help but kneel and touch that mystical part of Grizzly Hair. His legs were the most perfectly shaped of all men's. Oak Gall had mentioned that long ago, and it was true. The taut muscular calf between her hands made her want him. He smiled down and put a warm hand on her head. She wished she were not nursing.

Morning Owl signaled and Grizzly Hair waded into the river with the other men where so many dark fins creased the ripples. He liked to catch fish with his bare hands. She and Boy watched the circling ripples where the males chased each other around. Soon the heads would be boiled for glue. Tools would be repaired. The fingerlings would hatch and swim away.

Grizzly Hair lifted a big whipping fish out of the river. Etumu pointed for Boy to look. He squealed happily. He was a thoughtful child now and Grizzly Hair wanted to name him.

Etumu thought it was too soon, but there was something else. As she ran to the u-macha for her basket and knife along with other women, she reflected that a person's real name never changed. It was a lasting gift from parents. Grizzly Hair wanted to name the boy Crying Fox after his grandfather who had gone to the western sea and never returned—Grandmother Dishi's man. But that would forever link Boy with danger and tragedy. She didn't want that.

The herald called in a powerful voice: "A runner comes."

Meeting Grizzly Hair on the bank, she caught her breath. News from other places often meant he would leave. Excitement showed in his face as he handed her the thrashing salmon and went toward the dancehouse. Quickly she whacked the head on a beached tree, inserted the point of the knife and squeezed the roe into her little basket. Then she cut along one side of the backbone. The bigger ribs could be used for a comb. She hung the boneless halves over the drying rack by the attached tail. Several other salmon were already hanging there.

Worried, she went to listen to the runner. He had come from Little Cos. There had been a big fight. The Cosumne had killed some neophytes from Mission San José. "Little Cos invites you to attend the victory dance," he said looking around at the crowd. "He wants you to come as soon as possible."

"How many were killed?" somebody asked.

"More than twenty."

Amazed, Grizzly Hair asked, "Were black hats killed too?"

"No, only neophytes."

"How many of your people were killed?"

"None. No one injured either."

It had been a one-sided fight. "Why did you kill them?"

"We knew they were going to attack us."

"How many sleeps since the killings?"

"One."

Everyone looked to Grizzly Hair, who had explained why such attacks occurred and why unrelated peoples should help defend other villages. This was not the usual situation. Still, Grizzly Hair knew he should go. So should others help defend the Cosumne from avenging black hats.

He stepped up beside the runner and spoke to the assembled people, asking the men to come with him. Those who had been willing to go to Santa Barbara quickly agreed. Most others did not. The Cosumne lived far to the west, they said, and it would put the umne in grave danger to be associated with killers. He knew that meant spiritual as well as bodily danger. With the umne discussing it, he took the runner aside and asked him to notify Poo-soo-ne, Libayto and Topal. Pleased to hear that more help might be found, the runner rode north.

Everyone had taken the precaution of maintaining full quivers as well as a stash of extra arrows, so they were well prepared. Grizzly Hair went for his weapons and Etumu handed him his *Americano* knife.

As he was slipping it into his calf-thong, she said. "Wait, I'm packing my carrying basket. It won't take me long to get dry moss for the baby's bikoos."

Gently he said, "You shouldn't come."

She tossed the rabbit-skin blanket in the carrying basket and turned to him. Her expression said plainly that she had long ago decided to go the next time he traveled. She had told him many times that a man stays with his woman or a woman stays with her man. "We are all invited to the dance," she said firmly. "Women dance with their men."

"They are expecting retaliation," he pointed out, hating to frighten her too much; she wouldn't want him to go at all. "Besides, it is far and you have Boy to carry." He left to join the gathering men.

Etumu followed, telling him, "Straight Willow is going, and her daughter is heavier than our son."

Grizzly Hair didn't want any women to come, but could hardly tell Lame Beaver what to do. "This is no an ordinary dance," he said to all of them. "There could be great danger."

"I am not afraid," Etumu declared, the truth of that sitting on her stubborn young face. At that moment Straight Willow arrived with her big baby in her bikoos, which hung over the wide mouth of her carrying basket.

"We should run the whole way to get there before night," Grizzly Hair said. "You women couldn't keep up."

"Why hurry so?" Straight Willow said lightly. "The dance will last many sleeps. We can spend the night at Omuch's place on the way."

"This is important," he said. "We must get there as soon as possible."

"Then we'll run," Etumu declared, shrugging out of the bikoos, laying it in his arms. His son smiled at him, and Etumu ran toward the shaded boulders.

Hearing chuckles, he looked at Lame Beaver, Two Falcons, Falls-off-House and Scorpion-on-Nose. Even people who were not planning to go had gathered around.

He said to Straight Willow, "Women shouldn't come."

Lame Beaver's eyes flared and he spoke in a flat tone. "If you don't want my wife to go, speak to me about it."

Never before had Lame Beaver used that tone with him. Hurt, Grizzly Hair said to all of them, looking to Two Falcons for support, "We are hiding in this place to protect our women and children. It would be foolish to take them with us." He looked at the precious baby in his arms.

Some of the umne talked quietly among themselves, agreeing that they wouldn't go at all in this season of black hat raids.

Breathing rapidly, Etumu returned and retrieved the bikoos. She kneeled, hurriedly unlaced the bikoos, flicked out the wet moss and packed dry moss around the baby. Two Falcons said nothing to stop her. Hoping her mother would, Grizzly Hair allowed his glance to touch Nettles, but she said nothing. Etumu was lacing up the bikoos.

Lame Beaver spoke in a tone restored of its warmth. "Friend, my wife is coming. It will be good for the women to have each other on the long journey. We can watch closely to be sure there is no danger. We can take them to safety if there is trouble."

That's just what Grizzly Hair had thought when he allowed Oak Gall to travel with him. Etumu positioned the head-thong over her cap, shrugged to a standing position with the bikoos over the basket, and, as though going alone, headed down the wooded path. Straight Willow caught up and they walked swiftly, side by side. A hand landed on Grizzly Hair's shoulder. Two Falcons, giving him a comically helpless look, as though a man could never make a woman do his will.

Grizzly Hair couldn't talk to his mother-in-law, so he turned to Morning Owl. "Where is Red Sun? Maybe he can stop his daughter."

Morning Owl looked at Nettles, who left running. Meanwhile the other men who were going followed Etumu and Straight Willow. Grizzly Hair waited longer than he'd hoped, but Red Sun finally arrived, out of breath and striding toward Grizzly Hair with a troubled expression, Nettles trotting behind.

Embarrassed to have to ask Red Sun for help—he normally mentioned problems to his father-in-law only after he had solved them—he said, "Your daughter is determined and I could not stop her. But she and Straight Willow must stay here where it is safe. They could be killed."

For the first time in Grizzly Hair's memory, Red Sun's broad face conveyed indecision. He frowned through the trees, then motioned Grizzly Hair to one side and said in a low tone, "I know what she's like, when she's determined. She's your wife. I think you can change her mind better than I can."

"I already tried."

Red Sun motioned Nettles over. "Maybe we should go," he told her, "and help protect our daughter and grandson."

Grizzly Hair groaned inwardly. Red Sun was good with his bow, but another woman! Then he began to think it might solve the problem if they went. They could make sure Little Cos sent good scouts to warn of approaching black hats, and, if needed, Red Sun could take the women back to safety. He looked at his father-in-law, but couldn't make his tongue say the words. In his mind he saw Oak Gall in the ground.

He shook his head. "Too many tricks could be played on us. I have seen the enemy. No. I can't take her. But I'd be pleased if you would convince her to come back."

Red Sun said, "I'll bet she won't."

"She will if I tell her I'm not going." Grizzly Hair countered. "I don't need to be a warrior enough to risk losing my wife and son."

Red Sun looked at him and gave a sharp nod. "Let's go bring her back."

They trotted to where the women and the others were walking at a good pace. Grizzly Hair told them he wouldn't go if the women went. They stopped and looked at him. Whether it was his determination or Red Sun's presence, the two young women finally turned and went back, but not before Etumu gave Grizzly Hair the narrows of her eyes.

Putting that from his mind, he ran with the others, much faster without the women, not stopping except for a short rest at Omuch's place. When they left, Omuch and a few of his men accompanied them. Shalachmush and three of his men also joined them. It was dusk when they reached the brooding oaks that hung over the large town of the Cosumne. Passing through the several smaller villages, they had learned that many of the related peoples were already at the dance.

A large throng was there. Feathers decorated the dancehouse door. The herald announced them, and Little Cos greeted them with warmth and obvious pleasure. He turned to his people and said of Grizzly Hair, "This is the brave man who went to the Russians and returned with trade goods." Looking at all of them, he said, "Join us for food, then dance with us."

"Did you burn the bodies?" Grizzly Hair asked.

"In that trench." Little Cos pointed at a long furrow of turned earth.

"How many?" Omuch asked.

"Twenty and ten and four."

Grizzly Hair sat down to hear the story of the fight. The neophytes had come on a *lancha* from Mission San José. They arrived in the night and stealthily camped, planning to attack at dawn. "They made the mistake of picking up my uncle's cousin for a guide," said Little Cos. "In the late night he came and alerted us. He said they would take back the *cimarrones* who live here and any of the rest of us that they could overpower. We decided to fight. Why not?" The friendly lines crinkled around his eyes, "They expected to surprise us, so we surprised them."

Grizzly Hair liked him, a small, somewhat older man with a straight back and a smile always ready to break loose.

Another of Little Cos's men contributed, "We chased the survivors away. They were so scared they left their cannon." People chuckled and gleeful children jumped up and down.

"Cannon?"

"Yes." Little Cos nodded westward.

Another man said, "Our arrows flew like hornets and stung every one of those shits." All the people had crowded around.

"Your people weren't even wounded?" Two Falcons asked.

"That's right," Little Cos proudly declared.

"Can we see the cannon?" Falls-off-House asked.

Young people jumped up, hoping to lead, but half the people of the big town escorted them to the cannon. Among them were Te-mi and his three sons, from the Muquelumne. All walked through the forest, Grizzly Hair beside Elk Calf, who always allowed him to sleep in his u-macha when he was traveling.

They came to the cannon. The crowd parted to let the newcomers see it—smaller than the ones in Fort Ross, the wheels no bigger than the length of Grizzly Hair's foot. A torn-open wooden box of large iron balls lay beside it. The braver children were stroking the cannon.

"Do you have black powder?" Grizzly Hair asked Little Cos.

"We didn't find any."

He was sorry to hear that. "I've heard many stories," Grizzly Hair said, "but never heard of so many neophytes being killed at one time. Twenty and ten and four!" He shook his head. "Padre Durán will be very angry."

"That's why I'm glad to see you," Little Cos said. "The more bows the better."

Two Falcons asked, "Which way will they come from?"

"We'll send our best trackers to find them and report back to us. Last time they brought a *lancha* up the river and landed out of sight over there." Little Cos pointed.

"They wouldn't dare come back here," said a woman. "They ran like jackrabbits." Laughter rolled through the crowd.

"That's right," said another. "Those cowards won't try again."

Staring through the trees, Little Cos said, "*Españoles* always want revenge. But they won't arrive for many sleeps. *Cimarrones* know their ways." He motioned a man forward. "Tell them how long it takes them to make an *expedición* of revenge."

The man with long raised scars on his back stepped through the crowd and said, "They never leave before five sleeps after the return of a messenger. The bigger *expediciones* need more men and weapons and that takes more sleeps to get them from the presidio to the mission."

"Eight sleeps," said Little Cos, "if they come fast and ride horses over Alta Monte Pass."

"How long if they come by boat?" Grizzly Hair asked.

"Much longer. Maybe fifteen sleeps. They row the *lanchas* along the shore and camp along the way—many sleeps camping. Our scouts will see them either way." He paused and declared, "We have nothing to fear for at least six sleeps. We will dance for three nights, then hide in the tulares." He pointed to the marsh.

Grizzly Hair remembered another marsh where he and Oak Gall and Bowstring thought they'd be safe.

Lame Beaver was rubbing his belly, and soon everyone returned to the baskets of hearty food. As he ate Grizzly Hair recalled Etumu's last look, and wondered if he should have brought her after all. They could have danced. Red Sun could have taken them back. But now there was no use thinking about it.

The shadows of the big oaks stretched over the town like a comforting blanket.

Sunday Morning, Pueblo San José, Nov 12, 1826

With a quiet prayer for inner peace, Padre Presidente Narciso Durán raised the wings of his robe and intoned the *benedición* over the heads of the congregation, who kneeled before him on the clay floor of the little adobe church. He had rushed Mass. It couldn't be helped. He'd said it earlier this morning, then left the guards and alcaldes in charge of the mission. His anxiety to return would rush confessions too, for the military couldn't be trusted to do the right thing in a crisis.

Last night the survivors of the massacre had arrived at the mission, and this morning he'd sent a fast messenger to the presidio to report what had happened. The offenders on the Cosumnes River had to be punished immediately or their overweening confidence would foment general insurrection. Christians would be brutalized and killed, beginning, he knew, with Mission San José. Just look what happened in Santa Barbara. Two weeks ago in San Juan Capistrano, using vile and violent language, neophytes had tried to lock the padre in the stocks. Everywhere the Brothers had reported rising insubordination. A plan of action was needed. He must meet with Lt. Martinez.

He despised the ever-changing Mexican government. Recently it issued a statement announcing that the Brothers weren't to control neophyte punishments any more—the military would, thus obliterating a vital rule established by Brother Junipero Serra. On top of that, an idiotic *junta* had promulgated a declaration belittling the mission effort, Durán's life work. The opening lines stated that the members of the *junta* had been unable to reconcile the "principles of a *monastico-militario* system of government" with the spirit of political independence nor "with the true spirit of the gospel." As if they were authorities on that! How else could discipline be maintained over a large, childlike population? No wonder there was a brash new attitude among fugitives, with presidio authorities undermining discipline and lengthening the time between offense and punishment. And lately there was a growing reluctance to go after the fugitives.

Even crazier, Durán was officially under arrest. By order of a Mexican *junta* all priests born in Spain were to be expelled from the country, or more precisely, those who refused to swear loyalty to the latest version of the government. He'd sent a written oath declaring he would cooperate with the government on every point except one; he'd go to his heavenly reward before swearing to take up arms. Had he been less circumspect, he would have added: "not to defend one batch of misguided politicians against the next." That's how the infernal oath read: missionaries were to take up arms and lead their neophytes to battle against political insurgency. Predictably, the governor refused to remove the offending clause. Some of the priests, delighted to end their arduous service, immediately applied for passports. They were denied, of course. So the civil authorities had the amusing duty of explaining why the Brothers must remain at their posts after being ordered out of the country.

Unlike most missionaries, Durán viewed the challenges of mission life with a certain satisfaction—when left alone to do his work—and the truth was that despite everything, he was the master of the situation. Everyone knew the economy of Alta California depended upon mission produce. And anyone with sense knew that only the Franciscans could make the Indians work dependably. So as Padre Presidente of the missions, Durán held the power. Nevertheless, there were problems. Over time some of the Brothers had been released due to death or serious illness, and one who spouted nonsense like Echeandía had been declared insane and deported. But the vacant positions were not being filled. Very few new Mexican priests had been found to replace the Spaniards. So now, instead of two in each mission, many friars worked alone. By himself, Narciso Durán administered, taught and confessed over 1,850 neophytes. At times he had a visceral sense of tens of thousands of heathens battering down the fragile walls of civilization while, on his side, ignorant political appointees pecked away at the frail foundation.

His blood boiled at the thought of Governor Echeandía inciting the natives with ideas of independence and freedom. Without a doubt those statements had helped fuel the massacre on the Cosumnes. And there were other vexations, including the added duty of servicing the pueblo church—probably sixty people now, retired soldiers, criminals sentenced to Alta California, foreigners, adventurer craftsmen, ranchers who brewed *aguardiente* for barter with *cimarrones*, not to mention all their wives and children. Despite these troubles, his Latin flowed and the prayer came to a close. "*In nominae patri, filie et espiritu santu,* Amen."

"Amen," the congregation repeated.

At Durán's signal the door swung open and the boy in the yard began pulling the bell rope. Clang, clang, clang, clang. Children jumped up and ran for the door as men and women creaked to their feet.

Most of the congregation oozed doorward, but plenty lined up for confession. The altar boys gathered the sacred equipment. Durán shut the big Bible and led them out the side door to the lean-to where they locked the robes and church items. Checking to be sure Estanislao was watching the *carreta*, he re-entered the side door, strode without making eye contact past the line and opened the door of the confessional. The narrow bench affixed to the wall was, he recalled, a little weak, so he lowered his wide posterior by degrees. It held, and he peered into the shadowy black lace curtain that separated him from the person on the other side.

The creaky whisper of an older man came through. "Father, forgive me for I have sinned. It has been two months since you heard my last confession. This month I bought my wife cloth for a new frock and now have no money left for tithing."

Doubtless this was a retired soldier, one of the many who didn't exert themselves farming their retirement plots. Did they think they were the lilies of the field for which God would provide? He didn't blame old Pedro Amador, who was blind, but most were quite capable of doing more. Durán was about to absolve him but the man continued:

"By my oath, when I return with gold I will give ten percent to the church."

"You are forgiven your irresponsibility, but next time use better judgement. Your penance is to plant twice the crops you planted last year. Remember, my son, the Church gives you life." In the interest of time he almost swallowed the question leaping on his tongue, but as Padre Presidente he had broader duties. This reference to gold might shed light on an uproar he'd just settled. A friar in San Luis Obispo had been accused of shipping over $7,000 in gold nuggets out of the country while petitioning for a passport. Durán had quashed what he believed to be a mean-spirited rumor. Could it have been true? "Where do you expect to find gold?" he queried the supplicant.

The man hesitated for a long time, during which the bell stopped clanging and Durán imagined various types of mischief the neophytes might be getting into back at the mission. Then straight out of heaven it occurred to him how to handle the disaster on the Cosumnes. He would ignore the government orders and appeal directly to the presidio. He had a stash of savings with which to finance a well-equipped military expedition. He would pay for all the men Captain Martinez could spare, and for the ammunition for cannons and swivel-guns. He would assign a hundred and fifty neophytes to the *expedición*—to build tule boats and other tasks at the commander's direction. He would select these neophytes carefully for their grudges against the Cosumne Indians, for those were devious people who had hidden from the *lancha* when Durán himself accompanied the soldiers on the expedition in 1817. They hid *cimarrones* and had never been punished for their outrages as far back as 1813. It was time they were subdued and brought to the mission.

He could feel his smile turn crafty. The military couldn't refuse. He would feed them. Complaints of hunger in the presidio were probably lies to buy sympathy for further confiscation of mission coffers, but he knew it was normal for soldiers on *expedición* to be required to forage in the woods for their own food. He would tell his neophytes to pack large quantities of dried beef, beans and other food. And whether or not they were lying about chronic hunger, the soldiers hadn't been paid for over a year. He would pay each—

"Beyond the interior valley, Father," the old voice creaked. "In the foothills of the *sierra nevada,*" snowy range. "I know where to find *mucho* gold."

Ah, in THOSE hills! Brother Catalá of Mission Santa Clara, who in his infirm old age was believed by some to have prophetic powers, had predicted that large quantities of gold would be discovered in those very hills. Would the prophesy come true? Had the San Luis Obispo brother acquired a bit of that gold? The rules of the Order required Franciscans to leave the service as they arrived, in poverty. They were to take nothing but their staff and sack, meaning their robe. Durán hadn't called for an *inquisición* to uncover the truth. What was the point? It would only have invited more slander upon the venerable brothers who had served so nobly, on the whole. Nevertheless, he must remind them not to ship valuables, especially when applying for a passport to follow the valuables.

"Can you imagine, my son," Durán said quietly, "how much trouble the rumor of gold would stir up in Alta California? It would cause an ungodly stampede." All hope of a Christian utopia would fly. Miscreants of every nation would descend on the land and wipe out the traces of the Franciscans' hard-won achievements. The Devil, who thrived in the sewer of depravity called Europe, would reign supreme in California too.

"Maybe I shouldn't have mentioned it in the pueblo," the old man said timidly, "but most people don't believe me anyway."

Durán reflected that while most men had abandoned the search for gold, there was a rumor that one old man here in the pueblo kept looking—Pepe something. People said each time Pepe returned empty-handed, he vowed to try again. Fortunately the old man was regarded as a pathetic, even comic figure. Surely this was he. "Just remember," Durán said, "that it is difficult for a rich man to find his way to heaven. And say your prayers."

"Yes, Father. Please bless me, for the journey is long."

Durán delivered the blessing and waited for the shuffling on the other side of the curtain to cease, the next person sitting down.

After confessions Durán was about to open the little door of the *carreta* when he noticed a crowd at the *calabozo at* the opposite end of the plaza. Townspeople and grandees alike had gathered to pay the prisoners' fines in exchange for a week's labor. This had become a lucrative business. Lucifer's business.

Estanislao turned in the saddle and looked back at Durán with an enigmatic smile on his wide mouth. Often he appeared to be slightly amused, but always he seemed intelligent.

Distracted momentarily by it, Durán gruffed, "I'm going to see what's going on over there. It won't take long."

He walked along the water channel that supplied the houses, while naked Indian beggars, no doubt *cimarrones* who had sold their mission clothes for *aguardiente,* approached the *vecinos* with outstretched hands. The fugitives implored, *"Por favor, tengo hambre."* I am hungry. The *vecinos* had petitioned the Commissioner to keep such Indians out of the church, so *gente de razón* could find places to sit. Appalled that despite his presence in the pueblo, these destitute *cimarrones* boldly showed themselves, Durán angrily pressed his lips together. The governor's loose talk and lax policies had caused it.

Children darted around the houses, and groups of men squatted in the yards smoking *cigarros.* A rider startled him. Galloping eastward on a *pinto,* he wore a poncho and a presidio hat. He had bags behind the saddle and a gun at the side. Clearly a retired soldier. Old Pepe? Durán frowned. Despite all the difficulties, the *Indios* were the only hope for the new world. They didn't care about gold.

Sudden musical harmony came to his ears. He turned to look. A group of *Indios* stood singing mission music. Discipline had entirely broken down. Nevertheless, he had to admit that this bunch sang well. Even children came to a standstill then turned toward the lovely strains: *Agnus Dei, qui tolis pecatta mundi, dona eis requiem.* Yes, Lamb of God, who taketh away the sins of the world, give them rest—in their mission homes. The harmonies lifted and wove together like angels on gossamer wings. Soon, however, these *cimarrones* would fly elsewhere.

Gathering his robe he went to where the ten stood in two lines of five. A few *centavos* lay at their callused feet. He fixed his legendary stare on each one. One by one their voices faltered and the music died. It was quiet. They looked over his head, knees visibly quaking.

He used a tone that froze most people. "What mission do you belong in?"

Their eyes remained vacant but the quaking continued.

"I said, where do you belong?"

A man in the front stammered, "San Juan Bautista, Father."

"Go back there now. *Momentito!* There you will be fed and clothed." The useless military wasn't even trying to catch these people, who were obviously incapable of earning a living.

As one *Indio* bent to pick up the coins, others allowed their gazes to flicker across Durán's.

"God dislikes beggars," Durán explained in a quieter tone. "He wants people to work for their food. Now go back and do God's work." They didn't know the lesson of Adam and Eve. Making a mental note to use that in next week's catechism classes, he headed to the *calabozo.* The *rancheros* stood apart from the *vecinos.* Most had been at Mass. Durán wished he could make himself inconspicuous, but in his habit that was impossible.

The *vecinos* smiled and half-bowed at him. He smiled back at them—retired soldiers, Indian wives and a handful of the original gray-headed *negros,* their grown sons married to Indians and their lighter-skinned grandchildren running around. The Commissioner came from his house and approached the jail. Accompanying him, Roberto Livermore led a fine palomino.

The jailor with the greasy black curls jumped up and greeted *el Comisionado.*

"*Hola,* Flaco," said the Commissioner, "please unlock the door." The jailor pushed with both hands to make the huge key turn, then shouldered the heavy redwood door open.

A shout, a commotion and a stench rolled out of the adobe hut like the jaws of hell vomiting the damned. Hair askew, eyes protected by hands, the Indians stumbled out squinting into the bright autumn sun. Loose rags stained with vomit and excrement hung from their bony frames. How had the tiny room had held so many? How had they breathed?

Covering their noses, the *vecinos* stepped back. Even Durán, back in the crowd, smelled the stench. Most of the Indians lay down on the dirt sighing with relief. One woman wept quietly, asking the Commissioner, "*¿Donde están mis niños?*" Where are my children?

Where indeed? Many children were sold illegally to families to work as domestic servants. Bad as that was, at least they would be trained in Christian ways and taken to church along with the rest of the family. And young children could have died in that hell-hole of a jail. The *rancheros* were placing coins in the Commissioner's hand. Pocketing them, he signaled particular Indians to leave with this or that rancher. The commoners of the pueblo were last to receive attention. Few of them had any money.

Señor Livermore mounted and spurred his palomino up the road, herding his *Indios* toward his land grant forty leagues beyond the mission. *Indios*, Durán realized, were strong people to stand in that *calabozo* all night and half a day, then walk twenty leagues and work hard all week. But if they had strong constitutions, why did they die so readily of disease? Always the same question. Most of the remaining Indians followed don José de Jesús Vallejo. That rancher's *majordomo* mounted his horse and brought up the rear. Obviously disappointed not to receive any *Indios*, the *vecinos* dispersed.

"The Devil is here," Durán called in a loud voice. Many turned to look at him, including the departing Indians and the Commissioner.

Looking at the Commissioner's full pockets, Durán said, "I'd think you could find the money to pay a pueblo priest." Not wanting to hear the lying excuses, he left. He had no authority over what went on here. Soul-sick, he hurried back to the *carreta* with his head down to avoid conversation.

Estanislao's intelligent eyes and animal presence caused a forbidden sensation to rise up in him. "Go," he ordered, slamming the gate and settling himself on the cowhides. "Go down the Alameda. Take me to the presidio." This would make him a day late returning to the mission, but could save time in the long run. If his economic persuasion succeeded, Martinez would begin the expedition this very day, not muddling around for a week while they plotted how to account for the costs.

Nonetheless, Durán wept as the cart bounced over the ruts behind Estanislao's muscular back, his spread thighs guiding the running horse. Passing don José's Indians, their faces averted from the dust, he got himself under control. "Dear Santo Francisco," he prayed, "it has come to this. You, who care for the least of earth's creatures, are surely groaning in heaven. Nothing is harder to bear than impotence. How did you tolerate it? How can I? Show me the way. I told all who would listen and all who wouldn't that the policy of freeing neophytes would bring this result. I worked to get elected Padre Presidente so my voice would be heard. I thought it would be heard. I worked with the author of the ill-conceived Order and persuaded the Governor to alter it so it wouldn't apply indiscriminately. I have shown my neophytes the Christian way so they wouldn't want to leave their mission home, but though many remain, too many run away, dear saint. They run away to much poorer lives. They run away to lives barren of grace. Where have I failed? What more can I do? Teach me! And if I can't learn, teach me to bear it."

It was a twenty-league drive up the Camino Real—still called the King's Road despite the revolution. They left the sun and entered the fog that plagued the San Francisco Peninsula. Cold mist chilled the tears on his cheeks. He wiped them off with his sleeve and directed his thoughts to the task ahead.

There was an English captain by the name of Beechy anchored at the presidio waiting for some of his men to return from Monterey. They weren't expected back for some time and the captain had been amusing himself by mapping the bay. Yesterday he'd been at the mission. Durán figured that with moderate wind and full sail the H.M.S. Blossom could ferry a large expedition to the *Rio de los Cosumnes* in a day—not the seven or eight days it took *lanchas.* Captain Beechy was a trader. His purpose in Alta California was to make money. Why wouldn't he accept the proposal? But they'd have to come up the south bay to pick up the mission supplies and neophytes. He wasn't sure how much time that would take. A well-governed overland expedition could get to the rebel village in two days. In any case, Durán intended to impress the commander with the need for speed, and would mention this choice of transportation.

At last Estanislao dismounted before the commander's modest house. As Durán opened the *carreta* gate, the Indian offered his hand to steady him for the big step down. As he did so, Estanislao said, "Excuse me, Padre, but I think you are sad." His expression conveyed manly caring and, yes, an odd sense of equality.

"*Sí, mijo.*" Feeling almost giddy, he held the hand slightly longer than necessary.

"Are you sad about the *Indios* in the pueblo *calabozo?*"

"*Sí,* those poor deluded people have become slaves in this wicked world." But for now he steeled himself for retaliation upon the savages of the Cosumnes River.

55

Coming out of a perplexing dream, Grizzly Hair opened his eyes. Father sun was already high. People lay sprawled about, still asleep after dancing most of the night. Small noises caught his attention—snicks and muffled thuds.

He turned over and looked through the low-hanging branches west of the village. A wall of leather-clad men knelt there, quietly loading their guns. His stomach dropped. It couldn't be! Not for at least another five sleeps.

"Hide!" he yelled, voice breaking with shock. He ran before he was fully upright, nearly falling on his face. The scouts hadn't reported back. Where was his bow? Too recently in dream, he couldn't remember at first. Fear drove him and he dove behind the tule u-macha where he had left his weapons. The village was surrounded with leather-jacketed men and neophytes with clubs. Screaming women and children ran in every direction. The explosions of *fusiles* resounded in the trees. Hit by the balls, people flew through the air and fell bleeding.

A cannon boomed. Shrieking, an old woman somersaulted—arms and only one leg, blood showering. Frightened children wailed. Back in the trees Grizzly Hair remembered what O-se-mai-ti had said: *You must fight like cornered bears.* Unleashing that fierce anger, he crouch-ran from u-macha to u-macha, to get within bow range of the enemy.

A solder stepped in front of him—black *pantalones,* thick wrinkled rawhide jacket, rawhide hat. Grizzly Hair looked into the round black hole that would deliver his death. The white knuckle jerked.

Already diving, he saw the leather-jacket swallowed in a burst of light. He felt the heat of a bone-rattling blast. Something heavy landed on his back, burning. He rolled away in the dirt and lay on the ground in little pain trying to understand what had happened. An arm's length away lay the *Español*—a black hat in protective dress. The rawhide hat had fallen off and his short beard was gone. His face had been transformed into a pulpy red and black mass with a few teeth and white nose-bone showing. A tremulous moan came from him. Between them lay the bent iron tube and smoking stalk that had been a gun. It must have blown up in the *Español's* face.

Grizzly Hair was lucky. O-se-mai-ti had given him power. Neophytes in mission wool were running after people, beating them over the head with big sticks. Watching, *soldados* aimed *fusiles.* Neophytes yanked women out of their houses and dragged them toward the woods, where more people were fighting. Arrows came from the door of the dancehouse.

Two black hats suddenly loomed over him. He played dead. They took their injured friend by the armpits and pulled him toward the woods, retrieving the leather hat as they left. In the screaming chaos Grizzly Hair stealthily recovered his bow and quiver, arrows unspilled. Expecting to be shot, he jumped to his feet and darted behind an u-macha. No black hat was there. Luck was holding. He crouch-ran to the next u-macha and the next to the north edge of the village. The enemy swarmed around here like maggots on a dead animal. He would pay them back.

Suddenly knowing how to do this, he proceeded calmly, one enemy at a time. He felt alert, seeing things almost before they happened, somehow knowing where to look. He scanned the violence before him and every time a black hat came within range, he let fly.

The arrows bounced off the *cuero*—layers of wrinkled, unstretched cowhide dried in the sun, perhaps by him. He aimed at their necks and eyes, or if a neophyte was clubbing someone, shot him mid-torso. The defending men shot their arrows from cover in the surrounding trees. Many arrows flew, but with everyone in motion, none had felled any of the black hats that he could see, though more and more invading neophytes were falling, some with Grizzly Hair's arrows in them. Every boom of the cannon startled him, made him jump. Children continued to scream and cry.

Flames leapt from the dancehouse and muffled cries could be heard from inside. A black hat stood outside the door ready to shoot anyone who tried to escape. In the ring of trees around the village Two Falcons and Lame Beaver were helping several other men press against both sides of a black hat who had been trying to reload. Grizzly Hair joined another bunch of men using the same tactic on the black hat at the door of the dancehouse. The man swung his gun like a club. Grizzly Hair ducked along with the others and the black hat ran away. With balls zinging around him, Grizzly Hair ran back to cover. A new guard came to make sure no one left the dancehouse alive. He was covered by three club-swinging neophytes. Other neophytes ran around lighting all the houses on fire. Most of the defending men stayed under cover and let fly from hidden places.

All day long the injured and dead accumulated in the blackened town, bodies smoking where the dancehouse had been. The clubbing and dragging of people continued. Most of the dead were women and children, and it seemed all of the captured were women and children. Few if any had escaped through the forest. In some places the ground took on a glossy red sheen. As if to avoid the sight, father sun lowered himself into his house in the west. Gradually the screams diminished to moans and whimpers. Many were dead, and it was plain the black hats were taking people to the mission, and not just *cimarrones.* There had been only a handful of them.

A little boy ran to the bloody clearing and stared at a body. A woman darted after him. Whisking him to her arms, she started to run, but her feet left the ground as though she had been jerked by a rope. She landed a distance away. Blood gushed from a hole in her side. The *soldado* with the smoking gun ran over and pulled the screaming boy from the dying woman, probably his mother, and headed toward the captured people. Grizzly Hair let fly. The arrow bounced off the jacket.

He aimed again at his rapidly moving target. The arrow bounced again. All around, wasted arrows lay on the ground. Two neophytes in hip wraps came and took the boy, relieving the black hat. He turned around, eyes in shadow, clearly searching for the source of the arrows. Grizzly Hair released one, and another neophyte went down.

He pulled another arrow. A sharp blow to his head threw him forward on his bow, arrow breaking in the ground. Singing pain reverberated in his skull. Slowed by it, he turned to see what had hit him. A neophyte held a club over him, ready to bring it down again.

He rolled out of the way then uncoiled, striking the neophyte's knee with his heels. The crack of bone sounded over the din as the knee bent the wrong way and the neophyte collapsed, howling.

Jingling spurs approached. Still reeling from the blow, Grizzly Hair looked up and saw the black hat coming with a *fusil.* Grabbling his bow, he got to his knees and tried to sprint but his legs felt slow. A hard clout on his head extinguished sight.

Light returned with the next blow—on the back of his head. He rolled, seeing as if through disturbed water. The gunstock was swinging down again.

He caught it, deflecting the blow to his shoulder. He tried to wrench the gun away. They fought for it, the soldier kneeling over him with a knee in his belly. Their eyes locked. Despite being dazed, Grizzly Hair knew those mismatched eyes in the narrow face. He had fought this man before, in the tulares. He had lost then, and his amulet of O-se-mai-ti's hair had been thrown into the muddy water.

Now, however, rage burned in his stomach, not fear. It seared away the vertigo. Power inflated his chest, and he roared loudly. The black hats would not defeat him again.

One eye widened and the man leaned back, though he held the gun tightly.

Rocking on his back, Grizzly Hair jumped to his feet, jerking the smaller man up too, and nearly wrenched the gun from him.

Then, as a vaquero leaps on a horse, the black hat sprang to his back. Grizzly Hair nearly lost his balance. Spurs gouged his thighs and the man lunged forward, grasping the gun again with arms on either side of his neck. He reared back, slamming the gun into a choking hold on Grizzly Hair's neck. At the same time his legs gripped like iron pincers and he spurred Grizzly Hair like a reluctant horse, rapidly drilling his thighs and calves.

Staggering under the weight and pain, he tried to take the gun. The rider yanked it up over his head. Grizzly Hair kept his hands on it but couldn't stop the butt from coming down hard on his skull. The village swirled around him and he took lurching steps to stay upright as the spurs drilled his flesh. He strained with his arms trying to push up against the heavy, hammering butt with the iron strap around it. He tried running, whirling, shaking and bucking, but couldn't dislodge the rider. The legs squeezed with the strength of a practiced horseman and the spurs kept up their demonic rhythm.

He whipped his head back into the hot breath and contacted the chin. He heard the hollow sound of teeth, but his arms were weakening and it took all his strength to prevent the gun butt from breaking his head. It landed on his thumbs and the palms of his hands. If only he could get to his calf-thong, his knife.

The kick of spurs came hard and fast. Hoping to scrape the man off in the branches, he ran to the trees past hand-to-hand struggles and neophytes watching for escapees. He veered around them to protect his vulnerable belly from their clubs.

At an oak with low limbs he turned and pushed back into the big, half-dead branches. Cracking, some gave way. Summoning all his strength while his thighs, calves and shins were continually pummeled by the spurs, he planted his feet and swung his torso in lunging motions against the sharp broken branches. The gun snagged and pulled to the side, but continued to hammer his head. Arms burning with the effort, he pushed up and out, only to have the butt hit his forehead and nose in a painful glancing blow. Meanwhile the jacket protected the rider's back from the branches and the legs were too low.

With a loud "ahhhgghh," he ran backwards and collided with the trunk. Debris showered over his head. He stepped away and reared back again, ramming their combined weight into the trunk. The hiss of air warmed his neck and the gun wobbled. He jerked it forward into his grasp. Quickly transferring it to one hand, he twisted out of the four-legged grip and pulled his knife, now facing the *Español,* whose back and head were bumping down the tree bark, legs releasing his waist. The soldier came to a rest with his head forward on the trunk, legs kicking.

He wanted to cut the *Español's* throat but the spurs came at him furiously. He swung the gun by its barrel, bashing boots and spurs with the flat side and quickly slashed a leg above a boot. A spur caught his abdomen and groin.

Stunned with pain, he jumped back. The black hat flipped over and scuttled away. He ran in big limping hops, leaving a trail of blood. Watching him go, Grizzly Hair reinserted the knife in his calf-thong and picked some strands of brown hair from the bark. He had a piece of the enemy.

He glanced around, hearing only his own hard breathing and the thud of his heart. The attackers were gone. Trembling with the release from battle, he looked down and saw that he was covered with blood. Pain drummed in his head and the shredded flesh of his legs cried out with many tongues.

Falls-off-House was suddenly beside him, putting an arm around his shoulder to help him stand. It brought tears to his eyes. He hadn't been able to see what happened to the other men of the umne, but the spirits had protected this accident-prone friend. He appeared uninjured except for scrapes along his left side.

Grizzly Hair tucked the hair into his calf thong.

56

It was nearly nightfall. The few men left in the scorched village were staring at the dead women and children. It looked like more than two twenties. Some men squatted among the dead with their faces in their hands.

One pulled himself upright on his bow and said, "We have far to walk. Best go before dark." With a devastated expression he looked at Grizzly Hair and his friends. Weakly, he said, "Come to Newach's place. We'll sleep there. After the sleep we will return for the Burning."

Falls-off-House helped Grizzly Hair walk up the darkening river path. The footing through the big oaks was easy, the land flat and without rocks. Two Falcons and Lame Beaver joined them, neither wounded more than Falls-off-House. Scorpion-on-Nose had gone ahead with most of the Cosumne. Two Falcons supported Grizzly Hair under his other shoulder

Carrying the gun, Lame Beaver went searching for herbs. He seemed a small figure trotting beneath the stately oak people. The salmon light colored the bare-limbed trees revealing shapes and angles that silently told the secrets of their lives. Grizzly Hair *saw* everything. It was as though the jolt of the battle had improved his reception to the spirits. Everything had significance. "You didn't get hurt," he said to Falls-off-House and Two Falcons.

"I am a hunter," said Two Falcons. "You are a warrior. You attracted them."

He was still thinking about that when Lame Beaver came back with a bunch of fresh lacy yarrow leaves and white blooms. The men crushed the powerful healer and gently packed it into the gouges in Grizzly Hair's legs. They applied it to his head and other wounds. The blood became sticky enough to hold the medicine. It stopped most of the bleeding, but recurring dizziness made him stagger and he was grateful for the strong arms of his friends.

Lame Beaver said, "I'm glad our wives and babies weren't there." The sober expression on the flat bones of his face resembled Bowstring when he was being wry.

It nearly made Grizzly Hair smile to hear so great an understatement.

At last they arrived at the village of the Newachumne, a short distance that Grizzly Hair could have covered at his normal running speed between morning nu-pah and the end of bathing. He saw no women and figured they were all in their u-machas. He had consumed no food since before the previous sleep—nobody had—yet none was being prepared. Men were crawling inside the sweathouse, and Grizzly Hair and his friends followed them. Maybe those who arrived earlier had eaten. It was crowded inside. The heat hit him like a fist, and the fire's glow revealed wounded men lying on their sides or backs, several grimacing. Grizzly Hair's own wounds screamed at him as he waited for Yarrow to heal him. The smoking herbs on the fire would also help. No talk came for a long time, only quiet moans.

The voice of Little Cos said, "They surprised us."

Somebody said through his teeth, "Maybe the scouts led them to us."

An angry voice countered, "You are talking about my brother. That is an insult."

Little Cos used the soothing tone of a headman banishing disagreement, "None of the scouts would betray us. They must have been captured."

If so, they were not the best trackers, but this was no time for accusation. Grizzly Hair said, "People must be stealthier from now on." *We* would have seemed presumptuous coming from an outsider. "People must keep women and children safe, not allow them near the fighting. I agree with Little Cos. Next time people must be prepared, not surprised."

"Next time!" somebody exclaimed.

"Yes, next time," said a patient voice.

"I can't fight anymore," a new voice sadly declared. "I'm going to the mission to be with my wife and children."

After a long silence someone said in a raspy, skeptical tone: "Next time I suppose you'll fight against us."

There was a rude noise of air being blown through a flapping tongue: "No. They'll send him to fight the Ochejamne. They know we don't like those people. They like to fan the flames of hatred. Just like they brought the Anisumne here."

"That's right," said another. "You can't trust anyone from the other side of the Big Mo'mol."

A thin laugh responded. "I saw shits aplenty from this side of the river."

"Too many got away. I saw that stupid son of old Break Kindling from down there in Big Swamp strutting around here like a grand hy-apo. Thinks he's a new man because he lives in the mission. Why, he can't even piss straight."

The voice of the man about to go to the mission said, "If even the son of Break Kindling can be transformed, imagine how my sons will fare. They could become alcaldes. They will wear *pantalones* and shoot with *fusiles*. Your children will be ignorant h'nteelehs.

"Shut up!" somebody snapped.

Talk stopped for a while and there was nothing to distract Grizzly Hair from his pain. "My wife and son were not captured or killed," he said, "so I cannot speak for you who have lost your women and children. But I believe the mission neophytes will fight on our side someday and together we *Indios* will chase the black hats out of the Valley of the Sun, maybe back to where they came from. Then we can have the goods in the missions without living there. Estanislao says he will help fight, and he's a man mission people respect. But before that, I don't think any of us should go to the missions. It will only divide us."

"I'm going," the man declared.

Another growled, "I don't care what you say, those stinking turds who clubbed my wife are my enemies for all time."

Maybe this was a poor time to mention cooperating with mission people.

After a quiet space Little Cos said, "Our visitor from up the river is a warrior."

"Yes," two or three others quickly agreed.

Grizzly Hair appreciated that.

"That man who jumped on you is named Amador," said a familiar voice. "He was on our river not long ago. He rode a man like that, a man as strong as you, but Amador took his knife and reached around and stabbed the man's belly then pulled up and sliced him open. His guts fell out and that's the only reason he finally fell down. Nothing else stopped him."

The silence felt twisted and sick. Grizzly Hair twisted it back, "I have some of his hair."

Soft exclamations rasped around the sweathouse. "Give it to our doctor," a voice said. "He'll give him what he deserves."

Grizzly Hair had seen a doctor competition before one of the dances; the doctor of the Cosumne had won. Still, he would keep the hair and consider how to use it.

A husk of wood collapsed in the firepit, flinging sparks.

Finally he slept and dreamed of many animals walking around, but he couldn't find Eagle in the crowd. He had only a feather from Eagle, and though it was a precious gift, it wasn't enough. He searched for a long time and became very distraught, when Horse said, "I will go with you."

"But you are too big," Grizzly Hair countered.

As though to show him it wasn't true, Horse climbed into Grizzly Hair's arms, folded his long legs and curled up like a baby. And though he was very heavy and pulled him down with each step, Horse looked up with big loving eyes and Grizzly Hair felt a little better. However, he accidentally dropped the feather.

He awoke after restless sleep and knew it was a bad omen to lose Eagle. Horse could never supplant the Eagle wings that went back to the dawn of the world. He went to the river and gritted his teeth as the water loosened the yarrow and touched his raw flesh. But the pain brought clarity. It didn't matter that some neophytes were allowed to leave the missions, people were still being captured and the kind of war that had been underway for a long time continued. Now it was being waged on the home river. If the black hats were not resoundingly defeated, all the Cosumne would go to the mission and the battles would extend up the river to the home place.

He approached one of the medicine women who sat in the village center with baskets. Something about her pulled him. In a pleasant voice she asked, "Did you dream well?"

He thought about the sadness of losing Eagle and the solicitous caring of Horse and said, "I don't know."

"This is boiled from Sacayak," she said with a wise smile, touching the basket. "Do you know this plant?"

"Yes." He liked to sand his bow and arrow shafts with its hard-ribbed stalks. As a young child he had loved the way it popped and crackled when his mother threw it in fire as part of her ritual for rejuvenating elderly people, so for him it contained a remembrance of Eagle Woman's strength. After her death his eyes had opened to this unusual plant's second season, the branched phase of its life when it closely resembled a horse's tail. Thus for him it contained both Eagle and Horse.

"It will help heal you," she said, rolling out a clean tulare mat. He lay on his belly and let her pour the liquid on his wounds. Immediately it soothed the rawness.

"Let that dry in the sun," she said. "Do your people know the story of Sacayak?"

He did, but to encourage her to tell her version, he politely answered, "Maybe."

"Sacayak has power. People say that in First World a headman laid a stem of it across a path. He knew Coyote's daughter would come that way, and he wanted Coyote to feel sorry that he had made people stay dead instead of letting them come back to life. When Coyote's daughter walked down the path, Sacayak turned into a rattlesnake and bit her. She died. Later Coyote found her. He picked her up in his arms and cried. Now he was sorry she would not live again."

Grizzly Hair lay soaking up both sacayak and father sun's life-giving power. He thought about the shortness of life, and the loss to the world each time a person died. Many had died before the sleep. He thought about the riddle that Sacayak represented death never revived, yet was also associated with revitalization and healing. Maybe it would stop the vertigo. "You are good to me, Mother," he said in thanks.

"You look like my people," she said glancing slyly at him. "You have a certain look in your eyes and that handsome nose."

He suddenly realized his father had come from around here. Then he *saw.* Everywhere he looked he felt a dreaming recognition. The pattern of the oaks standing in a half-circle on the east side of the village, the distance from the dancehouse to the river, but especially the quiet feeling of knowing he was among friends. "I think I lived here when I was a very young boy," he told the medicine woman.

Her lips parted in amazement. "Who are your people?"

Unexpectedly, something blocked his tongue at this long-awaited moment of finding his father's people. He didn't want to mention Eats Skunk, who was widely disliked, or reveal the traits that would identify his father, a man who gambled too much and didn't care for his tools. "I live in my mother's home place, Morning Owl's people. There was a fight with the black hats. It must have been at the time when your men pushed a cannon into the mud. My father was killed."

The healer continued to scowl as though trying to place him. "I should come upriver and visit you," she said, no doubt fishing for clues.

He smiled. "Bring medicine for blindness, for Grandmother."

Little Cos, who had a bad bruise over half his face, his eye swollen shut, approached with Newach, the hy-apo of this small village, and offered Grizzly Hair cold nu-pah. He scooped hungrily three times. As he ate, Little Cos said, "Thank you for coming to help us. I am in the debt of all of you." He offered nu-pah to Lame Beaver and Two Falcons, who had come over.

Nodding at Grizzly Hair, the healer said, "He is a cousin-brother."

"My mother took me away from here a long time ago," he said, but with the clarity of his new *seeing*, he preferred his own earned reputation to the one he would have as his father's son. He also knew that he would not come here and do this again, not unless he had participated in careful planning. Next time he would not be surprised.

Several sleeps later he could walk without pain and dizziness and was preparing to return to his people. A runner came looking for the Cosumne. Finding the placed burned, he came upstream to the Newachumne and made a stunning announcement: "*Americanos* are in the Valley of the Sun."

People looked at each other and said it was the signal for war. "What are they doing?" Grizzly Hair asked.

"Trapping beaver, coming north very slowly."

"How many?"

"Sixteen."

"Where are they now?"

"Near where the San Joaquin River comes from the mountains and turns north."

"Do they have guns?"

"Many."

57

The drizzle from the featureless grey sky persisted. Etumu nursed Boy, who was growing big and saying a few words. He pulled in steady rhythm. Just outside, Straight Willow's daughter and her friend laughed over a mud village they were making, waiting for Boy to join them. It seemed only a few sleeps ago since Etumu had been that young.

Grizzly Hair had gone to check his snares. Thanks to the rain, the wide rivers and marshes kept him at the home place, but even now he often seemed quiet and preoccupied. Sometimes Etumu wished he was more like the men who never thought about the *Españoles.* Still, she wouldn't trade him for any other. Sighing, she leaned against the dark wall and watched the rain-slick heads of children. In the distance the muffled thump-thump of a pestle at the chaw'se was putting her to sleep.

A loud crack brought her upright and rang in her ears. A large tree branch breaking? Boy's eyes shot open and he released the nipple, twisting his head to avoid the spray of milk. Dogs barked and Straight Willow's children hugged each other in fear.

Boy wiggled off her lap and they both went outside. Morning Owl, Two Falcons, Lame Beaver and her father ran past. Would a gun sound like that? Grizzly Hair was suddenly there, pressing past her into the u-macha. He took his knife from the rafters and sat down tying his calf-thong. Boy was excited, obviously hoping his father would take him somewhere. Grizzly Hair looked at Etumu. She saw fear in his face. The truth jumped to her. It had been a gun.

He touched her shoulder and said, "Hill Boulders, quick." Grabbing his bow, he ran up the west path.

Boy started to cry and Etumu pulled him by the hand, "Run, run! The black hats are here." Grizzly Hair had told her the gruesome details of what happened at Little Cos's place. The rain hadn't stopped them from coming here. Panic nearly suffocated her. Boy's feet slipped in the mud and she whisked him up and tried to run up the slippery slope with him. Straight Willow was herding children as fast as they could go. All around, women and children headed toward Hill Boulders.

Rain streamed down Grizzly Hair's face and body as he approached the swollen brown river. The mat of leaves under his feet gave off the dank aroma of mold. He scanned both shores. In the river, the naked willows bent to the flow. A gray pine rode down the current, peaking and falling on the agitated waves. Big drops of water fell from the bare cottonwoods.

Something moved beyond a tangle of trees deposited by the river. Crouching, Grizzly Hair crept toward it, the noisy river covering his sound. Expecting black hats, he was surprised to see a floppy brown hat like Missouri's. A few steps closer he could see a man in fringed buckskin squatting beside the river, intent upon skinning a beaver. Then he saw the other man.

He lay face down in the water, legs on shore. His top half bobbed in the current. He was naked. One of the umne? Surely not. Grizzly Hair's stomach knotted with fear. He couldn't see enough from this distance.

The stranger slung an iron jaw of the type Missouri had used for trapping over his shoulder, picked up a long gun and stood up. Lifting his head as though sensing danger, he clutched the beaver pelt in the other hand and walked swiftly away from the river. Faded brown hair hung under his grease-stained hat and the wide brim darkened his face.

Silently Grizzly Hair took aim at the back of the buckskin shirt, but hesitated. Most men didn't travel alone. He looked up and down the shoreline on both sides, but saw nothing except trees and dark boulders. He must not provoke an ambush. Women and children were near. Besides, the man in the water could be an *Indio* from somewhere else, maybe a guide. An inner voice whispered *no*. Still, he lowered his bow and saw the other men do likewise.

The hoofbeats of a single horse running west rapidly faded. Grizzly Hair listened, but heard only the thrumming river. Signaling the men to cover him, he crouch-ran to the limp form. His breath caught as though hands choked him. Those narrow shoulders and tapered legs belonged to Falls-off-House. A line of pink matter floated from under the hair.

He rolled him over. Where the right eye had been, a hole stared vacantly. Matter oozed from inside. Shock and revulsion jangled through him. Hardly aware of the others gathering around, he dragged Falls-off-House out of the water. He had been unlucky once too often.

Morning Owl keened an unearthly sound. His orphaned nephew Falls-off-House was like a son to him. The man in buckskins had violated the umne and murdered a mild man with an ironic sense of humor. Fists clenched, Grizzly Hair told Morning Owl, "I'll kill him." The headman nodded grimly. "Yes. Go after him. You have a horse." Normally the next of kin took revenge.

Relieved to be moving, Grizzly Hair ran for Morena, then galloped west. Pounding hooves approached from behind. Two Falcons, grim-lipped, caught up on Milk.

The tracks led to a camp of cloth houses in an open treeless area below them, where Grizzly Hair had first watched Two Falcons hunt deer. They dismounted, hid the horses and watched from the boulders on the hill.

Around the camp about two twenties of horses grazed, and about the same number of mules. Grizzly Hair counted thirteen men, all dressed like the killer. They squatted around a fire or moved back and forth to the packs that had been removed from the animals. Their hats were pulled down. Some were cooking, steam and smoke mingling with the rain. Many skins were piled on one side of the camp.

"Did you see the murderer's face?" Two Falcons whispered.

"Only a moment." From habit Grizzly Hair had looked at the body rather than the narrow space between the hat brim and the end of the nose. The rest of the face was covered with flowing brown hair. Clothing disguised. "Did you see it?"

"No," said the master hunter. "They all look alike."

"Maybe I'd recognize him up close," Grizzly Hair said. But in this open place he couldn't get near enough.

Two Falcons said, "See that one? Tying the bundle on the horse? It's not him."

"No. Not him." The man's face and hands were black as charcoal, the beard and hair beneath his hat bushier than any Grizzly Hair had ever seen, including Missouri's. The other men looked as faded and high-nosed as the long robes. Some were taller than others, but how tall was the killer? One thing was sure. Missouri wasn't among them. No fleshy man was there.

These men were clearly beaver hunters with provisions for a long journey, probably the *Americanos* who had been coming north. But why had one of them killed Falls-off-House? Rage mixed with withering disappointment. He had hoped to make allies of these powerful men with good guns—that is if they didn't prove to be sorcerers like Missouri.

"They're leaving camp," Two Falcons whispered.

They were folding the cloth houses. "The killer probably told them what he did and they are afraid of us."

Two Falcons nodded to indicate that was likely. The cloth houses were quickly tied on the horses' rumps, and the piles of beaver skins on the mules' backs. "Maybe we can get closer to them at their next camp," Two Falcons said with a hunter's calm.

They followed the trappers north to the large river of Kadeema. Very high and vigorous, it would be dangerous to cross in this season. The tracks turned east along the river. Grizzly Hair and Two Falcons followed inside the line of trees. All day they headed into the wind-driven rain. In the evening they saw a fire on the plain, more than a bowshot from any cover. This was a sign of power, that they started a fire so quickly in the rain. Some of the trappers were setting up the cloth houses, others cooking. Still others stood watchfully around the camp with their guns.

As father sun's sad light rapidly faded, Grizzly Hair and Two Falcons hobbled the horses back in the trees beyond earshot of the many horses and mules that grazed on the plain. Then they settled where they could see the trappers. The thick branches of an oak sheltered them from the rain and its wide trunk stopped the southeasterly wind. The trappers took their food and crawled into their houses. But two well-positioned guards with guns over their knees stayed outside, hats down against the rain. Once in a while one of them would check on the horses, then return.

Grizzly Hair struggled to keep Falls-off-House out of his mind, and though he continued to feel hot rage, he couldn't help but admire the discipline of the trappers. They were obviously accustomed to traveling and protecting themselves.

"After the sleep when they defecate," Two Falcons said, "we'll watch and see which one is the killer. We'll cut his throat and throw him in the river. We'll be gone before they miss him."

Grizzly Hair agreed. "By the time they figure out what happened we'll have a good head start." Or so he hoped. The tree moaned as it stood against the wind, which drove rain between the sheltering branches. "It would be easier to lose them on foot," he admitted.

A warm, broad hand cupped his shoulder and Two Falcon's deep voice had a smile in it. "No one could track us on foot."

The compliment warmed him. The master hunter had taught him well. Things would work out.

A sharp crack made them both jerk, followed by a thud and an earth tremor. A branch had fallen out of their tree. "We are lucky," he whispered.

"Yes," Two Falcons agreed. "It was a sign."

Across the distance the storm snuffed out the campfire and darkness pressed upon them from all sides. Grateful for the nearness and warmth of his mentor, Grizzly Hair nevertheless longed for the sea otter cape Etumu had made, the warmest of furs. The river spirit rolled and thrashed and cried as she hurried through the dark, never exactly repeating herself. He listened for a long time, then flew with the storm. Half of him huddled beside Two Falcons while the other half entered one of the cloth houses. He began to *see* the dream of one of the trappers who lay sleeping below him. He saw the other side of the eastern mountains, a vast and lonely expanse with few trees and little water. Somehow he knew this man was indeed an *Americano,* a people as clever and powerful as the *Españoles.*

The trapper's spirit floated up and hovered with him. The two spirits looked at each other and Grizzly Hair saw that the *Americano* was troubled, in a hurry and afraid he would miss a big time of many, many people. This was important to him.

"Did you kill my friend?" Grizzly Hair's spirit asked.

The trapper's spirit said, "I am very sorry. One of my men shot him."

"We came to kill the murderer."

"We feared you might, but you'd have to kill us all first, and you can't do that."

"We only want the murderer."

"I won't give him up."

Grizzly Hair's spirit already knew this, and he asked the polite question. "Where are you going?"

"Over the mountains."

"Men cannot travel over those mountains when there is deep snow."

"We will do it."

"People say it can't be done."

"I have done many things people say can't be done."

Then Grizzly Hair was back at the tree, knowing he had spirit-tracked an *Americano.* His own feat impressed but puzzled him. Nothing linked him with that particular *Americano,* except that the man's friend had killed Grizzly Hair's friend. He shifted uncomfortably against the tree, goosebumps rising for reasons other than the cold. Two Falcons seemed to doze, but Grizzly Hair was alert, sick about Falls-off-House and desirous of avenging the murder. Yet as a warrior he wanted these brave and careful *Americanos* as allies.

Slowly the clouds changed from black to dark gray. The wind had stopped and the rain came straight down. Through the rain he saw the trappers stirring.

"Look, they don't spread their urine," Two Falcons said.

Fearless of spells that could be visited upon them, they didn't even use the high bunch grass standing all around them. They were confident in their power.

Two Falcons whispered, "Maybe we could take the urine to Drum-in-Fog."

But from this distance they didn't know which one it was. They would need urine from each one, and wet sandy earth would be hard to carry. They'd have to pay Drum-in-Fog for killing all of them. Grizzly Hair said. "It would cost too much." He watched the trappers fold their houses.

Two Falcons twisted his face and nodded. The trappers packed and headed east. They moved at the same determined pace, men going to an important big time.

"They don't even shit," Grizzly Hair remarked as he and Two Falcons ran to their horses. Grizzly Hair climbed on wet, shivering Morena, looked at the older man, who was mounting Milk, and said, "I know where they're going."

"Where?"

Self-conscious about his first spirit-tracking of a man, he said, "Across the eastern mountains."

Both horses stood with their heads down, tails between their legs. Rain streamed down their necks and ran from their jawbones. Appreciatively, Two Falcons glanced at Grizzly Hair, then gazed toward the heavy clouds obscuring the eastern mountains. Steam rose from his thick body and his long hair was plastered to his shoulders. "They will die," he said.

"Yes, ice and snow will finish them for us."

They reined the horses toward the home place.

Grizzly Hair stood before Morning Owl's u-macha watching streams of water cut channels through the dirt berm. Raven Feather looked out. Her blackened face blended with the gloom. Then Morning Owl came out with singed hair and eyes red with strong emotion.

Grizzly Hair told what had happened. Two Falcons nodded agreement. The headman said, "I should have gone after the murderer. It was mine to do." He turned and went back inside.

Grizzly Hair had failed. He tried to swallow the pain.

Crowding around, the umne tugged deerskin capes around their shoulders. Drum-in-Fog said, "The ghost will wander among us."

People sucked in breath and exchanged glances. Lame Beaver asked, "Was the killer a black hat"?

"Americano," said Grizzly Hair.

Sunshine-through-the-Mist asked, "Was it the evil doctor?" Whispers floated through the umne.

"No, Missouri wasn't among them."

Two Falcons said over the murmuring crowd, "They are going to the eastern mountains. The spirits in the ice and snow will kill the murderer for us."

Every day rain fell and the river rose almost to the village center. Domingo's place would be under water. No runner came from any direction. No horse could walk in the mud. During short periods when the clouds parted, people looked east and saw the mountains like a wall of teeth. Yet buttercups bloomed all around them.

More than a moon later the rains finally ended but water and deep mud still prevented travel. Nevertheless, a runner from Sucais somehow came through it. Grizzly Hair scooped up the tobacco he'd been pounding in a mortar hole and went to the crowd before the roundhouse, Boy close beside him. Etumu stood on his other side.

Gazing straight over the heads of the listeners, the runner recited a long, memorized message. "*Americanos* are camped in my village," he said. "Jediahsmith, the headman of the strangers, sends his apology. One of his men killed one of your men."

In stunned silence the umne stared at the runner. They had named the next river north for the men who had surely died on its shores, River of the Americans. A Cry for Falls-off-House had been held and everyone thought the murder had been avenged by the spirits of the ice and snow, but his soul could still lurk. People looked around with fear showing in the whites of their eyes.

The runner continued, "The *Americanos* tried to cross the eastern mountains but it was very cold. They ate their horses and wrapped themselves in the skins. They traveled down your river but crossed and went south before they got to your place. They didn't want to meet you. Now they are camping with us. Jediahsmith says your man was stealing a trap. The *Americano* hy-apo says he'll pay you for the loss of life in your village. Sucais asks that you not punish the killer or we could all be in danger. The *Americanos* are very strong. They have many guns."

They defeated the mountains. The thought hung unsaid in the air. Morning Owl used a disembodied tone that carried in the silence: "I should have killed him."

Maybe he should have. Grizzly Hair realized his own spirit had been torn between vengeance and the desire to befriend potential allies. It was a lesson. There was wisdom in the old ways. Sucais' runner stood waiting for a response.

Morning Owl spoke loudly. "The *Americanos* will pay for the death of my nephew." He frowned and drew black-faced Raven Feather aside for private talk. Everyone waited, and at last women went to their cooking baskets and lowered the hot rocks into their acorn water and listened for talk to resume. Shortly it became obvious that more thought was needed and everyone including the runner was hungry. Grizzly Hair knew the man slightly, so he invited him to his and Etumu's fire.

In the middle of supper Morning Owl stood up and said across two fires, "We want ten trained horses. My relative was shot in his family's own fishing place. He was not stealing the iron jaw, just looking at it. The *Americano* violated the fishing hole and murdered him."

The runner raised his voice to be heard at Morning Owl's fire, not part of his memorized message. "Jediahsmith is very sorry. I think he will pay it." Then he said to Grizzly Hair, "Jediasmith wants to trade with our people and your people. This is why I come to you. Sucais says we need to be allies with these strong men. Jediahsmith is headman of thirteen men, and later many more men might come to trap beaver. They have magical things and will bring more next time they come, like eye covers that make you see very far."

A chilly breeze flattened the flames of the fires. Women pulled deerskin robes closer over their shoulders and people quietly scooped nu-pah. Morning Owl called over his fire, "The killer might shoot more of our people." Throughout the village center people nodded and murmured as they ate.

"No, he will not," the runner protested across the space. "Jediahsmith's men are esteemed traders. They are polite guests."

Running Quail's voice resonated across the several fires. "It is not polite to kill people who look at their traps."

The runner responded in reassuring tones, and Grizzly Hair heard his keen hope for a peaceful solution. Talk continued after all had eaten their fill. Morning Owl showed ten fingers, indicating his unyielding price. Using the headman's repetitive, formal cadence, he announced, "After they pay, pay retribution of ten trained horses, Jediahsmith and all his men, except the murderer, all besides the murderer, are welcome here for trading. They are welcome for trading. But if the bad man comes, if he comes here, comes near our place, I will kill him, kill him myself. I, my men and I, will travel to Sucais' place and tell this to the *Americanos.*"

Morning Owl brought out his elderberry pipe and tobacco pouch, and Grizzly Hair joined the talk circle. Blowing out a mouthful, the runner said, "Many more neophytes have left the missions, many of my people."

Grizzly Hair looked at the man. "How many?"

"About *dos cien.* Ten twenties."

Now it comes, Grizzly Hair knew. All the more need for the friendship of the *Americanos.*

Two Falcons' eyes shifted, understanding the significance. He asked, "Where are those *cimarrones* camping?"

"Some are in Domingo's village, many are in my place. Some are camping with the Chilamne, some with the Cosumne. First Grass seed has been harvested and women are bringing baskets of it to the *Americanos.* There is a big time and dancing."

"Black hats will go after the *cimarrones,*" Grizzly Hair said. "Will the *Americanos* help us fight?"

The runner sucked smoke and said, "We hope so. People are dancing in their honor. War talk is everywhere. The mountain spirits sent them back to help us."

But Falls-off-House wouldn't be here to plan. Anger and sorrow and excitement pulled at Grizzly Hair from different directions. And uncertainty. Would the *Americanos* help or not? One thing was clear; he must talk with Jediahsmith, the hy-apo of the *Americanos,* a man his spirit already knew.

The next night Grizzly Hair and Etumu lay together listening to more rain dripping from the smokehole. The runner had gone with the message. She didn't want Grizzly Hair to go. He didn't want her to say it or lie there thinking it. He asked in a low tone, "What are people saying?" He had learned to trust her knowledge of the umne.

"Everyone is afraid of the ghost. I am too. Some say *Americanos* will sneak up and kill all of us. I don't want you to go." She put her hand on his chest beneath the rabbit blanket.

He closed his eyes. Dishi snored on the opposite wall and Boy's rapid breathing could be heard in the spaces between her loud pulls. "I must help bring the horses back," he said quietly. "Morena is a good herder." He didn't mention the significance of two hundred deserting neophytes, or the hope of making Jediahsmith an ally. He didn't tell her he must plan for the bigger fight that would surely come, or that after the victory she and Boy would be safer. Such talk would only set her up to worry.

Her palm made a circle on his chest. He felt himself stir and wished Boy were weaned. Instead he rolled off the mat and went to the sweathouse. A few stars winked in the clearing sky and though an occasional raindrop still fell, the night felt much warmer, as was normal in this season.

58

Dew glittered on every twig and leaf and blade of grass, and each droplet sparkled with brilliant Coyote colors. The beautiful sight portended well, and the cold water jolted Grizzly Hair to alertness. On the way back to the u-macha to retrieve his things, he encountered Etumu with her carrying basket.

"I am coming," she said.

He stopped where he stood. "But the *Americanos* are there. You are afraid of them."

"You said you are going to get the horses. That won't take long. Boy and I will be safe with you."

"Who will care for Grandmother?"

"Straight Willow is staying here; she will care for her."

Grizzly Hair was becoming uncomfortable. "I might need to stay longer. I need to talk to the *Americanos.* I need to talk with Sucais and Estanislao. It could take a long time." Before the words cleared, he saw his mistake.

With a twinkly smile she said, "Then you need me to cook for you."

She had Boy by the hand and started walking him toward the playing field. "We are going on the horse with Father," she told him. Boy gave a happy squeal and began to run on his short, fat legs. Grizzly Hair melted. Besides, Raven Feather was coming with Morning Owl, her big carrying basket on her back. Pretty Duck was packed to come with Scorpion-on-Nose too.

They all swam across the home river, then Grizzly Hair led Morena, with Etumu and Boy riding behind Raven Feather on Milk, Two Falcons leading. Morning Owl, Lame Beaver and Scorpion-on-Nose walked behind. Boy seemed to know he must be quiet and not wiggle. Newly released from his bikoos, he was accustomed to restraint and sat still in Etumu's arms.

The stream that had been small when Grizzly Hair had camped alone that first time he tracked the black hats was now wide and vigorous. They swam across it and for a time lost the two horses. Finding them downstream in the trees, they resumed the journey. Boy pointed at the grazing geese blanketing the land, and laughed. Sometimes he turned around and laughed at Grizzly Hair. He was happy. People of all ages enjoyed new adventures.

They swam the swollen river of the Muquelumne, then camped at Te-mi's place. Te-mi invited Morning Owl and Raven Feather to sleep in his u-macha. Grizzly Hair and Etumu slept with Elk Calf and his wife, nicknamed Swims Backwards. She had a young baby and the two women quickly became friends. In the morning, excited about the *Americanos*, Te-mi and his three sons, their wives and many more of the Muquelumne men and women joined the umne.

At last they arrived at the river of the Lakisamni. Sunlight came strongly from the west. They left Milk and Morena in a large brush corral with other horses and followed the path to the river bottom, much of it now occupied by the swollen river—transformed since Grizzly Hair had caught fish by hand in its separate pools.

Approaching the clearing where a dance was underway, the umne stopped and stared along with everyone else. Only in the mission had Grizzly Hair seen so many people in one place. The aroma of roasting horsemeat made his mouth water. Etumu smiled at him, thanking him wordlessly.

He touched her shoulder and tousled Boy's head.

"Look, Father," Boy said excitedly. He saw that the *Americanos* were unlike everyone else. Everyone continued staring at them as they danced around a fire. Skinnier than ever, they hopped to the beat of the log drum, fringe bouncing. The hairy beards on some of them covered the fronts of their shirts. They made sexual gestures at the dancing women, some of whom cheerfully gestured back, including women in red mission skirts.

Looking for the murderer, Grizzly Hair watched the faces of the *Americanos,* including the one with the black face. Then, as in a dream, the murderer advanced around the fire. Grizzly Hair was sure of it. He leaned toward Two Falcons and Morning Owl and pointed. Two Falcons saw the man and said, "He's the one." In the darkening shadows Raven Feather stood beside her man, the whites of her wide eyes all that could be seen in the pitch-blackened ball of her hairless head.

"When we tried to see him we couldn't," Two Falcons said, "and now he is revealed."

Morning Owl said, "It means we are asking the right amount of reparations." The killer's narrow backside retreated from view.

Te-mi's sons and their wives found relatives and melted into the crowd, all but Elk Calf. Grizzly Hair suspected he would stay with the umne to lend the support of his populous people and keep his people apprised of what was being said. Sucais came to greet them. Showing polite deference toward Morning Owl, he led them all to a place where a council would be held. He sat down in his saggy skin and patted the ground, indicating that he would play an important part in the council. He also beckoned an *Americano* from the shadow of a tree.

As the man came forward Grizzly Hair noticed brown hair falling from only one side of his floppy brown hat. He seemed a little older than Grizzly

Hair, maybe Estanislao's age, but his face was so gaunt and scarred that his age couldn't be guessed. His mustache and beard were trimmed, though the scars on one side of his face made the hair sparse. The point of his arrow-shaped nose came down to his upper lip. As he approached, the buckskin moved as though hanging from sticks.

"*Hola,*" he said, greeting them in Spanish. In the golden light from the west, his pale brown eyes sparked, and though he looked at them directly, Grizzly Hair felt at ease. Their spirits had talked, and he liked the man.

The American placed a fist on his chest and said, "Jed Smith. *Hablo poco Español.*"

He speaks little Spanish, Grizzly Hair translated in his mind. Another man came and sat beside Jed Smith. It was Narciso, the mission alcalde who whipped people, including the woman who was forced to carry the red doll. About Morning Owl's age, he sat there in a haughty manner as though Jed Smith were his best friend instead of a mere acquaintance, as he must have been in the short time they would have known each other. Narciso was obviously impressed with himself, and Grizzly Hair didn't like him any more now than he had in the mission.

Jed Smith started: "*Triste que el hombre de su familia está muerto.*"

Immediately Narciso said, "I will tell you what he says. He says it is sad that your man is dead."

Looking between Narciso and Jed Smith, Morning Owl corrected, "He was murdered. But first I must bathe." It had been a long ride and people needed purification before engaging in important talk.

Narciso rolled his eyes in a gesture that meant only h'nteelehs would bathe at this time, and he, Narciso, was far too knowledgeable for such foolishness. Nevertheless, Grizzly Hair and the others bathed, and when they returned, the *Americano* was waiting.

As they resumed their places in the talk circle, Jed Smith's lips turned up on the unscarred side, and he said, "That water is like ice. I think you *Indios* are *amphibious.*" Grizzly Hair didn't understand that, and it was obvious Narciso didn't either. So it was forgotten.

Jed Smith removed his hat, scratched his head and smoothed back several long strands of hair—the only hair on top. The last light of day revealed terrible scars, gnarled and raised, then he put the hat on.

Seeing the expressions, Narciso announced proudly, "He fought *Oso,* O-zoo-ma-ti." Pronounced a little differently, that was Grizzly Hair's spirit ally. Teeth had raked this man's scalp off, ripped the skin down the side of his face, and pulled off his ear. Grizzly Hair's own scalp prickled to think of his head in the mouth of a grizzly. He recalled what Jed Smith's spirit had said, that he often did what others said couldn't be done. O-se-mai-ti was his helper too. This was the powerful link that allowed Grizzly Hair to spirit-track him.

Sucais's wife and several other women approached with baskets of roasted elk and crisp seed bread. Gladly receiving the food, Grizzly Hair, Jed Smith and the others settled back and ate. Boy, tired from the long ride, snuggled against Etumu and closed his eyes.

Grizzly Hair saw that Morning Owl wasn't ready to begin talk. Maybe he was listening for Jed Smith's music, which Grizzly Hair couldn't hear either. Grizzly Hair filled in the blank time by asking Jed Smith, "Do you know Missouri?"

The *Americano* glanced at mother moon hanging like a torn fingernail in the dark blue sky, chewed a while, then said, "He is dead now. I didn't know him. There is palaber he came here. To this California valley, *muy rico en el piel de los animales.*"

As Narciso was translating, saying this place was very rich in animal skins, Grizzly Hair felt relieved to know Missouri was dead. People needn't worry about his bad medicine any more.

Morning Owl removed a handful of chewed sinew from his tongue, flicked the wad to a waiting dog, looked politely past the *Americano*, straightened his back and declared, "I want ten trained horses to pay for the loss of my nephew, or ten guns that thunder very well." The last part pleased Grizzly Hair. No doubt those thirteen men had ten guns.

The *Americano* responded through Narciso, "It was bad that my man killed your relative. Pardon, please. I want to trade with you. I am a friend of your people. But now I cannot give you guns or horses. Soon we will get many *caballos domesticados* from Padre Durán of Mission San José. We will give you ten of those." Throughout Narciso's translation Jed Smith maintained a serious, concerned expression. Narciso, however, gave Morning Owl a look that said, *You are too rude and ignorant to trade with my friend, the hy-apo of the powerful Americans.*

Morning Owl pointed toward the corral and said, "We saw horses over there. Give us ten of those, or ten guns." Narciso seemed reluctant to translate until Morning Owl gave him a superb stare.

"The good horses are not mine," Jed Smith responded without Narciso. "I have only six horses. Broken horses. Sick horses. No *manteca* on their bones." No fat.

Grizzly Hair had seen some bony horses. "You have goods. You can trade for good horses," Morning Owl stated.

"That's right," Grizzly Hair added before Narciso could translate. "We have seen your cloth houses and iron pots. Gabriel trades for horses." He glanced around the encampment wondering if Gabriel and Sick Rat were present. Instead he saw Estanislao acknowledging him with his eyes before joining the dance circle.

Jed Smith asked. "Does Gabriel steal horses from the *Españoles?*"

"*Sí,*" Grizzly Hair responded proudly. *Americanos* and *Españoles* were said to be enemies, and he thought stolen horses would be all the more attractive to the *Americanos.*

But Narciso said something about bad men and soldiers and Jed Smith said firmly, "I never trade for stolen goods." His lips made the firm line of a man not about to change his mind.

Grizzly Hair looked at Jed Smith and said in Spanish, "We don't need Narciso to talk for us. I speak Spanish. I will speak for my *capitán.*"

Narciso stood up, pushed out his chest and called Grizzly Hair and the umne a string of bad names in their own tongue, including h'nteelehs, which Grizzly Hair knew meant crude and ugly and unworthy of serious consideration. "I am a baptized Christian," he reminded Narciso, but the man rolled his eyes, knowing exactly how few sleeps Grizzly Hair had spent in the mission.

During this exchange Jed Smith's gaze moved from one to the other, and now he said to Narciso. "I will talk to this man without your help. Stay here if you wish.

Pleased, Grizzly Hair waited for Narciso—his face a mask of anger painted over with insincere tranquility—to sit down. And though Narciso wielded Padre Durán's authority in the mission and everyone there feared him, Grizzly Hair now ignored him and spoke directly to Jed Smith, "We want the horses or guns now," he said. "Because maybe you die. Then we have no horses for the death of our man."

Looking from the tops of his eyes, the *Americano* said, "I do not die easy." He leaned back and added, "But I am leaving for a little while. My men will stay here in this camp. They will get the horses for you while I'm gone."

The moment Grizzly Hair conveyed that, Morning Owl said, "No. We must have reparations before he goes."

Grizzly Hair struggled to say that in Spanish, and Jed Smith responded, "My palaber is my *seguridad.*"

He always used "palaber" for talk, but what did the other word mean? Smugly, Narciso explained, "His words are a tight bond. They don't break."

"Ten horses before you leave," Morning Owl said, "or ten guns. Otherwise we kill the murderer." Grizzly Hair added, "We know which one he is."

Jed Smith looked at the dancers, most of them deep in the rhythm and thick with ceremony, but the *Americanos* hopped around like awkward geese. He looked again at the umne. "I will get them myself if necessary, when I return. But probably my men can do it. I will write a *carta* to the *Españoles.*"

Carta? Before Grizzly Hair could ask the meaning, Narciso was explaining with the slow, cloying preciseness and exaggerated lip movements of an auntie telling a story to extremely young children. He described *papel,* upon which words were drawn so people who were far apart could talk by sending the *papel* back and forth. But though the insult of Narciso's tone stung, Grizzly Hair felt his anger erode like sand in a stream. He deserved it. He hadn't known what important people knew. He should have known. He had seen marks on sheets of thin material below the monsters on Father Fortuni's charts. He had seen such marks on the Russian glav-nyi's table. He shouldn't have needed Narciso's explanation. He recalled the unpleasant sensation, while talking with Padre Durán, of being a stumbling, bumbling man yearning for his home place so he could feel like a man again. Now something of that feeling returned.

Yet he had power. He had spirit-tracked Jed Smith, and wanted Narciso to know it. "You are going over the high mountains," he said to Jed Smith with a nod eastward. "You are going to a big time over there, beyond a wide and waterless land."

"Yes, the *rendezvous*, the *fiesta.*" He narrowed his eyes and examined Grizzly Hair with obvious interest—Narciso apparently subdued—and continued. "I can go faster alone. I will return *pronto.* By then you have your horses. Or if the *Españoles* won't sell them, I'll go to Father Durán and get them myself."

Grizzly Hair conveyed that to the home men, and Morning Owl looked at him like he wasn't speaking with enough force. Even Two Falcons appeared skeptical. Grizzly Hair said to Jed Smith, "Give us ten guns then. We know you have guns." One of them lay beside Jed Smith.

"I need my guns and my men need theirs. We will not part with a single one." The *Americano* pushed to his feet. "That's the best I can do. I hope we are *amigos.*" Narciso stood up too, both of them rudely ending talk before consensus had arrived.

Annoyed, but not wanting to be left sitting, Grizzly Hair also stood up. Morning Owl and the other men got to their feet, seemingly perplexed about whether the talk was finished. Alert to everything, the two women watched.

Motioning Jed Smith to wait, Grizzly Hair spoke to the umne in the home tongue: "He is leaving his men here. He knows we could kill them. They are his *seguridad.* I believe he will give us the horses, to keep the men safe."

"Maybe he doesn't care what happens to those men," Morning Owl pointed out.

"Then we'll kill the murderer."

Still sitting with his legs folded, Sucais said in a tone to end discussion. "There will be no killing of *Americanos* in my home place." He sat straight-backed, the host of many who wanted to be friends with the *Americanos.*

Jed Smith stood in his power, a man even O-se-mai-ti couldn't defeat.

Morning Owl and Two Falcons conferred, then Morning Owl said, "We will trade for the horses."

When this was conveyed, the *Americano* pursed his lips, squinted at the brightened fingernail of Moon and said, "Come to my camp in the morning. We will trade. Bring Gabriel." As he turned to leave, Grizzly Hair walked with him briefly and, because Narciso stayed nearby, said in a very low voice, "I want to talk with you about other things too, maybe *amigos de la guerra.*" Friends in war.

A flicker passed over Narciso's dark features as when a bobcat detects a rabbit, and the *Americano* said without hesitation, "*Palaber por la mañana.*" Talk after the sleep.

59

Boy's whimper and Etumu's stirring to nurse him woke Grizzly Hair. Bright light sliced through the openings in the willow shelter and he lay on his back remembering how good it had felt to dance, to pat the earth with his feet and find again the comfortable balance of earth and sky. By then all the *Americanos* had gone to their upstream camp, with women.

He rolled to his feet and went outside to scatter his urine in the dense green undergrowth. Soft snoring came from the willow shelters of Morning Owl and Two Falcons. Several children smiled up at him from their play. How quickly the air had turned warm, the sky blue! Pushing through fuzzy willows and green cattails, he skim-dived into the river he'd known when it was low, and swam upstream in the strong, cold current. It felt good to exert himself though he stayed in the same place. But swimming in place made him remember the reparations talk. He had wanted to be a man of knowledge. He wanted to be viewed as one of those few and had struggled as though to keep from washing downstream. It was like being a boy again, yearning to be accepted as a man of the umne. To a small extent he had wanted to be seen as more knowledgeable than the hy-apo and master hunter on account of having been in the mission. Yet Narciso had known the truth. Now the memory tasted bad and he swam hard to wash it from his mind, but stayed in the same place.

Back at the shelter Boy hardly noticed him; in his baby way he was playing with older children. He ducked his head like a fat little quail, thinking he was hiding. The children indulged him. Etumu was stirring a basket of bubbling nu-pah. He touched her wet hair and sat beside her to wait for the acorn pudding that kept him full all day. By the shape of the lumps, it appeared she had added some caterpillars.

"I want one of those red skirts," she said with a smile. "Can you get me one?"

Something fell out of him. How could he ever acquire such a valuable garment? No mission woman would part with hers. "You have a skirt," he pointed out.

"It's ugly. You can see through the cracks. It's made of willow bark!" She made a face like she'd tasted something bad.

Ugly. Anything h'nteelehs wore was considered ugly. He recalled a time when a ceremonial willow-bark skirt clacking around a woman made her exquisitely desirable. How *inocente* they had all been! But the red skirts were made from the hair of *ovejas*—wooly animals cared for by neophytes. Oak Gall had told him about a clever spinning device that spun thread so long it was wound into a large ball. She told him about the wondrous frame upon which the threads were strung and tightly woven. Only trained women were allowed near it. But he had no idea where the bright red dye came from. Typical of things in the mission, it was like nothing else on earth.

"I want a red skirt very much," Etumu repeated, looking at him like he could do anything he put his mind to.

"I'll try," he said. But the joy bursting on her face made him add, "It will be very difficult. Maybe I can't."

"Oh but I know you can," she bubbled. "Just imagine me in a red skirt!" She leaned over and rubbed her shoulder against his. "I would wear it at big times and every woman would want one." The smile never left her face, even when she took the tongs and removed the cooking stone. "Eat," she said, nudging the basket his way.

For a long time he scooped in silence, then said, "The easy way to get a red skirt is, go to the mission and live like a *Christiano*. A harder way is what I've been trying to do—get the neophytes and gentiles to fight together to defeat the black hats so they will leave and people like us can go to the missions whenever we want and leave without being whipped." He took a breath. "You could make a red skirt."

"These people," she made a broad gesture, "came from a mission and nobody is whipping them."

"What are you saying? You want to go to there?" He heard the irritation in his voice. Of course she didn't want to go where her sister had died; that went without saying.

She looked down. The blunt-singed hair fell forward on her narrow shoulders. Her joy was gone. This was the tender person he wanted most to protect from the *cuartas*. But now she had danced with the *cimarrones* and had begun to feel unworthy and lacking. He reached around her shoulder and pulled her to him. Needing her understanding, he confided his hope that this mass desertion of neophytes would lead to careful planning of a war against the black hats. He told her how helpful it would be if the *Americanos* joined them, and told her he must go now and talk with Jed Smith about it.

"I'm glad I came here," she said. "I like it when you talk to me like that." In a small voice she added, "I think you can get a red skirt."

Unexpectedly Sucais and Elk Calf silently fell into line as Grizzly Hair, Morning Owl and the other men of the umne went upstream on a freshly trodden path. Small rose plants and wormwood lay underfoot. Two Falcons led the way and the men spaced themselves out as they walked under a roof of new leaves. Grizzly Hair realized it was natural for the Lakisumne and Muquelumne peoples to watch how the talks proceeded. Estanislao was letting the gentiles handle reparations, though he remained present in his old home place.

Birds swooped through the trees with loaded beaks. Some carried nesting material, others beetles and worms. The recent cold had divided but not confused them. Neither was Grizzly Hair confused, though he might be temporarily divided from the other peoples in the matter of the *Americanos.* But when Morning Owl was satisfied, they would all speak with one voice.

The smell of the camp grew stronger. *Americanos* didn't bathe. They had a sharp, intense odor. Through the trees he saw the cloth houses standing in a circle with ropes strung from their peaks to the trees. A few people were visible but not the murderer. A woman wearing a red skirt stirred nu-pah near a fire. Narciso and Hipolito, a man Grizzly Hair had met during a pause in the dances, sat near one of the houses. Several dogs sniffed around the camp. Three *Americanos* with surprising chest fur—one crisply curled and reddish—leaned against a tree in their buckskin *pantalones.* One with black chest hair was maneuvering a salmon-rib comb through his tangled brown hair. Only Jed Smith wore the full regalia—hat, shirt, *pantalones* and foot coverings. He was half kneeling with one buckskin-covered foot on the ground, the other behind him in the soft earth. In his open hands, he held before him a strange thing. It overlapped his hands, dark where it lay against his palms, but mostly it was white and subtly curved up and over from a center line like the curving of long grass bowed over by wind and weighed down by rain. His eyes were closed and he was speaking softly over the strange thing, as a man speaks in private to his amulet. The only other time Grizzly Hair had seen anything approaching this was in the mission, on a high pedestal, but that had been much larger and lacked the graceful curvature of the white parts.

Jed Smith lowered his beard to his chest and remained in that posture for a short time, then closed the two halves of the thing, one side over the other. He put his other foot under him and carried the thing to a cloth house. Setting it on a hide blanket just inside the house, he sat down and folded his legs. Hipolito and Narciso had been sitting to one side, politely ignoring Jed Smith. But now the *Americano* took a square object from the house, put it on his lap, lifted the top off, removed a thin sheet of *papel,* restored the boxtop and placed the *papel* upon it. He picked up a yellow stick and began moving the end of it over the *papel*. Narciso and Hipolito scooted closer, watching. This continued for a long time. Jed Smith set the *papel* on the ground and began running the yellow stick over a second sheet.

Elk Calf flicked a mosquito. Seeing it, Narciso leaned toward Jed Smith and whispered. Jed Smith looked up and saw the umne. Grizzly Hair and Two Falcons stepped forward, followed by the others. Apparently satisfying himself that no one else was there, Jed Smith said, "*Un momento. Sientese.*"

"That means sit and wait," said Narciso, lowering his disapproving gaze to their nakedness.

Already Grizzly Hair felt irritated, but he reminded himself that Narciso was accustomed to ordering neophytes around for Padre Durán and seemed to think his favored position extended to the *Americanos*. He was upset at Grizzly Hair for speaking for Morning Owl before the sleep. It didn't seem wise to antagonize him further. Grizzly Hair and the umne sat down and watched the yellow stick mark the *papel* from one side to the other, then start again at the original side.

The stick was marvelously straight and cylindrical. Its marks were left by a dark tip. Jed Smith continued to mark the *papel*, ending with a tail that came up and crossed over previous marks. He picked the first sheet up and examined it carefully, making additional marks here and there. Then he laid the stick down, folded the *papel* and handed it to Narciso. "Take this to Father Durán," he said. "It is very important. Give it to him *pronto*."

Narciso accepted the *carta*—surely it was the paper that talked, the one telling Padre Durán to sell horses to Jed Smith's men. Narciso handed it to Hipolito, who inserted it into a clever little pouch sewn into his *pantalones*. "He goes faster," Narciso explained, "and he does what I say or he is punished." Hipolito jumped to his feet and ran up the path. Narciso scooted even closer to Jed Smith. The women stepped closer too, as though accidentally, but Grizzly Hair knew they hoped to hear what would be said.

Jed Smith put the box and yellow stick back on the hide blanket. Behind that were two finely woven, neatly folded blankets and a saddle. Jed Smith was looking at the umne. "No Gabriel?"

Grizzly Hair pointed up and slightly west. "Maybe he comes when the sun he is there."

"I will be gone by then," said Jed Smith. "We palaber now about trade." He gestured around the camp. "Things your chief takes so he will wait for the horses with tranquility in his heart." Judging by his awkward pauses, he was as new at speaking Spanish as Grizzly Hair. "You give them back when you have the horses."

Narciso explained the meaning to the umne as Morning Owl looked around the camp. In the home tongue Morning Owl said, surprising Grizzly

Hair, "A red skirt like that." He pointed at the woman making nu-pah. "And that." He pointed to an iron ax with a marvelous long handle lying beside a pile of split wood, then to an iron vessel with a graceful protrusion. "I want a buckskin shirt with fringes too," he said, "and three of those houses." He glanced at the listening women and said, "They have valuable beads. I want twenty beads."

Jed Smith had understood some of it. He got up and went to the fire-blackened vessel, slowly poured water out the protrusion to show its usefulness, lifted a lid, replaced it and ceremoniously carried the vessel by its clever, moveable handle and gave it to Morning Owl. Accepting it, the hy-apo maintained a well-guarded expression, but Grizzly Hair saw the light in his eyes as he put the vessel between him and Two Falcons. He pointed to the ax.

"He wants that," Grizzly Hair said.

"No," Jed Smith said. "We need it. I need it and my men need it, but that is our only ax. It is not possible to give it to you." His mouth drew a straight line.

Narciso explained it in the home tongue and Morning Owl indicated Grizzly Hair should demand the other items. Grizzly Hair pointed to the woman cooking the nu-pah and said, "We want two of those red. . ." He didn't know the word.

Slowly and with exaggerated lip movements Narciso said, "*Falda. Vosotros quieren dos faldas rojas.*"

Jed Smith leaned over, pointed and nearly touched the skirt. "*Falda?*"

"*Sí. Dos faldas,*" Narciso said.

Grizzly Hair whispered to Morning Owl, "Etumu wants one too. Morning Owl gave him a knowing nod.

"They are not mine to give," Jed Smith was saying.

Another *Americano*—not the murderer—crawled out of his house with a woman behind him. "You are a man of *fuerte,*" power, Grizzly Hair said to Jed Smith. "I think you can get two red skirts."

Jed Smith said, "*Un momento.*" He got up and swiftly walked to where several of his men were eating strange food. Rapid talk followed, sounding like the men's mouths were full of sticky nu-pah. Then Jed Smith returned and asked, "Are those *faldas* important?"

"*Sí,*" Grizzly Hair said after Narciso's translation. Morning Owl looked him solemn agreement. "*Una falda grande, una falda chica.*" One big skirt, one little one, Grizzly Hair told Jed Smith.

Jed Smith agreed, "*Dos faldas.*"

"*Dos faldas rojas.*"

"*Sí.*"

"Good." Very pleased, especially when he imagined Etumu's reaction, Grizzly Hair maintained a casual expression.

"Maybe you will get them after I go," Jed Smith added.

"No. We want them before you go."

Again Jed Smith went to his men and talked to them in their own tongue. Grizzly Hair could tell he cared about them very much. He would worry that the umne would kill or injure them while he was gone.

As Jed Smith returned to the talk circle, one of the *Americanos* approached the woman in the skirt and smiled. She got up and walked with him, and they disappeared into the trees. Women saw *Americanos* as more than men, and Grizzly Hair couldn't blame them. In his own way he wanted their favors too, as everyone did, and had to keep reminding himself that Falls-off-House was dead and he must bargain hard.

Jed Smith was saying, "We will get the red skirts later."

"Before you go."

"Maybe. I hope. Is that *todos,* all the things your chief wants?"

"No. He wants this." Grizzly Hair touched Jed Smith's shirt.

Jed Smith blew a little air and grabbed the bottom fringe, pulling the shirt over his head. Handing it to Morning Owl, he sat before them with every rib visible despite the curly dark brown hair on his chest. "Is that all?"

"He wants three houses," Grizzly Hair said.

Jed Smith sat for a moment, obviously thinking. "No. I cannot give you any houses."

Morning Owl insisted, and talk went back and forth several times. In the end they agreed on Jed Smith's own house. He crawled inside and carried his blankets and saddle outside, then untied the ropes from the branches and stakes and removed two interior poles. The house collapsed. He methodically folded it and signed that the umne should take it. Lame Beaver and Scorpion-on-Nose picked it up together, grinned a little at its weight, then set it down beside them.

Jed Smith asked again, "Is that all?"

Morning Owl asked for and received the yellow stick, two sheets of *papel* to draw upon, and a finely woven, striped blanket. Then he touched the strange thing on the hide mat, which had been removed from the house. Almost imperceptibly Jed Smith's hand jerked as though he wanted to stop Morning Owl from touching it but thought better of it. "What is this?" Morning Owl asked, withdrawing his hand.

Narciso repeated the question in Spanish.

Jed Smith seemed particularly awkward and hesitant as he tried to answer. In the end he appeared to give up. Narciso said, "It is the source of his power."

The nape of Grizzly Hair's neck prickled. All other goods meant nothing compared with this. It seemed right for this great power to be exchanged for the life of Falls-off-House, but of course the *Americano* wouldn't want to give it away.

"I want that," Morning Owl whispered. Grizzly Hair realized it might give the umne the power to defeat the *Españoles*. He saw the hidden excitement in the faces of Elk Calf and Sucais, and the men of the umne.

"My chief wants it," Grizzly Hair told Jed Smith.

"He isn't able to understand it," Jed Smith responded, shaking his head. Narciso said, "He won't give it to you." That wasn't the meaning.

Grizzly Hair told Narciso to tell Jed Smith that Morning Owl could learn to understand it.

"It is the Bible," said Jed Smith, "in English."

Grizzly Hair didn't understand *Bible* or *English*, but that didn't matter. "Teach him to use it," he said.

Jed Smith thought a while and said, "It speaks to me in the voices of *Dios* and Jesús and old men of knowledge."

Grizzly Hair grew more excited with every utterance. The voices of the great spirits of the powerful *Españoles* spoke from this object! But Narciso added, "*Dios* and Jesús cannot speak to him."

Jed Smith was frowning. "*Dios* and Jesús," he said, "speak to me without the Bible, but it. . . " again he was searching for words, "it helps me know them." He picked it up and fanned through its fabulously thin leaves—many papers that talked in spirit voices.

Narciso said, "*Dios* and María and Jesús cannot speak to him without a padre."

That contradicted what Grizzly Hair thought he'd heard, and he put it to the *Americano*.

A wry smile turned up the good side of Jed Smith's mouth. "*Dios* talks to me all the time. He talks to me in the mountains. He talks to me in the going down of the sun, and the coming up of the sun."

Narciso looked confused. "Are you a padre?"

"No."

Grizzly Hair explained to the umne that the great spirits of the *Españoles* talked to Jed Smith too, through the Bible. He then told Jed Smith that Morning Owl must have it. To his surprise and delight, Jed Smith handed it respectfully to Morning Owl. "No water on it," he stipulated.

Morning Owl accepted it with the ceremony of a dance doctor handling the condor robe. He repeated, "No water," and whispered to Grizzly Hair, "I have enough now."

Grizzly Hair conveyed that and added, "I will wait here for the *faldas rojas*."

Obviously satisfied with the trade, Morning Owl and the others walked down the trail toward the big encampment, the hy-apo using small careful steps as he carried the Bible before him on the palms of his hands. The others carried the folded house, buckskin shirt, kettle containing twenty beads, the yellow stick, two sheets of *papel*, and the blanket. Sucais and Elk Calf appeared to be glad that everything had been decided to the satisfaction of both sides.

Grizzly Hair waited to talk about war. Narciso hadn't left either. However, he acted less haughty and even sat beside Grizzly Hair like a friend. The footsteps of the umne had hardly receded when one of the *Americanos* gave his shirt to Jed Smith. He pulled it on, leaned down and picked up a feather and pushed it into the band of his hat. Then he sat down and marked another piece of *papel* with another yellow stick. This didn't take long.

Quickly—everything he did was quick—he walked over and handed the *papel* to Grizzly Hair. "This letter says we will give you ten trained horses." The marks resembled the precise squiggles of a scorpion crawling across a dusty path. Grizzly Hair folded it and put it in his calf-thong.

Jed Smith strode to where one of his men was leading three skinny horses into camp. He took and saddled a brown one. Another man saddled a darker one, and they began tying things on the rumps. Jed Smith leaned into a cloth house and called. A man crawled out—the murderer, hair askew. Glancing at Grizzly Hair they talked their mushy tongue.

Narciso, sitting cross-legged, leaned over and told Grizzly Hair, "Those two men are going with Jed Smith."

The killer was leaving. That was paid for. There was no reason for him to stay. Grizzly Hair asked Narciso, "Why did you bring the mission neophytes here?"

"We are on *paseo*."

Streaks of sunlight leaked through the green canopy as the *Americanos* strapped things on the three horses. "Talk straight with me," he told Narciso in a firm voice.

Narciso looked at him, and this time spoke without guardedness or haughtiness. "I heard many peoples were here. I wanted to see what was happening. Ten twenties of people left with me." He shrugged. "When Hipolito tells the neophytes in the mission what the *Americanos* were talking about, more will come. They are all excited."

"What did they talk about?"

"Before you came?"

"Yes, before I came." He looked at Jed Smith, who had finished packing his horse and now stood staring at the ax and rubbing his face. "What did they say?"

"Jed Smith wanted to know how many *soldados* live in the presidios and how many guns they have. He asked me what their guns look like. I told him. I also drew him an earth map showing the San Joaquin River and the presidio. He wanted to know how far apart they are. I told him one sun—true if you run the entire way. He copied the earth map onto his *papel* and told us we should fight if the *soldados* come to this side of the San Joaquin River. He said this is our land and we should not let them force people to go to the missions."

"Did he say he will help *Indios* fight?"

"He is careful with his talk."

The three *Americanos* were speaking by turns to each of the men who would stay—all shaking hands, the ax still on the ground. Grizzly Hair reconsidered his earlier desire to talk with Jed Smith about war. Now that Narciso had talked straight, why delay them? Anyway, Jed Smith would return and Grizzly Hair could speak to him in private. He asked, "Are you glad to hear talk of war against the black hats?"

The alcalde's guardedness returned. "If people are talking, I am glad to hear it."

"You brought the neophytes here."

"I didn't force anybody. I came and they came."

"Will they fight with us if there is a war?"

"Ask them."

"Will you?"

"I don't know."

"If the *Americanos* help us fight, will you?"

Narciso looked over with narrowed eyes. "If that happens everything will be different."

Jed Smith approached and said to Grizzly Hair, "You wanted to talk about *guerra*," war. "I am a man of trade. I want to be friends with the *misionarios.*" He was being careful.

Grizzly Hair said, "We will talk when you return."

"Good. Talk to Señor Rogers about the horses. Harry," he called, beckoning the man who had given him the shirt. The slim, hard-looking man joined them. His pale mustache curved around the ends of his mouth like a tapered, limp rope glued to his upper lip. The two *Americanos* spoke in their tongue.

"I told him," Jed Smith said in Spanish, "that if I have not returned in four moons, I am dead and they must continue the journey without me." He put a hand on his man's shoulder. "He will get the horses from Padre Durán, and see that you get the red skirts." The spark in his brown eyes was friendly, and Grizzly Hair liked him more than ever. But now the *Americano* was preoccupied with a big time across a waterless expanse of land.

"*Vaya con Dios,*" Grizzly Hair said. Go with God.

"*Gracias.* I will need the help of *Dios.*"

60

Morning Owl walked proudly in his buckskin shirt with long fringe dangling. His presence added weight to the councils that sprang up everywhere in the encampment. No one, however, walked prouder than Etumu in her red skirt. Grizzly Hair could see that she felt prettier, and maybe that's why she actually did look so pretty. Being older, Raven Feather hid her pride better but nevertheless showed her pleasure in her new appearance. Now many people didn't know that the home women were h'nteelehs.

The horses had not been delivered. It seemed Señor Rogers was having trouble convincing Padre Durán, through the *cartas*, to trade with him. It was as María had said. *Americanos* were not seen as esteemed traders. But Señor Rogers assured Grizzly Hair that Jed Smith could be trusted, and if he was killed and didn't return, he, Harrison Rogers, would somehow manage to get the horses. Nonetheless, Grizzly Hair felt pleased that Morning Owl had received the other goods. The hy-apo had already made a wooden platform for the Bible inside his cloth house. People walked out of their way just to peek at it, and often sat nearby for long periods. Sometimes Morning Owl could be seen on one knee holding the Bible before him. Just as Etumu seemed prettier, Morning Owl seemed more powerful.

More of Te-mi's people arrived, and councils sprang up. Wherever Estanislao went, groups of men and women talked about what *Dios* and María and Jesús would say about *Indio* peoples joining together to fight the black hats. Grizzly Hair sent word northward to Poo-soo-neh, Libayto, Topal, and those beyond to come and plan with them.

Four sleeps later, having received his message, several men came from each of those peoples, however Poo-soo-ne didn't come. He had counseled his people not to get involved in a dangerous fight. *Cimarrones* came from the mission in Sonoma. They informed the gathered peoples that a presidio was being built beside the *iglésia* in Sonoma. It was their strong opinion that the war should begin before new soldiers came to fill that presidio. The talks became more excited. Would the neophytes from Sonoma desert their mission and join the war? Most of them had gone willingly to the mission.

From the south came *cimarrones* from San Juan Bautista, together with their gentile relatives. The Cosumne arrived, and neophytes from Mission Santa Clara, relatives of Estanislao. Grizzly Hair felt the numbers like an ocean wave gathering strength, and he believed that if everyone present would fight, they could defeat the *Españoles* without the *Americanos*. But all agreed that a clever plan was needed, and as the sleeps passed, Grizzly Hair talked to them about the snare he had envisioned.

One evening before their willow shelter when they shared cold nu-pah, he admitted to Etumu, "I am glad you came here." They had just come from another all-day council that had begun with talk about whippings and ended with Grizzly Hair explaining his idea of trenches." She and Boy had stayed the entire time.

Now she looked at him sidelong and he saw her pleasure. "I am your woman," she said quietly. "I go where you go."

"Except when there is war."

She laughed at him. Scouts were positioned on both sides of the two rivers, and if the black hats approached, women and children would go upriver. They discussed this almost daily.

Then one day, two hundred more neophytes arrived from Mission San José. Shouts of joy could be heard throughout the encampment. Hipolito had told the people in the mission about the *Americanos,* and they assumed Jed Smith's men had come to help fight the black hats. The neophytes wanted the soldiers punished for the whippings and other outrages. They said they would "teach them a lesson they would never forget." Narciso laid low during such talk. Grizzly Hair and Etumu searched for Bowstring and Teresa, but were disappointed.

Estanislao explained, "They have become good *Christianos.* I don't think they would leave Padre Durán." A strange look came over him, as though he thought he too should return.

Alarmed, Grizzly Hair reminded him, "At the time of the war in Santa Barbara you told me true *Christianos* would want the black hats to leave this land. You said we *Indios* are the only ones who can punish the *soldados.* People say even Governor Echeandía wants them to stop forcing people to the missions."

Looking past him, Estanislao nodded. The downward creases of his broad face gave him a permanently sad expression. Obviously the mission people still held him in high esteem, but sometimes Grizzly Hair felt sorry for this man, who was divided within himself. "Why didn't you lead the neophytes from the mission when we were going to Santa Barbara?" He asked. "You went to the mission and stayed there."

"I heard that Andrés and all those people down there were losing. It was too late to help. If I had led our people away, the punishments would have been terrible." His wide lips made a straight line, his smile, and his amused, confidential tone returned. "They would have put me in the *calabozo* and no one would listen to me anymore. Instead, Padre Durán trusts me and so do the neophytes. So when we are ready to fight, the neophytes will join me in the war, and the *soldados* will be surprised."

Grizzly Hair put a hand on Estanislao's shoulder and said, "With all your neophytes and my gentiles, we will be strong."

Estanislao gave a solid nod. "And don't forget my father's many gentile friends and relatives." He paused. "But we must have enough arrows. More than they have *amunicíon.* The gentiles must bring the arrows." He flung a hand eastward. "Mountains of arrows. The gentiles must prepare what we neophytes cannot. Will you make sure we have arrows?"

"Of course I will." He already had the promises of elders in many villages.

Domingo was there too, in his blue three-cornered hat. His face showed faith in Estanislao. "We will need many runners with food and arrows, and medicine for the wounded." Little Cos agreed.

Gabriel snorted. "That snare you talk about? To surprise the soldiers?" Grizzly Hair nodded. "Could turn into a trap. They would surround us. Let's steal horses and attack them on their own horses. One well planned attack after another. In places where we can escape into the tulares."

Grizzly Hair had met this argument before. "You, Gabriel, would do most of the attacking. Many men can't ride horses. Many would fear riding into the black hats' home places, especially at night. They would fear the ghosts and they would fear capture. But with all the warriors in the same place, everyone would feel the strength in our numbers and fight more bravely."

"Yes," Little Cos said, "I agree with Grizzly Hair. But I still don't see how we can keep the black hats from surrounding us. They could stop the food and arrow runners."

"That's right," said Gabriel with a tilt to his chin, "you would be trapped."

Sucais straightened his back and looked around the circle of friends and elders of his people. Seeing that he would talk, they waited. "I like Grizzly Hair's snare," he said, "but I think we need better protection from the balls of the *fusiles.* We need to build something to kneel behind while we shoot our bows. We should also decide when to start the war, when to lure them into our snare. And we should decide which of us should send out the *pul.* I know these people." He made a gesture encompassing the entire river bottom. "They like to dance and have big times. They could talk until the end of Second World and still not be ready—not enough arrows, no trenches, no wall built. Let's decide when those things must be ready."

When to start the war. That had always been the question. Pomponio wanted to do it three *años* ago, but he had been tied up and made to sit on a high platform facing the *fusiles* of many soldiers. At a signal they all fired and Pomponio's daring was lost to the *Indio* peoples. In Santa Barbara the bravest warriors had been killed or fettered. Many others who might have been good warriors were gone. Maybe Grizzly Hair's father would have fought, and his grandfather. Malaca's men had burned themselves in their houses. Such bravery was everywhere and had been all along. People had been fighting for generations, but they hadn't fought together. Now, for the first time it seemed gentiles and mission neophytes would join together. But Sucais was right, they needed to decide when to fight.

One of the men who had been sitting at the outside of the circle said, "A good time to have the war is when the headman of the *Americanos* returns." A murmur of emphatic agreement arose and somebody muttered, ". . .show them we're not dogs who come when called."

Grizzly Hair spoke: "Sucais is a wise man and he is right. We should decide when to fight, and it should be soon. But we cannot prepare for war until we know where the battle will be. We need to dig trenches and build a wall." It occurred to him that this was the way of traditional war; the headmen decided where and when the arrow-dodging would take place.

Estanislao, who had been listening while drawing in the dirt with a finger, looked up and said, "Father, you and I have many friends to the north and south. This is a good meeting place, so maybe this should be the battleground. Right here at our place."

Sucais gazed across the heads of other men and women who had crowded closer to listen. "That would bring many deaths to our home place. Bad Ghosts would linger."

Domingo straightened a leg and cleared his throat. "Maybe my place. All of my people came from somewhere else. We don't need to live there."

"Where are the people who lived there first?" Little Cos asked.

"Most died in a big sickness at the mission." After a respectful pause he continued, "My place is broader than this. The trees are thick. It's easy to hide. And the river circles around, so the water would protect us."

Grizzly Hair had long thought Domingo's place was the perfect battleground, and had said so to Domingo and others. "We should go there and build a fort like the Undersea People made at Fort Ross," he said. "It should be made of strong tall poles, pointed at the top so men can't climb over."

Gabriel grunted in disgust and made a show of getting to his feet and leaving. Grizzly Hair was sorry about that. He had hoped Gabriel would help them no matter what plans were made.

Etumu, who had been listening, gathered Boy to her as the council dissolved, and the three of them went to the willow shelter. "Are we going to Domingo's place now?" she asked.

"That will take more talk," he told her, thinking aloud. "No one wants to leave the *Americanos*." Opportunities to touch their power abounded.

More sleeps passed, and more councils were held. People continued to talk about what wonderful warriors the *Americanos* would be. Since they were camped here and many people assumed they wouldn't move, Sucais finally agreed to allow his place to be used as a backup battleground. He and his brother walked around deciding exactly where to build the wall, examining the density of the river jungle and the availability of poles thick enough to stop the balls from *fusiles*. And because the enemy could come from any side, they realized the wall should be circular and the entrances underground, covered with brush, so food and arrow runners could go in and out but the black hats wouldn't see how to get in.

Even Morning Owl, a man of peace and consensus, agreed to help fight, which heartened Grizzly Hair. Two Falcons and the other men had already shown their willingness, but now the hy-apo added his voice to the growing belief that winning a war could make people safe in their villages. He even thanked Grizzly Hair for going to the mission and learning about the *Españoles.*

Throughout these talks, the eleven *Americanos* waited in their camp for the return of their headman. In exchange for grass seed and other food that the women brought, the *Americanos* hunted and shared large amounts of elk and deer with the encampment. The meat was roasted at many supper fires. Such friendship spoke. Grizzly Hair became infected by the general enthusiasm and belief that the *Americanos* would be allies. He was reluctant to insist that everyone leave them and go downstream, so he and the other men cleared berry canes and rotting logs to make room for a back-up fort. With many hands the work went quickly.

One morning when they were bathing Grizzly Hair asked Etumu, "Why do so many women want to couple with the *Americanos?*" He suspected that Pretty Duck had done it, and Elk Calf told him that Swims Backwards had sneaked off to the *Americano* camp.

Etumu's lips pressed down against a little smile. She grabbed Boy by the arm and scooped water over his sticky lower parts. "They want the *Americanos* to give them a *picaniña blanca.* White baby.

"Do you want a *picaniña blanca?*"

"Boy is nursing." She shot him a sidelong glance.

That didn't answer the question. Like bees to sweet flowers, women flocked to the exciting *Americanos.* Most men tolerated it for now, but eventually there could be trouble. And if many men became angry with the *Americanos*, the emerging consensus about the coming war could fall apart.

May 31, 1827, Mission San José

Commander Luis Argüello looked into the snapping black eyes of Padre Durán and promised to terminate the intolerable situation. He added, "With your permission, I need some writing equipment. I'll send a letter to the governor this afternoon with your fastest courier. I'll also write the presidio and order an expedition to round up the fugitives."

Padre Presidente Durán bowed in thanks. He motioned him down the corridor to a small room with a recessed window, and gestured Luis inside. This was the office where mission records were kept. Father Durán removed two big leather-bound volumes, the Book of Death and the Book of Baptisms, from the table. From the overhead shelf he took down a stack of blank paper, a vial of ink and a sharp little knife. He cut the point of the quill, handed it to him and said, "If there is anything else you need, don Luis, I will leave my trusted neophyte outside the door. Just tell him."

"There is one thing," the commander admitted. "Could you perhaps spare a little *aguardiente?*" Of late he couldn't pass too many hours without its comforting warmth.

The padre presented his bald pate and left to instruct the neophyte. Shortly after, alone in the tiny room with a cup and clay pitcher of aguardiente, Argüello fortified himself as he gazed out the window. On the wide road just outside people were coming and going—ranchers and their men, retired soldiers, two *Indias* in a wagon with many mixed-blood children riding on a pile of laundry. He was all but recovered from the insult of not being elevated from temporary to actual governor and now commanded San Francisco Presidio with, he hoped, the same moral weight as his father before him. This outrage in the interior cried out for decisive action. The government depended upon him. The liquor lived up to its name, imbuing his words with ardent passion as he addressed the American scoundrel who was left in command of Jedediah Smith's camp.

> *Señor Harrison G. Rogers,*
> *All civilized nations that have a wise government would be astonished at the very bad manner with which you have behaved, and continue to behave. You have entered territory in which your nation has no right, much less jurisdiction, to explore our possessions arbitrarily and with such lack of restraint, actually committing hostile acts, insulting the highest authority of this Territory with some ungrateful procedures—made more palatable and disguised maliciously as acts of nature.*

He swallowed more fortification. Padre Durán had it on trusted authority that Smith's men had shot and killed a native on the *Rio de los Cosumnes,* the very definition of a hostile act. And the deceit! Immediately after arriving, Smith had promised to go back over the southern *sierra* where he came from, yet had brazenly mapped his way up the interior valley. Too much snow, he had claimed, an act of God! Yet good men in that vicinity knew that the snow was no deeper than when they entered the country in the first place. The lying *malcreado* had even sweet-talked the padre of San Gabriel into vouching for his character.

> *You did this deliberately, because you had little or no need, nor have you had it, to make observations or discoveries in foreign territories that are truly well recognized by the owner who possesses them. Its natives are all well satisfied with the law that incorporates them into the Mexican nation, like branches of that trunk. No other may deprive them of this right, and much less with the treachery with which you have insinuated yourself, asserting your authority on the lands and wills of those*

same Indians. Yes my friends, all are insults. I am well informed by the natives themselves, who are observing your movements and watching your operations. Your object is none other than to win the goodwill of these natives, while at the same time you survey the land and rivers. Moreover, you give notice to these same natives that all that Territory, as far as the Columbia River, is yours... These actions are too insolent... Your usurpation fails to conform to international law which, we are well satisfied, completely prohibits you and any others from committing violence in foreign lands. I hope that you, persuaded of all that I tell you, carry out your withdrawal to your destination, leaving in peaceful possession and quiet these Indian natives who have become rather turbulent in the area where you are. I give you this notice in the name of the Commanding General of these Territories.

Mission San Jose, May 31, 1827
Luis Antonio Augüello

He felt a satisfying glow as he re-read the letter. All correct. The sharpness came through nicely. The exasperation. He would stay here in the mission and wait for word that the Americans had left the country.

Setting the first letter aside, he swallowed two slow draws of *aguardiente* and penned his orders to Lieutenant Ignacio Martinez. "With all haste," he wrote, "dispatch an expedition to Harrison Rogers in the camp on the river of the Lakisamni people, and learn his intent. I have here a letter from his superior, Jedediah Smith, but it is unintelligible, being written in English. Therefore your immediate recognizance is necessary. Meanwhile I will forward Smith's letter to Mexico City for translation. Second, round up those fugitives and herd them back to the missions. I await your response." He added that the expedition should consist of at least a dozen regulars and as many neophyte auxiliaries as Martinez thought prudent. "Select the neophytes with care," he added, "or they might be disposed to join the rebels."

61

JUNE 3, 1827

A lathered horse galloped into the encampment and the booming voice of the herald called the many peoples together. "Black hats are coming," the runner announced. "When I left they were crossing the San Joaquin River. I came as fast as I could, but they won't be far behind. We counted fourteen men with guns, twenty neophytes, but no cannon."

Grizzly Hair and Etumu grabbed their few belongings—weapons, baskets, stone mortar bowl—and mounted Morena. They rode alongside Two Falcons on Milk, crossed the river and galloped toward the Chilumne, who lived one river north on the River of Skulls. A Chilumne guide ran behind with Morning Owl, Raven Feather and the men of the umne. Two Falcons rode in the rear watching for danger. In every direction people were streaming away from Estanislao's home place toward prearranged hiding places. Runners would notify them all when it was safe to return, for it would require many sleeps to build the protective walls.

When he knew it was safe to travel slower, Grizzly Hair walked with the men, while Etumu continued to ride Morena. "The peoples are acting as one," he said to the men, not without a sense of pride.

"Ho," Two Falcons agreed.

Etumu said, "I am glad I am seeing this."

Grizzly Hair was glad too.

It was warmer than usual for this season and father sun burned overhead, bleaching the dry grass. Perspiration glistened on everyone, and Boy was fussing. When they arrived at the sleepy houses and shady oaks of the Chilumne, dogs barked. The guide, observing the time-of-pretending, went his own way as the herald announced them.

The headman came from the riverbank, dripping wet, and greeted them in the tongue of Estanislao's people. The Chilumne slowly gathered to listen in the shelter of a mother oak, though some continued to lie in the shade.

Morning Owl used the home tongue, which was known here. "We need a place to stay until the black hats leave the river of the Lakisumne."

As the headman offered his hospitality, Elk Calf rolled to his feet and approached. His dazzling smile had the confidence of a young man who could never fail at anything. He had arranged the hospitality of his wife's people.

"We have had many talks about a killing war against the *Españoles,*" Morning Owl told the Chilumne. "When it is safe for us to return to Sucais' place, you should come too. In the meantime I will tell you all that has happened."

"Good," said the headman brightly, "we needed something to wake us up. But first come to our swimming place."

Grizzly Hair was thirsty after the long ride. The cool water refreshed him. Morena also waded in, buckled her knees and rolled. Regaining her feet, she sucked long sips from the river. Several young women were standing to their waists in a shady backwater. They giggled and whispered among themselves. A young man took a running leap and dunked one of them. She came up spitting water, laughing.

People were petting Morena while she drank. "We want to ride the horse," said one of the boys. Before Grizzly Hair could stop them, an inexperienced rider was on her, a young man or perhaps still a boy. He ran her, then gave her to another, and three of them took turns riding. This unsettled Grizzly Hair, for Morena needed rest and shade, but he didn't want to appear impolite to his hosts. Then Elk Calf mounted and kicked her into a run. He nearly bounced off, grasping the mane and grinning back with a comical expression before disappearing into the foliage.

Grizzly Hair left Etumu and Boy and ran after him, following the trail of crushed nettles, poison oak and toyon. Three young men talked and laughed as they ran behind. A long distance east of the village, where the grass met the river vegetation, Grizzly Hair saw that Elk Calf had stopped in an open place beyond a screen of young evergreen oaks.

The others caught up, gasping for breath. Sweat ran down their bodies. The wing people had stilled in the heat. Grizzly Hair felt the presence of someone besides the young men. Behind Elk Calf, in the dark river vegetation, something bright winked. Few *Indios* had anything that reflected sunlight that well. He pointed. Elk Calf turned to look, then slipped to the ground and, after leading Morena back to Grizzly Hair, set off in a fast stalk from tree to tree.

Worried and wishing he could do this by himself, Grizzly Hair tied Morena to a branch and followed. Hearing the unskillful steps of the younger men or boys, he turned and made a sign for silence. The black hat expedition couldn't possibly be this far north. They were on Estanislao's river. It was quiet. Elk Calf crouched behind a mound of grapevines. Grizzly Hair joined him. Through the little spaces between leaves, something moved. Dark, with a streak of something very light. Not an animal. He heard sloshing above the river's murmur.

The approaching younger men covered their footsteps fairly well. Motioning them and Elk Calf to stay still, Grizzly Hair moved. From there he saw the back of a partly hidden man sitting beside the stream, a man in a black hat and pale shirt. He was bent forward, moving his arms like a woman washing acorn flour. Was this a black hat? Or an *Indio* dressed like one? Only *Indias* washed acorn flour, but he'd never heard of a woman wearing the clothes of a black hat. And if it was a black hat, what was he doing and where were his companions? They usually traveled in groups.

Very sorry that his bow and quiver lay back at the swimming place, Grizzly Hair was the only one of the four who carried a knife. For the safety of these unarmed men and their people, he decided to lead them away and tell their people to go into hiding.

A whinny shocked him—Morena in the distance. Nearby, a horse answered loud and long. The man at the river sat upright and turned around. It was an old black hat with dark *pantalones,* face pale, white mustache.
Stilling himself to become invisible in the oak leaves, Grizzly Hair listened for the approach of men or animals, but heard nothing except the single black hat thrashing awkwardly through the bushes. The old man didn't call out, as a man with companions would have; yet he was afraid enough to run.

Grizzly Hair glanced back at Elk Calf and his friends, whose eyes showed terrified fascination, and crouch-ran after the black hat. Quickly a saddled horse came into view. Only *Españoles* had saddles. This one would ride to his friends. He had to be stopped. Whistling a signal to follow, Grizzly Hair sprinted, easily overtook the man and dove on him just before he reached the brown and white spotted horse.

The man fell under his weight. Grizzly Hair clamped a hand tightly over his mouth, pulling his head to the side. The hat fell off, and a shiny iron bowl with a spike on the bottom lay on the ground with small gold nuggets and gold-flecked sand spilling from it. That bowl had glinted in the sun.

"*Por favor,*" mumbled the black hat through Grizzly Hair's hand. The rest he stifled. The man's face was lined with age and the droopy white mustache felt furry and moist on his hand. The hair on his head was the color of rusty iron salted with white, and it parted over a mangled hole where an ear had once been. This was the second man Grizzly Hair had seen lately with a missing ear, but this one showed no sign of a bear attack.

Fearing an ambush, Grizzly Hair pulled him upright, turning him around as a shield while he searched for movement in the trees. Elk Calf and the other three arrived and stared at the captive, and the horse. Tied on the saddle was a gun, a coiled *riata*, several hide bags and big wooden foot holders.

The old man kicked Grizzly Hair's shin with the flat toe of the boot. Stunned with pain, Grizzly Hair tripped him and fell on him again, and the man lay struggling to free himself.

"Cut his throat," said the youngest man, or boy.

Elk Calf asked, "Did this black hat whip you?"

"No."

"Did you fight him at Little Cos' place?"

"No. Did you?

"No. Elk Calf shifted to halting Spanish. "Let's cut off his feet and cook them for him to eat."

The man's eyes widened. Meanwhile the others rapidly removed the braided *riata* from the saddle, pulled off the man's boots, shirt and pantalones, then quickly tied his ankles together behind him, drawing the rope up through the tied wrists and yanking it tight.

The man moaned, but didn't try to yell. Grizzly Hair told them in his own tongue. "Killing a *soldado* would put your people in danger. Did you hear what happened to Pomponio? You would be *criminales de sangre.*" He shook his head. "Besides, killing this weak old man would bring no power. No honor." For some reason he felt sorry for him.

The black hat lay wide-eyed with his back arched and feet reeking. The boots emitted a stench as though he had been rotting from the ankles down. He didn't try to yell. It was almost certain he was alone.

Squatting over him, ready to cover his mouth again if he yelled, Grizzly

Hair asked in Spanish, "What are you doing here?"

"Washing gold," the man squeaked.

He was crazy. There was even less honor in killing a crazy man. "I think we should let him go so he can carry a message to the black hats."

"Maybe," said Elk Calf, looking at his younger in-laws with a happy expression. "A good message." The smiles of the others agreed with that.

Grizzly Hair looked into the old man's terrified gray eyes and said in Spanish, "Go home and tell your *soldado* friends that they are shit."

Elk Calf said, "I like that."

The others laughed and one observed, "Without his horse it will take him longer to deliver the message."

"His rotten feet will get sore," said another.

Still, the trembling black hat didn't yell. Clearly no other black hat was within earshot. Instead he began to speak in a rough voice, too rapid to understand. Elk Calf was stepping into the *pantalones,* pulling them as high as they would go and saw that the legs were much to long for his short, burly frame. He tore out the crotch and pulled them nearly to his armpits, then tightened the belt-thong around his chest and stood grinning proudly with his man's part hanging out. He then put the wide-brimmed hat on his head. One of the others pulled on the woolen shirt. The youngest picked up the smelly boots.

Grizzly Hair wiped the remaining sand out of the shiny vessel and said, "It looks like a cooking pot with a spike on the bottom." Except this had a moveable, hinged plate on one side with two slits in it. The pot wouldn't hold water.

Trussed like a kill, the old man managed to roll to his knees. "No, *por favor,*" he begged, "give it to me." He fell over.

Elk Calf picked up a fallen branch and ordered in a threatening voice, "What are you going to tell the *soldados?*"

The old man squeaked, "The *Indios* say you are shit."

"*Muy bueno,*" said Elk Calf. Giving the branch to one of his friends, he released the slip knot connecting the man's ankles, retied the wrists in front, and released his ankles. "*Adios,*" he said, but the man didn't leave. He fell to his knees and grabbed as much of the washed sand and gravel as he could hold in his bound hands.

Elk Calf easily forced the hands open and threw the contents into the brambles. The man gazed sadly after it, then looked longingly at the remaining pile. One of the younger men kicked it in all directions and laughed as tears welled in the old eyes.

Grizzly Hair felt certain the man was crazy. Perhaps he had encountered Bohemkulla on a night trail. "*Por favor,*" the old man pleaded, "Give me my *casco.*"

"*¿Qué es casco?*" Grizzly Hair asked.

The man extended his bound hands in a begging way. Looking at the vessel in Grizzly Hair's hands, he said, "*Sombrero.*"

"It's a hat," Grizzly Hair said, turning the spike side up. "A heavy hat." It would cover the nose. The plate with eye holes could be pulled down. No arrow could penetrate it, maybe not even a ball from a gun. He wiped out more gold-flecked sand and put it on. It fit snugly. This was a lucky find and a good omen. He would wear it to war, a clever hat stolen from a black hat, a hat that could protect him from guns.

"Go," the youngest man said, raising the branch, but before he could strike, the old man started running, tender-footed, pale buttocks jiggling. He looked at them over his shoulder. Still not yelling.

The man, or boy, heaved the branch and it grazed the old man's back, he jumped and continued running without losing a step. The others were laughing, but at that instant a falcon swooped low over Grizzly Hair's head, startling him. It coasted in a straight line through the trees and over the head of the black hat, nearly touching his hair. The man flinched but continued running. This was a messenger from Wek-Wek. The others felt the spirit presence too, each keeping his silence.

When the eeriness cleared and the old man was out of sight, Elk Calf said, "This is my horse. I found it in my wife's home place." His confident smile harbored a challenge as he patted the mare with large brown spots. Elk Calf's friends nodded in agreement. One untied the gun from the saddle.

Grizzly Hair had wanted the gun for Two Falcons and the saddled horse for Morning Owl. It seemed to him that without Morena no one would have found the black hat, but he was a guest on this river. He said, "I have seen a gun fired. I'll show you how." He picked up the powder horn and skin of implements and handed them to Elk Calf, who hung them around his neck.

Elk Calf belly-flopped over the saddle. He pulled himself up and put his wide dusty feet in the footholders, gun in hand. Grizzly Hair saw that Te-mi's son held himself like a warrior.

That night, in a makeshift willow house near the river, Etumu rubbed his calf, then his other calf. It made him want her and he wondered why she did it. "Boy eats many things now," she whispered. "I chew the food and he takes it willingly from my lips. He doesn't need milk anymore."

Grizzly Hair had hardly noticed. He'd been too preoccupied with war talk. Turning to her, he wondered why he was recalling the spirit messenger at this wonderful moment. Then the feel of her skin and the quiet lightning within her, dormant for so long, jumped to him and the world vanished.

62

June 5, 1827, Mission San José

Just after sundown Luis Argüello stood watching Sergeant Francisco Soto and the thirteen soldiers of his expedition dismount. He motioned Soto to follow. Inside the small record-keeping room, which Father Durán had provided for his use during his stay at the mission, the heavy door closed behind them. Soto removed an envelope from his pocket and handed it to Argüello. It contained two letters, both in English and therefore impossible to read except for the salutations and signatures, both signed Harrison G. Rogers for Jedediah S. Smith.

The first letter was dated: June 3, 1827, the second undated. The first was addressed to Capt. Luis Antonio Argüello at San José Mission, the second to Governor José María Echeandía. Both letters were several pages long and written in a terrible chicken-scrawl by the same hand. Both contained references to Soto, Jedediah Smith and "Saint Joseph Mission."

Folding the letters, Luis Argüello laid them aside, sat in the only chair and invited Soto to sit on the corner of the heavy table.

"*Gracias, Comandante,* but, with your permission, it has been a long ride and I prefer to stand."

"Of course. You helped him write some of this, didn't you?" He pointed to the letters, "Titles and names."

"*Sí, Capitán.* Señor Rogers requested it because he couldn't spell the names."

Argüello nodded. "Tell me everything that happened."

Standing nervously on the verge of attention in the tiny space between table and wall, the tough soldier rattled off every detail about the crossing of the San Joaquin River, the neophytes building tule boats to carry the gear, the swimming of the horses and mules and the loss of a fender off one of the saddles.

"Sergeant, *por favor,*" Argüello interrupted, "start with your arrival at the camp of the Americans."

"Yes, Captain. We counted eight men. They were well armed, not belligerent, but noticeably close to their weapons. Not to say they weren't respectful and polite. I asked why they were in the country. Señor Rogers pleaded that they were *pobrecitos* in need of clothing and food. The mission alcalde Narciso was there helping me understand the American's bad Spanish, not that it helped much, but a little I suppose. I tried to explain the meaning of your letter to him, the one I delivered. It upset Señor Rogers very much. One could see it in his eyes. He sat down right there in a high wind and wrote an answer, grabbing at the leaves of paper as the wind took them. He said these two letters explained his position. He made me understand that he is waiting for Jedediah Smith to return from finding a pass over the *sierra nevada* and expects him to arrive back at their camp in three or four weeks. He says they are trappers, trappers only, and never intended to get stuck in Alta California."

"You believe him then."

"Well, yes sir, I mean I believe he is caught in an unfortunate situation. I saw no evidence of charts and maps that would compromise us. It is true they have made themselves familiar with the local rivers but that is to be expected of trappers who hope to find their way out. With my own eyes I could see that those men have almost no supplies. They are eating Indian food, sir. Señor Rogers told me they tried to go over the *sierra* a month ago but nearly froze to death. Most of their horses died. They ate them." Soto shook his head in pity. "They are praying every day to return to their families. There is snow in the mountains even now, sir, as I could see from the distance, and this will slow señor Smith's exploration. Those men are desperate. I am convinced they have not caused the truancy of our *Indios.*"

Argüello didn't believe that. No sane men would embark on such a dangerous journey in the first place, just to trap beaver. Soto might be an experienced soldier, but he lacked understanding of human nature, and was therefore no diplomat. Martinez had sent the wrong man. "You mentioned that they were eating Indian food, and that Narciso was there. Were the rest of the *cimarrones* right there, camping nearby?"

"*Sí, Comandante,* most of them were nearby and as I learned, under the control of Narciso. The Americans said they didn't talk to them, didn't even look at them when they passed by."

"Did you interview the gentiles in the surrounding villages?"

"*Oh sí, Comandante.* They were entirely quiet. I saw no evidence of insurgency. At Narciso's word, the fugitives came readily with me, without incident. I saw nothing suspicious to implicate the *Americanos* at all. I could have looked beyond, but my orders—"

"Thank you, Sergeant. You did your duty." Nevertheless, something foul was afoot. Argüello had questioned Hipolito. For lying initially, he would receive twenty-five lashes each morning for five days running, and now that the remaining fugitives had been rounded up and were under guard at the mission, it wouldn't take long to get the whole story. He went out to procure it.

The next morning he took down paper, ink and quill and wrote to the Governor:

To Lt. Col. don José de Echeandía,

Yesterday, at eight o'clock at night, Sgt. Francisco Soto arrived at this mission. He returned without incident with his party, having satisfactorily completed his expedition. His commission, entrusted to him by

Lieutenant don Ignacio Martinez, was to approach the foreigners and round up all the Christians who had fled from these missions. In this he succeeded, and all have arrived at this Mission and appear to be tranquil.

I had also ordered Soto to visit all the closest Indian rancherías and to confer with them about how the behavior of these foreigners is affecting them. At the same time, he should inform himself thoroughly about the heathen Indians, if these foreigners have been the cause of the abortive flight of the neophytes and their disturbance. . .

Sgt Soto found them very tranquil and quiet in their lands. If the foreigners, shameful and cowardly, caused this disturbance of the neophytes, as is imputed to them, then Soto assures me that they did not find a way to verify it satisfactorily. . .

Nonetheless, I will not feel very satisfied until I have investigated the matter fully. . . I do not have the full story well investigated because this very day it has been revealed to me. Briefly I will outline to your excellency that which is being uncovered.

. . .The Christians of these missions, as far as San Juan Bautista, used to have or have had the wicked scheme or plan of rebelling simultaneously in order to deliver a definitive blow that would finish California and leave all of them in their old state of paganism. According to what is said, the Christians of the missions of the south are involved. They have only waited for those of one mission to raise an outcry for all to do it en masse. Thus, sir, at this time I find myself with this great danger. I want to investigate this infernal plan without losing a moment. . . The greatest secrecy and reserve must be maintained here in order that the ringleaders or plotters of the other missions do not succeed.

This is as much as I can quickly tell your excellency. I do not want to tarry over this and distract myself from looking into the substance of this serious matter.

God and the Law,
Mission San José, June 6, 1827
Luis Antonio Argüello

63

Grizzly Hair, Etumu, Scorpion-on-Nose and Pretty Duck returned to the river of Estanislao's people, having heard that the soldiers had left with most of the mission neophytes. Shortly afterward, a runner came from the mountains east of Monterey.

"The governor has changed his mind," he said in a tone of suppressed excitement. "All baptized Christians must return to their missions. Even married neophytes who were released must return. Any who hide or refuse will suffer severe punishment."

The hair prickled on the back of Grizzly Hair's neck.

Domingo leveled him a coyote look and said quietly, "Now the mission people will fight."

The runner continued, "Padre Durán appealed to Mexico and more soldiers are coming to help. But if you go to the missions without resistence, you will not be punished."

That evening O-se-mai-ti appeared to Grizzly Hair. "The people of the bull are tightening the ropes around your necks," she observed.

"We will trick them," he assured her. "We will grab them by the tongue and strike at their vitals. We will defeat them."

All during the long dry Grizzly Hair and too few men toiled to build a fort at Domingo's place. Instead of spending the hot languid afternoons floating and bobbing in the river, as sensible people did in other villages, they chopped down trees, dragged and upended them side by side in deep holes to make a stout protective wall. Only Domingo's men, some of the Muquelumne, and a few *cimarrones* from the south were there to help. Morning Owl and Raven Feather had folded their cloth house, taken their Bible and gone to the home place. Two Falcons and Lame Beaver went with them. Of the umne, only Scorpion-on-Nose and Pretty Duck remained.

September 18, 1827

The heat was stifling. Some of the grape leaves were curled and yellowed, but in the bottoms of the holes, down deep in the warm black soil made from generations of moldering leaves, a trace of moisture could still be felt. The tree people thrived here, enjoying the circling river and the absorbed moisture from the long-gone time of rain. Now, deeply grooving the earth, Grizzly Hair and nine men strained and sweated as they shoved the butt end of a freshly cut alder toward the wall of pointed poles until it bumped into its hole. In the welcome pause before upending this last pole of the day, Grizzly Hair looked at the golden light slanting through the stirred-up dust. Father sun was retiring earlier each day, but that didn't slow the construction. The men worked faster to cut and plant the allotted twenty poles each day. That rule had been established almost without talk. In the mission Grizzly Hair and Bowstring had skinned forty cattle each day under the guns of the guards. People made fifty adobe bricks each day; others had collected high numbers of grain bags each day. If they failed to meet the number, Narciso's spies would report and the guilty men and women would be chained to the church door and flogged. When that happened Narciso wielded the *cuarta* while the padres led the assembled neophytes to jeer at their fellow neophytes for their sin of sloth. Now these same men did exhausting, repetitive labor for their own purpose, and no alcalde or guard watched. Furthermore, even Narciso was expected to join the rebellion. This fueled the men's confidence and determination. A lump of pride caught in Grizzly Hair's throat to be one of them. He was a man of the *insurgentes* as well as a man of the umne.

At a signal from the man closest to the front, he braced his legs and lifted the far end of the pole. Men along the trunk grunted, pushed up, shifting in quick little dances of balance. Slowly, arms trembling, he pushed upward until his arms were fully extended overhead, then hand-walked down the trunk after the others, knowing that if he dropped his end, it could crush them all. He saw Elk Calf and Scorpion-on-Nose with their sturdy legs apart, nearly squatting, steadying the tree trunk from the opposite direction by means of braided ropes. A wash of stinging sweat obliterated Grizzly Hair's vision. Blinking, he felt more than saw that at last the point looked skyward and the pole stood firmly beside the previous pole. As the men whose turn it was to hold it steady moved around the excavated hole, Grizzly Hair picked some grape leaves and wiped his eyes and forehead. Then he and four others sat down and shoved dirt with the soles of their feet. They jumped inside and trampled the dirt, then shoved in more and trampled again it until the pole stood firmly by itself.

Men dropped to their knees. Grizzly Hair lay on his back. Hunger kneaded and folded his stomach and hurt up to his throat. Domingo asked, "Who carries the ax tonight?"

Señor Rogers had agreed that if women brought grass seed and cooked it for the *Americanos* every morning, the men could borrow the ax and bring it back every sundown. The *Americanos* needed it only in the morning for cutting firewood. The distance was long, half a day's walk each way from Domingo's place, half that for a horse, but the heavy, long-handled ax was well worth the trouble. "I did it last night," said one of Domingo's men. He lay flat on his back, eyes closed, hands on the ground.

One after the other inert men recited who had carried the ax before whom and slowly Grizzly Hair realized it was his turn. He had looked forward to bathing and lying with Etumu—not moving, just touching her with his hand. Love had been sweet between them all during the long dry.

"It's my turn," he admitted, wondering if he had the strength to walk to the corral. To make matters worse the ax had gone dull. He had noticed it on his turn chopping the last tree. That meant he'd have to sharpen it at Sucais' place. No stone could be found in the flatlands, where women used wooden mortar bowls and pestles.

Domingo said, "Somebody fetch Grizzly Hair's woman. He needs food for the journey."

"No, I'm on my way." He rolled over, enjoyed the four-footed position too briefly, then creaked to his feet. Sweating, dirt-streaked men lay strewn about like the treetops. Heat pressed upon them. But after the sleep they would swim and begin another day like this one. Only desperate men would do this, men determined to win the right to walk and live where they wished, like the Animal People made them. His talk about the wall around Fort Ross had given them hope that they too could fend off gun-bearing enemies. The presence of the *Americanos* also gave them hope. The *Americanos* wouldn't help build the fort, however, so it was left to desperate men. But sometimes in the night Coyote came and reminded him that all was not as it appeared.

"Watch Etumu tonight," Grizzly Hair said to Scorpion-on-Nose as he walked away. The master knapper signed that of course he would.

On the way to the river, Grizzly Hair acknowledged Etumu with his eyes. Before the willow shelter, she was placing a red-hot clay ball into a full basket. He took two running steps down the bank and splashed to his thighs. Even the water was too warm. He let himself sink, let the tepid river wash the sweat and the stickiness from his scalp. Then he returned to Etumu. He scooped up the congealed nu-pah̩ that remained from morning, filling his stomach as fast as he could.

She looked sad. "Wait for the stew," she pleaded.

"No, I need to travel while there's light."

"You should have told me you were leaving."

"I forgot it was my turn." Food was restoring calm to his insides. Looking up he saw Boy running happily toward him. As the strong little child hit, he hugged him and tipped over on the ground, rolling with him—Boy belly-laughing. After that he put Boy on his lap and told him, "I'm going to ride to Sucais' place tonight."

The soft little face fell, then brightened. "I go ride too?"

"No. You stay with Mother and keep her safe."

Jumping free, Boy ran to the shelter and picked up a toy bow and arrow. "See," he said, hurriedly fitting the stick arrow. "I shoot the bad men." He pulled back, released too soon and the stick fell to the ground.

"Good," Grizzly Hair said. "Soon you will be a man."

Boy's bright, clear smile was hard to leave. Etumu whisked the child to her hip and walked with Grizzly Hair toward the brush corral, passing the fort along the way. From a distance it was almost hidden among the trailing limbs and vines. Like beavers, they had fashioned points as they chopped the tree trunks. Not waiting idly for their turn with the ax, they used their stone axes on the next trees to be cut. Domingo had loaned one to Grizzly Hair.

"If only the *cimarrones* hadn't gone back to the missions," Etumu said looking at the gap in the circular fort. "You would be finished."

How often he had thought the same thing! Not only would this fort be finished, but the back-up fort at Sucais' place would be finished too. "If, if," he said, reminding her with a smile of Coyote schemes. "The black hats would have come after the *cimarrones* and we would have lost the war before we were ready." He picked up the *Americano* ax.

"Still, I can hardly believe how much it grows every day," she exclaimed. The place looked forlorn with the men gone and the earth trampled, and tree-tops littered about. Eventually that brush would hide the trenches. She was smiling at him. "I am growing bigger too."

He let his puzzlement show. "You look more womanly and I like that."

Her look was a tease. "I have a baby in my blood."

Another child! He loved being a father, and now another child was coming. He put a hand on her shoulder. Covering his emotion with a joke, he said, "You sure it's not a white pickaniño?"

She smiled with him. "This baby started when we were visiting the Chilumne."

"Did the *Americanos* make it stronger?"

Playfully she batted the air before him. "All right. You want me to say it. I never coupled with them." She gave him a look. "Any woman could have, and the ones who did say they are much stronger, and their men are too, so maybe you should be sorry I didn't."

He leaned down and rubbed noses with her, "I wish I didn't have to go tonight, and you would see I am strong enough." Already he had stayed too long.

Invigorated by the thought of a new child, he hurried to the corral and kicked Morena into a gallop. He realized that no matter the struggle of the *Indio* peoples, no matter the strategy for war, birth and children continued, and that was more fundamental. Sucais had said that. Grizzly Hair had learned many things from Estanislao's father and he hoped, someday, to be like him.

Weary in the backside he finally reined Morena to a stop at Sucais' place. Only a hint of purple-red remained in the western sky. Shadowy trees filled the river bottom and only one lonely fire twinkled where three moons before the big encampment had sprawled. An owl hooed. A dark figure approached. Sucais, walking faster than usual. "Where are you going?" he asked.

Grizzly Hair dismounted and wiped sticky clumps of wet horsehair off his inner legs. "I came to sharpen the ax, and sleep." He felt like he could drop where he was.

Sucais laid a hand on his shoulder and said with an air of excitement, "Jed Smith is here. With six more *Americanos*."

That shocked him awake. He had begun to think the hy-apo of the *Americanos* would never return. Four moons had passed and some of the *Americanos* had given him up for dead. The last ax runner had speculated the others would leave without him. Still, most people in Domingo's camp held to the belief that he would return and join them in war.

Sorry he had lingered so long at Domingo's, Grizzly Hair quickly honed the ax head while Sucais sat nearby. Moving the heavy iron back and forth over the stone, he noticed soreness in the thickening muscles of his arms. In the firelight they shone with sweat. Building the fort had made him leaner in some places and wider in others. His Spanish had improved too, as it was the tongue of Domingo's camp. That would help him talk to Jed Smith.

The trail upriver was dark, owls calling on all sides, and the ax felt heavy in his hand. A slight welcoming breeze lifted the hair off his damp forehead. Nearing the *Americano* camp, he almost gagged as the stench of excrement hit him in the face. They didn't bury it. The fire burned low and a few men sat in the path of the smoke to discourage mosquitos. "*Hola,*" he said in a fairly loud voice. The men sat up from their saddles. "Here is your ax." He used the *Americano* word.

"*Gracias.*" Señor Rogers' voice.

"I want to talk with Jed Smith," Grizzly Hair said.

"*Who's there?*" The voice sounded like Jed Smith.

"*Indian from the Cosommey River,*" Rogers called.

"*I'm plum tuckered,*" the voice called back. "*He can come back first thing in the morning if he wants, before I leave.*"

Señor Rogers repeated it in Spanish, telling Grizzly Hair to come *por la mañana,* in the morning.

He stood watching the tired flames and knew he was too weary for difficult talk anyway. The fort builders would have to use their stone axes for a while. He would bring something even more valuable than the ax—Jed Smith's intent in war.

When he entered the camp of the *Americanos* the next morning a lively little fire was popping. The ax lay beside freshly split firewood, and steam shot from the spouts of four *kettles* placed around the fire's edge. A strange new aroma, a little like burned nuts but rich and intriguing, covered the normal stench. It seemed to emanate from the kettles. Seven or eight women were there, and several unfamiliar *Americanos,* who sat eagerly scooping mush from the baskets, the murderer not among them. The new *Americanos* peered at Grizzly Hair from hooded brows, their beards obscuring most of their emaciated faces and scrawny necks.

Señor Rogers took a metal cup to the fire, poured dark liquid from a kettle, intensifying the nutlike aroma, and sat against an oak. He patted the ground inviting Grizzly Hair to join him. "Jed Smith *viene momentito.*"

As the words left the man's lips, Jed Smith's scarred face and floppy hat appeared on the south side of camp among high rose bushes decorated with tiny yellow fruit. He raised his chin in recognition, quickly walked to a cloth house and brought back a knife similar to the one on Grizzly Hair's calf. He was thinner and his brown eyes seemed to burn deeper in his head. Folding his legs beside Señor Rogers, he removed his hat, grabbed the few hairs that remained on his furrowed scalp and whacked them off. Then he began cutting his dark beard in small, jerky thrusts. Singeing would be simpler, but Grizzly Hair wouldn't make an impolite suggestion.

"Today I go to Mission Saint Joseph to get your horses," Jed Smith said as he sawed on the beard. In a shaft of morning sunlight, his eyes flashed orange. Something about him had changed.

Harrison Rogers mumbled in the mushy *Americano* tongue, "*Jed, I'm still of the opinion you'd oughta stay and rest a spell, after all you been through.*"

Stretching his cheek to the blade, Jed Smith scraped and it sounded like a mouse chewing wood. Scritch, scritch. "*No rest for the wicked,*" he muttered between scritches.

Señor Rogers gave him a look. "*Jed, if I didn't know better I'd think you meant that.*"

He kept scraping.

"*You know, of all the men in this world, I'd say you deserve a bit of slacking off.*"

Jed Smith continued scraping. Under his buckskin *pantalones* the bones of his thighs looked bird narrow. The hollow of the cheek being revealed looked like skin stretched over a skull. "*Deserving has nothing to do with it,*" he said.

"*Well, if you're so all fired hell-bent t'go,*" Harrison Rogers said—Grizzly Hair wondering how long this baffling talk would last—"*alla us oughta go with you. The men are goin' stir crazy in this bug-infested place. Two run off a'ready, as you well know. And we'd likely lose more.*"

The knife hung motionless over the cheek. "*Harry, from what you told me yesterday, and I didn't sleep much on account of it, we got ourselves an international situation here.*" He pointed the tip of the knife west. "*No telling what'll say howdy to me over that hill.*" He opened his mouth, shifted his jaw and started scraping the other cheek. "*The men are safer here. But keep your weapons handy.*"

For a moment Harrison Rogers sat still and Grizzly Hair hoped they were finished, but he continued. "*It's easier for grown men to face danger than sit and wait.*"

"*Take care of the ones I brought in. They been through hell.*"

"*Well then, I'd say you been to hell three times and back. The others was taken aback when them savages attacked back on the Colorado, but you're carrying the burden of those ten dead men. I know you pretty good, Jed. And I think it's got a hold on you.*"

"*Don't need nobody looking after me.*" Scritch, Scritch.

"*All I'm sayin' is, even the Lord rested after six days.*"

More impatient than he liked to be, Grizzly Hair shifted against the tree.

Jed Smith was exploring his cheeks with his finger tips. Satisfied, he stood up, lifted his shirt and inserted the knife in a leather holder on his waist. It hung beside a leather sling containing what appeared to be a very short gun. Did short guns exist? Guns that could be hidden? *"Thankee kindly for your concern, Harry, but we're headin' out."* Jed Smith looked at Grizzly Hair and said in Spanish, "You wanted to say something?"

He wished he could speak the *Americano* tongue and say this compellingly. "We need you to help us fight the *soldados*."

"No, no and no. Take that out of your head. Tonight I will tell Padre Durán I am NOT talking to you Indians about that. Somebody told him different. Now think, this is important. I never told your people I would fight. Did I? I never told you to make war." His eyes sparked.

Somebody had told Padre Durán. Narciso? Hipolito? No wonder Jed Smith wouldn't admit anything to Grizzly Hair; he thought it would be reported in the mission. Grizzly Hair wanted to deny that, compellingly, and keep the possibility of alliance open. He was searching for the words when Jed Smith jammed on his hat, walked rapidly to a cloth house, removed a gun, saddle and another Bible, and beckoned with his head to three men who in the meantime had dressed in full regalia and were holding guns and saddles.

Jed Smith looked back at Grizzly Hair and said in Spanish, "Palaber later." Then he announced to the remaining *Americanos*, *"I should be back in a few days."* He turned and walked swiftly toward the brush corral, his shrunken backside not even moving the folds in the rear of his *pantalones*.

When the four were out of sight, Señor Rogers gestured toward the piles of animal skins that the *Americanos* had collected in their hy-apo's absence and said, "When he comes back, we'll take those to the *Mexicanos* and trade for horses." He signaled Grizzly Hair to take the ax.

Grizzly Hair picked it up went to Morena. He had little to tell the fort-builders, but still believed the *Americanos* would join them in war—if only he could talk to their headman in a leisurely way. If they could both speak better Spanish. If, if, if. But like Coyote, Grizzly Hair would keep trying.

Jed Smith did not return in a few days. Two moons later he still wasn't there. A runner said he was locked in the *calabozo* in Mission San José, and soon afterward another runner brought a paper that talked from Jed Smith to Señor Rogers, telling him that. Grizzly Hair felt the horror of being locked in that dark, unhealthy place. Then a runner from Domingo's network said they had seen Jed Smith on the trail with his hands and feet in irons, being moved to Monterey. Pomponio had also been moved to Monterey, then shot to death. Grizzly Hair feared for the *Americano* as he and the others finished the fort at Domingo's. When they returned to Sucais' place and finished the back-up fort, he spirit-tracked Jed Smith and knew he was still alive. All he said aloud was that now Jed Smith would want to punish the black hats. Everyone agreed with that. Now the *Americanos* would help the *Indios* wage war.

With that hope and the cooler weather, and the ax closer at hand, the work went faster. Then it started to rain. Etumu felt homesick, even vomiting some mornings. She missed her parents. Everyone else missed the home place too, so Scorpion-on-Nose, Pretty Duck, Grizzly Hair, Etumu and Boy visited the *Americano* camp one last time to tell Señor Rogers they were leaving.

"When you have our horses," Grizzly Hair said, "bring them to my *ranchería.*" They well knew where it was. He looked at the hard, wiry man with the curved mustache, and said sincerely. "I hope Jed Smith and all of you have *buena suerta,*" Good luck. They shook hands all around.

The little group headed for the home place under a dark sky that seemed about to fall with the weight of the rain. Only magic held it up. The rain spirit was holding back, waiting, just as the *Indio* peoples were waiting for Jed Smith. Fortunately, the *Españoles* probably wouldn't try an expedition while the marshes were wet and muddy.

That turned out to be true. And, as fate would have it, even more rain fell than anyone could remember from seasons past.

64

Time of Early Flowers, 1828

A runner came from the Shalachmushumne and told the gathered umne: "The *Americanos* are coming with many horses. They are coming to visit you."

Excitement crackled all around and Etumu realized she would never wear the red skirt again. All the goods must be returned when they received the horses. But seeing the pleased smile on her man's lips, she knew she must be glad she'd had it this long. Now her father would have a horse. He would sit high upon it. She eased her swollen belly through the crowd and nuzzled up to Grizzly Hair's side. Boy trotted to his other side and convinced his father to pick him up so he could see. She loved the way he loved Boy.

"When will they be here?" Morning Owl asked the runner.

"Before the sleep."

Grizzly Hair said quietly to Etumu, "They are faithful like Cos." He reached around her and snuggled her to him. After the baby was born she couldn't couple with him again until the baby stopped nursing, so now she was very glad the baby hadn't come yet.

The crowd broke apart. Etumu and the other women returned to their previous activities, but the men stood in groups talking about how they would ride horses wherever they needed to go, and use them to hunt.

Father sun hadn't yet sunk in the west when she felt a slight earth tremor, a rumble up her bones. Then she heard a distant whinny. Nearby, Morena and Milk whinnied in return. Everyone ran toward the playing field. Ahead of the rest, Grizzly Hair, Morning Owl, Red Sun and Two Falcons went to greet the visitors. The rumble was suddenly louder. Etumu stopped in her tracks. Over the hilltop flowed a river of horses and mules that seemed as though it would never end. They came four and six abreast in shades of black and brown and acorn-tan, the herders still unseen. Boy squealed and ran toward them. Etumu almost didn't catch him in time to pull him out of the way. The herald was calling: "The *Americanos* are here."

In the village center, while the enormous herd eagerly grazed the green grass clothing the hillsides, the umne crowded around the *Americanos*. Etumu counted nineteen hairy skinny men in buckskins. Some she recognized, including the man with black skin and big laughing eyes, but the murderer had gone over the eastern mountains and never returned.

Talk began. Fortunately, Etumu had learned a lot of Spanish in Domingo's camp. Grizzly Hair talked for Morning Owl and she could see the shine of excitement in his eyes. Important allies were coming.

Morning Owl said to Jed Smith, "You have many horses."

"*Tres cien y diez.*" Three hundred and ten, said Jed Smith.

Etumu was trying to figure how many twenties that was when Jed Smith said, "But now I give you ten, so I will have three hundred."

At Jed Smith's gesture everyone got up again and walked back to the playing field. Jed Smith invited Morning Owl to select ten horses, but not the ones wearing saddles or packs. Two Falcons and Grizzly Hair helped—men who knew horses. Excitement was high as the umne rushed from horse to horse testing them by climbing on them and sensing their strength and willingness to carry people, and looking at the length of their teeth. The selected horses were marked by a twist of milkweed twine in their topknots.

Etumu felt out of breath with excitement. All around her the umne buzzed with happy talk as they returned to the village center and resumed their previous places. "Now," Grizzly Hair said, "we will give back the things you left us as *seguridad*."

Morning Owl and Raven Feather went to their u-macha, she for her red skirt and kettle. Morning Owl ceremoniously carried the neatly folded cloth house, the folded blanket and buckskin shirt with the Bible centered on top. Under the Bible lay the two sheets of paper, and beside it the yellow writing stick. "*No agua*," said Morning Owl, having learned a little Spanish. Grizzly Hair explained that the hy-apo hadn't allowed water to touch the Bible. That had been difficult on the ride to the home place when the sky had finally opened upon them. They had folded the Bible inside the shirt, wrapped the blanket around it, and put the package inside the folded cloth house.

Etumu went to the dim u-macha and brought the red skirt from the rafters—herbed so no worms would eat it. People were untying the thongs of their necklaces, ready to return the beads to the *Americanos.*

Jed Smith pushed the palms of his hands toward them. "No, you keep the frou-frou." To Morning Owl he said, "You keep this." He pointed at the buckskin shirt, *papel* and the kettle. "I will take these; he pointed at the cloth house, Bible and blanket. "You keep the beads and *faldas rojas.*"

Even the baby inside Etumu jumped with joy. The man was generous. Everyone gleefully restrung the frou-frou back on their neck thongs—wealth for future trading—and Raven Feather smiled Etumu a sisterly look. Etumu would wear the red skirt again after the baby was born, and keep the sense of being an important woman, she and Raven Feather together.

Grizzly Hair repeated the hy-apo's words for Jed Smith: *"Muchas gracias. Mi mujer está contento."* Both women were indeed happy.

Later, after the *Americanos* set up their cloth houses in the playing field, Grizzly Hair and Etumu were honored to eat at Morning Owl's fire with Jed Smith and Harrison Rogers. In addition to duck stew, they had a fresh salmon roasted on alder switches, a lingerer. Such lingerers came up the river much later than the big run. The other *Americanos* cooked the small brown fruits called *frijoles* and ate dried meat. Now Grizzly Hair would talk with Jed Smith about the coming war with the *Españoles.* Etumu almost wished it would vanish from everyone's mind, but how else would the umne be safe in their home place? That's what it always came back to. That's what Grizzly Hair said.

"Much water over there," Jed Smith said taking a bite of his salmon. He gestured west. "We had many problems coming this far. Many, many problems. Very bad. *Mucho malo. Mucha agua.* Much water, big rivers, much mud. Is there always this much rain?" His Spanish was more fluent since they had last talked. Four moons with the *Españoles* had made a difference.

Morning Owl shrugged. "Sometimes."

Grizzly hair added, *"Mucho malo en el calabozo, eh?"* Much bad in the jail. Etumu knew this was intended to bring the talk around to war.

The headman of the *Americanos* rolled his eyes. *"Mucho malo."* Briefly he pinched his nose, and went back to eating.

"I have been there too," Grizzly Hair said.

"*Malo.* No food or water for a long time."

"They never bring food and water to the *calabozo.*"

Jed Smith looked at him. "Did they use the *cuarta* on you?"

"Yes. Did they use it on you?"

"No. What bad thing did you do?"

Grizzly Hair thought a moment. *"Nada."* He and Jed Smith looked at each other. Red Sun, Two Falcons and others came to the hy-apo's fire and settled themselves comfortably within earshot.

Jed Smith, who had finished his salmon, wiped his mouth on his sleeve and pointed to the other *Americanos.* "My man, Thomas Virgen over there, nearly died in a *calabozo* in San Diego. He was sick and wounded with arrows when we brought him across the Mojave. I had to talk a long time to get them to let him go and meet us up here." He gaze lingered on his man, and Etumu saw that Señor Virgen was the skinniest one.

"Maybe you are *furioso* at the *Españoles* now." Grizzly Hair remarked.

Jed Smith looked into the darkening trees. Slowly and carefully he put the words together. *"Furioso no se producir benefício. Comprendes?"*

Anger does not produce benefit. Grizzly Hair nodded that he understood the words, but Etumu knew he didn't agree with them in this case. "The missions have corn and fruit trees," he said, starting in a new direction. "Good grapes. They make iron things there. Many good things. Maybe you would like to have a mission."

Jed Smith barked "Haw! Those padres are like a *kings* in their own separate *kingdoms.*"

"What is the meaning of kings?"

"Big chiefs."

"Maybe," Grizzly Hair continued, "*Americanos* and *Indios* could be trade friends. Make war together. If we won, you could live like a big chief in a mission." This was the enticement he had used on the Russian. Estanislao didn't want Russians to have missions, but these *Americanos* had been very friendly. Surely that was different.

Jed Smith narrowed his pale brown eyes. "You saw all those *Indios* from the missions, the ones on the Lakisamni River?"

"Sí."

"They call me *salvador.* You know what that means?"

"He who saves."

"Yes. They think I will save them, like Jesús saves the souls of *Christianos.* That's why I was locked in the *calabozo.*" He gave the hand signal for a chattering mouth. "That's why it took so much palaber to get liberated. "I don't want to make war with you. I don't want them thinking I am your ally. I don't want them coming after me."

Grizzly Hair looked at the tough man who had been scalped by a grizzly bear and gave rein to his persistence. "We made two *castillos* near where your men were camped. With you and *Americano* shooting guns, we will win and maybe you *Americanos* could get Mission San José and Mission San Francisco. Wouldn't you like that?" Sunshine-through-the-Mist came to the hyapo's fire and sat beside Straight Willow, and Etumu realized that the story-teller would tell the story of this night for a long time, and maybe one of the children would grow up and tell it after Sunshine-through-the-Mist. Etumu was sorry Boy wasn't older so he could stay awake and understand all that was being said.

Jed Smith had exchanged a long glance with Señor Rogers, and now addressed Grizzly Hair in a deliberate tone. "Yes, I know you used my ax every day to build it. More reason for me to quit this country immediately. The next *inquisición* will be about that. No. My men and I will not lift a gun against the Spaniards. It would start a war between Mexico and the United States. My country is not ready for that. It would be very bad for me. I want to trap beaver." He pointed at the other *Americanos*. "They don't want to fight either. Tom Virgen there, the one who nearly died, wants to go home to his wife and baby. We are traders, not men of war." His mouth made a firm hard line within the hairy opening.

Etumu felt a stab of sympathy for Grizzly Hair, that he had traveled far and wide trying to convince many peoples to join together and fight the *Españoles*, and now the *Americanos* were refusing, the ones who could bring sure victory. "The *soldados* are few," Grizzly Hair continued. "Tell your war chief to send *Americanos* who are warriors."

His persistence made her squirm. She tossed a stick of wood on the fire and sparks danced into the wind. Boy returned from play and snuggled next to her, no longer able to climb into her lap where he wanted to be. She stroked his hair.

"You don't quit, do you?" The *Americano* said, "I like that. But understand, Americans are peaceful people. Our men are making houses and clearing the forests for their families, far east of those mountains, beyond that wide desert." Again he looked at Grizzly Hair as though wondering how he had known about that. "Between here and my house is the Permanent Home of the *Indios*. Americans don't pass through it."

This was the first Etumu knew about *Indios* beyond the eastern mountains. "You passed through it," Grizzly Hair pointed out.

"We are *exploradores*. Understand?"

"No."

Jed Smith leaned back on an elbow. "We are different. Not afraid to travel."

"You are brave," said Grizzly Hair with perfect sincerity. "I think your people are brave. They can defeat the *Españoles*. And there are other ways to come to Alta California besides the way you came. Men come from the sea in big boats and they cross the mountains from the north, from *Rio Columbia*."

The *Americano* perked up. "You know the way there? Can you make an earth map of the *Rio Columbia?*"

Eagerly Grizzly Hair brushed away the debris and drew in the damp earth, showing the way to the Big Mo'mol where it split with the *Rio de los Americanos* and ran north all the way to mountains at the top of the big valley, as Missouri had shown it.

With a hand signal telling them to wait, Jed Smith went to the playing field. He returned with his box, sat down and put a sheet of *papel* on top, then copied Grizzly Hair's map, using the yellow stick. Morning Owl in particular showed an interest in the way the firm, flat box helped the stick make strong marks. "Will you come with us and be our guide to the Columbia River?" Jed Smith asked when he was finished.

Etumu caught her breath. It seemed whenever there was a chance to travel, Grizzly Hair jumped at it. But not this time. "I only know what Missouri showed me on an earth map," Grizzly Hair said. "Just follow this big river." His finger wiggled along the earth map. "Missouri went there." He pressed his fingertip into the dirt. "Very far north. I don't know that trail." He paused. "*Americano* warriors could come from there, or the sea."

Smith shook his head as if amused. "No. *Americanos* will not make war now."

"Later?"

"Maybe. Don't tell that to Durán."

Grizzly Hair's excitement was obvious, though he was trying not to show it. "My mouth is shut. Do you have a war chief?"

"Yes. He is a friend of the Big Chief in Washington."

"Good. Tell your Big Chief in Washington to make war on the *Mexicanos* now. Tell him to send a hundred warriors. Then you will defeat them and all *Indios* will be your friends. We will trade together and make things in the missions." Two Falcons, Morning Owl and the other elders nodded in enthusiastic agreement.

Jed Smith exchanged a look with Harrison Rogers. "We don't know the Big Chief," he said. "We can't ask him to do that."

It was the same with *Mexicanos* and Russians, Grizzly Hair had explained to Etumu. "How can a man be chief to people he does not know?" he asked the *Americanos.*

"An interesting question," said Jed Smith. "Interesting."

Etumu could see that Grizzly Hair liked this *Americano* very much. "Maybe the talking *papel* helps?" he suggested.

"Yes," Jed Smith agreed. "That helps. Some day your people will talk on paper." Etumu was trying to imagine that as he put his map and the yellow stick inside the wooden box, set it aside and reclined on his elbow again. It was even more difficult to see his skull face in the shadow of his hat.

"I thought you would want revenge on the *Españoles,*" Grizzly Hair said in an accepting tone.

"A trader must look forward," Jed Smith said. "Revenge makes no friends. Jesús said that if an enemy strikes us here" he touched his cheek, "we should turn our face the other way so he can strike the other side."

Morning Owl opened his eyes and mouth in surprise. "Jesús said that? He looked at the umne around the fire, showing his amazement.

"Yes. Jesús hates war. He says people should love each other."

It sounded good to Etumu. If people loved each other they wouldn't travel around all the time planning war. She formed the Spanish words, "The *soldados* should listen to Jesús."

Harrison Rogers and Jed Smith both smiled at her.

Lame Beaver tried out his limited Spanish, "Maybe Jesús say only *Indios* turn the face." He patted one cheek then the other.

Jed Smith shook his head, picked the Bible off the blanket and explained that the palaber of Jesús was on the paper leaves. Then, at the obvious interest of the umne, he told about the life of that spirit. Etumu quickly wearied of the difficult Spanish; she felt dizzy with it and longed for her mat in the u-macha. All day she had been waiting for Grizzly Hair to give more of himself to the growing baby inside her. If only he wouldn't display such fascination with everything the *Americano* said, the man might stop talking!

She took Boy to the u-macha and waited.

After everyone else left, Grizzly Hair glanced at Jed Smith, who reclined on an elbow beside the warming fire.

"We are both men of O-se-mai-ti," Grizzly Hair said. "Men of *Oso. Comprendes?*" Seeing only the shadows in the man's face, he tried to explain. "We are alike."

"A bear hurt me. You too?"

"No. Oso is my friend. Your friend too. She lets you live. She has a piece of you."

"Interesting," Jed Smith said. "*Oso* is a woman?

"The spirit. But many bears are men. Old Man of the Forest we call them. All bears talk to O-se-mai-ti and tell her if people treated them with respect."

Jed Smith chuckled and scratched his nose in the flickering firelight, and at that instant it seemed to Grizzly Hair that the barriers of tongue and custom vanished. He sensed that Jed Smith also felt their brotherhood of spirit. "I am sorry I cannot fight a war with you," he said, "but maybe I can tell you something that will help. Have you fought the Spaniards before?"

"They came to capture people on our river." He pointed southwest. "I went to help. The *soldados* surprised us." He told what had happened, and said there had been many such little wars. "But now we will join together and have a big war. We will not be surprised."

"Have your people fought big wars before?"

Grizzly hair laughed at the thought, but then remembered what Drum-in-Fog had said about people finding many arrowheads inside ancient human skeletons. Some people thought a big killing war had once been fought, but that would have been before the eight generations everyone counted in their families. Even the story of such a war had vanished. He described the arrow-dodging war when he was a boy.

Jed Smith whistled softly through his teeth. "You don't know what war is. And you want to fight professional soldiers."

"This time there will be many of us." He described the snare.

"I suppose that might work."

"Do you know how to fight big wars?" Grizzly Hair asked.

"My father's fathers fought many big wars. Some of them came across the sea to get away from those wars. I have never been a soldier but I have heard stories." He looked into the fire and said, "When I was a boy there was a man named Napoleon. Everyone said he was the best *general* that ever lived. He had four-hundred-fifty-thousand men. He fought the Russians, but he made some mistakes and was defeated."

Grizzly Hair didn't delay the story by asking the man to explain a number so enormous that it was more than four hundred, but he needed to know, "What mistakes?"

"He divided his men and they were not as strong. They were defeated one group at a time. And the cold *invierno* finished them, ice and snow."

Grizzly Hair could well imagine how cold could defeat warriors. "How do your people decide who wins a war?"

Jed Smith stretched his arms out to the side, yawned and said, "That depends. Sometimes you count the dead. The loser has more dead men. Sometimes it means capturing a place."

"Can a place be captured?"

"Oh yes." He appeared to smile. "The places around Mission San José and San Francisco have been captured. The original villages are deserted and the people who lived there now do what the *Españoles* tell them to. The area has been captured. Now the soldiers are coming farther east, beyond the San Joaquin River, toward your people. When the fighting is over, either you *Indios* over here will live as you wish, or you will lose and they will tell you what to do. I think you should stop them."

"This is why we wanted you to help us."

"War is very *serio*. Understand?"

"No."

"Not a little thing. Things are never the same again."

"We don't want things to be the same."

"You want *libertad*."

He wasn't sure of the meaning. "People free to go where they want?"

"Yes. You are fighting for *libertad*. My people fought for *libertad* and won. It is a good thing. But some people won't understand. They think *Indios* are different, not *gente de razón*."

"We want to be *gente de razón*. But we don't want their whips and *calabozo*."

"Punishment comes with being *gente de razón*. Catholics or not, it is the same. I whip my men when they disobey me. If I didn't, they wouldn't do what I tell them. But I don't think people can make other people love Jesús by whipping them. So that's where I think you're doing the right thing."

Grizzly Hair recalled Estanislao saying that Padre Durán wanted him to whip his people. But try as he might, he could not understand why powerful men like Jed Smith had to punish grown men. "What did your men do wrong? What *pecado?*"

"You mean why did I whip them?" Seeing his nod, he said, "Down south near Mission San Gabriel I had to whip a man for whipping a horse."

Grizzly Hair wasn't sure he'd heard well. "You whipped a man for whipping a horse?"

"Yes."

Grizzly Hair would have liked to turn that into a joke, but felt the barriers of tongue again, and a strong need for sleep. Instead he said, "I never whip my horse and our chief never whips our men."

"And you never have big wars." Jed Smith pursed his lips thoughtfully, then pushed to his feet and made the sleepy sign.

"Now we will have a big war," Grizzly Hair said, also standing up. He went to the sweathouse which had just stopped smoking. Settling at his usual place on the south wall, he considered all that the *Americano* had said. His talk about mistakes in war could be significant, but by far the most significant was his refusal to fight. This would discourage *Indios* far and wide. Despite what he'd just told Jed Smith, it might be impossible to bring the allies together again.

After the sleep the *Americanos* cooked and ate their food, packed the mules, saddled the horses, rounded up the herd and rode north. Jed Smith, who was the last to leave, ceremoniously gave Morning Owl the Bible, saying he had thought about it during the night and wanted the hy-apo to have it. Morning Owl nodded formally, accepting the magical object that had so much empowered him in recent moons. Then as the umne stood watching the *Americano* ride after the others, heading toward the river named for them, though they didn't know it, Grizzly Hair felt an emptiness worse than humger. Not only had Jed Smith rejected the idea of war, but all morning he'd had about him the foggy aura of death. All but one *Americano* had it; it had obscured their faces. Grizzly Hair went to the river to swim in place and try to forget what he had seen. He didn't want to spirit-track Jed Smith for fear he would *see* what would happen.

More rain pounded the home place and few runners came from the talk network in response to Grizzly Hair's message that Jed Smith had left California. The allies said it was an omen. They said even the talk of war was too dangerous and should cease altogether. They said people should accept fate: the *Españoles* had come into the world to stay. A message from Domingo added to the general discouragement. His place was under water and everyone had gone upstream. The fort at Sucais' place was flooded too. The Muquelumne were the only ones who thought everyone should go back and dig trenches and talk about war when the earth dried.

Then, in the time of golden poppies and purple larkspur, when the luxurious grass gladdened the spirits of all earth creatures, Etumu gave birth. The bright-eyed baby made Grizzly Hair laugh. Boy liked the baby too and everyone said she would bring happiness to the umne. The birth helper from the Omuchumne announced that the baby would live to be an old woman.

One night as they lay in the dark under the rabbit blanket, Etumu confided to Grizzly Hair that she wanted to name the baby after old María. "María helped me before you became my man."

"What help?"

"That's a secret." Her tone was light and friendly.

He told her, "I was thinking of naming the baby after my mother."

She lay quiet for a while, then said, "Maybe we should give her both names. María Howchia."

"It's too early to think about names," he said, poking fun at her for all the times she'd said that about Boy.

"Well then," she answered brightly, "let's name Boy Crying Fox, and wait to name the baby." She added in a serious tone, "María Howchia would be a powerful name. And a woman who will live long should have a strong name."

He stroked the side of her hip and got up to go to the sweathouse.

All during second grass, while the earth dried and the grass reached the horses bellies, Grizzly Hair received messages from the network. More soldiers had arrived to live in the presidios. Another brutal expedition had resulted in the round-up of *cimarrones* on Muquel's river east of Te-mi's place. Grizzly Hair hadn't gone to help because there had been no plan. His message back to Muquel was: We must fight together at the forts, places where we can win. We must show the black hats that the *Indio* peoples are not like the people of Jesús, who present their other buttock to the *cuarta*.

He sent a message to Estanislao, who was in the mission: "Will the fleas ever jump off the wolf?"

The response came on one of the hottest days of the long dry, when people could hardly bring themselves to get out of the river. Grizzly Hair had gone to help Scorpion-on-Nose where the trees of an ancient forest had turned to stone. He carried chunks of it to the knapper, who was flaking a large pile of arrowheads from the hard opal interior of the stone trees.

Then he heard the herald in the distance. He and Scorpion-on-Nose arrived at the dancehouse in time to hear the electrifying message.

V
Walking Into Fire

The men wore human skins
but removed them at night
and fell to the bottom of darkness
like crows without wings.

War was the perfect disguise.
Their mothers would not have known them,
. . .
That's why fire is restless
and smoke has become the escaped wings of crows,

From: "Skin"
— Linda Hogan, Chickasaw

65

Estonislao had led four hundred neophytes out of the mission. It was a signal. As a wind touches a smoldering branch that suddenly leaps into fire, the warrior bear lunged from the cool ashes of Grizzly Hair's soul.

"You and the children will be safe here," he told Etumu.

She and the other women had agreed to stay. The battle of the Cosumne had been a lesson, and this could be worse. Etumu looked down. He stroked her hair and tender shoulder, and felt a sense of unreality. Why should that be, when it had been clear for some time that his life had been fated for this? There would be no more false waiting for the *Americanos.* War could bring a safe future for the umne and many peoples. This was more than revenge for the whipping, more than avenging his father's death. Yet it seemed unreal because no one had done this before, except in story—El Cid and the fathers of the *Americanos* who had fought for *libertad.* But they were from another world.

O-se-mai-ti watched from the shadows of the trees along Berry Creek. Grizzly Hair tousled Boy's thick hair, then drew Etumu into his arms. Looking at the bear he said, "Thank you, spirits, for stopping the *Españoles* from coming this far." Now they never would, for the united *Indios* were about to show them what happens to people who don't leave them alone. And if they were completely successful, the black hats would go away and mission lands would revert to the people as Padre Duran had told Estanislao they would, as the fat long robe had told Grizzly Hair, as Governor Echeandía had told many people.

He donned his *casco,* put the little clump of Amador's hair in his neck pouch, and took one last look at his wife and boy. Then Morning Owl's warriors set out on their horses—Morning Owl in his buckskin shirt, Two Falcons, Running Quail, Lame Beaver, Scorpion-on-Nose and Grizzly Hair. They rode down the river trail, each with two full quivers and a vest of vertical blue-oak branchlets tightly woven with narrow strips of hide. Behind each rider bundles of arrows were tied on the horses.

In the villages along the way they collected more men, including Grub Log, who trotted behind on foot. It occurred to Grizzly Hair as he and Morning Owl and Two Falcons led the procession, that the umne spoke Spanish as well as anyone now, and were the only people north of the Chilumne who rode horses. No longer were they hill bunnies, *inocentes*, stupid h'nteelehs. They were, he thought as he surveyed the quiet oak grasslands, *gente de razón*, a people to be reckoned with, a people who understood what was happening in the world. That's what Drum-in-Fog had told him long ago, when he had seen the archway over the sky with many sad people walking across it, that he should go find out what was real in the world. He had done that. He had found something wrong and now was about to set it right—with the help of the united *Indios*. That had been the biggest hurdle, but his vision of unity had become real. Now they would fight together. O-se-mai-ti had stayed with him every step of the way on this long journey. She had often appeared to him and he felt her in his spirit. When the sudden thought stunned him, that his wife and son might never see him again, the bear said, "Often a parent dies protecting the young. That is natural."

They crossed the river of the Muquelumne and slept in Te-mi's village. After the sleep they were joined by fifteen Muquelumne men, as well as women who refused to be left behind. Women would be the food and arrow runners. They would also provide medicine at the fort. On the next river south, a number of Chilumne men and women joined them, and by the time they rode into Domingo's place, they were a strong band of *insurgentes*.

A big time mood prevailed. Hundreds of people milled around, some singing and gambling, but beneath the fun Grizzly Hair saw the resolve and purpose. Estanislao greeted him. He had changed. His wide lips were set in a seemingly permanent expression of determination, and his black eyes would have burned holes through a weak man. Cucunichi he had been named—he who will lead his people.

He introduced Grizzly Hair and Morning Owl to Bruno from Santa Cruz and Octavio from San Juan Bautista, who were talking nearby. Very fluent in Spanish, these men had the Spanish habit of looking a person directly in the eye. They admired Grizzly Hair's *casco*, particularly when he told them he had taken it from a black hat.

Estanislao said to all the dismounting men, "You have come a long way. Come and eat." He led them to a brush corral made of the old severed treetops. They carried the bundled arrows from the horses to the cleared area beside the fort, the tantalizing aroma of cooking meat drawing Grizzly Hair. He was glad to see an opened earth oven. A mission shovel lay beside the mound of dirt, and people were on their knees, bringing the steaming quarters of a cooked elk up to cooler earth.

"Put your arrows in there," Estanislao said, pointing to a pit under the fort wall.

Grizzly Hair jumped in, deep as his armpits, and ducked under the wall. As he climbed up inside the fort he was delighted to find a large hill of arrows stacked inside. He and the others laid their bundles beside it, then, stomachs rumbling, returned to the delicious smells.

Women had laid back the hide of the elk and were cutting hunks of meat from the haunches and flank. They sprinkled the meat with salt from little hide bags tied to their waist thongs—salt from the bay near Mission San José, he knew. Grapeleaf bundles of greens had been steamed with the elk. In addition to this communal feast, many people sat around eating their own fish stews, duck stews and grass-seed mush. Feeling lucky, he took an *Americano* bead from the thong about his neck and gave it to a woman with grasshopper balls. "Could you trade one of those for this?" he asked.

She examined the red and blue translucent bead with the perfect hole. "This would buy more than a grasshopper ball," she said truthfully.

He smiled. "But it's what I want. If it makes you feel better, I'll take two balls."

Solemnly the h'nteeleh woman—she wore a cattail skirt—handed him two balls. As he turned back toward his friends he overheard her excited talk and it made him smile. It had been a reckless thing, to give such a fine bead for only two grasshopper balls, but it made him feel good. So did the soft sweet-salt delicacy with crunchy bits of wing and leg.

"Help yourselves to the elk," Estanislao told him.

Grizzly Hair was cutting into the haunch when a group of men entered the clearing, Gabriel among them. Glad to see him, Grizzly Hair had worried that the horse-trader had abandoned the war plans when most men didn't want to fight his way. Then, somewhat to his surprise, he recognized Sick Rat among Gabriel's men, with a woman. Two Falcons saw him too and approached his son. Grizzly Hair joined them.

Sick Rat and the woman both wore woolen *pantalones*, and she had a shirt made of a light brown cloth that moved with her. One of the *Americanos* had worn such a shirt. A red cloth was twisted around Sick Rat's head. His long wispy hair had not been recently singed, and his ear ornaments were missing. He looked like a mission alcalde who was puffed up with self-importance.

Sick Rat smiled at them, but his music hadn't changed. "Well," he said to his woman, "Here are my people." The woman looked at Grizzly Hair brazenly in the eyes. Her eyes were too far apart and her was mouth uneven. She looked older than Sick Rat and her expression challenged. Grizzly Hair had seen men with that look, but not a woman. Sick Rat, without a word to his father, stared at the scars on Grizzly Hair's thighs. "Fall off your horse?"

"I fought the black hats," Grizzly Hair responded politely. "Where have you been?"

"Away." He leaned against the fort wall, arms folded as if he had learned the secrets of the universe. "What's that silly hat on your head?"

Something stopped inside Grizzly Hair. No longer would he soften Sick Rat's edge as he had done for so long, habitually excusing that rudeness as a product of his own closeness to Two Falcons. He was about to walk away when Two Falcons said to his son, "We want to know where you've been. Go get something to eat, then we'll sit and talk."

A hard gleam burned in Sick Rat's eyes. "I'll eat when I feel like it."

"Cousin-brother," Lame Beaver interjected, "Your father only meant to be friendly."

Two Falcons flared his eyes at Lame Beaver, a look that would have withered Grizzly Hair. But then Grizzly Hair saw that Two Falcons was more embarrassed for his son, than angry.

Not wanting any part of whatever would follow, Grizzly Hair left to join Morning Owl, Little Cos, Sucais, Estanislao and their women—Sexta and Estanislaa. Domingo was there in his now frayed and faded three-cornered hat.

Grizzly Hair waited until Sexta finished explaining how the food runners would extend their networks, then said, "We must dig the trenches."

"Yes, did you see the shovels?" Estanislao asked with pleased smile.

Grizzly Hair bit into his second grasshopper ball. "That was good, to bring shovels from the mission."

Domingo had a little smile. "We were waiting for you to tell us how the trenches should be laid out."

Grizzly Hair popped the remainder of the grasshopper ball in his mouth, set the hunk of meat on his thigh, and drew an earth map of Domingo's place with the river circling around and the fort in the center. "We must be able to get to and from the river," he said, drawing two lines from the fort to the river. "And to get in and out of the fort from several directions." Drawing an interconnecting line, he said, "The trenches should meet each other."

Little Cos's eyes were crinkled up in a smile. "He's thought about this before."

"Too much rain," Grizzly Hair shot back without looking up from the line he was drawing. "There was nothing else to do." Chuckles could be heard. He felt easy and lucky among these people.

When they had eaten their fill, Morning Owl stood up in his buckskin shirt, seized a shovel and took a practice scoop of earth. Others joined him, clearly remembering him from before the rains. Even mission people treated him with respect despite his being a gentile hy-apo.

Men took turns with the shovels. Men, women and children dug like foxes behind them. As the sleeps passed, chest-high trenches were carved through the dense river-jungle following Grizzly Hair's map. People appeared relieved to have something useful to do. Each day the trenches reached farther through the forest. Grizzly Hair easily ignored Sick Rat and his woman, though they dug now and then with the others. It appeared that Two Falcons had also begun to ignore his son.

Then Sick Rat told them one day that Juan, the big ugly man left behind after the horse raid, had died tied to the tree. Two Falcons straightened and stood breathing hard, the shovel like a walking stick in his hand. "Why didn't you untie him?"

"We left in a hurry," Sick Rat replied.

Grizzly Hair reflected that they had all left in a hurry. He knew the image of Juan tied to the tree would disturb him for a long time.

The next day a group of men arrived from Libayto's and Topal's and Putah's villages, and beyond, all pleased to see Grizzly Hair again and anxious to hear what was happening. Dance doctors arranged a big time and people brought food. During these dances Grizzly Hair found old Matías, who had taught him to make a club for the burl game and shown him how to make a tule boat. His back showed the scars of the twenty-five strokes of the *cuarta* he had endured every day for seven days. He smiled warmly at Grizzly Hair.

"Any day," Estanislao predicted, "a spy will come from Padre Durán. Our scouts will capture him and we will give him a message for Padre."

Little Cos suggested a message, "Come and try to find us. We have been waiting for you."

A young man, maybe a boy, from the southeast said, "Tell them we'll whip their asses."

Elk Calf and others threw out ever more insulting suggestions, and the competition for the best message kept people laughing and busy in their minds as they dug through the fluffy earth.

But no spy was captured.

After four nights of dancing, Grizzly Hair and Estanislao rode together to find a messenger. In addition, Grizzly Hair would warn María about the coming war, so she could tell her grandson not to fight. Cucunichi's old name fit him best now that he had removed his woolen *pantalones.* Polished crane bones swung in his earlobes as he rode his black horse. He had pierced his topknot with a dagger of elk cannon bone, as was typical of the men of his people. Strength came from this friend's appearance, and honor, that he traveled naked and wore the ornaments of a h'nteeleh.

They rode over windy Alta Monte pass and down the mountain toward the mission, talking from horse to horse. Sunlight washed across the gentle slopes and gullies. In a confidential tone, Estanislao said, "I am the most wanted fugitive since Pomponio. Padre will have me flayed raw, then the *militari*o will shoot me dead."

"But we will win and you won't be captured." That's how they ought to be talking. He took a breath. "What is the *militario?*"

"An umne of men only. It includes the guards at the missions and the *soldados*, even the governor and Luis Argüello."

"Most people call them black hats."

"Some of them wear different kinds of hats, but they are all part of the *militario.*"

"I thought they had women." María's son-in-law had a wife.

"Yes, but their women are not in the *militario.*"

"Not part of their men's people?"

"In the *militario* men obey the headman. The women don't. The soldiers are punished if they do not obey. They fear the *cuarta.*"

In some ways the *Americanos* and *Españoles* were alike. "Neophytes also obey orders for fear of the *cuarta,*" Grizzly Hair observed.

Estanislao nodded. "They are training us to be like the *Españoles.*"

Grizzly Hair had heard that before. "The long robes tell the black hats what to do," he said. "Does that mean the padres are of the *militario?*"

"No. Sometimes captains Argüello and Martinez don't do what Padre Durán tells them. Sometimes the soldiers act on their own. Remember in Santa Barbara? The padre down there didn't want the guards to beat the man as much as they did. That's how that war started." He looked into the shadows of the redwoods. Father sun sat on a ridge of hills on their right. "The padres have their own umne. They call them brothers. They are scattered all over the world. They obey their own headman and their special spirits."

"Are you saying an *Español* decides which people he belongs to? That he chooses his headman, and his umne don't live in his village?"

"That's right."

It would be difficult, Grizzly Hair imagined, for people who obeyed different orders to live together. How did they sort it out? Somewhere among them there had to be headmen who knew how to bring consensus. Men like Morning Owl.

Estanislao continued, "They say gentiles are like children with no parents, and that's why we need fathers to teach us."

Grizzly Hair could not bend his thinking that far. Adults were adults and children were children. That distinction was the sharpest in life, yet this talk stirred up memories of the mission. He had deeply resented being ordered around and not allowed to learn what he wanted. He had been treated somewhat like a child, yet even as a child he'd been more of a man.

Estanislao flicked away a mosquito and added, "Padre Durán says our headmen are stupid because they don't force people to obey them."

"I can't imagine telling men and women to obey me," Grizzly Hair said truthfully. He tried to imagine Morning Owl ordering the umne to do anything at all, but all that came to mind was derisive laughter. Morning Owl would forfeit his esteem and influence.

"Padre Durán told me punishment would make people respect me," Estanislao said. He fell silent. It was clear that one day Estanislao would become headman of the Lakisumne, in or out of the mission. Some people already called him an alcalde. Would he give orders in the Spanish manner? Would his people obey him? Would he punish them as Narciso had? Clearly that was the way of the new people.

"Maybe Padre Durán wants you to join the *militario* someday," Grizzly Hair suggested.

Estanislao chuckled and said in his quiet, confidential way, "I don't think *Indios* will ever be in the *militario.*"

"You said they want us to join their people." Seeing Estanislao's slightly annoyed shake of his head, he suggested, "Maybe he wants you to become a long robe."

Bitter laughter exploded from Estanislao, causing Morena to lose her walking rhythm.

"I've been thinking," Estanislao said at last. "In the beginning I liked the bargain of joining their people and was willing to wait to become one of them, but I have talked to old men and women who have made their homes in the missions most of their lives and they are still waiting. They are still treated like children. I could die there and never become a *ranchero* or a sergeant in the *militario* or a padre."

"You could become an alcalde."

That brought more bitter laughter. "They're whipped just like anyone else if they get up late or forget their prayers. They can't leave the mission unless Father gives them a *paseo.* Their wives are punished and ridiculed if Father suspects they lost a baby in their blood. Besides, I can never be a padre because I'm married."

"Is that what started this war?" He knew Estanislao would understand his meaning: why had he led the neophytes from the mission at this time, not before or later?

Estanislao looked ahead and Grizzly Hair waited, the hoofbeats the only sound in the long shadows of the tree-giants. The scent of cattle dung tinged the evening air, agitating his stomach with memories of shackles and skinning. "Yes," Estanislao finally said.

Grizzly Hair thought back to the question, and felt fairly sure that something had happened between him and Padre Durán. He wouldn't pry. "The men are having luck in hunting," he said. "We'll have enough dried meat for many days of fighting."

Estanislao's amused, confidential self returned. "Yes, I think the signs are good."

"We have fighting men all the way from the Lake of the Tulares to the river north of my place, and warriors from the hills of the eastern mountains. I am glad so many gentiles agreed to supply arrows, men all the way to Fort Ross."

"You have done well. You're a warrior. Your vision has never faltered."

Appreciating the compliment, Grizzly Hair ventured to say, "A warrior cannot doubt himself."

Estanislao looked over from his horse. They rode in silence, then he said, "Padre Durán is a warrior too."

"You said he is not in the *militario.*"

"But he is a warrior. His vision is never disturbed by what others tell him. My father taught me about warriors. Sometimes they use only their words to fight for what they believe."

"I think you are a warrior too." *Now,* he added in his mind.

Again Estanislao fell silent. The coral and red stripes across the western sky had deepened in color. Not far away a coyote howled and in the distance another coyote answered. On this entire journey they hadn't met anyone on the trail. Finding a place to camp in a wooded area beside a creek, they ate the meat and seed cakes Estanislaa had packed. In the morning neophytes would come into these hills to cut wood for the vat fires. One of them would be the messenger.

"I hope there aren't any bears around tonight," Estanislao remarked as he pulled his deerskin robe around him.

"I don't think a bear would hurt us," Grizzly Hair said.

He felt Estanislao looking at him and knew he might be guessing why Grizzly Hair bore the name of the great she-bear. Already he was feeling the subtle eclipses of sleep starting to pull him through the veil of spirits. Estanislao's quiet, confidential voice jerked him back. "Padre Durán wants neophytes to make babies."

That was a strange thing to say. Grizzly Hair let it pass, then bobbed at the edges of sleep again.

"He thought my man part didn't work right. He wondered why Estanislaa doesn't have a baby in her."

Grizzly Hair thought maybe he was dreaming.

"He took me in his room and told me to remove my *pantalones.* He wanted to see it work."

"Wanted you to do it?"

"No that's a *pecado.* Men are whipped for doing it to themselves."

"But—"

"He did it. I didn't want him to."

Unspeakably rude! This showed an appalling lack of respect for Estanislao. But, no one could oppose the will of the powerful long robe. Quietly, with the uncomfortable sense of invading his friend's privacy, except that Estanislao had brought this up, he dared ask, "Is that why you left?"

His voice was almost a whisper. "He told me to bring Estanislaa, so he could examine her too. I argued with him and told him she would get a baby in her blood if he let us go to our old home on *paseo.* He agreed. On the way out of the mission I spread the word that all the neophytes should follow us. Many did. I was surprised Padre gave them all *paseos.*"

A shriek owl made a ruckus and Grizzly Hair lay in the dark trying to imagine what he would have done in Estanislao's place.

After a while Estanislao chuckled and said, "Coyote would have peed on him." He added, "The real reason is, I can never be one of them. None of us can."

"Come here," Estanislao called to an older man who was separated from a group of wood gatherers. Turning confidentially to Grizzly Hair, he explained, "It's Flavio."

Arms full and clearly afraid, Flavio searched in the trees with his eyes. Estanislao stepped out. The man's fear dropped and he approached, exclaiming in an excited tone, "You are back already!" Taking in the length of him, he added, "Naked." It fell off his tongue like something sour.

"I am not coming back. Neither are the others. I came with a message for Padre. Tell him he can take his Christianity. I don't want it anymore. I am returning to my land to live as a gentile."

"But you can't!"

"I can and I will. All the rest are staying too. Tell him we have joined together with many peoples, all the way to Santa Cruz and San Juan Bautista. We have horses and will get many more. Tell him he can come and try to take us. But we are not afraid. We know the *soldados* are few in number and are very young. We know they do not shoot well. Tell him that."

Flavio's eyes had widened by degrees until they were perfectly round and surprisingly red—probably a fire-tender. "I will tell him but he will be *furioso.*"

"Good. After you deliver the message, gather your friends and join us. We are camped on my river just east of where it joins the San Joaquin River." Smiling slightly at the old man's astonished face, he said, "We will take over the missions. Everything will be different."

It was very dark when they dismounted on the hillside east of the pueblo not far from where Grizzly Hair had been sick. In the early dawn he touched Estanislao, who was still sleeping, and said he'd be back before father sun was straight overhead.

Estanislao sat up. "If anyone asks where you are going, say you are a gentile wanting *trabajo* for pay. Don't carry your bow or they will fear you. Tie your horse well outside of the pueblo and walk in. *Indios* are not supposed to have horses. And before you gallop away announce the war again." His lips straightened into a smile. "That will help Flavio."

Trusting Estanislao's knowledge, Grizzly Hair rode into a light mist. He passed through scattered drifts of long horns without seeing anyone. The fog had lifted and morning sun warmed his back. He stopped at a cluster of tule u-machas far outside the town. A pile of purple grapes rose higher than the u-machas. Eyeing him suspiciously, a mostly grown boy was stomping grapes in a wide wooden container. He wore a small hide apron that covered his man part. "Will you guard my horse?" Grizzly Hair asked in Spanish. A herd of horses grazed nearby.

The boy nodded.

"If you guard her well, I will give you this." He showed him an *Americano* bead on his neck thong. The boy looked at it. "Give me five *centavos,*" he said.

"I have no *centavos.*"

"Then give me two beads."

The brazenness flabbergasted him, but he had no choice. People were approaching. He was anxious to speak to María and be gone. "I'll give you two beads if my horse is waiting for me when I return." Tying her to the branch of an oak, he gave the boy a firm look.

Barely nodding, the boy continued high-stepping his purple feet. Three women were coming toward them pulling a *carreta* with more grapes.

Grizzly Hair was gone when they arrived. He saw that the pueblo was laid out exactly as María had described it, with about fifteen houses to a side with rock-lined ditches supplying water. On the north stood an adobe house with a cross on top and a bell in the yard. "My house is in the middle of the west row," María had said. "Stone up to here." She had indicated her shoulders, "adobes above that."

No one questioned him as he walked through the square, the shadow of his topknot before him. A woman almost as dark as the black *Americano* watched his progress from her door. Three small children pressed into her long dress. In the next door a pale woman wore a dress that billowed out from the waist but was tight on top. Such women had watched the bull fight the bear in the mission. He saw others like them carrying baskets piled with cloth or greens. One carried two wooden buckets of water. A very large number of children played and rode horses beyond a field of tended greens. He saw only a few men, none apparently much interested in him.

He found the half-rock house. On the ground before it sat an old man hunched under a tattered shawl of faded colors. His feet were wrapped in rags. "*Hola,*" Grizzly Hair said. Shock stole his breath as the man looked up.

His hair was white and tinted with orange, and it parted over his shoulder revealing a mangled, mostly missing left ear. This was the old man he and Elk Calf had robbed near the Chilumne village. Yet this had to be María's house. Could this be her son-in-law? The father of her grandchildren?

Slowly the watery eyes focused. "What do you want?" The same squeaky voice.

He tensed to run, but the man showed no sign of recognition. Perhaps he was blind now. Quietly Grizzly Hair said, "I am looking for María. An old woman."

Seemingly with enormous effort the man raised an arm and pointed. "Behind the house."

Relieved not to be recognized, Grizzly Hair recalled Wek-Wek's flight that day, connecting him with the old man. María had been the connection, as well as the baby girl who would be named for her. The baby had started that night. The families were linked by magic. Now Grizzly Hair wished he had brought the *casco* so he could give it back.

On the back side of the house he found María wearing the same earth-colored dress. She was pushing and pulling cloth from a tub filled with frothing suds. As she looked up her yellow face crinkled into a thousand wrinkles. The same old sunshine. She came over and hugged him, sudsy water trickling down his back. She was small inside her dress. The top of her head came to his breast bone, though stray white hairs tickled his chin.

"I promised I'd tell you when the war would start," he said pushing her to arm's length.

Her dark eyes looked inside him.

"It will be very soon. Please keep your grandsons away from the shooting. I don't want to hurt them." Yet he had humiliated their father.

"My grandson Pedro lives with the soldiers in Monterey Presidio. He does what they tell him, no matter what I say." She twisted her face in mock pain. "Is war necessary?"

"*Sí.*"

A fleshy woman in a green-striped dress appeared at the side of the house. Her face was pale like an *Español.* María said to her, "He is a friend." In a low voice she explained to him, "*Mi hija.*" My daughter.

The woman turned and left, and there was nothing more to be said. If Maria's grandson fought in the war and was killed, Grizzly Hair could only hope the arrow came from someone else's bow. But what of the old man?

"Is that your son-in-law in the front?"

"*Sí.*" At the next house two *gallos* flew at each other and put up a terrible squawk.

"Why is his ear gone?"

"It happened before I knew him, in a battle with the Saclan people. An arrow took most of his ear. An *Indio.*"

Grizzly Hair recalled meeting a man in Domingo's village who had come from the Saclan people. "What happened to the *Indio?*"

She wiped her hands on her dress. "Pepe killed him."

Gooseflesh rippled across Grizzly Hair's scalp, though he didn't know why. "Is he crazy?"

María grinned in her funny way. "No. But people think so."

"Tell him not to come to the war."

"He won't. He's too old."

Not about to linger like he had at their last parting, Grizzly Hair told her "*vaya con Dios,*" and walked away, across the pueblo square, out to the trail to the Indio village. Again no one stopped him. Maybe they were accustomed to strangers. Morena had pulled the branch to the breaking point to nibble the grapes in the big pile.

He handed the beads to the boy who was still stomping grapes and untied the horse. "I have a message for the black hats."

"Give me another bead and I'll deliver the it."

"I think you will deliver it without payment." Seeing a man in torn *pantalones* sleeping behind the next u-macha, he mounted Morena and announced in a loud voice, "The *cimarrones* and *gentiles* are ready for war. Tell Señor Argüello and his *soldados* to come and get us if they can. But we think they are too afraid."

Three men sat up blinking.

"Tell the *militario* we are waiting for them where the river of the Lakisumne meets the San Joaquin River. The soldiers cannot shoot straight enough to fight us." He kicked his heels into Morena and galloped away.

66

The Soto Expedition

The quill trembled in Fray Narciso Durán's hand as he wrote "November 9, 1828, Mission San José." He explained to Lieutenant Ignacio Martinez, acting commander of the presidio, that the Christians had not come back from *paseo* as they had agreed, the Lakisamni being the main miscreants. As he brought the quill back, too fast, from the bottle a drop of ink plopped on the paper. Sprinkling sand on it, he pondered how to adequately convey the magnitude of the festering sore in the interior. *Hadn't Estanislao seen that he loved him like a son?* He decided to repeat the exact words of the fire-tender and let them pierce the Commander's heart as they had his. Martinez was also a civilized man living in a howling wilderness, vulnerable to an attack by *Indios*. In addition he had a wife and family. He wrote:

> *They have declared themselves in rebellion and stated without reserve that they have no fear of the soldiers, because they, the soldiers, are few in number, are very young, and do not shoot well.*

A deep tremor shook him. How could this be happening? He had readily let them go on *paseo*, hoping the vacation would cure their homesickness so they would return to the discipline of the mission with smiles on their faces. Had he been too suspicious about the lack of pregnancies? Had he gone beyond the bounds? Were there bounds? Who had ever faced this before? There were no rules. He was a pioneer continually feeling his way through a labyrinth of wickedness—fornication outside marriage and abortion, abortion, abortion. Something had to be done and the practices at other missions seemed to work. By all reports women had finally begun to understand that the babes within them were holy, and it went without thinking that investigation must precede punishment. Tragically, despite the investigations and the penance, the records showed as yet no increase in births. Surely that would change, eventually producing the baptism of more mission-born children. But to ignore the problem was to stand idly by while the missionary effort crumbled around him. If *inquisición*, penance and instruction could solve the problem, such action was his duty before God. He must keep trying. The lives of the unborn were at stake, hundreds of innocent little children who should be entering the Christian world. Instead, he was continually training heathens reared in the filthy bogs of the Devil, people maddeningly prone to backsliding. Besides that, these frail mission outposts were surrounded by godless interests salivating to usurp mission lands. Time was growing short, perhaps too short, to develop a Christian stronghold with the integrity to withstand the mounting political pressures. He felt suspended between horns of devilish proportions—too few births on one side and too little political support on the other. Would the Devil win? Had too much sand already spilled from the hourglass? Trembling as he inserted the quill in the narrow neck of the ink bottle, he pushed the paper away and fell on his elbows.

"Dear Santo Francisco," he prayed grasping his wet face, "I have made mistakes. I am not perfect, but I have opened my life to you." A tear found its way around his fingers and splashed on the table. "Now I am about to endure death at the hands of those I have loved, those for whose salvation I forfeited the pleasures of the world. But if such a death is God's plan for me, strengthen me so I can walk the bitter path to Golgotha and draw my last breath with the humility to kneel before the cross. Mercy, dear saint, mercy. Grant me the peace to accept with God's grace that which I cannot change." He waited and slowly the trembling diminished. "I also pray for your intervention. Show the Christians in the wilderness the goodness of your ways and those of our Savior, so they will forget this savagery and return to the fold." He crossed himself, "In the name of the Father, the Son and the Holy Ghost, Amen."

With his sleeve he wiped the tears off the table, pulled the paper back, and wrote:

In view of the fact that the rainy season is approaching, I request the help of ten soldiers under command of Sergeant Soto, if it can be done conveniently, to go out on a combined expedition from the two missions, this one and Santa Clara.

He hoped a force of ten from the presidio would suffice. A hundred and fifty conquistadors armed with swords and muskets had, in Cortez' time, defeated twenty thousand Indians with bows and arrows. Ever since, the ratio of one to a hundred had proved adequate in the new world, so he judged ten to be enough. In addition, he would send some of the mission guards.

It could be seen as an overstep, he realized, to suggest the name of the leader of the command, but Sergeant Soto spoke some of the Lakisamni language, as Estanislao well knew, and that could prove pivotal to the success of this expedition. A seasoned Indian fighter, Soto also understood the need for restraint, as demonstrated on the previous expedition when, without bloodshed, he rounded up Narciso and most of the Lakisamnis. Besides, Durán couldn't abide that insolent Sergeant Sanchez, regardless of his touted military ability.

His heart constricted at the thought of Estanislao defying him. Sadly, there was one more thing left to write:

Above all, order must be restored. The leaders of this rebellion must be captured dead or alive, and they are a certain Estanislao from this mission and a person from Santa Clara called Cipriano.

November 20, 1828, San Francisco Presidio

Lieutenant Ignacio Martinez wrote to Governor Echeandía: "*I have arranged that a party of 20 men go out. . .*" The expedition, he continued, would be primarily for reconnaissance, to learn if any truth lay behind the message to Padre Durán from the fugitive Indians. He noted that Durán had, as before, offered the resources of the mission.

In the river jungle, council was held almost continuously for two suns after Estanislao and Grizzly Hair returned. "Soon they will come for us," Cipriano declared. He had arrived with two hundred more neophytes from mission Santa Clara. More came from San Juan Bautista, Santa Cruz and San José, expanding the enormous encampment. People who had not hunted or gathered for a long time went out with those who hunted or gathered every day. Everyone admired the solid fort, which the floods of the previous season hadn't undermined or damaged. Men from Grizzly Hair's network arrived with bundles of arrows. Cross-eyed Bear was among them, but not, Grizzly Hair was glad to see, Salmon Woman or her husband.

Some of them seemed to think war would be a big fandango. A man whose eyes were blurred with brandy told Grizzly Hair he had seen him in the pueblo and enjoyed hearing his war message. He had repeated it many times.

On the third sun after Grizzly Hair and Estanislao returned, Isadoro, Marin, Maximo and men who had ridden with Grizzly Hair at the time of the Santa Barbara rebellion arrived. In tule boats *cimarrones* and *gentiles* floated to the camp from south on the San Joaquin River. Tired neophytes poled in from missions San Raphael and Solano in Tso-noma. Men from all over the Valley of the Sun and the foothills of the eastern and western mountains delivered bundles of arrows.

Then a breathless scout told the gathered peoples: "The *soldados* are coming. They have a wagon with a cannon in it. They will cross the San Joaquin River and probably sleep there tonight, then come here after the sleep."

Twenty soldiers and twenty neophyte helpers led by Sergeant Soto was a small number, Grizzly Hair thought as he walked toward the edge of the thicket. He looked over the plain and tried to guess which way they would come. Grass had sprouted after first rain and was transforming the world from brown to green. A sooty gray cloud backed by a hard streak of pink slashed across the southwestern sky. At the pointed end of the cloud was the nose of O-se-mai-ti, and as he watched, the rest of her took shape and floated down. She stood before him in her luxurious fur and simple honesty.

"The enemy is coming," he told her. "They insult us by sending few warriors."

She gave a motherly growl. "This is no time to think about insults. Be glad you can deal them a crushing blow."

"But then they will return with many more warriors."

"Of course. That's when you fight like bears."

Feeling small before this spirit, he said, "Sometimes I am afraid we will do it wrong and fight poorly."

"You will defeat them." With that astonishing statement, she disassembled and floated up in a mist to join the dark cloud. Again her nose pointed northeast, toward the home place.

With his stomach strengthened, he looked across the grassland where women dug for roots. Etumu would be doing this at home. He missed her but was glad she was not here.

Back at the fort he helped the men shove one more pole into place. They had built a second wall, knowing two walls would protect them better than one. "Only twenty *soldados,*" Domingo remarked as they worked.

"The joke will be on them," Grizzly Hair said lightly.

On the sixth morning they waited. Most of the women had gone upstream to a hidden village. The remainder stayed to distribute arrows and food. In his polished *casco* Grizzly Hair hid in vegetation interlaced with a great quantity of runners and stems of grapevines. Even father sun could hardly penetrate, much less men on horses or a cannon. Unseen around him were Little Cos, Two Falcons, Lame Beaver, Morning Owl, Running Quail, Elk Calf with his useless gun and hundreds of others. Even Grizzly Hair's practiced eye saw only a foot here and a patch of skin there. Men waited behind heavily burdened alders that reared up like giant snakes toward the light.

The fungal odor of the jungle floor tickled his nose, and he recognized the thudding of his heart as excitement, not fear. The black hats's pride would defeat them. They would be surprised. With his senses sharp and tingling, he recalled dancing the Wok-ke-lah, war dance, before the sleep. He remembered the sweat where neophytes and gentiles together had sung to their bows. All had been strengthened by their spirit allies.

Crows croaked the warning. Shadows flickered down through several canopies to the jungle floor as they changed perches. The other birds quieted. The black hats had arrived.

Estanislao's voice rang over thicket and plain. "*Hola muchachos,* we have been waiting. Come in and visit if you are men." Even in full voice he sounded oddly confidential.

A man's shout responded in the distance. "Estanislao and Cipriano, surrender and your people will go free." Surprisingly, it was in Estanislao's tongue.

"Sergeant Soto, you are a coward," Estanislao retorted. "Are you shitting your pants with fear?"

A gun cracked.

"Poor little *niños* can't shoot straight," Estanislao yelled.

Nearly bursting with readiness, Grizzly Hair cupped his hands and yelled in Spanish, "See if you can find us."

Was Crane Beak out there? The guard who took pride in his shooting ability, the one who had killed a condor? Hearing sudden movement in the bushes, he gripped his bow tighter and called in a mocking tone, "*Pobrecito muchachos!* Poor little boys. You are scared. You don't dare find us."

A gun bang-thundered at close range. Unskilled men could be heard stumbling through the foliage. He waited, patient as a mountain lion. Estanislao, to his surprise, ran toward the oncoming *Españoles,* yelling in his own tongue, "Here's what we think of you." He twisted his body and pointed to his anus. Others yelled in their own tongue saying things Grizzly Hair couldn't understand, all in insulting cadence. The black hats had to be bursting with rage and the desire to prove their bravery. On the distant side of Domingo's place where most of the Muquelumne lay in wait, several guns were firing and a man screamed. The black hats had divided into smaller groups.

Beyond a fall of red and orange grape leaves, something moved—wrinkled, unstretched cowhide. He must aim for their faces and necks. Stepping through the tangled vegetation, arrow between his fingers, he and the others quietly surrounded four *cuero*-protected soldiers. At every sound the soldiers whirled this way and that, their faces dark beneath the pulled-down *cuero* hats. But though their faces couldn't be seen, their posture and jerky movements shouted fear, and afraid they should have been, for each step trapped them deeper in the canes and vines and rose bushes, and between their unseen stalkers. It had been stupid, when few men faced so many, to break into smaller groups. That was Napoleon's mistake.

Not a single twig snapped under Grizzly Hair's careful feet, not a leaf rustled. A flicker of brown skin here and there told him the four black hats were surrounded. A well-placed arrow from each bow would kill them all several times over. Like a red-winged blackbird, Sergeant Soto was marked by the red patches on his shoulders. Quietly Grizzly Hair knelt in good position, aiming at Soto's neck as he pulled the bowstring.

Soto whirled to the side, where Two Falcons suddenly stood before him about to release an arrow. With his eye to his gun, Soto pulled the trigger and jerked back. There was an ear-shattering bang. Smoke plumed from the gun and a ragged scream tore through the thicket. The sergeant dropped to his knees grabbing an arrow shaft that protruded from the same eye that moments before had been looking down the gun barrel. The *fusil* had guided the master hunter's arrow.

As the smoke cleared Grizzly Hair saw with relief that Two Falcons had vanished. Two more deafening bangs cracked at close range, clouds of acrid-smelling smoke filtering through the trees. Grizzly Hair released an arrow within a swarm of arrows flying from all points of the surrounding circle, and his arrow skewered the throat of a *soldado.* A grating, rasping sound came from him as he fell.

Arrows and balls thudded into the trees. He flattened himself on the ground to let them fly overhead. Hearing the soldiers thrashing back through the thicket, Grizzly Hair looked up. Two black hats lay motionless. Sergeant Soto was being helped through the bushes by the remaining black hat. Fletched arrows bristled from their legs and hips and they yelped when the arrows caught in the vines and bushes.

"Let them go," Estanislao called. "So they can report their defeat."

Grizzly Hair watched the black hats desperately trying to hurry back the way they had come. One tripped, fell and struggled back to his feet. The arrow in Soto's eye caught in the vines. The companion helped him quickly extricated it. Soto might not live long enough to announce his defeat.

In the distance more gunshots rang out. Arrow in hand, Grizzly Hair followed Sergeant Soto to the edge of the river jungle. He and others watched several soldiers with arrows protruding from their buttocks and legs awkwardly mount and lie upon their skittish horses. Soto flung himself over the saddle and his horse trotted after the others. The obviously terrified neophyte helpers pulled a loaded wagon after the horses. "*Piedad,*" they called over their shoulders. "*Merced.*"

Still wary, Grizzly Hair watched them leave. Many men from all sides of

Domingo's place now stood outside the jungle watching the enemy go. "They're running away," somebody said. From the far side of the Domingo's place, Little Cos called, "The ones that came in over here are gone. Any more over there?"

"No, not here." Grizzly Hair and several others answered. The last glimpse of the wagon vanished around the oaks, the neophytes still glancing over their shoulders.

"Is anyone injured," Estanislao called.

Men looked at one another. Talk circulated. No, no one was injured. Not even one? People checked.

Could it be over already? Hundreds of *Indios* now stood at the edge of the plain. Uncertainty gave way to laughter. Happy talk buzzed louder than the river, and happy tears ran down many faces.

Lame Beaver trotted to Grizzly Hair and his voice cracked with excitement. "It was easy. We should have done it long ago!"

"We weren't ready then," Grizzly Hair said looking into the broad, gleeful face with arched brows, so like Bowstring. He blinked back moisture. Relief and joy nearly overwhelmed him. "It was exactly as I imagined," he said, "the backsides of soldiers running away in fear." Wiping his face, he looked to the clear morning sky almost expecting O-se-mai-ti to appear. But his own power sufficed. The death of his father had been avenged. Malaca's men, who had burned in their houses, were starting to be avenged. The *Indios* had defeated the powerful *Españoles*. Within and around him joy mounted like an eagle rising from one thermal to the next.

Domingo sent men to follow the retreating *soldados* to make sure no more had assembled. He trotted out to catch the hobbled horses of the dead black hats that were attempting to follow their herd. Smiling women came from the fort talking excitedly.

Grizzly Hair went to where people were examining the ground, reliving the moment of the enemy's retreat. Pummeled by many hooves and slashed by the wheels of the wagon, the new grass told the story of wounded soldiers mounting jittery horses. The throng of happy people turned to itself, moving around touching friends and strangers alike. "We won," they said, confirming it over and over again.

A commotion caught Grizzly Hair's attention and he turned to see the youngest men and boys stripping the dead soldiers. They had dragged them outside the thicket and were distributing the garments. Most people cast them aside. Somebody yelled, "Help us hang him up in that tree."

A young man shimmied up an oak to a high limb where a thick brown stem of a grapevine hung down, and he waited while others made a human ladder against the tree, feet on shoulders. They shoved and pulled a dead *soldado* upward, many hands helping, and the man on top wrapped the vine around his neck and dropped him. They scrambled and jumped down. The naked body hung limp and pale as a skinned rabbit. "Target practice," a boy shouted.

Men and boys reached for their bows. "Wait," Elk Calf called. With a stick he gouged a line. "Here's the line for boys." He stepped farther back and drew a men's line. Competition was underway. Unspent arrows flew, unspent tension released.

Uncomfortable with that but knowing he couldn't stop the fun, Grizzly Hair cupped his mouth and called around, "Bring firewood. Find musicians. We will dance in the place where they ran away!" A boyhood memory flashed through his mind of the Kadeema-umne preparing their victory dance after they defeated the umne.

People conferred briefly then some ran for firewood. Others left to contact friends and relatives who had not fought. Lame Beaver, seemingly about to launch into the air with joy, said, "I'll ride home and get the umne and our women."

"Wait," Grizzly Hair said thinking fast. Etumu would want to stay here, but maybe she could. The upstream peoples had shown their willingness to hide women and children during the fighting, and the scouts were very good. "Yes," he said, "but take my horse and ask our men, here, if you can take and string theirs. That way the umne can come faster." It occurred to him that the victory dance could be used to gather more warriors for the next battle.

He caught up to Lame Beaver on his way to the brush corral and told him to send word up all the streams and rivers between here and the home place. This dance would give people courage. "This has never happened before," he explained. "Tell them it is a sign of great importance. All peoples are invited, even those who sent no one to fight. This victory belongs to all *Indios*. They should join us in the next battle and we will celebrate another victory."

Sucais sent the same message up Estanislao's river, and Tuol sent it up his river. Lame Beaver would spread the invitation up the River of Skulls—*Calaveras*—and beyond, and the big time would grow bigger.

By nightfall the dance was underway; women and children streamed in from other places. Never had Grizzly Hair imagined so much food in one place. There were mountains of acorns, the harvest having been bountiful, and enough steaming baskets of nu-pah to fill a roundhouse. Elk roasted in pits, and heaps of delicious bulbs and grapes waited in baskets. In addition, the salmon weirs were full.

By the next night the jubilant peoples were so numerous that more dance fires had to be built on the plain. Near one fire hung another soldier with a pike up his anus. He resembled a porcupine. Elk Calf took aim. The challenge was to find space for one more arrow point. He released. "You split an arrow!" shouted a little boy. Other children jumped up and down beside the pole, pointing.

Grizzly Hair went to a red willow near the water and cut a plug. He dug out the pith and soon had himself a whistle whose sides collapsed nicely as he blew a shrill note. Instrumentalists and singers came from far and wide. People came in their big-time feathers, shell money, skirts and capes. As mother moon moved silently across the night, flutes played intoxicating new melodies that made him think of Bowstring. After two strange songs in a row, he stepped beside the log drummer and raised his voice in his favorite song of the umne.

Many voices joined in the chorus. The spirits in the trees and grass and river sang too, and at the distant campfires in the sky the immortals joined in and danced around their own fires. The fullness of power flowed. Many seasons of uncertainty and fear had dissolved into riotous fun. In the shadows, even O-se- mai-ti frolicked and danced with her cubs. At one fire people sang as they danced:

Glo-ria in excelsis De-o
Gloh!-ria, heh, heh, heh.
Gloh!-ria in excelsis De-o
Gloh!-ria, heh, heh, heh.

"What does it mean?" he asked a woman.

"Happiness to God."

"Ho!" he exclaimed, blowing his whistle. He joined the dancing, bouncing on one foot then the other, blowing his whistle and singing, Happiness to God, Happiness to God! In the shadows he saw men pass bags of *aguardiente,* and men and women pumped sexual bliss into the victory.

After three more joyful days of feasting and dancing, he slept late and bathed in the languid river. When he returned to the camp center, there was Etumu in her red skirt. She had bright red toyon berries behind both ears. She pushed the bikoos into the ground and smiled at him. Nettles, Raven Feather, Straight Willow, Pretty Duck, Grasshopper Wing and the Omuchumne and Shalachmushumne women were removing their burden baskets.

Boy saw Grizzly Hair and ran to him. "You won, you won!" His eyes burned like fire as he looked up at him.

Grizzly Hair tousled the thick hair. "Crying Fox," he said, "I am glad you came to dance."

The boy looked perplexed. Then his eyes widened and his jaw dropped. He ran around in a tight circle, then squared his shoulders and with a huge grin, shouted, "I have a name!"

Smiling, Etumu told Grizzly Hair, "We heard you won." Her voice sounded as young as she looked, and she smelled of life and flowers. He pulled her to him and hugged her.

Throughout the next days men and women continued to arrive with arrows and food. Neophytes from different missions linked arms and strolled around the huge camp singing mission songs. Children raced through the crowds, Crying Fox among them.

Wrinkling and holding their noses, older boys took down the bodies of the dead soldiers and salvaged arrows. Later Crying Fox proudly told Grizzly Hair, "I pulled an arrow from his stomach. It smelled bad!" He made a face but his eyes sparkled with pride.

Etumu stared at him in horror. Grizzly Hair asked, "Have you washed yourself?" Crying Fox looked chagrined. Grizzly Hair whisked him to his shoulders and trotted with him, holding his calves. Etumu followed to the purifying river.

Stroking out to the current he held his son at arms length and let the water rinse him. Etumu marveled, "People here are not afraid of ghosts and bad luck."

"They learned that in the missions," he explained. "They don't believe the souls of the soldiers linger. They think they left immediately for a very hot place in the ground."

"Do you believe that?"

"I don't know," he admitted.

Treading water, she looked at him as though evaluating what he'd said. "No matter," she declared at last. "That is an abomination." She took Crying Fox, swam with him to shore and scrubbed his hands in the sand at the water's edge until he whimpered. "Never touch the dead," she scolded.

Grizzly Hair recalled that he had touched Oak Gall without purification, yet had the good luck to survive. Howchia had died soon afterward, but now power was on his side. The bad luck was over. When he returned to the field to help with the butchering of a moose, he heard that the larger boys had staked the torn bodies out on the plain where the black hats would pass when they came back.

Not going to the crowded sweathouse, as he had done each night, Grizzly Hair held Etumu and Crying Fox in either arm. The baby slept laced into her bikoos, which had been lined with rabbit skins. The nights were turning cold. By day he hunted for elk but killed a young wild horse. Tying the hind feet together, he dragged it behind Morena back to the big time.

During the sunny but cool days, vaqueros from the missions whirled *riatas* over their heads and made the older boys run across the playing field to be lassoed and dragged gently back, laughing, arms pinioned to their sides. Grizzly Hair saw the great value of roping, but when he tried it, realized it would take much practice.

On the sixth day the *aguardiente* was gone. In the brief sunshine between rain squalls, Poo-soo-ne, his wives and a dozen more men and women arrived. They clapped Grizzly Hair on the shoulders and grinned as though they had helped win the victory, as though they hadn't counseled against war.

"I never thought it could be done," Poo-soo-ne said with an admiring expression.

"We could have defeated many more," Grizzly Hair told them.

The entire encampment danced the Wok-ke-lah, the war dance, and later, despite his exhaustion, Grizzly Hair worried as he watched children and dogs curl up together wherever they found a quiet place. Were the scouts as vigilant as they had been before? After the moon set, it felt good to hold Etumu and run his hand down her slim backside, to feel again the perfect comfort of her. Somehow they both thought it would be all right to break tradition. All customs were broken here.

As she slept beside him, he tried to imagine the next battle. How many soldiers would come? The scouts had been wrong about the cannon. Either there hadn't been one, or it had been left behind and collected by the soldiers on the way back, but next time there would be a cannon. Would the fort hold up to heavy iron balls shooting with the magical gunpowder? Overhead the big trees thrashed. The wind plucked at the branches of their temporary shelter, and somewhere Coyote's howl reminded him that things were not always what they seemed.

67

The Sanchez Expedition

In the morning, father sun was hidden behind clouds and the west was a solid wall of black. A council was called. People came drawing capes over their shoulders.

"I don't think they will come back," an elder from Tuol's place threw out, starting the talk.

"I agree," added another, "Look at the sky. This is the seventh sun and the scouts have seen no one coming."

"You never know, they could fall on us while we're asleep."

"No. They never go on expedition in time of rain."

"This is why I wanted to talk," Estanislao said in his characteristic way, as though sharing an intimacy with each person. "I think we should send a special runner to the presidio to learn what they are planning."

People exchanged glances. Grizzly Hair knew he couldn't go without being recognized by José Amador, the *soldado* who had ridden him, or Crane Beak and the other guards at the mission.

Estanislao looked into the people. "I see a man here who I think could do it. Bartolo was never punished in the mission. He blended into the crowd and worked without complaint. I doubt the *soldados* would remember his face."

Everyone sat quietly in a big talk circle several people deep. Then a man looked up and said, "Maybe I could. I have a friend in the presidio. He takes supper to the *soldados* and washes their plates. He might help."

Estanislao straightened his wide lips, eyes shining through the gray day. "You are the perfect runner, Bartolo. *Gracias.* Did you eat well this morning?"

Before he could answer, grateful women pushed nu-pah baskets towards him and handed him strips of smoked salmon.

While Bartolo was gone game became scarcer every day. Men had to ride farther to hunt. Despite the bountiful acorn harvest only three moons ago, Etumu worried that the cha'kas didn't contain enough to feed this many people much longer. The herbs and forbs in a wide swath around Domingo's place had been overused. Even the huge salmon catch was diminishing at an alarming rate. There were simply too many people in one place.

Bartolo returned after the eighth sleep. The herald announced him and the crowd gathered as he climbed the mound and walked out on the roof, nondescript as before—a bird who would disappear in a flock. The anticipation of the crowd could almost be touched as people stilled themselves and gazed up at the man.

Bartolo spoke: "Sergeant Soto died one sleep after he arrived at Mission San José. Concepción Argüello used her medicine, but he died anyway."

Cheers exploded from the crowd.

"Even their doctors fail!" somebody shouted.

Bartolo waited for the laughter to fade, then said, "No expedition is planned."

Another shout went up. Everybody talked and laughed and whooped until Estanislao—seeing Bartolo ready to leave the roof—asked, "Would you tell us how you know that?"

Bartolo recounted his travels, how he skirted the mission and went directly to the presidio, how he hid his clothing and wore only the bone noseplug loaned to him by one of the gentiles here, and how he posed as a gentile seeking work for pay. Before long he was cooking beside his friend in the presidio *cocina.* "Three times a day we took food to the *soldados* in a big eating room. I was lucky. I overheard a *soldado* telling his friends he was glad they wouldn't be going to the interior to fight the *Indios.* His friend said the captain thought it was too dangerous to cross the San Joaquin River in time of rain. But another *soldado* disagreed. He said Captain Martinez would have gone immediately, but too many presidio horses had been stolen. He said it would take time to locate enough for the expedition, and the *rancheros* didn't want to go at all if they had to use their own horses. Too many of them had been stolen, too."

"Aiii!" one of Gabriel's men shouted. Laughing, they slapped each other. Bartolo waited as the buzz went around the crowd and smiles cracked many faces. Grizzly Hair stood amazed. He had thought horse stealing would annoy, but not cripple the *Españoles.* He had imagined the number of horses around the missions to be like blades of grass on the plain. María had said the *Españoles* had been forced to kill many of them. But that, he realized, was a long time ago, before Indios learned how to eat and ride them.

Bartolo continued, "I was lucky again the next day when I carried the plates back to the *cocina.* Different men were getting up from the table. One said that waiting until after the rains was good because the gentiles would leave Estanislao and go back to their home places. He said the gentiles would lose interest, and Estanislao's *insurgentes* could more easily be captured."

Grizzly Hair feared that might be true.

Estanislao said, "*Gracias,* Bartolo." As the mild man left the roof, Estanislao ascended. Without hesitation he addressed the crowd in his intimate manner. "Bartolo has done well. Now we know the soldiers will return. But we will expect them, won't we? And remember that they often change their minds. When the governor sends a message, everything can change. Our scouts are good. They will want to stay on the trail during the rains." He nodded to Grizzly Hair, who had pointed to his mouth in a signal to speak.

"All gentiles," Grizzly Hair said, "including my umne, should return to their home places." He wasn't finished when someone shouted:

"That's just what they want you to do!"

"Friend," Grizzly Hair replied, "there isn't enough food here. Send runners on good horses and we will return fast, with more arrows." He looked around the crowd and saw nods from men from several different rivers.

"He is right," Te-mi said. "My people will go home too." Nodding agreement, the hy-apos from many places exchanged talk.

Estanislao announced, using Grizzly Hair's Spanish name, "It is decided. Juan Gustavus is right. The elk and deer have gone elsewhere. But our runners are as good as our scouts. I trust you gentiles to return." He paused, then continued, "You *cimarrones* should leave too and hide with your relatives, if you have them. Tell them to come back and fight with you. We will send runners all the way to the Lake of the Tulares and the southern mountains."

Estanislao, Grizzly Hair realized, was the perfect headman for this mixed crowd, his father being a gentile. He had none of the arrogance that neophytes such as Narciso displayed toward gentiles, and his Spanish was fluent.

The last to speak, Gabriel mounted the dancehouse roof as Estanislao left it. "While you wait for your kind of war, my men and I will raid the ranches and missions from Monterey to San Francisco. We will herd horses to your villages, for trade. We will bring horsemeat and good riding horses." He smiled like a fox. "Sometimes we find horses with saddles left on them. A saddle would cost you ten strings of shell money." People chattered.

Grizzly Hair and the umne headed north with the Muquelumne and

Chilumne. Happy talk made the distance seem short, and as they traveled, it was comforting to see bears and herds of antelope, elk and deer. They also saw some wild horses north of the River of Skulls, farther north than they had been seen before. But as he led Morena, who carried Etumu and the children, Grizzly Hair wondered if the *Españoles* in the presidio were correct. Would the united front weaken when the peoples no longer shared talk each day? Would everyone return?

Lieutenant Ignacio Martinez,
Today the disagreeable news arrived that(neophytes fishing on paseo *on the San Joaquin River). . . were attacked by seven of the Indian rebels on horseback, with the renowned Estanislao at their head, and Macario was relieved of the horses, his saddle, harness and clothing. An even more lamentable circumstance was that the companion, named Benigno went over to the enemy. The latter, when they let Macario loose, gave him a message for me that now they are really going to become active, and soon they will try to fall upon the ranches and gardens.*

Fray Narciso Durán,
March 1, 1829, Mission San José

In the time of nesting birds Grizzly Hair and Etumu gathered with the umne to hear a runner from Domingo's place.

"Bartolo went to the presidio again," the runner announced. "He says the *soldados* are preparing an expedition. This time they will bring a cannon that works. Last time it broke. They have been waiting for Sergeant Rodriguez to return with stolen horses and saddles. Delfino, a runner from the south, told us that the Rodriguez expedition has been going from village to village on the San Joaquin River." Bartolo gave a detailed report on Rodriquez' movements as told by Delfino, concluding: "Rodriguez and his men are capturing horses and *cimarrones.* Some gentiles don't care about people they don't know, and they tell the soldiers where the *cimarrones* are hiding. They want the soldiers to leave in a hurry and not find where horses have been butchered." Bartolo told how Rodriguez and his men went to the Joyomi, Tache, Heuche, and Chowsila. "They went to the peoples at the Lake of the Tulares, Buena Vista Lake, and even across the southern mountains to the relatives of people who go to Mission La Purísima. About ten and two-twenties horses and over four twenties of people have been captured." The runner looked around at each person and said, "Estanislao wants you to return now to Domingo's place."

Every utterance of this long message drilled into Grizzly Hair. He hardly noticed Etumu putting her hand in his, squeezing his fingers, then removing her hand, only to do it again. Things would change now, possibly forever.

"Little Lizard Woman," he said, turning to her after the runner finished, "the fifty horses will be ridden by fifty black hats, the entire presidio of San Francisco. You must stay here with the children. If you want to help, take food to the downstream people, so they can run it to us."

She didn't like it, but stayed at the home place with Raven Feather and Nettles and the other women.

Domingo's Place, April, 1829

Grizzly Hair looked at the thin man standing near the double fort and wondered why Benigno seemed familiar. He had joined Estanislao rather than return to Padre Durán with Macario. Grizzly Hair walked through the mud that had been thrown up from the trench and on a whim asked in the home tongue, "Do you know me?"

The man looked up in surprise. "No. Not at all. But you sound like my home place." His talk was familiar too, as were his roundish eyes and flat nose. Then it came back. Lines had been added to his face and he had become thin and slightly stooped, though he retained the muscles of an active man. "I think you are Blue Snake," Grizzly Hair said.

A flash of shock hit the man's face. He had run in shame and trackers had never found him. Now he looked ashamed again, though he quickly recovered his calm.

Grizzly Hair told him truthfully, "When I was a boy I thought you were the most powerful man on earth. All I wanted in life was to dodge arrows like you, and run like you."

"I ran pretty well all right," he joked. "Who are you the son of?"

"My father came from far downstream on the home river, the Newachumne I think. He was killed by black hats and my mother took me to the umne. Her people became my people. The Lopotsumne."

"Ah yes. I saw Morning Owl here, didn't I? Wearing a buckskin shirt with fringe?"

Grizzly Hair nodded.

"You are the son of Eagle Woman."

Grizzly Hair looked away with an affirmative move of his chin. "Her heart is gone."

"Sorry. I didn't know."

"I am glad you will fight on our side. You are a warrior."

Blue Snake chuckled cynically. "Some people wouldn't agree. Didn't I see Running Quail too, my cousin-brother?"

"Yes, he is here." Seeing Blue Snake roll his eyes like the shame lingered in him, Grizzly Hair let a wry smile bend his lips. "After we win this war, I challenge you to a foot race." As a boy he had always wanted to do that.

Blue Snake smiled back and put a hand on his shoulder. "You name the place."

"It's muddy here," Red Sun observed, stepping carefully to join them. Mud lay around all the trenches. Red Sun, who had come with his brother Running Quail to fight the next battle, obviously recognized Blue Snake. Grizzly Hair always tried to act like Red sun's presence at Domingo's place was natural, but underneath he felt the unease of a boy who had unexpectedly convinced a man to do something. He told himself that Red Sun had made up his mind after listening to others of the umne, and he, Grizzly Hair, should accept that his father-in-law now saw him as a respected man. But under this conversation with himself he still felt himself in the presence of an elder who had once wanted to kill him. Not afraid, but never quite at ease.

This was the first time Red Sun had seen Domingo's place. With snow melting in the mountains, the river was at the top of its channel and the floods had lasted a long time. Scouts told of Sergeant Rodriguez and his men crossing the swollen San Joaquin River. It had taken them an entire day—horses drowning, gear lost. But now the rains had stopped and father sun gave vigorous new life to the grass on the plain. Rodriguez would soon be in the presidio with the trained horses.

Impatient for what would come, Grizzly Hair left the two men, who were discussing the best way to barb arrowheads, and went to the green plain. Again he wondered from which side of the river the soldiers would approach. The north sides of the tree trunks still wore thick coats of bright green moss, and everywhere a world of infant leaves had unfurled. Fluffy white clouds cast splotchy shadows over women digging corms and bulbs. Children frolicked around them. The tall blue brodiaea flowers marked the locations of the nut-like bulbs that he liked so well. Without a woman, a man ate poorly, and this was just one more thing that made him wish the black hats would hurry. If fate would have him die, he'd rather do it without watching other people eat better.

"I'll bet there aren't enough neophytes left in the mission to plant the maize," Estanislao said coming up behind him. "Another group will come in today."

Maybe Bowstring and Teresa.

Estanislao straightened his wide lips at him and said in his slightly amused, confidential tone, "Wouldn't you like to do something besides sit around here waiting for somebody else to do something? Let's go round up some new horses."

That sounded good to Grizzly Hair. He found Elk Calf, Two Falcons and several others, and they all rode the trail over Alta Monte Pass, heading for Las Positas—Señor Livermore's rancho. On the way, however, he learned that José

Amador's Rancho San Ramon wasn't far from Los Positas. The others agreed that Grizzly Hair and Elk Calf needed to pay Amador back. On a recent expedition, the one Grizzly Hair didn't help fight, Amador had ridden Elk Calf's cousin like a horse, spurring him cruelly. When they arrived at Amador's place, Grizzly Hair galloped at a daring speed, herding horses past helpless young vaqueros as he yelled, "Tell your *patrón*, next time we'll take the cows."

He dodged gunfire alongside the *insurgentes*, and like brothers they herded the horses to the valley and left them grazing on the plain outside Domingo's place. This excursion provided welcome activity, but also made Grizzly Hair's memory slip to big ugly Juan, who had ridden on the other horse raid.

The next day a hot north wind began withering the grass. Gone were the cooling breezes and rain showers, and with them the mood of a big time. With each passing day the earth hardened and a new little shelf was left beneath the many previous shelves that marked the receding shoreline of the river. Travel would be easier for the black hats.

At the same time, Grizzly Hair was relieved to see gentiles arriving every day from far-flung villages, all carrying bundles of arrows. Arrow deliveries came from villages that had not sent any to the first battle. Besides that, many arrows remained in the fort. Every day Grizzly Hair and other men went there to straighten warped shafts and repair fletching damaged by the floods.

One afternoon Egorov rode into the clearing on a black stallion, his long musket laid across a fine Spanish saddle. He looked at Grizzly Hair with clear brown eyes, but the rest of him was hard to recognize with his hair grown long and his beard shaggy. He wore a badly torn Russian shirt and frayed Russian pants. His boot tops were bound to the leather soles with cording frayed from having been walked on too much. Following the stallion, a pretty woman in a mission skirt rode a tan horse with a black mane and tail. It was burdened with many buckets and strange black baskets.

Grizzly Hair stepped forward to greet them as a crowd of curious people gathered, a few reaching to touch the thick black coating on the woman's baskets.

Egorov spoke. His Spanish pronunciation was so strange that most of it could not be understood. The woman translated into good Spanish. She said they came from Santa Barbara. Grizzly Hair recalled that Egorov had stayed in Santa Barbara after the war, and was said to live there with two women.

"When will the *Españoles* attack?" Egorov asked, looking directly at Grizzly Hair.

"Our runner says it will be another five to seven sleeps," he responded.

Egorov immediately set about building an oven of clay, which willing swimmers carried in baskets from the river bottom. He built the little dome downstream in a clearing where father sun could dry it quickly. Then Grizzly Hair watched the way he burned seasoned oak in the oven until the chunks were white hot, and the way he put chunks of metal called lead into a thick little pan with a furrow in its lip. With a new mother's delicacy he laid the pan on the hot firebed, then pushed dirt up to cover the small oven door. When he removed the dirt the lead had melted.

With several layers of elk skin, Egorov removed the pan and poured the liquid metal into a fold-out, hinged tray containing two rows of three evenly sized depressions, a half round on each side. He then closed the tray and with fire-hardened tongs tipped it upright so the furrows inside admitted the liquid metal into the six half rounds, now tightly together. He took the tray to the river and lowered it into a backwater where it sizzled and steamed between the tongs. When it was well cooled, he opened it to reveal perfectly round balls with only the slightest lines where the two sides of the tray met. As he looked at Grizzly Hair, his brown eyes moved down and up his length and he tried to stop the corners of his lips from turning up. Apparently he was now accustomed to naked men. It was the only time Egorov ever smiled at him. Grizzly Hair had no idea what was funny, unless it was his intense interest. Maybe he acted like a boy watching the butchering of a deer for the first time.

But though Egorov smiled, he could bring trouble. He might demand the four missions and the land between them.

"What are you looking at," Egorov asked. The woman translated, "Why do you look at him like that?"

"You didn't tell my runners you were going to Santa Barbara. I thought we were *amigos de guerra.*"

It looked as though an invisible demon filled the Russian full of red fluid. His face turned red, his brown eyes snapped and his unintelligible speech hurled small damp missiles. Somewhat shamefacedly, the woman translated, "No *negro* tells me what to do."

Grizzly Hair felt an urge to laugh at this strange little man who lacked the ability to cover his feelings. Instead he said in a dignified tone, "You brought no Undersea friends with you. You brought no cannon."

A spray of impossible sound hurled out of him. The woman said, "He asks if you want him to leave."

Grizzly Hair considered that. But though the question was meant more to taunt him, as though Egorov thought the *Indios* desperately needed him, it would be good to have a Russian gun shooting on the *Indio* side. The *Españoles* would tremble with fear and think there were more. He talked straight. "I am glad you came to help."

If Egorov still wanted the missions, he'd need to talk to Estanislao and the gathered hy-apos. Narciso and his friends might claim Mission San José, and Cipriano Mission Santa Clara. But that would come later. If they won.

May 7, 1829

With the bravado of the war dance fading, Grizzly Hair pressed his shoulder against the fort wall, unconsciously testing its strength. He noticed the faint rocking of his body, the beating of his heart. Fear bit into his stomach. The entire San Francisco garrison was on its way—wheeled cannon, four twenties of horses and a wagon heaped with ammunition and extra *fusiles.* More than three-twenties of neophyte helpers had built boats and ferried men and materials across the San Joaquin River. Scouts reported that Sergeant Sanchez and his men had slept near the river, then traveled during the night and camped again, still a distance from Domingo's village.

Hundreds of warriors waited in the trees. Hatchlings cried for food, and their parents coasted through the trees with insects in their beaks. A short time later these same birds flapped away, oblivious to the humans who would soon kill their own kind. He winced to think how the small bag of Egorov's balls shrank beside a wagon heaped with ammunition. Would arrows succeed now that the *soldados* were alert to the snare? Could his oak-branchlet vest stop lead balls? His sweating chest would test it. Could the fort stop the cannon balls and protect the women who had insisted on staying and helping run the arrows?

Caw, caw, Crow warned.

Estanislao's voice rang clear and penetrating. "Sergeant Sanchez, you are a coward and you can't get us."

They had arrived. Grizzly Hair cupped his mouth and called toward the plain, "We can smell your fear. You are shitting in your *pantalones.*" It settled his stomach and channeled the fear to its purpose. A man scurried through the trees and spoke to another man hiding nearby. The latter turned and said to Grizzly Hair and others, "They are putting the cannon together."

A Spanish voice called through the trees. "This is Sergeant Sanchez. You neophytes listen. We have instructions to kill you all, but if you come out now and go peacefully to the missions, you will not be harmed. This is your last chance. Put down your bows. Walk out with empty hands. I repeat, you will not be punished. Your friends and relatives are on our side, the side of God and people of reason."

"You are a turd," Estanislao answered in a cozy tone as though notifying Sanchez of that odd circumstance. It made Grizzly Hair smile through his high state of readiness.

A second voice called from the plain, familiar and resonant in the way of a practiced singer, in the home tongue. "This is José Francisco." Bowstring, heart-stoppingly Bowstring. "I know you gentiles from my river are in there. Come out and talk to me and Sergeant Sanchez. You will not be harmed. You are making a big mistake if you don't come out and talk."

Reeling with shock and sadness that his old friend had spoken for the black hats, it took a moment before Grizzly Hair saw Estanislao looking down from his perch in an oak.

"Maybe I should go talk to him." Grizzly Hair suggested.

Estanislao gave him a look of sympathy. "I can't go out there with you," he said, "but I know you are too strong to be twisted by the things they will say."

Another voice called from the plain, in the tongue of the Lakisumne. "All you gentile headmen, this is important. You are making a mistake. Sergeant Sanchez wants to talk to you. Come halfway and meet with him. He promises none of you will be harmed."

Quiet talk could be heard around the dense thicket: "What will they offer us?" "Maybe we should find out." "Is it a trick?" "Better find out. . ." In the end Grizzly Hair and about twelve other men, including Morning Owl, made their way through the vines and deadfall to the edge of the river jungle. Knowing that the hidden men were poised to kill the first enemy to injure any of them, Grizzly Hair put his *casco* and bow and quiver against a tree before he stepped out of the shade. Father sun struck with surprising force, his brightness dazzling Grizzly Hair's eyes.

Far away from the jungle edge were about two-twenties of *soldados*. Apart from them, about three times that many neophyte-helpers in woolen hip-wraps. Midway between there and the edge of cover stood three *soldados* in *cuero* jackets and hats, apparently without *fusiles*, and two neophytes. Something about the posture of the neophyte with stick-like legs and wide head told him it was Bowstring, though he had always been thickset.

Neither Lame Beaver nor Running Quail had come forward, but Grizzly Hair realized it would have been difficult for them, without a time of pretending. And what would they say to a son and brother who talked for the enemy? Running Quail had pronounced him dead.

Approaching the five, Grizzly Hair saw the red patches on the *cuero* jacket of Sanchez—another red-wing displaying his feathers. He also had metal dots running down his *pantalones*. Bowstring raised his head. Sorrow struck Grizzly Hair to see the arched eyebrows standing so harshly on his friend's gaunt face.

"I am Sergeant Sanchez," announced the red-wing. He had shot a dog in the head and nearly scared Grizzly Hair to death before the march to the mission. Now sweat glistened on his gray-streaked mustache and beard, and he was saying, "You *cimarrones* who are coming to our side, go over there and wait." He pointed at the neophyte-helpers.

Nobody moved. "We came to talk," Te-mi provided in his tongue. As the other neophyte-helper translated, father sun was frying Grizzly Hair's back and shoulders and cooking his hair. He couldn't stop looking at Bowstring, almost a ghost.

Sanchez spoke to the hy-apos and for a while Bowstring helped translate, but it became obvious that all the headmen spoke either Spanish or the Lakisumne tongue. Bowstring stepped to the side and said quietly to Grizzly Hair. "You look well, old friend."

"Looks like you haven't eaten for a while."

"I've been sick with watery stool but I'm better now."

"Do you and Teresa have a baby?"

"She will get one soon."

Delighted for him, Grizzly Hair felt his face crack into a smile. "You will like that. I have two children." As that left his lips he felt foolish, to be talking about children at a time like this. "I saw you after we raided Las Positas. Did they make you go back to the mission?"

"We went back when they told us to. We want no quarrel with Padre Durán."

Dismayed, Grizzly Hair looked at his friend's prominent kneecaps, no longer nestled in muscle, and changed the subject. "I heard there isn't enough food at the mission to feed all those people and the soldiers' families too." Most of the talk between Sanchez and the headmen was muffled, but he heard Sanchez say, ". . .leave Estanislao. Go to your homes. This isn't your fight."

Bowstring cocked his head, raised his eyebrows in the old joking way and asked, "Why are you making war against us?"

Us. It landed like a whip. Grizzly Hair spoke straight, though it sounded soft and apologetic to his ears. "If the black hats stayed in the presidio, there would be no war. You are making war against us." He leapt to the topic foremost in his mind. "Come with me now. Your father and brother are in there." He nodded toward the shade. "We are fighting to free you and drive the black hats from this land so all *Indios* can live where they want, in or out of the missions, without fear and suffering."

A covey of quail whirred to the ground and pecked for early seeds that had been threshed by many feet. Their fat bodies and jaunty topknots swam in the heat waves, a friendly scene that contrasted starkly with what the humans were about to do. "You should have gone to the home place when they let you leave," Grizzly Hair said, voice breaking with emotion. In a way Bowstring did seem dead. He could barely hear his music.

"I want to be near the orchestra. It is exactly as I dreamed." He looked past Grizzly Hair to the quail. "Your horse-stealing made the governor change his order and call everyone to the missions. Do you know that? You say you want to stop the suffering, but you cause it. Your raids make the guards upset and quicker to punish us." A mask of sadness contoured his perspiring features to such an extent that Grizzly Hair would have laughed had they been the same two friends who had entered manhood together, and had this talk not made him doubt everything he'd done since then. Various replies started to take shape in his mind, but the heat melted them before they got to his tongue.

The voice of Sergeant Sanchez filled the void. "Do you mean you are afraid of Estanislao?"

The hy-apos seemed to agree. This unnerved Grizzly Hair all the more, until he looked closely at Morning Owl's bland expression and realized that this excuse was as good as any for staying in the battle. Pomponio hadn't been the only *cimarrón* to harass gentiles who were friendly toward the missions. Morning Owl was being sly; he wouldn't desert Estanislao and that's all that mattered.

"Aiii!" a voice yelled from the forest. A gun discharged from that direction and the ball zinged past Sergeant Sanchez, causing him to jump back. Egorov.

"Come with me," Grizzly Hair whispered urgently as Sanchez ran toward his men. "Don't help kill your father." But Bowstring stood tragically in the heat.

Grizzly Hair walked away through the drying grass, showing strength alongside the hy-apos, who didn't run though the black hats could have guns in their hands by now. His head pulsed with the heat, and Bowstring's talk. Was war the problem, not the solution? It felt as though an infection had gathered itself to a throbbing boil and he was the point at which the boil would break. Was war useless? Would fighting continue even if the black hats left the land? Fighting stirred up by arrogant men like Narciso? Was it already too late for the old balances between peoples to reassert themselves? Or had the conversion of *Indios* into *Christianos* and *gentiles* changed the world forever? He picked up his weapons and hurried into hiding.

This was fated. The black hats had their guns ready. Even if O-se-mai-ti herself told him to stop, it was too late. Still, how much more human it would have been to settle this with arrow-dodgers! But the *Españoles* wouldn't follow the rules or abide by the outcome. They had, however, fulfilled their promise not to shoot the men who went out to talk. In that they had behaved like human beings. The warm breath of the musty earth and the fragrant expiration of young grape leaves cascading from dizzying heights stole the sharpness from the day as he knelt and positioned his first arrow.

The *cuero*-jackets formed a long, evenly spaced line and walked slowly toward the trees. The line wavered in the heat. They held big *cuero* shields. Behind the line, like a cloud in his mind, he saw Juan's face—eyes pleading, mouth lashed open by the tight thong. Juan had relished the idea of killing black hats and Grizzly Hair realized that his own private reparations to that man would be to kill them in Juan's stead. He would also fight in the place of Pomponio and Gonzalo and all those who had been bound and whipped and killed. He would fight so he could recover Oak Gall's bones. He would fight for his father and grandfather. He would fight to stop Durán from capturing the umne and locking Crying Fox in a house apart and teaching him to weave like a girl. He would fight for Falls-off-House, who would have given his all. If bees could sacrifice themselves to save the hive, so could men. He would banish Bowstring's talk from his mind. To kill was his fate. He would fight like a cornered bear. Hadn't O-se-mai-ti said they would win? The talk of spirits was not to be ignored, no matter how things might appear.

Estanislao's seductive voice came over the noisy birds. "You are slow, boys. We are waiting. Let's see if you are men. Come in and try to get us."

The long line of soldiers split three ways, two groups heading to opposite sides of Domingo's place. The third, with Sanchez in the middle, continued its slow march toward the edge of the thicket. *Soldados* behind Sanchez were pulling a small wheeled cannon.

Sanchez and his line of men stopped just out of bowshot. They held their shields between their legs, aimed their *fusiles* and fired. A cloud of white smoke issued from the many guns, hiding the soldiers for a while. Grizzly Hair had just let his first arrow fly. He couldn't see it land, though he was sure it must have landed short. He ducked behind his tree, ears hurting from the simultaneous blasts. Again the soldiers advanced one step at a time into the first trees, then stopped. They took turns tamping powder and balls into their long barrels, squinting down their lengths and firing at anything that moved. Occasional cries mingled with the booming guns. They were like demons controlled by something outside themselves. He heard a few bangs from his side and was glad Egorov was shooting. However none of the soldiers went down. The range of the guns was twice that of Grizzly Hair's bow, which was of the best yew wood, and the space was narrow between *cuero* hats and jackets. Each time Grizzly Hair scurried out, planted his knee and let fly, he was nearly hit by balls before he got back to cover. Bark chipped off the trees and rained down on him and he couldn't tell whether his excitement was fear or the crackling of magic. The *soldados* continued to fire, no longer in unison due to different speeds of reloading. Guns exploded continuously and their longer range all but stopped the flight of arrows.

Taunts were hurled at the *soldados* from here and there around the jungle, but they advanced no further. *They're not coming in*, Grizzly Hair realized. They had learned from the Soto expedition. Sanchez and another *soldado* stepped aside to make room for the cannon. A black hat inserted a burning stick into it. A horrific blast rattled Grizzly Hair's teeth. A plume of white smoke blew out of the cannon. He turned to look at the fort, but saw no damage and no one injured.

Egorov shot at the cannon-feeder, but many guns fired back at him and he failed to kill anyone. Meanwhile the *soldados* continued firing at the *Indios* and the few answering arrows dropped short of their targets.

Out of arrows, Grizzly Hair darted back to the trench and ducked under the double wall. "Are we winning yet?" asked one of the women who was sitting among the baskets of food and medicine.

"No." A gut-shaking boom followed, but no scream or sound followed, not even a thump on the fort. He filled his quiver, jumped in the trench and followed it out. As before, he couldn't get near enough and his arrows landed short.

The cannon spoke again. But its roar had no bite, and the cannon feeders pulled it away. Muffled talk could be heard from tree to tree around the thicket. This cannon was also broken. Good luck prevailed. Meanwhile the steady thunder and whine of passing balls continued, the reloading *soldados* always protected by those on either side.

But these men had to be killed so their bodies could be counted. Hoping to get closer, Grizzly Hair crouch-ran from tree to tree, hearing balls zing off the bark. One glanced off his *casco* with a high ringing noise that hurt his ears. The hat had saved his life. He was lucky. He crept around a wide oak and pulled the string to the breaking point and let fly at Sanchez's face. Again the arrow landed short. A hail of lead balls flew around him.

In the continuous thunder of *fusiles* and the intensifying heat, Grizzly Hair became more and more frustrated. Then he realized that a group of men might be able to circle around and attack the line of black hats from behind.

"Let's go shoot their rears," he said to the men around him.

Signaling, he made his way back through the trees and vines, the chink and thud of balls pursuing him until he was out of range.

Lame Beaver and Running Quail, Two Falcons, Grub Log, Eats Skunk, Blue Snake and others followed him down into the brush-covered trench. They ran along it to the end, then pulled themselves up to ground level. The gunpowder scent was fainter, though the guns sounded as loud as ever. Cutting through the vines with their knives, they went through a dense thicket, and with the noise of guns there was no need for stealth, or so Grizzly Hair thought.

Gunshots came from their right. He dropped to his belly, a hot sensation sizzling on his upper arm. Somebody moaned. "To the trench," he called, leaping to his feet. As he ran, balls thumped into the trees. This had to be one of the groups that had split off from Sanchez.

He jumped into the trench, others landing beside him. It looked like everyone was there. His arm bled where a furrow of skin had been removed. Again he'd been lucky. But one of the men had two bleeding holes in his side, one where the ball entered, the other where it left. Blue Snake ran back to the fort for medicine. Grizzly Hair and the rest let fly at the hidden soldiers. The enemy didn't advance and after a while Grizzly Hair realized this was their purpose—to stop the *insurgentes* from getting behind Sanchez. No doubt the third group was guarding the other side of the village.

"Stop wasting arrows," he said. "Let's make them think we've gone, and see if they come over here."

It didn't take long. The continuous noise of guns kept him from hearing it at first, but the black hats were breaking through the vines. He and the others waited in the trench, ready to spring up with their bows. But after a while they exchanged puzzled looks. The sounds had stopped. Cautiously rising to scan the trees and bushes, Grizzly Hair looked out, then climbed up to ground level. Where were they? He felt more than heard his heart pounding, but couldn't see any *cuero* jackets. His hands were slick with perspiration. That could interfere with good aim. Sweat also stung his eyes and he had to blink constantly. Even in solid shade the heat was intense. His mouth felt like cattail fluff and his throat was so parched it hurt to swallow.

The other men, all shiny with sweat, had climbed out too. They stood in fear-filled postures, blinking. "Where would they go?" Grizzly Hair asked no one in particular.

Lame Beaver whispered, "Back to Sanchez?"

"Where would you go?" Two Falcons asked, so like him.

"To the river. For a drink," Grub Log replied. "In those heavy costumes they must be hotter than we are."

Two Falcons said, "If they did that, we could get behind Sanchez. "I don't think they'd do it."

Talk came from the trench. Grizzly Hair looked down and saw Blue Snake back with a woman. She was poking something into the wounded man's side. He made two sharp yelps, then was silent. What should they do? The right thing would be to circle around to Sanchez, but the enemy could be lying in wait.

Blue Snake climbed out of the trench and said, "I need a drink. Let's go to the river." He added that the man in the trench needed to lie there and rest.

No one argued, though the river lay in the opposite direction. "Be quick about it," Grizzly Hair said, already slashing through the vines. "Then we'll get behind Sanchez."

Driven by thirst they cut rapidly through the interlaced runners and bushes, taking turns in front. When only a few trees stood before the open stretch of river beach, they saw four black hats sprawled on their bellies cupping water over the heads and necks. *Cuero* hats, shields, powder pouches and guns lay beside them.

Grizzly Hair positioned an arrow. Quickly and silently, the noise of

Sanchez' guns covering any sound, they stepped into the open and aimed at the four exposed necks. Grizzly Hair's arrow pinned one *soldado* to the wet sand. The three others were also as good as dead.

No other black hats were in sight. "Float them down the river," Two Falcons said, "or this place will stink." Grizzly Hair cut the arrow out of the man he had shot, washed it and returned it to his quiver. He didn't want the *pantalones* or shirt. Wool felt prickly and everyone knew the boots never fit. Black hats had narrow, misshapen feet. He pushed his dead man out into the stream and as the body floated away, submerged himself. Surfacing, he gulped water, thirstier even than he had realized. The other men were drinking, swimming or stripping the dead and pushing them into the stream. Teased by the current, one naked body seemed to move on its own.

Blue Snake said anxiously, "Somebody's coming."

Grizzly Hair ran from the water, swept up the gun, powder pouch, *cuero* jacket, hat, *casco,* bow and quiver and ran for the trees. Others ran trailing shirts and *pantalones* and shields. A *fusil* exploded, closer and louder than the background popping. No one was hit. As Grizzly Hair entered cover, dropping everything but his bow, he saw the backsides of Two Falcons and Lame Beaver disappearing into the bushes.

Grizzly Hair worked his way to another blind. He aimed at the neck of one of the black hats who was poking in the bushes with his gun. His arrow pierced the neck from the side, lodging up to its feathers, the point thrust out the other side. Teeth clenched and dropping his shield and gun, the black hat grabbed the feathers but made no sound.

Strangely, no more *fusiles* fired, and even in the heart of the village the popping of guns had grown sparse.

Sputtering and moaning, a naked man crawled out of the water a little downriver. The soldier with the arrow in his neck staggered toward him. The four black hats quickly gathered shields and followed, pivoting as they searched. They held shields and knives at the ready, the *fusiles* under their arms.

Afraid and out of amunición, Grizzly Hair knew. Besides, even if they weren't, they couldn't reload holding so many things. "Aiii! Let's get them," Grizzly Hair called, pushing out of the vines. Hesitantly, the others stepped out of hiding. "Give them more bodies to count," Grizzly Hair called, positioning an arrow.

The four uninjured *Españoles* were facing four different directions and moving slowly. They took small steps and held their shields in one hand, knives in the other. The two injured men, one with blood coursing down his wet body, crept along in the center. "Don't leave me," the naked man croaked as he fell on his knees. "Please don't leave me." He had seen Grizzly Hair aiming, and possibly his fellow *soldados* tensing to run.

But they did not run, and Grizzly Hair knew that knives in the hands of such desperate men would be dangerous. They were also calling loudly for help, voices carrying in the increasingly silent forest. They moved the big *cuero* shields skillfully over their faces and legs, and the arrows bounced off. It would only be a matter of time before a lucky crack opened, but Grizzly Hair had only two arrows left and didn't want to waste one. Fully drawn, he waited, and the *Españoles* continued moving in concert and yelling for help.

The gunshots had completely stopped, except for an occasional pop. Into that silence came the rushing footsteps of many men. Grizzly Hair turned. A larger group of black hats were charging down the freshly cut path with shields and guns. Were they loaded? Or were they bluffing, expecting that *Indios* would tremble with fear at the mere sight of them?

Grizzly Hair released his arrow into the thigh of one of the rescuers and melted into the thicket. Gunshots fired back but no bark or leaves flew. Now he had one arrow and the *cuero*-jackets were hurrying their friends toward the plain, the man with the arrow in his leg moving as fast as the rest. The injured men were being carried.

Grizzly Hair released his last arrow, only to see it bounce off a shield. "I'm going to the fort for arrows," he whispered to the others.

"Me too," more than one whispered back.

"I'll follow the black hats," said Two Falcons.

Back at the fort it looked like the soldiers were gone. Everyone was gone. Were both sides stalking the other in the jungle? Grizzly Hair and Lame Beaver and Blue Snake went under the fort wall. As they refilled their quivers, the same smiling woman said, "I think we won."

Figuring she couldn't know, he and the others returned to the outside. He was already thirsty again. It was the hottest time of day, when father sun hung over the western mountains like he would never go to his house. Lame Beaver went toward movement at the bright edge of the shade. Grizzly Hair and Blue Snake followed. Estanislao was there carefully pouring black powder from a soldier's pouch into a *fusil.* He walked out into the open, raised the gun and called loudly, "I was right. You cowards can't shoot straight." He leveled the gun and pulled back, laughing at the blast. He hadn't inserted a ball.

Grizzly Hair stepped into the searing sunlight. Many others did too. The black hats were small dark shapes retreating on horseback, some riding double with the wounded, some in the wagon. They still wore their black woolen clothing, heavy leather jackets and high boots. Maybe they didn't feel heat the way normal people did.

He looked at Estanislao. "Were they out of *munición?*"

"Yes."

"They are running away. Again!"

"Sanchez will report his disgrace," Estanislao cried.

Still disbelieving, Grizzly Hair looked at the crowds of curious people emerging from the shade like rabbits sniffing to see if the fox had gone. Among them was Two Falcons, Red Sun and Morning Owl, all uninjured. Women came from the fort and laughed. Many joined in the laughter, but not Blue Snake. He stood straight-faced in their midst. Recalling the laughter of the enemy when he had run from the battlefield long ago? Now Coyote had turned everything around. One of the Kadeema-umne, the former enemy, was standing here with Poo-soo-ne, whooping and laughing.

Luck had shifted. About to burst with pride, Grizzly Hair shouted at the top of his voice, "We won another victory!"

Others joined in: "We defeated San Francisco Presidio!"

"We defeated the *Españoles* again!"

"They ran away!"

"Let's dance where Sanchez danced!"

Estanislao's voice carried over the melee, "How many dead?"

The shouting and laughter diminished to a hum as people compared stories. Only four *insurgentes* had been killed. People thought there were sixteen or seventeen dead on the other side, including neophytes.

Egorov tapped powder from his pouch into the muzzle of his gun, tamped it down with his special stick and fired it in celebration. Estanislao yelled, "Mission San José runner! Where are you?"

A smiling man came through the crowd.

"Jorge, go to the mission by another route. Don't let the soldiers see you. Make sure Padre Durán hears of our victory from you before he hears it from Sanchez. Be careful, don't let them see you." Turning to the people, he said in a voice for all to hear, "Their disgrace will precede them. Prepare the victory dance. But leave room for me in the river!" With perspiration plastering his hair to his cheeks, he turned and headed for the water,

The entire whooping, yelling mass of people moved with him.

"I'm glad the war is over," a man said to Grizzly Hair.

But something told Grizzly Hair it was not over.

Scowling, Egorov pushed in front of Grizzly Hair and declared in his bad Spanish, "No time for *fiesta*."

"This is a good time," he countered. "They can't return before Sanchez tells his story and fresh soldiers travel here. At least six or seven sleeps." There was plenty of time to dance. And a dance would bring more warriors.

But the soldiers were wary of the snare. A council must be held on how to conduct the next battle.

68

Etumu arrived with the children. She looked pretty in her red skirt and fancy beads, and she wore a twisted headband of the pink roses that were blooming profusely throughout the thicket. Immediately Crying Fox ran to see the boys and men who were using the bodies of dead soldiers for target practice.

Many other women also arrived. Gabriel and his people, including Sick Rat and his woman, came for the big time. Some of them had helped dig the trenches, but not fought. They continued to disagree about how to fight the war. Grizzly Hair told Gabriel in detail what had happened at the last two battles. "Come to the council," he said. "We need to hear how you would fight the *Españoles* next time."

Gabriel seemed to appreciate that. He gave Grizzly Hair a straight-across look, man to man, without insult, and Grizzly Hair knew he was no longer a hill bunny in Gabriel's eyes.

Each day people awoke from sleep and ate their nu-pah, then searched for lead balls. Men chipped them out of the trees and the fort wall. Women and children hunted for them in the leaves and thick debris. Each discovery produced happy yells in the dense forest. Twelve guns and powder pouches had been removed from the dead black hats and every man who claimed one needed ammunition. This next battle would be different, with fourteen gun-bearing *insurgentes,* including Elk Calf who had a gun from María's son-in-law, and Egorov.

Egorov allowed no one else to melt and remake the damaged balls, but people brought fuel for the hot fire. A big stack of it stood beside his clay oven. But after four or five sleeps people grew tired of the search. Most felt that all the balls that could be found had already been located.

A flush of red hit the Russian's cheeks, the parts that could be seen through the dark facial hair. "No. Get these people to keep looking," he said, the Chumash woman translating.

"In the time we have," Grizzly Hair told him, "you could ride to Fort Ross and come back with new balls."

Egorov clenched his fists and sputtered in Spanish. "I cannot go back there and you know it." His face had turned dark red. He barked something and the Chumash woman softly explained, "He says you are not a war leader if you can't make women and children hunt for the balls."

Tired of this quarrelsome man, Grizzly Hair turned to leave.

"This is not enough balls," Egorov yelled after him, slapping the bag of balls he had remade.

"Then fire them only when it counts."

Egorov's face flushed even darker. Muttering in his fierce tongue he stomped away, the embarrassed Chumash woman walking behind. It was puzzling to see a grown man from a powerful people display weakness over things that couldn't be helped. His woman wasn't the only one who was embarrassed. Grizzly Hair was acutely aware that the Russian was here because of him. Egorov's gun had done little good. However, fourteen guns were a different matter.

When Ensign Mariano Guadalupe Vallejo received the letter from his commander, he took it to the room he shared with three other ensigns. As expected they were gone and he read the letter in private. He read it again, this time very slowly.

Ensign Mariano G. Vallejo,
The Indian rebels from Missions San José and Santa Clara have gathered together at the rivers, resolved to die rather than surrender. They are extremely insolent, committing murders and stealing horses, stripping bare the unwary, seducing the other Christians to accompany them in their evil and diabolical schemes, openly insulting our troops and ridiculing them and their weapons. They are relying upon the manpower of the wild Indians, on the terrain and positions which they are occupying (according to the reports which I have received from Ensign Don José Sanchez), and on the losses which we have suffered. In view of the reinforcements consisting of the three units which the military commander at Monterey has supplied me, and since we now can count on a sufficient number of troops plus the two pieces of artillery, you will proceed to these rivers with all the troops under your orders as commander in chief. The second in command will be Ensign Don José Sanchez. The objective will be to administer a total defeat to the Christian rebels and to the wild Indians who are aiding them, leaving them completely crushed. Finally, you and Don José Sanchez will operate in everything according to your best judgment and will retaliate in full for all damage inflicted.

God and the law:
Commandander Ignacio Martinez
May 16, 1829

Domingo's Place on Estanislao's River

Bartolo reported that two presidios would come on the next expedition. Ranchers from as far south as Mission San Carlos on the Carmelo River would fight with the soldiers, and hundreds of loyal mission neophytes would accompany them.

Why did that strike Grizzly Hair like an arrow to the stomach? Maybe the joy of the big time had overwhelmed his good sense and he had begun to hope the black hats would leave this land. Some of the dance doctors had predicted that would happen.

"Don't worry, their cannon doesn't work," someone yelled up at Bartolo, who stood on the dancehouse.

Bartolo looked around at the massed peoples and declared, "They will both work."

Estanislao asked, "When will Vallejo leave Monterey?"

"They are waiting while they repair the cannons. Vallejo won't leave until they work. He and the men of Monterey are also making large amounts of new *amunición.* Much more than Sanchez had. I think they will be here in eight or nine sleeps."

Grizzly Hair asked, "Will all the *soldados* of the two presidios arrive here at the same time?"

"Yes. Sergeant Sanchez is leading the ones from San Francisco but they will meet at Las Positas and the two presidios will come as one."

Estanislao asked, "Has Señor Vallejo fought killing wars before?"

The runner said, "No. He is very young."

People were whispering while Estanislao asked, "Did Sanchez and his men quit because they were out of ammunition?"

"Some say the heat defeated them."

"Did you hear?" people said to each other, "*calor* defeated the black hats." Cackling laughter could be heard sweeping like a wave through the large crowd. Grizzly Hair thought maybe it was true that heat had defeated them. Napoleon had been defeated by cold. Although Grizzly Hair had wished for cooler weather, he now hoped the heat would continue.

Bartolo was saying, "The men in San Francisco Presidio are ashamed we defeated them. They are afraid the Monterey soldiers will call them weak. They are afraid the Monterey soldiers will boast that they are braver and that Sergeant Sanchez was stupid."

Grizzly Hair glanced at Estanislao and saw his thin mustache spread in a ghost of a smile.

Crying Fox leaned into Grizzly Hair's elbow and whispered in a respectful tone, pointing up at the runner, "He knows what black hats say. But they are far away."

"He has friends in the village of the black hats."

The boy's plump unlined face showed intense concentration, as though memorizing each word.

Grizzly Hair raised his voice toward the runner. "Are the ranchers bringing their own horses and ammunition?"

"Yes. They hate the raids on their animals, so they're preparing to kill us all."

Other questions were asked and answered, and Crying Fox listened like a man. When the runner climbed down and the sober crowd was breaking up, the little boy announced to Grizzly Hair, "I will fight the soldiers with my bow."

Grizzly Hair had seen him practicing with his toy weapon. He picked him up and hugged him. "You must stay safe with your mother at the upstream village."

Crying Fox pushed back to lock glances with him. "But I came to help you fight."

Struck by his bravery, Grizzly Hair set him down. His son was worthy of his grandfather's name. He patted his hair, as thick as his life spirit, and said, "We are having council today. You may come and listen if you wish."

Many twenties of people squeezed into the clearing before the fort. Grizzly Hair softened his voice as he spoke to his son. "You might like it better at the river, playing with your friends."

Shaking his head, eyes flashing like stars, Crying Fox arranged his legs before him exactly like Grizzly Hair. His small chest swelled and he looked as sober as Morning Owl.

Speaking first, Estanislao detailed in heavy, ceremonial accents the *Mexicanos'* failures at war, the desertion of mission neophytes, and the joining of ever-more-distant peoples as news of the victories spread. "We were patient for a long time," he said, "but if our enemies spoke truth about giving mission lands to the people and giving us the right to sell the goods we make, they'd have done it by now. Now we will show them we are not *ovejas.*" Sheep.

"Ho!" Grizzly Hair said, rising to join Estanislao at the fort wall. Estanislao nodded for to him to speak.

Words sprang effortlessly from his lips and seemed to touch the quieted people. "The *Españoles* call me a *Christiano,* but I speak to you as a gentile. We gentiles fight to be safe in our villages, to go to the missions if we wish and leave them as we wish, and to trade for goods from the ships. The long robes are like ants. They want us to be their aphids so they can milk our *trabajo.* They make us feed the soldiers who hunt us down and whip us. Are they worthy traders?"

"No!" The roar of the crowd jolted the shady river jungle up to the highest oaks and cottonwoods. It heated Grizzly Hair's stomach. He used Estanislao's trick of looking into every face. He spoke of the indignities of punishment and the many who had died and walked the pathway of ghosts. "We will defeat them again and again, as many times as they come for us," he declared. "Our numbers are growing. As sure as I am standing here, the time will come when they will stop coming for us. They will leave us alone in our villages."

"Ho!" shouted the multitude. Grizzly Hair heard Crying Fox's high-pitched and somewhat late "ho." The boy leaned forward in rapt attention as Grizzly Hair nearly whispered, the intense quiet giving his voice the clarity of a rattler's buzz. "They are reaching farther and farther north. They are fighting on the river of the Muquelumne and Cosumne, and next they will start on the River of the *Americanos.*" He looked at Poo-soo-ne and Libayto and said strongly, "You will be next. Our grandfathers and our fathers were deceived. Many of you were deceived. But no longer!"

A chorus of *si, sí, sí, sí* rose like thunder in the heat. Every person stood and chanted. The unanimity sucked Grizzly Hair like a whirlwind. He felt the power of many. Then, knowing he had talked well, he walked back to where his son was still piping, "*sí, sí, sí, sí.*"

Egorov frowned, standing beside the Chumash woman in her red skirt and strings of Santa Barbara shell money. He walked to the fort wall and Estanislao indicated he should talk.

The woman clarified his impossible Spanish as Egorov orated about the need to find the lost lead balls. Grizzly Hair saw doubtful expressions. Many women and children had badly scratched themselves hunting as far as they could in the brambles. Egorov stamped up and down muttering in his fierce tongue. Then the Russian seemed to find his calm. "You were right to fight the enemy here, in a place you know well." People grunted sounds of agreement and wiped perspiration from their eyes. Grizzly Hair doubted it had ever been hotter this early in the long dry.

The woman translated, "But that was then. Now you must change your method of fighting. You must attack when they least expect it." Spurts of disagreement chopped through the crowd.

Egorov's voice hardened. "They do not expect you to attack, because you never have. Therefore, you have them at a disadvantage. You should ride out and shoot them in camp the night before they arrive here." He searched the doubtful faces. Several elders nodded in agreement and Grizzly Hair signaled that he wished to speak again.

"The Russian is right," Grizzly Hair said in Spanish. "We need a new trick. The soldiers have learned to avoid our arrows. The snare didn't work. Attacking them in camp at night could bring us the final victory. If we don't do that, what other trick will we use?"

Someone shouted, "No! Loose spirits and demons are abroad at night."

Another yelled, "It would bring death."

Domingo came forward in his tattered hat. "I am not afraid of spirits," he declared, "or the stinking soldiers. But we should not listen to a long-nose who comes here with a stolen woman. One whose impatience brought the disaster in Santa Barbara. Andrés rots in the *calabozo* because of him." The Chumash woman translated into Egorov's ear.

Gabriel spoke: "I don't trust him either. I don't think we can ever chase the black hats from this land, like Grizzly Hair thinks we can. The only way to defeat this enemy is to keep stealing their horses and attack them when they invade the valley."

Alarmed, Grizzly Hair realized Gabriel was still arguing against a big cooperative war. Eagerly he looked for and found frowns of disagreement.

"The long-nose's gun shoots crooked," someone said, and Grizzly Hair silently agreed. The Chumash woman did not whisper that into Egorov's ear.

A man of the Chowsila people went to the fort wall wiping the perspiration from his eyes, and faced the crowd. He urged, not a night attack, but a daytime blitz on horseback, a continuing, rotating attack after the soldiers arrived at Domingo's place. "Each of us would be exposed only a short time while galloping full speed. At the same time our men with guns would shoot at the soldiers. With so many attacking from two directions, they wouldn't have time to reload."

A handful of men raised their fists in support. Grizzly Hair had seen their bravery, and wondered if it would work. But he also wondered if riders would be cut off on the plain, facing a hundred guns. Would the *soldados,* all of whom were excellent riders, anticipate such an attack?

Cipriano thought that was too dangerous. "The snare gave us two victories," he pointed out. "Do not change a good thing. Grizzly Hair says we need a new trick. But we have two new tricks. Fourteen guns and a better fort to escape to."

Heads bobbed in agreement but Grizzly Hair saw furrowed brows on many men.

A Joyomi man, wearing only a short, sleeveless jacket of the decorated type ranchers wore over shirts, spoke more forcefully. "When I was in San Juan Bautista Mission, a soldier told of fierce *Indios* called Apaches who live on the other side of the eastern mountains. They attack *soldados* just as our Chowsila friend describes. All the soldiers are afraid of them."

Cipriano rose again. "Since the grandfathers of our ancient neighbors first fought the *soldados*, the only victories have been won in snares laid in plenty of cover. These trenches, these walls," he slapped the fort wall, "and the back-up fort and trenches at Sucais' place, these will defeat the soldiers. This time the black hats will stop coming for us. I know them well. Juan Gustavus is right about that." Grizzly Hair's Spanish name.

Someone yelled, "Ho! The spirits won't let them defeat us."

"Santa María will help," another called.

Morning Owl spoke: "The spirits have shown us that our way of fighting is good. And next time we will have guns. We should not separate into small groups to be cut off and killed. Some of you are good riders, but our enemies ride like dream-horses, part man, part horse. The *Americanos* warned us of splitting into small groups. Our strength is that we fight as one."

Cross-eyed Bear and Little Cos agreed with that.

Estanislao summed up: "More of you want to stay here and fight the way we did before." He waited for many sounds of agreement, many heads bobbing up and down, and was about to continue, but Egorov, who was pacing around, yelled and the Chumash woman said for him, "Juan is right." By this he meant Grizzly Hair. "You should follow your leader. A leader decides and you follow!" His face was as red as a toyon berry.

Once again the quarrelsome Russian was being a poor ally. Most people thought he had egged the Santa Barbara people to defeat. Were the fourteen guns enough of a new trick? Another thought struck Grizzly Hair and he had to say it fast before the council broke up. People were gazing longingly toward the river.

Estanislao nodded for him to speak.

"You are right that we should not change good tricks for bad. Our most important trick was to lure the *soldados* to this place. If needed, we will lure them even farther up the river to Sucais' place, and that is good. But if we are unlucky there, we should be ready to go father upstream. The farther they are pulled from their home place, the weaker they become. The *Americanos* told us that. They will use up their lead balls and will be as easy to attack as a nest of baby turkeys." He looked at Lone Goose, who lived upstream from Sucais in a place with caves in the riverbank. "We need another back-up place."

"There is no time to build a fort at my place," Lone Goose objected.

"Maybe we won't need one. Luring them that far with less ammunition could be enough. We will talk later."

As men and women stood up and stretched, Gabriel seized their attention. "My men and I will fight with you," he said, "but we will do it our own way. When the *soldados* stand in a line and shoot into the trees, we will rush them from behind on horseback. We will trample them before they can reload, and you can fall on them from the front. That will be our new trick." He turned and walked away toward the river.

Yes, Gabriel was right. Whoever had named him Flies-with-Storm knew him. Grizzly Hair felt much better about the coming battle.

Egorov yelled as he rushed into the dispersing crowd, "Find more balls. We need a hundred more." But people continued walking toward the river.

With father sun moving west, colors had softened in the river jungle. In the middle of the crowd, careful not to tread on the heels of a man in front, Grizzly Hair was wondering whether gold could be melted into shooting balls.

It had been easy to pound into a new shape. He dove into the river, lolled in the coolness, then pulled up on shore next to Egorov.

Sitting on the sand, still trembling, Egorov yanked off his boots and rolled up his pantlegs. He put a white misshapen foot into the water and looked at Grizzly Hair with angry eyes. Through the woman, who reminded Grizzly Hair she was only an interpreter, he said, "Your people deserve to lose if they insist on being stupid."

Grizzly Hair said the obvious, "Men do what they want."

"No! Not in war. You are one of the chiefs. Order them to follow you!" He glowered at him, seemingly about to hit him.

Grizzly Hair forced himself to remain calm. "It does no good to tell men to attack, and expect them to attack, only to learn in a dangerous situation they won't do it. It is better to know what men will do before the battle." He added, "Each man decides, then all agree."

Egorov jumped up and shouted in his face. Grizzly Hair wiped off the spit as the woman explained. "He says if the men of Russia and Europe acted like that, they would lose every war."

Not about to argue with him, Grizzly Hair started toward the supper fires where most people were heading, then, remembering his question, he turned to look back. "Can shooting balls be made of other kinds of metal?"

Swallows darted over the water, but Egorov stood like a pillar of stone.

Grizzly Hair repeated his question. The woman talked with Egorov, apologized and said, "He says he is too furious to talk."

Grizzly Hair covered a laugh. *The man openly admits this.* "Tell him there are metal nuggets in my home place that might be melted for balls. Yellow metal."

As the woman relayed this message, Egorov's brown eyes widened. He found his voice and it was surprisingly level. "He wants to know if the metal is gold," the Chumash woman said.

"*Si, oro*, gold."

Egorov spoke rapidly, his voice cracking like a boy's, the woman translating unnecessarily, "Where is this gold?"

"In my *ranchería*. My wife knows where." She had found a big pile of it somewhere beside the river. He suspected his mother had dumped it there before her death.

The river was beginning to reflect the gold of father sun. Some of the red in Egorov's face had softened. Through the woman he said, "Yes. We can make good balls of the gold. You must get your wife. I'll take her to get the gold tonight." The Chumash woman's expression had changed. Egorov stared at her with round eyes, displaying some kind of new emotion.

Puzzled, Grizzly Hair thought maybe Egorov overestimated the amount of gold. "We don't have much," he said. "Maybe it's not worth traveling so far."

"How much?"

"My wife knows. Maybe a basket this big." He circled his hands before him as if holding Howchia's cooking basket.

Egorov asked, "Is there more where that came from?"

"Yes, along the river, but it would take too long to find."

Egorov insisted on taking Etumu and leaving Grizzly Hair behind, but Grizzly Hair had little trust in this volatile man. "My wife and I will get the gold," he told the Russian. "We'll leave after this sleep."

"Take me there!" Egorov demanded.

Grizzly Hair didn't want to take the quarrelsome man on a long trip. Besides, he wished to be alone with Etumu, to convince her to stay at home during the coming battle. It was likely to be far worse than the last. Calmly he said, "If you insist on going, my wife and I will stay here and we will have no golden balls." Salivating, he turned toward the aroma of roasting cow.

Voices behind him rattled back and forth, then the woman called, "Egorov will wait for your return."

69

Grizzly Hair loaded the gold into his old otter-skin quiver. He wrapped it tightly with a thong and started tying it on Morena's rump. It seemed a long trip for so little metal, but shooting balls were precious and time was scarce. Soon the soldiers would start their journey from Monterey and he must hurry back to Domingo's encampment in time to help Egorov make the new ammunition.

Etumu came out of her parent's u-macha in her red skirt and a string of beads and shell money. She also had the baby's bikoos on her back. "I'll ride back with you," she said reviving the argument.

"No. I must get there in two sleeps or less. It would be too hard a ride for you and the baby. Besides your mother wants you to stay." Bracing for her unhappiness, he tied the knot over the otter-skin bag, which held the gold.

Her eyes glinted. "You tricked me into coming home, to stop me from being with you."

The harshness stopped him. He could say nothing, for he had indeed hoped she would stay. Crying Fox, who had not accompanied them home, would be cared for by Straight Willow at the village of the Tagualumne, upriver from Domingo's place.

"Maybe you like other women better."

He dropped the tail of the *riata* and laid his hand on her shoulder, gentling his voice. "If I didn't care about you, I'd ask you to fight beside me. But I want to bask with you when the fighting is over. I want you to live." He hoped his mention of Lizard would remind her of all the good times together.

Her head dropped. When she raised it, tears welled from under the pretty padded lids and her tattooed chin trembled. "Your spirit is there, where the war is. That is why I must be there too." She held out her palms. "Let these hands help your hands, so that we are man and woman together. Otherwise I am already dead."

They arrived at Domingo's place after hard riding, Etumu and the baby bouncing awkwardly before him. He was relieved to see the completion of the new trench. It lay in front of the area where the line of *soldados* had stood shooting.

Surprisingly, Egorov was waiting at the brush corral as though he'd been there the entire time. He nearly tore the heavy bag from Grizzly Hair's hands. As Etumu disappeared toward the village center, no doubt anxious to get away from the unvoiced tension of the long journey, he followed Egorov to a place with grapevines hanging all around, saw him plunge his arm into the bag and come up with a handful of nuggets. He bit into one, rubbed his thumb across it, and stood staring at nothing. The Chumash woman, who followed him everywhere, stood nearby. Puffy-eyed and subdued, she had large purple bruises on her cheek and neck.

Grizzly Hair said to her, "Tell him we must make the balls quickly." It would be impolite to ask, but he wondered what had happened to her.

Through her Egorov said, "I will do it tonight and I don't want any help." He left, walking swiftly on a narrow path in the direction of his oven. He stopped, scowled at the woman, hooked an arm, and she trotted after him.

"The black hats will come soon," Grizzly Hair called after them, perplexed that he didn't want help.

Egorov never slowed and the Chumash woman never turned to flash him a commiserating expression, as he had come to expect. Wherever Egorov went, she went. It was unnatural.

The next morning a scout reported that the soldiers were crossing the San Joaquin River. "They are setting up camp there, so they'll probably come at dawn."

Domingo announced the Wok-ke-lah and made the rounds telling people to eat plenty, for they might not eat again. Grizzly Hair felt something in the air, different than before the previous battles. The children were noisier, though fewer of them were present. Something quivered on the edge of bursting. He learned that the rotting bodies of two *Españoles* killed in the last battle had been hung in an oak on the trail where the black hats would pass. The tree was now blazing and smoking—a message to them.

Straight Willow came from the bathing place with a daughter in each hand. "I'm going now." To Crying Fox she said, "Come along."

His chin quivered and he beseeched Grizzly Hair with tearful eyes. Gently he said, "You must go," and swallowed a lump while watching his son's square little back as he walked with Straight Willow and her children.

He looked at Etumu. Instead of going with Straight Willow she pushed the stake of the bikoos into the ground. He went to her, put a hand on her shoulder and looked at another group of women and children who were leaving. "You should go now to the Tagualumne village."

She frowned and said, "Those women should dance tonight to make their men's spirits strong."

"The men might feel stronger knowing they are gone."

She gave him a disgusted look, watched the woman with the baby named Amerikano pass by, then declared, "I'll go at first light."

Something melted in him. He was tired of disagreement. He wanted peace on this last night before the big battle, and if she left early enough it would be safe.

Egorov passed by, alone for the first time.

Supper was quiet. Subdued talk hummed around the clearing before the fort. More than twenty supper fires burned. On the west side of the clearing Grizzly Hair ate with Etumu, Lame Beaver, Two Falcons, Morning Owl, Raven Feather, Red Sun, Cross-eyed Bear and Running Quail. In the twilight under the high canopy he felt the existence of each thing, each person, each tree with unusual clarity. A brush rabbit peeked from the undergrowth. He found himself looking at it, and the different shades of green melting into shadow. Perhaps the lack of sleep the last several nights affected him, or fear was showing him what he might never see again.

Etumu nursed the baby in one arm and delicately nibbled the jawbone of a fish with her other hand. Her smallness and the padded eyelids seemed tender to him now. He moved closer and put a hand on her thigh.

She shot him a sidelong glance and continued eating. The still evening air was warm with the aromas of meat, fowl and bulbs and grains. A cock quail cried *kikágo, kikágo*, the *o* fading along with the light. Tree frogs beeped and their big brothers in the backwaters began to bellow.

Cross-eyed Bear wiped an arm across his mouth and said to Grizzly Hair, "I have a message from Salmon Woman. Remember her?" His mischievous look was intended to tell Grizzly Hair, once again, that he had known about them. "It is about the man who fell down the hollow redwood. She said you shouldn't worry too much about the truth of stories." He shrugged in his gap-toothed way as if to say he had no idea what that meant, but he'd made good on his promise to a strong woman. He flicked a seed cracker into his mouth and crunched.

Etumu, who had never heard of Salmon Woman, looked at Grizzly Hair like he was a stranger. He thought back to the story of the starving white man who had eaten a frog. The frightened rescuer had climbed the redwood and fallen to his death. Grizzly Hair had told Salmon Woman that no one would have been left to tell the story. How, he had asked her, did they know it happened? She said back, "It doesn't matter." Now he wondered if anyone would be left to tell the story of this war. Did it matter?

The baby girl looked at him and a slow toothless grin spread over her tiny features, the nipple lying slyly on her tongue in a mouthful of milk that ran down her chin. She held the other nipple between her small thumb and fingers, released it, held it, released it, demonstrating that though she was full now, the milk would be in its place the next time she wanted it. Would it?

Etumu straightened, plunked the baby on Grizzly Hair's lap and brushed dirt off her own backside. "It's getting dark," she told him. "I'm going to get cattail fluff for the bikoos." Her expression said she disliked hearing a message from a woman he had known on his travels. Did she care that he had coupled with her? With other women? Is that why she insisted on being here tonight?

The baby laughed at him. She was chubby and strong, and he could feel her trying to balance herself on his knees. Her thatch of black hair stuck up like a surprised bird, and her sparkling eyes, so like Etumu's, made him smile. She was always wakeful and happy in the early evenings. Would there be more evenings for her, for him?"

He raised a finger for her to grasp and felt grateful for her company. A horse neighed. Cross-eyed Bear glanced that way. When war was imminent, Grizzly Hair knew, even the trill of a redwing could startle a man. No doubt it was one of Gabriel's horses being brought into the special corral in the heart of the jungle.

The fires threw winking light on the dark faces. Crickets and other night animals sang. On the other side of the shadowy clearing, men began to sing haunting mission music, and it made him think of Bowstring. Morning Owl was down on one knee holding the Bible before him exactly as Jed Smith had held it. A chill came up from the ground though the air was generally warm. It was getting darker. Grizzly Hair looked around, expecting Etumu. The baby grew restless too, so he walked her to Poo-soo-ne's fire and visited.

Then he realized something had happened to Etumu.

70

The Vallejo Expedition, First Battle

The fires of the Wo-ke-leh leapt on the plain but Grizzly Hair raced from fire to fire and to each of the sleeping enclaves asking whether anyone had seen Etumu. He accidentally scraped the baby's face on a thorny tendril. She screamed and howled and wouldn't stop though he patted her. It seemed she cried for Etumu. The people all shook their heads and shrugged. They didn't know her.

She wasn't in the tulares. She was nowhere.

"She'll come back," men said. "Don't worry."

"The big woman in charge of the supply runners frowned. "Does she often walk alone at night?"

"Never."

Another food woman remarked, "But she went to the cattails when it was almost dark. A ghost could have taken her."

He had never feared the spirits much. Maybe they stole Etumu to teach him a lesson. No, he thought, I will find her. If only I could see her tracks!

He went downstream to Egorov's oven and quickly saw that no one was there. Back at the dances and the conflicting heartbeats of the log drums, he continued to ask questions but received no answers. He needed to dance away his jitters and dream before the big battle, but instead trotted in circles covering the same ground. Surely Etumu wouldn't hide, or deliberately cause him this anguish on this important night. He kept seeing her expression when Cross-eyed Bear mentioned Salmon Woman. No, she wouldn't do that, even though she was still upset with him. Would someone want to hurt her? The crickets didn't answer, nor did anyone else.

Estanislao patted him on the shoulder asking, "Is anyone else missing?"

"How would I know in this tangle of people?" Then he began to understand Estanislao's look. He thought she had gone with another man. That's what women did. Simply left. He had been gone too often to know whether she looked at other men.

The distant dancefire lit the long tired lines of Estanislao's face. "Sleep," he said, "and maybe she'll be there in the morning. Or maybe your dream will tell you where she is."

Stomach tight, head throbbing, Grizzly Hair stumbled into the willow shelter they shared with Lame Beaver and Running Quail and laid the drowsy baby beside him. He lay as rigid as the bikoos, a stick man staring into the dark, hands at his sides. When he closed his eyes, fantastic colors and shapes came swelling and exploding at him. Too exhausted for that, he opened them and recalled the edge in Etumu's voice. But, no. She wouldn't do this. She wouldn't leave the baby.

Some time later he heard excited voices. Suddenly hopeful, he crawled out. The guttural speech of the men from the southern San Joaquin River led him through the dark. "Something's happening over there," one of them explained. All avoided the trenches as he did, from deep knowledge of their locations. When they got to the open plain, Gabriel and Sick Rat and other men were there.

"What happened?"

"They captured our horses," Gabriel said. "We were herding them to the corral in there."

"Every last one?" somebody asked in a low tone.

"Every last one."

Another bad omen. Somebody muttered. "Maybe the black hats are still around here.

"No," Sick Rat said. "They came in fast on horseback and herded them out fast. We were off our horses opening the corral."

"That's right," Gabriel added. "I'm sure we surprised those *hombres.* I think the *expedición* had just camped downstream. Probably sent that bunch up to scout the place and got lucky. Herded them down there, west of here."

Somebody asked the question on Grizzly Hair's mind. "Are you going to get the horses back tonight?"

Gabriel hurrumphed and said, "They'll have guards watching all night. You want to go down there?"

No one answered. "Maybe they stole my wife," Grizzly Hair said. Again he explained that she had disappeared at suppertime. Then he remembered the way Gabriel had looked at Oak Gall and talked about buying women. Could he have taken Etumu?

"No," Gabriel was saying, "I heard about that. But I'm certain they traveled after dark and got to their camp just a little while ago." His voice had a tone of resignation. "They just got lucky. Now they'll be waiting for us to come after the horses, like a hive of stirred-up hornets." It rang true. Gabriel was too preoccupied to steal a woman. But what about Sick Rat? Maybe he wanted revenge for his father's attentions to Grizzly Hair.

No, No. His thoughts had warped from anguish and lack of sleep. Neither of them could keep her hidden and quiet. The horse disaster was bad enough without accusing his fellow warriors of stealing his wife. Now there would be no horseback attack from the rear. "Will you still fight with us?" he asked them.

"Oh yes," Gabriel said without thinking. "We're in this just like you are." He snorted. "But we sure could have done a lot of damage on horseback." Low grunts of agreement came from all sides.

"My horse is up at the Tagualumne village." Grizzly Hair said. "I don't know how many more are there. Maybe you can go get them. Use my horse."

"I already took your horse."

That shocked him. "You didn't tell me."

"I tried but you were running around. I was going to ask you to ride with me in the morning."

Morena was gone. In the dark only fleeting impressions of the men could be seen—placid, accepting fate. Bad luck upon bad luck. They could all die when father sun rose again. All that mattered now was fighting well with what was left. He retraced his steps through the river jungle. Even the crickets had gone silent. Etumu might be on the mat, ready to explain herself. With rising hope he crawled in, knelt, ran his hands lightly over the bikoos and around to where Running Quail and Lame Beaver lay sleeping. She wasn't there. His temples pulsed painfully. He lay down with his eyes open wider than ever. Maybe, he thought, if I can find my calm I could spirit-track her. He put a hand on the bikoos that she had woven with her deft hands, and tried.

The next thing he knew he was hunting with Two Falcons in a foggy place. With every step the mist thickened. They bent forward, examining the ground for tracks. Grizzly Hair saw little. Which way should they go? All was cushiony, white, eerie. "I'll go find sign," he said. But as he left his mentor, father sun became ever more hidden in the fog and Grizzly Hair became chilled and disoriented. He looked around, but saw no landmark. He took a step and the fog stirred around his foot. Nothing else lay underneath! His heart jumped to his throat. The earth was gone! In panic, he turned back, but terror stopped him. It seemed he would fall to his death if he moved. Even in dream he knew he had dreamt this before and wondered what it meant, but that didn't help. "Two Falcons," he called, but the fog swallowed the sound. He was alone. His ears hurt from listening to nothing. Then something large and dark took shape. Stepping toward it, miraculously not falling, he felt warmth, then saw O-se-mai-ti standing before him in her strength. Like a tearful child he reached for her and cried out with joy.

May 30, 1829

His own cry awakened him. Etumu was absent. Fear skittered across his scalp, just as in the dream. The gray, eerie light was the same too. Soon the baby would cry for milk and the *Españoles* would start shooting. He glanced at the place where the iron hat was supposed to be. It was gone. Omen upon omen, all bad. What had the bear meant to tell him? He felt certain she had a message, but he hadn't been calm enough to hear her, and when people didn't listen to spirit messengers, terrible luck would surely follow.

He left Lame Beaver and Two Falcons, who were beginning to rise, and stepped away to relieve himself. His throat was dry and sore from talking to so many people. He needed a drink, needed father sun's strength, needed calm, for he must inspire others to be brave. But first he ran to the stand of cattails and immediately saw, among the many tracks, Etumu's small even-toed prints leading through the mud to the water. He couldn't find her tracks coming back. Many other people had made tracks here too, and a horse had gone by. Egorov had removed his boots and waded in, apparently bathing at long last. But where had she come to shore? He searched the waterline to no avail. Grinding his teeth at the lack of time to cross the river and track her on the other side, he ran to where the big arrow-supply woman slept. At his touch her eyes flew open.

She waddled after him to the brush shelter and picked up the baby. The bikoos dripped with sweet-smelling urine. He had forgotten to replace the fluff. "Don't worry any more," the woman said. "I'll take care of her."

In a rush of gratitude for this near stranger, he hugged the big soft woman as he would have hugged O-se-mai-ti in his dream. Between them the surprised baby opened her eyes.

Bits of talk came from people around them: "Across the river. . ."

"Horses. . . downstream."

". . . surround us first."

Lame Beaver and Two Falcons were gone, other men putting on bows and quivers. "Go," he said urgently to the woman. "Take her to the Tagualumne." He saw doubt, then assent in her eyes, and she waddled up the path as fast as her bulk would move.

Suddenly craving violent action, he picked up his gun, powder, bow and quiver and hurried to the vantage place where he could see the shallow ford. A long line of *cuero*-clad *soldados* were wading across, guns and shields overhead. All beyond gun range. Looking for the front of the line, he saw that it was circling Domingo's place with the steady determination of ants. Farther downstream a tule boat was being guided across by many men. The cannon? Ammunition? It was then he realized he had no balls for his gun.

In frustration he yelled louder than he thought he could. "You *soldados* can't even piss straight."

Nearby, men stirred in their hiding places and he saw several grins. From a nearby tree crotch, Estanislao raised a fist and called just as loudly, "*Muchachos*, did you see our *bienvenido* on the trail?" Our welcome.

Grizzly Hair showed his gun and asked Estanislao, "Do you have some extra *amunición?*" He'd been too upset before the sleep to remember that Egorov was supposed to give him most of the golden balls.

"I don't have enough for my own gun." Estanislao lifted a big leather pouch hanging from his neck.

Gabriel ran past and kept running outside the protective cover. He stopped, quickly fanned his behind to the *soldados* and yelled, "You can't even fart straight." A *fusil* popped. Laughing the whole way, he ran back to the underbrush.

Good for Gabriel. "I need *amunición,*" Grizzly Hair said to everyone nearby. "Egorov," he called softly, "where are you?"

The Russian didn't show himself. He had loudly insisted on more than his share of the lead balls, arguing his greater shooting experience, so even if he'd heard Grizzly Hair, he might not have responded. Every man with a gun had wanted more balls than he was given. Sadly, there weren't even any pebbles in Domingo's place, even at the river—only sand and mud.

Nor was there a plan, now that Gabriel's horses had been captured. Originally the men with guns were to hide in the first brush and surprise the soldiers when they approached in a shooting line, firing before they did. The balls would have penetrated the *cuero*. While the survivors reloaded, Gabriel's horsemen would have attacked from behind, and arrows and knives from the front would have finished them.

Now, the *Indios* were spreading throughout the jungle. Some were calling insults and taunts to lure the black hats to the interior. Sanchez was visible in his red shoulder patches, but either Vallejo had gone around to the other side or he was the one with a large brownish feather in his hat standing beyond the line of men where he could watch the cannon being unloaded from the boat. A knot of *cuero*-jackets reattached the cannon to its big wheels and began pulling it toward the river jungle. Behind them came a long line of neophytes with boxes on their heads—all out of range. Closer by, he noticed neophytes carrying dry brush.

Did they intend to set a fire? The deadfall was dry, but he doubted this much young foliage would burn. Unless, after the extreme heat of the last moon—maybe. He hoped Etumu wasn't—No. He must stop thinking about her. He had a war to fight.

Gunfire blasted from the *Indio* side. Neophytes dropped their brush and ran. He realized he could scare them even without balls. Recalling the *Español* whose gun had exploded in his face, he tapped a limited amount of black powder into the gun. Then he worked his way closer to the fire-starters and pulled the trigger. The gun spoke loudly and more neophytes ran. The black hats called them back against their will.

He positioned an arrow and aimed for the nearest black hat, one of those searching the trees with their eyes but not seeing him. The target was narrower than ever. Standing collars had been added to the *cuero* jackets. He let fly. The man moved and the arrow missed the ear and bounced off the collar. Instantly a gun barked and he dove behind the tree under the whine of a speeding ball. A hail of missiles discharged from both sides.

The black hats tamped and fired into the trees by methodical, protected turns. This went on for a long time. Grizzly Hair couldn't show himself long enough to take aim, though he fired his useless gun a few times. Frightened nestlings rained from their nests, slipping from branch to branch until they gained purchase or fell all the way to the ground.

Where was Egorov and his golden ammunition? Why hadn't Grizzly Hair come across him while looking for Etumu? With sudden clarity he recalled a horse whinnying just after she went for cattail fluff. There had been fresh hoofprints nearby. Egorov had not been at his oven melting gold. It had looked cold. Other things flashed back: Egorov's insistence on riding with Etumu to get the gold, the terrible bruises on the Chumash woman, and Egorov being alone before the sleep. What did it all mean? A foggy trail seemed to be emerging in Grizzly Hair's mind.

Estanislao yelled, "*Loco cholos!* We know you can't shoot straight."

Grizzly Hair fired again. The fire-starters ran a little but returned. The ominous-looking cannon was pulled up to the edge of the thick foliage. Boxes were set down and opened. Powder was stuffed up the cannon's snout with a long-handled tool. He fired his gun again, but though the neophytes looked nervous, none ran. There were too many black hats protecting the cannon handlers. In the thin trees he couldn't get close enough to use his bow.

The ha-boom of the cannon punched his lungs and made the ground jump. The crack and snap of trees breaking told him the cannon worked. Panicked men flushed from their hiding places pushed wildly but too slowly into the thicket. They made easy targets for the guns of the black hats. Elk Calf's Chilumne uncle-in-law flew through the air and landed near Grizzly Hair with blood spurting from his back.

White gunsmoke hung like fog in the air. Watching for an opportunity, Grizzly Hair maintained his hiding place. For a while the cannon handlers fired their *fusiles*, but they laid them down and, covered by their companions, began to put things in the cannon again.

Another boom from the big gun knocked the tree into his head. Sharp pain and engulfing blackness made him reel. There had been a loud crack. As sight returned, he saw that he was barely hidden beneath the tree, which had broken like a knee over him. He ran with the others flushed from hiding and desperately struggled to penetrate the brush as the *cuero*-jackets calmly and regularly fired.

Heart jumping in his ears, he crawled through intertwined vines and thorny canes, dragging the long gun. It snagged repeatedly, as did the bow over his chest and his quiver. As he extricated them, he expected a ball in his back, and each bang of the nonstop guns made his limbs buzz with fear. The next cannonball could pulverize him. Where was his power?

Estanislao's voice came from the direction of the fort: "Monterey boys! You are no different than the San Francisco cowards. We will laugh at your rumps running away." Would they?

Through the acrid gunsmoke he detected ordinary smoke. He looked up and saw dark wings of it floating through the green understory. He listened for the crackle of fire, but near and far heard only the constant reports of guns. However in the distance he heard a cry: "Fire!" In the other direction another cry: "Fire." More bad luck.

Escaping the guns and cannon, he made his way toward the southern side of Domingo's place to see if he could do anything useful there. The black hats had surrounded Domingo's entire place. Here in the southern side, *Indios* were shooting at them with guns and there was no cannon. Diving into the brush near a patch of brown skin, he asked, "Did you kill any?"

Surprisingly it was Two Falcons who answered. "I think I got one, but just about got my head blown off." His face did seem blacker and his buckskin pouch looked empty of ammunition. "Morning Owl's over there." He pointed with his head.

"I need ammunition," Grizzly Hair said. "I've been firing the gun to scare them."

"I think most of us are out of balls. Watch out!" A ball zinged through the wall of roses.

Grizzly Hair worked his way steadily to a place where he could see better. Like the *cuero*-jackets from the first battle, these stood just inside the brush line firing methodically. When they ran out of ammunition they went back to where the neophytes held boxes of balls. They reloaded their pouches and guns and returned to shoot again. Estanislao yelled another insult. Grizzly Hair realized that while he and others were holding the soldiers at bay out here, Estanislao had been trying to lure them inside where they could be surrounded. That would be much better than trying to get off an occasional arrow from the perimeter.

He returned to Two Falcons and beckoned Morning Owl over. "Let's go back there and try to lure them in."

"But they're trying to start fires. We were trying to stop them," Morning Owl said.

Did Estanislao know they were starting fires? Then, about eight guns came swinging through the brush. Grizzly Hair, who was already hidden from that direction loaded an arrow, stilled himself and let the enemy pass by. More appeared, dressed like rancheros.

Two Falcons and Morning Owl and the other men in the bushes waited patiently, letting them pass.

Carefully, Grizzly Hair stood up, aimed at the last invader and released his arrow into the shirt that was unprotected. The enemy fell without a cry. His unsuspecting companions, one with flashes of red showing on his shoulders, crept forward until more arrows flew and a soldier yelped. Two Falcons had driven an arrow through the cheeks of a surprised soldier, pinning his mouth open. The other *soldados* whirled and fired into the brush and vines, reloading in turns.

A ball dislodged a flurry of dirt into Grizzly Hair's eyes. Shoot through the leaves, he told himself, the way Gabriel's men practiced shooting at unseen targets. As a hidden soldier reloaded, Grizzly Hair stood erect and let fly into a fall of grapevines. Two musket balls nearly hit him before he thumped back to the ground, but he heard a cry behind the vines.

He motioned the others to keep shooting into the leafy curtain while he circled behind the black hats. The sounds of his movement were covered by guns, yells, cannon booming and, yes, the snapping roar of a big fire. With smoke catching in his throat he drew his bow at the legs of *soldados* not more than two man-lengths away. A ball sang past his head from the other direction and he dove to the earth. More *soldados* had come to prevent the first group from being surrounded!

Balls whizzed over his head and thunked into trees. Arrows and balls flew back and forth for a long time. His ears rang from the noise. There were too many black hats here now. More *Indios* had come to help, but none with a working gun. Then the ha-boom of a cannon compressed his chest.

"To the trench," he called, weaving back and forth as he ran a twisting course through the thicket. With enormous relief he jumped in. From the opposite direction Grub Log thumped in alongside him, grimacing, holding a bloody leg. Two Falcons and Morning Owl were already there, Morning Owl with the Bible strapped to his chest.

"You need medicine," Grizzly Hair said to Grub Log, who painfully started crawling on hands and one foot. It looked like his kneecap was missing.

Two Falcons called after him, "Tell them we need more men here."

Morning Owl said to Grizzly Hair. "Better we carry him. You take his shoulders." He slung the bow over his shoulders and picked up Grub Log's good leg.

They carried him until they came to a supply woman who was coming the other way with a huge armload of arrows. They stopped to fill their quivers then continued up the trench. The smoke thickened, bad smoke that clogged a man's throat.

"Look out!" Morning Owl dropped Grub Log's leg, whipped his bow around and positioned an arrow.

Quickly laying Grub Log down, Grizzly Hair saw the black hat standing over him at the side of the trench, aiming. He sprang forward as the ear-shattering gun discharged, then pulled and released an arrow into the fog of the smoke. With a cry, the black hat fell grabbing the arrow, which had driven into his groin under the *cuero* jacket. He scuttled away sidewise. Grizzly Hair looked back. Morning Owl lay sprawled against the trench wall. His surprised eyes were wide and fixed. Brain matter ran out of a hole in his caved-in forehead.

"More coming," Grub Log whispered excitedly, up on one leg, peering out of the trench. He still had his bow, and was readying an arrow.

Pulling an arrow, Grizzly Hair joined him. Three soldiers were coming. Both released. The arrows hit the *cuero* and fell away. The soldiers grabbed their scuttling friend and quickly carried him back through the smoking foliage, which suddenly burst into flame.

Grizzly Hair sank down beside Morning Owl, disbelieving, unconsciously pushing his headman's shoulders to make him live. But his head was ruined. The Bible hadn't protected him.

Awareness of the gunfire and yelling and the roar of the fire dropped away. The white smoke became the fog of his dream. He was alone, beyond the world. The hy-apo's soul was leaving the body and Grizzly Hair sang it on its way to the pathway of ghosts.

Finishing his song he saw that Grub Log had painfully moved himself up the trench. Grizzly Hair took the wrists and dragged Morning Owl's body after Grub Log. A vision of long ago came back—Morning Owl smiling as he stood at the side of the dance circle while Grub Log and Grizzly Hair, champions of the ti-kel game, enjoyed the attentions of many women. Half the sky had been blue, the other half black with double arches of coyote pee blazing colorfully before it. In that magical moment he hadn't imagined he would drag Morning Owl's dead body out of a hot place smelling of sulfur where death lay on every side and a man couldn't tell whether his side was winning or losing.

Many people were inside the fort. He pulled Morning Owl to one wall. A women came and scowled. "Take him out. He is dead." He almost objected, but pulled the hy-apo's body back outside and laid him beside the wall, covering him lightly with loose earth from the trench, Bible and all, so people wouldn't be disturbed. Back inside, he saw Grub Log being treated by the medicine women. He climbed the deadfall piled along the inside of the wall and joined a row of men standing on top with bows in hand, looking out, ready to defend the heart of Domingo's place. From there he could see dark smoke boiling from several places around the perimeter. It wheeled skyward, and bright fire crackled in the interstices.

"Let's get out of here," one of the men said.

"Yes," said another. "The other fort is better."

"First," Grizzly Hair said pointing, "Sanchez is over there with about twelve *soldados* and some ranchers. Let's show them what we think of them." For killing Morning Owl, he added in his mind.

They hurried with him back up the trench, but where the black hats had been, an orange wall of fire blazed. Two Falcons and about ten other men approached in the trench. "They're gone," Two Falcons reported in a yell to be heard over the fire.

"I think we should swim out of here now." Another man said, "There's no enemy left to fight here."

Everyone could see that the new enemy, heat and smoke, would soon overcome them.

"Spread the word," Grizzly Hair said to everyone. "I'm going to Sucais' place."

The perspiring men turned as one and headed back the other way, Grizzly Hair in the middle, men jumping in the trench to join them. They continued on toward the river, but he stopped for Morning Owl. He dragged him by the shoulders, letting others pass. Ahead, men were throwing off the brush cover, which was dry and catching fire from sparks. Chased by the fires, men were feeding into the two trenches that led to the water. Was it almost night? He couldn't tell. This was a naturally dark and shady place, but the smoke further dimmed the light, and it became difficult to breathe, to draw enough air.

A logjam of people stopped the flow. Somebody shouted over the snapping and roaring—big trees having caught fire—"They are shooting people in the river. They're shooting from the other bank. Pass the word. Swim underwater." Condor's dream had taken a new turn. The *soldados* were killing everyone and trying to make the rest burn to death. They were not capturing people for the missions.

Estanislao's voice came from behind. "Swim out after dark."

Grizzly Hair coughed and strained to breathe. He needed two lungsful for each breath. This was more than smoke, it was the absence of air. The fire was stealing the air. He looked up and down the trench. Men and a few women were packed together both ways, all coughing. Then Raven Feather was suddenly pushing through, staring at her husband with eyes so full of shock and horror that Grizzly Hair could hardly say, "I will make sure he is returned to the home place."

She climbed out of the trench before he could stop her and walked into the fire. The trench protected people from the fire. He thought of going after her, but knew he wouldn't be able to breathe, wouldn't get the hy-apo back to the home place, wouldn't find his wife and children. Raven Feather was going where her spirits told her.

He put his face near the dirt, sucking air that came from earth mother. Morning Owl would never see father sun again. Tears stung Grizzly Hair's eyes for the man whose body he protected, the man who had called himself a peace chief, and had proudly worn his leather shirt and strings of shell money, the man who said all that a man needed to learn could be learned at home, the man who would have stayed there bringing consensus to the umne if Grizzly Hair had not talked him into this. He moaned aloud. The fort, which had been so hard to build, and the hills of arrows inside it, meticulously made and delivered by so many—arrows that would have lasted a long time—would now burn. The people would burn. The trench started to spin, and he drifted to the bottom of darkness.

"You didn't help him," I say.

"What could I do?" O-se-mai-ti asks.

"Give him courage."

"He already had courage. They all had courage."

"But he lost his calm and could not hear his allies. He was surrounded by frightened people who had been surprised by the fire and stunned by the cannon. They could not see the whole war from where they were inside that fire. He needed help."

With a deeply troubled expression, the bear sits looking over the river. "Strength and bravery were not enough," she says.

Coyote, who is still here, says, "That's why you're extinct in California." But he adds in all humility, "I am not particularly brave. I would have run from that war."

Bear speaks in a mournful tone: "The *Españoles* were like bear hunters, men who spent their lives devising tricks to confuse me. When they were called to a village, they would hold council and pick about ten men. In the middle of a fight, if I caught on to their trick, they would change tricks. They got their cunning from you, Coyote." She hangs her head. "The *insurgentes* fought like bears."

"But they won," Coyote says, enlivened by this conversation. He rises, shakes dirt and hair off his coat and sits on his haunches looking at the bear with a pointed expression. "Things happened that no one expected. In war you never know what will happen."

In the decaying leaves and debris Ant is waving her front legs and feelers. To stand taller she props herself on her four hind legs and the point of her smooth abdomen. Her people climb my trunk to milk the scale on my twigs and they burrow out enormous underground houses that aerate and fertilize the earth around my roots. Coyote and Bear point their snouts down at Ant, their ears forward.

"The new people are allied with me," Ant squeaks. "Their warriors do what they are told and never stop until their leader tells them. They don't need to worry about what's happening where they can't see. They are a big body made of separate little parts."

Bear growls. "Strength and courage would have been enough, except for the cannon and *fusiles*."

"The time of the bear is over," Coyote remarks without a trace of sentiment.

I feel sorry for this ally of my son, and realize that I made a thoughtless remark a little while ago. Of course she was doing her best to help him. The bravery of my great shaggy spirit-friend should not be forgotten. To protect her cubs she drove off male grizzlies twice her weight, and they were loathe to get near her cubs again. "My son was lucky to have you," I tell O-se-mai-ti.

The calm returns to her voice. "Watch. I did something neither of you could do, and it helped a great deal."

When Grizzly Hair's spirit returned, Estanislao was yelling over the roar of the fire, working his way past others and approaching Grizzly Hair. "We killed a lot of them."

Yes, but most had been left standing and the fire blazed with increasing fury. The *Indios* had lost the ground. That could be seen as defeat. He thought about Etumu, and that also felt like defeat. Had she left him? For her sake he was glad if she had gone, but she might well be somewhere in the fire. He tried to make his throat swallow. It was too dry.

Estanislao pushed his way to Grizzly Hair and talked into his ear to be heard over the roar. "You and Egorov were right about attacking. We should circle back tonight and kill them in their camp."

At the thought, new strength flowed into Grizzly Hair, and he stood up on his knees shouting to be heard over the roar, "Let's go back tonight and attack those murderers in their camp." Morning Owl, however, lay quietly beside him.

Estanislao touched his shoulder. "If the men were all like you, we could win this war."

That brought sudden anger. "We are not defeated. You should not talk that way. We'll swim out of here and get them."

Estanislao cupped his mouth to Grizzly Hair's ear. "We'd better, or they will follow us and do the same thing at my place."

Grizzly Hair jumped to his feet to call to the men, but in the sucking absence of air, swayed and fell against Estanislao, who was crouched at the bottom of the trench. Smoking grapevines reeled before his eyes and went black, but he put his nose to the dirt and recovered.

People moved ahead. The logjam was breaking up and people were going into the water.

Grizzly Hair tried to yell over the fire's roar, "Let's ride. Tonight. Attack like wasps." Then he remembered, he didn't know how many horses were left at the Tagualumne village.

Two Falcons and Lame Beaver would ride, if they had horses. But where were they? He saw no one he recognized, except Eats Skunk.

"Yes. I'll do it," Eats Skunk shouted in answer. "But I don't know how to ride."

Grizzly Hair winced. A novice rider couldn't do it. Crawling ahead, Estanislao dodged a falling firebrand and threw it out. Then he returned and fitted his cupped his hands to Grizzly Hair's ear. "There aren't enough men," he said, "or horses. We need at least twenty."

If only talk weren't so difficult! "I can get four very fast," Grizzly Hair yelled back. "Four can do damage." He coughed, unable to stop, each spasm forcing him to inhale green smoke. He couldn't hear his own coughing against the coughing of others and the full-bodied roar of the fire.

"Four would do nothing," Estanislao shouted. He coughed out, "Talk later."

On Grizzly Hair's other side Eats Skunk was yelling, "How many will ride with us?"

Grizzly Hair shook his head and dragged the dead hy-apo forward. It was hard to separate the fire from the grief within. He didn't even know if it was day or night. Until he got the body to the cutbank and saw that it was dark. The river was orange from the fire. The Bible had slipped out its straps somewhere along the way. Eats Skunk slid ahead into the river. Grizzly Hair secured his bow and quiver over his back, and pushed the body ahead of him down the short, steep slope, then dove and pulled it below the surface. The water here was deep. This too had been planned. He had a free arm to swim against the current. Underwater he kicked and pulled until his lungs nearly burst, then allowed the body to surface and stole a breath from beneath Morning Owl's armpit.

Gunshots cracked and a jolt rippled through the body. Nearby Eats Skunk jerked and disappeared. Underwater again, he labored with difficulty through a swifter narrowing of the river, surfacing to breathe only when about to lose his spirit. In this way he swam past several bends of the river, then put the body over his back, holding the arms, and carried it ashore. Bowed forward with the weight, he headed through the thicket, now in the eerie half-dark of the towering fire on his right.

Finding the trail outside the jungle that led eastward toward the Tagualumne village, he kept up a fast, steady pace. He walked in the midst of dark human shapes strung out before and behind him. Hundreds of brave men and women were ready to fight again, not retreating, merely moving in an orderly fashion to the next battleground. The part of him not smothered by grief and anxiety felt proud, like a father when his son behaves like a man. The hy-apo's head was flopping around and he began to realize that the soft slippery matter on his cheek and neck came from the head. He stopped and made a plug of twisted grass, for body parts must not be separated from the whole or the soul would not find its way to the immortals. He began to trot. Strength powered his back and legs. Etumu might be there. Surely she'd know the baby would be there. Moving faster, he tried not to think how different it would have been if he had seen the black hat sooner and pushed Morning Owl out of the way. He also tried not to think how he could have carried Oak Gall like this if he had escaped sooner from the mission. If, if, if. Everything that happened in the world was a dream of Condor, and dreams could not be changed.

"My headman is dead," he told the Shalachmushumne boy at the horse corral at the place of the Tagualumne. "Can you ride?"

"I learned today," the boy said.

"Can you take him to my home place?" The boy would fear night travel, but everything was different now. Things had to be done that had never been done before.

"Which horse is his?"

"You are brave." In gratitude Grizzly Hair touched the boy's shoulder and counted the few animals in the corral, not enough for an attack. They all looked the same in the dark. He went to the nearest one—a horse could be returned—and placed Morning Owl over its back, hanging face down. "Do you remember my wife?"

"No."

"Etumu disappeared before the sleep, before the battle. I thought she would come here, to be with my little son and the baby, with Straight Willow, Lame Beaver's wife."

"Oh, I know. Straight Willow was asking about her at supper. She's not here."

He felt strength draining out. The boy mounted and rode east into a quarter moon that had just risen, and, suddenly very tired, Grizzly Hair pulled himself up on the nearest horse and left for Sucais' place. Very quickly he realized this horse would have ruined an attack on the black hats. Continually he had to force his will upon the reluctant animal. Another bad omen.

71

Sick about Etumu, frustrated by the horse, and tender as though sunburned, Grizzly Hair rode up the trail. He couldn't stop thinking about doubling back, waiting for dawn and tracking Etumu. But he couldn't desert the brave people on the trail.

The reluctant horse stopped. He struggled to make it go. If the black hats returned to their presidios, he would go back and track Etumu. A soft-voiced owl hoo-hooed, giving him a terrible thought. Egorov might have stolen her. No one had seen him since before the battle either. Which way would he take her?

The owl reminded him that he had coupled with Katya, and Egorov might have learned of it. This was the way of some men, to steal a wife in return. All he knew for sure was that she had walked into the river and not come out. Egorov had gone in and come out at about the same time. At the sight of the gold Egorov had behaved strangely. Grizzly Hair had thought about asking why, but hesitated, not wanting to make the Chumash woman talk, because on that day her words seemed to upset her man. So Grizzly Hair imagined he had helped the woman by keeping quiet.

The other thing that puzzled him was Egorov leaving after his rude insistence on keeping more than his share of lead balls. He'd seemed determined to wage war, so why would he leave on the eve of the battle?

The horse stopped and jerked its head around as though trying to throw off the reins. He had to kick hard to make it go forward, and the braided horsehair cut into his hands as he struggled to control the head. Worsening his sense of lost power, his throat and lungs were sore from coughing. Raven Feather was surely dead. There would be no night attack on the black hats, unless there had been more horses and others had already ridden back. This he doubted. These thoughts were constantly interrupted by vivid sensations of Etumu. It seemed as though her determined spirit also rode under mother moon's quartered light and she also heard the morbid hoots of owls.

Something worse struck him. Maybe Etumu wanted Egorov. Maybe they loved each other. In his weakened state that was more than he could bear, and it shook the tears loose.

The arm clamped around Etumu hurt her ribs, and the breath on the back of her neck stunk like greens rotting in putrid water. She'd been astride the saddle for a long time, hard against the man as he kicked the horse west, and she ached all over and yearned to be free of him. He had hit her and threatened to kill her if she made a noise, then carried her to the horse. She had never been so afraid. Now mother moon had moved across the sky, and it felt to Etumu that the horse's every step stretched an invisible cord between her and the baby, but no matter how far she went, it would never break. She would rebound. The baby needed her milk.

Most of the journey had been on flat ground, and the horse had walked fast. Now it climbed and picked its way slowly through rocks and uneven terrain. Sometimes it stumbled in the dark and the man's arm tightened. At the first loosening, she intended to slip down and run, and hide. Then, if he didn't find and kill her, she'd return to the baby and Grizzly Hair. If the war had gone badly, Grizzly Hair would ride up the river to Sucais' place. She wasn't sure where the baby was, but would find them both.

Planning how she would hide in the shadows of rocks, she strained to see in the dim light. There were a few widely scattered trees. At the sound of running water the man stopped and allowed the horse to drink, but the arm clamped her tightly. He spoke his tongue into her ear, laughing strangely, and then he said in thick, barely intelligible Spanish something about "*rico,*" rich, and his people coming to her *ranchería.* But she lived east and they were traveling west, so it made no sense.

He kicked the horse up the hill and when the gait was regular, dropped the reins and twisted around in the saddle, pulling her around too, the hard pommel hurting her thigh, then settled back. By the meat smell and the bumping on the back of her head and the smacking and gnawing and scraping of teeth on bone, she knew he had taken out the hunk of bull leg from Grizzly Hair's otter-skin bag, which had contained the gold and was now lashed behind the saddle. This was the third time he had taken out the meat, but this time as he ate he also moved his fingers over her right breast, never releasing the grip of that arm. She leaned forward to keep the meat from her hair and he pinched her nipple—fortunately toughened from the baby's sucking.

Smacking his lips, he extended the leg of meat around her face, smearing it across her cheek. Her stomach would not accept meat now. She turned her head away. Removing it from her face, he continued gnawing, but grabbed her entire breast and breathed bull meat and Russian talk into her ear, low like the babbling of the stream they had left. Small dark oaks jutted from the hillside, better hiding places. On increasingly rocky footing, the horse clattered slowly along, and a slight breeze cooled her forehead while the greasy lips moved in her ear.

The man suddenly released her breast and jammed that hand down her backside with his knuckles furiously digging at his crotch fasteners. She was poised to leap from the horse without alerting him, when behind, she heard the gruff cough of what sounded like a big animal.

The man's body slammed into her. The horse screamed and dropped its head. She was thrown over the saddle horn, and as the horse stretched into a wild run, she was barely able to hold onto the mane. Afraid to let go, she slipped far to one side. More and more terrified, she dug her fingers deep into the coarse hair and held on, one leg hooked over the neck, the other loose, whipped by the wooden foot-holder.

There came a cry, inhuman and lengthy. The horse slowed, then bucked her up and down. She lost her grip and flew through the air and hit the rocks. It took a moment to feel the pain in her shoulder and hip. The horse was gone in a clatter of rocks. She lay still, not knowing what had happened, not knowing if she was hurt.

She got to her knees and looked down the trail. A massive shape, high at the shoulders and low at the haunches, stood moving its big head in the way of an animal eating meat. It was a grizzly bear, not a bowshot away. It had snorted just before the attack, and the man's death cry lingered like a ghostly echo.

Heart pounding and looking back frequently to check the location of the bear, she ran toward an evergreen oak with multiple trunks and limbs. Rapidly she hoisted herself from branch to branch, higher and higher, knowing bears could climb. Inside the canopy she found an opening, looked back and noticed something strange in the bear's stance as it nosed around its kill seeking better purchase on the meat—a limp, useless foreleg. Maybe a bear with a limp foreleg couldn't climb. Nevertheless, she stood on her toes, hooked a knee on a higher branch and pulled herself up until the branches thinned. She felt the scratches, not as pain but relief to be safer. Sometimes a bear pushed a tree down or shook it to dislodge its prey, but she judged this tree to be too strong for that, and for now felt much better.

Below, in the dim light of the quarter moon, the black hulk jerked and shook its kill like it was very hungry and the meat was tough. The crunch and crackle of bone and the smacking and slurping came clearly to her ears. She knew the bear had been attracted to the bull meat, and had come from behind when the horse was upwind.

Now it was eating the Russian. Stomach quivering and not wanting to see any more, she worked back on a limb where she could sit firmly against the trunk with her feet before her, and tried to find her calm. The crunching and slurping continued, but her heart slowed and her trembling subsided.

Bad as this was, it was better than traveling with the frightening man, better than feeling the distance stretch behind her, better than being bruised and possibly killed, as she suspected the Chumash woman had been. Now she could return to her children and her man. The bear had saved her, assuming it didn't eat her too.

Screech owls plied the hillside for night animals until mother moon splintered in the canopy then disappeared behind the hill. The eating sounds stopped. She heard only the soft patter of small leaves touching each other in the faint breeze. Then the breeze died and the world went silent.

The tree spirit enfolded and protected her so she wouldn't fall, and she floated in and out of dream.

The horse jerked off the trail and stopped. The back of Grizzly Hair's neck bristled as he listened, the horse's belly expanding and contracting under him. Was this horse trying to tell him something? The big oaks loomed like scattered demons harboring owls who brought the messages of evil doctors. Coyotes yipped and sang near and far. From behind, a horse approached.

Reining back to the trail, he told himself that the supposed demons that haunted night trails could be as harmless as the Kashaya demons that ran down hills with burning pitch on their heads.

"Is that you?" It was the voice of Cross-eyed Bear.

Relieved and realizing that this old man had been one such demon,

Grizzly Hair answered in the Kashaya tongue. "Miwok, from the river of the Cosumne."

The older man caught up, and as the two horses walked together, said, "It is bad luck to travel at night. I'll be happy to get to Sucais' place." There was no hint of the usual childlike glee in his tone.

"This horse is bad, but I think we should ride back and attack the soldiers on the trail, if they come after us. If we have enough horses." If, if.

"When? At night?"

"Maybe. Or before dawn. Go back and surprise them on the trail. Would you join me?" He knew Cross-Eyed Bear would need time to think. As they rode in silence a white owl swooped low through the trees, wings outstretched. Grizzly Hair's horse reared and stepped around crazily.

The older man's voice was raspy. "Sounds like you don't believe that fort will protect us."

The fort at Sucais' place was better built. The *Americanos* had advised them to space out three separate walls about ten man-lengths apart. "But did you see what the cannon did to the trees?"

The old man made a thinking noise. "I'll dance, then decide," he said. His spirit allies would advise him.

This was as it should be. People needed to dance and put the world back in order. His failure to do that before the last sleep might have brought bad luck. "I'll talk to you there," he said.

Then after a while he asked, "What happened to the Chumash woman?" Cross-eyed Bear was a good observer. He might know something that would help Grizzly Hair find Etumu.

"People say she disappeared, maybe went home."

"Do you think Egorov would follow her back to Santa Barbara?"

"I don't know. He was angry with her and she was afraid of him." He rode in silence, then said, "He needed her to talk for him, but resented the power it gave her. That's why some of my men don't like their women to learn other tongues."

"Did Egorov talk about the *oro?*"

"What is *oro?*"

"Yellow metal. I went to my home place to get it so he could make more balls." Apparently no talk had circulated. "I was thinking, if a woman left a proud man, maybe he wouldn't trail after her like a puppy. Maybe he would be ashamed that she left him and would go somewhere else. Where he could talk without anyone's help." Fort Ross.

Cross-eyed Bear said, "Egorov might have killed her."

Horror struck Grizzly Hair's stomach, for a man who would kill one woman could kill another. Again the horse pulled off the trail, sharply jerking its head down and nearly unseating Grizzly Hair. He yanked the rein back and forth. The animal danced, and as he struggled with it, Cross-eyed Bear rode ahead.

Riding alone, Grizzly Hair recalled the many sleeps he'd left Etumu unhappily alone. All the way to Sucais' place her loss throbbed like a wound through which his strength poured. For many seasons he had thought his journey to war would protect her. Now his actions had brought her to danger, possibly death. Just as his actions had killed Oak Gall. And Morning Owl.

The war dance was underway though only about half the people had arrived. There was no council. Grizzly Hair tried to pull the men out of the dance line to talk and find out how many horses there were, but in the darkness and dancing firelight, the men looked at him glassy-eyed, even Cross-eyed Bear. Their faces showed the fatigue of the battle and the long night journey. They didn't want to think about anything difficult now. It was more important to connect with their power. The mesmerizing log drums soothed spirits and quenched talk.

Exhaustion hung on Grizzly Hair too, for he had ridden for the gold and slept poorly even before the battle, and now had ridden much of the night on a fractious animal. As new people arrived and joined the dance, others curled up to sleep. Nobody talked.

This too was fated. Awareness of self dropped away as he danced, and it felt like someone else weaving and staggering, then collapsing. The earth came up like a cloud to meet him. The log drum faltered and ceased, and he sank into dreamless sleep.

~

At the first graying of the eastern horizon, Etumu scooted out along the branch and strained to see in the dark, but couldn't see the bear. All was still. She backed up to her sleeping place and dozed again, until the pink of a new day wakened the wing people. She looked again. Not far down the hill lay a red lumpy pile of twisted flesh. A severed piece of it terminated with a boot. The rocks around there were red. As she stared, the topmost rim of father sun flashed from the summit of the distant eastern mountains, and bits of bright yellow gold winked all around the grisly sight. Her stomach turned and she forced her gaze away.

Where was the bear now? Gone far away she hoped. Sleeping in its den. She looked around. To the west rose a hillside of grass and rocks and occasional evergreen oaks. North lay more grass and boulders. Something moved. The bear? She watched with pounding heart. It moved again. Instead of the bear, into view came the long smooth line of the horse's tan back with the saddle in place. Its nose was to the ground, grazing.

Overjoyed, she knew she could catch the horse and ride back to where she belonged. The bear had gone or the horse would have seen or smelled it.

Quickly she lowered herself from limb to limb, careful of her tender, heavy breasts that were already scraped and full of milk. It was time for the baby to suck. The thought conjured the baby's sweet mouth, and the milk lurched forward, nipples blindly spraying in all directions as she descended the tree. She vowed not to treat Grizzly Hair badly again. The silliness of her anger when he had wanted her to stay at the home place shamed her now. She had acted like a child when, to the best of her reckoning, she had seventeen *años,* as the *Españoles* counted.

She stretched a leg down to a branch near the ground, and as her weight followed, her breath caught and her heart stumbled. Directly beneath her lay the bear. After its supper it had curled up to sleep under the tree. Running across the big furry back was a slash of bald skin. O-se-mai-ti had fought a battle, perhaps with the one who had injured its leg. But what animal could injure a grown grizzly bear? None that she knew. Until she remembered the story of the bear and bull fight. Long horns could have done it.

A slight breeze wafted from west to east, or the horse would smell the bear. Grizzlies also had excellent hearing. Could it hear her heart? She was afraid to move, afraid to climb, for it would take too long to get out of reach of the good paw, the long curved claws. She tried to calm her heart, and was so still that a mourning dove perched almost within grasping range, oblivious as though she were part of the tree. It gripped its twig tightly and sang the downward call of doves. Ah-coo-coo-coo.

The song alarmed her, but the bear slept on. It slept though the dove called again and again. At last the noisy bird flew away. The fire of father sun, redder than usual, had seared away the smoky haze that had stretched across the giant valley floor. It would be another hot day.

The heat could wake the bear. Or the wing people, anything could. It was dangerous to wait. She must leave while the big head lay quietly between the forepaws, and while the horse was still there. She must climb down, step beside the big jaws, and silently flee. She must get to her baby.

Slowly, she extended her leg down to the lowest fork of the tree, almost at the ground. To still her noisy heart she called upon Oam'shu, Angelica Root. She shifted her weight to one instep, until the arches of both feet were secure on the tree crotch below. Then she put a foot down next to the bear. Carefully releasing the branch, she shifted her weight to the ground, big toe, ball of the foot, heel, other foot. Without a sound. At last she stood beside the mountain of fur. The bear breathed noisily, almost snoring. The deep animal scent of fur made her giddy, as though she were a cub in a world of bears. The limp foreleg of this bear might prevent its running faster than a deer, but certainly it could outrun her, if it didn't decapitate her in the first instant. Oam'shu wasn't calming her heart!

Lightheaded with rapid heartbeat, she stepped to a well-anchored rock.

Then she chose a second rock, and another, and another, always checking to make sure they wouldn't teeter. She avoided whispery vegetation.

She went north toward the horse, but not by the shortest route, for it was necessary to pass beneath other trees in case she needed to climb in a hurry. Glad she wore no entangling, rustling clothing, she felt as though she wore a he-u-to, target, between her shoulders for the bear to strike, a blow to stop a moose's heart. She looked back frequently to see the motionless fur under the tree. *Thank you mother tree*, she said in her mind. *Thank you, O-se-mai-ti. Sleep well.*

She must not frighten the horse either, or it would awaken the bear. The bear would terrify the horse and it would run away. She'd be left facing a man-eating grizzly bear. Fortunately, in the morning heat the breeze had entirely quit. Her scent would not be blown into the nostrils of either horse or bear.

As she moved her foot toward a new rock, the stabbing, metallic trill of a nearby meadowlark caused her to lose balance. She caught herself, but the rocks rattled. Her stomach dropped and she whirled toward the bear, waited for it to rise, waited for death.

But the bear lay still. She released her breath just as the careless lark trilled again. Another lark took up the cry, making her heart bang louder. Here and there, on all sides, the birds stood on rocks greeting father sun with their yellow breasts and loud gossip, and still the bear slept. *Dream well, O-se-mai-ti.* Father sun burned her shoulder, though he had only just risen. Perspiration ran between her breasts. Fear had long since stopped her milk. When her booming heart seemed a little more muffled, she resumed her slow progress thinking, *Perhaps I will not meet my death today.*

Ahead, the female horse with black tail and mane nibbled grass that was still a little green on the shady side of a boulder. This had been the Chumash woman's horse. Where was she? Etumu stood behind an outcropping of rocks surrounded by upthrust poison oak vines. She hummed a little tune, a soft but distinctly human sound that she hoped would arouse the horse's curiosity without alarming it. The horse continued nibbling. All around, more raucous wing people chattered and trilled. Cupping her hands to focus the sound, she hummed louder.

Still chewing, the horse lifted her nose, the rein falling from it. Half standing, Etumu turned her head slowly from side to side to show the horse that she was a person. Looking back, she saw that the bear was still out of sight, below the fall of the land. Waking up? It would be better to see the bear and meet her death than have it pounce on her unexpectedly.

The horse remained calm, and by degrees she approached, holding her hand out the way Grizzly Hair sometimes got Morena to come. The horse never moved. Arriving, Etumu put her nose in the good smelling cowhide saddle, stepped into the wooden foot-holder and pulled herself up. The foot-holders hung far beneath her feet. Glancing back from this height, she saw the canopy of the tree that had saved her and just the crest of the dark fur still at its foot. Touching her amulet and taking a deep breath, she gently pressed her heels to the horse's sides.

Another meadowlark emitted a shrill song. Frightened by her fear, the horse jerked forward. She pulled back the reins, leaned down and patted the sensitive animal on the side of her neck, telling her head-to-head about the carelessness of meadowlarks. Nothing moved in the direction of the tree.

Again she breathed deeply and started the horse. Not a good rider, she nevertheless knew how to direct a horse. She tried to avoid rocks, for a horse was a noisy walker. As the distance lengthened between her and the bear, she put more pressure on her heels and they moved a little faster.

Out of the bear's hearing and suddenly euphoric, she realized that her escape was not unlike the feat that had given Grizzly Hair his name. He would be proud. She was proud. She felt powerful.

Squinting into the blinding sun, she imagined the baby would be crying for milk now. The cries came magically to her ears and the milk rushed down, filling her breasts until they were painfully hard and seemed about to break. Milk sprayed in fine streams. It ran down her arms and legs and down the horse's sides. It fed the dry grass and insects on the valley floor. "I am coming," she told the baby across the distance.

As the enormous sun rose higher, the pressure in her breasts intensified almost beyond endurance, for the baby had missed three meals, including the big one of the early morning. The horse's gait worsened the pain. With her arm she supported her breasts to ease the jolting, and guided the horse with the other hand.

Where was Domingo's village? The baby would be frantically screaming by now, unless they had found a wet nurse. But when she saw Etumu, the lovely sucking would commence. The pain would stop. Anticipation propelled her, mindless of hunger and fatigue and the black hats and the long dark smudge running north-south in the otherwise perfectly blue sky.

72

A scant twenty-one years of age, Ensign Mariano Guadalupe Vallejo leaned against the wagon wheel sipping his morning chocolate. His personal servant had added vanilla. He was conscious of his round face and had been trying to connect his sideburns to his beard in a way that would outline his face and make him look older. His sister had told him that would do it. Ignoring the prisoner chained tightly by the hands and feet to the opposite wagonwheel, he looked toward the *ranchería.* The smoke still rose from the dense forest where most of the rebels remained hidden. He felt slightly wet from having waded into the river to get cool at least once in what promised to be another scorching day. The ticklish relations between the two presidios and between him and José Sanchez, a soldier with much Indian fighting experience, had to end, and he hoped it would end today. Now, having buttoned his double-breasted officer's jacket, he was ready to finish off the rebels and justify Lt. Martinez's faith in him. This was Vallejo's first command, the largest military force ever mobilized in Alta California, and a heady moment in his life.

By appointing a second-generation Californian to lead the combined troops, Martinez had done more than deliver leadership to a new generation, he had signaled the onset of new thinking. Now it was up to Mariano to win the respect of the older generation, and military achievement was the primary route to political success, land grants and invitations to the big *casas.* In short, this was the opportunity of a lifetime, but more than personal success was at stake. In his eyes the smoking ramparts of Estanislao's stronghold represented the end of a creaking, medieval, church-dominated world. A global revolution was underway. Across the continent British colonists had shed the yoke of a distant government. The French had thrown off a long established monarchy, Mexico had declared itself free of Spain, and he knew that someday Alta Californians would break away from Mexico and seize control of their own destiny. He drank in this change like the good chocolate. Cousin José Castro and Nephew Juan Bautista Alvarado had talked with him in excited tones. The Vallejo name was respected. Together they would work toward making California an independent land in which the Church would be less prominent. Civil authorities would rule in an enlightened manner. Schools would be established—not the excuse for a school he had suffered in Monterey, where the cruel and ignorant one-legged sailor stumped back and forth like a crazed rooster beating boys on the head with his cane. This would be a California where marriageable girls like his sisters would not pine for the social life of other lands. Cultured people would settle here willingly.

He drained his cup, handed it to the servant and stretched. First things first. Now he would finish proving himself on the field of battle.

The number of rebels had surprised him, probably around two thousand, but now this nest of insurgency would be nothing but a gap in the line of vegetation marking the river's path. Too bad the Christians couldn't behave themselves. He placed the black *chapeau de bras* on his head and prepared to count bodies. Still this could be dangerous.

"Roust the men, Sergeant," he said to Sanchez. "Let's finish this." He forced himself to ignore the older man's insolent glance. Didn't he realize that he had already perfectly conveyed his dislike of taking orders from a man half his age? But he had botched the last expedition, and such was life. Monterey Company had poured salt in the wounds, joking about Sanchez' rout. Not overtly—if they did Vallejo would stop them. All were disciplined soldiers. But the truth was, he felt uncomfortable giving Sanchez orders and worse avoiding giving them. But if Sanchez crossed a certain line, Vallejo would send the little game cock back to San Francisco in disgrace.

Watching Sanchez muster San Francisco company, Vallejo hoped for a lessening of hard feelings. If he could laud him publicly and make him look good in the report of this expedition, it would go a long way toward mending the rift between generations and garrisons. In point of fact, Sanchez had demonstrated valor and tenacity yesterday.

Now Vallejo ordered the handles be put on all the axes for clearing brush. He told the cavalry, artillery, and infantry to replenish their ammunition. When all was in good order, he led the troops the league and a half to the scene of yesterday's battle, stopping just outside the burned forest. The night guards rode over and reported, "No one came out in the night." They had been stationed around the periphery of the *ranchería.*

"Cavalry dismount," Vallejo called. As they handed the horses to the neophytes, Vallejo gave the Indian alcalde instructions to establish a horse camp out of harm's way. He then ordered the field piece to be put into position behind the ax-bearing infantry, and gave the signal to penetrate the forest. Yesterday he had dealt the rebels a devastating blow. Today they would surrender.

Carbine in hand, he and the other cavalry, along with uninjured ranchers Pacheco, Suñol and Espinosa, followed the infantry and artillery into the dark spiderweb of runners, the bare stems still smoking. The scent of gunpowder lingered. An eerie silence prevailed. He stopped and called, "Estanislao and Cipriano, surrender and your people will not be harmed."

No insolent voices answered. No voices at all. The only sound was axes chopping through the scorched vines. He felt increasingly apprehensive as they approached the partly burned palisade that Sanchez had described—a truly wondrous structure, considering the ignorance of Indians in military matters. Still, no human voice could be heard. The smell of smoke and ash was overpowering, and in places little fires still burned. Where were they? The sharpshooters had reported killing only a few as they tried to escape into the river, and since they had been posted there all night, Vallejo had assumed the Indians would be in the stockade or the unburned portions of the forest. But quite suddenly, why he didn't know, he felt certain all had somehow escaped.

Maybe they had swum out. All his life he'd heard stories of Indians fishing by swimming the bottoms of rivers with spears, holding their breath for five minutes or more. Had he underestimated how long they could stay under if their lives depended on it? Or maybe they had all drowned trying to escape.

The cannon was now within ten yards of the stockade, positioned to blow it to bits.

"Nobody's in there, Ensign," Sanchez reported.

Vallejo began to feel foolish. Somehow the Indians had outsmarted him. "Withdraw the cannon," he called. "Cavalry, go back and recover your horses. The rebels are hiding somewhere else. Monterey Company, we'll examine every part of these woods from here to the edge of the plain. Sanchez, take San Francisco Company around to the river side and examine everything. Count the dead and report back to me."

With the infantry he stepped carefully into the heart of what had been the stockade. No bodies were there. Then he examined the ingenious system of trenches criss-crossing the battleground. In increasing awe, he saw no bodies. One section of a trench had been deliberately filled in, no doubt to hide bodies.

"Look at that, Commander," said a young soldier, "The bastards suffered." Two roasted bodies lay curled in a trench. But he had expected to find hundreds.

His voice sounded more whispery than he intended. "They were brave. Clever too." He cleared his throat. "A great deal of thought went into those trenches." He clucked his tongue in amazement. People didn't think Indians were capable of planning.

"They popped out like ghosts, sir," one of the men added.

"With respect, *Comandante,*" said a garrulous old soldier from Monterey, "My father was stationed in San Francisco when I was young. He told us about some battles where the Indians dug pits and trenches to keep the horses out of their *rancherías.* Saclanes, I think those Indians were called. On the east side of the Bay. They dug trenches to make the cavalry dismount and fight on foot."

"That is interesting history," Vallejo said truthfully. His own father, a pioneering soldier in Alta California, had fought Indians but hadn't talked much about it around Mariano, who was one of the youngest children. His father had been quite old when he was a boy. A bowl-shaped object caught his eye. Picking it up and dusting out the ashes, he was astonished to find an old helmet.

A *vecino* from Pueblo San José stood close by, peering at the helmet as Vallejo wiped it off. "I think that belongs to old Pepe," the cobbler said.

"Is he here?"

"No. He's retired, old. He claimed Indians stole it."

"Does Pepe have a son of military age?"

"One is here, Pedro Valdez." He turned and looked around.

"Pedro Valdez," Vallejo called, remembering a young recruit by that name in Monterey Company. A boy of about thirteen years stepped forward to accept the helmet. He expressed extreme gratitude to have it back in his family.

San Francisco Company was returning from its reconnaissance, and Sanchez reported, "They're completely gone, Ensign. We found only one woman, a Christian."

"Where is she?"

"My men killed her."

Vallejo's face and ears heated. Her disposal was his prerogative. "The battle on this site is over, Sergeant, and she was a woman. She could have been questioned. I would not have had her killed." The orders had been clear; he would make the decisions. Some of Sanchez' men were looking at him in a way he didn't like.

Sanchez' reply was devoid of expression. "She was running away, sir. We had no choice."

Swallowing anger and insult, Vallejo raised his chin and said, "I've seen enough. "Return to the horse camp. Scouts, find the trail of the rebels. We'll follow and engage them until they surrender."

"Sí, Comandante."

The horse camp was half a league from the *ranchería*. The neophyte auxiliaries were taking their ease in the shade. By the position of the sun, it was about two o'clock in the afternoon, and Vallejo was hot, sticky, thirsty, hungry and tired. He wondered if he'd made a mistake in not giving Sanchez a thorough reprimand. *Madre de Dios*, this valley was one big oven, a veritable Hades. How did the Indians tolerate it? Oh for the much-maligned fogs of Monterey! One thing was sure, when it came to choosing land for his grant, it would be in a pleasing climate where a man could feel like a man instead of a sweating amphibian yearning to sink in the mud.

He decided they should eat cold food, take siesta, then travel all night for however long it took to locate the rebels. They would surround them before they woke. This was turning out to be more difficult than he'd hoped.

The scouts returned with reports of the tracks of large numbers of Indians heading upstream, along a well-worn path. Thanking them, Vallejo went to the prisoner, who had been chained to the wagonwheel since the previous afternoon. Pointing at the smoking battlefield, he said, "Tell me where they went."

The naked man, who claimed to be a gentile, didn't respond. He'd been caught taking a basket of pudding to the rebels for their succor, but protested his innocence of insurrection.

Taking a breath, Vallejo said, "Let's start at the beginning. Where is your *ranchería?*"

The *Indio* looked stoically ahead. Yet he was a Christian, or he wouldn't be able to understand Spanish. Vallejo raised his quirt, but only the eyes flinched. "Answer me or you'll be sorry. Where is your *ranchería?*"

"He is Tagualumne," said a quiet neophyte auxiliary, stepping forward.

Vallejo gave him a stern look. "When I ask this man a question, I expect him to answer, not you. Understand?" He turned back to the shackled man. "Now, I think you have quite a lot to tell me."

Etumu followed the smoke. Guiding the horse inside the line of shade, she rode up the south side of Estanislao's river. Father sun was high and hot, and if she hadn't needed to find the baby so urgently, she would have stopped to nap in the shade. But then she began to make out something in the distance, insubstantial in the wavy heat of the flat land.

Riding deeper in the trees, she continued toward it and watched until she was sure there were wagons ahead, and many horses and *Españoles.* What did it mean that they were still there? Had the war gone badly? Was Grizzly Hair dead? Was the baby dead? Until she found the baby and ended this pain, she decided, she couldn't think of anything else, so she forced herself to pretend that finding the baby was all she had to do.

Seeking a way to the river so she could swim across and ride unseen on the north side, she worried that the plant people would prevent the passage of a horse. That had been an advantage of fighting in a river jungle, the men had said, to keep the Spanish horses out. But to her surprise, this horse slightly arched her neck and lowered her head so she was looking from the tops of her eyes, and rapidly pushed through the snapping, cracking stems and bushes as though entirely certain which way to go. Etumu wouldn't have known. She realized her human understanding was limited by her size and the fear that the obstacles ahead would defeat her. However, the horse saw the weak places and knew her strength. Fortunately her eyes were located on the sides of her flat, bony forehead and she could ram through the brush without injuring them. Perhaps knowing they were going to water, she displayed horse wisdom that had been hidden from Etumu. All Etumu had to do was lean down so she wouldn't get scraped off the saddle, hold the reins to keep them from snagging, and pull her feet up out of the brush and thorns. This horse was moving fast.

To Etumu's further surprise, she began to recognize the place as being near Egorov's oven, which was a fair distance downstream of Domingo's village. Why were the black hats camped so far upstream? That and the silence told her the war was over. *Don't try to figure it out,* she reminded herself. Go to the baby.

She and the horse enjoyed a long drink, then she swam the river with the reins in her hand. She led the horse until she found a very narrow, overgrown pathway running east along the elevated north bank of the river. The horse looked at her with those big brown eyes and conveyed that she could do this better, so Etumu mounted and once again the horse pushed rapidly through the high rose bushes. They came to an opening where she could see across the river. Most of the place was blackened. The smell of smoke was strong. So many trees and bushes were burned that even from this distance she could see the half-burned fort. It didn't appear that anyone could have lived, and for the first time she seriously considered the likelihood that Grizzly Hair could be dead. She loved him as she always had, but in that clear-eyed moment knew that she would go on, despite what she'd told him about life being nothing without him. Her children needed her. They would need her all the more if he were dead. Being a mother had changed her.

Something caught her eye—a human shape sprawled in an unnatural position on the sandy beach. A big woman. It almost looked like Raven Feather. Did she dare swim across to look? No. More black hats could be lurking over there. She was going to the baby, and the baby was most likely with Straight Willow at the village of the Tagualumne. That wasn't very far upstream. Later she would think about this. First, the baby's little mouth must end her pain.

She rode on a trail outside the river jungle. Father sun was low and burning her back when she realized the Tagualumne village had to be across the river. Again the horse bashed her way through the thicket and they swam the river.

On the south bank a young woman sat washing a basket of acorn meal. "Is my baby here?" Etumu asked.

"I think so." The woman set the basket aside and led Etumu up another narrow path and pointed to a brush corral. Etumu left the horse there with about ten others, and followed the woman to a camp of mostly temporary shelters in a small clearing densely surrounded by thick jungle.

"Mother," Crying Fox shouted. She saw him break from a large group of children. He hit her running and his strong little body smelled fresh in her arms. She lifted him and wept to see him again, this bright-eyed boy who didn't know how close he had come to being motherless.

Women crowding around were asking, "Where have you been?"

She put the boy down. "First, where is my baby?"

With a wonderful smile, Crying Fox seized her hand and pulled her into one of the u-machas. The baby lay like a rose bud, closed and asleep in her bikoos. Fingers trembling with the need for her, Etumu unlaced the cording and woke her up, hugging her, milk spraying everywhere. Curious women crowded inside until there was no more standing room. Straight Willow pushed through and the shine in her eyes spoke of her joy to see her friend. But as Etumu anxiously tried to connect mouth with breast, the baby only played at grabbing the spray and turned away with a squinting face when it got in her eyes.

"She's probably not very hungry," Straight Willow explained. "I've been feeding her with my youngest." She had never been apart from her children and couldn't know this pain, a pain hinted at in story but which had to be felt to be understood.

Etumu touched her in thanks, then suddenly exhausted and disappointed beyond endurance, lay down uninvited on the nearest mat and closed her eyes. The baby wiggled beside her and Crying Fox squeezed into the crook of her other arm.

Then she remembered. Pushing to her elbows, she announced in a loud voice, knowing she should have said it first, "There are wagons and horses and many black hats downstream on this side of the river."

This produced a loud stir, people speaking rapidly to each other in different tongues. Even men poked their heads into the crowded u-macha and many people collected outside, mostly women, for there were few men here. Talk went on for a long time, with strenuous gestures and frowns and strong opinions that she couldn't understand. Then they started asking questions. Had she been captured? How she had gotten around the *Españoles?* Were they leaving to go west? One woman said her man was missing and asked whether Etumu had seen him. But of course she hadn't, and wouldn't know him if she had.

She asked her own questions. How had the battle gone? Had anyone seen Grizzly Hair? Most people escaped the fire, women said, turning to ask others. Talk spread outside the u-macha, then came back to her. Grizzly Hair was known by many people, but no one here had seen him. However that didn't mean anything because most of the men had gone upstream on foot, or come for a horse late at night without disturbing anyone.

A tense and somber mood prevailed. She could tell people were afraid, as well they should be, located between one battleground and the next. She knew she couldn't rest and was about to get up, but then the baby, as though slowly deciding to be nice, toyed a little then began to suck in earnest. Etumu shut her eyes and let tears of relief run with the milk. People backed out and left them alone.

Afterwards, she went out to help with supper, cutting cold strips of salmon and greens so no smoke would signal their presence. Straight Willow remarked that she wished she'd stayed in the home place. "Maybe we should hide," she said in a voice heard by everyone.

An elder said, almost with a smile, "We are hiding. They will pass by, out where horses and wagons can travel."

"But we are hiding Christian children," said a younger women who looked just as worried as Straight Willow.

A man joined in with a reassuring tone. "They won't come here. They never have. They don't know people are here. It's our old place. They'll go right past. There isn't even a trail into here from out there."

"But we sent food to our men," Straight Willow pointed out. "Won't that make them angry?"

The man was adamant. "No, they wouldn't care about that. And the runners are careful. We are safe here. This is a hidden place. The woods are very thick from here out to the plain. They'll track the people directly to Sucais' place."

But in the softer light and the relief of the first cool ground-air, mosquitos—ashes of the cannibal giant—sucked Etumu's blood with unusual vigor. It was a bad portent.

A bang like a lightning strike knocked her over and left her shaking on the ground, more frightened than she'd been with Egorov and the bear combined. More gunshots followed as *soldados* rushed into the village from all directions shooting people. Nearly paralyzed with fear she forced herself to creep on her hands and knees, bikoos under one arm, toward the shelter of the nearest u-macha. The man who'd just said they were safe fell back with blood gushing from a large hole in his abdomen. His cry stood her hair on end. The baby screamed too and Etumu kept her head down as she crawled through the maelstrom of death. Shaking with fear, she made it to the u-macha and peeked out, her heart leaping to escape from her ribcage.

In the twilight she saw bloody people lying on the ground. The *soldados* continued to fire their guns. Sharp-smelling smoke floated in the air. Children stood in a huddle, crying and stamping their feet as children do when frightened and helpless. Little Crying Fox, his face a twisted mask of terror, was hugging the legs of an older girl. An *Español* suddenly loomed over them—short black vest, flared *pantalones*—and pushed the huddle apart. He grabbed Straight Willow's girls and strode away with one under each arm. A *soldado* took two little boys, kicking and screaming in his arms. They were stealing the children! No one was shooting at them. The men of the village were dead.

Something like fire leapt inside Etumu. Throwing the bikoos over her shoulders, she ran out, jumped over a man with half his face blown away, ran to Crying Fox, grabbed him and ran down the trail toward the horse that knew how to walk through a jungle.

Frantically she yanked aside the entangled brush, then, with *Españoles* running up behind her, ran among the nervous horses and found the tan one with black mane and tail. She plopped Crying Fox in the saddle, heaved herself up, kicked the horse into a run and leaned forward to cover her son with her body.

With a whinny that made the screaming baby pause then scream louder, the determined animal leaped through the opening, nearly trampling the *Españoles.* In all directions the panicked horses ran out with her.

The *Españoles* made high-pitched chirping noises and loud shouts of "ho, ho." She caught a glimpse of them holding their arms wide as though trying to surround the horses. But her horse, immediately understanding what was wanted, was already bashing her way through willows and alders and grapevines, heading upstream toward Grizzly Hair. The sound was covered by the commotion, and the plant people closed discreetly behind them.

Mariano Vallejo had acceded to the wishes of the valorous civilian volunteers, who wanted what was often termed "a harvest of children." Boys and girls captured on expeditions were used in the households of their captors or sent to the captors' friends and relatives. Indian houseboys and housekeepers made life more gracious for the women. It was one of the few luxuries of the frontier. Indian children were also utilized to pay people back for good deeds past. So Vallejo was pleased that the men had found so many children all in one place. It had taken a while to get the prisoner to talk, but had been worth it. They killed him for his insolence; devious men like that had made this expedition necessary in the first place.

The crescent moon provided enough light and the neophyte guides were good, so everything looked propitious for a rout at dawn. The Tagualumne man, when he hoped to buy his life, had described in detail the place and fortifications.

Yesterday they had suffered casualties and grave injuries, but over a hundred and twenty-five soldiers and civilian volunteers were ready to attack again. Some of the Indian auxiliaries had gone over to the enemy but plenty were left, and they still had 19,000 rounds of ammunition as well as half the cannonballs and grapeshot. That ought to suffice. The field piece was being hauled very carefully, slowly, so as not to break the wheels. As Vallejo followed the neophyte scouts, he reviewed the purpose of the expedition: to deliver a decisive, punishing blow to the Christian rebels and their gentile allies, and to capture Estanislao and Cipriano dead or alive.

He turned around and rode back to Joaquin Piña, Monterey Company's superb cannoneer, and asked, "Will the old lady do her job as well as yesterday?"

"*Sí, Comandante.* The new bed and sheet was all she needed."

Sanchez seemed happier too, now that they had found so many children, and a dozen more horses besides. He also expected a decisive win tomorrow. The number of men under Estanislao was astonishing, but they were armed with bows, most of which had a range of about thirty yards, against guns with a range of seventy yards, for good aim. Furthermore, Sanchez had agreed with him that the rumored Russian guns, said to be on the side of the rebels, were in actuality the guns that had been salvaged from previous expeditions. That meant they wouldn't have any ammunition, or whatever powder they had yesterday would have been spoiled in the river. This expedition was too important for Vallejo to be over-confident, but he had every reason to believe things would go well.

73

It seemed to Grizzly Hair that he had just closed his eyes. Somebody was moving around outside the sweathouse, and he thought he'd heard a familiar voice. Or had that been a dream? He stepped over a sleeping man, feeling his way toward the doorway. Outside, all was dark, except overhead where a few bright stars sparkled through small cracks in the canopy. The river spoke loudly of the places she was going, and the air had the expectant feel of profound dark before first light.

"Grizzly Hair?" The quiet female voice electrified him.

"Etumu?"

Trying to find her he stumbled into sleeping men who hadn't been able to squeeze inside the sweathouse. Surprised grunts a short distance away told him she was doing the same thing. Guided by the grunts, they found each other and he pulled her to him. Her body against him made him moan with relief. His little woman was back, not dead after all. Her music thrilled him, and she was hanging on to him like she'd never let go. He feared only that this was a sorcerer's trick and he would wake up to find her gone. His throat tightened with such strong emotion he could hardly say, "Where were you?"

"There's no time. The black hats are coming. They traveled all night. I got here just ahead of them."

This made his heart race. When they didn't show up before the sleep, some thought they'd gone back to the presidios. However, the scouts hadn't reported, and he had known it was likely that this would happen. "Did you find the baby?"

"Yes, and Crying Fox. The black hats were killing people and stealing the children, but I escaped and brought them here."

"Escaped? Killing—at that little village?"

She trembled in his arms and her talk became choked. "I thought we'd all be killed. Straight Willow's children were stolen."

"Stolen! Where are our children?"

"With the horse, asleep."

"What horse?" He couldn't keep up with the surprises.

"Egorov's, ah, his woman's. There's no time. Wake these people up. Soon it will be first light. I'm sure the shooting will start then."

"Take the children and go upstream. There's a village up there."

"I finally found you and I'm too tired to ride any more with the children. I'll take them into the fort. We'll be safe there."

He pushed her to arm's length and looked into her face though he couldn't see any part of it. "Etumu, I'm afraid the cannonballs will go through wood. Go. Take them to safety." He felt weak confronting this old argument. He doubted he could change her mind, and had no time to try.

Quietly she said, "I'll go. Is there a path?"

Relief let him breathe again. "Yes, outside the trees, south side. Go up there."

"The black hats will camp out there," she said, "but I'll find a way. I believe O-se-mai-ti is helping me."

"O-se-mai-ti?"

"I slept in a tree and walked beside a bear, close as we are now."

"Tree? Walked with a bear?"

"The bear ate Egorov. I've got to go. Maybe I can get to the trail before they get here." She pulled away, hands skimming down his forearms and hands and fingers. "Spirits, be with my husband," she murmured.

Then she was stumbling over the sleeping men, and he stood at a loss in the dark. *Ate Egorov?* But the feel of her lingered on his skin and he knew she had not left him of her own volition. Could O-se-mai-ti be her ally too? It had never occurred to him.

"I heard you talking," somebody said from the sweathouse entrance. "Who was that?"

"A brave woman. The black hats are coming. They might be here now. She alerted us. Get up and get ready. Pass it on."

Men began moaning and staggering in the dark, finding bushes. Estanislao's voice approached. "Was that the Tagualumne scout?"

"No, Etumu." Sensing Estanislao's surprise, he went on. "She said the *soldados* traveled all night. They'll attack at first light. They stole children and killed the Tagualumne. They took José Francisco's nieces." Bowstring's.

Muttering something unintelligible, Estanislao's voice rose in elevation as he stood up. He called quietly to everyone within earshot: "The enemy will be here at first light. Keep quiet. Don't let them know we're awake. No taunting until later. Spread out. Attack if they try to start fires. Pass it on."

74

The Vallejo Expedition, Second Battle, June 1, 1829

Men crept quietly through the tangled forest. Grizzly Hair, Two Falcons and others went toward the east side, where light would reach sooner. The separate trees on the plain could already be distinguished. He settled beside a tree in a nest of old dry leaves and pondered the mystery of his woman being helped by O-se-mai-ti. The magic of it brought strength. His power was back. Etumu was back, stronger than he'd imagined. She had saved both children from guns. Now the warrior bear in him relished the opportunity to kill more black hats. He could hardly wait. And if the fight turned bad, Lone Goose had invited everyone to go upriver and fight in his place. A council had been held and all the warriors agreed to go. They also discussed how best to defeat the *Españoles* in that river gorge, if they were driven out of Sucais' place.

A shadowy, upright figure moved past. Several others followed. Men. He crept as close as he could get to the now stationary shadows. If his fellow warriors followed they made no sound. At ground level a flash of fire commanded his attention. A flame no bigger than his little finger lit the face of a *cuero*-clad *Español.* A fire-starter. They were trying to roast them while they slept. Instant fury leapt to his stomach. He wanted to pull his powerful claw, his knife, and rush at that face, but guns protected the fire-starter. The bear was in him, but so was Coyote. He positioned the first arrow of the day, anchored his right knee on the ground, and began to pull.

The flame went out. The shadows moved and ducked and moved again. He waited, his arm not trembling though the yew-wood was strong.

Another flame brightened the same face, the same mustache. He pulled the oiled sinew to the fullest. He had sung to the bow and now it sang back, twanging as the point of the arrow drove beneath the fire-starter's left eye.

The cry and answering gunshots ended the pretense that the *Indios* were asleep. Lead balls thunked into the tree as Grizzly Hair dove behind it. Bark ricocheted and pinged into other trees. More arrows flew. In other places around the periphery of Sucais' place, gunfire told the same story. The fire-starter with the arrow in his eye was carried away, but another took his place, this time protected by even more *soldados* holding *cuero* shields over him.

Every time he tried to aim, the *cuero*-jackets fired, reloaded and covered each other. They watched his tree. It was struck several times, and each time the tremor in its strong trunk told him how useless his blue-oak vest would have been. He had discarded it after the first battle.

The eastern horizon was blushing and the wing people were trying to talk, but the jungle crackled with gunfire and the air sharpened with acrid gunsmoke. As before, the guns shot farther than the best arrows from the best bows in the hands of the strongest men. But this time none of the gunshots came from the *Indio* side, the powder having spoiled in the river.

None of this dampened Grizzly Hair's spirit. No cannon was booming, and *Indios* were not being flushed from hiding. He thought the cannon must be broken. Etumu might have been safe in the fort after all. Everyone might be safe there. Men could stand on the scaffolding and shoot down at the enemy. He looked forward to it. A retreat to the fort would assure victory, if they could get the soldiers that far inside the forest.

Feeling unneeded here, and being lucky today, he dashed back into the thicket toward the south side near where the trail came down the bluff. He kneeled behind a wall of blooming roses. Two Falcons had accompanied him, he was glad to see. Out of bow range, black hats were backing away from where they had started a little fire. Their movements reminded Grizzly Hair of neophytes working in the mission, without manly taunts, without joy, but with the steady purpose of ants.

"They're doing it again," Two Falcons said in a discouraged tone.

"But this time there's no cannon," Grizzly Hair countered.

On the bluff Mariano Vallejo sat his horse in the already hot sun and watched the sharpshooters lead the way. Next, twenty soldiers swung axes in diligent rhythm to widen a path so the cannon could be brought down the long bank and put into use. Incredibly, the bushes and runners seemed even tougher here than at the first battleground. As the procession inched its way down the incline, Vallejo caught glimpses of the destination—a large, apparently three-layered stockade in the heart of the *ranchería*. At first he hadn't believed his eyes. The last stockade seemed more than ignorant savages could construct, but this one looked even more impressive. Furthermore, from the pattern of engagement, he could tell they had dug trenches here too. This gave the rebels the advantage of protection and unseen mobility. But, as the artillery had delivered success in the previous battle, so it would today. Judging by the difficult ax work, the artillery piece would arrive at the first fortification about noon.

He wiped his sleeve across his eyes, stinging sweat already bothering him, and rode back to tell Corporal Piña, the level-headed leader of the artillery group, to prepare to follow the axes. He also retrieved a captured food supplier and tethered her to his horse, making her walk before it.

With the infantry escort, he then rode his horse down the narrow trail. Shaking with fear, the *India* glanced back at him every other minute. When they got to the heart of the *ranchería*, he ordered her: "Convince your people to surrender now, and you'll not be punished."

The woman called to the hiding people in their Lakisamni language.

"Tell them again," he ordered. She did, but no rebels came out of the thicket. He was about to take her to a different location when an old Indian came from the bushes. "I would speak to the soldier chief privately," he said.

Vallejo called him over to the other side of his horse, where the old Indian spoke in a low tone, in good Spanish. "The woman tells the people to surrender, but her hand signs tell them to keep fighting."

"Sanchez," Vallejo said, "have the woman shot."

Without hesitation Sanchez shot her. Her body jerked until a second shot to the head quieted her.

"What is your name, old man," Vallejo asked.

"Matías."

"Stay with me, Matías. I will need you."

Whipping brush caught Grizzly Hair's eye. Long guns pushed through, connected to *cuero*-jackets. Behind them came swinging axes and the familiar sound of chopping. Were they making an easier retreat for the soldiers?

With Morning Owl's caved-in forehead a vivid memory, he vented his rage, "You can't kill us. You're too stupid." To demonstrate, he ran a weaving course to different cover, balls poofing into the ground and chipping off a piece of the alder he squirmed behind. War was fun when you were lucky.

He slithered unseen to another wall of roses and from there to the nearest trench. Head down, he made his way to the center of the action. How he'd like to rush at them one at a time with his knife!

A number of friends were already there, including Two Falcons and Lame Beaver. Covered by the noise of the *fusiles*, Grizzly Hair pulled himself out of the trench and up through the brush cover. With so much noise there was no need for stealth. Hidden by cascades of grape leaves with tiny clusters of green fruit, he anchored his right knee, stilled himself, and let fly. The arrow entered the target ear so neatly that the *soldado* didn't even scream. By the time the other black hats saw the falling *soldado*, he had released another arrow under a *cuero* jacket. With a satisfying cry, the black hat dropped his gun and clutched the arrow in his groin.

Laughing, Grizzly Hair jumped back in the trench. The hair of his top-knot yanked painfully as a lead ball passed through it, but that was only hair. He was lucky. The snap of fire could be heard as masses of dry deadfall ignited beneath the green wood. These Spanish offal had to be defeated quickly, he realized, before the fires became too fierce.

Wordlessly following Grizzly Hair's example, Lame Beaver and other men climbed out into the smoke. They got off several arrows. One entered a black hat's throat but not before a ball threw the bowman into the air. He dropped to the ground with his chest opened. He and the *Español* lay near each other, both moaning and gurgling. Several black hats pushed through the roses. Grizzly Hair and several others released arrows, but the enemy's heads were down and the *cuero* hats deflected the points. They dragged their wounded away.

Big flames suddenly shot into the overhanging trees and smoke roiled upward. At ground level, very small as viewed against the tree giants, he saw O-se-mai-ti. She had come to him like this a long time ago, standing small against a column of smoke that reached the top of the sky. She had come in a dream when he and Oak Gall and Bowstring were in the brush corral on their way to the mission. Soon after that a real bear had frightened the horses of the soldiers. Now she was here in a different kind of dream. Too distant to talk, she apparently meant to stoke his rage and fierceness, however, something about her small size against the column of smoke bothered him.

Despite the fire, the ax-men continued chopping and the *soldados* continued reloading and firing. The fire ignited the dry brush over the trench and it crackled quickly toward Grizzly Hair. Injured men and men in need of arrows were trying to go to the fort before the fire reached them, so everyone went, Grizzly Hair included. This too was fated. It was time to retreat to the fort. He felt like a mythical demon snorting gunsmoke. It fed his strength.

Behind the first wall there were already many people—men, women and even a few children. A quick look told him Etumu wasn't there. He hoped that meant she had made it safely to the trail before the black hats arrived. He filled his quiver from the piles of arrows and hurried up the loose logs, the makeshift scaffolding, as fast as he could without slipping. From the top, he looked out and caught a glimpse of the reason for the wide path. His stomach dropped. Behind the ax-men a team of *soldados* were pulling a cannon. Relentlessly it came toward the fort, moving faster as more *Indios* abandoned the skirmishes and headed to the fort. It wouldn't take long before the *soldados* were within bow range; and the closer they came to the fort, the less brush they needed to clear. The fort-builders had done it.

A familiar voice called out in Estanislao's tongue, ". . .last chance. . . neophytes come. . . not be punished. . . back to your missions." It sounded like old Matías.

"We would rather die," Estanislao's replied.

Glad to hear that, Grizzly Hair nevertheless felt it was a bad omen if Matías had gone over to the enemy. Maybe he had become certain the *insurgentes* would lose and he wanted to avoid daily whippings. Grizzly Hair and others watched through the cracks between poles, prepared to pop up and release arrows when the *soldados* came within range. Two Falcons climbed up the scaffolding and said, "Red Sun and I will take some men down to the trench near the cannon. You shoot from here. We'll attack them from both sides." He left with Red Sun, Lame Beaver and about ten other men.

Grizzly Hair appointed two young men to spread the word among those now entering the fort, to hide along the scaffolding until they were ready to release arrows. Other men guarded the entrances to the fort.

The vanguard of *soldados* entered the largely cleared area, but were not yet within bow range. They seemed preoccupied with arrows coming from behind—Two Falcons and Red Sun. It even appeared that there was hand-to-hand fighting. This went on for some time, then most of the soldiers turned around and came forward. Others pulled the cannons to within bowshot of the fort, the cannon feeders shielded by the other *soldados*. Why hadn't Two Falcons and the others slowed them down more? Then he realized gunfire was coming from farther behind. Two Falcons, in turn, had been attacked from behind.

Grizzly Hair and others popped up, released and ducked before the black hats could get good aim. The fort wall proved to be good protection. Each time before he released an arrow, Grizzly Hair moved a little to confuse the black hats. But the *cuero* hats with the flared brims protected the *soldados* from above, and it was impossible to shoot past them to kill the busy cannon feeders. If only they had big rocks such as lay littered around the home place! They could throw them.

The cannon ha-boomed, jerked back on its wheels and issued a heavy cloud of smoke. He heard loud snaps and cracks and screams. The scaffolding shifted under his feet and some men fell. The logs under his feet settled. He regained his footing and balance. People were crying. He looked down inside the fort. One of Te-mi's men was howling, stabbed in the buttock by a stake that had apparently been torn from the wall by the cannonball. He was on his knees. An old man lay as though pinioned to the earth by a large wooden dagger in his stomach. Pain had opened his eyes very wide and he held the stake in his hands. The brittle poles hadn't even slowed the big iron ball. It had flown through the first wall, across the open space and cracked the second wall. Confused, excited people were scurrying around, talking in many tongues.

Grizzly Hair looked at Cross-eyed-Bear, who was crouched near him looking down in obvious horror. "We've got to kill the cannon feeders," he said. One of them, protected as they all were by *cuero*, was stuffing a mass of dripping rags into the cannon's nose by means of a long stick. He pulled the stick out, steam rising from the cannon-barrel, and as he jammed the rag end of the stick into a bucket of water, the backs of his legs were exposed. Grizzly Hair released an arrow into a leg and ducked down.

The scaffolding pile shifted again, trapping some of the men. Cross-eyed Bear scampered down safely. Lame Beaver stood beside the east exit tunnel wildly motioning Grizzly Hair and everyone else to come down. Why wasn't he behind the cannon? This still could work with enough men surrounding the men who surrounded them. *Indios* far outnumbered the enemy, but nobody was directing them. Nobody could see the entire place at the same time. People had expected the fort to be a magic shelter.

Carefully he stepped down from log to log. When he was halfway down, he teetered on a half-rotten log, put his arms beneath the shoulders of a man and pulled with all his strength, freeing his legs. He freed three more men and was pulling out the fourth when more underlying logs shifted and somebody yelled, "Watch out!" He couldn't help but drop the man he had just helped. He managed to stay upright only by springing off a moving log and leaping out to the ground beyond the logs.

He went to Te-mi's man, who held his bleeding buttock after yanking the big splinter out. Blood spilled over his hands. "Medicine," he called to the huddled women. One of them had a big sliver through the droopy flesh of her upper arm. An uninjured woman crept across the open ground with a basket of medicine, clearly frightened that another cannonball would annihilate her.

When the acorn-paste medicine had been daubed on the man's wound, largely stanching the flow of blood, Grizzly Hair helped the man to his feet. "Go behind the third wall," he said to everyone. First they had to go under the second wall, which had been cracked but not penetrated. The wounded man put his arm over his shoulder and limped with him toward the pit between the walls. As they passed by, Grizzly Hair momentarily locked glances with the man with the dagger through his stomach.

"Sing my spirit on," the man requested in a thin voice.

"I will sing," he replied, "from behind the third wall." He knew the cannon needed rest and a bath between blasts, but didn't know how long would it rest.

He jumped into the underlying pit, helped the injured man down, then climbed up inside the second fort. It too was crowded with excited people. He looked around, assuring himself that Etumu and the children were not there. Cross-eyed Bear was on the west side bending over the trench that led to the outside. Two heads came up—Lame Beaver and Two Falcons. They were lifting Red Sun.

Grizzly Hair shouted to Two Falcons, "He's my father-in-law. Let's trade. Take this man."

Two Falcons relieved him of the limping man and Grizzly Hair knelt beside Red Sun, now stretched out on ground. He appeared to be surprised, like he didn't know his hand was dangling from the mass of broken bone and blood that had been his wrist. He would never use a bow again, even if he didn't bleed to death. He was pale, and from the look of the spurts of blood, would soon die. Grizzly Hair untied Red Sun's calf-thong, inserted Red Sun's Russian knife beside his *Americano* knife, and tied the thong very tightly just above Red Sun's wrist. The pulsing blood slowed to an ooze. Then he got up and brought the woman who had paste medicine for open wounds.

"We thought he should rest in here," Lame Beaver said, watching her.

"Water," Red Sun whispered.

The water baskets were empty. Grizzly Hair also felt thirsty. "I'll take you to the river," he said.

BOOM. Grizzly Hair dove to his belly. With a loud cracking and snapping and a whir like a monster hummingbird, a cannonball whooshed across the open area accompanied by a flock of huge splinters. It slammed into the third wall, somewhat caving it in. The ball then bounced to the ground and rolled a short distance. Still smoking, it came to rest. People stared at it like it might jump up and kill them. The explosion echoed in Grizzly Hair's head and stomach, shaking and loosening his power. Screams and cries filled the fort. More people had been wounded by the splinter-spears. A man who had been about to jump into the pit under the third wall fell slowly into it, a stake protruding from his back. This fort was supposed to protect people. It was supposed to bring victory. But now it was attacking its own people.

Somebody started singing. Many moaned in fear and pain. Grizzly Hair crept to the center of the yard and looked through the ragged hole in the second wall into the round dark circle of the cannon barrel, which had been pushed through the first wall. Dripping rags were shoved into it, steam rising from the snout when they were pulled out. The next blast would demolish the third wall.

Two Falcons was helping the man with the bleeding buttock walk toward the third wall. Grizzly Hair called to him. "The fort is killing people. Let's go to Long Goose's place. I'm taking him to the river." He pointed at Red Sun. Many people were listening, and with the reports of the *fusiles* somewhat lessened, they could hear.

He put Red Sun over his back, good and bad hands dangling over his shoulders and lowered himself into the trench that led outside to the burning forest. As he left he sang the dying souls onward, and others joined in, all coughing, for the bad smoke was thickening and the fires were raging more quickly than last time.

Once again the smoke and lack of air made his heart beat too rapidly. He could hardly breathe at all. Red Sun was heavy. But despite the fire, *cuero*-jackets came through the brush from all sides, firing into the trenches. Everyone kept their heads low and unencumbered men popped up and let fly at the faces. This held the *saldados* back.

Throughout the blazing hot afternoon Vallejo watched the cannon demolish the stockade. When the first and second palisades were blown to bits, they moved it to the third. Despite this and the steady din of muskets, the Indians were amazingly tenacious, still shooting at the cannoneers from hidden places. The hot air reeked of gunpowder.

A red-faced young soldier reported to Vallejo, "Corporal Piña said to tell you he will soon be out of ammunition."

"Go to the ammunition camp and bring all that remains, for artillery and muskets."

As the young man hurried up the widened path, Vallejo watched the fires igniting in different parts of the forest. They spread faster than he had expected, faster than last time, possibly due to the higher elevation and drier soil. Today these rebels would breathe their last.

A little later, the red-faced soldier approached Vallejo's horse, breathlessly reporting, "This is all we have, *Comandante.*" He pulled two mules laden with boxes, too little. It was hard to believe that nearly thirty-five thousand rounds had been fired. This changed things.

The day was hot. He was hot. The guns were hot. His horse was hot, sweaty and increasingly skittish about the fire, which further elevated the hellish temperature. The cannon would fry a man's arm. If Piña wasn't careful it would split apart. All the men's faces were red and wet. Having long ago finished his *bota* of water, Vallejo was growing lightheaded. He knew that Monterey and San Francisco companies were equally unaccustomed to the heat, yet they continued to fight valiantly in this impossible terrain. He steeled himself.

Sanchez came over. "Want me to engage them, Ensign? Some are leaving the stockade."

"No, we're about out of ammunition. We need what's left to protect ourselves on the way home."

"We can't leave without a decisive victory," Sanchez said with maddening sincerity, as though he hadn't left his battle in total defeat.

"By the looks of that fort, I'd say we've won a decisive victory," Vallejo disputed, holding in his irritation.

"Too many are left alive, sir." Insolent emphasis came through the final word.

Vallejo lost his temper. "Well if that's it, Sergeant, go ahead. Be my guest. Get in the trenches and fight hand to hand."

"All right, watch me."

He should have known Sanchez would take him up on it. Quickly the tough, wiry sergeant selected a score of men who, like him, were straining at the bit to prove their manhood. These were the kind of men who would think the hotter, the dirtier, the more difficult the fight, the better. Vallejo recalled such boys in the school with the peg-legged teacher. He also realized that this kind of courage made Spanish fighting men the most formidable in the world. This very spirit and fervor had emboldened Spanish peasants to drive Napoleon's famous army out of their villages time and again, with the help of British armaments. Seasoned armies in other countries had failed to stop their progress. Sanchez needed to prove himself, and if he didn't worry about the fire, Vallejo wouldn't either.

Heading toward the river Grizzly Hair saw fighting ahead in the trench, *Indios* and black hats battling with knives. Grimly determined, he left Red Sun, pulled his *Americano* blade and crept up on the melee. From behind he clamped an arm around the forehead of the nearest black hat and before the man could raise his knife, the *Indio* in front slit his throat. He moved to the next fights, one after the other. Two Falcons and Lame Beaver fought with their Russian knives, and after several brutal knife fights in the thick, choking smoke—Lame Beaver slashed across the face—the black hats finally started chinning themselves out of the trench, kicking with spurs to prevent being crippled by knives. Maybe they hadn't known that many *Indios* outside the mission now carried iron knives. As the enemy ran or limped through the fire, Grizzly Hair realized that, like Napoleon's men, they had split up and become vulnerable.

His feet slipped in a bloody slick as he pulled Red Sun through it. He passed a slashed, naked body—Narciso. Even he had not been spared. Beside him lay two more *Indios.* In the heat all their woolen clothing had been discarded and it was impossible to tell *Christianos* from *gentiles.* But that didn't matter now. The important thing was to stop the *Españoles* from counting the dead. Grizzly Hair pulled himself out of the trench and shoved the excavated dirt in with his feet over the bodies. Others helped. The trench was a ready grave. The people coming behind would have to climb over it. Then he continued hauling Red Sun toward the river.

Vallejo regretted his impulsive order. He couldn't see what was happening in the trenches. Only an occasional yell, a glimpse of a *cuero* hat or movement flagged the location of the struggles. Overhead, however, the menace was clear. Their own fire was roaring down on them. He had already ordered the artillery to retreat. It was almost too late. The blazing underbrush had cut Sanchez off. But suddenly Sanchez and his men emerged from the fire. Approaching, they slapped their steaming clothes with their *cuero* hats. Maybe their sweaty clothes had saved their lives.

It had been another close call, one that could be criticized. Vallejo sat on his fidgety horse above the steaming men and gave the order to retreat to the ammunition park. As he guided his anxious horse around men and artillery, the roar of the fire astounded him. Hot wind riffled his hair. Sweat dried instantly on his face. He looked back at the blazing forest. The fire would finish the Indians this time.

But there never had been a frontal engagement, and now that his fire was driving him from the battlefield, he must prevent any escapes, tighten the net he'd arranged last time. He would station more sharpshooters in and around the river. He would camp, post guards and count bodies in the morning. No doubt about it, this firestorm would kill every living thing.

Giving the necessary orders, he had the ammunition distributed.

Smoke grabbed the inside of Grizzly Hair's throat like a nest of crawdads. Coughing continuously, he looked up through the flames. Sparks wheeled like red stars loosed from their moorings. The big limbs were burning, the smaller branches and lighter wood raining down in fiery streaks to the forest floor. On all sides strings of green leaves curled into flame. The fire after Coyote killed the Ké-lok must have been like this. Everyone said Ké-lok couldn't be defeated, but Coyote had thrown a red hot rock and hit the winged giant on the only place where he could be killed, a white spot on the inside of his arm. No one thought it could be done. But as Ké-lok died, his faithful little supper fire leaped up in vengeance and burned the entire world. Ké-lok had killed Wek-Wek for no reason, but Coyote's vengeance had brought total destruction.

Word came down the trench that no one could leave until dark because the soldiers were shooting from across the river. They were also standing in a line across the shallow place to kill all who swam downstream. Knowing most people lived downstream, they had guessed, but these people said they would go upstream. Waiting, Grizzly Hair kept his nose low in the trench. The previous fire had taught him that these passageways served more than one purpose. Red Sun spoke incoherently, then seemed to fall unconscious. Grizzly Hair put his father-in-law's nose on the earth.

Men were tossing out burning limbs as they landed in the trench. Through the noise and confusion, he heard a voice calling, "They are leaving." It was Estanislao standing in the trench, shouting. Only a few heard it over the roar.

With a jolt Grizzly Hair realized he had lost sight of the possibility of victory. But here it was: the enemy leaving the battleground. Were they out of ammunition? Even three wagons of musket and cannon balls would eventually be exhausted. In contrast, the piles of arrows had been sufficient. That was a measure of victory.

He stood up, called and motioned to Estanislao, feeling the scorching heat on his back. Cucunichi approached slowly through the crowded trench, eyes reflecting the flames all around. "I'll bet they make camp," he said, kneeling beside Grizzly Hair, putting his face down low to the earth. His voice conveyed his excitement. "I think they're out of ammunition."

Strength and power and exhilaration rushed back full force. "Let's go after them," Grizzly Hair bellowed. "Kill them all."

Coughing, Estanislao nodded. "Swim two bends upstream and get out. We'll talk there. Pass it on." He balanced his bow and quiver on his back and crawled up the trench toward the river.

Carrying Red Sun, Grizzly Hair looked around for men he knew. Where was Tuol, Cross-eyed Bear? Little Cos? Anyone who could convince others to follow? Now that they had seen the failure of the stockade, they might be discouraged. But two twenties of men could suffice, and surely more than that would join them now. Clear victory could be seized.

Lame Beaver and Grub Log were behind him, coughing and gasping. Lame Beaver was bleeding badly, but he would live. Grub Log, the bravest of men, had ridden all night and fought all day with a shattered knee wrapped in cloth. Grizzly Hair yelled to be heard over the roar, "They might be out of ammunition. Let's follow them tonight. Kill them while they sleep." A burning stick fell on his head. Tossing it away, he smothered the fire in his hair with his hands.

Under the sucking firestorm, no one answered.

"Meet two river bends upstream," Grizzly Hair yelled. He realized Estanislao would talk to the men in this trench when they got to the river, and he should go to the west trench to spread the message. Nodding at unconscious Red Sun, he asked Lame Beaver and Grub Log to care for him.

It was difficult to move through the oncoming people, and required more breath than he had. In the west trench he crawled beneath hotter fire. Movement had stalled. People were waiting for dark, noses down. The burning coals were thick on the forest floor around them, making the trenches the only way to the river.

His lungs felt scorched, and his excitement ebbed beneath soft, dark feathers that seemed to be settling upon him. Fear looked at him through the orange eyes of others, all reflecting fire. When his thoughts straightened, he yelled over the thundering fire, "Where is Gabriel? Cipriano? Little Cos? Tell them to meet upstream. Two bends of the river. Estanislao thinks they're out of ammunition."

Men looked past him like he wasn't there. Some shook their heads. Some were too wounded. Some were caring for the dead and injured.

"Join us," he started to yell, but the crawdads grabbed his voice. Coughing used up his air, and the feathers came down again. He sucked air from the earth and when thought returned, said to all around him, "Attack with us. Spread the word. Meet two bends upstream."

Some time later, the coughing people began to move again. Some had to be slipping into the river. Or were they being killed? He could hear gunshots through the fire. Either they had ammunition or they were bluffing with powder. Careful not to hurt others with his bow, he crawled in the slow-moving crowd toward the exit where he would stay and convince each person who went into the water to meet upstream.

Trying to see how far it was to the river, he stood up in the firewind. It lifted his scalp. His hair was burning. He got down, beat it with his hands and rolled against the side of the trench, but he had inhaled too much heat and too little air. He spun in a slow circle though he lay still. His mouth was open but he forgot what to say. A wild-eyed man squeezed past, painfully scraping his burned skin. Far above, the flaming oaks whirled. The feathery blackness came down over him.

How long had his spirit been gone? As the booming, snapping roar returned, he realized he must hold tightly to his spirit and get to the healing water. But where in the jungle was he?

Hairless men came from behind and crawled past, dragging others. The crush of people pushed him along. They knew where they were going, so he followed. Had he left Lame Beaver and Grub Log helping his father-in-law? Why would he do that? He should go back and help. No. That was wrong. Why was he here? His power was evaporating in the heat, his thoughts flying away with the smoke. Like migrating salmon people pressed from behind, heading for water. Continuing to crawl, he gritted his teeth. His skin felt tight and alien.

All light was red. The stench of burning flesh and hair nauseated him and he coughed bile. Then he remembered. "Meet upstream," he called to a strange man. "We're going to—"

A ripping crack overpowered the fire's thunder. He looked up to see a huge oak branch tearing away from a trunk in a burst of popping, spitting sparks. The branch careened straight down toward him and his yell joined others, became a single scream as he clambered back against the human tide.

The limb bounced and rebounded across the trench, ripping his shoulder. It made the earth jump. The branch settled over the people ahead. Their screams ended, but those around him increased. Flames shot three times as high as his head, blocking the way to the river. "This is our death," said the man next to him. His eyelashes were flaming.

About to burn up, Grizzly Hair pushed and climbed over people who had been pushing from behind, only dimly aware of faces, arms, backsides, feet, bows, the crunching of quivers. His size and strength took him from the worst of the heat while weaker people roasted beside the burning limb. He neither noticed the pad of flesh hanging from his shoulder nor saw the tip of pearly bone through the blood. He realized that he must run around the obstruction and get to the trench on the other side.

A man beside him relaxed as though going to sleep, eyes rolled up. The pressure from the people who knew nothing of the obstruction pushed the man toward the fire. The giant might be dying, but his fire continued to fight for him. Grizzly Hair had lost his bow and quiver. He had lost the gun and *cuero* jacket. He had lost the *casco.*

Moon Woman, Grasshopper Wing, appeared beside him, cupping her mouth on his ear, "Where is Grub Log?" She stared at the wall of flame.

"In the east trench." If he hadn't died trying to save Red Sun. Inhaling some air from the earth, he vaulted out of the trench and pulled her up. She seemed surprised but willing as he threw her arm over his neck, grabbed a handful of wilted, steaming grape leaves, covered his nose and ran into the bright weave of fire. Their feet crunched upon the white-hot coals. With his uninjured left arm around her and his right hand outstretched, he broke through the flaming runners and bushes. Only power and speed would save them. Into the dark empty trench beyond the burning limb he jumped with her. They rolled in the dirt and cooled their skin. Her hair was gone. No doubt his was too.

"Grub Log," she murmured to him. She was Grub Log's wife and the smoke was scrambling her thoughts.

He put her knees under her and pushed her forward. Quickly they came to the cutbank. The wonderful scent of water wafted up, and he saw red and gold riffles reflecting the fire. Otherwise it was dark. Men slid down the slope ahead of them. Out of the dark came small starbursts of flame accompanied by the barks of *fusiles.* Cries told him the *soldados* had *amunición*. No attack could be attempted. This war was over.

People huddled behind the willows. Afraid of the shooters, they kept glancing at the fire above and behind them. But others were sliding or running down to the river. He took Grasshopper Wing's hand and ran with her down the steep bank. Lead balls splashed in the water around them as he slipped into the stinging embrace, his burned skin feeling as though he'd been whipped. The water hit his shoulder like ten arrows. In agony he pushed deep underwater. Grasshopper Wing was fending for herself.

The current was stronger here than at Domingo's place. Swimming hard against it, he held what little air he could in his scorched lungs until ready to burst. Then he dropped his legs, pushed his mouth carefully to the surface, sucked air, then pushed down under again, swimming upstream.

He continued underwater past the second bend in the river, came up, looked around and stroked to shore. Heavy as stone, he pulled himself up on slippery, mossy rocks. He slipped, caught his balance, then slipped again. A few dark silhouettes of horses were visible on the high bank. In the red light he saw human shapes sitting against the trunk of an oak.

Heading toward them, he pressed the flap of muscle to his shoulder. Water sheeted off him as he climbed onto dry grass and small bushes. On his right the firelight colored the sky-dome. The big tree people stood black before it. It was too dark to identify anyone. "Who is there?" he asked. They all appeared to be bald.

"I am here," Estanislao's voice said.

"I am here too," said Two Falcons. The rest of the men were silent.

He joined them and looked down to the river where dark heads moved against the current. Salmon swimming upstream. No other fish did that. All would have died in the fire had they not been tough people. Like him, most had probably lost their weapons. Again the shameful realization hit him that he had left Red Sun with injured men.

Estanislao touched his shoulder. Grizzly Hair jumped, then pressed the flap into place.

"Sorry. I didn't know you were injured."

"It's little."

Estanislao leaned his head back against the tree where the red light illuminated the defeat in the long downward lines of his face. He said, "I talked to many men, but they were finished fighting. The *soldados* were shooting with *amunición.*"

"But our people are swimming upstream," Grizzly Hair countered, but without strength. Some were walking east along the shoreline.

Estanislao lowered his tone. "They are finished." After a moment he added, "I'm glad you found your woman."

Grizzly Hair didn't dare ask about Estanislaa. He didn't know whether she had been in the fort or had been with the Tagualumne. Probably the former because she had no children. But either way, she most likely was dead."

"You're lucky you have a village to go to," Estanislao said.

But Grizzly Hair didn't feel lucky any longer. And for all he knew Etumu had been behind the third wall. No, he forced himself to think, she could have made it to safety. "Where will you go?"

The silence was long. "Back to the mission."

Grizzly Hair's stomach constricted painfully and he cried, "You told Padre Durán you didn't want his Christianity. You said he could have it. Come with me and live with my people."

"No. The *militario* won't rest until I am dead. No village would be safe hiding me. Your people would be killed."

"But they'll kill you in the mission."

"Probably."

"Don't go."

Estanislao looked over with eyes of fire. "I want Padre Durán to forgive me before I die. Then I won't go to the Devil's fire for all *eternidad*."

"Aiii," he couldn't keep the bitterness from his voice. "So it was useless. After all the planning and waiting and suffering. Useless."

Estanislao's voice was soft, confidential. "They might be satisfied to get me." He gestured toward the fire. "They think I made all this happen. They want me punished. I don't think they'll care as much about the rest of you. They expect gentiles to be bad." He looked down. "Padre might forgive me. Maybe he won't let them kill me."

Sick with the knowledge that this would be taken for surrender, Grizzly Hair watched another dripping shape emerge from the water. It picked its way up the bank, and he recognized Gabriel's legs. He had no hat, no shirt, no weapon.

Squatting beside them, Gabriel said, "What's the matter. You're sitting there like lost pups."

The river spirit thrummed and the silent survivors continued swimming upstream, pulling the dead and injured. Would they ever fight again if Estanislao returned to the mission? Would Grizzly Hair? Did it matter? Somebody else was approaching—Blue Snake.

Gabriel looked toward the fire and said in a steady, gravelly voice, "In the beginning I thought this kind of war was stupid. But now that you've done it, I see it was good. Now they know we are not sheep."

No one spoke and Gabriel continued, "In the morning when they find us gone, they'll run for the presidios checking over their shoulders. Every time the padres talk of raiding our villages, the soldiers will fear an attack by hundreds of warriors. They will stop hunting people in the Valley of the Sun. This means we won the war."

Already dry and pounding with heat and pain, Grizzly Hair felt anything but victorious. "Are you going to Long Goose's place?"

"No. I'm going after those shits. I lost my weapons, but I have a horse. I'll set a fire while they sleep and aim it at their powder kegs. But if I'm wrong and the expedition comes this way, I'll ride up there and tell you. I'll be your scout." He paused. "But I'll bet you three horses they are finished fighting."

No one took the wager. Gabriel sat down carefully, but though he was clearly in some pain, his talk sounded like a hy-apo orating at a big time. "We should keep fighting, even if they leave. I'll keep up the horse raids, but there is much more we can do." Turning to Grizzly Hair, he said, "I've been thinking about you. You did something I thought couldn't be done. You unified the gentiles. People respect you. You speak like a chief. People want to follow you. You could gather the warriors again and we could push the *Españoles* off the ranchos and out of the missions. That's what you always wanted. You can do it now. Now that we've done this. You have *fuerte.* You are a warrior chief."

But Grizzly Hair felt only the loss of Morning Owl and probably Red Sun and Grub Log, as well as many friends. Many would be crippled if they lived. He hadn't seen Lame Beaver or Running Quail or Scorpion-on-Nose. Etumu and the children could be dead. He told Gabriel, "Estanislao is going back to the mission."

Silence fell. After a while Estanislao said, "My wife is dead. My father is dead."

Sucais's wisdom was lost to the world. Grizzly Hair moaned. He had hoped to learn more from that elder. Then a sudden sharp need to find Etumu and the children gripped him and he couldn't think about anything else. He wanted to believe that she had managed to go east before the black hats arrived. In a hurry, they hadn't decided exactly where to meet, but surely she had known to go to Lone Goose's place.

One-handed, unable to tolerate any movement of his right arm, he stood on his burned feet and stepped carefully toward the horses. His stomach trembled as he pressed the flap of muscle back into his shoulder. Pain was weakness. Weakness was illness. Illness was the lack of power. "Whose horses are they?" he asked.

"All mine," came Gabriel's quick reply—somehow another signal of the end of war. "But you can borrow one, to get you to Lone Goose's place. Talk to the people there, and think about what I said."

He didn't want to go there, except to find Etumu.

75

"I can do it, Mother." In the dawn light his black eyes flashed with pleasure at the responsibility.

Etumu saw something of his father's sober steadfastness in him. He was capable beyond his years. "Tell me again what you will do if you see *Españoles* coming."

He planted his feet and recited, "I stay hiding right here." He gestured around the secluded place where they had slept, where she had stockpiled greens and brodiaea corms. "I sit down like this and don't move."

"And what about the horse?"

"I let them take the horse. I don't make any sound."

"Good. And what do you do if a normal kind of person goes to the horse?" The mare was hobbled a good distance away, not directly visible to Crying Fox.

"I say, 'That is my father's horse. He is coming to get her now.'" With transparent pleasure, he accepted Etumu's smile and her rewarding pat on the head.

"If a bear or wolf comes," he volunteered, "I let them kill the horse. And I climb up this tree." An accomplished climber like most children, he pointed to the oak that formed the backdrop of the nest.

"That's good. Watch their eyes and climb fast if they see you. But remember, they want the horse more than you." She hadn't mentioned mountain lions because they were climbers and there was no reason to frighten him unnecessarily. She hugged him, then took a breath, pointed to the west side of midday, and asked, "What if father sun gets over there and I am not back?"

"I walk a *very* long way to the first people who live that way." He pointed east. "I will wait there."

"Good, son. That is a lot to remember, but you are a little man. I am sure I will return before sunlight comes straight down." The good-luck scent of wormwood was strong around him. She turned from his brave eyes and, with the baby on her back, headed south toward the edge of the jungle. Every little while she moved the foliage in an unnatural way so she could readily find her way back to him. She had rubbed him with wormwood, even the bottoms of his feet, and hers, and sprinkled the nest with it to eliminate the human scent.

Now she allowed herself to think about the terrifying previous day, when they had heard the booms of the cannon and constant popping of guns. Grizzly Hair had wanted her to go upstream, but she hadn't made much progress. By the time she collected the children and rode up the long angling bank of the river, the *Españoles* were camped on the trail. Afraid and keeping to the trees, she rode eastward. When the guns started she knew the *Españoles* were busy. The horse was skittish. She was too, for every gunshot could mean the death of her husband and her father. She went deeper into the jungle to find a resting place, for the baby had started her hungry-cry. The guns were still audible, but far enough away that the horse was calmer. And while the baby nursed, all three of them fell asleep.

The baby's funny little talking noises had awakened Etumu. The sounds of gunfire continued, but she didn't want to make the horse walk through any more brush. She feared going out to the trail during daylight where the *Español* scouts might see her, so she stayed there the entire day hoping the *Indios* would win and the black hats would leave. She and Crying Fox had gathered greens and roots. He thought it was fun to be alone in the woods like bears or coyotes. To keep her mind off the guns, she told him stories.

In the night the sky told its own story, and now she felt an urgency to see what had happened. It worried her to leave a boy that young, but at his age he could stub a toe and cry out unexpectedly. She could muffle one mouth, but not two. And if the worst happened and they saw her, he couldn't run very fast. But this was only a precaution; she would return very quickly, intending to go only to the edge of the thicket and see if people were on the trail.

She hid in the trees where she could see both ways. Looking east, she saw the backs of several walking people—naked, normal skin color. In the west two more naked men were helping each other walk toward her. She waited for them to approach. Both hairless and without weapons, one had vines wrapped around a thigh, with herbs sticking out, maybe yarrow. Injured stragglers. Their willingness to walk on the trail in daylight told her they didn't fear the *Españoles.*

She stood up at the side of the trail where they could see her. "Where do you come from and where are you going?" she asked politely.

"We come from Sucais's burned place, and we're going to Lone Goose's place," the uninjured man said in a mix of the Lakisumni tongue and Spanish. "Where are you going?"

"I am looking for Grizzly Hair. He is my husband."

"He was looking for you."

"Did you see him this morning?" Hope cracked her voice.

"No. When we were down at Domingo's place."

"Oh, you haven't seen him then."

The injured man spoke for the first time. "I think I saw him over there before the sleep." He nodded back toward the smoke. "He was helping an older man, his father-in-law I think."

She caught her breath. "Is my father wounded?"

"I'm not sure. Maybe worse than that." He gazed past her.

"Maybe they're both—" She had tried to harden herself but couldn't continue. "Grizzly Hair, was he all right?"

"Nobody was all right in that fire." With black faces they looked ahead.

"Are the *Españoles* gone?" she asked.

"Oh yes," Quinconul said, —now she recognized the injured man as Sucais's brother. "Somebody said they were out of *munición*."

Hope rising that she could help, she said, "Maybe I should go there and look for Grizzly Hair and my father."

"Maybe," Quinconul said. Most people went to Lone Goose's last night. A few of us rested under cover last night. If they did, sooner or later they'll come out on this trail. They could be anywhere." The two continued limping eastward.

Wary and anxious, Etumu hurried west to look for her men. If she found them in need of being carried, she would run back for the horse.

A little while later she was approaching the clearing of smoking ash when she heard men's laughter and a voice crying, "*Mátame, por favor.*" Kill me, please. Stealthily, she moved a little closer and crouched behind a tree. Many black hats, she was shocked to see, had surrounded a kneeling man, and very near to him they were shooting arrows into him. Not knowing if it was Grizzly Hair or her father, she watched in sick horror as they continued releasing arrows, avoiding the places that would kill the man. She couldn't see him well enough through the surrounding black hats, and his voice was strained and unnatural. Mutilated people hung in the trees. They were too bloody to identify. The food she had eaten earlier lurched up. She hurt her insides forcing herself to make it come out without noise.

She was removing the bikoos to hold the baby's mouth if necessary, when the bushes whipped nearby. Then *Soldados* were coming! Weak with fear and nausea, she almost got up and ran. Then she saw that they were chasing another woman with a bikoos. That woman tripped and fell. They easily grabbed her, then carried her, screaming and kicking, back near the kneeling man, who continued to beg for death.

In a brief glimpse Etumu saw that it was Swims Backwards. Unable to help, Etumu cried silently as they removed the baby from her back and laid her on the ground. Men held her ankles and another held her hands, which were stretched over her head. Not far away two *Español* riders sat on horses.

Vallejo reined his horse from the ugly sight. At dawn the men had howled, "The damned *malcreados* got away again!" And now they were punishing the luckless stragglers and curious onlookers. He too was appalled that most of the rebels had escaped like a magic trick. But that was no excuse for atrocities. And he feared repercussions. The governor was known to be soft on Indians.

No doubt San Francisco Company thought him squeamish on account of his lack of field experience. For permission, they had turned to Sanchez. Dangerously, the command was slipping from Vallejo's control. But when the suffering Indian cried out again, "*¡Máteme!*" he rode over, aimed at the man's head, saw the grateful look in the eyes and blew his brains out.

The men turned and gave him a look, then began counting the number of arrows in the body. A few unburned bows had been found along the river, and some of the men knew how to use them. Vallejo had been equally unable to stop the maimings and hangings.

Now the men had a young Indian woman and were holding her on the blackened ground by her wrists and ankles. He rode over. They had her crying baby. Terror was stamped on her features. "Put this women under guard and protect her with your lives," he said in his deepest, sternest voice. Wasn't it enough that they had killed three women? Now they were starting on another. "If any of you hurts her, all are responsible, and I'll see to it that you suffer the extreme penalty. If I have to kill you myself."

With an eyebrow insolently hiked, José Sanchez brought his horse alongside. "Ensign," he began as though talking to a child, "the females were the arrow suppliers, rebels as much as the men." In a reasonable tone and voice pitched for the surrounding men as well as Vallejo, he added, "You allowed the killing of the other women. This one is no different."

The audacity of *you!*

The arrow-counters were still busy and Sanchez was looking fondly at the group of his men who had circled around.

"That's enough, Sergeant," Vallejo ordered. "It's time to get out of here. No more of this." Gesturing at the bloody remains of the hanging Indians and the bodies of dead women sprawled on the ground, he added with greater volume, "I absolutely forbid any more torturing and killing. Period. Men or women."

But he knew that an order was only as good as the respect of the men. The men of both companies, even those kneeling over the young woman watched and waited. Maybe they smelled a new sport, the long awaited fight between Sanchez and him. Sanchez had made himself borderline insolent the entire expedition and Vallejo had half a mind to put him in irons. But confronting him could intensify the mutinous sentiment of San Francisco Company. Each incident influenced Monterey Company too, like poison spreading in a well. Vallejo had tasted it in jokes repeated to him with innocent expressions, about his boyish appearance. And now all the men were frustrated to have been defeated again by Indians. Every man here had grown up steeped in stories about the laughable attempts of Indians to defend themselves against Spanish fighting men. This was a new reality, and their frustration could turn to blame, he being the object of it. The danger was palpable. He must regain full control, right now, or his career was forfeit, if not his life.

"Seventy-eight," came a happy cry. "We shot seventy-eight arrows into him without killing him!"

Pitching his voice low and authoritative, Vallejo addressed Sanchez.

"Sergeant, I need to talk to you, alone." He reined his horse away and waited. Meanwhile, the naked *India* struggled and the baby screamed.

The sergeant took his time, but joined him, sitting loosely in the saddle, hands crossed over his Sinaloa horn. He looked at the woman as the soldiers ran their hands over her. The soldiers kept an eye on Vallejo and Sanchez.

Vallejo, who still held his carbine, opened the frizzen, slipped in the paper cartridge containing both powder and ball, and clicked it shut. All watched as he rested his new-style gun over the saddle horn, a gun that had been ordered from a specialty gun-maker in the United States through a friendly ship captain. He pointed it casually toward the men.

"Sergeant," Vallejo said without taking his eyes from the scene, "our objective was to crush the rebellion and return any stray neophytes to the missions. Not torture and mutilate them."

Sanchez looked at his men, one of whom laid the cradleboarded baby a meter away behind the woman's head. She twisted around, struggling against the hands that held her, straining to see the sobbing baby. Her breasts were full and her brown stomach sank slightly beneath the wings of her rib cage. The rounding of her hips was a perfect frame for the dark slit between her firm young thighs, parted as the men held her knees and ankles. Watching Vallejo, one man slowly placed his hand over a breast, then drew it down over her pubis and thighs. A challenge.

In the larger picture Vallejo knew he needed Sanchez, and he adjusted his tone to one of comradery. Gesturing with his gun toward the mutilated Indians, he said, "When Padre Durán hears of this, he'll report that *we* are the savages. He'll say these atrocities prove that we are incompetent to police the frontier. I know you don't like him. That's no secret. But Durán is a strong Padre Presidente. This won't help either of our careers." Career was Sanchez's sensitive spot. Unlike Vallejo, he had no Certificate of Pure Blood. He had the reputation of being too chummy with his men, disrespectful to the holy fathers, and now he had been defeated by Indians, twice. Padre Durán had made no secret of his feelings against Sanchez when he complained to Lieutenant Martinez that the military should never have entrusted a soldier of low character to command an expedition to the interior.

Sanchez tore his gaze from the young *India* and looked at Vallejo. Pretending not to notice, Vallejo continued to watch the man named Avelino, who was now manipulating the flap in front of his *pantalones*, one slow button at a time.

"Commander," Avelino said with a borderline rude expression and a tone of false pleading, "I will not hurt her."

"None of us will hurt her," said another with an ingratiating smile as he too unfastened himself, "She will like it." Down the sides of the woman's face, tears ran in sunlit streaks.

The intense morning light also revealed the pock scars on Sanchez' face. He had to be considering his career. Vallejo wondered if allowing the men this one pleasure would seem weak. He'd said nothing about rape, just torture and mutulation. Rape was a routine part of war. Would even that erode their respect? Would it encourage more violence and mutiny? Or would it defuse the situation and serve as a token that he was a reasonable man? He wished he'd had more experience, or a younger father who could have given him more pointers.

There was one thing, however, that his aging father had impressed upon him. Beyond obeying orders, the duty of an officer was to think bigger than any of the men under him, to hold his country's needs before all other considerations. This was his challenge. The objective here was to bring unity between garrisons and win the respect of all the men, so that even though this expedition might have failed, he would be respected for his part in it. Then eventually his vision for Alta California would have a better chance of becoming a reality.

He had decided not to follow the rebels further east and expose his men to danger when they lacked sufficient ammunition. He had also decided the interior, which was flooded in winter and hellish in summer, wasn't fit for man nor beast, and to the extent anyone asked his opinion, which they might if all went well, he would counsel against any more military expeditions to the interior. He would tell them that the rebel Indians knew the terrain too well and were rapidly learning strategies of defense. The governor was anxious to end what he called the *monastico-militario* system of government, and Vallejo couldn't agree more. If ranchers wanted to recover their stolen horses, they should do it themselves without government involvement. And as for labor, he'd seen on his father's rancho that gentiles could work as well as neophytes and learn the necessary skills. But the first step in gaining political support was to smooth over this debacle and, yes, compromise a little.

Avelino's gaze darted between the girl's *poza* and Vallejo.

"Sergeant," Vallejo said firmly, "we have a won total victory here. A complete rout with only a few casualties on our side. Understand? On the Indian side hundreds have died. I am devoting a paragraph in my report to your exceptional valor and competence." Though Sanchez never took his eyes off the brown girl, his hard face registered interest.

Vallejo continued, "The government sent a military force into the field poorly equipped. With adequate supplies and up-to-date armaments we would have annihilated the rebels. In spite of that we won a great victory and have no reason to act like savages ourselves, and *this never happened.*" He jabbed his gun around at the dead Indians, including the one whose head he finally had to blow off. "We are heroes, you and I. Too disciplined to allow atrocities. I guarantee you, we will be rewarded if we stick together and get our stories straight. This was a resounding victory against an insurgency of enormous proportions. The only time Christians and gentiles ever united against us. We succeeded by dint of our military competence, discipline and bravery." He kept looking at Sanchez for signs of comprehension.

Much as a day dawns, slowly and with growing clarity, Sanchez' face lost its hard edges. The graying temples seemed almost distinguished, and he looked at Vallejo for the first time as a man ought to look at his commanding officer.

Vallejo pressed his advantage, "I believe you have a petition for a *rancho,* and I'm sure they will consider your heroism here. Now I would like you to look at this," he motioned with his head, "through the eyes of those who are likely to hear of it from some disgruntled soldier."

Sanchez' expression already told Vallejo he was a fellow conspirator, and as Vallejo waited for the words, he considered the other thing. Avelino had asked permission, and by his silence Vallejo had all but granted it. Still Avelino waited, as did all the men. This was a delicate moment. They were showing their compliance, at least momentarily. Now it seemed that allowing them this one small pleasure might seal an unspoken bond. And if they let her go afterwards, what was the harm?

Extending his bony hand, Sanchez leaned forward in his saddle and said, "It was a complete rout. Hundreds of casualties on their side. No atrocities this morning."

Vallejo shook the hard hand with a lifetime of military experience and breathed easier. The California of his dreams might yet be advanced by this unpleasant affair. Sanchez called to Avelino and the men, "Don't hurt that woman. When you're done, give her the baby and let her go."

76

San José, June 4, 1829

A month before his seventy-eighth birthday Pepe lay on his bed facing the wall. He sank within himself as a rag drifts downward in a still pond. Part of him was a boy in Mexico.

"Old man," said a voice.

He was too deep. Behind his shut lids he saw poinsettias blooming in February and his patient *India* mother sweeping the corridors of Loreto Presidio. His Spanish father was away on expedition.

"Pepe." A hand rubbed him. Human life forcing itself upon him. "You were my friend for many years. I am sorry I couldn't make you happy. I pray Angelita did." It was María, the *India.*

In his mind he saw them together on the wind-swept cliff above the gunnery esplanade of the presidio as the dark water of the bay heaved below them. She had lain with a governor before him. The *cholos* envied him. People cared about love. People who were alive.

"Pepe, I have a confession."

Was she still there?

"I know where there is gold, but I never told you."

His mind stumbled back over the decades—soldiers churning up the steep hills near the presidio, men who thought of nothing else. Then he found it. He saw himself begging the Indians to give the gold back, but they threw it away and took his helmet, a gift from his father—their only link. That's when he started to sink. People would assume that familiar posture, touching their forehead. The word *loco* formed in their mouths. But that no longer mattered.

"I've only known about it a few years." She was rubbing his hand. María, not Angelita. Not his daughter María Encarnación. María, the old woman, his *India.* Why was she trying to pull him up? Once he'd cared about returning to Mexico rich and famous, to make his father's legitimate family proud of him. But now life was cold.

"Pepe, can you hear?"

His eyes were rolled up.

"I am going to young Pedro. He is wounded, in the mission infirmary. Remember? He fought the rebellious Indians."

For María he would turn over. He began the struggle and she helped, then he faced her and breathed hard but not hard enough. She was blurred. *"Qué?* What did you say?"

"I am taking medicine to young Pedro, your son. I will stay at the mission for as long as he needs me. Understand?"

He forced his eyes to focus, and saw that she was old. It was too late for her too. He released his eyes.

"I promised to tell you if I heard about gold in California. But I also promised Eagle Woman I wouldn't tell anyone. I hope she forgives me, if she can hear this. No one else will hear it from my lips. Only you, Pepe."

She had waited until it was too late.

"Who is it?" Durán called through the door of his office.

"A poor woman come to confess."

Concepción Argüello, he knew from the voice. "A few minutes. Meet me in the confessional." He must finish the letter to the governor and get it on the ship this afternoon. Saint Francis had intervened and shown him the way. It had been wrong to request that Estanislao be punished by death. The poor burned man had come to beg his forgiveness, and Durán's heart had opened.

He had forgiven him with tears and embraces. At his insistence Estanislao was hiding in his apartment. The military considered him a murderer and likely would want him executed.

He worded the last sentences carefully to let the Miraculous Intervention speak through his words. The governor must hear his heartfelt sincerity in requesting a full and unconditional pardon for Estanislao.

There was also the matter of the harvest of children, about which Estanislao had spoken so movingly. Clearly the Christian children must be returned to their missions, but gentile children should also be returned to their parents. This hadn't been done before, so procedures had to be established. He offered his services in any way needed to effect the transfer of children.

Signing the letter, he folded it, sealed it with wax and handed it to the waiting neophyte. Then he went to the sanctuary, noticing as he opened the door, the tail of the bay far below where the ship was anchored. The courier would be starting down the long trail that connected the mission to the embarcadero, with instructions to put the letter into the hands of the captain. The governor, who now resided in San Diego, should receive it within a month, guessing the time it would take for the brig to make its commercial stops.

Shutting himself in the dark box, he reflected that Concepción didn't come here often, usually only to help in the infirmary. Once again he heard her confess the same old sin with Count Rezanov, though she didn't mention that *malcreado's* name. He figured she had confessed it to other priests too, but this time she told of a published diary. She wept softly through her words and he knew that her honor as an Argüello had been shattered by the diary. She had waited many long years for the Russian to come and marry her, and now his diary, found in Siberia after his death, apparently announced to the world that he had used her in hopes of gaining Alta California for Russia.

"My daughter," he said as he had before, "he is dead and it is finished. God has forgiven you. A published diary makes no difference, especially when printed in Russian. And you were absolved long ago."

"But I didn't know the full consequences of it then." Her voice caught in a sob. "I can't look my brother in the eye. I can't live in his *hacienda* any longer."

Luis Argüello's Las Pulgas.

"Father, it is not my shame, but that which I have brought upon my brother and my family that gives me such pain."

Pride was indeed a tenacious sin among Spanish people. "Have you considered joining a convent? You could go to Mexico. Or maybe the east coast of the United States. There are some nunneries there."

"Do you think I would make a good nun?"

"I think you are finished with confession." He blessed her and they walked outside, where he learned that she had indeed come to help the wounded soldiers in the infirmary. At a leisurely pace they walked that direction, and talked. "Yes, Concha, a nunnery would give you a blessed profession." He added, "And a new place to live."

"I would like that, and I want to give up the Argüello name, which I used so badly. But Father, I love this land. When I was a girl I dreamed of leaving for a more civilized country, but there is a gentleness in the land of my birth that tugs at my heart, and I don't think I could bear to leave. Won't Franciscan nuns come to Alta California?"

Red roses twined up the corridor posts and the young olive trees were beginning to provide welcome shade. "Not Franciscans," he explained, "but I heard that a Dominican nunnery might be established in Alta California."

"Then I will wait for the Dominican nuns."

He strolled beside her with hands clasped behind his back. His sandals were silent on the packed earth and the habit whispered of a simple life. However his life was not simple. His nature was too passionate and active, too involved in the world. At night, as penance, he sometimes flogged himself with the *cuarta de hiero* until he was bloody and weak.

"Mariano Vallejo is a hero, isn't he," Concepción remarked lightly, jarring his heart. "I can hardly believe how quickly he grew up. I have fond memories of the Vallejos coming from their Rancho Pajaro to visit us in the presidio. I remember Mariano asking me to dance the Borrego with him in our parlor." She chuckled. "I must have been about nineteen and he was five."

Not wishing to say too much, but not able to resist setting her straight, he heard himself mutter, "The military calls it a victory. I'm sure your brother does too," *if he hasn't drowned in aguardiente.* "Even Sanchez is being rewarded for his part in the affair, but that was no victory. And they are not heroes." Watching his toes poke from beneath the habit, he clamped his tongue in his teeth.

Clearly shocked, Concepción slowed to a standstill. "But didn't Estanislao come back here and beg your forgiveness?"

"I suppose everyone knows that. Yes, and I granted it."

"Well, that's wonderful! It's surrender."

"Concha, not while over a thousand dangerous rebels remain at large." He couldn't not add, "They are running with gangs of wild gentiles. No matter what the military reports say, this was no victory. Now people will claim we failed to civilize the heathen and they'll use that to stoke the argument that mission lands should become secular ranches. The Indians' souls are not looked after at the ranches. My work here would be ruined. Besides, only Estanislao and a few others returned to me. In Santa Barbara, all the surviving rebels were brought in. No, this was no victory. And terrible atrocities were committed. They were not heroes."

As they arrived at the door, two people converged upon them from different directions. All four came to a halt as though waiting for someone else to open the door. One was a wrinkled old *India* whom Durán had seen here before, a Christian from the pueblo. She carried a lidded basket. The other was José, his wonderful musician from the Cosumnes River.

"Is *Comandante* Luis well?" The *India* asked of Concepción.

Concepción looked carefully at the old crone, and her startled expression changed to pleasure. "María? Is that you?"

"Yes *niña.*" A loving tone.

"It must be twenty-five years! Father, this woman was my *abuela.* She was our housekeeper and took care of me when I was young." Turning back to the *India*, she said, "You've been living in the pueblo. I heard Angelita had children." To Durán she added confidentially, "Her Angelita was my age—half white."

María smiled and said, "Yes, I am bringing medicine to one of my grandchildren now, Pedro Valdez."

"Valdez," Concepción said, thinking. "Isn't that the name of the girl who will marry Sergeant Sanchez next month."

"Yes, María Encarnacion, Pedro's sister."

"Well," Concepción said in amazement. "Sergeant Sanchez's new rancho is near Las Pulgas. Don Luis and I and all his family will attend the *fiesta de matrimonio.* Your granddaughter will be my new neighbor!"

José moved slightly toward the door. "Where are you from?" The old woman asked him, then uttered something in a gentile language.

José's mobile face twisted into an irresistible grin, possibly at hearing his heathen language. "The Cosumnes River."

"I have friends on the Cosumnes River," she said with a funny smile.

"How far up the river?"

"At the start of the boulders in the low foothills. She spoke more heathen words, and Durán might have stopped her except José's face lit up with obvious pleasure, and it was a joy to see such a smile on the face of any neophyte.

"He was my best friend," José said.

The old woman tilted her head and narrowed her eyes at him. "You must be José Francisco, the musician."

"*Sí.*"

"I danced with your parents and brother at two autumn fandangos and the *fiestas* in between. They were kind to me. And sorry to lose you."

This came as a shock to Durán, that a Christian would participate in heathen rituals. José's face had folded into the picture of tragedy, then he sank into that unfocused look that newcomers to Alta California often mistook for stupidity.

"I know very little about gentiles," Concepción said brightly, but María, it sounds like you're related. Wouldn't it be wonderful if his relatives could go to the wedding fiesta?"

María looked puzzled, but not as puzzled as Durán. Then he saw that Concha's heart had opened to these simple people, as his had long ago, and it pleased him despite the impracticality of her idea.

María said it for him. "It wouldn't be safe here for gentiles, so soon after the war."

Compelled to clarify, Durán said, "War isn't the word. It was a misguided rebellion, a passing thing."

Concepción was infused with an excitement of a kind that had long gone dormant in her. "I know that's unrealistic, silly I guess," she continued. "I was just thinking of a wedding as the kind of celebration that could bring gentiles more readily to the Church. Maybe the methods of the military are too harsh." She looked at Durán. "Don't you think so?"

"Possibly," he said, completely taken aback to be hearing this from the daughter of Brevit Captain José Argüello and the sister of Luis and Santiago—a family who had long dominated the military leadership of Alta California.

"I'm going to be a nun," Concepcíion explained to María. "I will make it my special work to bring harmony to my native land in every way I can."

Durán turned José aside and spoke confidentially to him, "I am doing what I can about the children, but I will need your help in getting your brother's children back to him."

77

In the long dry, cool breezes often dance in from the southwest pushing out smoke and stagnant air. They usually arrive in the evening and last all night, and in the morning carry the freshness of the plains and marshes. The wing people sing for no reason. Mother bobcat stalks more crisply and turns to look at an intruder with eyes like sunlight on water. Everyone sniffs the air and notices subtle fragrances that had been covered up—grass in seed or something new blooming. The air is so transparent that the Spirit Peak looks big and blue. On such a morning Grizzly Hair was ready to talk again.

He handed two ducks to Red Sun.

"I can still hunt," Red Sun said, "but the ducks are nice."

"I want you to have them." Grizzly Hair had vowed to provide food for his maimed father-in-law for the rest of his life.

Nettles went away to skin the ducks where she wouldn't be tempted to look at or speak to her son-in-law.

"Sit," Red Sun said. He gestured with his good hand. Raven Feather had cut the rest of his left hand away, except for the skin, and applied medicine to keep it from putrefying. She had threaded fine sinew through a bird-leg awl and sewed the living skin over the stub as best she could. Still, it remained swollen, lumpy and ugly, and at times the pain could be seen in the squint of his eyes.

Grizzly Hair sat for a while then left, but the silence had been broken.

Later, the early night air was warm and fragrant, alive with the music of frogs and crickets and distant wolves. The campfires of the immortals sparkled in the black sky-dome. Grizzly Hair and Etumu were leaning back on their u-macha. Crying Fox and the baby who would be named María Howchia were sleeping. Several people had gathered around Red Sun's fire—Drum-in-Fog, Raven Feather, Straight Willow, Scorpion-on-Nose, Pretty Duck, Lame Beaver, Sunshine-through-the-Mist and Running Quail. Bereft of her children, Straight Willow had singed off her hair. Lame Beaver's was already burned off. Two Falcons joined them, whole but badly burned. He had arrived at the home place only the sleep before, after helping Grub Log to his home place where Grasshopper Wing had been anxiously waiting.

Some distance away a wolf sang high then let his voice slide seamlessly downward until it disappeared in the night. "Lizard Woman," Grizzly Hair suggested to his wife, "let's go sit with the umne."

The people moved to accommodate them. An owl hooted but that was to be expected. Magic was everywhere, good and bad, unpredictable. Drum-in-Fog threw a handful of sacayak into the fire. It popped and crackled in energetic little explosions. "This will renew you," the doctor said to no one in particular. Eagle Woman had been the last doctor to use sacayak in this way.

Watching the excited fire, Grizzly Hair spoke. "We didn't thank them for their lives."

For a while people watched the fire. Then in the slightly uncertain tone of one who doesn't wish to be contrary, Red Sun said, "They didn't thank us either." He rested his stub on his thigh.

Everyone was contemplating that when Two Falcons said, "We walked into fire."

Only Drum-in-Fog and some of the women had eyebrows and lashes. Blackfaced, Raven Feather stared at the fire. She had walked to the home place after seeing her man dead, and her spirit allies had protected her from the shooters at the river. A Cry had been held when Morning Owl's body was burned. Over and over Grizzly Hair had cried out the names of the dead, unable to stop thinking of how they died. His feet and the feet of many others had been too sore to dance as much as they liked. Blue Snake's relatives had keened when he left again for the mission. He said the mission was his home now, even though he would be punished.

"I saw a bear in the smoke, Grizzly Hair said. "It looked so little beside the tall smoke that I almost didn't see it. I dreamed that too, a long time ago."

"Was the smoke black?" Drum-in-Fog asked with obvious interest.

"Yes. It had swirls on it going straight up."

"Maybe crow feathers," the doctor said.

Sometimes the smoke had looked like wings. Coyote had marked with dark feathers the places where human villages sprang up. Now, much had burned. Would Coyote recognize the survivors? Did Drum-in-Fog recognize them? Did Grizzly Hair recognize himself? That question had silenced him since his arrival six or seven sleeps ago. Etumu had caught up with him as he limped on burn-tender feet. He had never been so happy as he was to see her on the Chumash woman's horse. He had thought she and the children were dead. She told the story of Three-Legs eating Egorov, but not why she wasn't waiting for him at Lone Goose's village. Beyond that, they had spoken very little, but he knew that someday when it felt right, she would tell him why tears sometimes ran down her face for no reason. But no matter what it was, he rejoiced to have her and the children here with him, whole and unburned.

Drum-in-Fog tossed more sacayak into the fire. The pops and sparks transformed the faces, making the old appear younger. Sacayak was a plant of startling transformations. In its first season it was slim, unbranched and crisply jointed. In its second season it bushed out like a horse's tail, and in fire it exploded like the magic powder fed to guns.

Running Quail looked up at Grizzly Hair and said, "You should go visit the gentiles and get them to attack the missions and ranches. You are the only one who can do that."

By the postures of the umne it was obvious that Gabriel's opinion had been discussed here, as it had been at Lone Goose's place. Grizzly Hair knew his talk could influence people when he let the spirits speak through him. Had not the umne gone to war? Wasn't that the reason Morning Owl was dead? And why Grub Log would never walk right again, and Red Sun never pull a bowstring? Etumu was looking at him, waiting for an answer to the unspoken question.

"Gabriel thinks we defeated the *Españoles,*" Grizzly Hair said. "He says they won't come up the rivers any more to capture people. Maybe he is right. Maybe that is a victory." O-se-mai-ti, his honest and straightforward ally, had told him they would win.

People shifted in their places, maybe expecting him to be the warrior he had always been, but he was not. He had defeated a more devious enemy, his own clarity. He now understood the wisdom of the old ways. Not that he would forfeit, even if he could, his knowledge of the *Españoles;* but in the aftermath of the war, his eyes had opened wider and he knew that his hard-won warrior's clarity had blocked broader knowledge.

"If Gabriel is wrong and they come up this river to kill or capture people," he continued, "I would fight." The bear would always live in him. "But killing does not stop killing. It brings more killing. I will not lead gentiles to attack missions and ranches."

Lame Beaver sounded upset. "But you could do it. People listen to you." His voice broke. "They took my children."

He had known some would be disappointed in him, maybe including Raven Feather because he wouldn't avenge her man's death, and Running Quail and Hummingbird Tailfeather whose grandchildren had been stolen, but each man had to find his own way to power. He was sure about that. "I told Estanislao about the children," he said. "He is a friend of Padre Durán and Bowstring. Maybe they can get the children back."

Straight Willow and Lame Beaver looked at him intently. Raven Feather looked down and he couldn't see her eyes.

Several evenings later he was in the river bottom. The claws of Etumu's dog clicked on the warm, smooth stones. Still singing to the river baby spirit, Grandmother Dishi was leaving for the u-macha with her drilled shells. As they met he stopped and rubbed her shoulders. Drum-in-Fog had cared for her. He said she paid for it by keeping the river spirit happy. In her abrupt way she turned and continued toward the u-macha and the leftover supper.

The heat of the day was lifting from his burned skin. Panting, the bitch scanned the river bottom. "We are not hunting now," he told her. This was the time of day when he was most likely to absorb power from father sun. He faced the life-giver, whose golden brightness lay on the water in the canyon of trees. Waiting for a surge of power, he looked at the beauty around him with the eyes of one who had nearly left the world. His lungs stretched to the sweet fragrance of the white ball flowers hanging over the deep fish hole. He released his air and turned, without thinking why, the opposite direction.

His stomach twisted and a sound escaped his lips. Fire behind the hill made black silhouettes of the oaks. The *soldados* had followed! The home place was aflame. He must save Etumu and the children. Running before he was fully upright, he fell on his face in the sand. As he lifted his head he knew why the eastern sky was orange, and though fear still buzzed in his extremities, he laughed aloud at himself.

Mother moon was rising, big and full and orange. He rolled on his back and laughed in great loud guffaws. The dog peered down, checking him. Saliva splashed on his nose. Wiping it, he scratched her ears and noticed a coyote behind her, outrageously close, camouflaged in the bushes, tail hanging, grinning at him. It had been a Coyote trick. What was the meaning of it?

This was not the first time he had seen the moon big and orange while the sun sank into his western house, but every time he marveled that she could have sneaked so silently that near to the earth. It looked as though she might be touching the trees. The dog sat down to wait, not hearing Coyote fade into the brush.

He felt a subtle change, a lift, power flowing in this place where Eagle Woman had loved the gold nuggets and the sweet scent of lupin, where Oak Gall had told him she was going with him to the mission, where Etumu had first held his hand, where Jedediah Smith's man had killed Falls-off-House. Power was here. He must purify himself to receive it. He stepped into water as warm as the air. Stringy tendrils of moss threaded between his toes, and tadpoles and minnows scurried away as he waded to where the little river was slow and deep. Not far downstream it tumbled over the rocks, but here it was quiet. He floated with his feet dangling. The pain in his shoulder subsided. Etumu had sewn it with sinew and it was healing well. A fish rose up. Small waves traveled across the water and pulsed on his neck—its spirit touching him. Sagey wormwood, moss, and peppermint scented the air. Frogs sang loudly to their mates, and he could hear the deer stepping through the grass, talking in rough whispers. *Horeh, horeh.*

Moon floated serenely upward, changing to yolk yellow in a dark blue sky. Almost unbreathing in his respect for her magical transformations, which reminded people of the transformation of all things in their worldly journeys, he admired her round yellow twin in the water. Even his spirit allies were changing, not deserting him but shifting in some way.

CRACK. Gunfire! His heart hit his ribs. He took a swimming stroke toward shore, but then saw the wet head and glittering eye of a beaver looking at him from the opposite side of the pool. She had slapped her tail to scare him away from her home place. Weak with relief, he let himself sink into the full embrace of the water, then surfaced and told Beaver, "You have nothing to fear. I will not harm your family." In a short time he had been twice tricked. The spirit messages were strong.

Coyote, who was standing in the brush, said, "What if a hostile, gun-bearing enemy came here in an unstoppable flow and took your home place?" The confusion and horror of that terrible vision fractured the quiet beauty of the evening.

"I would kill them," the bear in him answered without hesitation. "And I would get many others to help."

Coyote looked at him with amber eyes aslant. "You said killing doesn't stop killing."

"We would push them back to the west and make them afraid to return. We would move upstream to the place of granite and higher hills."

"Not if they came from the east." Coyote said.

East! *Americanos* lived in the east, so many that their number could not be understood. One of them had killed Falls-off-House with no more hesitation than a boy spearing a frog. But they had made reparations. Was Coyote tricking him again?

It seemed that much of the war had been tricks—his hopes for Russian and American allies, Pomponio and Egorov ruining the possibility of helping the people in Santa Barbara, the false confidence of the early victories at Domingo's place, the feeling that people's lives were less important than they had been before, riding hard for the gold only to have Egorov steal his wife, the fort killing the people it was built to protect, the black hats severing people's body parts and shooting so many arrows into a living man. Etumu had seen it. She told him what happened to Swims Backwards, Elk Calf's wife. He climbed up the bank and sat in the sand watching Moon changing from yellow to white. "People are clowns," he told the dog. Only power and proper living could restore balance.

In need of Etumu, he returned to the quiet village. Under the willow porch of the u-macha, he groped toward the mat and lowered himself carefully beside her.

"Are you all right?" she whispered.

He had wondered if she'd be awake. He kept his voice low, "Yes, are you?"

She nuzzled her cheek on his good shoulder, and the baby made a small dreaming noise.

He whispered, "Do people say I made a mistake to talk for war?" She always knew what the umne were thinking.

"They are sad about the dead, and worried the soldiers will attack us here. Raven Feather says she will never be washed of her mourning in the Molah-gumsip."

"It is to be expected that they blame me."

Her voice became sharper, more than a whisper. "No. You followed your spirit allies. The umne followed theirs. They could have stayed here." In a softer voice she added, "No one was forced to go."

He knew she included herself. He thought about Estanislao's last words to him, that no one would be safe unless he went back to the mission. Had he sacrificed himself for others? Or was he a meadowlark flitting from one tree to the next? Or maybe he thought that someday Padre Durán would give Estanislao's people the missions.

"We should celebrate our victory," he said turning to Etumu. "Hold a big time and invite all the related peoples. Then people will know we won the war." He knew she would be surprised, for he had been very quiet. Feeling restless, he said, "The river is warm and the air smells sweet. I'd like to bask there with you, even if lizards prefer sunshine. Come and see how lovely mother moon is." His lips moved lightly against her cheek as he added, "I'd like to share talk."

"Bohemkulla might be on the path." Her voice had a welcome smile in it.

He gave back, "Bear-woman would have nothing to fear."

Quietly they left the house and her presence soothed him like the balmy air. They walked past the nickering horses—Milk and Morena gone forever, Chumash with a baby in her—and up the west hill. "Did you know," he said, "I will never leave you again?"

She stopped walking and he listened to her music.

Unable to see her eyes, he resumed their slow walk up the hill and spoke as he had once spoken to her sister, almost talking aloud to himself. "I have been thinking about the people who survived the war. Many have no place to go now. Some will go back to the missions, like Blue Snake. But many will not return to the missions. Quinconul and his people might stay at Lone Goose's place, now that their place is burned down. I think more men than ever will ride with Gabriel. They have learned to live a new way. Horses have changed them. But some people might want to come and live here. I think we should welcome them. We are lucky. Our place is not ruined and we can live as our ancestors lived. But the others are also our people." Some things had changed forever.

She walked in silence, then said, "You are right. Things will never be the same." She had heard his thought.

He asked the question she normally asked of him. "What are your thoughts?"

She stopped and turned to him, and it seemed there might be a smile on her lips. "You asked what people say about the war, but you didn't ask about their other talk."

"What are they saying?"

"Raven Feather says her deceased man would have wanted you to be hy-apo. The umne agree with that."

Gooseflesh ripped through him. This was the last thing he had expected to hear. A boy still lived under his skin, one who had tried to learn more, track better and do all things to prove himself worthy of the umne. "Why not Two Falcons?"

"They see that you have changed. Two Falcons says you have wisdom about the old ways, and the new. You are more than a warrior. You have trade allies and many friends across the land. You know the new people—*Españoles, Americanos* and Russians. The Horse Trader *Indios* respect you even though you won't join them." She paused. "The umne are proud of you. Crying Fox will be proud too."

Emotion choked him. In his mind he saw the boy's tear-pinched face when he confessed he'd played with the *casco* before the last battle at Domingo's and forgot to put it back. Grizzly Hair hadn't cared half as much as the boy.

All he wanted was for his son to know deep in his stomach that he belonged to the umne. Too overcome with surprise and gratitude to speak, he took her hand and continued up the hill.

At the top, they turned back and looked down on the home place. Cool light streamed from moon's shining face, now far overhead. She paled the big oak behind the dancehouse and lit a slim smoke line connecting the village to the sky people. Very nearby, Coyote warbled in full throated laughter.

Suddenly laughing with Coyote, he pulled Etumu into his arms and lifted her and turned around with her.

They had a big time to plan.

Epilogue

To: Mariano Guadalupe Vallejo
From: Lieutenant Ignacio Martinez
June 5, 1829

I have just received at 6:00 P.M. the report which you sent me concerning the attack made by you on the Christian Indian rebels of San José and Santa Clara missions. I rejoice exceedingly that this scum has been chastised and I congratulate you, your second in command, and all your troops, that you have well upheld the honor of our nation's arms.

Just as I have been gratified in this manner by your message, I have felt regret that due to lack of munitions and supplies you did not inflict a complete rout upon those rebellious and insolent Christians. For this reason I counsel you to maintain your troops in their present position until, meanwhile, you can come to this Presidio in order to confer upon what has to be done to expurgate the infection which may remain in the high country back of the rivers."

From: Governor Echeandía
To: The Commandant of Monterey
June 9, 1829

I have received the letter sent to me by Ensign don Mariano G. Vallejo relative to the expedition which he conducted to the tulares. I am surprised that you did not send me a copy of the orders which you gave the Ensign. . . neither he nor you in your report said anything about distributing prisoners to private individuals, as I have since been led to understand. . .

From: Governor Escheandía
To: The commandant at San Francisco
August 7, 1829

It has come to my attention that among the events which occurred during the recent campaign prosecuted by Ensign don Guadalupe Vallejo against the malefactors of the departments of Monterey and San Francisco was the following. Three men and an equal number of women having been captured, or encountered, at a long distance from the field of battle, were shot, stabbed with spears and arrows, and finally choked to death. Three other women who were caught after the battle were going to be sacrificed. . . these acts (are to be) investigated with the greatest care and speed. . .

From: Governor Echeandía
To: the Commandant at Monterey
October 23, 1829

I understand that on the expeditions made recently among the wild Indians by the troops of your garrison and that of San Francisco a harvest of children was secured who, without my knowledge, were distributed throughout your neighborhood and I do not know in what other localities. Therefore I strongly urge you to identify each and every one of these children. Acting in collaboration with the Reverend Father Prefect (Durán) let them be assembled at San Carlos or Soledad mission. Those who have been Christianized and who have blood relatives who will claim them shall go as neophytes to the mission or missions nearest their villages. Those who have not been Christianized shall be returned to their relatives, or in case the latter do not appear, they shall remain in San Carlos or Soledad and learn the catechism unless there are private individuals who will adopt them formally as their children. If so they shall be delivered to these persons, according to governmental orders. Notice is likewise given that any who have been Christianized but who have no relatives, or whose relatives give consent, may also be allocated to private persons to be adopted as stated above.

". . .(T)he minutiae of the campaigns are of very secondary importance. What is important is the general picture of the desperate and effective struggle of the lowly California Indian against a vastly superior military machine." (S. F. Cook, 1962, p. 169.)

"These (expeditions and reports about them) bring to an end an era. They were probably the last formal, official *entradas* into the valley. . . Thereafter the penetration of the San Joaquin region, whether officially sanctioned or not, was carried out on a completely informal basis, the outcome of campaigns being conveyed by brief letter, word of mouth, or probably in many instances not at all." (S. F. Cook, 1962, p. 181.)

Consequences Of The War

Dislocation and unrest continued on the native side. After the final battle, many settled upstream of the battles in Knight's Ferry, which continued to be an important center for peoples of mixed Miwok and Yokuts origins well into the 20th century (Gray). Individual ranchers like José Amador made forays to the interior to recover stolen livestock and punish the thieves. Atrocities against Indians were described by the Mexican vigilantes. In retaliation, mounted natives organized in a quasi-military fashion to become a large mobile strike force. José Jesús, thought to have been born in present Farmington, became the most feared Indian leader. For the remainder of Mexican sovereignty, the "interior" was a dangerous area to be avoided by Mexican settlers. In the 1840s Mexican policy encouraged foreign settlers such as Sutter and Jared Sheldon, who agreed to help pacify the interior.

During this time, imported diseases such as measles, mumps, small pox, tuberculosis and syphilis continued to spread throughout California. In 1833 a party of trappers came from the Columbia River with wives and children, carrying a deadly disease, perhaps malaria. Having no immunities, the natives rapidly perished, especially throughout the mosquito-ridden central valley. Estimates are that between one-third and one-half of the population died within a few months. Retracing their route back to Oregon Territory, the puzzled trappers wrote of the eeriness of finding entire villages now deserted, and the dead lying about with no one to bury them.

Emancipation Won

Despite disease, unrest and dislocation in the 1830s, it was becoming apparent that Indian resistance had helped emancipate them from a reluctant colonial system. A measure of that victory is that no further military expeditions to the interior were ordered by the government. Another measure is that most of the Indians left the missions, crippling them economically. Private ranching quickly supplanted the missions as the economic backbone of California.

History traditionally credits mission secularization and the emancipation of the neophytes to a change of policy in Mexico. While true at one level, it doesn't explain the timing. Under the Spanish and Mexican regimes, neophytes were to receive full rights as citizens after ten years of "training;" yet after 60 years, freedom hadn't been granted. Finally ordered in the early 1820s, it still didn't occur for another ten years, about 1833. The timing closely follows what is now called Estanislao's Rebellion, but which could be called the Indian Wars of the California Central Valley.

World History Influenced

The long-term effects of the war favored the United States. Far from being a matter of slight import, as it is traditionally treated, the native victory and continuing guerilla warfare prevented Mexico from discovering California's gold. Mexican settlers feared penetrating the Central Valley and therefore didn't get far enough east. John Sutter established his fort in the heart of Indian territory and made peace pacts with José Jesús and others. Often illegally, Sutter encouraged the settlement of immigrants from the U.S. and Europe. Thus the sadly ironic consequence of the native victory was to "save" the gold for a far more ruthless invader, a people who viewed Indians as vermin to be exterminated rather than valuable laborers and souls to be saved.

Not until 1846 was the U.S. politically and militarily ready to fight a war to acquire Mexican territories, nor were Americans numerous enough in California and the far west to affect its events. Had the native people been satisfied participants in Mexican society, Mexican ranchers might have settled the interior years earlier and found the riches in the Sierra foothills. The gold would have activated and enriched the Mexican government. Arms could have been purchased, armies raised, the land protected from other countries. Russia might have exerted her claims and engaged Mexico in war. Had she won, Russia could have used the gold to settle Oregon, Washington and British Columbia, thus connecting those valuable lands to Russia's Alaskan/Aleutian colony. Other imperial countries and maritime powers like England or France might have joined the fray—all before the U.S. was positioned to play a major role. Instead, the gold went to U.S. banks, where it funded the Union side in the Civil War, accelerating the importance of the West and helping to bring about a strong and unified United States.

Author's Acknowledgments

Not all of my sources will agree with all my interpretations of the native people or the missions and missionaries. Different interpretations abound and much has vanished into the mists of time.

I owe an enormous debt to self-publisher Hubert H. Bancroft for his 1886 multi-volume *History of California.* Compiled from every available document and detailed interviews with men who lived during the chronicled time, this towering work will continue to be a treasure trove for historians. He is inclusive to a fault. Unless otherwise noted, references are from the 1966 facsimile of the first edition published by Wallace Hebberd.

For the native side of the story I am particularly indebted to Albert Hurtado, *Indian Survival on the California Frontier* (1988), George Harwood Phillips, *Indians and Intruders* (1993), Thorne Gray *Stanislaus Indian Wars* (1993), and Randy Milliken, *Time of Little Choice: The Disintegration of Tribal Cultural in the San Francisco Bay Area 1769–1810* (1995). Dr. Milliken shared his time, sources, computerized mission records and evolving map of native villages (yet to be published). Other useful works by Milliken include his contributions to environmental impact reports, including, "Native American History Studied for the Los Vaqueros Project" (1977, Mount Diablo area). Indispensable were the primary historical documents in translation compiled by Sherbourne F. Cook, *Expeditions to the Interior,* 1820–1840 (1962, U.C. Berkeley and Los Angeles).

Other valuable sources: Malcolm Margolin's introduction to the *Journal of Jean Francois de la Pérouse* (1989) showing the psychological impact of missionization on the natives, and the diary itself; Richard J. Orsi (ed) *California History: Contested Eden: California Before the Gold Rush* (1997); Richard B. Rice, Willam A. Bullough, and Richard J. Orsi (eds) *The Elusive Eden: A New History of California* (1988); James J. Rawls, *Indians of California: The Changing Image* (1984); Antonio María Osio who, rather than contribute to

Bancroft's works, wrote his own *History of Alta California: A Memoir of Mexican California*—saved for generations by family and the University of Santa Clara and first published in 1996; Alan K. Brown, "Pomponio's World" in *The Argonaut*, a publication of the San Francisco Corral of Westeners, Vol #6 (1975); Kyrill T. Khlebnikov *Colonial Russian America: Reports, 1817–1832*, translated and published by the Oregon Historical Society (1976); Richard A. Pierce, *Russian America: A Biographical Dictionary* (1990); David Weber, *The Californios versus Jedediah Smith 1826–1827* (1990); Harrison Clifford Dale, *The Explorations of William H. Ashley and Jedediah Smith, 1822–1829* (revised edition 1991); Auguste Dehaut-Cilly, *A Voyage to California, Sandwich Islands, Around the World in the Years 1826–1829* (reissued in 1997 and 1999); Robert S. Smilie, *The Sonoma Mission: San Francisco Solano de Sonoma (1975);* Ruy E.Kern, *The Vallejos of Mission San Jose (1983);* Edwin Bryant, *What I saw in California* (1848, reissued in 1985); and Mead Kibby's preliminary chapter, "Explorations and Visits Before 1839" in *A History of Sacramento 1851*," California State Library Foundation (2000).

For cultural information I am indebted to James A. Bennyhoff, *Ethnography of the Plains Miwok* (1977 UC, Davis); Frank F. Latta, *Handbook of Yokuts Indians*, 2nd edition, (revised and enlarged, 1977); Stephen Powers, *Tribes of California* (1871), a collection of monographs on native societies beginning in the north and journeying down California's length; R.E. Heizer and M.A. Whipple (eds) *The California Indians: A Source Book* (1971); Lowell J. Bean and Thomas C. Blackburn *(eds), Native Californians: A Theoretical Retrospective,* 1976; C. Hart Merriam's collection of Miwok myths, *The Dawn of the World* (1993); Richard Burrill's *River of Sorrows* (1988) presenting Nisenan stories, including an arrow-dodging war near the Cosumnes River; Louis Payen's unpublished paper, *The Walltown Nisenan* (1961); Malcolm Margolin's *The Ohlone Way* (1978) presenting the daily life of the Bay Area native people in their lush, cared-for environment; Margolin (ed), *The Way We Lived,* stories in authentic native voices (1981); Jennie Goodman, Claudia Lawson, Vana Perris Lawson, *Kashaya: Pomo Plants* (1980); and Carolyn Niethammer (ed) *Daughters of the Earth,* a pan-Indian collection (1977).

California Grizzly by Tracy I Storer and Lloyd P. Tevis, Jr.(1955) describes bull and bear encounters.

In addition to my teachers at UC, Berkeley, I wish to thank Jerald Johnson of California State University, Sacramento, Edward Green of the former San Francisco Presidio Army Museum, the California Department of Forestry and Fire Protection for explaining the uniqueness of fires in California's "river jungles," California Museum Resource Center and Fort Ross State Park Interpretive Center, California Division of Mines and Geology for information about melting gold and the gems and geology of Del Puerto Canyon, the Cosumnes River Conservancy, Craig Bates of Yosemite State Park Museum, Dena Boer and Marge Brooks from the McHenry Museum in Modesto for leading me to the battlefields, Ralph Virgen for sharing his insights into native spirituality, María Angeles de la Pisa Marcos for Spanish editing, the writers who commented on the various drafts, and the many readers of *River of Red Gold* who let me know that history is important to them.

Glossary of Terms

ALTA CALIFORNIA - the name of California prior to U.S. acquisition. *Baja* (Lower) California, was politically attached to *Alta* (Upper) California. Today an international boundary separates the two.

BLACK HATS - a fanciful name for Mexican soldiers. They wore black Spanish-style caballero hats with stiff brims. Red bands bore the black numeral of their presidio: 1 San Diego, 2 Santa Barbara, 3 Monterey, 4 San Francisco.

CANNON - a type of artillery. Normally spelled cannon in the plural, it is spelled here with an "s" to make certain passages clearer.

CANNON BONE - the metacarpal bone of a hoofed mammal, extending from hock to fetlock—a favored hair ornament among the men of the Yokuts linguistic area.

GENTILES Sp. *gentiles.* Hen-teélehs - people outside the ritual inclusiveness of a religion. In her youth the author was called a gentile by her Mormon neighbors. In early California the term meant non-Christian Indians, or unbaptized Indians, and was used interchangeably with heathens, savages and wild Indians.

LEAGUE - an antiquated unit of linear measurement equal to a little over two and a half miles.

MIWOK (also MEWUK) - the language of Grizzly hair's people. Originally it didn't connote "tribe," any more than Yokuts, Wappo or Maidu did. Those names were bestowed by anthropologists who were mapping languages around the turn of the 20th century — inadvertently imposing paper unity over many independent "tribelets." Several of those linguistic areas are encountered in this book. Now that the government has given the term "tribe" economic import, unity and leadership ties have been forged, and Miwok now signifies an actual tribe in the political sense, as do the other California tribal names.

NEOPHYTES Sp. *neofites* - novice Christians. Today this usually denotes children apprenticing in the Catholic or Anglican churches. During the mission era it meant baptized Indians of any age in missions where Indians were the only neophytes.

OAK GALL - a smooth round growth on an oak twig caused by a wasp sting. Its interior substance is like hardened foam.

PRESIDIO - Sp. military garrison. The Presidio of San Francisco continued to be used for military purposes through 1994. Now it is part of Golden Gate National Recreation Area. In the Southwest the term has gone into English.

SPANISH Sp. *Españoles* - For many years the Mexican Revolution was little noticed in Alta California. Settlers called themselves Spanish rather than Mexican well into the 20th century. The native peoples would have used that term in the 1820s..

MIWOK TERMS (hyphens added)

Cha'ka - family-sized storage silo for acorns, woven of vines and pine branches around stakes. It stood on short legs and was roofed with branches to discourage birds and squirrels.

Chaw'se - mortar rocks, holes in hard rock created by pounding acorns, common in California's gold country. Indian Grinding Rocks State Historic Park in Pine Grove is a spectacular example, with 1,185 holes in huge slabs of granite.

Hy-apo - headman.

H'nteeles - ugly, stupid, hick, backward. Discovered in several native languages, it is derived from the Spanish for gentiles.

Lopots - knotty tree. Lopotsumne - Knotty Tree People. The fact that Bennyhoff mapped the "Lopotsimni" living on the author's ranch while Rancho Sacayak was its historic name, points to the pine as the source of their identity. See Sacayak.

Miwok - people, human being. In the northern range, the *i* was short and the *k* was silent or nearly so. The father south, the more the "Mewuk" was heard. These and other variant spellings appear on roads and establishments. None are wrong.

Nu-pah - thick acorn mush, the staple food among California natives.

Oo-lah - thin acorn soup eaten at big times.

O-se-mai-ti - grizzly bear. Pronounced like u-zoo-mi-tey in the southern Miwok range. In nearly all Animal People stories this bear is female. Yosemite National Park clearly derives its name from this animal, with Spanish spelling.

Sacayak - the plant that changed into a rattlesnake and bit Coyote's daughter. The elderly informant Mike Cleanso, who lived beside the American River in the early 20th century, identified it as horsetail — a plant believed to have healing and rejuvenating powers. Located after this book was finished, Catheryn Callaghan, an expert in the Miwok language, says Sakkyjiak meant gray pine, and the Sacayakumne of Gold Rush times would have meant "Gray Pine People." The gray pine, formerly called the digger, also had healing powers. The author's ranch is at an elevation where the gray pine begins to be seen. See Lopots.

Ti-kel - a game somewhat resembling "Indian football."

U-macha - house in northern Miwok, made from handy materials — clay, slabs of pine, cedar, or redwood, tulares or combinations thereof.

Umne (um-ney) - people, the people of. Linguistic variations recorded among neighboring peoples, include imne, amne, and ume.

SPANISH TERMS

Alcalde - leader or representative. All Spanish/Mexican communities had alcaldes. Whether to allow neophyte alcaldes in the missions was debated, and ultimately accepted. Possessing limited authority, they notably administered punishments.

Calabozo (kala-bóso) - jail. Calaboose is an English corruption.
Castigo - punishment
Cimarrón - pl. *cimarrones*. Fugitive from the law, wild man, criminal. In the 1800s the term meant Indians who escaped from the missions. Once baptized, they were not free to leave.
Cuero - leather
Dios - God
Domingo - Sunday
Frio - (freé-o) cold
Gente de razón - people of reason, civilized people. In early California this meant Mexicans, Europeans, and their Christian Indian wives and children. Census data were collected for *gente de razón* and neophytes, but not gentiles (heathens).
Hombre - man
Iglésia - church
Inquisición - investigation, not necessarily involving torture
Insurgente (een-soor-hénteh) - insurgent, rebel
Mi hijo - (mee ee-ho) my son. *Mijo* is a contraction
Merced - gift of mercy
Nada - nothing
Padre - Father, priest, missionary. The padres of early California belonged to the Franciscan Order and were therefore more appropriately termed Brothers, or friars. However, in historic as in modern times that distinction often gave way to the convention of Padre, a term of respect.
Paseo - holiday, permission to travel outside the mission
Pecado - sin
Piedad - kindness, mercy, pity
Pueblo - town. Three existed in California in the 1820s.
Ranchería - Indian village
Rancho - tract of land, often with a dwelling
Tulares - (tu-lár-es) a specie of giant hollow-stemmed marsh grass, often shortened to *tules* (tú-les), as in California's Central Valley "tule fog"
Sábado - Saturday
Vaquero - cowboy. In 19th century California skillful vaqueros garnered enormous respect. In the West the term has gone into English. The Spanish *v* sounds like *b,* causing English speakers to spell it baquero or bucarro. Not knowing the accent was on the middle syllable, some pronounced (and spelled it) it buckaroo.
Vecinos - townspeople

LATIN from the Catholic Mass
Agnus Dei, qui tollis peccata mundi - Lamb of God, who taketh away the sins of the world
Salve me - save me
Rex tremendae majestatis, salve me fons pietatis - Great majestic King (God), save me with mercy

Endnotes

PROLOGUE. All characters are historical except Ensign Valdez. Neither Governor de Neve nor Commander Pedro Fages participated in the actual council, but their viewpoints, as presented, would have been discussed. Shortly afterward, Fages "El Oso" was relieved of his command, however the viceroy later appointed him to replace de Neve as governor. A few years later Doña Eulalia de Callis went to Monterey to live with her husband and discovered his Indian mistress. Instead of quietly enduring the infidelity, as wellborn Spanish women were expected to do, she trumpeted it, sued for ecclesiastical divorce, and petitioned to have her husband removed from his position. Neither that nor the divorce was granted. In early 1790, in declining health, Fages resigned and sailed to Spain (Bancroft, Vol I, 479-485). **Overland migrations.** In January, 1774, Captain de Anza led the first 20 soldier-pioneers with their families from Sonora, across the Gila and Colorado rivers to Mission San Gabriel in the Los Angeles area. In October, 1774, de Anza led another party of pioneers from Sonora, this destined for San Francisco Bay—235 people of both sexes, driving over 800 head of livestock. They suffered illness, storms, drought and a long delay at San Gabriel while de Anza and his soldiers helped quell a rebellion of up to 1000 Indians at San Diego Mission and Presidio — a padre found dead. After more delay in Monterey, de Anza returned to Sonora, and Moraga led the pioneers to San Francisco, as shown. The exact date of the founding of the presidio and first mission are uncertain. Bancroft presents various contentions in a ¾ page footnote. Also in dispute is the July 4th date of the signing of the U.S. Declaration of Independence. Whatever the details, these two events occurred very close to the same date, on opposite shores of the continent.

PEPE was probably a retired soldier. In the early 1820s Russian diplomat and linguist Dimitry Zavalishin met him in Pueblo San José. Pepe told him there were large amounts of gold in the Sierra foothills. People in the town regarded him as crazy. Zavalishin writes, "... he was a tall, lean old man with wild, roving eyes... almost naked and barefoot, in a threadbare cloak... but he gave very definite answers to my questions and displayed no insanity at all." Judging by Pepe's age, he could have accompanied the first pioneers to San Francisco (Zavalishin's memoirs). In *River of Red Gold*, Pepe's son Pedro is a major character.

GRIZZLY HAIR and his people are fictional representatives of the Lopotsumne or Sacayakumne. Until recently the California natives did not speak of their deceased relatives and had no written language; therefore their history was not accessible except through mission records and occasional references by travelers and visitors. Russians in Fort Ross mentioned an Indian approaching them for help in an Indian rebellion; I made Grizzly Hair that man. **María Howchia,** the infant girl born to Grizzly Hair and Etumu will become the "Indian Mary" of gold rush times, who lived to old age near the author's ranch. She is a major character in *River of Red Gold (River)*. **Crying Fox,** the son of Grizzly Hair and Etumu, will become Salvador of *River*, an Indian guide recorded to have been killed and eaten during the Donner Party ordeal. Grizzly Hair is also a character in *River of Red Gold.*

MARÍA, a fictional character representative of the many native people who accommodated to Christianity and Spanish life. I have made her the mistress of Commander (later Governor) Fages. The actual Indian mistress was a Mohave.

BOWSTRING, a fictional representative of native people who assimilated into a mission and stayed after its secularization. Briefly he appears in *River of Red Gold.*

GABRIEL, a fictional representative of the so-called Horse Thief Indians of the 1830s and 40s—seen here as such a man might have been prior to the rebellion. Yokuts and Miwok speakers, likely veterans of the wars depicted herein, contiued guerrilla warfare with Mexican settlers. Contact with missions and American horse traders transformed them into a mobile melting pot of social change.

TE-MI, a rare gentile (Moquelumne River) whose name survives, is mentioned in Jedediah Smith's records. The Ione Miwok people believe the famous rebels of the post-Estanislao era, Rafael and Maximo, were sons of Te-mi, a term they believe meant elder or leader. Elk Calf is my fictional name for the younger brother, who likely went to the mission just after the 1833 "plague" and acquired the name Rafael. In the early 1840s Rafael angered John Sutter, who had him beheaded, the head piked on the gate of his fort where it rotted as a warning to others.

PROKHOR EGOROV, a *promyshelnik*, Russian serf who took seasonal employment in distant places. He sailed to Fort Ross in 1820. Pierce credits him with leading the Indian uprising in Santa Barbara. "With the scanty information available no one can say how a Russian fur hunter got involved in this disturbance, what he sought and how he met his end" (p. 133). Rumor said he died in 1824 at the hands of his Indian allies while abducting the wife of one of them. There were also reports of a Russian gun firing in Estanislao's rebellion. Egorov might well have been the shooter.

NARCISO DURÁN, from Catalonia, Spain, arrived in the new world in 1806 with Friar Fortuni. After training in the Franciscan college in present Mexico, they traveled to Alta California and served in Mission San José, Durán for 39 years. He was known for his Indian orchestra and his unique system of musical notation with color-coded harmonic parts. He was also known as a stern taskmaster and strict disciplinarian. He wrote: ". . .one must consider them (the natives) the poorest, backward, and most stupid of the people of America" (Rice et al, p. 48). He was fond of amusing himself at meals by tossing tortillas to Indian boys, who scrambled like dogs to catch them in their teeth. He locked all girls over the age of 11 (some say 9) in the *monjería*, a building with few windows placed high on twenty-four-foot walls to prevent entry or escape. In his words this was because they were so "obstinate in their evil intercourse" (Rice et al, p. 48). One of the more aggressive priests, Durán traveled inland with the soldiers to recover fugitives, sent teams of neophytes—some belligerent—to bring in new converts, and financed punitive military expeditions. Brother Altimira filed a complaint that Durán broke the rules in procuring neophytes in the North Bay area, but nothing seems to have been done about it. The 1826 attack upon the village of the Cosumne is one of the few documented incidents in which vanquished gentiles were forced to Mission San José for baptism—40 women and children. Forced baptism was not condoned by the Catholic Church or the Franciscans. After Fortuni replaced Friar Altimira in Sonoma, Durán served alone at Mission San José. He complained to Lt. Martinez that Sergeant Sanchez had made a poor showing against Estanislao. Later he criticized Martinez for the atrocities against captured Indians. Durán penned in the margin of his Registry of Deaths: "*So many sick and dying Indians, who are more fragile than glass.*" He is said to have loved Estanislao like a son, and was quick to petition for amnesty for the rebels. As Padre Presidente after 1824, Durán vigorously resisted emancipation of the Indians. Unlike many Spanish-born missionaries who left as soon as possible, Durán stayed in Alta California until his 1846 death in Santa Barbara.

ESTANISLAO (born Cucunichi), whom Gray calls the best military leader among the natives of California, was a man of two worlds. Some believe he died in 1829 shortly after the last battle and soon after receiving Durán's forgiveness (Hurtado). Gray and Philips believe he lived in the mission 10 more years, often going on extended *paseos,* during which he participated in raids against the coastal settlements. Osio says Durán hid Estanislao in his apartment at the mission to protect him. It is not well known that there were other Estanislaos at the mission, including a relative of the famous rebel (Milliken). Records and recollections might have been confused, or, for Estanislao's protection, Durán might have wanted people to believe he was dead when he wasn't. In these ambiguities Estanislao precedes the California bandit Joaquin Murieta, whose death was variously reported. It is not unusual for heroes of the common people to outlive their reputed deaths. Juan Bojorques described Estanislao as very intelligent, tall, light-skinned and heavily bearded—an alcalde born in the mission or raised there since early childhood. This description is repeated in nearly every writing about the man. Milliken found that Estanislao arrived in the mission only three years prior to the rebellion, when he was about 28, and Narciso was alcalde. Born of native parents in the interior valley, he would have resembled his own dark-skinned people. It was common at that time for Europeans to attribute European traits to indigenous leaders who defeated them. This fiction helped "explain" the success of a supposedly inferior race. Some people attributed the native success in battle to the coaching of Jedediah Smith and his trappers. Smith vigorously denied it. There were precedents for stockade-building (Fort Ross) and a tradition of pits and trenches in earlier battles. Additionally, serious rebellions had occurred without Smith in San Diego and Santa Barbara.

GOVERNOR ESCHEANDÍA, his desire to liberate the native people and his vacillation under political pressure are shown in Bancroft. His ideas echoed those of Governor de Neve a generation earlier.

CONCEPCIÓN ARGÜELLO, younger sister of Luis Argüello. The story of her romance and wait in vain for Count Nikolai Rezanov were once known to all California school children. She eventually joined a Dominican nunnery in Benecia where she became known as an "angel in black," and is buried there. Prior to her death, the young daughters of George Donner of the ill-fated wagon train met her when they attended school at St. Catherine's convent. The youngest recalled helping that nun walk up the stairs—"bowed by age and wasted by disease, (and) patiently awaiting the final summons." (Eliza Donner Houghton, *The Expedition of The Donner Party and its Tragic Fate*, 1911, reissued 1997, p. 301-2)

LUIS ANTONIO ARGÜELLO, commander of San Francisco Presidio, was California's first California-born governor. Born in 1784 in San Francisco Presidio, he might have played a more important role in history had he accepted the offer of mutinous soldiers from Monterey Company who marched to him *en masse* in 1825 and begged him to become the leader of an independent Northern California. Soldiers from San Francisco joined the cause, but after consideration, Argüello refused. He established trade with the Russians, contrary to Spanish law, and entered into a business partnership with Karl Schmidt, manager of Fort Ross. In 1818 Argüello explored the interior valley on his launch with Padre Durán. Argüello became provisional governor and served until 1826. When replaced by Echeandía, he seems to have developed a drinking problem and didn't actually command San Francisco Company again, though he was the nominal commander. Lt. Ignacio Martinez performed that duty. Argüello's visit to Fort Ross with Canónigo Fernandez occurred in October 1822, a year earlier than shown here. Arroyo Verde (Green Creek, present Salmon Creek) was in fact named by Argüello after the Canónigo vomited there (Bancroft).

CANON FERNANDEZ, the Mexican Emperor's diplomat, was selected to visit Alta California to assess the loyalty of the officials, inspect Fort Ross, and give the Russians 6 months to depart. Bancroft describes him as a "rosy-cheeked bon-vivant" who was always ready to borrow — a gambler with an "unclerical fondness for wine and women." The missionaries were "scandalized" by him. Iturbide lost favor in Mexico shortly after the visit, and Fernandez was imprisoned. (Vol II, pp. 469). Mexico was developing a republican style of government.

KARL SCHMIDT, an ethnic German of Lithuanian birth, served as manager of the Russian American Company as shown. His service ended in 1825 when Pavel Shelekhof became the company manager. Schmidt was best known for his shipbuilding, first using redwood, then oak. These California-made trading ships plied the coast for many years.

PADRE FORTUNI (or Fortuny) served in Mission San José with Padre Durán, leaving in September 1926 to assume sole responsibility for Mission Solano at Sonoma. He was slim, brown-haired, brown-eyed, and pockmarked. While at Mission Solano, French ship captain August Duhaut-Cilly visited with Fortuni, who told him a different account of the 1826 attack on the Cosumne village. Duhaut-Cilly and F.W. Beechy, an English captain, wrote about the "ridiculousness" of religious establishments pretending that neophytes were "on vacation" or "visiting their old homes" when they were traveling on gunboats and bullying gentiles into going to the missions.

POMPONIO, a mission renegade born of Coast Miwok parents, probably from Bolinas. Baptized in Mission Dolores in San Francisco at the age of 4, he became the most wanted man in northern California in the early 1820s. His people left San Francisco, where the death toll was heavy, joining the runaways who habitually returned to the north side of the bay. The Franciscans founded San Rafael, a "hospital mission" on the north shore, thus "regularizing what they could not prevent," possibly as early as 1811 (Brown, p. 5.) A padre rowed to San Rafael to perform services, returning to San Francisco. Thus until 1819 there was no resident padre, no guard and few records. Pomponio would have been 21 years old when discipline arrived in the form of Padre Gil, with guards. Pomponio began his career as a *cimarrón*. With a small gang of renegades, he terrorized missions as far south as Soledad, infiltrating them and extorting food from the neophytes. At least once he absconded with a woman. He made daring escapes, including the one shown herein, but was finally captured in Nicasio (Marin County) and executed in Monterey on September 6, 1824 by firing squad. A creek, a beach, and a ridge are named for him in San Mateo County. Brown writes in his final footnote:

> "Among the survivors of the Sierra Miwok in the 1930s, an anthropological linguist recorded the word-stems *pompomjo* . . .and *sunhente* with the meanings "sneak thief" and "burglar." The second word is recognized to come from a Spanish form which must be *surgente*."

GONZALO, a follower of Pomponio from Mission San Carlos in Carmel. According to Bancroft, he was captured and confined with a heavy iron ring around each ankle. "He well knew that death or some terrible punishment awaited him. I have it on good authority, incredible as it may seem, that while the guard was asleep, Gonzalo deliberately ...cut off both of his heels, so as to slip his feet out of the rings, and thus effected his escape." (Vol I, 1888 printing: 682-683). Gonzalo died in a horse accident while he and Pomponio were eluding soldiers. A number of sources mention different Indians cutting off their heels, one or both, in order to escape. Story inconsistencies have led some to doubt it ever happened. On the other hand it might have happened more than once. I split the difference with Bancroft by having Gonzalo amutate only one heel.

JOSÉ MARÍA AMADOR was born in San Francisco Presidio, son of Pedro Amador. His mother taught the presidio children to read. Bancroft describes J. Amador as a crude and violent man, less civilized than his father. Most of the present city of San Ramon lies within Amador's Rancho San Ramon. Amador city and county are named for him—he took his ranch workers there to mine gold in 1848. A portrait of him, showing his mismatched eyes, hangs in Mission San José.

SERGEANT JOSÉ ANTONIO SANCHEZ of San Francisco Presidio, later made brevet alférez, was known for his skill and courage as an Indian fighter. Duhaut-Cilly calls him a "fiery spirit." Bancroft writes that Sanchez was "denied the comforts of religion on his deathbed, and . . .Christian burial, through some quarrel with the friars to whom he was always hostile. He was a good man, of known honesty and valor, but very ignorant and unfit for promotion" (Vol.V, p. 710).

JEDEDIAH STRONG SMITH, born in New York in 1798 of parents of modest means, self-educated and a Methodist by choice, was among the rugged trappers called mountain men. He is the first recorded North American to explore the Central Valley of California, cross the Sierra (then in 4-8 feet of snow—present Ebbett's Pass, Hwy 4), cross the Nevada desert to Salt Lake (he carried a man the last lap), and go overland from central California to Oregon. Six-feet tall and partly scalped by a grizzly bear, he appeared on the California scene at a sensitive time and was thought by the Mexican officials to have exacerbated a seething rebellion. The leader of 16-18 trappers, some of whom deserted, he carried a Bible and agonized over his "wicked heart" (Dale). His adventures in California were as shown here. One of his trappers killed an Indian on the Cosumnes River; no record exists of reparations. His men also shot Indians on the American River. After talking his way out of incarceration in San Jose and Monterey jails, he received permission to trade his 1500 lbs. of fur and acquired a passport to leave California. Late in December he and 17 men (with 100 horses) left San Francisco under a guard, whom they soon eluded. Instead of going directly to Fort Ross, thence northward out of California, they visited the Cosumnes River and other streams before heading north. At the Umpqua River (present Oregon) Indians killed 14 of his men. Smith and 3 other survivors reported to Hudson Bay HQ on the Columbia River. Amazingly, Smith later returned to the Umpqua Indians and talked them into giving back his maps and journals. Quitting the trapper's life, he joined a trading company on the Sante Fe Trail, where in 1831, alone and searching for water, he was shot and killed by Comanches.

MISSOURI is a fictional representative of Bancroft's contention that before Jed Smith, there were rumors of an American trapper in the central valley, possibly from the Columbia River. Missouri is portrayed as a carrier of typhoid fever, suffering bouts of pain in the gall bladder. The disease was prevalent in the U.S. at the time, and about 10% of infected adults became carriers. Among Indians who lacked immunities, the mortality would have been high. Contagion is passed by fecal contamination of water or hand-to-food contact. Typhoid fever was probably one cause of the extraordinary mortality in the California missions, where the death rate of women far outstripped men, perhaps because of the greater crowding in the women's lockups (Hurtado, Margolin).

MARIANO GUADALUPE VALLEJO, 8th child of 13, was 21 years old when assigned the command of the expedition against Estanislao. His father Ignacio, who was proud of his Certificate of Pure Blood from Spain, had come to Alta California in one of the first overland emigrations. Assisting the wife of another soldier when she gave birth, Ignacio asked as payment the baby girl's hand in marriage when she came of age, and returned to marry the baby when she turned 13. That was Mariano's mother. The family settled on a land grant in the Pajaro Valley near Monterey; they had the first glass windows in Alta California (Kern). Mariano Vallejo was criticized for the atrocities after the last battle—the live Indian with

78 arrows in his body a case in point. However, no punishment seems to have ensued. Mariano became a major force in California history, receiving a large land grant in the north Bay Area, near Petaluma and Sonoma. He commanded a paramilitary force and helped establish a presidio at the Mission in Sonoma. He gained the cooperation of Solano, an Indian leader from the Suisun people, who in turn controlled hundreds of Indian laborers. Later Vallejo played a role in the diplomatic victory of the United States against Mexico. Today, Vallejo's *Casa Grande* is a state park, and the city of Vallejo is named for him.

THE NATIVE LANGUAGES OF CALIFORNIA "show greater linguistic variety than all of the known languages of the continent of Europe." Charlton Laird, *Language in America* (1970). Many researchers estimate around 300—depending on the criteria. Powers records that as he walked the length of California, the language changed about every twenty miles, judged by key words.

SPELLING of native villages varies between sources and will appear differently in different books. Milliken found that the native peoples tended to be multilingual and married outside their group, thus giving various names to the same villages. Often villages were named for the headmen, who changed over time. Sometimes they used a nickname (Kashaya = "good gamblers") or simply the location of a village — northern people, southern people. Transliteration caused more confusion. A Spanish speaker hearing native sounds might transcribe "Guala." Hearing the same thing, an English speaker would write "Walla." The Spanish "j" is pronounced like a soft English "h." Junisumne is also Unisumne. Other variants stem from the many different sounds of English vowels. Handwriting also caused problems. In some instances "i" apparently became "l" or visa versa, and "u," "o" and "a" were interchanged. So the Chilamne of this novel are also the Chilumne. And Grizzly Hair's people, the Lopotsimni after Bennyhoff, are clearly the Lopotsumne. The Moquelemne are the Mokelumne. In Spanish and English "s" makes a noun plural, thus being added to words that were already plural—but not always.

CULTURAL PRACTICES were used in this book when known, but from time to time material was borrowed from the Nisenan, who bordered the Lopotsumne on the north and were likely intermarried with the Cosumnes River Miwok. Birthing practices were borrowed from the southwest (Niethammer). In California, the native cultures were largely destroyed prior to Euro-American interest in them. Missionization took the first toll, then came the "plague" of 1833, followed by the unrest caused by Sutter's mini-empire, then the violence, massacres and dislocation of the Gold Rush. At the end of the 19th century anthropologists finally recognized what was being lost and went out to interview elderly survivors. They spoke in broken English. These fragmentary responses formed the major pool of knowledge about the indigenous cultures. Little was gleaned about women's lives. Fortunately, journalist Stephen Powers vividly described some practices and ceremonies in 1871. Captivated by the music, he regretted his inability to make musical notation. We are left to wonder, and to admire the rapidity with which the natives excelled at the European music taught in the missions.

SEXUAL PRACTICES of the California native people were regarded by 18th and 19th century Europeans (Protestants and Catholics alike), as promiscuous and ungodly. Captain Pedro Fages writes of their "unspeakable vice of sinning against nature." He says there were men in every village who encouraged the "unnatural abuse of their bodies." These men were "held in great esteem" (In Heizer and Whipple, p. 255, 259). The sexual behavior of girls and women was a major target of the priests, and the reason for locking females in the *monjerías.* Stephen Powers describes the natives as extremely sensual. He describes "wild, extravagant" dances celebrating the joy of spring. Girls "begin a voluptuous, dithyrambic dance. Faster and faster, wilder and wilder grow the motions. . . They "run riot over the whole place. They break asunder with screams and laughter, and every one of the spectators finds himself pelted with girls and flowers." The third "act" of this dance ends in bevies of "young maidens" dancing around two chosen young men. (p. 325). "Kindly," he writes of one such dance, "liberal night draws her sable curtain over the scene that ensues" (p. 287). Harrison Rogers, Jedediah Smith's second in command, writes of the women:

> "The women here are very unchaste. . . . They think it an honnour (sic) to ask a white man to sleep with them; one came to my lodgings last night and asked me to make her a blanco Pickanina, which, being interpreted, is to get her a white child, and I must say for the first time, I was ashamed, and did not gratify her or comply with her request, seeing her so forward" (Dale, p. 217).

PUEBLO SAN JOSÉ DE GUADALUPE, established 1777 on the Guadalupe River about 20 miles from the mission, was the first chartered town in Alta California. The second was Los Angeles in 1781. Branciforte at Mission Santa Cruz in 1797 was the third and last. Craftsmen and retired soldiers received town plots and were encouraged to grow specific crops. Gentiles came there to work for pay, though that created conflict with the missions. Before the Indians began to steal them, horses became so numerous around Pueblo San José that mass slaughters were ordered and herds were driven into the central valley (Bancroft).

ALTA MONTE PASS (present Altamont) was a major route over the coastal range, used by the soldiers in pursuit of *cimarrones.* Now it is a busy freeway linking the Bay Area with the Sacramento-San Joaquin Valley. *Alta monte* means high forest. Today the only forest is a thicket of electricity-generating wind machines, as the pass is also the route of coastal winds that make the interior habitable in summer. Robert Livermore's rancho, just west of the pass, is now the city of Livermore.

RIVERS were variously named by the native peoples. Mostly they referred to the "northern river" or "southern river," using their own river as the referent. ***Rio de los Americanos*** (American River) was called Wild River by Jedediah Smith. Moraga had previously named it *Las Llagas,* The Sores. The native people were so astonished by Smith and his trappers that the name could well have originated with them. In 1833 more American trappers (bearing disease) camped along the banks, and that could also be the source of the name. ***Rio de los Cosumnes*** was named by Padre Durán. Gabriel Moraga had already named it the *Rio de San Francisco,* but Durán's name stuck (long u). English-speaking pioneers spelled the river "Cosumney" (accent on short u). Both are considered correct. ***Rio de los Muquelemnes*** was also named by Durán. The modern spelling is Mokelumne, the present pronunciation is Muckélumee, short "u" in both places, the silent "n" consistent with the pronunciation of neighboring Yokuts speakers. In 1841 Northamerican settler Jared Sheldon mapped his land grant as terminating at the *"Ranchería de los Muquelemnes."* **The Calaveras River** (Sp. River of Skulls) was originally named *Rio de la Pasión* by Gabriel Moraga, but the unearthing of skeletons along its banks led Moraga to revise the name in 1808. **The Sacramento River,** formerly the Jesus María, seems to have been named by Gabriel Moraga in 1808, as he led an expedition from the south on horseback, searching for mission fugitives and a suitable site for a valley mission. He left no journal entry that day, but legend says he likened the beauty of the huge oaks and grassy plain to a holy sacrament. **The Stanislaus River** was named the *Guadalupe* in 1808. Durán referred to it as the *Rio de los Lakisamnis* for Estanislao's people, and Jed Smith called it the Appillaminy after another people on its shore. By the 1840s Estanislao's military fame and his association with that river led John Frémont to map it as the Stanilaus River for use in the United States.

RIVER JUNGLES are so called by the California Department of Forestry because of the dense vegetation. It is difficult to set a fire when the foliage is green, but once started, it can hardly be checked. The oxygen is quickly depleted, which kills along with the thick smoke. Today, levees channel the rivers, and underground aquifers are pumped for agriculture and urban uses. The once-common jungles have all but disappeared in the Central Valley. An exception worth visiting is Caswell State Park, the site of three battles in this book.

MOUNT DIABLO, the 3,849 ft. "spirit peak" of this novel, can be seen from many directions in an otherwise flat landscape. Native peoples up and down the valley and in the Bay Area saw it as a spiritual site involved in creation. It was said to be the birthplace of Coyote and Raven or Condor, three important spirit-beings. The Miwok of the Jackson Rancheria tell the story that Mount Diablo was the place where Raven and Coyote perched in the time before people, when water covered the rest of the land. They decided to go east to Jackson Peak in the Sierra foothills, Coyote swimming and Raven flying above him. (Rachel Ortiz, in "Native American History Studies for the Los Vaqueros Project"). In the mission era the peak was named *Monte del Diablo*, Forest of the Devil, reflecting the native people's respect for its power. Christians credited the Devil with any spiritual power different from their own. Spanish and Mexican soldiers believed a feathered monster would roar down its slopes and kill them. Soldiers were said to disappear in the vicinity of the mountain. The native people, however respectful, feared no such monster.

MISSION SAN JOSÉ, founded in 1777, the 14th of 21 missions in Alta California, was considered the most successful of the northern missions judged by the quantity of agricultural produce and the number of baptisms. More than 6,000 Indians were baptized there during the 39 years of its operation. Professor Richard Orsi wrote for the Bicentennial of the Mission in 1997, "It was the most unhealthy of all the missions. The death rates there were horrendous." Bryant describes Mission San Jose in the 1840s as covering about fifty acres of ground. The massive walls were of adobe, the roofs of baked tile.

> "I passed through extensive warehouses and immense rooms, once occupied for the manufacture of woolen blankets and other articles, with the rude machinery still standing in them, but unemployed. Filth and desolation have taken the place of cleanliness and busy life. The granary was very capacious, and its dimensions were an evidence of the exuberant fertility of the soil, when properly cultivated under the superintendence of the *padres.* The calaboose is a miserable dark room of two apartments, one with a small loophole in the wall, the other a dungeon without light or ventilation. The stocks, and several other inventions for the punishment of offenders, are still standing in this prison" (p. 312).

José Amador, a military guard under Padre Narciso Durán, wrote in his memoirs:

> "The treatment accorded the Indians was stern. Their shortcomings were pardoned but rarely... A very minor dereliction was punished with 15 lashes, a more serious one with 25. A person who was absent from work over 2 weeks without permission or through laziness or anything else not thoroughly justified suffered 50 lashes. Other serious infractions, such as quarrels at the rancherias, fights or the use of arrows brought 100 lashes and a set of shackles in the guard house for 1 or 2 weeks during hours off from work, while at the same time (working as usual) during the daily hours of labor." (Rice, et al 1988, p. 49)

Osio criticizes, not the punishment, but the poor instruction in Christianity when he relates an incident at Mission San José:

> "A custom had been established that a neophyte who had not appeared for work or who had committed some minor crime during the week would receive a dozen or more lashes at the church door after Sunday mass. Then, as a sign of submission, he would go and kiss the Father's hand. Among those to whom this happened was one of the Cosumne. . . When he approached the Father, he took off his shirt and wrapped it up in the blanket. Then he threw them both at the reverend feet and said, 'Father, take your Christianity. I don't want it anymore because I am returning to my land as a gentile." (Osio, p. 67).

Osio adds that many natives submitted to baptism mainly to obtain knowledge about the Devil, the spirit most feared by Christians.

Today, the restored mission is open to the public, functioning as a church and museum. The displays are changed from time to time.

GENITAL INSPECTIONS were recorded in Santa Cruz and Santa Gabriel missions. Padre Olbes at Mission Santa Cruz, not Narciso Durán, inspected the penis of the husband of an infertile couple to determine if it was "in good order." Olbes also ordered the couple to have sexual intercourse in his presence to investigate why they were not having babies. He then attempted to inspect the woman's genitalia. She refused, fought with and tried to bite him. Olbes had her bound, lashed fifty times, shackled and locked in the *monjería*. He gave her a *monigote* (doll painted red to signify blood) and ordered her to "treat the doll as though it were a child and carry it in the presence of everyone for nine days." The husband was also humiliated. A set of cow horns—heavy longhorns—were tied to his head with leather thongs, and he was herded to daily Mass in these horns and fetters. Reports of intransigence and punishment were sent to the administrator (Padre Duran) from the padres themselves. They were all schooled to care for their Indian charges, including the most intimate aspects of their health and lives. Genital inspections would have fallen within that scope and not been noteworthy in themselves. Hugo Reid, an early naturalized Mexican citizen in the Los Angeles area, wrote that the priests at Mission San Gabriel, when a woman miscarried and they suspected abortion, ordered the women flogged, head-shaved, and shackled for three months. She was made to appear every Sunday in church on the steps leading to the altar with a hideous painted wooden child (monigote) in her arms representing the dead infant. (Antonia Casteñeda, "Women, Conquest, and the Production of History," in Orsi, p. 234-5.) The low birth rate was a matter of grave concern. In combination with the high death rate it meant the padres had to procure large numbers of new converts to maintain the missions. Unrest is mentioned by all writers as the cause of Estanislao's rebellion. No specific triggering cause is recorded.

PUNISHMENT was a part of neophyte education. Bancroft mentions many charges of excessive cruelty brought by Spanish and Mexican observers. To mention two: Padre Horra wrote a detailed petition requesting that the severity of punishment be reduced for specific misdeeds, and the working hours for the heavy labor of adobe-making be reduced for pregnant women. He was declared insane and deported. Govenor Fages's departing letter to his successor criticizes Padre Peña for whipping neophytes with chains at Santa Clara. Visiting ship captains remarked on the cruelty of punishments, though some praised the Brothers. (See Margolin's discussion of international motivations — 1989). The compulsion to work was "unrelenting" (Rawls), but the neophytes were often sick and found it hard to comply with the work hours. In the 1830s Dr. Marsh wrote on the condition of mission Indians:

> "All these Indians . . . are weak and unvigorous; spasms and rheumatics, to which they are so much subject. . . .what most injures them, and prevents propagation, is the venereal disease, which most of them have very strongly." (Quoted in Bryant)

Contrast these descriptions with Power's observations of Indians beyond the reach of the missions as "large, vigorous, healthy Indians." And Bryant's description of Indians encountered north of mission influence: ". . .Indians running toward us with an apparent speed, greater than could be achieved by any of the animals we were riding. Notwithstanding we proceeded at our usual gait, they soon came up to us, and holding out their hands as we did to them, greeted us with much kindness and cordiality" (Bryant, 194).

While modern people tend to be shocked at the treatment of mission Indians, the friars knew their punishments were light as compared to the boiling in oil and drawing and quartering that were common in Europe. Whipping, shackling and confinement in stocks and dungeons for minor infractions were ordinary punishments in Europe, but this would not have impressed the California Indians, who had never encountered institutionalized punishment for social control. The Franciscans genuinely tried to help the natives by bringing them "civilization" and saving their souls. Fearing for their own lives, the friars wanted the protection of the military, but also saw its counterproductive influence. To control sexual contact, Junipero Serra succeeded in separating the garrisons from the missions. The order to punish came primarily from the padres. It is sadly ironic that the Franciscans hoped to cultivate a new world based on the peaceful teachings of Jesus and St. Francis, but carried within themselves some of what they wished to leave behind.

MISSION SAN FRANCISCO DE SOLANO at Sonoma was founded in 1824 under the republican government of Mexico, initially without the approval of the Franciscan authorities. This mission was the dream of Padre Altimira, who worked with Governor Argüello to shut down Mission San Rafael and build a new mission at the new site. Church authorities, pushed by Padre Amarós, reopened San Rafael but, after deliberation, authorized the new mission in addition, with the stipulation that neophytes could go to San José, San Rafael or San Francisco de Solano. This gave the neophytes unintended freedom, because they continually chose to go to other missions, thus eluding the guard. The beauty of the pristine environment and natural springs was described by Padre Altimira in his reports on the siting of the mission (Smilie). The area was also admired by ship captains who came for "elk butter." Vaqueros of "inconceivable skill" hunted the elk when they were at their fattest and had lost their "lightness of foot." ". . .Mounted on the fastest horses and armed with hunting knives and the fatal lassos" they "snare" the animals, throw them on the ground and cut their hamstrings, avoiding the sharp antlers and pointed hooves" (Duhaut-Cilly, p.136). The fat was sweet and fine, and traders bought it by the barrel.

MISSION LANDS in California were loosely defined as territories formerly occupied by the Indians who became neophytes at those particular missions. These were vast, unfenced holdings of indeterminate size, grazed upon by immense herds of livestock. The natives were to be given title to those lands, however, after 1833 mission lands were given or sold to secular administrators (ranchers), who exploited the labor of the displaced Indians. A handful of Indians received land grants, but nearly all were forced to sell. When the U.S. won California, most of the former mission lands were acquired by North Americans through a court system favoring them over the former Mexican citizens. The native people continued working on the hunting grounds of their ancestors, much of which had become wheat fields, until many were displaced in the late 19th century by mechanization. Utilizing the railways, the survivors became California's first migrant labor force.

SPANISH/MEXICAN LAW excluded Indians from some of the normal rights of citizens, such as the right to buy and sell goods and move about freely, however they enjoyed important legal protections. Killing an Indian was a crime, and murders were rare. Indians were called to testify in court. In contrast, under California's first constitution as a U.S. territory, the native people lost all protections under the law. Not only was it legal to kill them, a federal bounty could be collected for their scalps. Indian testimony was not allowed in court, so they couldn't defend themselves. If found "vagrant" they were subject to arrest, and often "worked off" the bail paid by those who wanted their labor. Many became virtual slaves. It was not until after vast numbers had been killed and/or died of hunger, disease and hardship, that the native people were given full citizenship.

FORT ROSS. In early history Russians were known as "the people of Ross" (pronounced Roash). Their country was called Rossiia, or Russia in English. The fort was established in 1812 on the California coast by the Russian-American Company (RAC) for the initial purpose of hunting sea otters. Khlebnikov (trans. 1976) provides detailed information about environment, agriculture, costs of goods, and the international situation. The RAC employed Aleuts to hunt sea animals in native kayaks. They hunted the otters to depletion and the RAC sold their belongings to John Sutter in 1841, who never completed payment. Ironically, the Russians left 7 years prior to the Gold Rush to pursue other enterprises including mining for precious metals in Siberia.

GRIZZLY BEARS were remarked upon by most visitors to early California. They were numerous from the Sierra Mountains to the sea, adapting to all climates except deserts. Captain Duhaut-Cilly tells of men rowing a small boat across San Francisco Bay when a large grizzly, apparently tired of swimming, caught up to the boat and attempted to board. Soldiers firing directly into its head finally killed it. Bears preyed upon Spanish livestock, becoming more common along the coast the longer the settlements were there. The last grizzly was killed in California before the 20th century, at about the time the grizzly bear was designated the state animal. Their feet were considered most delicious and are remembered in today's bakery pastry: bear claws.

GOLD. A San Luis Obispo padre was accused of shipping gold out of the country, and a priest in Mission Santa Clara predicted that large amounts of gold would be discovered in the Sierra foothills (Bancroft). Dimitry Zavalishin wrote decades later from Siberia where he served a life sentence that he had met a man in Pueblo San José who talked about rich gold discoveries in the foothills of the Sierra. (See "Pepe"). Other stories of gold survive; the padres were apparently loathe to spread the word about California's gold.

THE BATTLES were described by a number of soldiers, officers and other observers, all compiled by Cook. **The Soto Expedition** according to Bancroft, didn't occur, but contrary evidence is provided by Cook. Soto's painful death the day after his battle and his consequent failure to write an official report probably contributed to the confusion. The detail of the arrow aimed up the gun barrel into Soto's eye was recorded by soldier José Galindo. **The Sanchez Expedition,** as described in Sanchez' official report, was heavily used here. Sanchez writes that the gentile headmen with whom he conferred beforehand claimed to fear Estanislao. The method used by the soldiers to shield their injured comrades at the end of the battle is told by Corporal Pacheco. **The Vallejo Expedition** as described in Mariano Vallejo's official reports was used here, along with Piña and Osio. On the eve of Vallejo's first battle his men captured a number of horses being moved near the *ranchería*. From that, the rebels' intent to use horses in the battle was surmised. Between Vallejo's first and second battle, his men captured about twelve more horses from the Tagualumne village, presumably upstream on the Stanislaus River. None of the reports disclose where the "harvest of children" occurred. During the night while the Mexican troops were camped on their way back to the presidios, they were awakened by a fire, but managed to move the powder before it exploded. **Battle locations.** From sketchy diary descriptions and tales of rusty cannonballs on private property, it seems that the battles of Soto, Sanchez and Vallejo #1 occurred on the south side of the Stanislaus River on the opposite shore from today's Caswell State Park. A plaque in the park marks Caswell as the site of the battles and commemorates Estanislao. The south side cannot be approached except through a private vineyard. Because Caswell Park has been left in its pristine condition, it is much closer environmentally to the actual site than the vineyard. Furthermore, Caswell could well be the site. Cannonballs could have been moved. Bancroft thought Vallejo's second battle was fought on the Tuolumne River about ten miles south of the first battleground, based largely on the pronunciation of Tagualamne, which in Spanish sounds like Tuolumne. However, even if it was the same people, they could have been camped on the Stanislaus for the battle. Estanislao's people, the principal "hosts" of the war, would have been likely to travel up their home river, particularly since a back-up strategy had been planned in advance and an elaborate stockade built. For these and other reasons, including the failure of contemporary reports to mention a different river, Gray and others conclude that present-day Riverbank or Oakdale, or some place between the two, was the site of Vallejo's second battle.

Of splinters Osio writes:

> "(the Indians) expected to obtain good results from their method of fortification which consisted of primary, secondary and tertiary stockades, quite well designed to protect them from the carbine fire... Even though they were dislodged from these . . . the(y) would reach a labyrinth of wide and deep trenches, communicating with each other, where as a last resort the defenders had resolved to die fighting . . .
>
> "But the first discharge of the cannon, fired at them to open a breach, caused a lot of heavy splinters to fly out which killed several Indians. The second had the same effect and consequently the Indians were suddenly disillusioned. They found that the palisades mentioned were of no value for defense against artillery, for even though the shot did no damage, the splinters which were driven out of the logs of the stockade were lethal." (Osio, p.92-93)

Oak "splinters" had the same effect upon the crews of ships during cannon broadsides at sea.

Photo: Sirlin Photographers, Sacramento, CA

About The Author

Naida West was born in Idaho Falls, Idaho. In her early years she lived in towns and farms and ranches mostly in Idaho, and often with relatives. She attended many schools, including a one-room schoolhouse in Divide, Montana. In 1953 her mother moved the children to Carmel, California, where Naida graduated from high school. She worked in Germany, received a B.A. in sociology from the University of California, Berkeley, a master's degree from the California State University in Sacramento, and a Ph.D. in sociology from U.C. Davis.

In 1982 West and her husband Bill Geyer moved to their 12-acre remnant of a once-large ranch on the Cosumnes River in California's Gold Country. She researched obscure documents and interviewed old timers to learn about the people who had lived there before her—native people and Mexican era ranchers, including Elitha Donner of the ill-fated wagon train. In 1990 West quit her teaching and consulting careers to became a full-time writer. Her published articles became the backbone of her first history novel, *River of Red Gold* (1996). She is working on a third novel in the series. The mother of three grown children, she frequently speaks about California history, and about writing and publishing.

If you liked this book and would like to pass a copy on to someone else, or would like a copy of the sequel, *River of Red Gold*, please check with your local bookstore, online bookseller, or use this form:

Name____

Address ____

City ______________________ State _____ Zip _________

Eye of the Bear ____ copies @ $18.98 each $ __________

River of Red Gold ____ copies @ $18.49 each $ __________

California residents, please add applicable sales tax $ __________

Eye of the Bear $1.47

River of Red Gold $1.43

Shipping and handling:

$3.00/first copy; $1.60 each additional copy* $ __________

Total enclosed $ __________

For more than 5 copies, please contact the publisher for quantity rates. Send completed order form and your check or money order to:

Bridge House Books
P.O. Box 809
Rancho Murieta, CA 95683

Email: west@bridgehousebooks.com
Phone: 916-985-7411
Fax: 916-354-2788

For additional books see:
www.bridgehousebooks.com

---

*International shipping is extra. Please contact us for the shipping rates to your location, if outside the United States.